Fifth Edition Foes

Authors: Scott Greene, Matt Finch, Casey Christofferson,
Erica Balsley, Clark Peterson, Bill Webb, Skeeter Green,
Patrick Lawinger, Lance Hawvermale, Scott Wylie Roberts "Myrystyr",
Mark R. Shipley, "Chgowiz",
Developer: Steven Winter
Editors: Steven Winter, Merric Blackman, James Redmon
Layout and Typesetting: Charles A. Wright
Cover Art: Artem Shukayev

Cover Design: Charles A. Wright
Interior Art: Peter Bergting, Ed Bourelle, Brian LeBlanc, John Bridges,
Chris Curtin, David Day, Andrew DeFelice, Jim DiBartalo,
Talon Dunning, Tom Gianni, Jeff Holt, Llyne Hunter, Veronic Jones,
Chris McFann, Chet Masters, Gary McKee, Cara Mitten, Jim Nelson,
Claudio Pozas, Erik Roman, Chade Segesketter, James Stowe,
Rich Thomas, Tyler Walpole, MKUltra Studios, UDON Studios

Necromancer Games is not affiliated with Wizards of the Coast™.
We make no claim to or challenge to any trademarks held by Wizards of the Coast™.

NECROMANCER
GAMES

5th Edition Rules,
1st Edition Feel

Table of Contents

FOREWORD

Fifth Edition Foes is a first step into supporting the Fifth Edition of everyone's favorite roleplaying game. The monsters in this book should be familiar to anyone who enjoyed the *Tome of Horrors* supplements (all four volumes of it) published by Necromancer Games during the Third Edition era. Many of these monsters reach back further than those books, though, since they're culled from First Edition volumes such as the *Fiend Folio* (1981) and *Monster Manual II* (1983)—and those books drew material from the even older pages of magazines like *The Dragon* and *White Dwarf*. So while the stat blocks and powers of these creatures are as up-to-date as we could make them, they also harken back to the very early years of roleplaying games, when any addition to the game—every new monster, spell, or magic item—was completely new and exciting.

I remember well the thrill that ran through the offices of TSR when a new book like the *Fiend Folio* arrived from the printer. Any pretense at trying to work was set aside as everyone tore into the latest shiny volume, examining stats, commenting on illustrations, discussing how the new creatures could be worked into upcoming adventures and which existing creatures and spells they could be paired with to produce really nasty surprises for players.

Updating these monsters to the latest edition brought back much of that same excitement. The rules of the game have changed in big ways and small over the decades, but the fundamental idea—a group of thrill-seeking roustabouts relying on their prowess and their wits to survive in an imaginary world filled with magic and monsters—is still the same. Ideas and concepts that were challenging, frightening, or amusing to players' imaginations in 1981 have the same potency today. Imagination never becomes obsolete because of new technology. As G. K. Chesterton wrote, "There are no rules of architecture for a castle in the clouds."

We're not relying on nostalgia to make these monsters interesting. This book lines up well with the Necromancer Games philosophy that the challenges faced by our imaginary heroes should be interesting and tough. Many of these creatures don't fit neatly into level-specific challenges. Some of them punch well above their weight class. Others have an alarming ability to keep swinging long after other monsters would flee or perish. Shocks like those are what keep the game fresh and surprising. When there was doubt about how to rank a monster's challenge rating, we intentionally erred on the low side, because players are resourceful. If they take a beating in their first meeting with a "level-appropriate" monster, they can fall back, dress their wounds, learn from the defeat, and come back the next day armed with a better plan that leads to victory. That refusal to admit defeat is, after all, part of the fabric of heroism.

— Steve Winter

Aaztar-ghola

Aaztar-gholas are ancient creatures originating from some other dimension, foul things that have established themselves in the prime material plane. They attire their tall, hideous bodies in flowing, richly embroidered robes, adorning themselves with strange, baroque jewelry.

Aaztar-Ghola

XP 1,100 (CR 4)
CE Medium humanoid
Initiative +0

DEFENSE
AC 13 (*mage armor*)
hp: 38 (7d8 + 7)

OFFENSE
Speed: 40 ft.
Multiattack: The aaztar-ghola attacks twice with its scimitar.
Melee Attack—Scimitar: +4 to hit (reach 5 ft.; one creature).
  Hit: 1d6 + 2 slashing damage.

STATISTICS
Str 14 (+2), **Dex** 11 (+0), **Con** 12 (+1),
Int 16 (+3), **Wis** 11 (+0), **Cha** 12 (+1)
Languages: Common, Abyssal
Skills: History +5

TRAITS
Arcane Fatigue: An aaztar-ghola gains 1d3 levels of exhaustion when it uses its *finger of death* spell-like ability. It recovers fully after taking a short rest and consuming a fresh human body part.
Dominate Ghouls (3/day): As a bonus action, an aaztar-ghola can try to dominate all ghouls within 60 feet. The aaztar-ghola makes a DC 8 Cha check; if it succeeds, it charms every ghoul in the area. The aaztar-ghola establishes a telepathic link to affected creatures, and they do their best to carry out its simple commands. This charm lasts for one hour. Ghouls under this affect have tactical advantage on Wis saving throws against being turned. If any ghouls the aaztar-ghola is trying to charm are currently turned by a cleric, the aaztar-ghola has tactical disadvantage on its Cha check.
Mage Armor: An aaztar-ghola always has *mage armor* cast on itself.
Spell-like Abilities: The aaztar-Ghola can use the following spell-like abilities, using Intelligence as its casting ability (DC 13, attack +5). The Aaztar-Ghola doesn't need material components to cast these spells.
2/day: *inflict wounds* (range 50 ft.), *fear*
1/day: *dispel magic, finger of death, fly, see invisibility*

ECOLOGY
Environment: Any
Organization: Solitary

Aaztar-gholas find human flesh delectable, especially when it is cooked with the strange spices of their distant homeland. An aaztar-ghola lair often contains cauldrons, skewers, and more alien and disturbing culinary implements.

Aaztar-gholas have a necromantic affinity with ghouls and ghasts, which obey their commands without any perceptible reluctance. The lair of an aaztar-ghola is 90% likely to be guarded by a pack of 2d6 + 6 ghouls. In the presence of an aaztar-ghola, ghouls are highly resistant to being turned; they have tactical advantage on saving throws against turning. Ghasts are also willing to serve aaztar-gholas, but they do so for their own purposes. They are unaffected by the strange control that aaztar-gholas have over ordinary ghouls. Aaztar-gholas themselves are not undead and can't be turned, although as creatures not inherently native to the prime material plane they are affected by *protection from evil*.

These horrid creatures are natural adepts of the necromantic arts, and all of them have inherent spellcasting powers. The most fearsome of these is *finger of death*. Because of its debilitating effect on them, however, aaztar-gholas save it as a last resort, using it to destroy a final enemy, to ensure their escape from a bad situation, or as a last, spiteful act before dying. They always have *mage armor* cast on themselves, whether or not they expect trouble. Aaztar-gholas are capable of speaking with any sort of undead creature, even those that have no intellect at all such as zombies. This ability to communicate with the undead does not imply the ability to control; ghouls are the only undead creatures that automatically follow commands given by an aaztar-ghola.

Credit
  Author Matt Finch

Adherer

This creature appears to be a withered humanoid wrapped in decaying bandages. Upon close inspection, what appeared to be bandages are actually loose folds of the creature's rotting skin. A sour odor fills the air around the creature.

Adherer
XP 450 (CR 2)
LE Medium aberration
Initiative +1

DEFENSE
AC 13 (natural armor)
hp: 45 (7d8 +14)
Vulnerability: Fire damage

OFFENSE
Speed: 30 ft.
Multiattack: The adherer slams twice.
Melee Attack—Slam: +4 to hit (reach 5 ft.; one creature). *Hit:* 1d8 + 2 bludgeoning damage, and the target creature is grappled and restrained (see Adhesive).

STATISTICS
Str 14 (+2), **Dex** 12 (+1), **Con** 14 (+2),
Int 4 (–3), **Wis** 11 (+0), **Cha** 8 (–1)
Languages: Common (understands but can't speak)
Skills: Stealth +3
Senses: Darkvision 60 ft.

TRAITS
Adhesive: An adherer exudes a sour smelling, gluelike substance that is a powerful adhesive. Any creatures or items that touch it, except for items made of stone, become stuck to the adherer. The adherer automatically grapples and restrains any creature it hits with its slam attack. It can grapple up to two opponents at one time. Gtrappling does not reduce the adherer's number of attacks. Creatures grappled this way can break free with a successful DC 15 Str check.

A weapon that strikes an adherer is stuck to the creature unless the wielder succeeds on a DC 12 Dex saving throw. Pulling a stuck weapon free requires a successful DC 12 Str check.

Boiling water thrown on the adherer deals 1d6 points of damage to it and to any creature grappled by the adherer. It also grants tactical advantage on Dex saving throws and Str checks to free a weapon or to escape from the adherer's grapple; this bonus lasts for one round. Inflicting fire damage on the adherer also weakens the adhesive, granting tactical advantage on Dex saving throws and Str checks for 1d3 rounds. *Universal solvent* dissolves the adhesive instantly. An adherer can dissolve its adhesive at will, and the substance breaks down naturally one hour after the creature dies.

ECOLOGY
Environment: Temperate forests and subterranean
Organization: Solitary or gang (2–4)

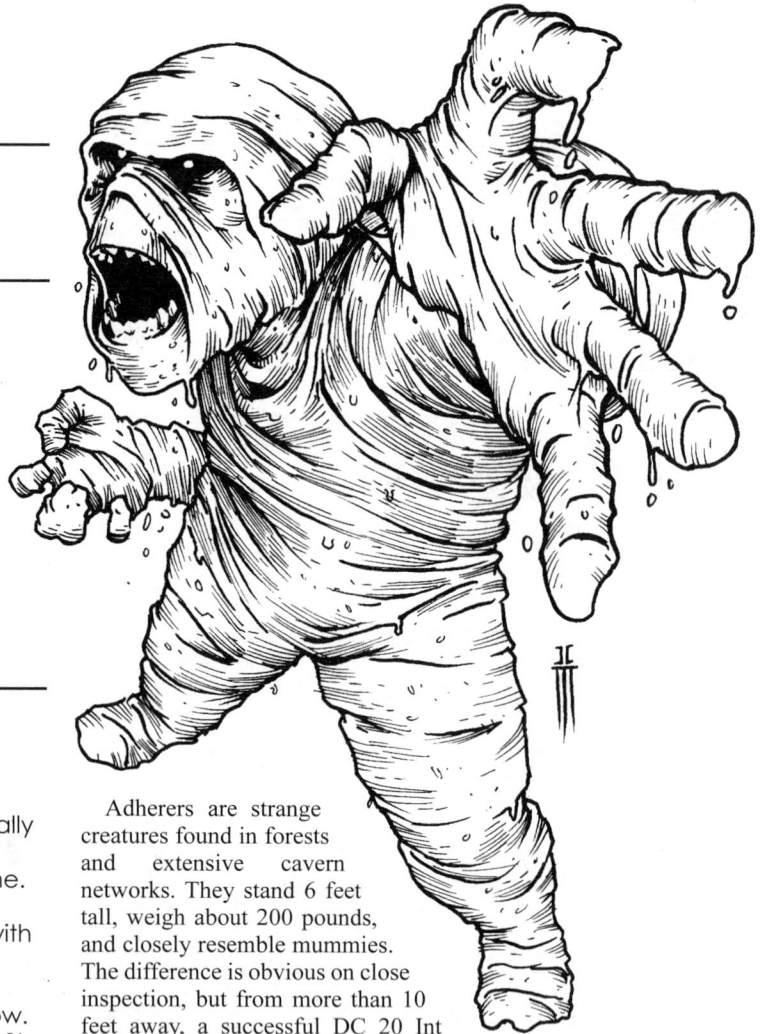

Adherers are strange creatures found in forests and extensive cavern networks. They stand 6 feet tall, weigh about 200 pounds, and closely resemble mummies. The difference is obvious on close inspection, but from more than 10 feet away, a successful DC 20 Int (Nature) check is needed to discern the difference. They are not in fact related to mummies, nor are they undead. Adherers are malign, living creatures that attack just about any other creature they encounter.

Adherers always attack from ambush. When lying in wait, an adherer covers its body with leaves, sticks, or other natural debris to blend with its surroundings. When prey wanders too close, the adherer springs to the attack. In this type of ambush, adherers always have tactical advantage on their Stealth checks to determine surprise (+5). They are cowardly creatures, however, and if spotted before they can spring their ambush, they flee.

Credit
The Adherer originally appeared in the First Edition *Fiend Folio* (© TSR/Wizards of the Coast, 1981) and is used by permission.

Copyright Notice
Authors Scott Greene and Clark Peterson, based on original material by Guy Shearer.

Aerial Servant

This creature appears as a man-sized humanoid composed of grayish white vapor.
No facial features can be discerned.

Aerial Servant
XP 5,000 (CR 9)
N Medium fiend
Initiative +4

DEFENSE
AC 18 (natural armor)
hp: 152 (16d8 + 80)
Saving Throws: Dex +8, Wis +4
Resistance: Bludgeoning, piercing, and slashing damage from nonmagical weapons
Immunity: Poison damage; grappling, paralysis, petrification, poison, prone, restraint, unconsciousness

OFFENSE
Speed: 60 ft., fly 60 ft.
Multiattack: The aerial servant slams once and constricts once, or uses its wind blast.
Melee Attack—Slam: +9 to hit (reach 5 ft.; one creature). *Hit:* 2d10 + 5 bludgeoning damage, and the target creature is grappled.
Melee Attack—Constrict: automatic hit (one creature grappled by the aerial servant). *Hit:* 2d10 + 5 bludgeoning damage.
Area Attack—Wind Blast (recharge 5, 6): automatic hit (80 ft. line; creatures in the line). *Hit:* 4d10 bludgeoning damage, and creatures of Medium size or smaller are knocked prone and pushed 2d10 feet away from the aerial servant. Affected creatures that make a successful DC 17 Dex saving throw take half damage and are not knocked prone, but they are pushed away.

STATISTICS
Str 20 (+5), **Dex** 18 (+4), **Con** 20 (+5), **Int** 4 (–3), **Wis** 10 (+0), **Cha** 11 (+0)
Languages: Common, Primordial
Skills: Perception +4, Stealth +8
Senses: Darkvision 60 ft.

TRAITS
Flawless Tracking: An aerial servant can track any creature on the same plane of existence as itself across any terrain automatically.
Link with Caster: When summoned, an aerial servant creates a mental link between itself and the caster who summoned it. Should the aerial servant fail the mission it was assigned, it returns to the caster and attacks him. The aerial servant can find the caster as long as they are on the same plane of existence. If the caster leaves the plane, the link is temporarily broken. If the two are again on the same plane of existence, the link is immediately reestablished and the aerial servant moves at full speed toward the caster's location. The link is broken permanently only when the aerial servant or the caster is destroyed.
Natural Invisibility: An aerial servant is permanently invisible, and it remains invisible even when attacking. This ability is inherent and can't be magically cancelled or dispelled. Invisibility is not factored into the aerial servant's +8 Stealth modifier; it gains the benefits of invisibility in addition. An aerial servant is visible on the Astral and Ethereal Planes, but it is always lightly obscured in those locales.

ECOLOGY
Environment: Any (Plane of Air)
Organization: Solitary

Aerial servants are semi-intelligent creatures from the Plane of Air that often roam the Astral and Ethereal planes. One is seldom met on the Material Plane unless it was summoned by a spellcaster and commanded to perform some task. Typically, such tasks involve retrieving objects or tracking the summoner's enemies. Though an aerial servant performs whatever task is asked of it, it resents being summoned and forced to do another's bidding; therefore, it looks for ways to pervert the conditions of the summoning and its mission. An aerial servant that fails or is thwarted in its mission becomes insane and immediately returns to the caster who summoned it, either killing the caster or carrying the caster back to the Plane of Air with it.

Aerial servants are always invisible on the Plane of Air. On other planes, they can be seen when they wish, though only vaguely, appearing as humanoids composed of whitish-gray vapor. Sometimes eyes, a nose, and a small mouth form in the vapor. They can't become invisible on the Astral and Ethereal Planes, but their appearance is always indistinct there.

Aerial servants attack with a shearing blast of wind or by grabbing and crushing an opponent in their powerful grasp.

Aerial servants can be killed only on their native Plane of Air. If slain elsewhere, they simply dissolve into wisps of vapor and return to their home plane.

Credit
The Aerial Servant originally appeared in the First Edition *Monster Manual* (© TSR/Wizards of the Coast, 1977) and is used by permission.

Copyright Notice
Authors Scott Greene and Clark Peterson, based on original material by Gary Gygax.

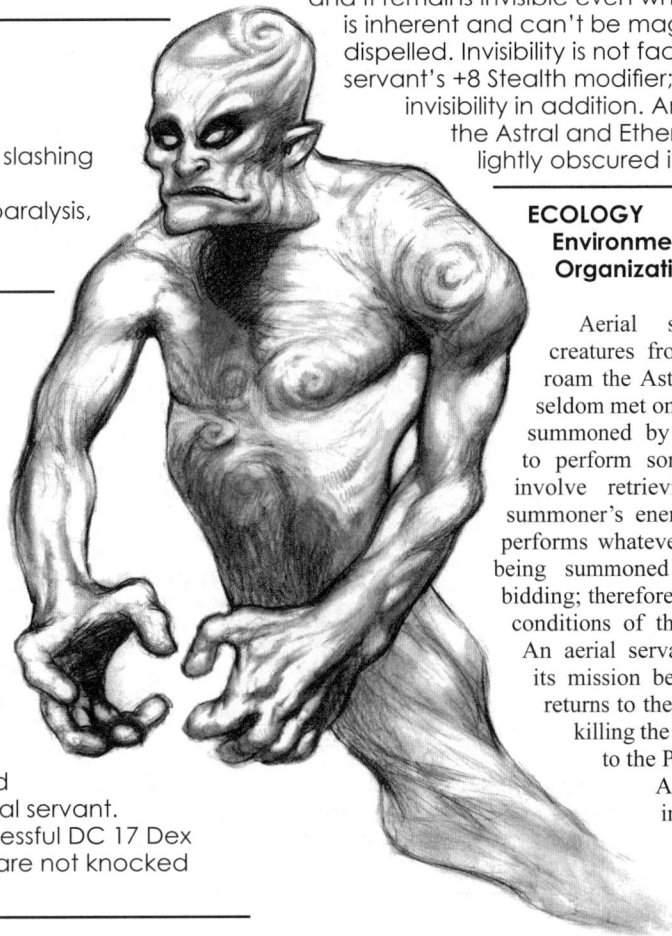

Algoid

This stocky, man-sized creature seems to be composed of nothing more than algae and murky, stagnant water.

Algoid

XP 700 (CR 3)
N Medium plant
Initiative +0

DEFENSE

AC 14
hp: 52 (7d8 + 21)
Saving Throws: Con +5
Resistance: Slashing and piercing damage from nonmagical weapons
Immunity: Lightning and fire damage; prone

OFFENSE

Speed: 20 ft.
Multiattack: The algoid slams twice or attacks once with its mind blast.
Melee Attack—Slam: +6 to hit (reach 5 ft.; one creature). *Hit:* 1d8 + 4 bludgeoning damage. If an algoid scores a critical hit with this attack, the target must make a successful DC 14 Con saving throw or be stunned. The stunned creature can repeat the saving throw at the end of each of its turns; the condition ends on a successful save.
Ranged Attack—Mind Blast: automatic hit (range 60 ft. cone; creatures in the cone). *Hit:* creatures in the cone must make a successful DC 13 Int saving throw or be stunned for 3d4 rounds.

STATISTICS

Str 19 (+4), **Dex** 10 (+0), **Con** 16 (+3), **Int** 4 (–3), **Wis** 10 (+0), **Cha** 10 (+0)
Languages: Common (understands but can't speak)
Skills: Stealth +4
Senses: Darkvision 60 ft., Tremorsense 120 ft.

TRAITS

Animate Trees: An algoid can innately cast the *animate objects* spell at will, requiring no components. Each casting animates two trees, which are all the algoid can control at a time. A newly-animated tree takes one full round to uproot itself. Once free, trees act on the algoid's turn.
Vulnerability to Water Magic: *Control water* and *destroy water* spells deal 3d6 piercing damage to an algoid (no save).
Water Camouflage: An algoid has tactical advantage on Stealth checks when it has any type of standing water to blend into.

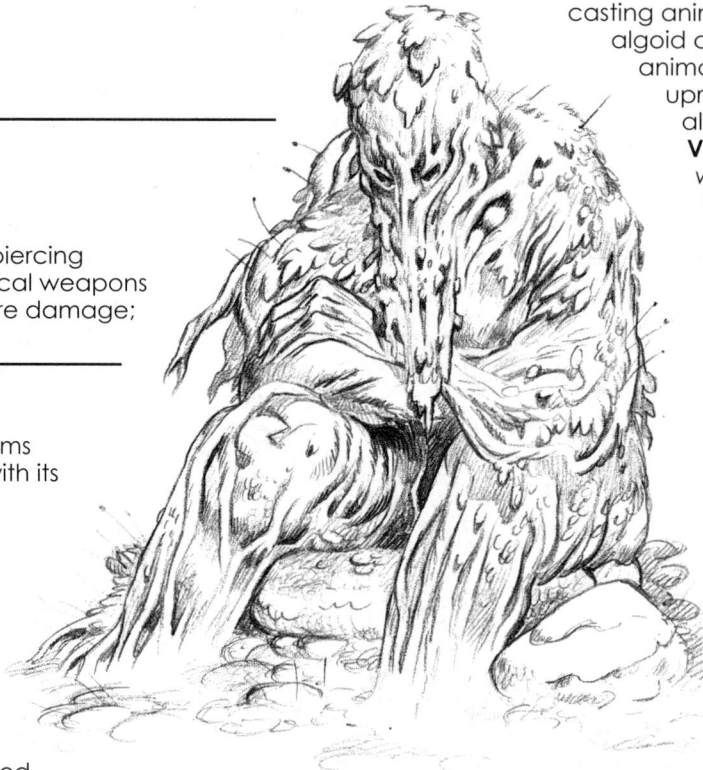

ECOLOGY

Environment: Temperate marshes
Organization: Solitary, pair, or cluster (3–6)

The algoid is a living colony of algae that has developed some semblance of intelligence and mobility. It is dark green and roughly humanoid in shape. Algoids make their lairs in marshes and swamps. They are often encountered with other marsh-dwelling sentient plants, but never with shambling mounds (algoids hate them and usually attack them on sight).

An algoid is 7 feet tall and weighs about 300 pounds. The "skin" of an algoid is coarse and rough with a leafy texture. In its natural surroundings, it is nearly invisible until it attacks. Algoids use this natural camouflage to gain tactical advantage on Stealth checks when prey is nearby. The algoid lies in wait, submerged in water or a bog, locating prey with tremorsense. When a potential victim passes nearby, the algoid springs to attack.

Credit
    The Algoid originally appeared in the First Edition *Fiend Folio* (© TSR/Wizards of the Coast, 1981) and is used by permission.

Copyright Notice
    Authors Scott Greene and Clark Peterson, based on original material by Mike Ferguson.

Amphorons of Yothri

The creatures have jointed, metallic shells, clanking limbs, and one glistening, glassy eye.
Clearly, they are not of this world.

Amphoron of Yothri (Worker)

XP 100 (CR 1/2)
N Small construct
Initiative +0

DEFENSE
AC 17 (natural armor)
hp: 13 (3d6 + 3)
Resistance: Damage from magic spells and spell-like effects
Immunity: Piercing damage from nonmagical weapons; poison damage; charm, fright, paralysis, poison, stun, unconsciousness

OFFENSE
Speed: 30 ft.
Multiattack: The amphoron attacks twice with pincers.
Melee Attack—Pincer: +2 to hit (reach 5 ft.; one creature).
Hit: 1d8 piercing damage.

STATISTICS
Str 9 (–1), **Dex** 11 (+0), **Con** 12 (+1), **Int** 8 (–1), **Wis** 9 (–1), **Cha** 6 (–2)
Languages: Common

Senses: Darkvision 60 ft.

TRAITS
Flicker: Roll 1d6 for every amphoron in play at the start of its turn. On a roll of 1, the amphoron "flickers" due to a momentary interruption of the connection across time and space. Flickering lasts until the start of the amphoron's next turn. While flickering, the amphoron can't be attacked and can't inflict damage. It regains 2 hit points when it rematerializes. A controller flickers only on a roll of 1 on 1d20, but if it does, all amphorons under its control also flicker.
Highly Charged: Worker amphorons carry a high static electrical charge. Any living creature that begins its turn within 10 feet of a worker amphoron takes 2 electrical damage from static discharge.
Levitate (1/day): Once per day, a worker amphoron can cast *levitate* on itself as an action. No components are required.

ECOLOGY
Environment: Any
Organization: Work gang (1d4 workers) or crew (1d4 – 1 workers, 1d3 – 1 warriors, and 1d2 – 1 juggernauts)

Amphoron of Yothri (Warrior)

Warrior
XP 450 (CR 2)
N Medium construct
Initiative +0

DEFENSE

AC 17 (natural armor)
hp: 33 (6d8 + 6)
Resistance: Damage from magic spells and spell-like effects
Immunity: Piercing damage from nonmagical weapons; poison damage; charm, fright, paralysis, poison, stun, unconsciousness

OFFENSE

Speed: 30 ft.
Multiattack: The amphoron attacks once with pincers and once with its flamethrower.
Melee Attack—Pincers: +4 to hit (reach 5 ft.; one creature). *Hit:* 1d10 + 2 piercing damage.
Area Attack—Flamethrower: automatic hit (range 100 ft. line; all creatures in line). *Hit:* creatures in the line must make a successful DC 11 Dex saving throw or take 2d6 fire damage.

STATISTICS

Str 14 (+2), **Dex** 11 (+0), **Con** 12 (+1),
Int 10 (+0), **Wis** 10 (+0), **Cha** 6 (–2)
Languages: Common
Senses: Darkvision 60 ft.

TRAITS

Flicker: Roll 1d6 for every amphoron in play at the start of its turn. On a roll of 1, the amphoron "flickers" due to a momentary interruption of the connection across time and space. Flickering lasts until the start of the amphoron's next turn. While flickering, the amphoron can't be attacked and can't inflict damage. It regains 2 hit points when it rematerializes. A controller flickers only on a roll of 1 on 1d20, but if it does, all amphorons under its control also flicker.

ECOLOGY

Environment: Any
Organization: Work gang (1d4 workers) or crew (1d4 – 1 workers, 1d3 – 1 warriors, and 1d2 – 1 juggernauts)

Amphoron of Yothri (Juggernaut)

Juggernaut
XP 2,300 (CR 6)
N Large construct
Initiative +0

DEFENSE

AC 17 (natural armor)
hp: 102 (12d10 + 36)
Resistance: Damage from magic spells and spell-like effects
Immunity: Piercing damage from nonmagical weapons; poison damage; charm, fright, paralysis, poison, stun, unconsciousness

OFFENSE

Speed: 40 ft.

Multiattack: The amphoron attacks twice with whirling saw blades and once with its crane.
Melee Attack—Whirling Saw Blades: +7 to hit (reach 5 ft.; one creature). *Hit:* 2d8 + 4 slashing damage.
Melee Attack—Crane: +3 to hit (reach 15 ft.; one creature). *Hit:* target is grappled and lifted by the crane to be dropped into the juggernaut's processing chamber on the juggernaut's next turn (see Processing, below).

STATISTICS

Str 18 (+4), **Dex** 10 (+0), **Con** 16 (+3),
Int 6 (–2), **Wis** 10 (+0), **Cha** 6 (–2)
Languages: Common
Senses: Darkvision 60 ft.

TRAITS

Processing: The juggernaut amphoron is equipped with a large, moving crane mounted on its back. In addition to attacking with its whirling saw blades, the juggernaut can pick up one creature per round with its crane and hoist it aloft. On that creature's turn, it can make a Str (Athletics) or Dex (Acrobatics) check (with tactical disadvantage if the creature is wearing metal armor, because of the magnets in the crane), opposed by the juggernaut's Str check. If the creature wins the contest, it struggles free from the crane and drops harmlessly to the ground. If the juggernaut wins the contest, then on its next turn, it drops the creature into the processing chamber. Any creature dropped through the hatch is immediately reduced to 0 hit points and must make a death saving throw each turn until either it dies or the juggernaut amphoron is destroyed; a dying creature can't stabilize inside a juggernaut's processing chamber. If the creature dies, it emerges from the juggernaut's ejection hatch on the juggernaut's next turn as a brick of processed concentrate. A death saving throw is not required on a turn when the juggernaut flickers.
Flicker: Roll 1d6 for every amphoron in play at the start of its turn. On a roll of 1, the amphoron "flickers" due to a momentary interruption of the connection across time and space. Flickering lasts until the start of the amphoron's next turn. While flickering, the amphoron can't be attacked and can't inflict damage. It regains 2 hit points when it rematerializes. A controller flickers only on a roll of 1 on 1d20, but if it does, all amphorons under its control also flicker.

ECOLOGY

Environment: Any
Organization: Work gang (1d4 workers) or crew (1d4 workers, 1d3 – 1 warriors, and 1d2 – 1 juggernauts)

Amphorons of Yothri are mechanisms created by the artificers of that plane using their strange magic-science. Amphorons on the material plane are physical projections of a model that remains on Yothri; the artificer's mind, possibly using a lens apparatus of some kind, projects the device into the material plane, where it has a physical reality.

These projections can fail momentarily, a phenomenon known as "flickering." A flickering amphoron is visible as a faint, static-shrouded shape. Moreover, the artificer's control of more than one amphoron at a time depends on his mental connection to a single, controlling amphoron. If the artificer attempts to switch his mental connection from one amphoron to another, the process takes 1d6 rounds to complete.

The controlling amphoron has only a 1 in 20 chance of flickering, but if it does so, all of the amphorons under its control also flicker. Any amphoron can serve as the controller, but a single controller can't control more than six other amphorons, and an artificer can project his mind to only one controller at a time. Thus, unless the artificer has projected some apparatus (the possibilities are many, and left to the Referee's creativity) to allow remote controllers or auto-controls, the maximum number of amphorons encountered at time is seven (six controlled and one controller). When the artificer's nefarious schemes on the material plane are complete, he will likely not bother to disintegrate his amphorons, so their material substance remains on the material plane: operating randomly, remaining completely inert, or proceeding independently with their rudimentary intelligence.

An amphorons metallic insides are filled with wires and a gel-like flesh that allows the mental connection with the distant reality of Yothri, and also gives the creature its basic intelligence.

Worker amphorons are smaller than humans, and they move on four crablike legs. Warrior amphorons are usually used to protect worker amphorons or in situations where the artificer's schemes involve violence. The juggernaut amphoron is a harvester/processor the size of a semiattached trailer truck, with a moving crane mounted on its back and two huge circular saws mounted on its articulated arms. Exactly what the artificers of Yothri do with the bricks processed through their juggernauts remains a mystery.

Ant Lion

This creature resembles a giant gray or brown ant with leathery skin covered in coarse, black bristles. Its deep, inset eyes are black and its mouth is filled with rows of jagged teeth.

Ant Lion

XP 1,100 (CR 4)
Unaligned Large beast
Initiative +0

DEFENSE

AC 15 (natural armor)
hp: 93 (11d10 + 33)
Saving Throws: Con +5
Immunity: Charm

OFFENSE

Speed: 30 ft., burrow 10 ft.
Melee Attack—Bite: +4 to hit (reach 5 ft.; one creature). *Hit:* 3d10 + 2 piercing damage, and the target is grappled.

STATISTICS

Str 14 (+2), **Dex** 11 (+0), **Con** 17 (+3),
Int 2 (–4), **Wis** 10 (+0), **Cha** 4 (–3)
Languages: None
Skills: Stealth +2
Senses: Darkvision 60 ft., tremorsense 60 ft.

ECOLOGY

Environment: Warm deserts
Organization: Solitary or nest (mated pair plus 1d4 noncombatant young)

The ant lion is a vicious insectlike creature that lurks at the bottoms of pits and holes, feeding on those unfortunates that fall in.

An ant lion is about 9 feet long and weighs nearly 700 pounds. Ant lions dig deep, funnel-shaped pits in which to trap their prey. An ant lion pit is about 60 feet across and about 20 feet deep. A creature that steps on the pit must make a successful DC 16 Dexterity (Acrobatics) save or slip and fall into the funnel. It is there the ant lion waits, buried just under the surface of the ground. When prey falls to the center of the funnel, the ant lion surfaces and attacks, using its mandibles to grab and tear its prey. An ant lion never releases its grapple voluntarily.

Credit

The Ant Lion originally appeared in the First Edition *Monster Manual II* (© TSR/Wizards of the Coast, 1983) and is used by permission.

Copyright Notice
Author Scott Greene, based on original material by Gary Gygax.

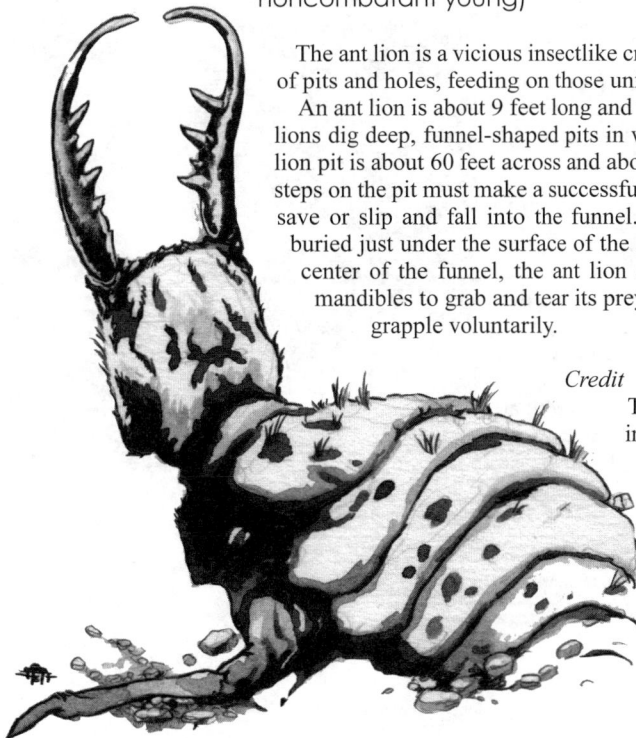

Ape, Flying

The creature's leathery wings blot out the sun, allowing your dazzled eyes to see that it's a great, hairy ape with enormous leathery wings. That's all you see before it dives into you.

Ape, Flying

XP 450 (CR 2)
CN Large monstrosity
Initiative +2

DEFENSE
AC 13 (natural armor)
hp: 45 (6d10 + 12)

OFFENSE
Speed: 30 ft., fly 60 ft.
Multiattack: The flying ape attacks twice with its fists.
Melee Attack—Fist: +6 to hit (reach 5 ft.; one creature). *Hit:* 1d6 + 4 bludgeoning damage. If both fists hit the same target, the ape also rends, doing another 2d6 slashing damage and the target is grappled and restrained.

STATISTICS
Str 18 (+4), **Dex** 14 (+2), **Con** 15 (+2), **Int** 6 (−2), **Wis** 11 (+0), **Cha** 7 (−2)
Languages: None (some flying apes understand Common but can't speak)
Skills: Perception +2

ECOLOGY
Environment: Temperate
Organization: Solitary

Flying apes are larger and more muscular than gorillas. Most have leathery wings similar to a bat's, but some have feathered wings like a bird's.

If a flying ape hits the same target with both of its slam attacks, it can either rend its foe for additional damage or gain a hold secure enough to carry the foe into the air, either to drop on a following round or to deliver the victim to the ape's evil overlord, as applicable.

Typical flying apes are considerably less intelligent than humans, but smarter ones are not uncommon. It has been observed that as their intelligence increases, so does their tendency toward cruelty and evil behavior.

Aranea

As the monstrosity approaches across its web, you notice that unlike other giant spiders, this one has a pair of diminutive arms and hands, and an oddly brain-shaped hump on its back.

Aranea
XP 700 (CR 3)
CE Large monstrosity
Initiative +3

DEFENSE
AC 14 (natural armor)
hp: 39 (6d10 + 6)
Saving Throws: Int +5

OFFENSE
Speed: 30 ft., climb 30 ft.
Melee Attack—Bite: +5 to hit (reach 5 ft.; one creature). *Hit:* 1d8 + 3 piercing damage, and the target must make a successful DC 11 Con saving throw or become poisoned (see Paralytic Poison, below).
Ranged Attack—Webs (recharge 5, 6): +5 to hit (range 30 ft./60 ft.; one creature). *Hit:* The target is restrained by webs. A webbed creature can use its action to attempt a DC 12 Str (Athletics) check to escape. The web can also be destroyed by 5 points of slashing or fire damage against AC 10.

STATISTICS
Str 14 (+2), **Dex** 16 (+3), **Con** 12 (+1),
Int 16 (+3), **Wis** 12 (+1), **Cha** 6 (–2)
Languages: Common, Deep Speech
Skills: Stealth +5
Senses: Blindsight 10 ft., darkvision 60 ft.

TRAITS
Paralytic Poison: The poisoned creature has tactical disadvantage on attack rolls and ability checks. At the end of each of its turns, the poisoned creature must attempt a Con saving throw. On a result of 16 or higher, the poisoned condition ends and the character becomes immune to this aranea's poison. On a result of 11–15, the poisoned condition continues. On a result of 10 or lower, the creature becomes paralyzed and no more saving throws are needed. Paralysis lasts for 1 hour or until the poison is neutralized.
Shapechange: An aranea can use its action to polymorph into a Medium beast or humanoid creature of CR 2 or lower, or from another form back into its own form. The aranea retains its Int, Wis, and Cha scores and its current hit points while polymorphed; otherwise, it takes on all the attributes of the adopted form. It can cast spells if the adopted form can provide the spell's verbal and somatic components, and it retains its paralytic poison trait if the adopted form has a bite attack. A shapechanged aranea reverts to its natural form when slain.
Spellcasting: All aranea are 3rd-level wizards. They use Intelligence as their casting ability (DC 13, attack +5) and require no material components for their spells. Typical known spells are listed below, but individual aranea can know different spells.
Cantrips (at will): *dancing lights, poison cloud, shocking grasp*
1st Level (x4): *charm person, sleep*

2nd Level (x2): *invisibility, mirror image*
Spider Climb: Aranea can climb any surface without making ability checks.

ECOLOGY
Environment: Temperate forests, caves, subterranean
Organization: Solitary or cluster (1d6 + 1)

An aranea is an intelligent, shapechanging spider with sorcerous powers. In its natural form, an aranea resembles a typical giant spider, with a humpbacked body a little bigger than a human torso and venomous fangs. Although considered a Large creature, an aranea's mass is no more than a typical human's; its size comes from its long legs. An aranea can be distinguished from other giant spiders by the hump on its back that houses its brain and by the fact that, in addition to eight legs, it has a fifth pair of limbs, each about 2 feet long, located ahead of the first pair of legs. These limbs end in hands, each equipped with three clawed fingers and a double-jointed thumb.

When aranea are encountered in groups, some might be young: identical in all respects to adult areanea but without the spellcasting trait.

Aranea often use their shapechanging ability to lure unsuspecting victims into ambushes. Less often, they assume humanoid form to infiltrate human societies, where they conduct research and gather information for their inscrutable purposes.

Arcanoplasm

This creature resembles a giant, pale amoeba shot through with stripes of dark gray.
Caught within its protoplasmic form are half-digested creatures of various types and sizes.

Arcanoplasm

XP 1,100 (CR 4)
N Large monstrosity
Initiative −2

DEFENSE

AC 12 (natural armor)
hp: 103 (9d10 + 54)
Saving Throws: Con +8
Immunity: Poison damage; paralysis, poison, polymorph, prone, stun, unconsciousness

OFFENSE

Speed: 40 ft.
Multiattack: The arcanoplasm slams once and constricts once.
Melee Attack—Slam: +4 to hit (reach 5 ft.; one creature). *Hit:* 1d6 + 2 bludgeoning damage plus 1d6 acid damage, and the target is grappled.
Melee Attack—Constriction: automatic hit (one creature already grappled by the arcanoplasm at the start of the arcanoplasm's turn). *Hit:* 1d6 + 2 bludgeoning damage plus 2d6 acid damage.

STATISTICS

Str 15 (+2), **Dex** 6 (−2), **Con** 22 (+6), **Int** 10 (+0), **Wis** 14 (+2), **Cha** 14 (+2)
Languages: Common, draconic (understands but can't speak)
Skills: Athletics +4, Stealth +0
Senses: Darkvision 60 ft.

TRAITS

Absorb Arcane Energy: Any arcane spell targeted at an arcanoplasm is automatically absorbed into its body. This cures 1 point of damage per 3 points of damage the spell would otherwise deal; nondamaging spells cure 1 point of damage per spell level. Spells that affect an area are not absorbed, but neither do they affect the arcanoplasm. The arcanoplasm can't absorb magic from spells that it cast itself using arcane spell mimicry, and it can't absorb divine magic, which affects it normally.
Amorphous: An arcanoplasm can move through gaps as small as 1 square inch without penalty.
Arcanesense: An arcanoplasm can automatically detect the location of any arcane spellcaster within 100 feet. This ability is not blocked by any material.
Arcane Spell Mimicry: As an action, an arcanoplasm can mimic any arcane spell of 4th level or lower cast within 30 feet of it on its next turn. The spell takes effect as if cast by a 7th-level sorcerer (DC 13, attack +6) and requires no components. Because of its innately magical nature, an arcanoplasm adds both its Con and Cha modifiers to concentration checks when it takes damage.

ECOLOGY

Environment: Underground
Organization: Solitary

Thought to be the result of a failed magic experiment, wizards and sorcerers alike have tried for years to gather information on this alien creature, but thus far such information has eluded even the most resourceful of researchers.

Arcanoplasms are found in areas where the residual energy of arcane magic lingers. Such areas include abandoned wizard's towers, keeps, dungeons, and so forth. Here they feed and remain until disturbed. Most encounters with these monsters take place in such locations, as the arcanoplasm rarely travels far from its lair. Because it lairs in ruins and similar places that attract adventurers, it rarely has to wait long between meals.

Arcanoplasms always target arcane spellcasting creatures first. Thanks to its ability to replicate spells cast near it, the arcanoplasm always tries to stay within 30 feet of a hostile arcane caster. Mimicked spells are cast at the foe deemed most threatening.

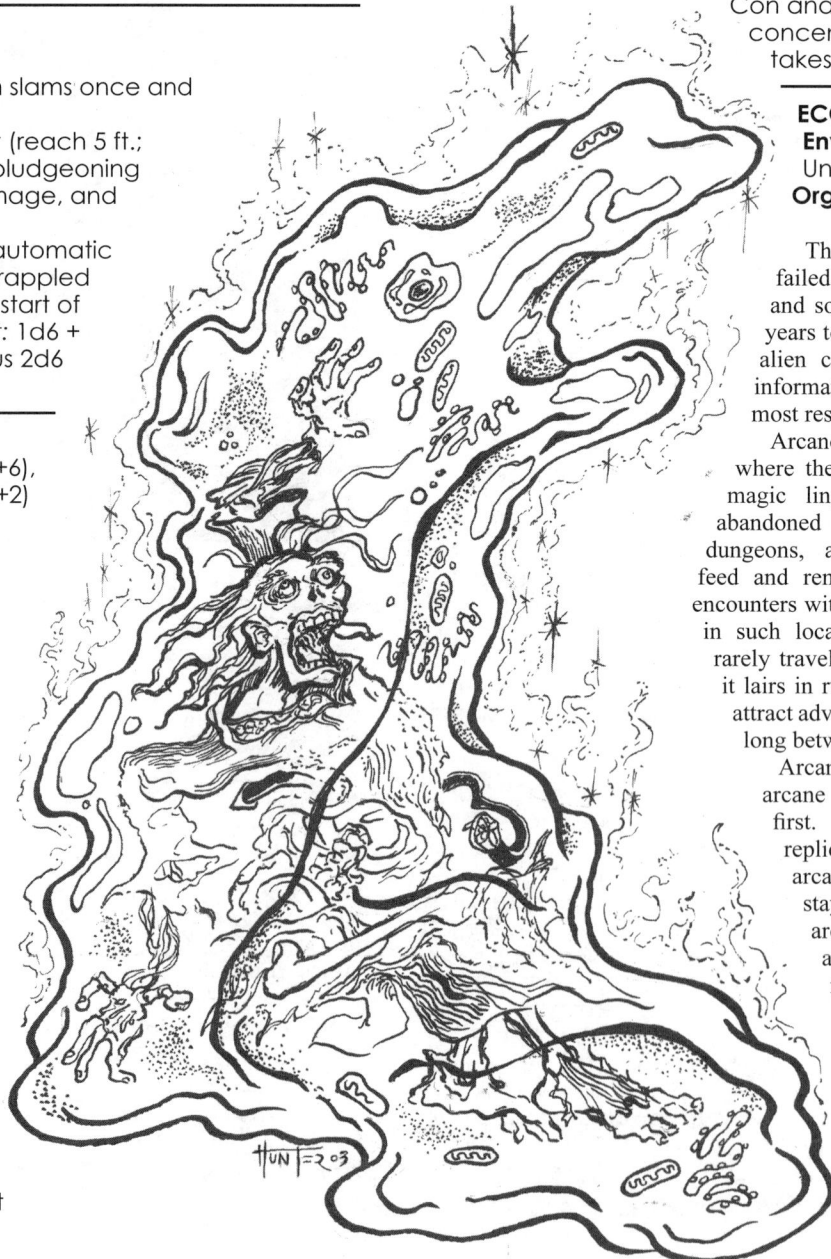

Artificer of Yothri

The artificers of Yothri are tall and skeletal, a construction of dark-hued metalloid bones acting as the framework for artificial tubes and organs. They wear hoods and long, black robes—perhaps a necessity on the dead world they inhabit in a distant and eroding reality.

Artificer of Yothri

XP 1,800 (CR 5)
CE Medium aberration
Initiative +2

DEFENSE

AC 16 (natural armor)
hp: 66 (12d8 + 12)
Resistance: Damage from magic spells and spell-like effects
Immunity: Nondamaging effects from magic spells and spell-like effects

OFFENSE

Speed: 20 ft.
Multiattack: An artificer of Yothri attacks twice with claws.
Melee Attack—Claw: +5 to hit (reach 5 ft.; one creature). *Hit:* 1d12 + 2 slashing damage.

STATISTICS

Str 8 (−1), **Dex** 14 (+2), **Con** 12 (+1), **Int** 20 (+5), **Wis** 11 (+0), **Cha** 15 (+2)
Languages: Any
Skills: Intimidation +5, Stealth +5
Senses: Blindsight 60 ft.

TRAITS

Spellcasting: The artificers of Yothri replicate the effects of magic with their alien science (that only they are capable of understanding). They have the spellcasting capability of 9th-level wizards, but their spellcasting requires no components. They use Intelligence as their casting ability (DC 16, attack +8). Typical spells are listed below, but individual artificers can know different spells.

Cantrips (at will): *mage hand, shocking grasp*
1st Level (x4): *charm person, mage armor, ray of sickness, sleep*
2nd Level (x3): *mirror image, see invisibility*
3rd Level (x3): *counterspell, protection from energy*
4th Level (x3): *dimension door, wall of fire*
5th Level (x1): *telekinesis*

ECOLOGY

Environment: Any
Organization: Solitary or expedition (1 artificer plus a work gang of amphorons)

The artificers originate on Yothri, a distant world—perhaps an alien dimension—where reality itself is crumbling. They live in baroque palaces of green glass and alien metal, twisted into unnatural shapes, domes, and bubbles. The artificers are mutually hostile, each coveting the others' resources and knowledge. It is remotely possible that player characters might be kidnapped to serve an artificer by attacking the citadel of a rival artificer in the barren, suppurating wastelands of Yothri.

Artificers employ the Science of Yothri, which is a mix of psychic power, alien magic, and unfathomable technology impossible to achieve outside the decaying physical reality of Yothri itself.

An artificer might be encountered alone if he or she hopes to avoid attracting attention, but more often, they travel with a work gang of amphorons for protection and to handle all physical labor. They can maintain a mental connection with a controller amphoron anywhere in the universe, including on other planes of existence. (See the entry "Amphorons of Yothri" for more information on such connections.)

Credit
Author Matt Finch; first appeared in *Knockspell* Magazine #1

Ascomoid

This creature appears as a large, wide puffball of living fungus. Its surface is brownish-green. Small pocks dot its form, seeming to function as some sort of sensory organs.

Ascomoid
XP 700 (CR 3)
Unaligned Large plant (fungus)
Initiative +1

DEFENSE
AC 12 (natural armor)
hp: 76 (9d10 + 27)
Saving Throws: Con +5
Resistance: Bludgeoning and slashing damage from nonmagical weapons; fire and lightning damage
Immunity: Charm, prone, stun, unconsciousness

OFFENSE
Speed: 40 ft.
Melee Attack—Slam: +6 to hit (reach 5 ft.; one creature). *Hit:* 3d8 + 3 bludgeoning damage.
Area Attack—Spores (recharge 5, 6): automatic hit (20-ft. radius sphere within 30 ft. range; creatures in sphere). *Hit:* creatures in the sphere must make a successful DC 16 Con save against poison or take 2d6 poison damage and become nauseated (incapacitated) for 1d4 rounds. A successful save negates the poison damage but not the incapacitated condition, and also makes the creature immune to further spore attacks from the same ascomoid for 24 hours.

STATISTICS
Str 19 (+4), **Dex** 13 (+1), **Con** 17 (+3),
Int 0 (–5), **Wis** 11 (+0), **Cha** 1 (–5)
Languages: None
Senses: Tremorsense 60 ft.

TRAITS
Trample: As the ascomoid moves, it can enter spaces occupied by enemies but can't stop there. Creatures in spaces the ascomoid enters can attempt DC 15 Dex saving throws. On a failed save, the creature takes 2d10 + 4 bludgeoning damage and is knocked prone; on a successful save, the creature moves 5 feet to get out of the ascomoid's path and can make an opportunity attack if it's allowed to react. An ascomoid can attempt to trample any number of creatures during its move, but it can't trample the same creature more than once per round.

ECOLOGY
Environment: Underground
Organization: Solitary

Ascomoids are subterranean fungus monsters. They feed by sitting atop a slain creature and absorbing its body fluids into the ascomoid's own form. Creatures slain in this manner appear as rotting husks.

Ascomoids generally avoid light and the surface world, though they have no adverse reaction to sunlight or bright light. The typical ascomoid lair is a large, damp, dark, natural cavern with only one way in or out. Bones from its victims are strewn about the lair. The monster has no use for treasure, but the possessions of those it killed tend to be scattered loosely all over its lair. Fragile items tend to be destroyed by the ascomoid's great weight as it feeds.

The average ascomoid is 10 feet wide and weighs 300 pounds.

Credit
The Ascomoid originally appeared in *Dragon #68* (© TSR/Wizards of the Coast, 1982) and later in the First Edition *Monster Manual II* (© TSR/Wizards of the Coast, 1983) and is used by permission.

Copyright Notice
Author Scott Greene, based on original material by Gary Gygax.

Assassin Bug

This large insect has a narrow head ending in a segmented beak or proboscis. The creature's carapace is dull brownish-black, and its front jackknife legs are covered in thousands of small hairs. Two long segmented antennae jut from its head.

Assassin Bug

XP 1,800 (CR 5)
Unaligned Medium beast
Initiative +3

DEFENSE

AC 16 (natural armor)
hp: 120 (16d8 + 48)
Immunity: Charm

OFFENSE

Speed: 30 ft., climb 20 ft., fly 50 ft.
Multiattack: The assassin bug attacks once with claws and bites once.
Melee Attack—Claws: +6 to hit (reach 5 ft.; one creature). *Hit:* 2d6 + 3 slashing damage, and the target must make a successful DC 13 Dex saving throw or be grappled by the assassin bug.
Melee Attack—Bite: automatic hit (reach 5 ft.; one creature grappled by the assassin bug). *Hit:* 2d8 + 3 piercing damage plus 1d8 poison damage, and the creature's maximum number of hit points is reduced by the amount of the poison damage. The creature's maximum number of hit points returns to normal after a long rest or when the poison is neutralized.

STATISTICS

Str 14 (+2), **Dex** 17 (+3), **Con** 16 (+3),
Int 0 (–5), **Wis** 12 (+1), **Cha** 9 (–1)
Languages: None
Senses: Darkvision 60 ft.

ECOLOGY

Environment: Temperate forests
Organization: Solitary, cluster (2–5), or colony (6–11)

Assassin bugs are predatory insects that feed on the blood and tissue of living creatures. Actively hunting or passively waiting for its prey, an assassin bug is a formidable killing machine that has few enemies.

Although often encountered alone, assassin bugs are communal creatures. Nests containing up to 20 creatures have been found. Most nests contain at least one female of mating age. During mating season, the female deposits a sticky clutch of 2d4 eggs in a narrow nest scraped into the forest floor. The eggs hatch within two weeks. Newborn assassin bugs look exactly like their adult counterparts (other than being smaller). An assassin bug goes through several growth stages before finally reaching adult stage within one year.

An assassin bug stands 5 feet tall. Its body is segmented, and most are dull brownish black (though red and black or even yellowish-brown assassin bugs have been reported). Its front, curved legs (called jackknife legs) are black and covered in tiny hairs that aid it in climbing as well as capturing its prey. An assassin bug has two pairs of wings that it keeps folded against its back when not flying.

Depending on the disposition of the assassin bug, it might wait in ambush for prey to come close, or it might actively seek out live food. In either case, when a victim is within range, the assassin bug leaps to the attack, attempting to grapple its prey so it can inject its organ-dissolving saliva. A victim that dies is kept in the assassin bug's lair for several weeks as it and any others in the nest slurp up the liquefied internals of the victim.

Astral Moth

The creature moves like a dream on mothlike wings that flutter gracefully in a breeze only it can feel.

Astral Moth

XP 25 (CR 1/8)
(alignment varies) Large monstrosity
Initiative +2

DEFENSE

AC 12
hp: 32 (5d10 + 5)

OFFENSE

Speed: 10 ft., fly 30 ft.
Melee Attack—Bite: +5 to hit (reach 5 ft.; one creature). *Hit:* 1d6 + 3 piercing damage.

STATISTICS

Str 16 (+3), **Dex** 14 (+2), **Con** 12 (+1), **Int** 4 (–3), **Wis** 10 (+0), **Cha** 10 (+0)
Languages: Any (understands via telepathy but can't speak)
Senses: Darkvision 60 ft.

TRAITS

Interplanar Flight: Astral moths can fly into the spaces between realities and travel effortlessly between planes of existence and dimensions. The time required for such travel varies in accordance with the intended destination, but it would be rare for a trip of any distance to take more than 24 hours.

Mount: An astral moth can carry a single Medium rider, two Small riders, or up to ten Tiny riders.

ECOLOGY

Environment: Any
Organization: Solitary or eclipse (2d6)

Astral moths are large, mothlike creatures with the bizarre ability to carry other creatures between planes of existence or into other dimensions.

The origins of these rare creatures are lost in the sands of time, but three varieties are known. The dark and white varieties are both semiintelligent, with the dark-colored moths being Chaotic Neutral in alignment and the white ones being Lawful Neutral. There is also a grey variety which is believed to be closer to the original breeding stock, having only animal intelligence and Neutral alignment. All three varieties are capable of planar travel and of receiving instructions by means of rudimentary telepathy.

Training is essential for an astral moth that is intended for use as a mount, because poorly trained and untrained astral moths may try to throw off a rider mid-journey—a significant hazard in some of the realms astral moths can cross.

The creatures themselves are relatively harmless. The true threat from an astral moth is whatever strange being might be riding it. Astral moths have been used by many lost and forgotten nonhuman civilizations that existed in different times, planes, and dimensions.

They are, of course, greatly prized by wizards. The egg of an astral moth can fetch 5,000 gp from the right buyer. Capturing a wild adult is possible, but care must be taken to keep it from getting airborne: if the creature is able to take wing, it will simply escape into unknown dimensions, possibly dragging its would-be captor along into distant realms with no hope of a safe return.

Credit
Author Matt Finch

Astral Shark

This creature resembles a shark with sickly white skin, tinged here and there with smears of pink. Its dorsal fin is jagged and slightly curved, and the creature's eyes are large, bulbous, and lidless.

Astral Shark
XP 1,800 (CR 5)
N Large fiend
Initiative +2

DEFENSE
AC 14 (natural armor)
hp: 102 (12d10 + 36)

OFFENSE
Speed: 60 ft.
Melee Attack—Bite: +6 to hit (reach 5 ft.; one creature). *Hit:* 2d12 + 3 piercing damage.

STATISTICS
Str 16 (+3), **Dex** 15 (+2), **Con** 17 (+3), **Int** 6 (–2), **Wis** 12 (+1), **Cha** 6 (–2)
Languages: None
Skills: Stealth +5
Senses: Darkvision 60 ft.

TRAITS
Astral Scent: An astral shark is highly attuned to the energy of a traveler in the Astral Plane. It automatically detects all living creatures within 180 ft. of itself.
Sever Silver Cord: When an astral shark scores a critical hit with its bite, in addition to the normal effects of a critical hit, the target creature must attempt a DC 10 Dexterity saving throw. Failure indicates that the astral shark severed the silver cord connecting the target's astral form to its material body, and the target creature dies instantly.

ECOLOGY
Environment: Astral plane
Organization: Solitary or school (2–5)

An astral shark is a sleek creature that resembles a shark but spends its entire life in the Astral Plane; astral sharks can't materialize on any other plane. Among the lower life forms of the Astral Plane, the astral shark is near the top of the food chain. When astral sharks detect extraplanar visitors nearby, the astral sharks attack them in preference to any other prey and seldom stop attacking until they're killed. It is unknown if the astral shark is drawn to the visitors' strange energy or if it somehow gains special nutrition from them or from the silver cord that connects an astral traveler to its material body.

Most astral sharks are 10 to 15 feet long, but they can grow to lengths of nearly 30 feet. An astral shark's tactics resemble those of its Material Plane counterpart: circling its prey, then darting in and biting with its powerful jaws. Astral sharks are greatly feared by experienced astral travelers.

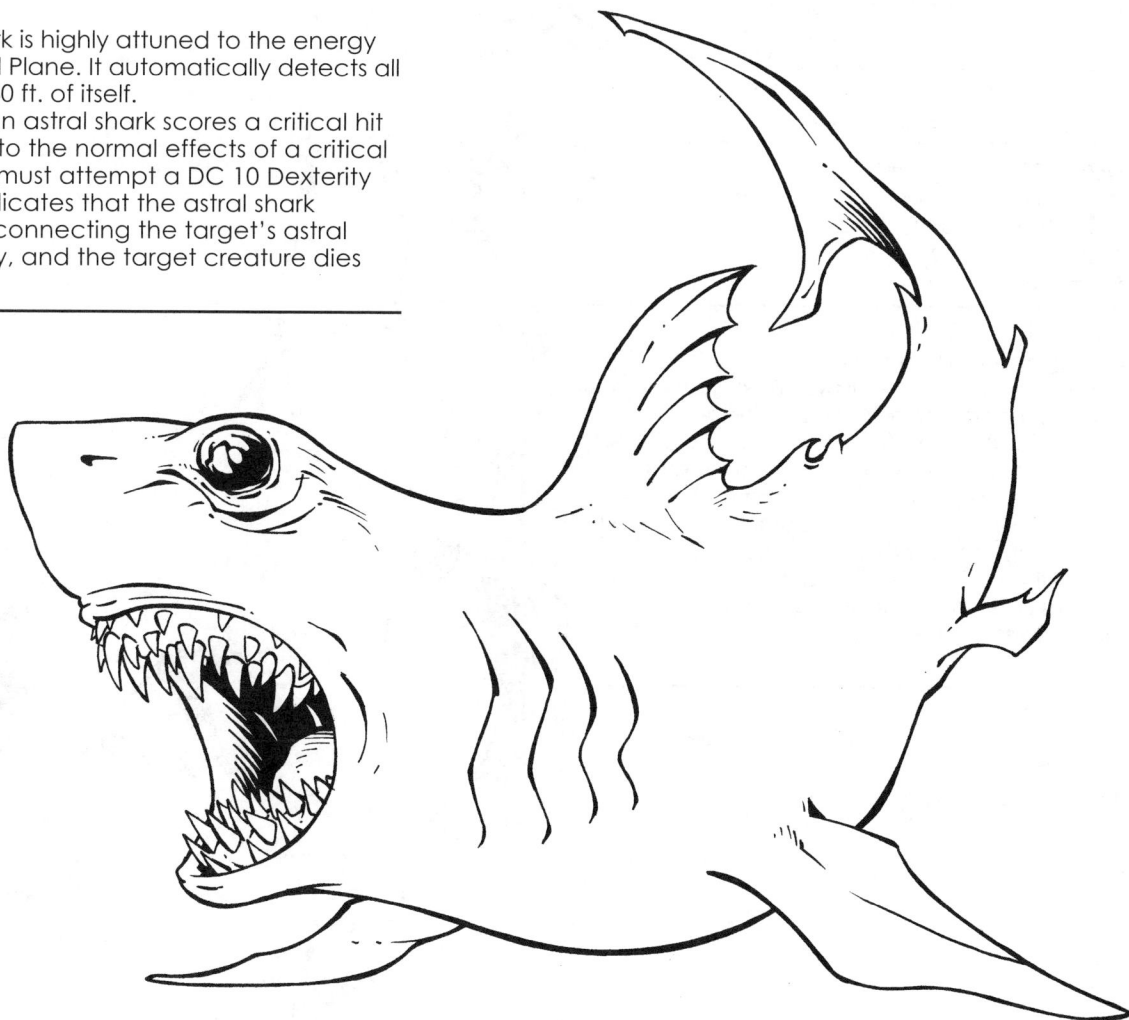

Aurumvorax

This small, feral creature resembles an eight-legged wolf with bright golden fur.

Aurumvorax (Golden Gorger)
XP 1,800 (CR 5)
Unaligned Small monstrosity
Initiative +5

DEFENSE
AC 16 (natural armor)
hp: 78 (12d6 + 36)
Resistance: Fire damage
Immunity: Poison damage; poison

OFFENSE
Speed: 30 ft., burrow 10 ft.
Multiattack: The aurumvorax bites once and attacks twice with its claws. If the aurumvorax has its jaws locked onto a target, it rakes that target instead of biting.
Melee Attack—Bite: +8 to hit (reach 5 ft.; one creature). *Hit:* 1d8 + 5 piercing damage, and the aurumvorax locks its jaws onto the target (see below).
Melee Attack—Claws: +8 to hit (reach 5 ft.; one creature). *Hit:* 2d6 + 5 slashing damage.
Melee Attack—Rake: automatic hit (reach 0 ft.; one creature the aurumvorax's jaws were locked onto at the start of the aurumvorax's turn). *Hit:* 4d6 + 5 slashing damage.

STATISTICS
Str 12 (+1), **Dex** 20 (+5), **Con** 16 (+3), **Int** 2 (–4), **Wis** 13 (+1), **Cha** 11 (+0)
Languages: None
Senses: Darkvision 60 ft.

TRAITS
Locking Jaws: When the aurumvorax bites a creature and locks its jaws, the aurumvorax enters that creature's space. The aurumvorax can't move on its own while its jaws are locked, but it moves with the other creature. To get free from the aurumvorax, the target creature or an adjacent ally must use its action to make a successful DC 16 Str (Athletics) check. The aurumvorax can't use its bite attack again until it releases its jaws, which automatically moves it out of that creature's space.

ECOLOGY
Environment: Temperate plains, hills, or forests
Organization: Solitary or pair

The aurumvorax (also called the golden gorger) is an extremely vicious creature. It will attack any living prey it meets in its territory, and its territory often extends up to a mile in all directions from its lair.

Despite being just 3 feet long, an aurumvorax weighs between 100 and 150 pounds. The creature's copper-colored claws are razor sharp. Its eyes are silver with gold pupils, and its whiskers are bronze in color.

The aurumvorax attacks by biting a foe, locking its jaws, then leaping onto the creature and shredding it with a tornado of claws. Once its jaws are locked onto an enemy, an aurumvorax doesn't let go until either it or its prey is dead.

Credit

The Aurumvorax originally appeared in the First Edition *Monster Manual II* (© TSR/Wizards of the Coast, 1983) and is used by permission.

Copyright Notice

Author Scott Greene, based on original material by Gary Gygax.

Basilisk, Crimson

This creature looks like a stocky, eight-legged, crimson-scaled reptile. A row of bony spines juts from its back and runs the length of its body. Its eyes have a ghostly blue glow.

Crimson Basilisk

XP 700 (CR 3)
Unaligned Medium monstrosity
Initiative +0

DEFENSE

AC 13 (natural armor)
hp: 60 (8d8 + 24)

OFFENSE

Speed: 20 ft.
Melee Attack—Bite: +5 to hit (reach 5 ft.; one creature). *Hit:* 2d8 + 3 piercing damage plus 1d8 acid damage (also see Blood Frenzy below).

STATISTICS

Str 16 (+3), **Dex** 10 (+0), **Con** 16 (+3),
Int 2 (−4), **Wis** 12 (+1), **Cha** 10 (+0)
Languages: None
Skills: Perception +3, Stealth +2
Senses: Darkvision 60 ft.

TRAITS

Blood Frenzy: A crimson basilisk that detects fresh blood within 30 feet enters a frenzied state at the start of its next turn, as do any other crimson basilisks within 30 feet of the frenzied basilisk. Frenzied crimson basilisks fight until they are slain or until 1 minute has passed without the basilisk being attacked. While frenzied, they gain tactical advantage on attack rolls and saving throws, their acid damage increases to 2d8, and their armor class decreases to 11.

Stone Camouflage: A crimson basilisk has tactical advantage on Stealth checks in a stony environment or when it has a stony background.

Wounding Gaze: A creature within 30 feet of a crimson basilisk that meets the monster's gaze must make a DC 13 Con saving throw. Failure means the creature takes 1d6 points of damage as blood weeps from the victim's eyes, ears, nose, and mouth. Creatures without blood and other crimson basilisks are immune to this effect. A creature that is capable of taking actions can look away at the start of its turn to avoid the basilisk's gaze, but if it targets the basilisk

while averting its gaze, it suffers all the usual penalties for attacking an unseen target.

ECOLOGY

Environment: Underground
Organization: Solitary or pack (2–5)

Crimson basilisks are variants of the common basilisk, and in some cases more dangerous. Adventurers might be relieved that they won't be turned to stone, but such relief is usually short-lived when they meet the creature's gaze.

Crimson basilisks are subterranean carnivores with a voracious appetite that is only whetted when they get the thing they desire most—blood. While they can survive on a diet of plants, mosses, and meat, they prefer blood above all else, and they will even attack their own kind when food is scarce.

A typical crimson basilisk lair is a stony cavern that reeks of blood and whose walls and ground are covered and caked in dried blood. The lair usually contains up to five of these creatures, with an equal chance of males and females. Up to four young are likely to be present as well. Young crimson basilisks do not fight.

A crimson basilisk can grow up to 6 feet long and weigh over 400 pounds. Its tough, armored scales are dull crimson, but it can change its color (as a bonus action) to match its surroundings. Its eight legs are stout and end in sharpened claws. The spines on its back are a darker crimson than its body, especially in males. Its eyes glow with a ghostly blue light.

A crimson basilisk most often attacks from ambush, using its ability to camouflage itself against its surroundings and lying in wait for prey to wander close. They automatically sense the presence of blood within 30 feet; any wounded character is detected automatically within that range. Fortunately, only very fresh blood prompts a frenzy; a basilisk must cause fresh bleeding with its bite or its gaze to trigger the frenzy.

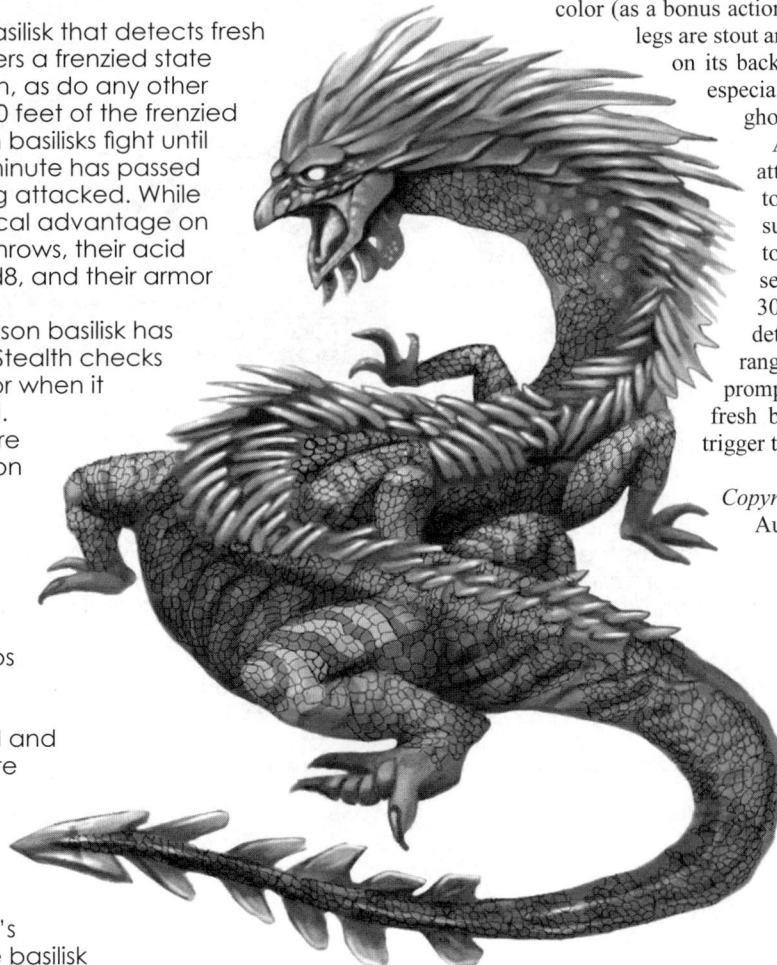

Basilisk, Greater

This creature is a thick-bodied reptile with eight legs.
Its eyes glow with an eerie, pale green incandescence.

Basilisk, Greater
XP 1,800 (CR 5)
NE Large monstrosity
Initiative −1

DEFENSE
AC 16 (natural armor)
hp: 95 (10d10 + 40)
Saving Throws: Con +7

OFFENSE
Speed: 20 ft.
Multiattack: The greater basilisk bites once and attacks once with claws.
Melee Attack—Bite: +7 to hit (reach 5 ft.; one creature). *Hit:* 3d6 + 4 piercing damage plus 3d6 poison damage.
Melee Attack—Claws: +7 to hit (reach 5 ft.; one creature). *Hit:* 2d6 + 4 slashing damage plus 2d6 poison damage.

STATISTICS
Str 19 (+4), **Dex** 8 (−1), **Con** 18 (+4),
Int 6 (−2), **Wis** 10 (+0), **Cha** 7 (−2)
Languages: None
Skills: Perception +6, Stealth +5
Senses: Darkvision 60 ft.

TRAITS
Foul Breath: A greater basilisk's breath is extremely foul. Any creature adjacent to a greater basilisk's head (within 5 feet of its head—this applies automatically to anyone targeted by the basilisk's bite) must make a DC 15 Con saving throw. Failure indicates the creature is poisoned (per the condition) until it moves more than 5 feet away from the basilisk's head and then makes a successful save at the end of its turn. A successful save means the creature is immune to this basilisk's breath for 24 hours.

Gaze: A living creature that starts its turn within 30 feet of a greater basilisk must make a DC 15 Con saving throw. Failure indicates the creature begins turning to stone; it immediately becomes restrained, and it must make another DC 15 Con saving throw at the end of its next turn. Success on the second saving throw ends this effect. Failure on the second saving throw means the creature is petrified. A creature that is capable of taking actions can look away to avoid the greater basilisk's gaze, but if it targets the basilisk while averting its gaze, the creature suffers all the usual penalties for attacking an unseen target. Creatures that are blind, unconscious, or unable to see the greater basilisk for any other reason are immune to this attack.

ECOLOGY
Environment: Warm deserts
Organization: Solitary or pair

A larger, malevolently intelligent cousin of the basilisk, the greater basilisk is a 12-foot long reptilian monster with dull brown skin and a yellow underbelly. Sages believe the greater basilisk hails from the Elemental Plane of Earth.

Greater basilisks rear up on their hind legs and slash opponents with their poisonous claws while also using their deadly petrification gaze. They have a fearsome bite and breath so foul that all living creatures within 5 feet can be affected by it just by entering or remaining in the area.

Credit
The Greater Basilisk originally appeared in the First Edition *Monster Manual II* (© TSR/Wizards of the Coast, 1983) and is used by permission.

Copyright Notice
Author Scott Greene, based on original material by Gary Gygax.

Bat, Doombat

This creature appears as a giant black bat with glowing yellow eyes.

Bat, Doombat

XP 700 (CR 3)
Unaligned Large monstrosity
Initiative +5

DEFENSE
AC 15
hp: 59 (7d10 + 21)

OFFENSE
Speed: 10 ft., fly 50 ft.
Multiattack: The doombat bites once and attacks once with its tail.
Melee Attack—Bite: +7 to hit (reach 5 ft.; one creature).
   Hit: 2d8 + 5 piercing damage.
Melee Attack—Tail: +7 to hit (reach 10 ft.; one creature).
   Hit: 1d8 + 5 bludgeoning damage.

STATISTICS
Str 17 (+3), **Dex** 21 (+5), **Con** 17 (+3),
Int 2 (−4), **Wis** 12 (+1), **Cha** 6 (−2)
Languages: None
Skills: Perception +3
Senses: Blindsight 60 ft.

TRAITS
Shriek (recharge 5, 6): A doombat can emit a piercing shriek as an action. All creatures that can hear the doombat's shriek (except other doombats) within a 100-ft. radius must make a DC 13 Wis saving throw. Failure indicates that the creature has tactical disadvantage on all attack rolls and ability checks. An affected creature can repeat the saving throw at the end of each of its turns, ending the effect early with a successful save. A successful saving throw also gives the creature immunity to the shrieks of that doombat for 24 hours.
Yip: Doombats yip constantly while in combat, and the noise interferes with spellcasters' concentration. Creatures within 100 ft. of any number of yipping doombats must make a DC 13 Int saving throw every time they attempt to cast a spell. Success indicates the spell is cast. Failure with a result of 9 or higher indicates the spell is not cast, but the spell slot is not expended. Failure with a result of 8 or lower indicates the spell is not cast and the spell slot is expended.

ECOLOGY
Environment: Underground
Organization: Solitary or colony (2–5)

The doombat is a nocturnal hunter that desires living flesh to sustain it. The yipping of doombats can be heard long before the creatures arrive on the scene.

The doombat has a 10-ft. wingspan, though specimens with wingspans reaching 25 feet have been reported.

Doombats attack any living thing they encounter. They typically shriek before entering melee and again whenever possible. Their yipping is constant for the duration of the fight.

Credit
   The Doombat originally appeared in the First Edition *Fiend Folio* (© TSR/Wizards of the Coast, 1981) and is used by permission.

Copyright Notice
   Author Scott Greene, based on original material by Julian Lawrence.

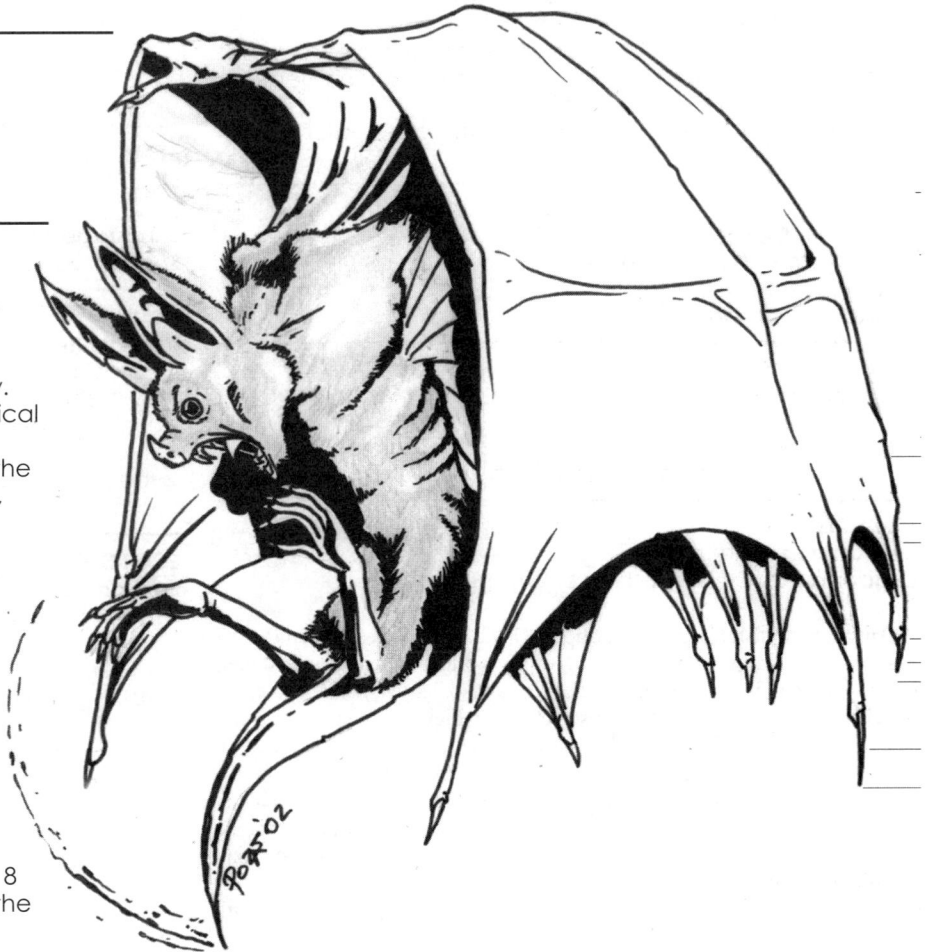

Beetle, Giant Rhinoceros

This creature is a giant beetle with a grayish-brown carapace and wing-covers. A large, brownish-black "horn" is positioned between its mandibles.

Giant Rhinoceros Beetle

XP 1,100 (CR 4)
Unaligned Large beast
Initiative +0

DEFENSE
AC 18 (natural armor)
hp: 95 (10d10 + 40)

OFFENSE
Speed: 20 ft.
Melee Attack—Gore: +7 to hit (reach 5 ft.; one creature that was not adjacent to the beetle at the start of the beetle's turn). *Hit:* 3d8 + 5 piercing damage.
Melee Attack—Bite: +7 to hit (reach 5 ft.; one creature). *Hit:* 2d6 + 5 piercing damage.

STATISTICS
Str 20 (+5), **Dex** 10 (+0), **Con** 18 (+4),
Int 2 (–4), **Wis** 10 (+0), **Cha** 6 (–2)
Languages: None
Senses: Darkvision 60 ft.

TRAITS
Symbiotic Vermin: Any living creature other than another giant beetle that ends its turn adjacent to a giant rhinoceros beetle must make a successful DC 15 Con saving throw or be poisoned until the end of their next turn.

ECOLOGY
Environment: Temperate forests
Organization: Cluster (2–5) or swarm (6–11)

An adult rhinoceros beetle is about 10 feet long. These creatures are found in the warm jungles and forests of the world, where they spend their days searching for plants, fruits, berries, and other creatures—some of which are ferocious predators themselves—on which to sustain themselves. They also scavenge the carcasses of dead animals, wading into the carrion as they shred the remains with their mandibles. In the process, the beetle inevitably becomes smeared with blood and gets chunks of carrion caught in its carapace. Consequently, giant rhinoceros beetles are accompanied everywhere by clouds of flies, gnats, and other tiny, buzzing, stinging vermin that make them very unpleasant to stand near.

A giant rhinoceros beetle charges heedlessly into melee, slashing with its horn whenever it can charge up to an opponent and biting with its razor sharp mandibles if it has a target already adjacent.

Credit
The Rhinoceros Beetle originally appeared in the First Edition *Monster Manual* (© TSR/Wizards of the Coast, 1977) and is used by permission.

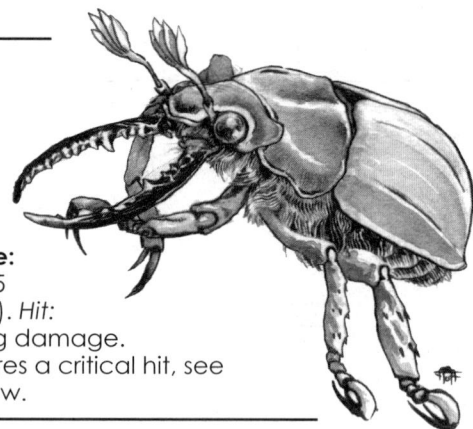

Beetle, Giant Slicer

This creature is a giant beetle with a triangular head and two long, razor sharp mandibles. Its body is jet black.

Giant Slicer Beetle

XP 700 (CR 3)
Unaligned Large beast
Initiative +0

DEFENSE
AC 15 (natural armor)
hp: 59 (7d10 + 21)

OFFENSE
Speed: 20 ft.
Melee Attack—Bite: +7 to hit (reach 5 ft.; one creature). *Hit:* 2d10 + 5 piercing damage. If this attack scores a critical hit, see Vorpal Bite, below.

STATISTICS
Str 20 (+5), **Dex** 10 (+0), **Con** 16 (+3),
Int 2 (–4), **Wis** 10 (+0), **Cha** 9 (–1)
Languages: None
Senses: Darkvision 60 ft.

TRAITS
Vorpal Bite: The mandibles of a slicer beetle are extremely sharp. It scores a critical hit if the attack roll is a natural 19 or 20. If a slicer beetle scores a critical hit on its attack roll, the affected creature must make a DC 10 Dex saving throw. Failure indicates the slicer beetle severed one of the opponent's extremities (roll 1d8: 1–4 = arm, 5–8 = leg; even = right, odd = left).

ECOLOGY
Environment: Temperate forests
Organization: Solitary or cluster (2–5)

The slicer beetle closely resembles a large stag beetle and is often mistaken for one. However, the slicer beetle is more aggressive than the stag beetle. The creature dines on carrion, fresh meat, and leaves.

Slicer beetles are about 10 feet long, but they can grow to lengths of 20 feet or more.

The slicer beetle attacks by biting with its razor-sharp mandibles. Their lairs are often littered with the severed limbs of its victims.

Credit
The Slicer Beetle originally appeared in the First Edition *Monster Manual II* (© TSR/Wizards of the Coast, 1983) and is used by permission.

Beetle, Giant Water

This giant beetle has a cylindrical and hydrodynamic body that tapers to a pointed tail section.
Its wing covers and carapace are brownish black, and its legs are dull yellow.
A silver stripe runs lengthwise along its back.

Giant Water Beetle

XP 100 (CR 1/2)
Unaligned Medium beast (aquatic)
Initiative +1

DEFENSE
AC 14 (natural armor)
hp: 30 (4d8 + 12)

OFFENSE
Speed: 10 ft., swim 60 ft.
Melee Attack—Bite: +4 to hit (reach 5 ft.; one creature). *Hit:* 1d10 + 2 piercing damage.

STATISTICS
Str 15 (+2), **Dex** 13 (+1), **Con** 16 (+3),
Int 2 (–4), **Wis** 10 (+0), **Cha** 9 (–1)
Languages: None
Senses: Tremorsense 60 ft. when underwater

TRAITS
Ink Cloud (recharge 6): As a bonus action while it is underwater, a giant water beetle can emit a cloud of jet-black ink that fills a sphere centered on itself with a radius of 10 feet. The area inside the ink cloud is heavily obscured.
Water Dependent: Giant water beetles can survive out of water for eight hours. After that, they gain one level of exhaustion every 10 minutes until they die or return to fresh water.

ECOLOGY
Environment: Fresh water
Organization: Cluster (2–5) or colony (6–11)

These highly aggressive beetles make their home in deep fresh water such as slow-moving rivers, lakes, large pools, and inland seas. They can be found in any climate, from the warmest to the coldest. Giant water beetles are predators. They sustain themselves on fish and other aquatic animals. They spend most of their lives in the water, rarely emerging onto land. In the rare cases where they are encountered on land, a giant water beetle is seldom more than 30 feet from water. They are diurnal creatures, hunting during the day and sleeping in deep water at night. They dive with blinding speed when they spot a potential meal in the water. When not actively hunting, they sometimes simply drift along with the current.

The giant water beetle normally uses its ink to escape from attackers, but thanks to its tremorsense, it can fight inside the ink cloud without penalty.

Giant water beetles lair on the bottoms of lakes, rivers, and inland seas. A colony always contains at least one female giant water beetle and 2d4 eggs. Eggs hatch within three weeks after the female deposits them and reach full maturity in six to eight weeks.

When hunting, these creatures prefer to attack by ambushing their prey. They usually drift near the water's surface and dive down onto targets below them with surprising speed, but they have also been known to drift in darker water at greater depth and lunge upward to seize prey with their tough, sharp mandibles.

Copyright Notice
Author Scott Greene.

Biclops

At first glance this monstrosity appears to be a filthy ettin of huge size. Closer inspection reveals the true nature of the creature, as it has but one eye in the center of each ugly head.

Biclops

XP 2,300 (CR 6)
N Huge giant
Initiative +1

DEFENSE

AC 13 (hide armor)
hp: 115 (11d12 + 44)

OFFENSE

Speed: 30 ft.
Multiattack: A biclops attacks twice with its longsword or twice with spears.
Melee Attack—Longsword: +9 to hit (reach 10 ft.; one creature). *Hit:* 2d8 + 6 slashing damage.
Ranged Attack—Spear: +9 to hit (range 20/60 ft.; one creature). *Hit:* 2d6 + 6 piercing damage.

STATISTICS

Str 22 (+6), **Dex** 12 (+1), **Con** 18 (+4), **Int** 9 (−1), **Wis** 9 (−1), **Cha** 10 (+0)
Languages: Giant
Skills: Intimidate +3
Senses: Darkvision 60 ft.

TRAITS

Rock Thrower: A biclops without spears can throw boulders, tables, or any other large objects instead, with the same attack and damage statistics as its spear attack.
Two-Headed Action (recharge 4, 5, 6): After taking its normal action, a biclops can use a bonus action to attack (attacking twice, as normal), move, or search.
Two Heads: A biclops has tactical advantage on Wis and Int saving throws and on saving throws against being charmed, deafened, stunned, and knocked unconscious.
Wakeful: A biclops never falls fully asleep; one head always remains awake while the other sleeps.

ECOLOGY

Environment: Temperate and warm mountains
Organization: Solitary, pair, gang (2–4), or clan (5–8)

Despite their ferocious appearance, biclopes are generally peaceable creatures who live by hunting and herding giant longhorn sheep, which they keep for milk and wool. They are feared by less intelligent giants such as hill giants and trolls, whom most biclops will beat to death on sight. Biclopes have good relations with stone giants, with whom they trade finished metal weapons and goat cheese in exchange for raw ore and gold.

Adult male biclopes stand about 16 feet tall and weigh about 4,500 pounds. Females are slightly shorter and lighter. Both males and females dress in clothes of dark or dull colors (browns, greens, and dark reds are typical). Biclops skin ranges from ruddy brown to cinnamon, and their eye color is usually blue. Hair color is almost universally dark, though occasionally a fair-haired biclops is born (such a biclops is viewed as special among his or her kind). Warriors and protectors wear hide armor (sometimes with human-sized breastplates and other armor bits riveted on), and they always carry weapons.

A biclops can live to be 350 years old.

Biclopes fight with twin longswords. Each arm is controlled independently by a separate head. If given advanced warning, they prefer to chase off intruders with well-aimed spears and boulders hurled from great heights. They've also been known to rig controlled avalanches to crush invaders.

Biclopes live in tribelike communities in remote hills and mountains. They construct their homes from the stones and lumber of their environment. A typical biclops home has three rooms: a communal area where the family meets, a sleeping room, and a kitchen. Biclops families rely on each other for protection, food, and trade. External trade is often set up between biclopes and other races, particularly stone giants and dwarves. Less reputable tribes take prisoners for forced labor or even cannibalize humanoids and monstrous humanoids. In such a case, there is a 20% chance that a biclops lair contains 1d4 captive humanoids or monstrous humanoids.

Biclops leaders are usually fighters or barbarians. Most groups of biclopes include clerics (sometimes called shamans among the biclops race). Sorcerers, warlocks, and wizards are extremely rare among biclopes.

Copyright Notice
Author Scott Greene.

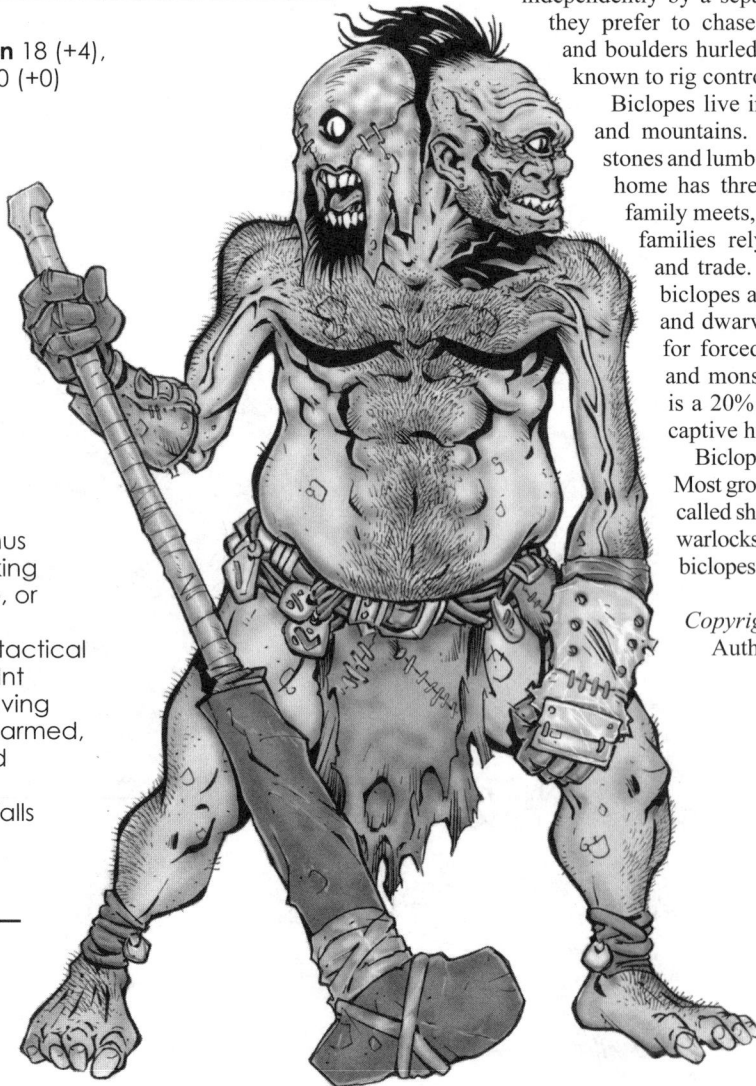

Blood Hawk

This creature appears as a hawk with red talons and a dull red beak.

Blood Hawk
XP 50 (CR 1/4)
Unaligned Small monstrosity
Initiative +3

DEFENSE
AC 13
hp: 5 (2d6 – 2)

OFFENSE
Speed: 10 ft., fly 60 ft.
Melee Attack—Talons: +5 to hit (reach 5 ft.; one creature).
Hit: 1d4 + 3 slashing damage and the target must make a successful DC 13 Dex saving throw or be blinded until the end of its next turn.

STATISTICS
Str 8 (–1), **Dex** 16 (+3), **Con** 8 (–1),
Int 2 (–4), **Wis** 14 (+2), **Cha** 6 (–2)
Languages: None
Skills: Perception +4
Senses: Darkvision 60 ft.

TRAITS
Keen Sight: A blood hawk has tactical advantage on Perception checks based on vision.

ECOLOGY
Environment: Any forest, hills, plains, and mountains
Organization: Flock (6–11)

The blood hawk is nearly identical to a normal hawk and is often mistaken for one, but a blood hawk is stronger and far more aggressive than a normal hawk. Blood hawks love the taste of human flesh and are relentless in their hunt for human prey. They often steal gems from the corpses of their humanoid prey, which they use to decorate their nests.

Blood hawks are fierce combatants that quickly swoop down on their prey to attack with their razor-sharp talons and beak. Once they attack and get the taste of flesh in their beaks, blood hawks seldom retreat.

Credit
The Blood Hawk originally appeared in the First Edition *Fiend Folio* (© TSR/Wizards of the Coast, 1981) and is used by permission.

Copyright Notice
Author Scott Greene, based on original material by Ian Livingstone.

Blood Orchid

This beast has three downward curving "petals" of flesh with a dark, pebbly outer hide and a pallid whitish underside. The petals end in split tips that converge beneath the blood orchid's bulbous body. The body is flexible and squishy, about one foot long and six inches in diameter, and terminates with a sphincter-shaped mouth front and center. A swarm of writhing, pallid tentacles dangle from its underside: there are 16 manipulator arms and eight thinner tendrils with red eyes at the ends. A second cluster of eye tendrils rises from its back.

Blood Orchid

XP 1,800 (CR 5)
CE Large aberration
Initiative +1

DEFENSE
AC 14 (natural armor)
hp: 85 (10d10 + 30)
Saving Throws: Wis +4
Resistance: Acid, cold, fire, and lightning damage
Immunity: Thunder damage

OFFENSE
Speed: 5 ft., fly 30 ft.
Multiattack: The blood orchid attacks six times, in any combination of tentacle slams and blood drain.
Melee Attack—Tentacle Slam: +5 to hit (reach 5 ft.; one creature). *Hit:* 1d6 + 2 bludgeoning damage, and the target is grappled.
Melee Attack—Blood Drain: automatic hit (reach 5 ft.; one creature already grappled by the blood orchid at the start of the blood orchid's turn). *Hit:* 1d8 piercing damage, and the target must make a successful DC 13 Con saving throw against poison or become unconscious. Unconscious characters can repeat the saving throw at the end of each of their turns; they regain consciousness on a successful save. A creature that makes a successful save against this attack becomes immune to the blood drain's unconsciousness effect for 24 hours.

STATISTICS
Str 15 (+2), **Dex** 12 (+1), **Con** 16 (+3),
Int 11 (+0), **Wis** 12 (+1), **Cha** 13 (+1)
Languages: Common (via telepathy)
Skills: Perception +7
Senses: Darkvision 60 ft.

TRAITS
All-Around Vision: A blood orchid sees in all directions at once. Enemies never gain tactical advantage or bonus damage against a blood orchid because of the presence of allies.
Telepathic Bond: Blood orchids communicate through a nonmagical telepathic bond. They can sense emotions in other blood orchids at distances up to 100 feet, can communicate fully with each other through telepathy at a distance of 20 ft. or less, and can share vast amounts of information almost instantly when touching each other. They can sense emotions in other types of creatures when touching them or within 5 feet.

ECOLOGY
Environment: Underground
Organization: Solitary, brood (3–8), or colony (9–20)

Blood Orchid Savant

XP 2,900 (CR 7)
LE Large aberration
Initiative +2

DEFENSE
AC 15 (natural armor)
hp: 82 (11d10 + 22)
Saving Throws: Wis +6
Resistance: Acid, cold, fire, and lightning damage
Immunity: Thunder damage

OFFENSE
Speed: 5 ft., fly 30 ft.
Multiattack: The blood orchid savant attacks six times, in any combination of tentacle slams and blood drain.
Melee Attack—Tentacle: +6 to hit (reach 5 ft.; one creature). *Hit:* 1d6 + 3 bludgeoning damage, and the target is grappled.
Melee Attack—Blood Drain: automatic hit (reach 5 ft.; one creature already grappled by the blood orchid savant at the start of the blood orchid's turn). *Hit:* 1d8 piercing damage, and the target must make a successful DC 12 Con saving throw against poison or become unconscious. Unconscious characters can repeat the saving throw at the end of each of their turns; they regain consciousness on a successful save. A creature that makes a successful save against this attack becomes immune to the blood drain's unconsciousness effect for 24 hours.

STATISTICS
Str 16 (+3), **Dex** 14 (+2), **Con** 14 (+2),
Int 13 (+1), **Wis** 16 (+3), **Cha** 18 (+4)
Languages: Common (via telepathy)
Skills: Perception +9
Senses: Darkvision 60 ft.

TRAITS
All-Around Vision: A blood orchid sees in all directions at once. Enemies never gain tactical advantage or bonus damage against a blood orchid because of the presence of allies.
Spellcasting: Blood orchid savants are spellcasters who can cast the spells listed below. They use Charisma as their casting ability (DC 15, attack +7) and don't require material components.
Cantrips (at will): *chill touch, light, mage hand, minor illusion*
1st Level (x2): *burning hands, cure wounds, magic missile*
2nd Level (x1): *phantasmal force*
Telepathic Bond: Blood orchids communicate through a nonmagical telepathic bond. They can sense emotions in other blood orchids at distances up to 100 feet, can

communicate fully with each other through telepathy at a distance of 20 ft. or less, and can share vast amounts of information almost instantly when touching each other. They can sense emotions in other types of creatures when touching them or within 5 feet.

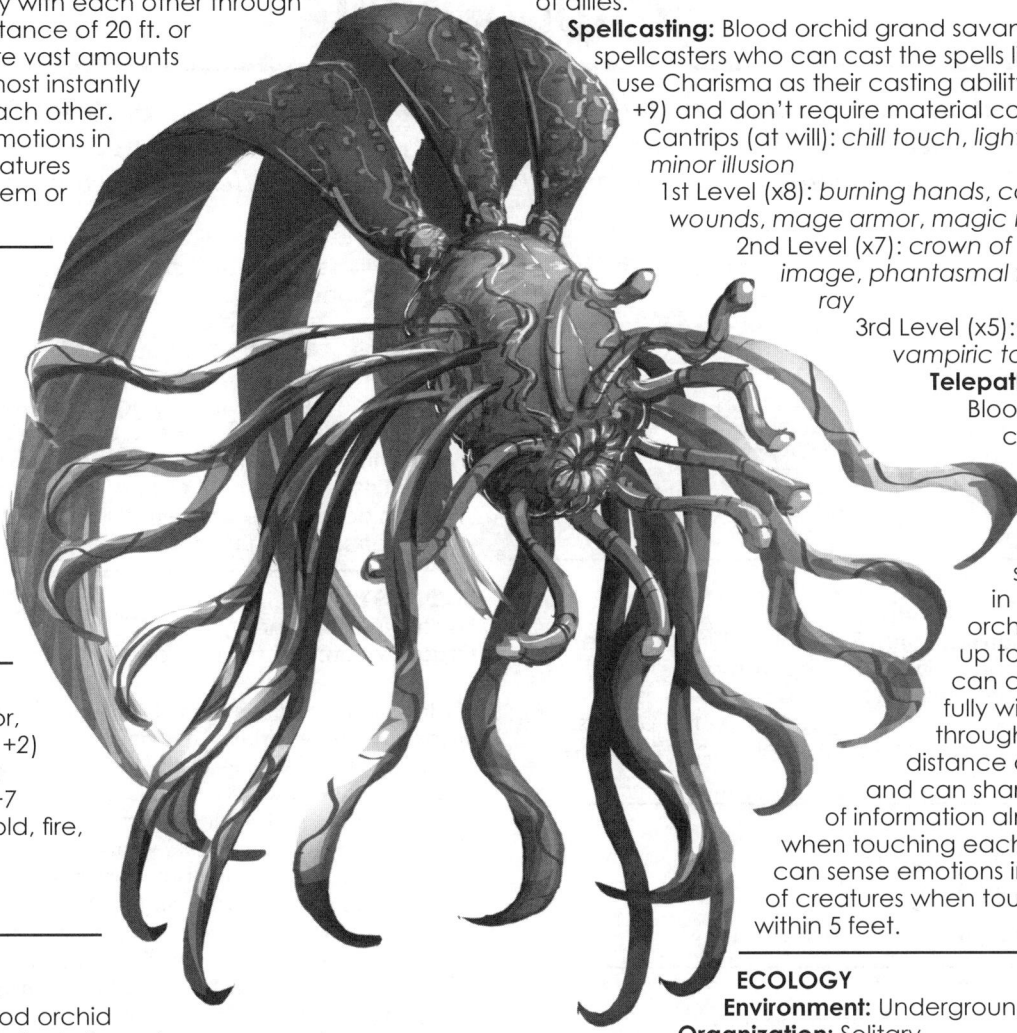

ECOLOGY
Environment:
  Underground
Organization:
  Solitary or brood
  (3–8)

Blood Orchid Grand Savant
XP 5,000 (CR 9)
LE Huge
  aberration
Initiative +1

DEFENSE
AC 16 (natural armor, *ring of protection* +2)
hp: 136 (13d12 + 52)
Saving Throws: Wis +7
Resistance: Acid, cold, fire, and lightning
Immunity: Thunder damage

OFFENSE
Speed: 5 ft., fly 30 ft.
Multiattack: The blood orchid grand savant attacks six times, in any combination of tentacle slams and blood drain.
Melee Attack—Tentacle: +8 to hit (reach 5 ft.; one creature). *Hit:* 1d10 + 4 bludgeoning damage, and the target is grappled.
Melee Attack—Blood Drain: automatic hit (reach 5 ft.; one creature already grappled by the blood orchid grand savant at the start of the blood orchid's turn). *Hit:* 2d8 piercing damage, and the target must make a successful DC 16 Con saving throw against poison or become unconscious. Unconscious characters can repeat the saving throw at the end of each of their turns; they regain consciousness on a successful save. A creature that makes a successful save against this attack becomes immune to the blood drain's unconsciousness effect for 24 hours.

STATISTICS
Str 19 (+4), **Dex** 13 (+1), **Con** 18 (+4),
Int 13 (+1), **Wis** 16 (+3), **Cha** 20 (+5)
Languages: Common (via telepathy)
Skills: Intimidation +9, Perception +11
Senses: Darkvision 60 ft.

TRAITS
All-Around Vision: A blood orchid sees in all directions at once. Enemies never gain tactical advantage or bonus damage against a blood orchid because of the presence of allies.

Spellcasting: Blood orchid grand savants are spellcasters who can cast the spells listed below. They use Charisma as their casting ability (DC 17, attack +9) and don't require material components.
  Cantrips (at will): *chill touch, light, mage hand, minor illusion*
  1st Level (x8): *burning hands, color spray, cure wounds, mage armor, magic missile, shield*
  2nd Level (x7): *crown of madness, mirror image, phantasmal force, scorching ray*
  3rd Level (x5): *lightning bolt, vampiric touch*
Telepathic Bond: Blood orchids communicate through a nonmagical telepathic bond. They can sense emotions in other blood orchids at distances up to 100 feet, can communicate fully with each other through telepathy at a distance of 20 ft. or less, and can share vast amounts of information almost instantly when touching each other. They can sense emotions in other types of creatures when touching them or within 5 feet.

ECOLOGY
Environment: Underground
Organization: Solitary

Blood orchids are territorial, xenophobic, and possessive. They rarely form alliances with other creatures, as their alien mindset keeps them from forming any common ground. They regard other races as aberrant and not to be trusted, even other lawful creatures.

Communication for blood orchids is through a means of empathy/telepathy. They have no sense of hearing, which helps render them immune to sonic effects. The blood orchid can close its outer petals downward and rest on the ground, where it resembles a rocky nodule or fungus of some kind.

Blood orchids occasionally develop sorcerous talents and transform into savants. When their abilities reach a certain level, they can evolve into a grand savant. Normally, each colony of blood orchids is led by a single grand savant, and another can't evolve while one is present. A blood orchid savant ready to become a grand savant leaves the colony with a few followers and sets out to establish a new brood elsewhere.

Credit
  Originally appearing in *Rappan Athuk Reloaded* (© Necromancer Games, 2006)

Bloodsuckle

This is a nightmarish plant consisting of a bulbous root and several vinelike tendrils, each ending in a hollow, needlelike point. Woody limbs as thick as a human's leg sprout from the trunk. Its leaves are a vile greenish color and constantly drip a sticky, foul-smelling sap.

Bloodsuckle

XP 700 (CR 3)
Unaligned Large plant
Initiative +0

DEFENSE
AC 13 (natural armor)
hp: 57 (6d10 + 24)
Saving Throws: Con +6
Immunity: Blindness, charm, deafness, fright, prone, stun, unconsciousness

OFFENSE
Speed: 0 ft.
Melee Attack—Constriction: +5 to hit (reach 10 ft.; one creature). *Hit:* 1d4 + 3 bludgeoning damage plus 1d12 piercing damage, and the target is grappled. If this attack deals 9 or more piercing damage, the bloodsuckle releases this victim and seeks another. Also see Create Host, below.

STATISTICS
Str 16 (+3), **Dex** 10 (+0), **Con** 18 (+4),
Int 6 (–2), **Wis** 11 (+0), **Cha** 11 (+0)
Languages: None
Senses: Blindsight 60 ft.

TRAITS
Create Host: A bloodsuckle that grapples a living target injects its poison sap into the victim. The target creature must make a successful DC 14 Wis save or become dominated by the bloodsuckle, as if the plant had cast *dominate person* on the victim. Immunity or resistance to poison applies normally to this sap. Domination is permanent until broken by a successful save or by the death of the bloodsuckle. The host does not get additional saving throws when it takes damage; instead, a host with an Intelligence of 3 or higher is allowed another DC 14 Wis saving throw with tactical advantage to break the bloodsuckle's control when it is commanded to act in a manner inconsistent with its alignment or to turn against its allies.

Host Sense: A bloodsuckle automatically senses the location of any hosts within 100 feet.

Seed: Once per month, a bloodsuckle generates a walnut-sized seed that it implants in one host's body. The host's maximum number of hit points reduces by 1d10 per day. When its maximum hit points reach 0, the host dies and a new bloodsuckle plant erupts from the corpse. A *greater restoration* or *blight* spell destroys the seedling.

ECOLOGY
Environment: Temperate
Organization: Solitary or orchard (2–20)

Bloodsuckles are semi-intelligent and immobile plants that gain nourishment from the blood of living creatures. Unlike other carnivorous plants, the bloodsuckle maintains a herd of living hosts that it feeds on.

Bloodsuckles are found in forests, swamps, and rolling hills in temperate climes. They are never found in arctic regions, but a variety of this plant is suspected to exist in tropical regions.

When a bloodsuckle detects movement within 30 feet, it sends out its long, vinelike tendrils toward the disturbance. When the tendril strikes a living target, one set of needles sucks blood from the victim while another set injects sap into the victim. The sap brings the creature under the plant's control. A bloodsuckle automatically recognizes its own hosts and never attacks them. Rather, it lets the host approach so it can embrace it with its tendrils and consume more blood.

A victim that becomes a host returns to the plant whenever the plant calls. Such hosts are normally used by the bloodsuckle for feeding purposes, but if the plant comes under attack, it will also summon nearby hosts for defense. Once per month, it summons a host that it senses is near death and implants it with a seed, then typically commands that host to walk until it dies. Thus the bloodsuckle spreads far and wide across the land.

Bloody Bones

*This creature appears as a skeletal humanoid with bits of muscle and sinew hanging from its body.
Four long, sinewy tendrils writhe from its midsection.
The entire creature oozes a mixture of blood and mucus. Its eye sockets are hollow and dark.*

Bloody Bones

XP 450 (CR 2)
CE Medium undead
Initiative +1

DEFENSE
AC 13 (natural armor)
hp: 27 (6d8)
Resistance: Fire and necrotic damage
Immunity: Poison damage; Exhaustion, fright, poison, unconsciousness

OFFENSE
Speed: 30 ft.
Multiattack: A bloody bones attacks twice with claws or four times with tendrils.
Melee Attack—Claw: +5 to hit (reach 5 ft.; one creature). *Hit:* 1d8 + 3 slashing damage. This attack hits automatically if the target is grappled by the bloody bones.
Melee Attack—Tendril: +5 to hit (reach 30 ft.; one creature). *Hit:* 1d4 bludgeoning damage and the target is grappled and can be dragged (see below).

STATISTICS
Str 17 (+3), **Dex** 12 (+1), **Con** 10 (+0),
Int 11 (+0), **Wis** 13 (+1), **Cha** 14 (+2)
Languages: None
Senses: Darkvision 60 ft.

TRAITS
Slippery: Bloody bones are difficult to grapple or snare because of the constant flow of blood and mucus across their bodies. Webs, magic or otherwise, do not affect bloody bones. A bloody bones has tactical advantage to escape from a grapple, and enemies trying to escape from its grapple have tactical disadvantage.

Drag with Tendril: As a bonus action, a bloody bones can drag each creature grappled by its tendrils 10 feet directly toward the bloody bones. When a creature grappled by the bloody bones's tendrils is within 5 feet of the bloody bones, it can be clawed automatically (no attack roll is necessary). The bloody bones's tendrils can be attacked separately (AC 13); 6 points of slashing damage severs the tendril. This damage affects only the tendril, however, and doesn't reduce the bloody bones's hit points. The monster generates a new tendril to replace the severed one at the start of its next turn.

ECOLOGY
Environment: Any caves and ruins
Organization: Solitary or gang (2–5)

Bloody bones are evil undead spirits that haunt caverns, caves, and other desolate places. Their origins are unknown, but they are believed to be the undead remnants of adventurers who desecrated evil temples and were punished by corrupt gods for their actions.

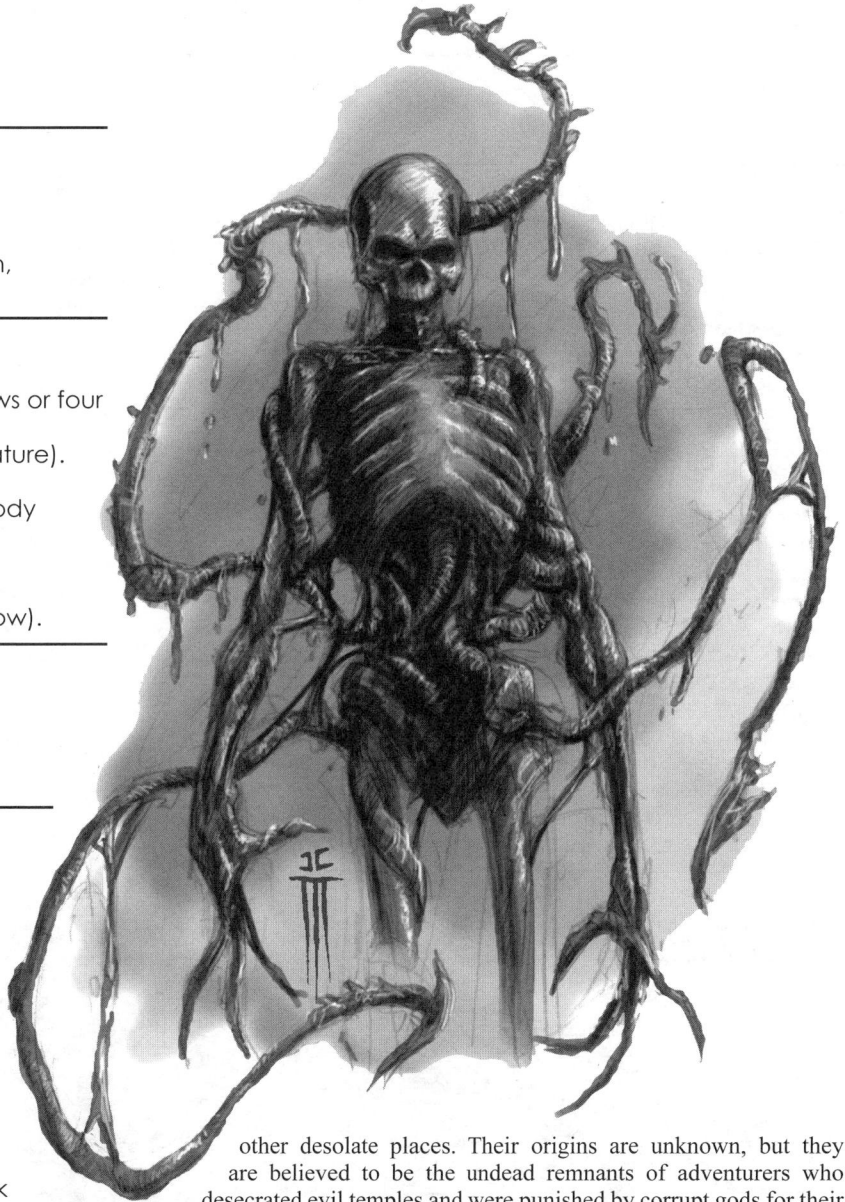

From a distance, they are likely to be mistaken for skeletons. Those who make this mistake often regret it, for the bloody bones is far worse than the undead creature it resembles.

A bloody bones stands about 6 feet tall. It is unknown if they can speak, but they never do. A bloody bones prefers to hide in the shadows and wait for its prey to pass nearby. It then leaps to the attack, entwining its opponents with its tendrils and clawing its prey to death.

Boalisk

This creature appears as a vile serpent with dark scales and reddish eyes.

Boalisk

XP 200 (CR 1)
Unaligned Large monstrosity
Initiative +2

DEFENSE
AC 12
hp: 39 (6d10 + 6)

OFFENSE
Speed: 20 ft.
Melee Attack—Bite: +5 to hit (reach 5 ft.; one creature). *Hit:* 1d8 + 3 piercing damage and the target is grappled and restrained.
Melee Attack—Constriction: Automatic hit (reach 0 ft.; one creature grappled by the boalisk). *Hit:* 1d10 + 3 bludgeoning damage.

STATISTICS
Str 16 (+3), **Dex** 15 (+2), **Con** 14 (+2),
Int 1 (−5), **Wis** 10 (+0), **Cha** 4 (−3)
Languages: None
Skills: Stealth +4
Senses: Darkvision 60 ft.

TRAITS
Gaze: Creatures within 30 feet that meet the boalisk's gaze must succeed on a DC 12 Con saving throw or contract black rot disease. Creatures with black rot can't spend hit dice to recover lost hit points. A diseased character repeats the Con saving throw at the end of every long rest. On a failed saving throw, the disease continues. With a successful saving throw, the disease ends. The disease can also be cured with a *lesser restoration* spell.

ECOLOGY
Environment: Warm forest, aquatic
Organization: Solitary

The boalisk is a vile serpent that lurks in misty jungles and along dark riverbanks. It can cause a disease with its gaze that prevents a body from healing itself.

A boalisk is a constrictor snake 12 to 30 feet long with dark scales interspersed with pale green and yellow daubs of color to help it blend in with its surroundings. The eyes of a boalisk are large and reddish in color.

A boalisk hunts by grabbing prey with its mouth and then squeezing with its powerful body. More powerful opponents (or if the boalisk has recently eaten) will be attacked with the boalisk's gaze attack.

Credit
The Boalisk originally appeared in the First Edition module *S4 Lost Caverns of Tsojcanth* (© TSR/Wizards of the Coast, 1982) and later in the First Edition *Monster Manual II* (© TSR/Wizards of the Coast, 1983) and is used by permission.

Copyright Notice
Author Scott Greene, based on original material by Gary Gygax.

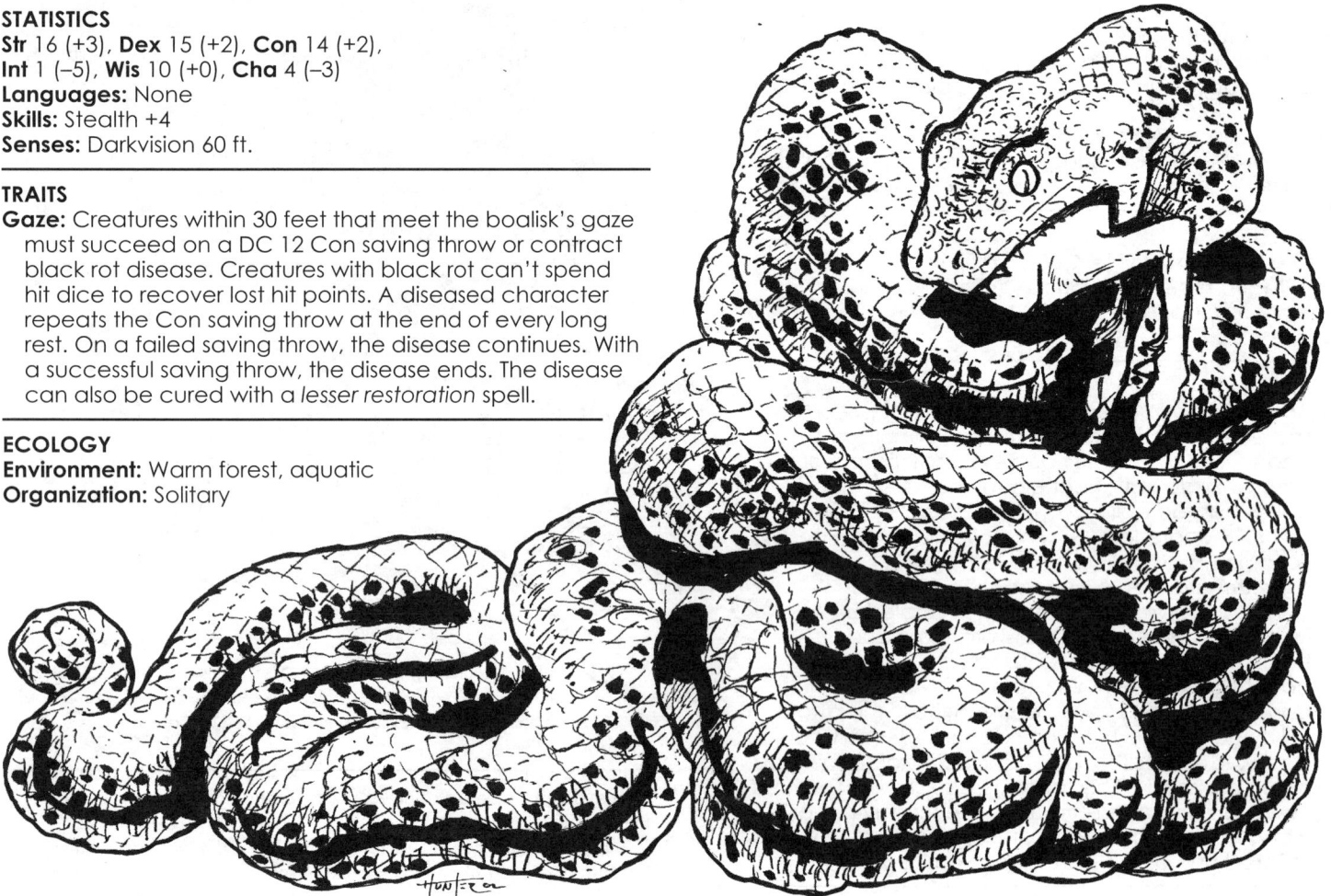

Bone Cobbler

This creature appears as a tattered and desiccated humanoid with grayish flesh drawn tight over its bones. Its eyes are hollow sockets of darkness, and its clothes are rags.

Bone Cobbler

XP 450 (CR 2)
CE Medium aberration
Initiative +2

DEFENSE

AC 13 (natural armor)
hp: 22 (5d8)

OFFENSE

Speed: 30 ft.
Multiattack: The bone cobbler attacks twice with light hammers or twice with claws.
Melee Attack—Claws: +4 to hit (reach 5 ft.; one creature). *Hit:* 1d4 + 2 slashing damage.
Melee Attack—Light Hammer: +4 to hit (reach 5 ft.; one creature). *Hit:* 1d4 + 2 bludgeoning damage.
Ranged Attack—Light Hammer: +4 to hit (range 20 ft./60 ft.; one creature). *Hit:* 1d4 + 2 bludgeoning damage.

STATISTICS

Str 14 (+2), **Dex** 15 (+2), **Con** 11 (+0), **Int** 10 (+0), **Wis** 14 (+2), **Cha** 8 (−2)
Languages: Deep Speech, Undercommon
Senses: Darkvision 60 ft.

TRAITS

Animate Bones (1/day): Once per day as an action, a bone cobbler can animate up to five skeletal statues within 30 feet of itself. These creatures use the stat block of skeletons, though their forms and structures do not need to resemble humanoids or anything remotely humanoid. The skeletal statues remain animated until destroyed, until the bone cobbler wills them back into statues, or for 24 hours.

Bonestripping: A bone cobbler can strip all the flesh from the corpse of a Medium creature in three minutes using its claws and hammers. For each size category larger or smaller than Medium a corpse is, add or subtract 1 minute. Once stripped, the bone cobbler devours the flesh and collects the victim's bones to use in its sculptures. A creature slain in this manner can be brought back to life only by a *wish* or *resurrection* spell.

ECOLOGY

Environment: Subterranean
Organization: Solitary or gang (2–5)

The bone cobbler is a tattered and desiccated humanoid that is easily mistaken for a zombie. The bone cobbler, however, is not undead, but is thought to originate from another plane or dimension of existence. It delights in slaying opponents, stripping the flesh from their bones, and then assembling the bones of various creatures into nightmarish sculptures of creatures that never existed.

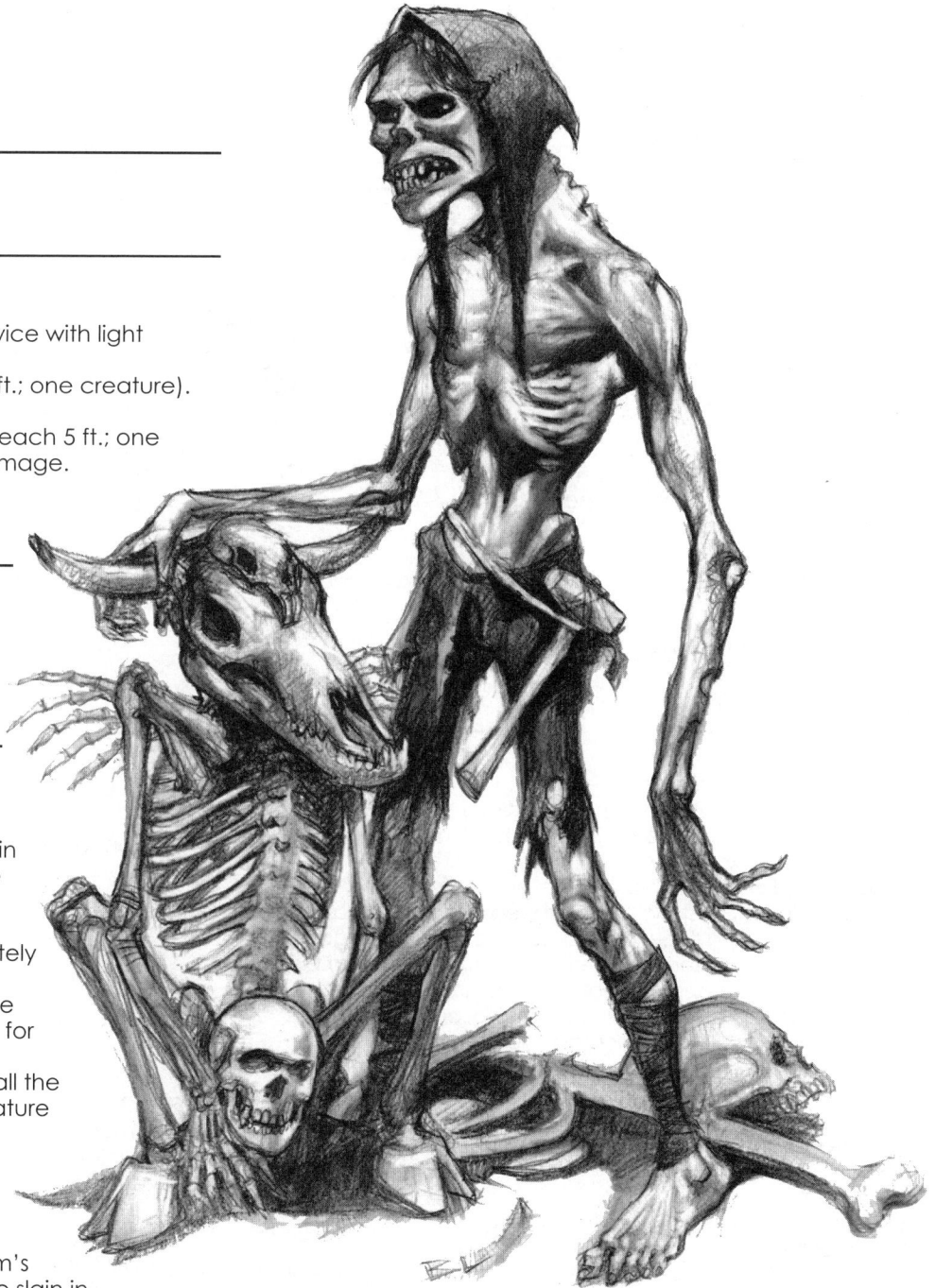

Bone cobblers stand 6 feet tall.

Copyright Notice
Author Scott Greene.

Boneneedle

This creature is about 5 feet in diameter and resembles a bloated yellow bag of pulpy flesh with eight spidery legs. It has two long, sharply-curved mandibles protruding from one end of it that you can assume is the front, though the creature seems to lack both eyes and a mouth.

Greater Boneneedle

XP 200 (CR 1)
Unaligned Medium beast
Initiative +3

DEFENSE

AC 13
hp: 31 (7d8)
Immunity: Psychic damage; charm, fright

OFFENSE

Speed: 30 ft., climb 20 ft.
Melee Attack—Bite: +5 to hit (reach 5 ft.; one creature). *Hit:* 2d8 + 3 piercing damage and the target must make a successful DC 12 Con saving throw or suffer the effect of boneneedle poison (see below).

STATISTICS

Str 8 (–1), **Dex** 16 (+3), **Con** 11 (+0), **Int** 1 (–5), **Wis** 12 (+1), **Cha** 3 (–4)
Languages: None
Senses: Darkvision 60 ft.

TRAITS

Aversion to Daylight: Boneneedles shun light. While exposed to natural (not magical) sunlight, they have tactical disadvantage on all attack rolls, saving throws, and skill checks.
Boneneedle Poison: The bite of a boneneedle injects a syrupy neurotoxin that destroys flesh and weakens bone. A creature that fails its saving throw against boneneedle poison gains the poisoned condition. While the creature is poisoned by boneneedle poison, it also takes an extra 2 points of damage whenever it takes bludgeoning, piercing, or slashing damage. Cumulative bites do not increase the extra damage. The poisoned creature can repeat the saving throw after a long or short rest, ending the poisoned condition with a successful save. A *lesser restoration* spell or comparable magic also neutralizes the poison.

ECOLOGY

Environment: Subterranean
Organization: Solitary, pack (1–3 plus 3–6 lesser boneneedles), or nest (2–4 plus 12–24 lesser boneneedles)

Lesser Boneneedle

XP 50 (CR 1/4)
Unaligned Small beast
Initiative +2

DEFENSE

AC 12
hp: 13 (3d8)
Immunity: Psychic damage; charm, fright

OFFENSE

Speed: 20 ft., climb 20 ft.
Melee Attack—Bite: +4 to hit (reach 5 ft.; one creature). *Hit:* 1d6 + 2 piercing damage and the target must make a successful DC 12 Con saving throw or suffer the effect of boneneedle poison (see below).

STATISTICS

Str 5 (–3), **Dex** 14 (+2), **Con** 10 (+0), **Int** 1 (–5), **Wis** 10 (+0), **Cha** 3 (–4)
Languages: None
Senses: Darkvision 60 ft.

TRAITS

Aversion to Daylight: Boneneedles shun light. While exposed to natural (not magical) sunlight, they have tactical disadvantage on all attack rolls, saving throws, and skill checks.
Boneneedle Poison: The bite of a boneneedle injects a syrupy neurotoxin that destroys flesh and weakens bone. A creature that fails its saving throw against boneneedle poison gains the poisoned condition. While the creature is poisoned by boneneedle poison, it also takes an extra 2 points of damage whenever it takes bludgeoning, piercing, or slashing damage. Cumulative bites do not increase the extra damage. The poisoned creature can repeat the saving throw after a long or short rest, ending the poisoned condition with a successful save. A *lesser restoration* spell will also neutralize the poison.
Crowd: Up to three boneneedles can occupy the same 5-foot space.

ECOLOGY

Environment: Subterranean
Organization: Pack (3–6), cluster (5–8), or nest (12–24 plus 2–4 greater boneneedles)

Boneneedles are eyeless, bone-white creatures that resemble a blob of semi-translucent flesh with eight spindly, spidery legs colored black or gold. These creatures feed on bone marrow, so their lairs are always scattered with the cracked, deformed bones of their victims, both humanoid and animal. A greater boneneedle is a larger version of the lesser, They appear to be nothing more than lesser boneneedles that have survived long enough to grow larger than their nest mates.

They make their lairs deep underground to avoid natural daylight, though some brave the surface world by venturing from their lairs at night. Such surface encounters are rare, and will always be with at least a pack of greater and lesser boneneedles. Boneneedles flee from natural daylight if at all possible.

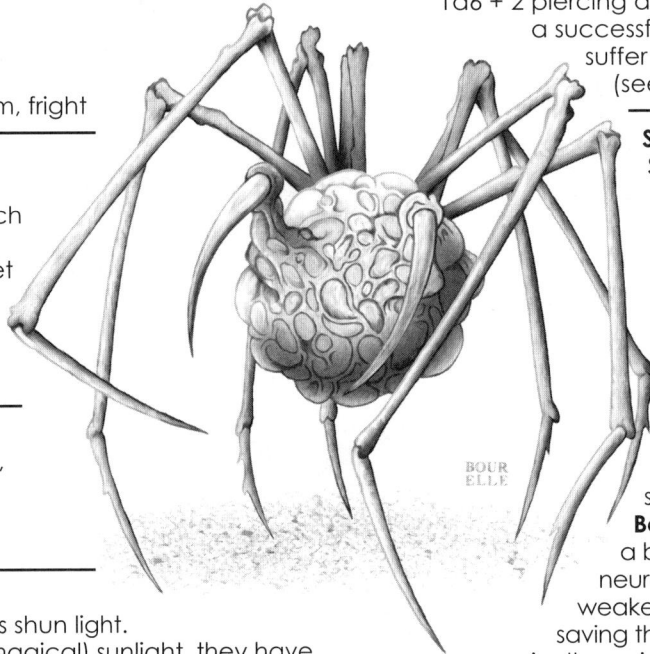

Other than the nest, boneneedles have no particular social structure, though they do cooperate when hunting and feeding. Very young boneneedles are generally nonthreatening, as they lack the deadly poison injectors that adults possess.

A boneneedle's mandibles are glossy-black and hollow, both to inject poison and to siphon out the dissolved flesh and bone from a victim's corpse. While feeding, the boneneedle's fleshy form pulsates and expands. After feeding, its form becomes less translucent and takes on a greenish yellow color.

These creatures are highly aggressive and opportunistic hunters. Using their coloration, they hide among piles of bones in their lair and wait for living creatures to wander close by. When prey comes within 20 or 30 feet, the boneneedles dart from their hiding places to swarm the victim.

Copyright Notice
Author Scott Greene.

Bonesucker

This bizarre creature resembles a fleshy tree trunk. Atop its main body protrudes a mass of writhing tentacles that constantly ooze and drip a brownish-yellow fluid. Beneath these is a ring of black, unblinking eyes.

Bonesucker
XP 1,100 (CR 4)
NE Large aberration
Initiative +1

DEFENSE
AC 15 (natural armor)
hp: 68 (8d10 + 24)
Resistance: All nonmagical damage

OFFENSE
Speed: 20 ft.
Multiattack: The bonesucker attacks four times, using any combination of tentacle attacks and bonesucker poison attacks.
Melee Attack—Tentacle: +6 to hit (reach 10 ft.; one creature). *Hit:* 1d6 + 4 bludgeoning damage and the target is grappled and restrained.
Melee Attack—Bonesucker Poison: automatic hit (reach 10 ft.; one creature already grappled by the bonesucker at the start of the bonesucker's turn). *Hit:* 1d6 + 3 poison damage and the target becomes poisoned until it escapes from the bonesucker's grapple.

STATISTICS
Str 18 (+4), **Dex** 13 (+1), **Con** 17 (+3), **Int** 10 (+0), **Wis** 12 (+1), **Cha** 13 (+1)
Languages: None
Senses: Darkvision 60 ft.

TRAITS
All-Around Vision: Thanks to its 360-degree vision, the bonesucker has tactical advantage on all Perception checks and attackers never gain tactical advantage or bonus damage against it from the presence of nearby allies.

ECOLOGY
Environment: Subterranean and any land
Organization: Solitary

A bonesucker is a bizarre creature that stalks the darkness dank caves and remote wastelands. The body is encased in a thick, rubbery sheath of flesh and muscle that makes the bonesucker highly resistant to injury. The bonesucker moves through the use of five thick tentacles at its base.

Bonesuckers consume only the bones of an opponent by grabbing it and piercing its flesh with hollow tentacles. The tentacles inject digestive enzymes into the bones, which break down and are sucked up as a pasty meal for the bonesucker. The process is horrifyingly painful for victims. Experienced adventurers always know they are nearing the hunting grounds of a bonesucker, because the creature leaves the boneless carcasses of its meals lying where it finished them.

Bonesuckers stand about 10 feet tall.

A bonesucker attacks with its tentacles. Initially, the tentacles appear to be only a foot or two in length, but the bonesucker can extend them to a length of approximately 10 feet. It can attack with up to four of its eight tentacles in a single round.

A bonesucker's natural weapons are treated as magic weapons for the purpose of overcoming resistances and immunities.

Copyright Notice
Author Erica Balsley.

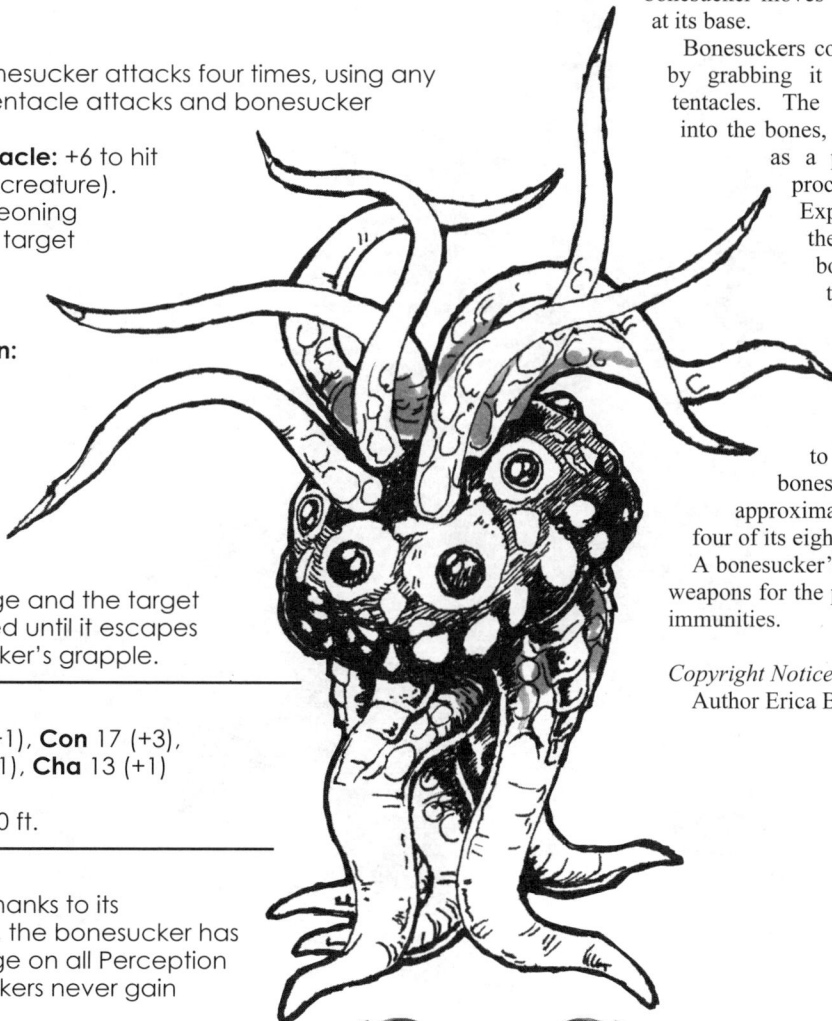

Borsin

*The borsin closely resembles a centaur but with the upper body, arms,
and head of a great ape rather than a human.*

Borsin (Ape Centaur)
XP 700 (CR 3)
CE Large monstrosity
Initiative +2

DEFENSE
AC 12
hp: 60 (8d10 + 16)

OFFENSE
Speed: 40 ft.
Multiattack: A borsin attacks twice with claws and bites once.
Melee Attack—Claws: +7 to hit (reach 5 ft.; one creature). *Hit:* 1d6 + 5 slashing damage. If both claw attacks hit the same target, the second attack inflicts an additional 2d6 slashing damage and the borsin gains tactical advantage on its bite attack, if that attack is made immediately against the same target.
Melee Attack—Bite: +7 to hit (reach 5 ft.; one creature). *Hit:* 1d8 + 5 piercing damage.

STATISTICS
Str 20 (+5), **Dex** 14 (+2), **Con** 15 (+2), **Int** 4 (–3), **Wis** 11 (+0), **Cha** 8 (–1)
Languages: None
Skills: Athletics +7

ECOLOGY
Environment: Temperate
Organization: Solitary

A borsin is a creature with the head, arms, and upper body of an ape joined to the body and legs of a quadruped. The lower half may be that of a boar, equine, or hound. In that regard they resemble centaurs, but they are less massive and far more brutish than those majestic creatures. They are suspected to have been magically crossbred as battle-beasts in antiquity. Unlike a centaur, a borsin has only a savage, animal cunning, though they are capable of problem-solving and setting crude traps. They fight only with their teeth and claws, never their hooves.

They do not use weapons or tools, or carry treasure. Pack leaders have been seen to drape themselves in the skins and furs of creatures they have killed, including those of humanoid adventurers.

Borsin form packs led by the strongest member. They use pack tactics to drive opponents and prey into traps, kill zones, or natural hazards such as cliffs and ravines. Borsin packs stake out their territory by raising small cairns of stone topped with the skulls of their kills, and they patrol their borders regularly. They often grunt, howl, and gesture to each other, but whether they have an actual, simple language is unknown. Borsin are omnivorous and hardy, capable of surviving on plants but much preferring freshly-killed meat.

Author
Scott Wylie Roberts, "Myrystyr"

Brass Man

This creature resembles a humanoid constructed of brass.
Its features are exquisite and delicate. Ancient runes and symbols adorn its body.

Brass Man

XP 2,300 (CR 6)
Unaligned Large construct
Initiative +0

DEFENSE
AC 18 (natural armor)
hp: 95 (10d10 + 40)
Resistance: Bludgeoning, piercing, and slashing damage except from adamantine weapons
Immunity: Fire and poison damage; paralysis, petrification, poison, stun, suffocation, unconsciousness
Vulnerability: Cold damage

OFFENSE
Speed: 30 ft.
Multiattack: A brass man attacks twice with its fists, or twice with its greatsword, or once by spitting molten brass.
Melee Attack—Fist: +8 to hit (reach 10 ft.; one creature). *Hit:* 1d10 + 5 bludgeoning damage plus 1d10 fire damage.
Melee Attack—Greatsword: +8 to hit (reach 10 ft.; one creature). *Hit:* 2d12 + 5 slashing damage.
Ranged Attack—Molten Brass (recharge 5, 6): automatic hit (range 30-ft. line; all creatures in line). *Hit:* 6d8 fire damage. Targets that make a successful DC 15 Dex saving throw take half damage.

STATISTICS
Str 20 (+5), **Dex** 10 (+0), **Con** 18 (+4), **Int** 3 (–4), **Wis** 11 (+0), **Cha** 1 (–5)
Languages: None
Senses: Darkvision 60 ft.

TRAITS
Immunity to Magic: A brass man automatically succeeds on all saving throws against spells and spell-like effects. If a successful saving throw reduces damage by half, the brass man takes no damage instead. In addition, certain spells and effects function differently against the creature, as noted below (these effects override its immunity).

- A magical attack that deals lightning damage automatically slows a brass man (as the *slow* spell) for 3 rounds.
- A magical attack that deals fire damage automatically ends any *slow* effect on the brass man and repairs 1 point of damage for each 3 points of damage the attack would normally inflict deal. If the amount of healing would cause the brass man to exceed its hit point maximum, it gains the excess as temporary hit points.

ECOLOGY
Environment: Elemental plane of fire
Organization: Solitary or squad (2–4)

Brass men are humanoid-shaped constructs built by the powerful efreet of the City of Brass. Most are created for the sole purpose of guarding secrets within the walls of the city, with a few serving as war machines to aid the efreet in battle against their enemies. They are rarely encountered elsewhere, though on occasion one is sent to the Material Plane by its efreet creator to retrieve an object or creature.

Brass men are very tough opponents and difficult to stop. Typically, a brass man begins combat by spitting molten brass onto the closest opponents before moving into melee with its huge greatsword or its powerful fists.

Construction

The construction of the brass men is a highly guarded secret among the efreet. No one outside the City of Brass has ever discovered the proper method of constructing a brass man, and the efreet certainly won't share the secret.

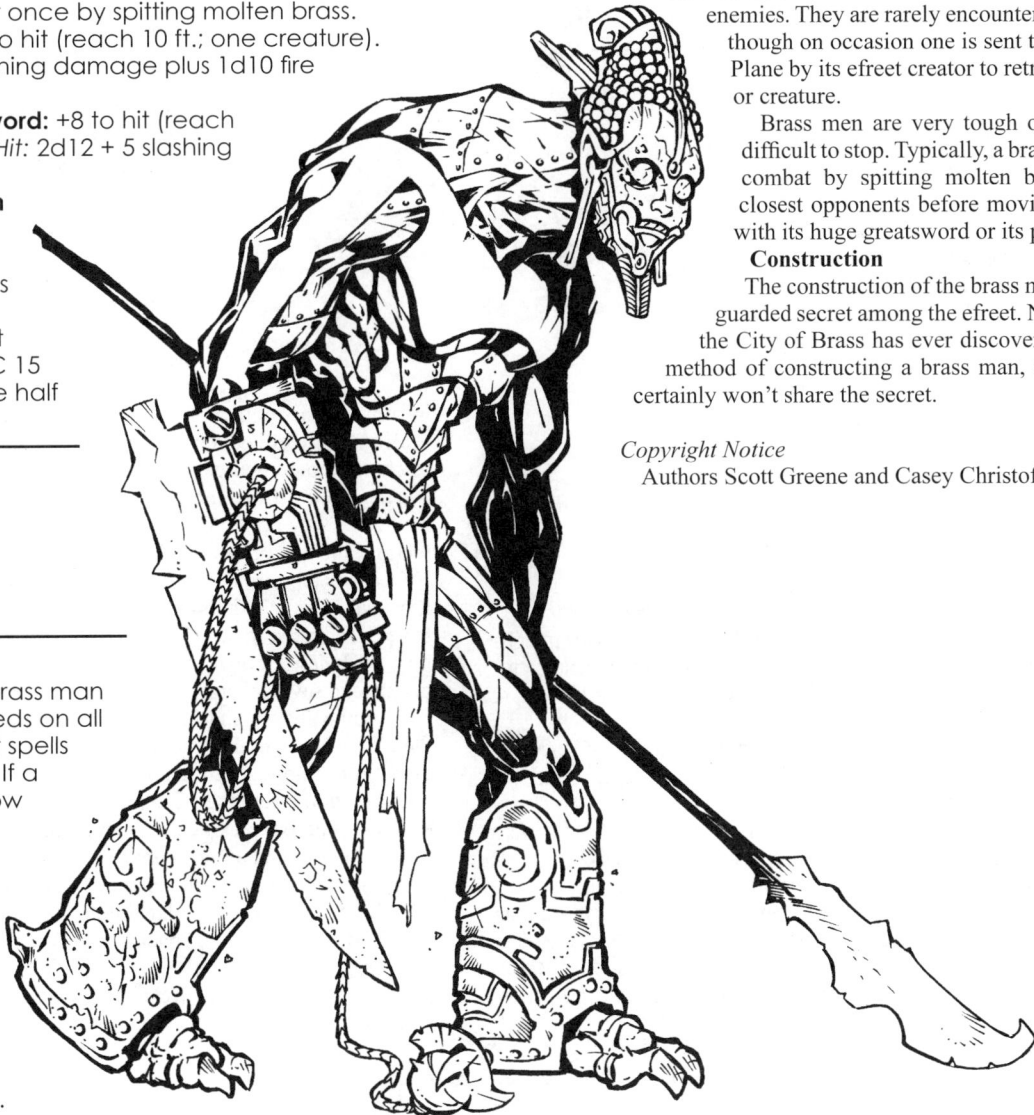

Brume

The semi-transparent brume has the appearance of a humanoid wrapped in a soggy funeral shroud. Long claws extend from the arms of the shroud. When its hood is thrown back, a noseless, earless face filled with needlelike fangs and sunken black eye-sockets that glow with two wicked golden points of light is revealed. The creature has no apparent legs, but instead hovers inches above the ground on its "feet" that are nothing more than foul, swirling vapors.

Brume

XP 2,300 (CR 6)
NE Large aberration
Initiative +3

DEFENSE

AC 16 (natural armor)
hp: 90 (12d8 + 36)
Saving Throws: Wis +5
Resistance: All nonmagical damage
Immunity: Poison damage; poison

OFFENSE

Speed: 20 ft., fly 40 ft.
Multiattack: The brume attacks twice with claws.
Melee Attack—Claws: +6 to hit (reach 5 ft.; one creature). *Hit:* 1d8 + 3 slashing damage and the target must make a successful DC 14 Con saving throw or lose one point of Charisma. The target is also subject to memory loss (see below).

STATISTICS

Str 13 (+1), **Dex** 16 (+3), **Con** 17 (+3), **Int** 14 (+2), **Wis** 14 (+2), **Cha** 17 (+3)
Languages: Understands Common and most other languages, but does not speak
Skills: Perception +8, Stealth +3
Senses: Darkvision 60 ft.

TRAITS

Incorporeal: A brume can move through solid objects and living creatures at half-speed. If it ends its turn inside another object or creature, it takes 1d10 force damage. This damage is not reduced by the brume's resistance to nonmagical damage.
Lifesense: A brume can automatically pinpoint the location of any living creature within 120 feet, and it knows how close to death the creature is.
Memory Loss: A living creature struck by a brume's claw attack must make a DC 14 Int saving throw. Failure indicates the creature is affected as if by a *confusion* spell for 1d4 hours and it forgets everything that happened in the preceding 1d6 hours. If the target is a spellcaster, he or she also loses spell slots equal in value to the sum of those two die rolls (d4 + d6). The spell slots are treated exactly as if they'd been used to cast spells already. The largest spell slots possible must be lost; e.g., a 6th-level wizard who forgets five spell slots must lose a 3rd-level slot (the largest possible) and a 2nd-level slot (to reach five slots lost). The

confusion effect can be removed with a *dispel magic* spell, but the memories of the last few hours are gone forever. Lost spell slots are recovered normally through rest.
Natural Invisibility: A brume is always invisible in fog, smoke, or mist. It can't become visible in such an environment.
Misty Surroundings (recharge 6): The brume can create an area of fog around itself as if it cast the *fog cloud* spell. It does not need to concentrate to maintain the fog. The fog cloud has a radius of 40 feet.

ECOLOGY

Environment: Any
Organization: Solitary

These strange creatures of extraplanar origin dwell within the mists of the Styx, where they are known to strangle the life from any living creatures that find themselves lost there. Brumes track and observe enemies that enter their territory before attacking them, seeking to steal personal effects from the intruders to gain information about their strengths and weaknesses.

Brumes are effectively invisible in fog and they can generate their own fog banks, making them almost impossible to spot.

They feed off the energy of lost souls, devouring the dead of Styx as readily as they do the living, absorbing whatever energy remains in their victims and leaving a dried husk in their wake.

Occasionally brumes find their way into the material plane, where they lurk near planar conduits and crossing points that lead into the Styx. Brumes have been bribed to act as guides into Styx, but they usually demand some form of living sacrifice in return for this service. Brumes are believed to understand several languages, but they are not known to speak.

A brume always attacks at the time and place of its choosing; between their fog and their ability to move through solid obstructions, brumes are essentially impossible to force into combat. They strike from the mist, attempting to throw their enemies into confusion and set them to fighting each other before picking them off in isolation. They have been known to track a large group of intruders over great distance, until such time as they could strike at just a few separated from the main group. They've also been known to strike at isolated individuals, stripping their memories and then letting them wander back amongst their friends, who they attack in their *confusion*.

A brume's claws are treated as magic weapons for the purpose of overcoming resistances and immunities.

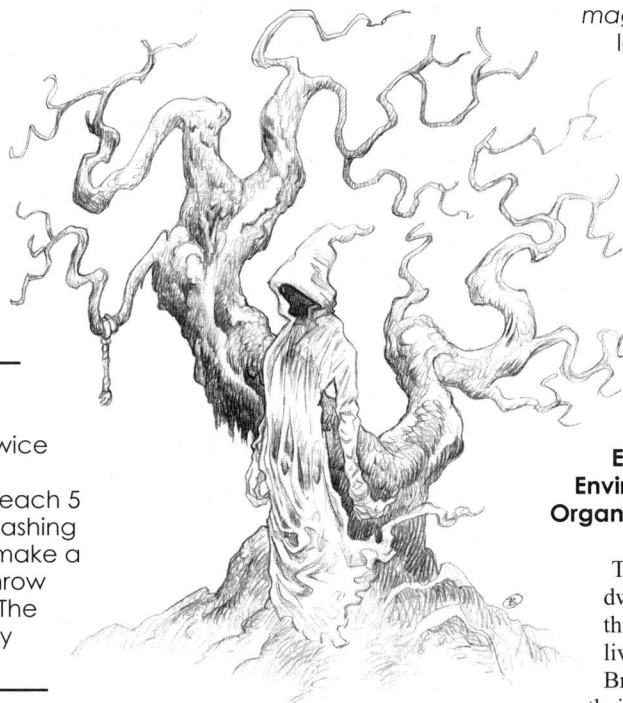

Burning Dervish

This creature looks like a normal human but with symbols and tattoos of alien design covering most of its flesh.

Burning Dervish

XP 700 (CR 3)
LE Medium fiend
Initiative +3

DEFENSE

AC 16 (natural armor)
hp: 65 (10d8 + 20)
Immunity: Fire damage
Vulnerability: Cold damage

OFFENSE

Speed: 30 ft., fly 20 ft.
Multiattack: The burning dervish attacks once with its falchion or twice with fists (fist attacks are possible only in flame form).
Melee Attack—Falchion: +6 to hit (reach 5 ft.; one creature). *Hit:* 2d8 + 4 slashing damage.
Melee Attack—Fist (flame form only): +6 to hit (reach 5 ft.; one creature). *Hit:* 1d10 + 4 bludgeoning damage plus 1d6 fire damage.

STATISTICS

Str 18 (+4), **Dex** 16 (+3), **Con** 14 (+2), **Int** 13 (+1), **Wis** 15 (+2), **Cha** 15 (+2)
Languages: Common, Infernal
Skills: Perception +6, Stealth +7
Senses: Darkvision 60 ft.

TRAITS

Spell-like Abilities: A burning dervish can use the following spell-like abilities, using Charisma as its casting ability (DC 12, attack +4). It doesn't need material components to use these abilities.
At Will: *fire bolt, produce flame*
3/day: *invisibility* (self only)
1/day: *enlarge/reduce, flaming sphere, plane shift* (Elemental, Astral, or Material Planes)
Elemental Endurance: Burning dervishes can survive on the Elemental Planes of Air or Earth for up to 48 hours and on the Elemental Plane of Water for up to 12 hours. Failure to return to the Elemental Plane of Fire after that time deals 1 point of damage per hour to a burning dervish until it dies or returns to the Elemental Plane of Fire.
Flame Form (3/day): Three times per day, a burning dervish can use its action to change its form to that of a column of fire. In this form it can attack with its fists. The transformation lasts indefinitely; changing back requires another action.

ECOLOGY

Environment: Elemental plane of fire
Organization: Solitary, company (2–4), or band (6–15)

Burning dervishes are the fanatical minions of the Sultan of Efreet (see the *City of Brass* by **Necromancer Games**). It is said that the burning dervishes were once a noble tribe of jann who sold their souls to the Sultan of Efreet in exchange for greater power over the Elemental Plane of Fire.

Burning dervishes are virtually indistinguishable from human. They spend a great amount of time in the Material Plane as agents of the Sultan of Efreet, seeking to spread worship of the Sultan as the true god of Elemental Fire. They also operate as assassins and spies, often leading daring surprise attacks against foes of the Sultan or procuring powerful relics for his pleasure.

The burning dervishes have a citadel atop the Great Ziggurat of the City of Brass that serves as the central temple to their zealous faith. It is from this ziggurat that the Sultan communes with his worshippers, sending them out on raids throughout the planes to further his name and power.

Burning dervishes usually turn themselves invisible before attacking, the better to catch their foes by surprise. In combat, a burning dervish usually fights with its falchion. Depending on the power of its opponent, the burning dervish can either use *enlarge* on itself or *reduce* on its opponent. A burning dervish that is outclassed or overmatched either takes to the air and flies away or attempts to *plane shift* to safety.

Cadaver

This monster resembles a humanoid dressed in tattered rags. Rotted flesh reveals corded muscles and sinew stretched tightly over its skeleton. Hollow eye sockets flicker with a hellish glow. Broken and rotted teeth line its mouth, and its hands end in wicked claws.

Cadaver

XP 100 (CR 1/2)
CE Medium undead
Initiative +1

DEFENSE

AC 11
hp: 15 (2d8 + 6)
Resistance: Bludgeoning, piercing, and slashing damage from nonmagical weapons; necrotic damage
Immunity: Poison damage; exhaustion, fright, poison, unconsciousness

OFFENSE

Speed: 30 ft.
Multiattack: The cadaver bites once and attacks once with claws.
Melee Attack—Bite: +3 to hit (reach 5 ft.; one creature). *Hit:* 1d8 + 1 piercing damage and the target may be infected with cadaver fever (see below).
Melee Attack—Claw: +3 to hit (reach 5 ft.; one creature). *Hit:* 2d6 + 1 slashing damage and the target may be infected with cadaver fever (see below).

STATISTICS

Str 13 (+1), **Dex** 13 (+1), **Con** 16 (+3), **Int** 3 (−4), **Wis** 10 (+0), **Cha** 10 (+0)
Languages: None
Senses: Darkvision 60 ft.

TRAITS

Cadaver Fever: At the end of a battle against cadavers, anyone who was clawed or bitten by a cadaver must make a DC 13 Con saving throw against disease. Failure indicates the character is infected with cadaver fever. An infected character gains one level of exhaustion immediately and must repeat the saving throw at the end of every long rest. Each failed saving throw adds one more level of exhaustion; a successful saving throw at the end of a long rest means only that the character's condition doesn't worsen. The character recovers fully when he or she makes successful saving throws at the ends of two consecutive long rests or when *lesser restoration* or comparable magic is used on the character.

Reanimation: When reduced to 0 hit points, a cadaver is not destroyed; rather it falls inert and begins regaining 1 hit point per round. Hit points lost to magical weapons or spells are not regained. When the creature reaches its full hit point total (minus damage dealt by magical attacks and weapons), it reassembles itself and stands up, ready to fight again. Scattering or even destroying the pieces of its body don't prevent it from magically reassembling and reanimating. If *gentle repose* is cast on the cadaver when it is at 0 hit points, it can't reanimate. A *bless* spell delays the reanimation, causing the creature to regain 1 hit point per minute instead of per round.

ECOLOGY

Environment: Any
Organization: Solitary or gang (2–5)

Cadavers are the skeletal remains of people who were buried alive or given an improper burial (an unmarked grave or mass grave for example). They can be found haunting graveyards and cemeteries.

Cadavers are infused with a hatred that rivals many other undead creatures. This hatred is directed toward its own existence as well as the existence of all living creatures. Thus, the cadaver attacks all creatures it encounters. They have a distinct hatred for light, but it does not damage them. All encounters with cadavers are at night or in places cloaked in darkness.

Encounters are most often with a solitary creature. Multiple cadavers do not work in concert with each other, though they do not attack each other. Being mindless, they simply charge into combat with no thought for tactics or finesse.

Cadavers are sometimes found in the employ of greater undead such as wights or ghasts.

A cadaver attacks by raking with its filthy claws or biting with its sharp, disease-infested teeth. They often lie in shallow graves waiting for potential victims to wander too close, where they immediately spring to the attack, raking and biting until destroyed or until all foes are dead.

Cadaver Lord

The rotted flesh and tattered garments of this creature do little to hide the savage gleam of intellect in its burning eyes nor the grin of anticipation that crosses its features as it advances.

Cadaver Lord
XP 700 (CR 3)
CE Medium undead
Initiative +2

DEFENSE
AC 15 (chain shirt)
hp: 45 (6d8 + 18)
Resistance: Bludgeoning, piercing, and slashing damage from nonmagical weapons
Immunity: Cold, necrotic, and poison damage; fright, poison, exhaustion, unconsciousness

OFFENSE
Speed: 30 ft.
Multiattack: The cadaver lord bites once and attacks once with claws.
Melee Attack—Bite: +5 to hit (reach 5 ft.; one creature). *Hit:* 1d8 + 3 piercing damage and the target may be infected with cadaver fever (see below).
Melee Attack—Claw: +5 to hit (reach 5 ft.; one creature). *Hit:* 3d6 + 3 slashing damage and the target may be infected with cadaver fever (see below).

STATISTICS
Str 17 (+3), **Dex** 15 (+2), **Con** 16 (+3),
Int 10 (+0), **Wis** 12 (+1), **Cha** 14 (+2)
Languages: Any language it spoke while alive; communicates telepathically with all undead within 100 feet
Senses: Darkvision 60 ft.

TRAITS
Aura of Desecration: All undead within 20 feet of a cadaver lord gain tactical advantage against attempts to turn undead.
Cadaver Fever: At the end of a battle against cadaver lords, anyone who was clawed or bitten by a cadaver lord must make a DC 12 Con saving throw against disease. Failure indicates the character is infected with cadaver fever. An infected character gains one level of exhaustion immediately and must repeat the saving throw at the end of every long rest. Each failed saving throw adds one more level of exhaustion; a successful saving throw at the end of a long rest means only that the character's condition doesn't worsen. The character recovers fully when he or she makes successful saving throws at the ends of two consecutive long rests, or when *greater restoration* is cast on the character.

Create Spawn: A creature slain by a cadaver lord rises in 1d4 minutes as a cadaver under the control of the cadaver lord.

Reanimation: When reduced to 0 hit points, a cadaver lord is not destroyed; rather it falls inert and begins regaining 1 hit point per round. Hit points lost to magical weapons or spells are not regained. When the creature reaches its full hit point total (minus damage dealt by magical attacks and weapons), it reassembles itself and stands up, ready to fight again. Scattering or even destroying the pieces of its body don't prevent it from magically reassembling and reanimating. If *gentle repose* is cast on the cadaver lord when it is at 0 hit points, it can't reanimate. A *bless* spell delays the reanimation, causing the creature to regain 1 hit point per minute instead of per round.

Spell-like Abilities: The cadaver lord can use the following spell-like abilities, using Charisma as its casting ability (DC 12, attack +4). The cadaver lord requires no material components to use these abilities.
1/day: *darkness, fear*

Summon Undead (1/day): Once per day as an action, a cadaver lord can summon five cadavers. They arrive in 1d6 rounds (shambling from nearby chambers, digging up from their shallow graves, etc.), and are under the cadaver lord's control.

ECOLOGY
Environment: Any
Organization: Solitary or troupe (cadaver lord plus 1–4 cadavers)

Cadaver lords are rare examples of cadavers that arose from creatures that were uncommonly powerful in life, making them extremely dangerous opponents. They are stronger, tougher, and more intelligent than the cadavers they command. They are rarely encountered by chance and rarely encountered alone. Most maintain a lair far away from civilization where they plot and plan, sending their minions on missions to further their goals.

Copyright Notice
Author Scott Greene.

Carbuncle

This creature resembles a cross between an anteater and an armadillo. Embedded in its head is a large, red jewel. The creature has a long snout and a low-slung body protected by thick bands of leathery hide, which are dappled gray and brown, shading to lighter colors of gray on its underbelly.

Carbuncle

XP 25 (CR 1/8)
Unaligned Small aberration
Initiative +0

DEFENSE
AC 11 (natural armor)
hp: 4 (1d6 + 1)
Saving Throws: Dex +2

OFFENSE
Speed: 10 ft.
Melee Attack—Bite: +2 to hit (reach 5 ft.; one creature). *Hit:* 1d4 piercing damage.

STATISTICS
Str 7 (–1), **Dex** 10 (+0), **Con** 12 (+1),
Int 10 (+0), **Wis** 18 (+4), **Cha** 8 (–1)
Languages: Telepathy within 100 ft.
Senses: Darkvision 60 ft.

TRAITS
Discord: As an attack, a carbuncle can telepathically sow discord in one creature within 30 feet. An affected creature must make a successful DC 14 Wis saving throw or fall into loud bickering and arguing with those around him or her. Meaningful communication is impossible. If creatures of different alignments are affected and bickering, each has a 30% chance that they feel compelled to attack the person they are bickering with who is the most different in alignment. Bickering lasts 5d4 rounds. Fighting (if it occurs) begins 1d4 rounds into the bickering and lasts 2d4 rounds.

ECOLOGY
Environment: Temperate forests
Organization: Solitary

Deep in the tangled underbrush of forests and in the remote regions of dismal swamps and bogs lives a strange creature called the carbuncle. It is a shy creature that seeks to avoid encounters. Should it seek interaction, a carbuncle often begins by proudly announcing the value of the gem in its forehead just to watch the reaction the information arouses.

Despite its shy nature, the carbuncle has a mischievous side as well. It sometimes joins travelers so it can play pranks on them and observe the reactions of the unfortunate victims of its curiosity. After joining with a party, a carbuncle eventually seeks to breed hostility and suspicion between party members. They have been known to telepathically contact nearby monsters and draw them to the party, so that it can watch the battle and read the thoughts of the party under attack before slipping away.

A carbuncle can be coerced to surrender the gem in its forehead with a successful DC 20 Cha (Deception) check. If the attempt fails, the carbuncle sees through the deception and flees. If the carbuncle relinquishes its gem, it grows another one within one month. When a carbuncle is slain, its forehead gem crumbles to dust.

Though fascinated by combat, carbuncles are nearly helpless in melee. They enjoy setting up encounters using their powers and watching the brutal scenes unfold, but they surrender immediately if attacked themselves. In a lethal situation, a carbuncle first tries to bargain for safety with its gem. If that fails, it can will itself to die rather than suffer torment (and rather than giving up its gem to someone it suspects will only kill it anyway).

Credit
The Carbuncle originally appeared in the First Edition *Fiend Folio* (© TSR/Wizards of the Coast, 1981) and is used by permission.

Copyright Notice
Author Scott Greene, based on original material by Albie Fiore.

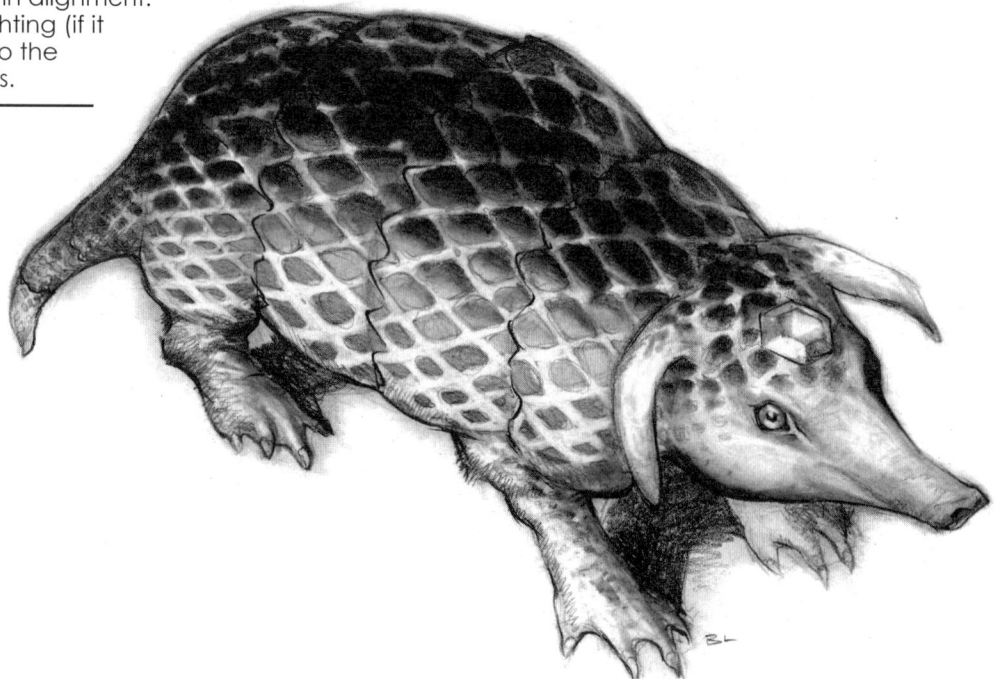

Caryatid Column

An exquisitely sculpted and finished statue of a beautiful female warrior, longsword in her hand.

Caryatid Column
XP 200 (CR 1)
Unaligned Medium construct
Initiative –1

DEFENSE
AC 14 (natural armor)
hp: 30 (4d10 + 8)
Resistance: Bludgeoning, piercing, and slashing damage from nonmagical weapons
Immunity: Necrotic, poison, and psychic damage; disease, fright, paralysis, petrification, exhaustion, stun, unconsciousness

OFFENSE
Speed: 20 ft.
Melee Attack—Longsword: +4 to hit (reach 5 ft.; one creature). *Hit:* 1d10 + 2 slashing damage.

STATISTICS
Str 14 (+2), **Dex** 9 (–1), **Con** 14 (+2), **Int** 10 (+0), **Wis** 11 (+0), **Cha** 1 (–5)
Senses: Darkvision 60 ft.

TRAITS
Immunity to Magic: A caryatid column automatically succeeds on all saving throws against spells and spell-like effects. If a successful saving throw reduces damage by half, the caryatid column takes no damage instead. In addition, certain spells and effects function differently against the creature, as noted below (these effects override its immunity).
• A *stone shape* spell cancels the caryatid column's immunity to magic for 1d4 rounds.
Shatter Weapons: Whenever a character strikes a caryatid column with a melee weapon and the attack roll is a natural 1, 2, or 3, the character must make a Str check. The character's Str bonus is added to the roll, but the character's proficiency bonus and the weapon's magical bonus (if any) are subtracted from the roll. If the result is 15 or less, there is no effect. If the result is 16 or higher, the weapon shatters and becomes useless.

ECOLOGY
Environment: Temperate
Organization: Solitary

A caryatid column is akin to the stone golem. Both are magical constructs created by spellcasters, but caryatid columns have a much narrower purpose. They are always created for a very specific defensive function. The caryatid column stands 7 feet tall and weighs around 1,500 pounds. The column always wields a weapon (usually a longsword) in its left hand. The weapon itself is constructed of steel, but is melded with the column in such a way that it is indistinguishable from stone until the column animates. When melded, the sword blends into the column in a way that makes it difficult to notice at all (a DC 20 Wis [Perception] check is needed to see it).

Caryatid columns are programmed as guardians and activate when certain conditions or stipulations are met; for example, when a living creature passes through a doorway or tampers with a locked chest guarded by a caryatid column. A caryatid column can't move more than 50 feet from the spot it guards.

Credit
The Caryatid Column originally appeared in the First Edition *Fiend Folio* (© TSR/Wizards of the Coast, 1981) and is used by permission.

Copyright Notice
Author Scott Greene, based on original material by Jean Wells.

Cat, Feral Undead

This creature looks like an escaped house cat that died weeks ago.

Undead Feral Cat

XP 25 (CR 1/8)
CE Small undead
Initiative +2

DEFENSE

AC 12
hp: 3 (1d6)
Resistance: Necrotic damage
Immunity: Poison damage;
exhaustion, poison,
unconsciousness

OFFENSE

Speed: 30 ft.
Multiattack: The feral cat attacks
twice with claws.
Melee Attack—Claw: +4 to hit
(reach 5 ft.; one creature). *Hit:* 1
slashing damage and the target
creature must make a successful
DC 8 Con saving throw or suffer
the effect of paralyzing poison
(see below).

STATISTICS

Str 4 (–3), **Dex** 15 (+2), **Con** 11 (+0),
Int 3 (–4), **Wis** 12 (+1), **Cha** 6 (–2)
Languages: None
Senses: Darkvision 60 ft.

TRAITS

Paralyzing Poison: Every time a
character is clawed by a feral
undead cat, he or she must make
a DC 8 Con saving throw. On the
first failed save, the character
becomes poisoned; on the
second failed save, the character
becomes restrained; and on the
third failed save, the character
becomes paralyzed. Each effect
lasts for 1d6 x 10 minutes, and
the lengths add together as the
character's condition worsens.

ECOLOGY

Environment: Graveyards and ruins
Organization: Group (2–5) or pack
(4–24)

Feral undead cats look like they were created by zombie-raising magic, but they are quite unlike mindless undead such as skeletons or zombies. These cats possess an animal cunning akin to that of ghouls (although with less intelligence overall), and they are not slow moving as zombies are. Like ghouls, they tend to form into packs. A lone undead cat is almost certainly scouting or keeping watch for a larger group.

Feral undead cats sometimes hide in plain sight by lying alongside the road, in ditches, along fencerows, or in abandoned buildings—places where people wouldn't be surprised to see dead cats. The surprise comes when the cats leap onto the characters' legs and backs with their filthy, razor-sharp claws extended. Malevolent witches and other evil spellcasters who sometimes need dead cats for their magic can be caught unaware by these creatures and overcome by their poison. The cats eat what they bring down, but slowly, while it's still alive and paralyzed. They've been known to use one victim as bait to lure more victims into their territory.

Credit
Author Matt Finch

Caterprism

This creature looks like an immense, crystalline caterpillar.

Caterprism

XP 1,100 (CR 4)
Unaligned Large monstrosity
Initiative +1

DEFENSE
AC 14 (natural armor)
hp: 87 (8d10 + 32)
Immunity: Petrified, prone
Vulnerability: Thunder damage

OFFENSE
Speed: 30 ft., burrow 20 ft.
Multiattack: A caterprism attacks four times with claws, or once with mandibles, or spews its crystal saliva.
Melee Attack—Claw: +7 to hit (reach 5 ft.; one creature). *Hit:* 1d8 + 5 slashing damage.
Melee Attack—Mandibles: +7 to hit (reach 5 ft.; one creature). *Hit:* 2d8 + 5 piercing damage. This attack has tactical advantage against targets in armor. If the bite scores a critical hit, the target must make a successful DC 15 Con saving throw or be reduced to 0 hit points instantly.
Area Attack—Crystal Saliva (recharge 6): automatic hit (range 20 ft. cone; creatures in range). *Hit:* 3d6 piercing damage, or half damage with a successful DC 14 Dex saving throw, and the affected area becomes difficult terrain for all creatures except caterprisms.

STATISTICS
Str 20 (+5), **Dex** 12 (+1), **Con** 18 (+4), **Int** 4 (−3), **Wis** 13 (+1), **Cha** 11 (+0)
Languages: None
Senses:
Darkvision 60 ft.

ECOLOGY
Environment:
Elemental plane of earth

Organization: Solitary, pair, or nest (2–5)

Caterprisms come from the Elemental Plane of Earth. They resemble gigantic caterpillars made of crystal, with hexagonal body segments and twelve sharply-angled legs. Each body segment is about two feet long and contains a single pair of legs. The head of a caterprism contains its large, faceted eyes and huge, crystalline mandibles that can snip the head off an armored warrior as easily as scissors snip the head from a paper doll.

Besides its crystalline claws and mandibles of unearthly sharpness, a caterprism can also spew a silklike substance in a 20-foot cone. This substance instantly solidifies into rock-hard, needle-sharp spears of crystal.

Although caterprisms prefer to consume the rich minerals of their home plane, they sometimes wander through natural portals into the Material Plane. There they create long, winding tunnels as they eat their way through solid rock. Dwarves have been known to bring caterprisms under some degree of control and use them to help carve out mines and new dwelling places. A caterprism can eat through 1 foot of solid stone per minute, leaving behind a tunnel 5 feet in diameter.

If it feels threatened, a caterprism's first action is to spew its silklike saliva at opponents. It then closes in to bite or rears up and stabs at opponents with the first four of its razor sharp legs.

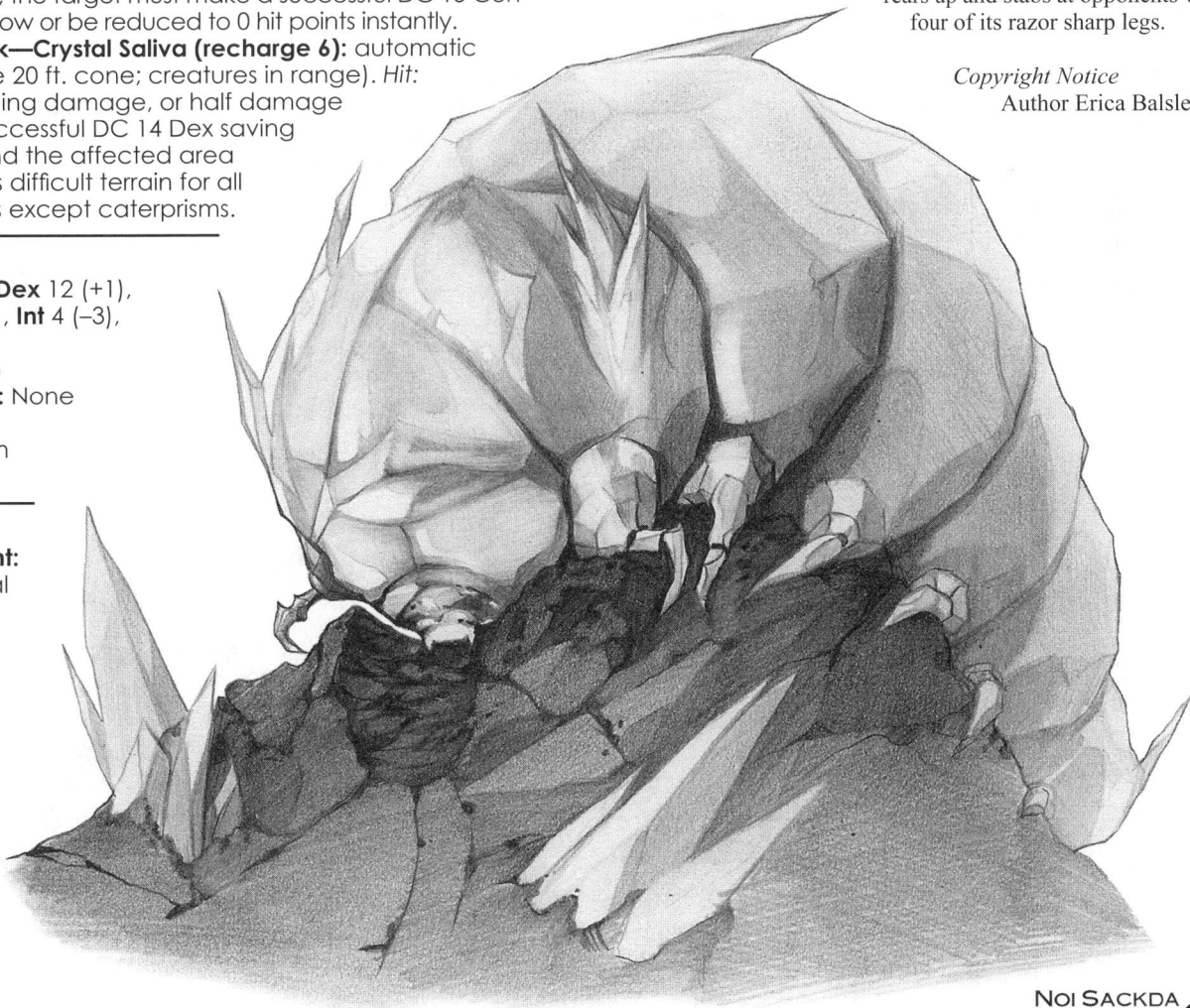

NOI SACKDA
UDON

Catfish, Giant Electric

A wide mouthed, goggle-eyed fish with slippery grey skin and a puffy, bloated body.

Giant Electric Catfish

XP 700 (CR 3)
Unaligned Large beast (aquatic)
Initiative +2

DEFENSE
AC 12
hp: 68 (8d10 + 24)
Immunity: Lightning damage

OFFENSE
Speed: Swim 40 ft.
Multiattack: The giant electric catfish bites once and uses its electricity discharge (if available), or it swallows a grappled creature. It can't bite another target while it has a creature grappled.
Melee Attack—Bite: +6 to hit (reach 5 ft.; one creature). *Hit:* 1d10 + 4 piercing damage and the target is grappled and restrained.
Melee Attack—Swallow: +6 to hit (reach 0 ft.; one Medium or smaller creature grappled by the giant electric catfish). *Hit:* 1d8 + 4 acid damage and the target is swallowed (see below).

STATISTICS
Str 19 (+4), **Dex** 15 (+2), **Con** 17 (+3),
Int 2 (–4), **Wis** 12 (+1), **Cha** 2 (–4)
Languages: None
Senses: Tremorsense 60 ft. (in water)

TRAITS
Electricity Discharge (recharge 6): A giant electric catfish can generate a pulse of electricity. Every creature within 10 feet of the giant catfish takes 2d6 points of lightning damage and is stunned until the start of the giant catfish's next turn. A successful DC 13 Con saving throw reduces damage to half and negates the stun.
Swallow: A swallowed creature is blinded and restrained but no longer grappled. It takes 1d8 + 4 acid damage automatically at the start of each of the giant catfish's turn. Only one Medium creature or two Small creatures can be inside the giant catfish at one time. A swallowed creature is unaffected by anything happening outside the giant catfish or by attacks from outside it. A swallowed creature can get out of the giant catfish by using 5 feet of movement, but only after the giant catfish is dead.

ECOLOGY
Environment: Non-arctic aquatic
Organization: Solitary or school (5–8)

Giant electric catfish make their homes beneath submerged logs and in streambed pits where they face upstream with their mouths open, swallowing everything resembling food that tumbles or floats into their toothless maws. They favor dank, dark, slow-moving water with limited visibility. They are nocturnal hunters and venture out a few hours after sunset to hunt.

Giant electric catfish are about 8 feet long but can grow to lengths of 12 feet or more. Their bloated bodies are generally gray or brown in color, fading to a dull white or cream on the underbelly. Their eyes are small and positioned on either side of a wide, round snout. Three sets of barbels (feelers) are located around the mouth. Unlike many fish, a giant electric catfish has no dorsal fin.

Giant electric catfish are territorial, and the defend their realms with great ferocity. Before engaging in combat, when threatened or facing a potential enemy, an electric catfish generates a pulse of crackling electricity in an effort to intimidate or discourage would-be predators. Failing this, the giant electric catfish enters combat and bites its foe.

Catoblepas

This creature resembles a bloated hippopotamus with a whiplike tail,
a long neck like the body of a snake, and the most repulsively ugly head imaginable.

Catoblepas

XP 1,800 (CR 5)
Unaligned Large monstrosity
Initiative +0

DEFENSE

AC 13 (natural armor)
hp: 76 (8d10 + 24)
Immunity: Poison damage; poison

OFFENSE

Speed: 30 ft.
Multiattack: The catoblepas attacks with its tail and uses its rancid breath (if available).
Melee Attack—Tail Sweep: +6 to hit (reach 15 ft.; up to 3 creatures in a 10-ft. square). *Hit:* 1d10 + 3 bludgeoning damage and the target is knocked prone.
Area Attack—Rancid Breath (recharge 5, 6): automatic hit (60 ft. cone; creatures in the cone). *Hit:* creatures in the cone must make a DC 15 Con saving throw against poison or be stunned. Stunned creatures can repeat the saving throw at the end of each of their turns, recovering with a successful save. If a creature that is currently stunned by the catoblepas's breath is stunned again by a second rancid breath attack, that creature immediately drops to 0 hit points.

STATISTICS

Str 17 (+3), **Dex** 10 (+0), **Con** 19 (+4),
Int 4 (−4), **Wis** 8 (−1), **Cha** 4 (−3)
Languages: None
Senses: Darkvision 60 ft.

TRAITS

Stunning Ugliness: The catoblepas is so shockingly ugly that just glimpsing one can blind the viewer. Characters fighting a catoblepas must either either avert their eyes and take tactical disadvantage on attack rolls against the catoblepas, or make a DC 15 Con saving throw before making their attack roll. Failure on the saving throw means the character is blinded until the start of his or her next turn. Anyone who rolls a lower initiative result than the catoblepas must attempt this saving throw immediately at the beginning of combat.

ECOLOGY

Environment: Swamps
  Organization: Solitary, pair, or herd (3–6)

The catoblepas is loathsome beyond description, with no positive qualities whatsoever. It resembles a bloated hippopotamus with a long, whiplike tail and a snakelike neck topped with the oversized head of a diseased warthog with bloodshot eyes. For all its ungainliness, its tail is tremendously quick and accurate when whipping around to strike at enemies anywhere near the creature.

The deadliest weapon of the catoblepas, however, is its rancid breath, which can leave creatures helplessly gasping for air, or even kill with too large a dose. Fortunately, its metabolism is so slow that it exhales only infrequently.

Catoblepases live only in swamps, and the more fetid, the better. They are territorial, ill-tempered, and aggressive when encountered, but they spend most of their time slumbering, digging for roots, or hunting for small prey or fish in shallow water. On those rare occasions when they venture to the edges of their fens, they've been known to devastate entire villages simply by standing at the outskirts and letting their rancid breath waft through town.

Cave Cricket

This creature appears to be a giant cricket, about the size of a dog. Its body is pale gray in color.

Cave Cricket

XP 50 (CR 1/4)
Unaligned Small beast
Initiative +2

DEFENSE

AC 13 (natural armor)
hp: 5 (2d6 – 2)

OFFENSE

Speed: 30 ft., climb 30 ft., leap 30 ft.
Multiattack: The cave cricket kicks twice.
Melee Attack—Kick: +4 to hit (reach 5 ft.; one creature). *Hit:* 1d4 + 2 bludgeoning damage.

STATISTICS

Str 10 (+0), **Dex** 14 (+2), **Con** 8 (–1),
Int 1 (–5), **Wis** 10 (+0), **Cha** 7 (–2)
Languages: None
Senses: Darkvision 60 ft.

TRAITS

Chirp: Creatures within 20 feet of a chirping cave cricket can't be heard unless they scream. Spellcasters in the area must make a successful DC 9 Con saving throw to cast a spell correctly. Failure indicates the spell is not cast, but the slot is not expended. The chirping doubles the chance of attracting wandering monsters, if applicable.

ECOLOGY

Environment: Underground
Organization: Solitary or cluster (2–5)

Cave crickets are larger versions of normal crickets and, like the smaller crickets they resemble, they are mostly harmless. Their chief danger comes from their chirping, which they do when alarmed, because other monsters recognize that sound as indicating there might be fresh prey nearby. The chirping travels up to 300 feet through the tunnels and caves where these crickets are normally found.

Cave crickets are about 3 feet long.

These giant insects rarely attack living creatures larger than themselves. If attacked, a cave cricket uses its powerful legs to kick opponents before hopping away.

Credit

The cave cricket originally appeared in the First Edition module *S4 The Lost Caverns of Tsojcanth* (© TSR/Wizards of the Coast, 1982) and later in the First Edition *Monster Manual II* (© TSR/Wizards of the Coast, 1983), and is used by permission.

Copyright Notice

Author Scott Greene, based on original material by Gary Gygax.

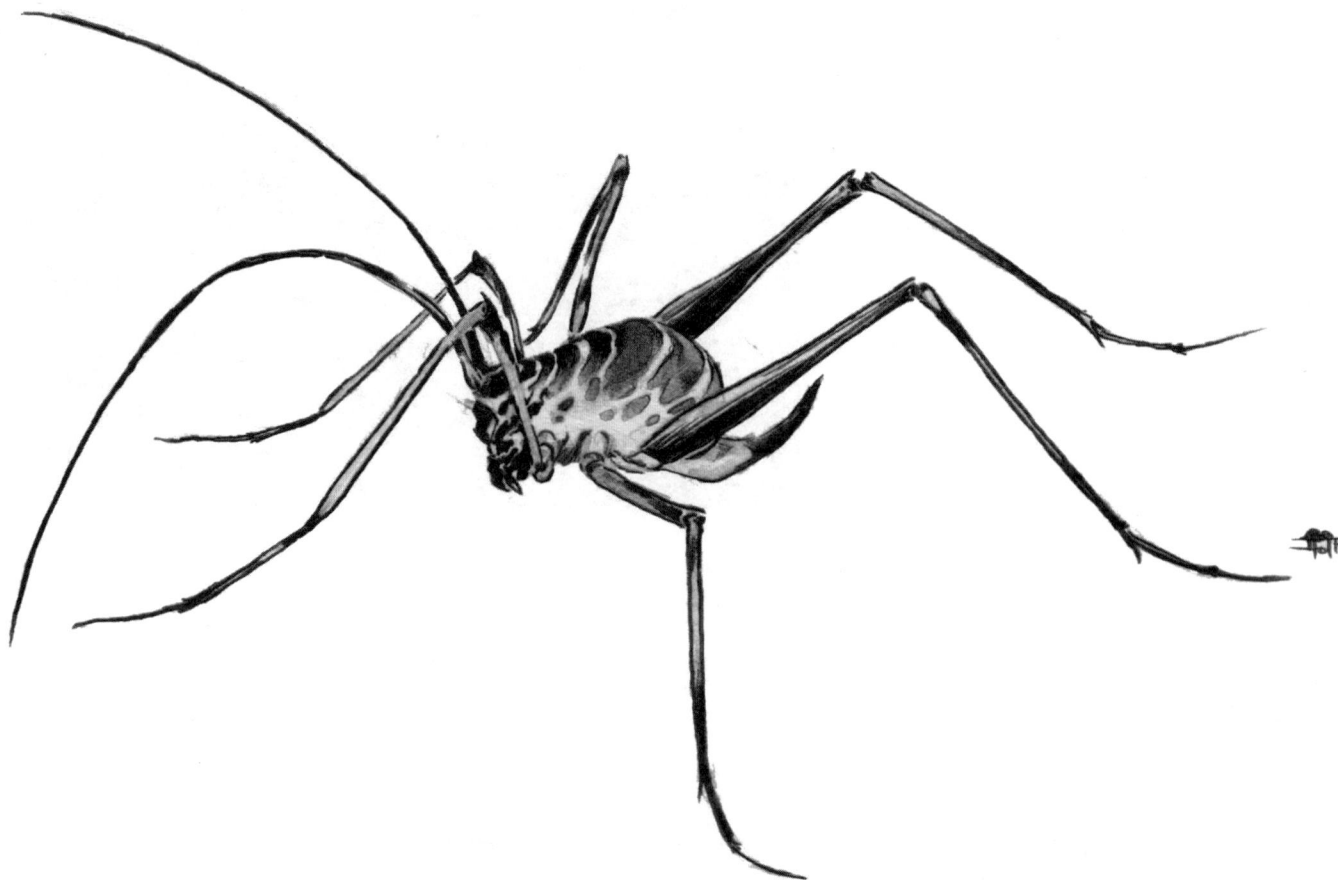

Cave Eel

This creature resembles a cross between a snake and an eel,
but that's only if you see it before it bites into you with its steel-hard teeth.

Cave Eel

XP 50 (CR 1/4)
Unaligned Medium beast
Initiative +2

DEFENSE

AC 12
hp: 9 (2d8)

OFFENSE

Speed: 25 ft.
Melee Attack—Bite: +4 to hit (reach 5 ft.; one creature). *Hit:* 1d8 + 2 piercing damage and the target is grappled and restrained (see Viselike Jaws, below).

STATISTICS

Str 13 (+1), **Dex** 14 (+2), **Con** 11 (+0), **Int** 1 (−5), **Wis** 10 (+0), **Cha** 3 (−4)
Languages: None
Skills: Stealth +4
Senses: Darkvision 60 ft.

TRAITS

Concealed Burrow: Cave eels conceal their burrows skillfully, so they have tactical advantage on Dex (Stealth) checks to be hidden at the beginning of an encounter. An attacking cave eel lunges from its cave, bites a victim within 5 feet, and then withdraws back into its burrow without triggering an opportunity attack. While in a burrow, a cave eel has three-quarters cover (+5 bonus to AC and Dex saving throws). The only way to negate this benefit is for a character to ready an action and attack the cave eel with a reaction as it extends its body to strike.

Viselike Jaws: When a cave eel withdraws back into its burrow with a grappled character in its jaws, that character's body effectively becomes a shield protecting the eel, giving it total cover inside its burrow (it has only three-quarters cover against the character it grapples). While the eel has a character grappled this way, it doesn't need to extend from its burrow to attack the grappled character, who it bites automatically.

ECOLOGY

Environment: Caves and other subterranean areas
Organization: Group (2–5) or swarm (3–24)

Cave eels resemble large, air-breathing eels, but they have armored snouts and tremendously tough teeth with which they can chew tunnels through rock. They wait in these tunnels for potential prey to walk near, then lunge out to take great bites from whatever's in front of them. They usually pick narrow cave passages for their ambushes, where prey has little room to back out of reach of the cave eels' long, sinuous bodies.

These unusual creatures have even been known to chew burrows into earth elementals and stone golems and take up residence in those constructs, to the mutual benefit of both. They don't collect treasure for any purpose, but because they drag the slain bodies of their victims (including unfortunate adventurers) into their tunnels to eat them, treasure can sometimes be found if one follows their tunnels to their lairs. Cave eel tunnels are just barely big enough for an unarmored human or tiefling to squeeze through; halflings, gnomes, and elves have an easier time of it, while dwarves, half-orcs, and dragonborn are too big to fit.

Cave Fisher

This man-sized creature resembles a cross between a lobster and a spider.
It has eight legs, two of which end in serrated pincers. Its snout is long and pointed.

Cave Fisher
XP 450 (CR 2)
Unaligned Large monstrosity
Initiative +2

DEFENSE
AC 12 (natural armor)
hp: 51 (6d10 + 18)
Immunity: Psychic damage; fright

OFFENSE
Speed: 20 ft., climb 20 ft.
Multiattack: The cave fisher attacks once with its filament or twice with claws.
Melee Attack—Claw: +5 to hit (reach 5 ft.; one creature). *Hit:* 1d6 + 3 slashing damage.
Ranged Attack—Filament: +3 to hit (range 60 ft.; one creature). *Hit:* the target is grappled and pulled 20 feet closer to the cave fisher (see below).

STATISTICS
Str 17 (+3), **Dex** 12 (+1), **Con** 17 (+3),
Int 1 (–5), **Wis** 10 (+0), **Cha** 4 (–3)
Languages: None
Skills: Perception +2
Senses: Darkvision 60 ft.

TRAITS
Filament: A creature struck by a cave fisher's filament becomes grappled by the sticky thread and is pulled 20 feet closer to the cave fisher. A grappled creature can use its action to rip the filament free with a DC 13 Str check, or can attack the filament directly (AC 12, 5 hp, resistant to all but slashing damage). Alcohol or *universal solvent* dissolves the adhesive and releases the creature caught by the filament. A cave fisher can have only one creature grappled at a time.

ECOLOGY
Environment: Underground
Organization: Solitary or gang (2–4)

The cave fisher is a 7-foot long creature with a hard outer shell that makes it resemble a large beetle. It can shoot a strong, sticky, weblike filament from its extended snout. The creature uses this filament to trap and drag prey to within range of the cave fisher's slicing claws.

The cave fisher lairs on ledges and cliffs underground, where it can quickly strike passing prey and reel it up to its mouth. Its lair is always littered with bones and gear from previous victims, and hanging shreds of spent filaments.

The cave fisher's preferred method of attack is to anchor itself to its ledge and string filament across the ground of its lair. When a living creature touches or passes near the filament, the fisher attempts to trap it and reel it in, all while remaining safely sheltered on its ledge. If this initial trap fails, the cave fisher can move forward to the lip of the ledge and launch its filament like an anteater's tongue at an opponent up to 60 feet away, but this exposes it to attack from below. Another favored method of attack for the cave fisher is to hide itself in a crack or a ledge above a cavern and dangle its filament down onto unsuspecting creatures passing below it.

Credit
The cave fisher originally appeared in the First Edition adventure *A4 In the Dungeons of the Slave Lords* (© TSR/Wizards of the Coast, 1981) and later in the First Edition *Monster Manual II* (© TSR/Wizards of the Coast, 1983) and is used by permission.

Copyright Notice
Author Scott Greene, based on original material by Lawrence Schick.

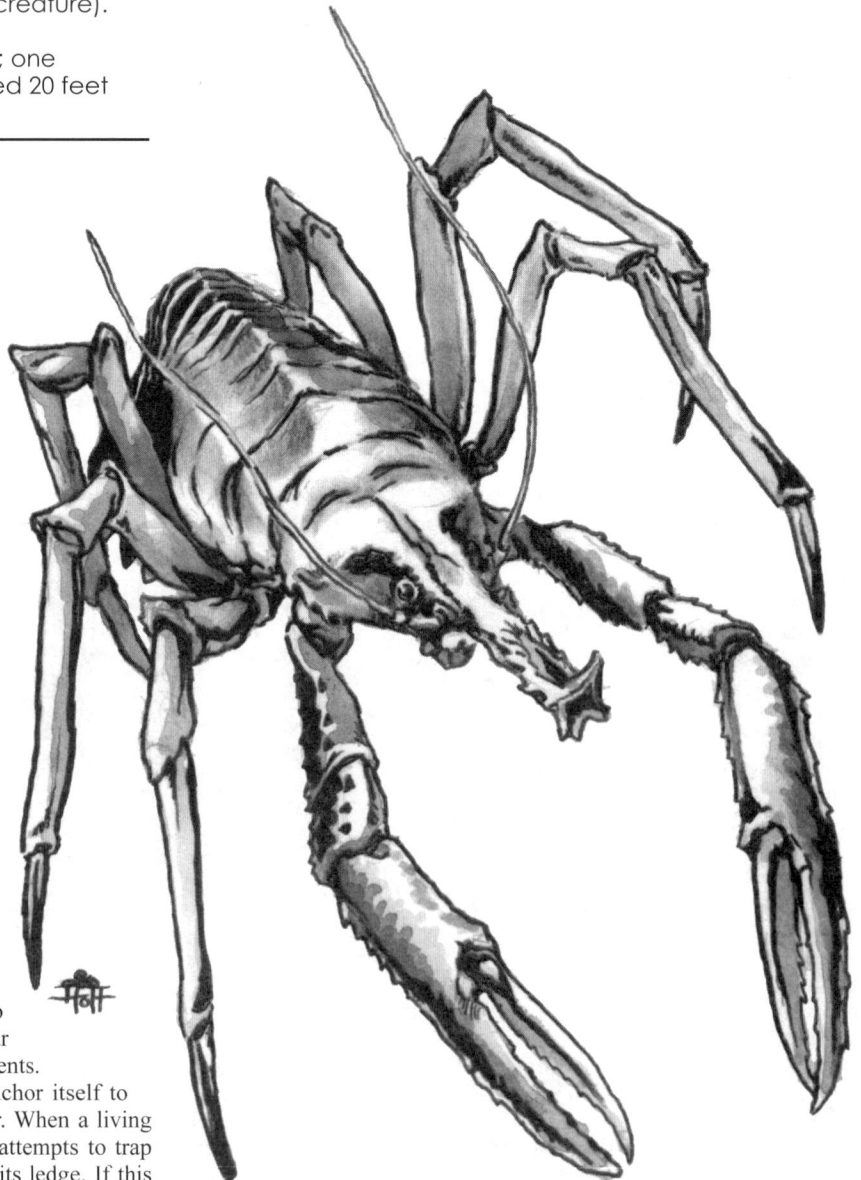

Cave Leech

This large, bloated creature has a flattened, semitranslucent body of sickly yellow. Eight whiplike tentacles protrude from the monster's front, near its head. Hundreds of smaller tentacles line its body and seem to aid in locomotion. Its mouth is rounded and ringed with dozens of needlelike teeth.

Cave Leech

XP 2,300 (CR 6)
CE Large beast
Initiative +2

DEFENSE
AC 10
hp: 102 (12d10 + 36)
Resistance: Bludgeoning damage

OFFENSE
Speed: 20 ft., swim 30 ft.
Multiattack: The cave leech attacks eight times, in any combination of tentacle attacks and constriction attacks.
Melee Attack—
Tentacle: +7 to hit (reach 10 ft.; one creature). *Hit:* 1d6 + 4 bludgeoning damage and the target is grappled and restrained.
Melee Attack—Constriction: automatic hit (one creature grappled by a tentacle). *Hit:* 1d6 + 4 bludgeoning damage and the target can be dragged to the cave leech's mouth to be drained of blood (see below).

STATISTICS
Str 18 (+4), **Dex** 11 (+0), **Con** 17 (+3), **Int** 3 (−3), **Wis** 12 (+1), **Cha** 6 (−2)
Languages: None
Senses: Tremorsense 60 ft.

TRAITS
Blood Drain: Immediately after making a constriction attack against a grappled creature, the cave leech can try to drag that creature to its mouth, where it bites the creature automatically and drains its blood, inflicting 1d8 piercing damage. The target can resist being dragged with a Str contest against the cave leech; the cave leech must win the contest to drag the character to its mouth.

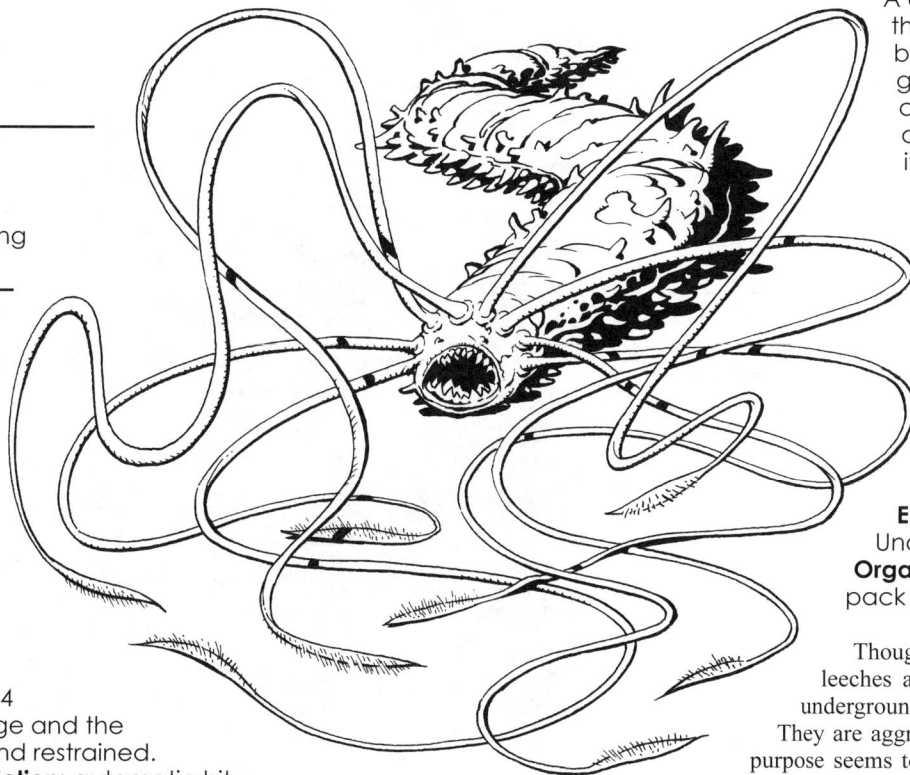

A character who wins this contest does not break the cave leech's grapple. The cave leech can try a Str contest against every creature it makes a constriction attack against until it wins a Str contest and drains one creature's blood. It can drain blood from the same creature or a different creature each round, but it must win a Str contest each time.

ECOLOGY
Environment: Underground
Organization: Solitary or pack (2–5)

Though not aquatic creatures, cave leeches are often found lairing near underground rivers, lakes, and streams. They are aggressive monsters whose sole purpose seems to be to kill and devour any living thing that stumbles into their territory.

Cave leeches aren't social animals, but they are seldom found alone. Food is not shared among them, so each leech is effectively on its own when hunting prey. When one catches something, however, others are likely to show up quickly. Quarrels often erupt over prey, with grappled victims being caught in the middle of a tug-of-war between two or more leeches, all trying to suck out their blood.

An adult cave leech grows about 8 feet long, and its whiplike tentacles are each about 6 feet long. Cave leeches are easily mistaken for ordinary giant leeches, especially when at rest, when the creatures fold their tentacles back against their bodies. They also do this when waiting to strike.

When a meal comes within range, the cave leech lashes out with a tentacle and grabs its target. Grabbed prey is pulled to the cave leech's mouth and bitten by its horrible teeth. A victim that is completely drained of blood becomes a pale, shrunken husk. Leathery, mummifying carcasses of the leeches' victims litter their hunting grounds or lairs, where victims are sometimes dragged to feed the leeches' young.

Centipede Nest

These centipedes aren't larger or hungrier than any other, normal centipedes; there are just more of them.

Centipede Nest

XP 100 (CR 1/2)
Unaligned Medium swarm of Tiny beasts
Initiative +2

DEFENSE
AC 11
hp: 22 (4d8 + 4)
Resistance: Bludgeoning and slashing damage
Immunity: Piercing damage; fright, paralysis, petrification, prone, restrained, stun

OFFENSE
Speed: 15 ft., climb 15 ft.
Melee Attack—Bite: automatic hit (reach 0 ft.; one creature). *Hit:* 1 piercing damage, and the target might suffer the effect of Centipede Poison; see below.

STATISTICS
Str 2 (–4), **Dex** 12 (+1), **Con** 12 (+1),
Int 1 (–5), **Wis** 5 (–3),
   Cha 1 (–5)
Languages: None
Senses: Darkvision 10 ft.

TRAITS
Centipede Poison: The first time a character takes damage from a centipede nest, the character must make a successful DC 11 Con saving throw. On a successful save, the character is immune to the poison from that swarm. On a failed save, the character becomes paralyzed. A paralyzed character repeats the saving throw at the end of each of its turns; on a successful save, the paralysis ends and the character becomes poisoned instead. The character remains poisoned for 5 minutes.

Swarm: The swarming nest can occupy another creature's space and vice versa. The swarm can move through an opening large enough for an individual Tiny insect. The swarm can't regain hit points or gain temporary hit points. Once a character takes damage from a centipede nest, the centipedes are on him or her, and the character continues taking 1 piercing damage every round at the start of the centipede nest's turn, even if the character moves away from the swarm. This continues until three actions have been spent smashing, sweeping, and plucking off all the centipedes that crawled onto the character.

ECOLOGY
Environment: Any nonarctic land
Organization: Solitary or colony (2–8)

A nesting of centipedes is a vast collection of normal centipedes, often combined with a few other sorts of bugs that share the same living space: cockroaches and spiders, generally. Such vermin are not dangerous individually, but when a great number of them are disturbed at once they can present a serious threat.

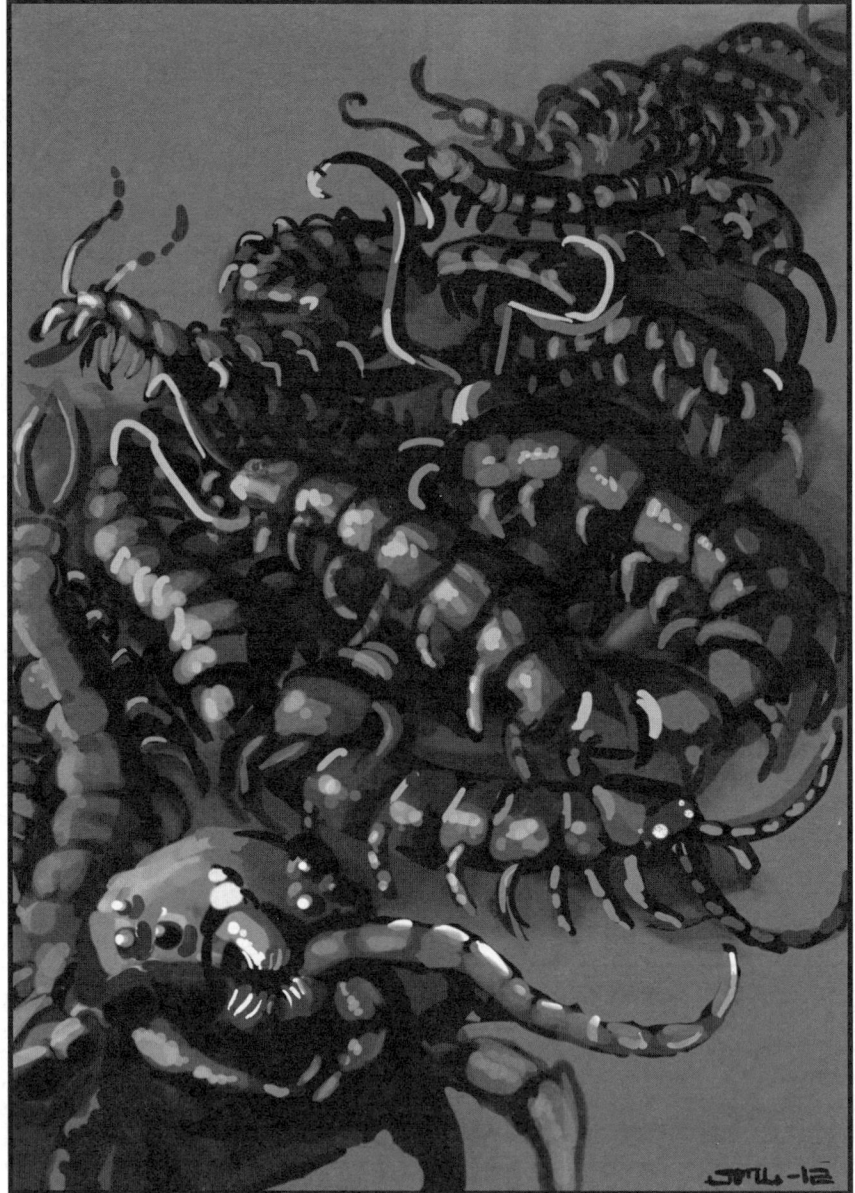

A party will normally encounter a nest of centipedes by accidentally disturbing the nest itself. Moving large wooden beams and prying into ancient masonry entail the risk of arousing one of these huge colonies. The centipedes can swarm up through the floor or drop from the ceiling. When they attack, they clamber all over the character from head to toe, even getting inside the person's armor and clothing.

Author
   Matt Finch (first appeared in *Monsters of Myth*, published by First Edition Adventure Games)

Cerebral Stalker

This humanoid creature has blackish-gray scales covering its semireptilian body. A thick layer of glistening mucus drips from its flesh. Its bestial head sports slate-gray eyes with vertical pupils and a wide mouth lined with sharp teeth. Its hands end in filthy claws.

Cerebral Stalker

XP 1,800 (CR 5)
CE Medium aberration
Initiative +2

___

DEFENSE
AC 16 (natural armor)
hp: 85 (10d8 + 40

___

OFFENSE
Speed: 30 ft., burrow 20 ft. plus earth glide (see below)

Multiattack: The cerebral stalker bites once and attacks twice with claws, or it uses its fear gaze or cocoon ability.

Melee Attack—Bite: +6 to hit (reach 5 ft.; one creature). *Hit:* 1d10 + 3 piercing damage.

Melee Attack—Claw: +6 to hit (reach 5 ft.; one creature). *Hit:* 1d8 + 3 slashing damage and the target is grappled and restrained.

Ranged Attack—Fear Gaze: automatic hit (range 30 feet; one creature that can see the cerebral stalker). *Hit:* Target must make a successful DC 14 Wis saving throw or become frightened for 1d4 rounds.

___

STATISTICS
Str 16 (+3), **Dex** 15 (+2), **Con** 19 (+4),
Int 11 (+0), **Wis** 15 (+2), **Cha** 16 (+3)
Languages: Believed to understand Common and possibly others, but never speaks
Skills: Perception +8
Senses: Darkvision 60 ft., tremorsense 60 ft.

___

TRAITS
Cocoon (3/day): As an action, a cerebral stalker can cocoon a grappled foe with sticky webbing. The webs completely encase the victim, excluding the top of the victim's head, its eyes, and its nose. The cocooned victim is restrained and anchored by the webs to the cerebral stalker's body. The cocooned creature can, as an action, attempt to break free with a successful DC 20 Str (Athletics) check or Dex (Acrobatics) check. The webbing can be cut open enough for a trapped character to escape with 8 points of slashing damage against AC 10.

Consume Brain: Once it has its victim underground, the cerebral stalker begins gnawing on the victim's head, rapidly chewing through bone and tissue, dealing 2d8 + 4 points of piercing damage each round. When the victim dies, the cerebral stalker reaches its goal: the victim's brain, which it promptly devours. A victim slain in this manner reanimates in 1d4 rounds as a zombie. Typically, the cerebral stalker "tosses" them back up to the surface of the ground so their traveling companions can witness the reanimation and deal with their newly undead friend. Zombies created in this manner are under no one's control.

Earth Glide: A cerebral stalker can glide through any sort of natural earth or stone as easily as a fish swims through water. Its gliding leaves no sign of its passage or hint of its presence to creatures that don't possess tremorsense. It can bring cocooned victims along with it, but they have no special capacity for breathing while underground. Getting into the ground, however, is not as easy for the cerebral stalker as moving underground. It must spend four moves on four rounds (no dashing) melding into the ground. On the first round, the creature sinks to its knees; on the second round, to its waist; on the third round, to its neck; and on the fourth round, the stalker and any creature it has cocooned disappear completely underground. Melding into the ground does not provoke an opportunity attack. If the cerebral stalker is grappled while sinking into the ground, it must win a Str contest against its grapplers to sink farther that round. *Dispel magic* or a similar spell cast on a sinking cerebral stalker paralyzes it the same as a *hold monster* spell. The spot where the cerebral stalker sank radiates magic for one hour.

ECOLOGY
Environment: Any land
Organization: Solitary

A cerebral stalker is a carnivorous predator that lies in wait just below the surface of the ground for an unsuspecting victim to pass over or near it. When it detects prey with its tremorsense, the stalker bursts through the ground in a shower of rock and earth, seizes and cocoons its victim, and disappears into the ground to devour the victim's brain at its leisure. Companions of the cerebral stalker's intended victim are held at bay with its fear-inducing gaze—but the real terror is reserved for those the creature drags below ground, where they're destined to have their skulls chewed open and their brains devoured.

The lair of a cerebral stalker is a large, hollow chamber underground, often littered with skull fragments, bits of webbing, and chunks of desiccated brain matter. A cerebral stalker has no use for or interest in treasure, but the belongings of its victims—especially weapons and magical implements they were clutching in their hands when the cerebral stalker grabbed them—sometimes fall loose in the creature's lair, making it worthwhile to locate the lair if possible. The only way in is to dig, however; the cerebral stalker needs no tunnel or doorway of the usual variety.

Cerebral stalkers are solitary creatures; they despise others of their kind. They do not team up or hunt in concert, and they even attack others of their race if one invades their territory. The typical stalker's hunting ground covers an area of 5 square miles, though an individual rarely journeys that far from its lair. The lifespan and reproduction method of these creatures is completely unknown.

Chain Worm

This creature looks like a massive centipede with a bright, reflective silver carapace. Its legs are dull silver and its oversized mandibles are black. A dull black stinger is located at the rear of its body.

Chain Worm
XP 8,400 (CR 12)
Unaligned Large beast
Initiative +3

DEFENSE
AC 21 (natural armor)
hp: 161 (17d10 + 68)
Immunity: Psychic damage; fright

OFFENSE
Speed: 30 ft., climb 20 ft.
Multiattack: The chain worm bites once and stings once with its tail.
Melee Attack—Bite: +10 to hit (reach 5 ft.; one creature). *Hit:* 2d10 + 6 piercing damage, and the target is grappled. While the chain worm maintains a grapple, it can only bite the grappled creature.
Melee Attack—Tail Sting: +10 to hit (reach 5 ft.; one creature). *Hit:* 2d8 + 6 piercing damage plus 2d8 poison damage, and the target is poisoned (see below). This attack has tactical advantage against targets that are grappled by the chain worm.

STATISTICS
Str 22 (+6), **Dex** 16 (+3), **Con** 19 (+4),
Int 1 (−5), **Wis** 12 (+1), **Cha** 4 (−3)
Languages: None
Senses: Darkvision 60 ft., tremorsense 60 ft.

TRAITS
Poison: A creature poisoned by the chain worm must make a DC 16 Con saving throw at the end of each of its turns. On a failed save, the creature takes 2d8 poison damage and remains poisoned. On a successful save, the poisoned condition ends.
Trilling: By rapidly vibrating its carapace as a bonus action, a chain worm emits a high-pitched trilling sound that stuns and deafens creatures within range. All living creatures within 30 feet that can hear the trilling must make a successful a DC 16 Con saving throw or be stunned and deafened. Stunned characters can repeat the saving throw at the end of each of their turns; a successful save ends the stunned condition, but the deafness lasts until the end of the creature's next long rest.

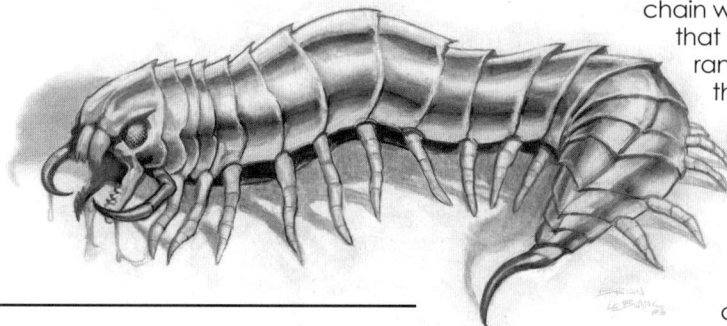

ECOLOGY
Environment: Any land or underground
Organization: Solitary, pair, or pack (3–5)

Chain worms are terrifying subterranean predators with an insatiable appetite for meat. The creatures have a particular fondness for dwarf, gnome, and bugbear flesh. Chain worms often build their nests near communities of these creatures. Though not particularly fond of cold or damp weather, chain worms can be found almost anywhere, as their bulky, heavily armored exoskeletons offer ample protection against almost any environment.

A chain worm's nest is a hole or tunnel littered with rocks, bones, refuse, and debris, and often located on a rocky outcropping or ledge where it is nearly inaccessible to most creatures. Any valuables found in its lair are simply the remains of previous meals that the chain worm couldn't digest or didn't bother eating.

Chain worms stand nearly 6 feet tall and are about 10 feet long, with silver carapaces and dull silver legs. Their heads sport oversized, dull black mandibles that constantly drip brownish-gray saliva. A chain worm's tail stinger is almost a foot long and jet black. As they age, their tail stingers fade to dull gray.

A chain worm lies in wait for a meal, attacking whenever its target comes within range. Once it grabs a foe in its mandibles, it stings the victim repeatedly until the unfortunate creature dies.

Chaos Knight

The chaos knight appears to be a faintly glowing, ghostly suit of animated armour.

Chaos Knight

XP 700 (CR 3)
CE Medium fiend
Initiative +2

DEFENSE
AC 16 (chain mail)
hp: 78 (12d8 + 24)
Resistance: Bludgeoning, piercing, and slashing damage from nonmagical weapons
Immunity: Cold and psychic damage; fright, stun
Vulnerability: Fire damage

OFFENSE
Speed: 30 ft.
Multiattack: The chaos knight attacks twice with its greatsword.
Melee Attack—Greatsword: +6 to hit (reach 5 ft.; one creature). *Hit:* 2d6 + 4 slashing damage plus 1d6 cold damage.

STATISTICS
Str 18 (+4), **Dex** 14 (+2), **Con** 15 (+2), **Int** 10 (+0), **Wis** 12 (+1), **Cha** 16 (+3)
Languages: Common
Skills: Perception +4
Senses: Darkvision 60 ft.

TRAITS
Icy Incorporeality: By using an action, a chaos knight can make itself incorporeal until the start of its next turn. While incorporeal, it can pass through solid objects such as a wall, or other creatures, as if they were difficult terrain. It leaves behind an icy outline where it passes.
Spell-like Abilities: The chaos knight can use the following spell-like abilities, using Charisma as its casting ability (DC 13, attack +5). The chaos knight doesn't need material components to use these abilities.
At-Will: *chill touch, ray of frost*
3/day: *dimension door, protection from good*
2/day: *ice storm*
1/day: *telekinesis, wall of ice*

ECOLOGY
Environment: Temperate
Organization: Solitary

No features can be discerned within a chaos knight's helm, save for a dim blue glow. Although the creature seems insubstantial, a chaos knight has a real physical presence. Intense cold radiates from its being; any fire within 20 feet sputters, struggles to remain lit, and gives off no noticeable heat. Liquids in that radius turn cold and quickly freeze.

The chaos knight's *dimension door* portal appears as a kaleidoscopic passage of jagged energy bolts and whirling, ever-changing elemental matter. Any being other than the Chaos Knight that passes through the portal suffers 10 points of cold damage.

Chupacabra

This fur-covered, bipedal creature is 3 or 4 feet tall with a hunched back, red eyes, and a mouth filled with sharpened teeth. A flexible rows of spines runs down its back.

Chupacabra

XP 200 (CR 1)
CN Small humanoid
Initiative +2

DEFENSE

AC 12
hp: 27 (6d6 + 6)

OFFENSE

Speed: 20 ft.
Multiattack: A chupacabra attacks once with claws and bites once.
Melee Attack—Claws: +4 to hit (reach 5 ft.; one creature). *Hit:* 1d4 + 2 slashing damage and the target is grappled. The chupacabra can't attack with its claws while it has a creature grappled.
Melee Attack—Bite: +4 to hit (reach 5 ft.; one creature). *Hit:* 1d4 piercing damage. If the target is grappled by the chupacabra, it takes an extra 1d6 + 2 piercing damage.

STATISTICS

Str 10 (+0), **Dex** 15 (+2), **Con** 12 (+1), **Int** 3 (–4), **Wis** 11 (+0), **Cha** 10 (+0)
Languages: None
Skills: Stealth +4
Senses: Darkvision 60 ft.

TRAITS

Wings: One in ten chupacabras have leathery wings that give them a flying speed of 40 feet.

ECOLOGY

Environment: Warm forests and hills, decaying urban areas
Organization: Solitary or pack (2–12)

Chupacabras are small, terrifying bloodsuckers that lurk on the fringes of society. They emerge from their hiding places at night to drain blood from warm-blooded creatures. Though they aren't particularly selective when it comes to who or what they feed on, chupacabras prefer to attack creatures they can easily overpower (such as small livestock or children). Many chupacabra attacks are blamed on vampires, wild dogs, or wolves (because they often tear a victim's corpse into pieces in a rage if the creature dies too soon). If the chupacabra leaves any tracks, however, a skilled observer can readily tell the attacker was small, bipedal, and barefoot.

A chupacabra is a vaguely humanlike creature, but if there is any true relationship between the species, the chupacabra is a frighteningly degenerate cousin. They stand only 3 or 4 feet tall but look even shorter because of their severely stooped posture. A chupacabra's body is covered in patchy, dark, filthy fur. Their eyes are bright red and appear to glow when they catch the light from a lantern or torch. Their arms and legs end in four digits with dull black claws.

A chupacabra cannot speak in any intelligible way. Instead, it utters a baleful moan when frightened, or howls when threatened. If a chupacabra grabs a foe, it slashes at the victim's throat and greedily slurps up the blood.

A small proportion (10 percent) of chupacabras have fur-covered, batlike wings that enable them to fly, albeit somewhat clumsily. They seldom use their wings in combat, but instead use flight to seek victims far from their lairs, making it more difficult for enemies to track them back to the safety of their hidden dens.

Church Grim

This creature resembles a large, ghostly black dog with glowing red eyes.

Church Grim
XP 200 (CR 1)
LG Medium monstrosity (incorporeal)
Initiative +2

DEFENSE
AC 12
hp: 32 (5d8 + 10)

OFFENSE
Speed: fly 40 ft.
Melee Attack—Bite: +4 to hit (reach 5 ft.; one creature).
Hit: 1d8 + 2 piercing damage plus 1d6 radiant damage. The church grim gains temporary hit points equal to the radiant damage inflicted, and the target's maximum hit points are reduced by that amount.

STATISTICS
Str 13 (+1), **Dex** 14 (+2), **Con** 15 (+2),
Int 12 (+1), **Wis** 15 (+2), **Cha** 14 (+2)
Languages: Common
Skills: Perception +4
Senses: Darkvision 60 ft.

TRAITS
Howl: The howl of a church grim forces any evil creature within its limited domain (see below) to make a successful DC 12 Wis saving throw or become frightened for 2d4 rounds. Good or Neutral creatures are unaffected by the howl as long as they are not intending to steal anything or attack the church while inside the church grim's domain. Once a character succeeds or fails at this saving throw, it need not make another against the same church grim's howl until after the character takes a long rest.

Incorporeal: A church grim can pass through solid objects such as a wall, or other creatures, as if they were difficult terrain. It takes 1d10 force damage if it is still inside an object at the end of its turn.

Know Alignment: A church grim automatically knows the alignment of any creature that enters its churchyard.

Limited Domain: The realm of a church grim encompasses the churchyard it defends and no more. It can wander freely in its cemetery and any adjoining church grounds, but it can't move beyond; it must stop at the boundary of consecrated land.

Rejuvenation: It is difficult to destroy a church grim. A slain church grim restores itself to full health after lying "dead" for 24 hours. The only sure way to get rid of a church grim permanently is to raze the church it protects and desecrate the churchyard so it is no longer consecrated land.

Soul Defender: It is the sacred duty of a church grim to defend the bodies and souls of those buried in its churchyard. Casting *animate dead* or a similar spell within the confines of a church grim's domain requires a successful DC 15 concentration check by the caster. If the check fails, the spell slot fizzles away just as if it had been cast. Whether the check succeeds or not, the caster immediately attracts the attention and the wrath of the church grim.

ECOLOGY
Environment: Any graveyard or cemetery
Organization: Solitary

Church grims are good spirits that guard cemeteries from those who seek to steal from graves, reanimate the dead, or desecrate the sanctity of the graves there in any other way. The eyes of a church grim see all evil that crosses into its territory, and it has no mercy for such trespassers. The precinct of a church grim is the cemetery and church it has chosen to protect; it can't leave that holy ground for any reason. A church grim can't be destroyed without also destroying the place it protects. If dispatched, a church grim returns 24 hours later to resume its duties.

Only churches or temples dedicated to good deities attract the service of a church grim guardian. The holier the locale, the more likely a church grim is to be present.

Often, these entities are not well understood even by those who serve in the churches protected by church grims. Many pastors and deacons speak fearfully of "a ghostly hound" that prowls the ground around their churches without realizing that the spectral being they fear means them no harm and will protect their temple more ferociously and more tenaciously than any real guard dog could.

A church grim does not attack or harm anyone who enters the churchyard or the cemetery to worship, pay their respects, and go about normal business. It only attacks evil creatures and those who intend to rob from the dead. Church grims also attack undead creatures on sight.

Copyright Notice
Author Erica Balsley.

Churr

The trees and underbrush in front of you explode in a hail of leaves and brush that showers down around you. From the tangled mess emerge feral, apelike creatures with wickedly long claws and fangs.

Churr

XP 1,100 (CR 4)
NE Large monstrosity
Initiative +2

DEFENSE

AC 14 (natural armor)
hp: 57 (6d10 + 24)
Saving Throws: Dex +4

OFFENSE

Speed: 30 ft., climb 20 ft.
Multiattack: A churr bites once and attacks twice with claws, or it howls once.
Melee Attack—Bite: +6 to hit (reach 5 ft.; one creature). *Hit:* 1d8 + 4 piercing damage.
Melee Attack— Claw: +6 to hit (reach 10 ft.; one creature). *Hit:* 1d8 + 4 slashing damage and the target is grappled and restrained.

STATISTICS

Str 19 (+4), **Dex** 15 (+2), **Con** 18 (+4), **Int** 6 (−2), **Wis** 12 (+1), **Cha** 10 (+0)
Languages: Giant
Skills: Stealth +4
Senses: Darkvision 60 ft.

TRAITS

Howl: A churr can unleash a frightening howl as an action. Creatures within 60 feet of the churr must make a successful DC 10 Wis saving throw or become frightened for 1d6 x 10 minutes. A successful saving throw renders a character immune to the howling of churrs until after the character's next long rest.

ECOLOGY

Environment: Temperate and tropical forest
Organization: Pair, mob (3–6), or pack (7–12)

Churrs are savage, apelike creatures that dwell in warm, heavily forested areas. They are reasonably intelligent; some churrs are known to use primitive clubs or even to fashion spears with which to hunt. A typical adult churr stands 8 feet tall and has arms that are nearly as long as its body.

In rare instances, stone-age tribes have been known to adopt churrs as guardians. The creatures take to sign language readily. Among themselves, they speak a debased, pidgin form of Giant. They can learn to understand Common but they seem unable to speak more than the simplest words, and even those come out with a thick, guttural accent that takes practice to understand.

Churr can interbreed with some humanoid and most ape species, making them a "missing link" or bridge species. Mixed progeny are usually smaller but more intelligent than a typical churr, and they have an easier time learning and speaking Common and other languages.

Evil bands of churr are known to kidnap humanoids to keep as slaves— until such time as the slave inadvertently enrages a churr and is killed and eaten on the spot.

Churr begin combat by unleashing their horrific howl and beating their chests. They then charge opponents, attempting to get their meaty paws around them and choke or smash the life from them.

Churrs congregate in small bands or packs of less than 20 individuals. Males dominate the pack and females are tasked with menial chores, childbearing, and raising the young. Usually the strongest and most powerful churr becomes the leader. Fights to the death are not uncommon when a leader dies, as ambitious replacements vie for the open command. Churrs are omnivorous. They hunt small game as well as gathering fruits and vegetables in season.

Cimota

A figure materializes out of the surrounding shadows. It has the black cloak and cowl of a monk, but the cloak floats in the air, seemingly enclosing no visible body. Only menacing green eyes glare from inside the dark hood.

Cimota

XP 450 (CR 2)
LE Medium undead
Initiative +3

DEFENSE
AC 15 (natural armor)
hp: 44 (8d8 + 8)
Immunity: Cold, lightning, necrotic, and poison damage; fright, poison, exhaustion, unconsciousness

OFFENSE
Speed: fly 60 ft.
Multiattack: A cimota attacks twice with claws.
Melee Attack—Claw: +5 to hit (reach 5 ft.; one creature). *Hit:* 1d8 + 3 slashing damage.

STATISTICS
Str 16 (+3), **Dex** 16 (+3), **Con** 12 (+1), **Int** 13 (+1), **Wis** 14 (+2), **Cha** 19 (+4)
Languages: Common, Infernal
Skills: Intimidation +6, Perception +4, Persuasion +6
Senses: Darkvision 60 ft.

TRAITS
Lifesense: A cimota notices and locates all living creatures within 60 ft., without effort or error.
Magic Proof: A cimota automatically succeeds on saving throws against spells and magic effects unless it chooses not to.
Manifestation: As an action, a cimota can transport itself from any point on the Material Plane to another point within its defined area or within 300 feet of the artifact to which it is bound. A cimota can also lurk on the Negative Plane, prepared to manifest on the Material Plane if certain conditions are met, such as trespassers entering the area the cimota is doomed to guard. A cimota can't attack or move in the round in which it manifests—it is effectively stunned until the start of its next turn. When it manifests, it appears as a shifting cloud of shadows that coalesces into its cloaked and hooded form. Until the start of its next turn (the round after it manifests), its shifting form has the effect of a *blur* spell.
Unholy Existence: Although it is possible to temporarily destroy a cimota's physical form, it will return in 1d6 days, manifesting again to continue its unholy existence. The only way to permanently destroy a cimota is to disrupt its existence by consecrating the ground to which it is tied or by destroying the artifact to which it is bound. Sometimes, significant alteration of an unholy place, such as demolition of an evil temple or burning a haunted forest, could cause cimota to fade away permanently.

Unnatural Aura: All animals, wild or trained, become frightened when a cimota is within 30 feet. Trained animals will approach closer if their master makes a successful DC 20 Wis (Animal Handling) check. The check allows trained animals to approach the cimota but does not eliminate the tactical disadvantage on ability checks and attack rolls because of fright.

ECOLOGY
Environment: Any
Organization: Solitary, pair, or haunt (3–6)

Cimota Guardian

XP 1,100 (CR 4)
LE Medium undead
Initiative +3

DEFENSE
AC 16 (natural armor)
hp: 71 (11d8 + 22)
Immunity: Cold, lightning, necrotic, and poison damage; fright, poison, exhaustion, unconsciousness

OFFENSE
Speed: fly 60 ft.
Multiattack: A cimota attacks twice with scimitars.
Melee Attack—Scimitar: +6 to hit (reach 5 ft.; one creature). *Hit:* 1d8 + 4 slashing damage plus 1d8 necrotic damage.

STATISTICS
Str 18 (+4), **Dex** 16 (+3), **Con** 14 (+2), **Int** 13 (+1), **Wis** 14 (+2), **Cha** 20 (+5)
Languages: Common, Infernal
Skills: Intimidation +7, Perception +4, Persuasion +7
Senses: Darkvision 60 ft.

TRAITS
Lifesense: A cimota notices and locates all living creatures within 60 ft., without effort or error.
Magic Proof: A cimota automatically succeeds on saving throws against spells and magic effects unless it chooses not to.
Manifestation: As an action, a cimota can transport itself from any point on the Material Plane to another point within its defined area or within 300 feet of the artifact to which it is bound. A cimota can also lurk on the Negative Plane, prepared to manifest on the Material Plane if certain conditions are met, such as trespassers entering the area the cimota is doomed to guard. A cimota can't attack or move in the round in which it manifests—it is effectively stunned until the start of its next turn. When it manifests, it appears as a shifting cloud of shadows that

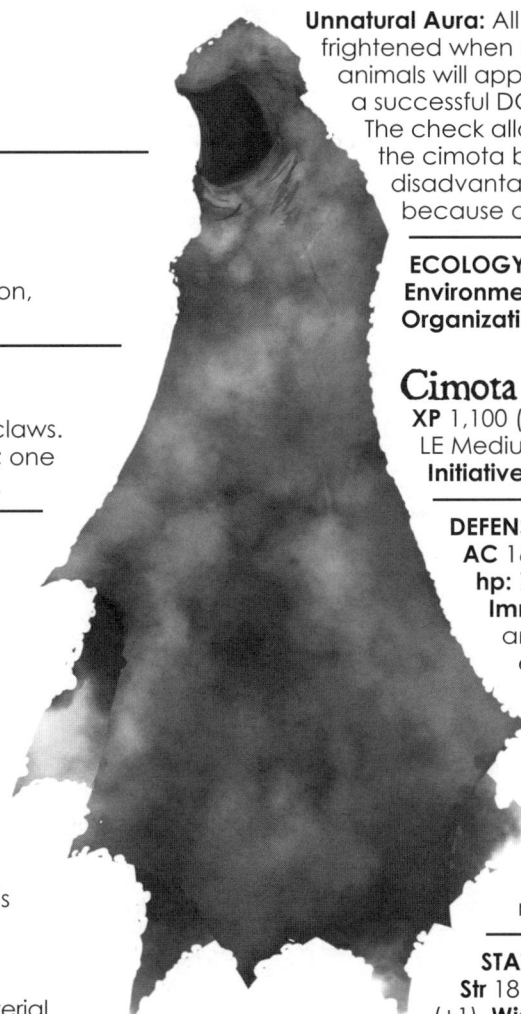

coalesces into its cloaked and hooded form. Until the start of its next turn (the round after it manifests), its shifting form has the effect of a *blur* spell.

Unholy Existence: Although it is possible to temporarily destroy a cimota's physical form, it will return in 1d6 days, manifesting again to continue its unholy existence. The only way to permanently destroy a cimota is to disrupt its existence by consecrating the ground to which it is tied or by destroying the artifact to which it is bound. Sometimes, significant alteration of an unholy place, such as demolition of an evil temple or burning a haunted forest, could cause cimota to fade away permanently.

Unnatural Aura: All animals, wild or trained, become frightened when a cimota is within 30 feet. Trained animals will approach closer if their master makes a successful DC 15 Wis (Animal Handling) check. The check allows trained animals to approach the cimota but does not eliminate the tactical disadvantage on ability checks and attack rolls because of fright.

ECOLOGY
Environment: Any
Organization: Solitary, pair, or haunt (3–6)

High Cimota
XP 2,300 (CR 6)
LE Medium undead
Initiative +4

DEFENSE
AC 17 (natural armor)
hp: 99 (18d8 + 18)
Immunity: Cold, lightning, necrotic, and poison damage; fright, poison, exhaustion, unconsciousness

OFFENSE
Speed: fly 60 ft.
Multiattack: A cimota attacks twice with scimitars.
Melee Attack—Scimitars: +7 to hit (reach 5 ft.; one creature). *Hit:* 1d8 + 4 slashing damage plus 1d8 lightning damage.

STATISTICS
Str 16 (+3), **Dex** 18 (+4), **Con** 13 (+1),
Int 14 (+2), **Wis** 16 (+3), **Cha** 20 (+5)
Languages: Common, Infernal
Skills: Insight +6, Intimidation +8, Perception +6, Persuasion +8
Senses: Darkvision 60 ft.

TRAITS
Dark Fury (recharge 5, 6): As a bonus action, a high cimota can generate a field of necrotic energy in the form of black lightning. This energy can be shaped into either a 20-foot radius sphere with the high cimota at its center, or as a 100-foot line extending from the high cimota's fingertips. Dark fury inflicts 6d8 necrotic damage on every living creature in its area of effect; a successful DC 15 Dex saving throw negates the damage. Undead, constructs and other nonliving targets are unaffected by dark fury.

Lifesense: A cimota notices and locates all living creatures within 60 ft., without effort or error.

Magic Proof: A cimota automatically succeeds on saving throws against spells and magic effects unless it chooses not to.

Manifestation: As an action, a cimota can transport itself from any point on the Material Plane to another point within its defined area or within 300 feet of the artifact to which it is bound. A cimota can also lurk on the Negative Plane, prepared to manifest on the Material Plane if certain conditions are met, such as trespassers entering the area the cimota is doomed to guard. A cimota can't attack or move in the round in which it manifests—it is effectively stunned until the start of its next turn. When it manifests, it appears as a shifting cloud of shadows that coalesces into its cloaked and hooded form. Until the start of its next turn (the round after it manifests), its shifting form has the effect of a *blur* spell.

Unholy Existence: Although it is possible to temporarily destroy a cimota's physical form, it will return in 1d6 days, manifesting again to continue its unholy existence. The only way to permanently destroy a cimota is to disrupt its existence by consecrating the ground to which it is tied or by destroying the artifact to which it is bound. Sometimes, significant alteration of an unholy place, such as demolition of an evil temple or burning a haunted forest, could cause cimota to fade away permanently.

Unnatural Aura: All animals, wild or trained, become frightened when a cimota is within 30 feet. Trained animals will approach closer if their master makes a successful DC 16 Wis (Animal Handling) check. The check allows trained animals to approach the cimota but does not eliminate the tactical disadvantage on ability checks and attack rolls because of fright.

ECOLOGY
Environment: Any
Organization: Solitary, pair, or haunt (3–6)

Cimota are the physical manifestations of evil thoughts and actions. They exist on the Negative Plane, manifesting in the Material Plane as indistinct, cloaked figures. Their existence is always tied to a specific area or artifact that is imbued with ancient and highly malevolent evil. A cimota is able to manifest anywhere within an accursed locale that has given it life or within 300 feet of an evil artifact to which it is attached, but it can't leave that area on the Material Plane.

The physical form of a cimota is a floating figure in a monk's cassock. Green eyes glow deep within their raised cowls, but their bodies are entirely invisible. S*ee invisibility*, *true seeing*, or similar abilities to see invisible objects reveal a ghostly human figure seemingly made of shadow within the cloak. Cimota are manifestations of evil that can be touched like any other creature, and even injured by nonmagical weapons, though magic has reduced effect against them. When a cimota is destroyed, only a few shreds of tattered black cloth remain to show that they ever existed.

Cimota are bound to repeat the evil thoughts and actions that created them. When they manifest, they endlessly repeat the deeds that spawned them. So, for instance, a group of cimota might haunt a ruined temple where they endless reenact evil rituals. Cimota might guard an unholy site such as a city, forest, or building. They fight to the death to defend these places. Cimota who are bound to an artifact might act out the intentions of that artifact. A cimota might follow the owner of an artifact, for example, slaying the owner's friends and associates (to prevent them from stealing the artifact, in their greed) while keeping its existence a secret. Within the parameters of their creation, cimota are capable of strategy, deception, and highly intelligent tactics.

Cimota are capable of speaking Common and Infernal. Their voices are either hollow, ringing, and unnatural, or malevolent whispers. Most often, cimota use their voices to chant or to shout dire condemnations at intruders. They do not parley and they never negotiate unless it is to deceive mortals to their deaths.

Credit
Original author Mark R. Shipley
Originally appearing in *The Black Monastery* (© Frog God Games/ Mark R. Shipley, 2011)

Clam, Giant

A large, brightly-colored shell shifts in the current. Seemingly split or divided down the middle, its interior is a dazzling golden brown.

Giant Clam

XP 50 (CR 1/4)
Unaligned Large beast
Initiative +0

DEFENSE

AC 14 (natural armor)
hp: 22 (3d10 + 6)
Immunity: Psychic damage; fright, stun
Vulnerability: Fire damage

OFFENSE

Speed: Swim 5 ft.
Melee Attack—Swallow: automatic hit (reach 5 ft.; one Medium or smaller creature). *Hit:* Target creature must make a successful DC 13 Dex saving throw or be grappled and restrained inside the clam's shell (see Swallow, below).

STATISTICS

Str 16 (+3), **Dex** 1 (–5), **Con** 15 (+2), **Int** 1 (–5), **Wis** 10 (+0), **Cha** 9 (–1)
Languages: None
Skills: Stealth +2
Senses: Tremorsense 60 ft.

TRAITS

Camouflage: The rough shell of a giant clam is draped with barnacles, anemones, and bits of coral, which help it to blend into its environment. A giant clam has a +2 bonus on normal Stealth checks despite its low Dex score, and it gets tactical advantage on Dex (Stealth) checks to conceal itself before an encounter (since they have nothing but time, lying there on the sea bottom).

Swallow: A swallowed creature is blinded and restrained. It takes 1 acid damage automatically at the start of each of the giant clam's turns. Only one Medium or smaller creature can be inside the giant clam at one time, and a giant clam can swallow only one creature per 24 hours. A swallowed creature is unaffected by anything happening outside the giant clam or by attacks from outside it. A swallowed creature can get out of the giant clam by winning a Str contest against it— the swallowed character has tactical disadvantage in this contest—or by using 5 feet of movement after the giant clam is dead.

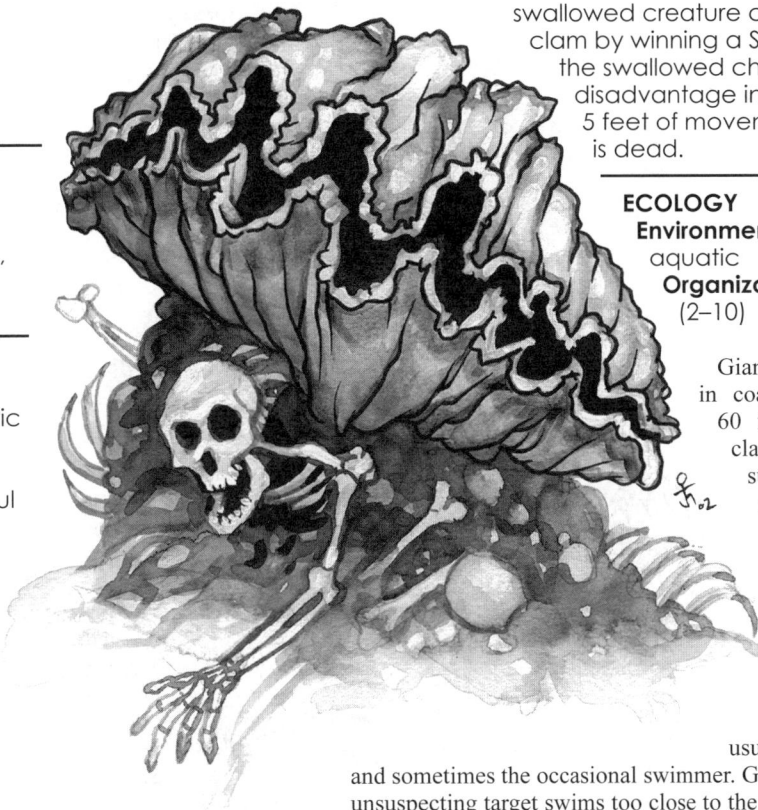

ECOLOGY

Environment: Warm or temperate aquatic
Organization: Solitary or cluster (2–10)

Giant clams are generally found in coastal waters no deeper than 60 feet. Many species of giant clams subsist strictly on a diet of sunlight, and as such are never found at depths where sunlight can't reach. Such giant clams typically live in shallow seas or attached to coral reefs near the surface.

Some species of giant clams feed not only on sunlight but also on what they can filter from the water, usually small plants and animals, and sometimes the occasional swimmer. Giant clams simply wait until an unsuspecting target swims too close to the clam. When a creature at least one size smaller than the clam comes within reach, the clam sucks the prey into its interior and clamps its shell shut. It slowly digests its meal and expels any indigestible material (such as metal, stone, jewels, and coins) into the surrounding water. Air-breathers trapped by a giant clam face the danger of drowning as well.

A giant clam moves by pushing out a small "foot" and sliding itself along the sea bottom.

Credit

The Giant Clam originally appeared in the First Edition module *EX2 Land Beyond the Magic Mirror* (© TSR/Wizards of the Coast, 1983) and is used by permission.

Copyright Notice

Author Scott Greene, based on original material by Gary Gygax.

Clamor

A series of garbled voices, clicks, grinding noises, and other less discernible sounds seem to emanate from empty air, with no apparent point of origin.

Clamor

XP 450 (CR 2)
Unaligned Medium aberration (extraplanar, incorporeal)
Initiative +7

DEFENSE

AC 17
hp: 45 (6d8 + 18)
Immunity: Nonmagical damage; thunder damage

OFFENSE

Speed: fly 50 ft.
Melee Attack—Thunder Touch: +9 to hit (reach 5 ft.; one creature). *Hit:* 1d8 + 7 thunder damage and the target is pushed 5 feet away from the clamor.
Ranged Attack—Sonic Ray: +9 to hit (range 120 ft.; one creature). *Hit:* 1d6 + 7 thunder damage and the target is deafened until the start of the clamor's next turn.
Area Attack—Sonic Burst (recharge 5, 6): automatic hit (range 100 ft. sphere centered on clamor; all creatures in range). *Hit:* every target must make a successful DC 13 Con saving throw or be stunned for 1d3 rounds. Living creatures within 50 feet of the clamor are also permanently deafened if this saving throw fails. *Greater restoration, wish,* or comparable magic can restore a creature's hearing.

STATISTICS

Str 1 (−5), **Dex** 25 (+7), **Con** 17 (+3), **Int** 5 (−2), **Wis** 12 (+1), **Cha** 17 (+3)
Languages: Unknown—seems to understand a bit of most languages
Senses: Darkvision 60 ft.

TRAITS

Incorporeal: A clamor can pass through solid objects such as a wall, or other creatures, as if they were difficult terrain. It takes 1d10 force damage if it is still inside another object at the end of its turn. It can move in total silence when it chooses to.
Natural Invisibility: As creatures of living sound, a clamor is naturally invisible, even when it attacks. This ability can't be "switched off" or negated by any means. *See invisibility* adds a ghostly outline around a clamor, but *true seeing* reveals nothing, because the clamor has no visible form to reveal.
Sound Mimicry: A clamor can duplicate any sound it has ever encountered with perfect accuracy. It can duplicate speech, music, or any other auditory phenomenon, although sounds with magical properties (such as *power word* spells) lose their magical effects when duplicated.
Speed of Sound (1/day): Once per day, a clamor can fly at the speed of sound for four minutes, an effective speed of 6,730 feet per round. It can't attack or use any other abilities when moving this way. In four minutes, it can cover 51 miles (82 kilometers).
Sound-Related Vulnerabilities: Any magical *silence* effect or effect that creates a vacuum deals 3d8 force damage to a clamor and forces it to make a successful Con saving throw against the spellcaster's DC or become frightened for one minute. In addition, any spells or abilities that deal thunder damage require the clamor to make a successful Con saving throw or be affected as if hit by a *confusion* spell for one minute. Spells or abilities that manipulate sound in pleasing or at least nonlethal ways (such as a bard's countercharm ability) require the clamor to make a successful Cha saving throw or be affected as if charmed for one hour. The DC of both saving throws equals 8 + the attacker's applicable ability score modifier + the attacker's proficiency bonus. The DM has final say whether a specific spell or ability affects a clamor, and how.

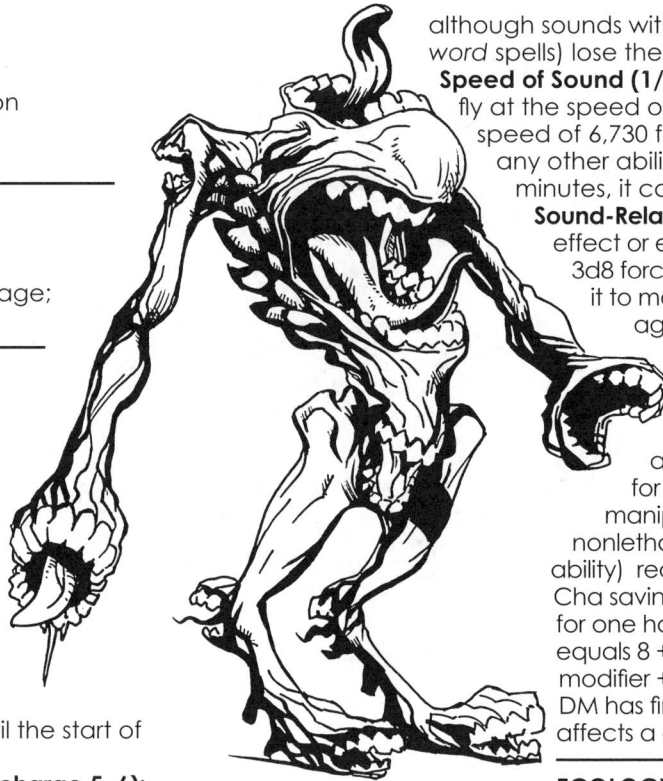

ECOLOGY

Environment: Any land
Organization: Solitary

Clamors have a playful kind of intelligence, and they appear to desire communication with humanoids. Being able to mimic any sound they have ever encountered, clamors wander the Material Plane emitting a nonsensical cacophony of voices, crashes, clicks, roars, and music. Since they are usually invisible, most adventurers that encounter a clamor walk away from the din without ever having realized that they just met one of the more enigmatic creatures in existence. Many a sentry on duty has heard only his own voice in response to what he thought was someone walking around out in the darkness; what he really heard was a clamor trying to talk to him.

Most bards are fascinated by these odd creatures. Many a bard has gained a clamor as a companion of sorts, thanks to the effect music has on clamors. A bard of at least 5th level can communicate with these creatures on a rudimentary basis, but working out the basics of such communication takes several hours of patient work by the bard and the clamor, interspersed with frequent soothing, musical interludes by the bard. The intelligence and patience of a clamor are comparable to those of a young child, so complex communication and long stretches of concentration are not feasible.

Despite their curiosity, clamors tend to keep their distance from other intelligent creatures until some level of trust has been established. They emit random noises and "play back" interesting sounds made by the creatures they are observing. Once provoked to attack, clamors strike at their foes with high frequency sonic beams. If cornered or overwhelmed, a clamor uses its sonic burst ability before fleeing at the speed of sound, an ability that almost ensures its escape.

Cobra Flower

This tall, slender plant has a large flowering bulb topping its brownish-green roots.
Two green, winglike leaves flank its flowering top, giving the appearance of a cobra's hood.
Its leaves are thin and have transparent blotches on them.

Cobra Flower

XP 450 (CR 2)
Unaligned Large plant
Initiative +1

DEFENSE
AC 11
hp: 51 (6d10 + 18)
Saving Throws: Con **+5**
Immunity: Psychic damage; fright, exhaustion, stun, unconsciousness
Vulnerability: Necrotic damage

OFFENSE
Speed: 5 ft.
Melee Attack—Bite: +5 to hit (reach 10 ft.; one creature). *Hit:* 1d10 + 3 piercing damage plus 1d8 acid damage, and the target is grappled. This attack hits automatically if the target is already grappled by the cobra flower.

STATISTICS
Str 17 (+3), **Dex** 13 (+1),
Con 16 (+3), **Int** 1 (−5),
Wis 13 (+1), **Cha** 9 (−1)
Languages: None
Senses: Tremorsense 30 ft.

ECOLOGY
Environment: Temperate and cold forests
Organization: Solitary or patch (2–4)

Cobra flowers draw nutrients from sunlight, soil, and water, but they also enjoy a diet of insects, rodents, animals, and even humanoids when they can catch one. These plant-creatures can be found nesting in forests, and they sometimes take up residence near small population areas to feed on humanoids who wander into their reach. Many a child's or adult's disappearance can be attributed to a cobra flower.

When a cobra flower detects a living creature, it remains motionless until its prey is within 5 feet. It then spreads its leafy hood, opens its flowery bulb, and bites its prey, injecting acidic enzymes to break down and digest the victim.

Coffer Corpse

This creature appears as a desiccated humanoid shrouded in rotting, tattered funerary clothes. Its fingers end in sharp, enormously long fingernails.

Coffer Corpse

XP 450 (CR 2)
CE Medium undead
Initiative +1

DEFENSE

AC 12 (natural armor)
hp: 45 (6d8 + 18)
Saving Throws: Wis +3
Resistance: Bludgeoning, piercing, and slashing damage from nonmagical weapons; necrotic damage
Immunity: Poison damage; exhaustion, fright, poison, unconsciousness

OFFENSE

Speed: 25 ft.
Melee Attack—Claws: +5 to hit (reach 5 ft.; one creature). *Hit:* 1d8 + 3 slashing damage and the target is grappled.
Melee Attack—Strangulation: automatic hit (one creature already grappled by the coffer corpse at the start of the coffer corpse's turn). *Hit:* the target must make a successful DC 13 Con saving throw or it runs out of breath and begins suffocating. If the strangled creature escapes from the coffer corpse's grapple, suffocation ends immediately but the creature is incapacitated until the end of its next turn.

STATISTICS

Str 16 (+3),
Dex 12 (+1),
Con 16 (+3),
Int 6 (−2), **Wis** 13 (+1),
Cha 14 (+2)
Languages: None
Senses: Darkvision 60 ft.

TRAITS

Death Grip: A creature that is grappled by a coffer corpse can't speak or cast spells that have verbal components.
Deceiving Death: The first time a coffer corpse's hit points are reduced below 20, the creature collapses to the ground as if slain. A grappled creature is released. To all inspection, the coffer corpse appears destroyed. At the start of its next turn, the coffer corpse regains 3d6 hit points and rises again as if reanimated. Every creature that sees the coffer corpse rise must make a successful DC 12 Wis saving throw or be frightened for 2d4 rounds or until they see the coffer corpse destroyed.
Magic Weapon: A coffer corpse's claws are treated as an attack from a magic weapon.

ECOLOGY

Environment: Any land, subterranean
Organization: Solitary or crypt (2–12)

The coffer corpse is an undead creature formed as the result of an incomplete death ritual. It is often found haunting stranded funeral barges or in situations where a corpse has not been delivered to its final resting place. Because of the manner of their creation, most coffer corpses are sealed inside coffins or sarcophagi until they are released by unwitting tomb robbers. Coffer corpses hate life and attack most living creatures on sight.

At a distance, a coffer corpse is often mistaken for a zombie. They are quicker, however, and display a level of anger and hatred that indicate they are more than mindless automatons.

In combat, a coffer corpse attacks with its filthy, ragged fingernails. They always try to grab a victim by the throat and strangle it to death. Once a coffer corpse gets its hands around a victim's throat, it doesn't let go until the victim is dead, or the coffer corpse is either destroyed, or damaged enough to trigger its deceiving death.

Credit
The coffer corpse originally appeared in the First Edition *Fiend Folio* (© TSR/Wizards of the Coast, 1981) and is used by permission.

Copyright Notice
Author Scott Greene, based on original material by Simon Eaton.

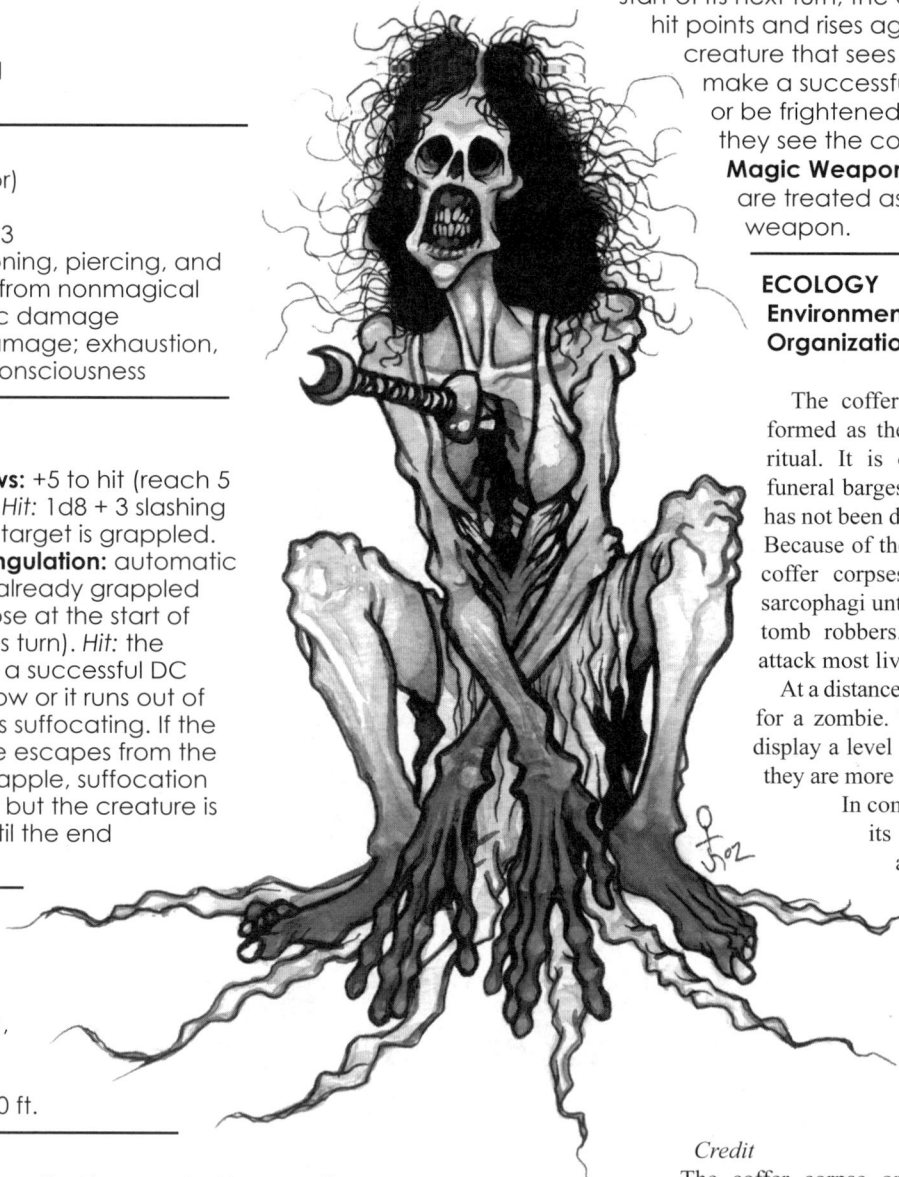

Cooshee

This creature appears as a large green- and brown-spotted dog with slightly elven features.
It has a long, curling tail and ears that taper to points above its head.

Cooshee
XP 200 (CR 1)
NG Medium monstrosity
Initiative +3

DEFENSE
AC 13
hp: 13 (3d8)

OFFENSE
Speed: 40 ft.
Multiattack: A cooshee bites once and attacks once with claws.
Melee Attack—Bite: +5 to hit (reach 5 ft.; one creature). *Hit:* 1d10 + 3 piercing damage and the target is knocked prone and grappled and restrained (see Dominate below).
Melee Attack—Claw: +5 to hit (reach 5 ft.; one creature). *Hit:* 3d6 + 3 slashing damage.

STATISTICS
Str 14 (+2), **Dex** 16 (+3), **Con** 11 (+0),
Int 4 (−3), **Wis** 12 (+1), **Cha** 8 (−1)
Languages: None
Skills: Perception +5, Stealth +5
Senses: Darkvision 60 ft.

TRAITS
Dominate: A cooshee that has its opponent restrained and prone makes it very difficult for that foe to stand up again. To stand up, the creature must break the grapple, which also ends the restraint. If the creature fails in its attempt to break free, it takes 1d4 piercing damage.
Sprint: Once per hour, a cooshee can move ten times its normal speed (400 ft.) for one round. When sprinting, it gains tactical advantage on Stealth checks.

ECOLOGY
Environment: Temperate forests
Organization: Solitary, pair, or pack (4–9)

Cooshees are large, 200-pound, 4-foot tall hounds. They are known throughout the world as elven dogs, for their features resemble those of elves and they are often found in the company of elves, who train them as guards. They bark only to warn their masters or other cooshees, but their bark can be heard clearly up to one mile away.

Cooshees attack by biting and tripping their foes. Once down, an opponent is held down. A cooshee trained as a guard can hold a person down until help comes; wild cooshees are more likely to tear the foe to pieces.

These dogs are also legendary for their ability to race like the wind in almost perfect silence. This is how cooshees launch most attacks; they begin their charge from so far away that they either haven't been spotted yet or their intended victims believe they're safe. If the cooshees weren't spotted before they charged, odds are they'll be among their foes and attacking without anyone hearing their approach.

Credit
The cooshee originally appeared in *Dragon #67* (© TSR/Wizards of the Coast, 1983) and later in the First Edition module *S4 Lost Caverns of Tsojcanth* (© TSR/Wizards of the Coast, 1982) and still later in the First Edition *Monster Manual II* (© TSR/Wizards of the Coast, 1983), and is used by permission.

Copyright Notice
Author Scott Greene, based on original material by Gary Gygax.

Corpse Rook

This creature resembles a gigantic three-headed raven with oily black feathers and bright silver talons and beak. Its wings are tipped with silver feathers. A pungent, almost sulfuric odor emanates from the creature.

Corpse Rook

XP 1,100 (CR 4)
NE Large monstrosity
Initiative +2

DEFENSE

AC 14 (natural armor)
hp: 45 (6d10 + 12)

OFFENSE

Speed: 10 ft., fly 60 ft.
Multiattack: A corpse rook bites three times and attacks once with claws.
Melee Attack—Bite: +5 to hit (reach 5 ft.; one creature). *Hit:* 1d10 + 3 piercing damage.
Melee Attack—Claw: +5 to hit (reach 5 ft.; one creature). *Hit:* 2d8 + 3 slashing damage.

STATISTICS

Str 17 (+3), **Dex** 15 (+2), **Con** 14 (+2),
Int 5 (–3), **Wis** 10 (+0), **Cha** 11 (+0)
Languages: None
Senses: Darkvision 60 ft.

TRAITS

All-around Vision: A corpse rook's three heads allow it to see in all directions at all times. It has tactical advantage on sight-based Perception checks, and opponents never gain tactical advantage or bonus damage against it from the presence of nearby allies.
Combat Mobility: Opportunity attacks against a moving corpse rook always have tactical disadvantage.

ECOLOGY

Environment: Temperate or warm plains

Organization: Solitary, pair, or nest (pair plus 1d4 nonfighting young)

Corpse rooks are giant, three-headed birds of prey that devour anything they can catch. Their preferred diet consists of horses, giant lizards, dire rats, giant frogs, cattle, sheep, and humanoids of all kinds. They build their nests at the tops of sturdy, broadleaved trees, or on high, rocky outcrops in less forested terrain. A corpse rook's nest is constructed from mud, grass, hair, leaves, and the bones of their victims. These creatures do not associate with other avian creatures. They are often hunted by red and green dragons, rocs, and wyverns, who savor the taste of their flesh.

Corpse rooks are solitary hunters with a hunting territory extending 5 miles in every direction from their nests. Hunting is done during the day. During spring and early summer months (mating season), both male and female corpse rooks hunt for food—sometimes together, but most often they fly off in separate directions from the nest. Creatures killed by a corpse rook are carried back to the nest and either devoured or fed to hatchlings. A nest typically contains 1d4 silver and gold-flecked eggs (or hatchlings later in the season) along with the chewed and dropping-spattered belongings of slain prey.

Corpse rooks attack from the air, slashing with their claws and biting with their sharpened beaks. They rarely land on the ground during battle, preferring to swoop in and out of melee to keep their opponents off balance and limit their vulnerability to melee. Although they generally hunt individually, a lone corpse rook will call for help from others of its kind if it spots a group of delectable prey that it suspects it can't handle alone. The spotting bird then circles high above the potential victims until more corpse rooks arrive. When working together this way, it's common for one or two corpse rooks to land and draw the attention of the prey, while others swoop in from multiple directions.

Corpsespinner

A massive, bone-white tarantula is the only way to describe this monster. Bands of gray and silver ring
its abdomen and legs, and its body is covered in short, bristly hairs of white and silver.
A large, skull-like marking appears on the creature's thorax. Its eight eyes are stark white.

Corpsespinner

XP 1,800 (CR 5)
Unaligned Huge
monstrosity
(extraplanar)
Initiative +3

DEFENSE
AC 17 (natural armor)
hp: 114 (12d12 + 36)

OFFENSE
Speed: 40 ft., climb
20 ft.
Melee Attack—Bite:
+8 to hit (reach 15
ft.; one creature).
Hit: 2d10 + 5
piercing damage
plus 1d10 poison
damage and the
target is poisoned.
A poisoned
creature makes a
DC 14 Con saving
throw at the end
of each of its turns;
a successful save
ends the condition.
Ranged Attack—Web
(recharge 5, 6):
+6 to hit (range 80
ft.; one creature).
Hit: the target
is restrained. A
restrained creature
can use its action
to attempt a DC
14 Str (Athletics)
check, becoming free of the
webs on a success. A character has tactical
disadvantage on this check on the Astral Plane. These
webs can be destroyed with slashing damage (AC 12, 10
hp), but they are immune to all other damage, including
fire.

STATISTICS
Str 20 (+5), **Dex** 17 (+3), **Con** 17 (+3),
Int 7 (−2), **Wis** 15 (+2), **Cha** 10 (+0)
Languages: Deep Speech
Skills: Perception +5
Senses: Darkvision 60 ft.

TRAITS
Astral Jaunt: A corpsespinner can shift between the Astral
and Material Planes in either direction as a move. This
does not trigger a reaction.
Astralsense: A
corpsespinner can
automatically sense the
presence and location
of anything within 200
feet of it on the Astral
Plane.
Create Corpsespun:
Creatures that die
while affected by a
corpsespinner's poison
(and not devoured
by the corpsespinner)
rise in 1 hour as a
corpsespun.

ECOLOGY
Environment: Astral
Plane
Organization: Solitary
or troupe (1 plus 4–9
corpsespun)

Corpsespinners are highly
aggressive extraplanar spiders
originating on the Astral
Plane, where they hunt and
devour astral sharks and other
native creatures. Only rarely
do they enter the Material
Plane to hunt all types of giant
spiders and humanoids.

On the Astral Plane,
corpsespinners spend their
time constructing elaborate
webs. They enjoy using
unusual anchor points for
their constructions, such as
bizarre outcroppings of rare
materials, the corpses of deceased
astral travelers, drifting astral ruins, and
just about anything else the corpsespinner
finds intriguing or unique.

When not constructing webs, the corpsespinner is usually hunting—
and this sometimes leads it to the Material Plane. If encountered on the
Material Plane, there is a good chance the corpsespinner has its most
recent victims with it as corpsespun.

Corpsespinners seldom associate with others of their kind. Their
ecology and reproduction cycles are unknown by outsiders, though
intrepid interplanar adventurers have talked of seeing huge webbed lairs
on the Astral Plane containing young corpsespinners.

When hunting on the Material Plane, a corpsespinner uses its ability to
shift back and forth between the planes to confuse and stymy its foes. If
facing defeat, the corpsespinner retreats to the Astral Plane and seeks the
safety of its lair.

When accompanied by corpsespun, the corpsespinner focuses on trapping foes in webs and then lets its minions soften up the trapped enemies. The corpsespinner wants to ensure that their veins are filled with its poison when they die, to keep its supply of corpsespun high.

Corpsespun

XP 200 (CR 1)
N Medium undead
Initiative +1

DEFENSE

AC 11 plus armor worn
hp: 44 (8d8 + 8)
Immunity: Necrotic and poison damage; exhaustion, fright, poison, unconsciousness

OFFENSE

Speed: 30 ft., climb 20 ft.
Melee Attack—Claw: +5 to hit (reach 5 ft.; one creature). *Hit:* 1d6 + 2 slashing damage plus 1d4 poison damage and the target is poisoned. A poisoned creature can make a DC 11 Con saving throw at the end of each of its turns; a successful save ends the condition.
Ranged Attack—Spider Spray (recharge 5, 6): automatic hit (range 20 ft. cone; all creatures in cone). *Hit:* target must make a successful DC 11 Dex saving throw or take 1d6 piercing damage plus 2d6 poison damage.

STATISTICS

Str 15 (+2), **Dex** 13 (+1), **Con** 13 (+1), **Int** 3 (–4), **Wis** 10 (+0), **Cha** 6 (–2)
Languages: None
Senses: Darkvision 60 ft.

TRAITS

Spider-Infested: Spiders continually crawl out of corpsespun, swarm over them, and fall to the ground around the undead's feet. All creatures other than a corpsepinner or other corpsespun that are adjacent to a corpsespun at the end of the corpsespun's turn take 1d4 poison damage from spider bites. This damage is cumulative from multiple adjacent corpsespun.

ECOLOGY

Environment: Astral Plane
Organization: Troupe (4–9 plus 1 corpsespinner)

Corpsespun resemble zombies that are infested with spiders. Spiders crawl in and out of their bodies through their mouths, ears, nostrils, eye sockets, and wounds, and the creatures can vomit out a stream of spiders as an attack. They tend to be draped in webbing. Corpsepun follow the commands of the corpsespinner that created them, which they receive telepathically. If a corpsespinner is killed, its corpsespun minions continue carrying out their last instructions, and they fight to protect their master's body or its home web; otherwise, they have little purpose and are not innately hostile without a corpsespinner telling them who to kill.

Crabman

This giant-sized creature is a bipedal humanoid with a crablike head, large hands that end in powerful pincers, and splayed feet. It is covered with chitinous plates that are reddish-brown in color. Two smaller humanoid arms protrude below its pincers.

Crabman

XP 200 (CR 1)
Neutral Large monstrosity
Initiative +0

DEFENSE

AC 14 (natural armor)
hp: 22 (3d10 + 6)
Resistance: Slashing damage from nonmagical weapons

OFFENSE

Speed: 30 ft., swim 20 ft.
Multiattack: A crabman attacks twice with pincers.
Melee Attack—Pincer: +5 to hit (reach 5 ft.; one creature). *Hit:* 1d8 + 3 slashing damage and the target is grappled.

STATISTICS

Str 16 (+3), **Dex** 11 (+0), **Con** 15 (+2), **Int** 10 (+0), **Wis** 10 (+0), **Cha** 8 (−1)
Languages: Unique (crabman)
Senses:
    Darkvision 60 ft.

TRAITS

Amphibious: A crabman spends most of its life in water, but they are equally at home on land or in water. Crabmen do not treat water as difficult terrain, and they breathe comfortably in air or water.

ECOLOGY

Environment: Temperate aquatic
Organization: Gang (2–12)

Crabmen inhabit coastal water, where they hunt for fish and other food. Their language is unique, relying on buzzes and clicks that can be produced underwater without the distortion that makes breath-based language unintelligible. Those with Intelligence 12 or higher sometimes learn Common from land-dwelling traders and sailors.

Crabmen make their homes in sea caves and coastal cliffs. They spend most of their time hunting, filtering algae for food, or scavenging along rocky shores and beaches for flotsam from shipwrecks. They can subsist by gathering wet sand from the seashore and filtering it through their mouths, sucking out all organic material, but they prefer not to. The hardened, dry balls of sand left behind can be a clue that there is a crabman community nearby.

Some communities excavate expansive burrows into sea-facing cliffs. Within such a warren, each individual has a lair set off from a centralized meeting area.

Each crabman tribe is led by an elder that can be of either sex. Most crabman tribal elders are at least 3rd-level warriors.

Crabmen have no regular breeding or mating cycle. Each female seems to have her own phases of fertility and infertility. A fertile female produces about 100 eggs over a span of two weeks. Crabman eggs are released into the ocean, where they hatch into translucent larvae with soft shells. These larvae vaguely resemble the adults but can be mistaken for normal crabs. After six months, these larvae molt, develop more humanoid body structure, and develop the harder shell required for life on land. Before their first molting, crabman larvae are largely defenseless; they hide in coral reefs and among kelp beds for safety. They receive no protection or parenting of any kind until after they emerge onto land.

Crabmen rarely engage in commerce with other humanoid communities around them, including other crabman tribes. Crabman artisans produce only ephemeral goods made of driftwood, shells, and seaweed, but they are quite capable of producing what more aesthetic races would call works of art.

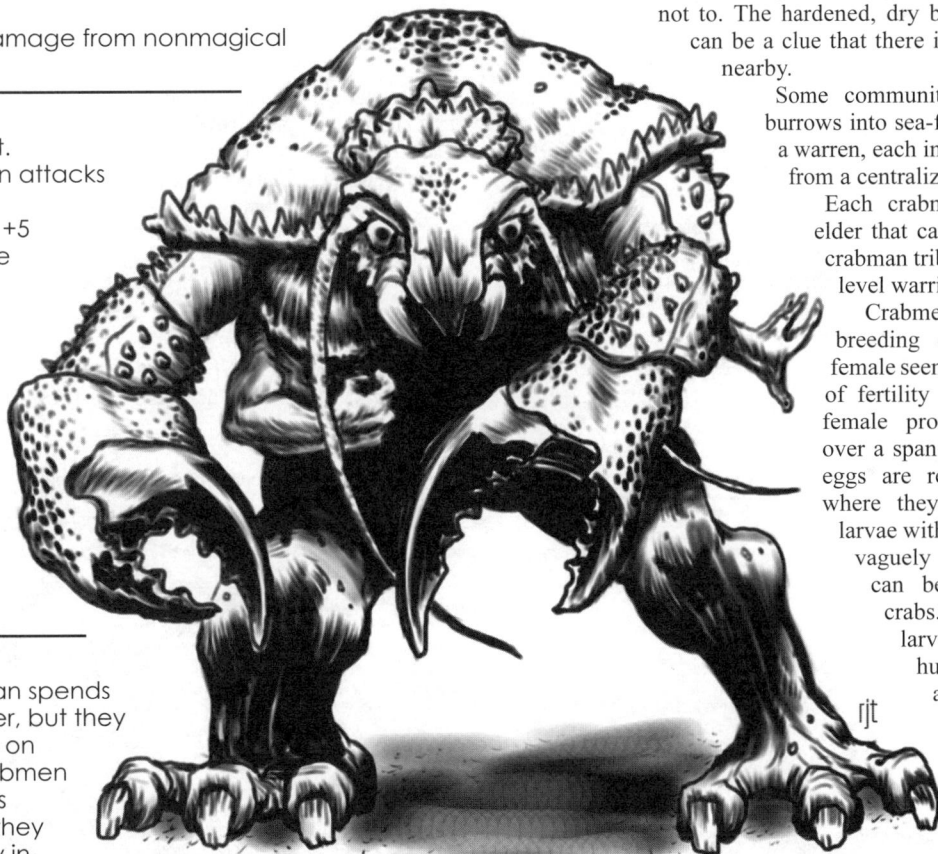

Crayfish, Monstrous

This creature looks like a giant lobster with a sharp snout and eyes on movable, flickering stalks. Two large claws extend from its thorax in front of four smaller pairs of spindly walking legs. Its exoskeleton is dark brown.

Monstrous Crayfish

XP 450 (CR 2)
Unaligned Large beast (aquatic)
Initiative +0

DEFENSE

AC 14 (natural armor)
hp: 45 (6d10 + 12)
Immunity: Fright

OFFENSE

Speed: 20 ft., swim 40 ft.
Multiattack: A monstrous crayfish attacks twice, using any combination of pincer and crush attacks.
Melee Attack—Pincer: +5 to hit (reach 5 ft.; one creature). *Hit:* 1d8 + 3 slashing damage and the target is grappled.
Melee Attack—Crush: automatic hit (one creature grappled by the monstrous crayfish). *Hit:* 1d8 + 3 piercing damage and the target is grappled.

STATISTICS

Str 16 (+3), **Dex** 10 (+0), **Con** 14 (+2), **Int** 1 (–5), **Wis** 10 (+0), **Cha** 2 (–5)
Languages: None
Senses: Darkvision 60 ft.

TRAITS

Water Dependency: A monstrous crayfish can survive out of water for 7 hours. After this limit, a monstrous crayfish begins suffocating, with the same effect as if it were drowning.

ECOLOGY

Environment: Any freshwater aquatic
Organization: Solitary or colony (2–5)

Monstrous crayfish are freshwater creatures that dwell on the bottoms of seas, lakes, ponds, and other shallow water. They are predators and scavengers that exist on a diet of decaying flesh from dead fish, algae, snails, worms, and other animals, including swimmers who venture too close to the monstrous crayfish's lair.

These giant crayfish make their homes under rocks or in underwater tunnels that are dug by the crayfish. Their flooded tunnels extend over long distances and always include a "chimney" through which the monstrous crayfish can enter and exit its home via dry ground. These exits have been found as far as 100 feet inland from the lake shore or river bank.

Giant crayfish are often hunted as food by dragon turtles, humans, storm giants, and giant turtles.

Credit
The Monstrous Crayfish originally appeared in the First Edition *Monster Manual* (© TSR/Wizards of the Coast, 1977) and is used by permission.

Copyright Notice
Author Scott Greene, based on original material by Gary Gygax.

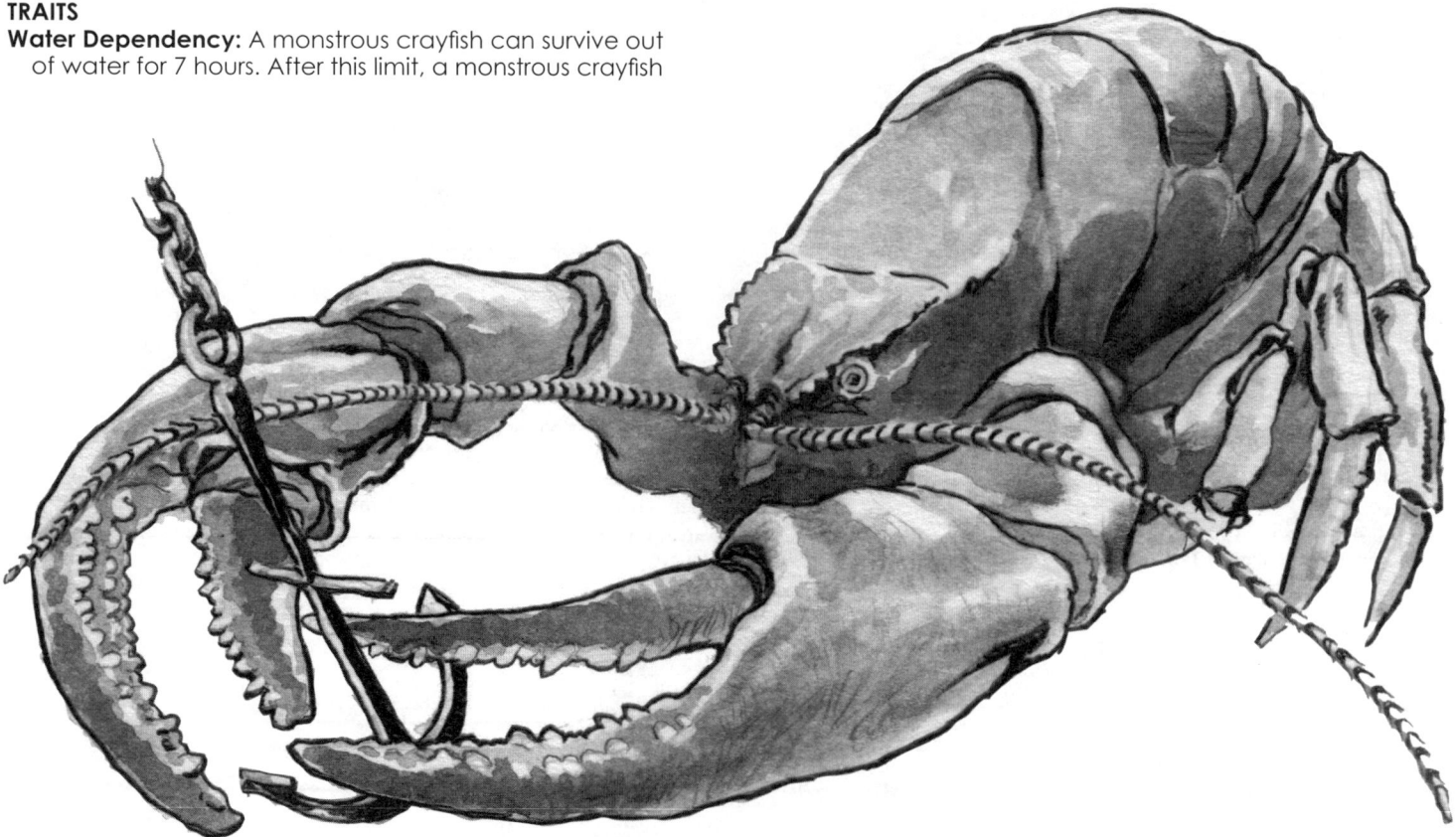

Crimson Mist

*Seemingly made of red vapor, the crimson mist is an outstanding stealth hunter.
It is vaguely humanoid in shape, with what appear to be arms, a torso, and a
head, but where a humanoid would have legs, the crimson mist's body trails away into crimson vapor.
The creature has no distinct facial features, other than two glowing points where eyes should be.*

Crimson Mist

XP 2,900 (CR 7)
NE Medium aberration
Initiative +4

DEFENSE
AC 17 (natural armor)
hp: 127 (17d8 + 51)
Resistance: Nonmagical damage except from silver weapons
Vulnerability: Bludgeoning, piercing, and slashing damage from silver weapons

OFFENSE
Speed: fly 60 ft.
Multiattack: A crimson mist attacks twice with tentacles.
Melee Attack—Tentacle: +7 to hit (reach 5 ft.; one creature). *Hit:* 1d8 + 4 bludgeoning damage and the target is grappled and engulfed (see below).

STATISTICS
Str 11 (+0), **Dex** 18 (+4), **Con** 16 (+3),
Int 17 (+3), **Wis** 16 (+3), **Cha** 16 (+3)
Languages: Deep Speech (understands but doesn't speak)
Skills: Perception +6, Stealth +7
Senses: Darkvision 60 ft.

TRAITS
Engulf: When a crimson mist strikes a target with one of its tentacles, it can immediately make an engulf attack by entering the opponent's space. The engulfed creature can attempt a DC 15 Dex saving throw to evade the attack. Success indicates the character avoids the attack entirely by retreating or stepping aside as the crimson mist moves forward. Failure indicates the crimson mist's body encloses the target, trapping the target inside. An engulfed character is restrained, takes 2d6 necrotic and psychic damage at the start of each of its turns, and immediately begins suffocating. An engulfed character can escape by winning a Dex contest against the crimson mist. A crimson mist can engulf only one Medium or smaller creature at a time, and doing so prevents it from attacking with one of its tentacles.

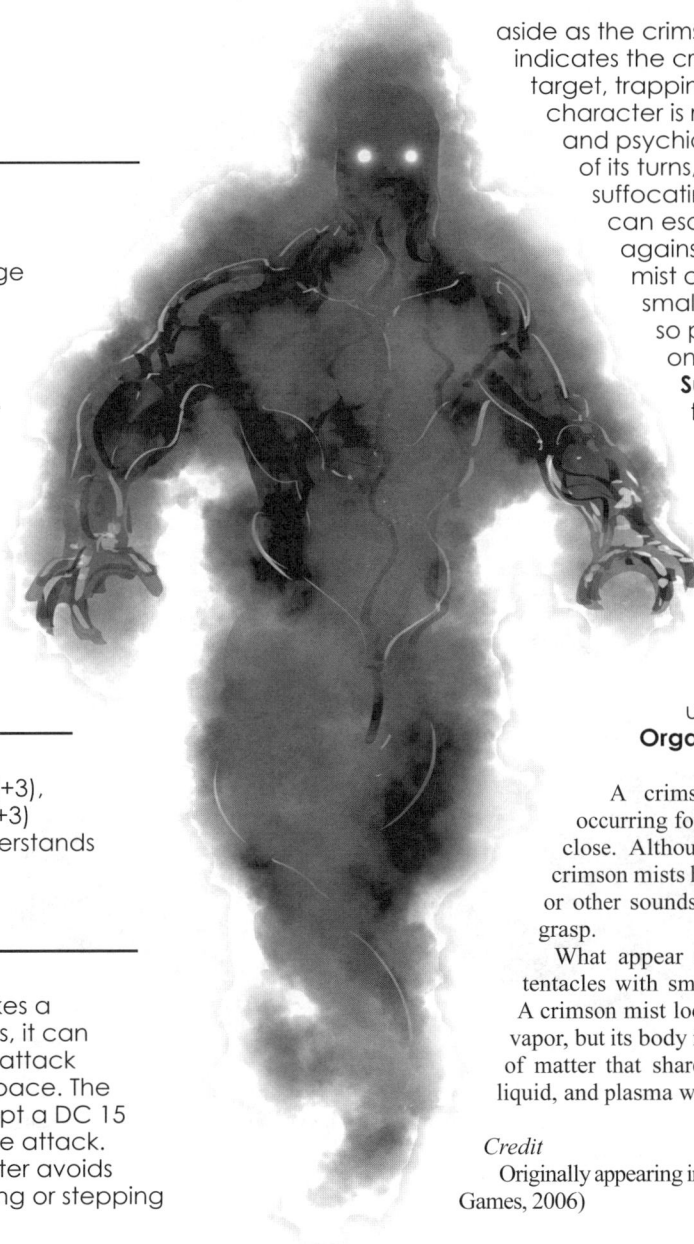

Susceptibility: If a creature dies from the crimson mist's engulf attack, the crimson mist's speed drops to 30 ft., its Stealth bonus drops to +3 (it flushes crimson, hence the name), and attacks against it have tactical advantage. These effects last for 1 hour.

ECOLOGY
Environment: Swamp or underground
Organization: Solitary

A crimson mist usually hides in naturally occurring fog and waits for potential prey to wander close. Although they are not known to converse, crimson mists have been known to mimic cries for help or other sounds in an attempt to lure a victim into its grasp.

What appear at first sight to be arms are actually tentacles with smaller, fingerlike tentacles at their ends. A crimson mist looks s if it's composed of thick, swirling vapor, but its body is surmised to be an unknown, fifth state of matter that shares some of the qualities of solid, gas, liquid, and plasma without actually being any of those.

Credit
Originally appearing in *Rappan Athuk Reloaded* (© Necromancer Games, 2006)

Crypt Thing

*A skeletal humanoid wearing a dark, hooded robe sits in a high-backed chair before you.
Its eyes appear as small pinpoints of reddish light. As you approach,
the creature raises a bony hand and points at you.*

Crypt Thing

XP 700 (CR 3)
N Medium undead
Initiative +2

DEFENSE
AC 15 (chain shirt)
hp: 52 (8d8 + 16)
Resistance: Bludgeoning, piercing, and slashing damage from nonmagical weapons
Immunity: Necrotic and poison damage; exhaustion, fright, poison, unconsciousness

OFFENSE
Speed: 30 ft.
Multiattack: A crypt thing attacks twice with claws.
Melee Attack—Claw: +4 to hit (reach 5 ft.; one creature). *Hit:* 1d8 + 2 slashing damage.

STATISTICS
Str 12 (+1), **Dex** 14 (+2), **Con** 14 (+2),
Int 12 (+1), **Wis** 14 (+2), **Cha** 16 (+3)
Languages: Common
Skills: Insight +4, Perception +6
Senses: Darkvision 60 ft.

TRAITS
Teleport Other (1/day): Once per day as an attack, a crypt thing can teleport all creatures within 50 feet of it to another location. A targeted creature resists teleporting with a successful DC 13 Wis saving throw. Affected creatures are teleported a random distance (1d10 x 100 feet) in a random direction. Roll separately for each creature that fails its saving throw. A teleported creature arrives in an open space as close as possible to the determined destination spot. A creature can teleport into midair rather than onto a solid surface, if the crypt thing wishes. A creature that teleports into midair takes falling damage normally unless it has some means to prevent falling.

ECOLOGY
Environment: Underground, burial sites
Organization: Solitary

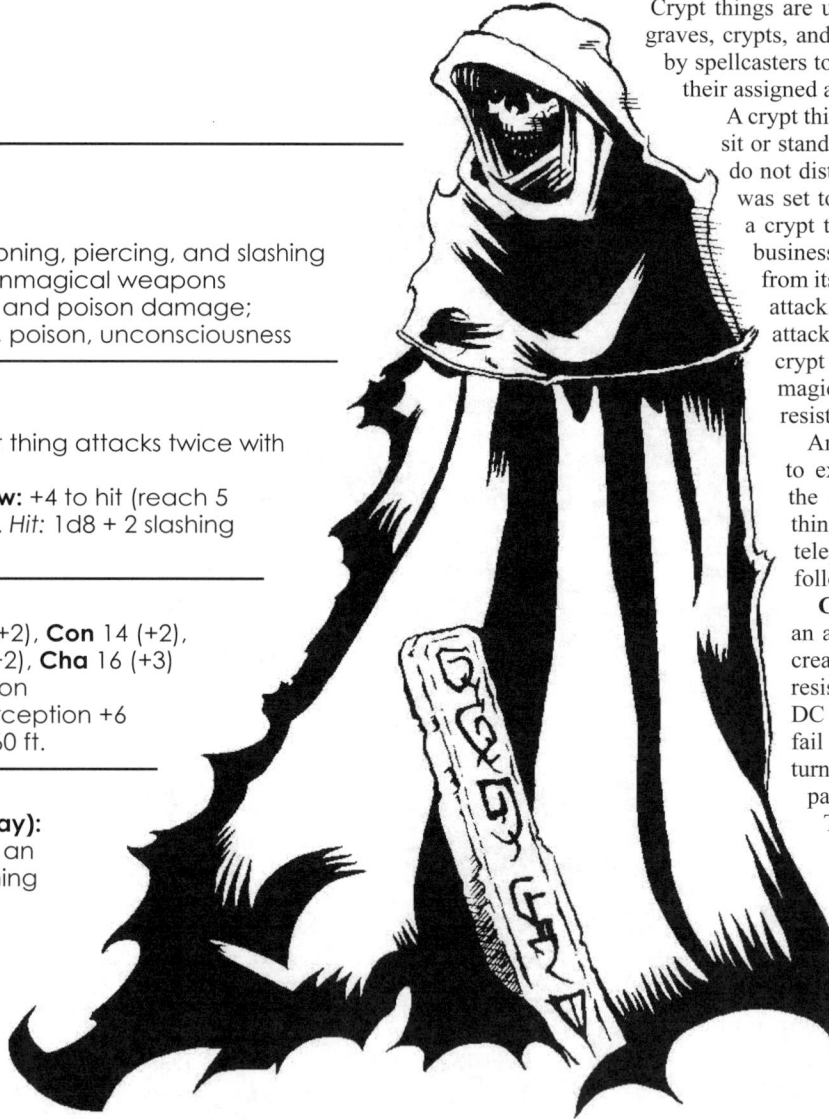

Crypt things are undead creatures found guarding tombs, graves, crypts, and other such structures. They are created by spellcasters to guard such Areas, and they never leave their assigned area.

A crypt thing never initiates combat. It is content to sit or stand in its assigned area so long as intruders do not disturb it or violate any of the conditions it was set to guard. At the first sign of disturbance, a crypt thing springs to action. Its first order of business is to attempt to remove the interlopers from its assigned area by using its *teleport other* attack. Opponents that resist teleportation are attacked by the crypt thing with its claws. A crypt thing's natural weapons are treated as magic weapons for the purpose of overcoming resistances and immunities.

Another variety of crypt thing is rumored to exist, called a crypt guardian. It has all the same abilities and statistics as a crypt thing, with one change. The crypt thing's teleportation ability is replaced with the following *cloak other* ability.

Cloak Other (1/day): Once per day as an attack, a crypt guardian can paralyze all creatures within 50 feet. A targeted creature resists paralyzation with a successful DC 13 Con saving throw. Creatures that fail the saving throw are paralyzed and turned invisible. Affected creatures remain paralyzed and invisible for 2d4 days. The saving throw can be repeated at the end of each 24-hour period, with both conditions ending early on a successful save.

Credit
The crypt thing originally appeared in the First Edition *Fiend Folio* (© TSR/Wizards of the Coast, 1981) and is used by permission. According to an article by Don Turnbull in *Dragon #55* (© TSR/Wizards of the Coast, 1981), the crypt thing was never intended to be an undead creature, though somehow it evolved into that over the years.

Copyright Notice
Author Scott Greene, based on original material by Roger Musson.

Dagon

This creature has the upper body, arms, and head of a green-skinned humanoid, and the lower torso of a great, scaled fish. A thin, almost translucent fin runs the length of its back, and a long mane of black hair falls from its head and down its finned back. Its eyes are crimson.

Dagon

XP 25,000 (CR 20)
CE Large fiend (aquatic)
Initiative +4

DEFENSE

AC 19 (natural armor)
hp 287 (25d10 + 150)
Saving Throws: Con +12
Resistance: Acid, cold, and fire damage; all damage not inflicted by good-aligned attackers or good-aligned weapons
Immunity: Lightning and poison damage; all damage from water-based or water-effecting spells

OFFENSE

Speed: 20 ft., swim 60 ft.
Multiattack: Dagon attacks once with its trident and twice with its claws.
Melee Attack—Trident: +13 to hit (reach 10 ft.; one creature). *Hit:* 3d13 + 7 piercing damage.
Melee Attack—Claw: +12 to hit (reach 5 ft.; one creature). *Hit:* 3d10 + 7 slashing damage and the target is poisoned.

STATISTICS

Str 25 (+7), **Dex** 18 (+4), **Con** 22 (+6),
Int 18 (+4), **Wis** 20 (+5), **Cha** 19 (+4)
Languages: Abyssal, Celestial, Common, Draconic, Giant, Infernal; telepathy to 100 ft.
Skills: Athletics +13, History +10, Insight +11, Intimidation +10, Perception +11
Senses: Truesight 120 ft.

TRAITS

Deadly Critical: Dagon scores a critical hit whenever its attack roll is a natural 19 or 20. A creature struck by a critical hit from Dagon is also poisoned for one minute and must make a successful DC 20 Con saving throw or immediately begin drowning. This affects all creatures, even those that can ordinarily breathe underwater or are benefiting from a *water breathing* spell or similar magic. The target can repeat the saving throw at the end of each of its turns; drowning ceases with a successful save. Drowning continues until a successful save is made, the target dies, or the effect is dispelled as a 7th-level spell. A successful saving throw does not make the target immune to this effect from another critical hit.
Legendary Resistance (3/day): Dagon can opt to automatically succeed on a saving throw it just failed.
Spell-Like Abilities: Dagon can use the following spell-like abilities, using Charisma as its casting ability (DC 18, attack +10). Dagon doesn't need material components to use these abilities.
Constant: *speak with animals* (aquatic animals only)

At will: *cloudkill* (works underwater only), *dominate monster, darkness, detect evil and good, detect magic, detect thoughts, dispel magic, fear, magic missile* (6 missiles), *teleport, telekinesis, tongues, water breathing*
3/day: *blur, conjure elemental* (water only), *enhance ability*
1/day: *confusion, feeblemind, finger of death, hold person, hold monster, lightning bolt, stoneskin, time stop, web, wish*
Unholy Aura: An unholy aura surrounds Dagon to a radius of 40 feet. All creatures must make a DC 17 Wis saving throw with the effects shown below. Evil creatures have tactical advantage on the saving throw. (Most evil creatures know better than to approach within 40 feet of Dagon.)

Level or CR	Successful Save	Failed Save
25	No ill effect	Stunned 1 round
21–24	Frightened 1d4 rounds	Stunned 1 round, then frightened 2d4 rounds
16–20	Paralyzed 1d6 rounds, then frightened 1d4 rounds	Paralyzed 1d10 minutes, then frightened 2d4 rounds
0–15	Paralyzed 1d10 minutes, then frightened 2d4 rounds	Instant death

Water Mastery: Dagon always has tactical advantage on attack rolls, ability checks, and saving throws when he is even partly in sea water.

LEGENDARY ACTIONS

Dagon can take up to three legendary actions per round. Legendary actions are taken at the end of another creature's turn, and only one can be taken after each turn.
Claw Attack: Dagon attacks once with a claw.
Spell-like Ability: Dagon uses one of its at-will spell-like abilities.

Trident Attack: Dagon attacks once with its trident.

ECOLOGY

Environment: Any aquatic, the Abyss
Organization: Solitary, but can also be accompanied by any number of aquatic creatures, monsters, or fiends

Dagon is the demon prince of sea creatures. He is worshipped as a deity by legions of sahuagin, locathah, lizardfolk, tritons (those that have accepted the ways of evil), and some merfolk. His Abyssal lair resembles the Elemental Plane of Water in that it is composed entirely of water. Pockets of air are rumored to be trapped in invisible bubbles throughout his lair to allow non-water breathing demons to exist comfortably. His home is a great underwater citadel made of rusting iron and sunken ships called Thos, located at unimaginable, crushing depth in a near-bottomless trench of his home plane.

Dagon appears as a 10-foot tall merman weighing 2,000 pounds. He can move on land using his fists to drag or pull his body, but prefers to remain in water whenever possible. One of his favorite "pranks" is grabbing an air-breathing opponent and diving as deep as he can in the sea, until the unbearable pressure collapses the victim's lungs and it drowns.

Followers of Dagon are mermen, locathah, sahuagin, lizardfolk—any evil humanoids that revere the seas and oceans. Devout followers of Dagon are called scaled ones. Many of them sign a pact of evil with Dagon, which gives them the ability to breathe underwater and a swim speed of 20 ft. (unless they naturally have a swim speed faster than that). Over time, they develop physical similarities to the most alien, frightening creatures of the mysterious deeps, until eventually they can no longer pass even as freakish members of their original race.

Dark Folk

This creature resembles a small humanoid with a light, thin frame.
It has gray skin and stark-white eyes with gray pupils. It dresses in filthy, brownish-black clothing.
The smell of dung and rotted meat hangs in the air around it.

Dark Creeper

XP 50 (CR 1/4)
CN Small humanoid
Initiative +3

DEFENSE

AC 15 (rag armor; see below)
hp: 16 (3d6 + 6)

OFFENSE

Speed: 30 ft.
Melee Attack—Dagger: +5 to hit (reach 5 ft.; one creature). *Hit:* 1d4 + 3 piercing damage and the target must make a successful DC 12 Con saving throw or be poisoned (see below).

STATISTICS

Str 11 (+0), **Dex** 17 (+3), **Con** 14 (+2),
Int 9 (–1), **Wis** 10 (+0), **Cha** 8 (–1)
Languages: Deep Speech, Undercommon
Skills: Sleight of Hand +5, Stealth +7

TRAITS

Death Throes: When a dark creeper is slain, its body combusts in a flash of bright light, leaving its gear in a heap on the ground. All creatures within 10 feet of the slain creeper must make a DC 12 Con save or be blinded for 1d6 rounds. Other dark creepers within 10 feet fail the saving throw automatically.
Poison: Dark creepers are skilled in the use of poison. They favor a foul-smelling, dark paste called black smear that they distill from fungi that grows only in deep caverns. Creatures poisoned by black smear take 1d4 poison damage immediately and suffer the usual effect of the poisoned condition. Poisoned creatures repeat the DC 12 Con saving throw at the end of each of their turns. On a successful save, they are no longer poisoned; on a failed save, they take 1d4 poison damage and the poisoned condition continues. Each dark creeper carries three doses of this poison, and they train from childhood to reapply it to their daggers as a bonus action after a successful hit.
Rag Armor: A dark creeper's multiple layers of filthy rags function as hide armor when worn by one of their kind.
See in Darkness: Light conditions are reversed in effect for dark creepers. They treat complete darkness as bright light and bright light as complete darkness. A dark creeper sees perfectly in darkness of any kind, including magical darkness.
Sneak Attack: A dark creeper's dagger attack does an extra 1d6 piercing damage if the dark creeper has advantage on the attack or if another dark creeper or dark stalker is within 5 feet of the target.

ECOLOGY

Environment: Any underground
Organization: Solitary, pair, gang (3–6), or clan (20–80 plus 1 dark stalker per 20 dark creepers)

Dark Stalker

XP 450 (CR 2)
CN Medium humanoid
Initiative +4

DEFENSE

AC 15 (hide armor)
hp: 48 (6d8 + 12)

OFFENSE

Speed: 30 ft.
Multiattack: A dark stalker attacks twice with shortswords.

Melee Attack—Shortsword: +5 to hit (reach 5 ft.; one creature). *Hit:* 1d6 + 4 piercing damage and the target must make a successful DC 12 Con saving throw or be poisoned (see below).

STATISTICS
Str 14 (+2), **Dex** 18 (+4), **Con** 14 (+2), **Int** 9 (−1), **Wis** 11 (+0), **Cha** 13 (+1)
Languages: Deep Speech, Undercommon
Skills: Sleight of Hand +5, Stealth +7

TRAITS
Death Throes: When a dark stalker is slain, its body combusts in a flash of flame. All creatures within 20 feet of the slain stalker take 3d6 fire damage, or half damage with a successful DC 12 Dex save. The stalker's combustible gear is burned to ash, but other items (shortswords, poison vials, coins, gems) survive the burst of fire.
Poison: Dark stalkers are skilled in the use of poison. They favor a foul-smelling, dark paste called black smear that they distill from fungi that grows only in deep caverns. Creatures poisoned by black smear take 1d4 poison damage immediately and suffer the usual effect of the poisoned condition. In addition, they must repeat the DC 12 Con saving throw at the end of each of their turns. On a successful save, they are no longer poisoned; on a failed save, they take 1d4 poison damage and the poisoned condition continues. Each dark stalker carries six doses of this poison, and they train from childhood to reapply it to their shortswords as a bonus action after a successful hit.
See in Darkness: Light conditions are reversed in effect for dark stalkers. They treat complete darkness as bright light and bright light as complete darkness. A dark stalker sees perfectly in darkness of any kind, including magical darkness.
Sneak Attack: A dark stalker's shortsword attack does an extra 2d6 piercing damage if the dark stalker has advantage on the attack or if another dark stalker or dark creeper is within 5 feet of the target.
Spell-Like Abilities: Dark stalkers can use the following spell-like abilities, using Charisma as their casting ability (DC 11). Dark stalkers don't need material components to use these abilities.
At will: *darkness, detect magic, fog cloud*

ECOLOGY
Environment: Any underground
Organization: Solitary, pair, gang (3–6), or clan (20–80 plus 1 dark stalker per 20 dark creepers)

Dark creepers lurk in lightless places deep below the surface of the world, venturing forth at night or into neighboring societies when the urge to steal and cause mayhem grows too great to resist. Endless layers of filthy, moldering black cloth shroud these small creatures, leading some to believe that the creature inside is smaller still. Dark creepers flee from bright light but are quite brave in the dark. They stand just under 4 feet tall and weigh about 80 pounds. Their flesh is pale and moist, and their large eyes are milky white. Dark creepers exude a foul stench of sweat and spoiled food, owing primarily to the fact that they never take off their clothing—instead piling on new layers when the outermost one grows too ragged.

It is known that subterranean cities of dark creepers exist. Most creatures that have seen these cities venture no closer than necessary, for the route to the city will be lined with traps, snares, and other deadly devices to bedevil trespassers. Each city is a large circular pit with a spiraling staircase leading down through the multi-layered city. A dark creeper city is constantly shrouded in impenetrable darkness. The actual habitat and details of dark creeper society remain a mystery, as few who venture into a dark creeper city return to testify about what they've seen (if, indeed, they saw anything in the stygian darkness).

The strange and mysterious dark stalkers are the undisputed leaders of dark creeper society. Deep underground, these creatures dwell in remote villages (some rumors suggest entire cities) built of stone and fungus in caverns where they are served and worshiped by the coarser, smaller dark creepers. Dark stalkers come to the surface rarely. When they do, they are on a mission, and accompanied by a small army of dark creepers.

Dark stalkers are tall, frail humanoids with incredibly pale skin. They wear multiple layers of dark cloth and blackened hide armor, but unlike their lesser kin, a dark stalker's garb is always clean and spotless. Each dark stalker carries a pair of short swords—they prefer these weapons to all others. Dark stalkers are 6 feet tall and weigh 100 pounds. In a fight, dark stalkers are not above sacrificing lesser creatures, including dark creepers, to win the day or to cover their retreat if things go poorly. They never fight to the death if they can escape by sacrificing others. Dark stalkers hate light and prefer to fight under the cover of *darkness*.

For all the mayhem and trouble a pack of dark creepers can cause, this is nothing compared to the danger a tribe led by the sinister dark stalkers represents. Dark creepers treat their tall, lithe masters almost like gods, presenting them with offerings and obeying their every whim. All of the heavy work and labor falls on the shoulders of the creepers, freeing the dark stalkers for their own decadent pleasures. Yet the dark creepers themselves see no inherent imbalance in this arrangement—to a dark creeper, a life in servitude to a dark stalker is a life fulfilled.

The origins of the dark stalkers and dark creepers are shrouded in mystery, made even deeper by the fact that these folk do not keep records of their history. Many scholars believe that, just as the drow descended from elves, so too must the dark folk have descended from humanity; their eerie powers and spell-like abilities grew over generation upon generation of devotion to profane and sinister magic. Alas, the truth of the race's history may never be known.

Credit
The Dark Creeper originally appeared in the First Edition *Fiend Folio* (© TSR/Wizards of the Coast, 1981) and is used by permission.

Copyright Notice
Author Scott Greene, based on original material by Rik Shepard.

Darnoc

*This entity appears as a translucent humanoid whose face is twisted in an evil scowl.
Its eyes burn with a hellish red glow.*

Darnoc

XP 450 (CR 2)
LE Medium undead
Initiative +2

DEFENSE
AC 12
hp: 52 (8d8 + 16)
Resistance: Necrotic damage
Immunity: Poison damage; exhaustion,
fright, poison, unconsciousness

OFFENSE
Speed: 30 ft.
Melee Attack—Slam: +4 to hit (reach
5 ft.; one creature). *Hit:* 1d8 + 2
bludgeoning damage, and the
creature's maximum number
of hit points is reduced by the
same amount. Hit points
lost to this attack can't be
healed by any means until
the darnoc's curse is
broken with a *greater
restoration* spell or
comparable magic.

STATISTICS
Str 12 (+1), **Dex** 14 (+2),
Con 15 (+2), **Int** 12 (+1),
Wis 12 (+1), **Cha** 14 (+2)
Languages: Common
Senses: Darkvision 60 ft.

TRAITS
Create Spawn:
Any humanoid
slain by a
darnoc
reanimates as
a darnoc in 1d4
rounds. Spawned
darnoc are under the
command of the darnoc that created them and remain
enslaved until its death, when they become independent.
They do not retain any of the abilities they had in life.

Ghost Form: As an action, a darnoc can become
incorporeal for up to 10 minutes each day. While
incorporeal, the darnoc has resistance to bludgeoning,
piercing, and slashing damage from nonmagical
weapons, it gains tactical advantage on attack rolls, its
slam attack does an extra 1d6 necrotic damage, and it
can move through creatures and solid objects as though
they were difficult terrain. The darnoc takes 1d10 force
damage if it is still inside another solid object or creature

at the end of its turn.

Symbol of Discord (1/day): Once per day
as an action, a darnoc can scribe a
symbol of discord in the air. All creatures
with an Int score of 3 or higher within
60 feet who see the symbol must
make a successful DC 12 Wis save or
immediately fall into loud bickering
and arguing with those around him
or her. Meaningful communication
is impossible while bickering. If
creatures of different alignments
are affected and bickering, each
has a 30% chance that they feel
compelled to attack the person
they are bickering with who is
the most different in alignment.
Bickering lasts 5d4 rounds.
Fighting (if it occurs) begins 1d4
rounds into the bickering and
lasts 2d4 rounds. Once drawn,
the darnoc's symbol lasts
two hours, making it useful
as a temporary trap or
delaying tactic.

ECOLOGY
Environment: Any
Organization: Solitary or
gang (2–4)

The darnoc is a corrupting evil
presence whose very touch sucks
the life from an opponent bit by
painful bit. Darnocs are said to be
the restless spirits of oppressive,
cruel, and power-hungry
individuals cursed forever to
an existence of monotony
and toil, forbidden by the
gods to taste the spoils
of the afterlife they so
desperately craved in life.
Darnocs often walk the same
halls and repeat the same actions of their insipid existence over and
over again while dressed in the clothes they wore in life. Because of
their great greed, many darnocs are found in treasury vaults endlessly
counting coins. Another common haunt is a graveyard, where the darnoc
endlessly gloats at the headstones of the business foes it bested in life.
When distracted from its reverie of remembered life, the creature
flies into an inconsolable rage, which usually leads to it lashing out
without provocation at the first individual who approaches it or tries to
communicate with it.

Copyright Notice
Author Scott Greene.

Death Dog

This creature appears to be a two-headed hound with rich black fur and piercing yellow eyes.
Each set of jaws constantly drips foul-smelling saliva.

Death Dog

XP 100 (CR 1/2)
NE Medium monstrosity
Initiative +2

DEFENSE

AC 13 (natural armor)
hp: 26 (4d8 + 8)

OFFENSE

Speed: 40 ft.
Multiattack: A death dog bites twice.
Melee Attack—Bite: +4 to hit (reach 5 ft.; one creature). *Hit:* 1d8 + 2 piercing damage plus rotting death (see below).

STATISTICS

Str 13 (+1), **Dex** 15 (+2), **Con** 15 (+2),
Int 4 (−3), **Wis** 12 (+1), **Cha** 6 (−2)
Languages: None
Skills: Perception +5
Senses: Darkvision 60 ft.

TRAITS

Flawless Tracker: A death dog has tactical advantage on Wis (Perception) checks to follow a trail by scent.
Rotting Death: A creature bitten by a death dog must make a successful DC 12 Con saving throw or be infected with rotting death, which is both a curse and disease. An infected character repeats the saving throw at the end of every long rest. On a failed save, the character's maximum number of hit points immediately drops by 1d8; on a successful save, it drops by 1d4. Rotting death can be cured only by first removing the curse, then curing the disease; attempts to cure the disease while the curse is still in effect fail automatically.

ECOLOGY

Environment: Warm deserts
Organization: Hunt (2–4) or pack (5–10)

Death dogs resemble mastiffs, but with two heads. They are nocturnal killing machines that hunt their prey without hesitation across the desert sands and wastelands. Death dog packs have been known to share territory with other packs with little friction, although they do engage in dominance battles if food or water become scarce. Death dogs are strictly carnivores. They hunt and attack creatures much larger than themselves if they have the numbers to bring down a big opponent, but they are leery of hunting foes that outnumber the pack.

Credit
The death dog originally appeared in the First Edition *Fiend Folio* (© TSR/Wizards of the Coast, 1981) and is used by permission.

Copyright Notice
Author Scott Greene, based on original material by Underworld Oracle.

Death Worm

*This creature is a long, slender (relative to its length), reddish-brown monster
with yellow mottling across its back. Its body tapers toward its head, which is mostly mouth
—a circular maw lined with multiple rows of steel-hard teeth
that allow it to chew through rocks and earth as it burrows underground.*

Death Worm
XP 700 (CR 3)
Unaligned Large monstrosity
Initiative +1

DEFENSE
AC 15 (natural armor)
hp: 59 (7d10 + 21)
Saving Throws: Wis +2
Immunity: Blindness, prone

OFFENSE
Speed: 20 ft., burrow 10 ft.
Melee Attack—Bite: +6 to hit (reach 5 ft.; one creature). *Hit:*
1d10 + 4 piercing damage plus 1d8 acid damage.
Ranged Attack—Acid Spit (recharge 5, 6):
automatic hit (range 30 ft. line; creatures in
line). *Hit:* 4d6 acid damage, or no damage
with a successful DC 13 Dex saving throw.
Ranged Attack—Lightning (recharge 6):
automatic hit (range 20 ft. line; creatures
in line). *Hit:* 4d8 lightning damage, or half
damage with a successful DC 13 Dex
saving throw.

STATISTICS
Str 18 (+4), **Dex** 13 (+1), **Con** 16 (+3),
Int 3 (–4), **Wis** 11 (+0), **Cha** 5 (–3)
Languages: None
Senses: Tremorsense 60 ft.

ECOLOGY
Environment: Temperate
Organization: Solitary

The death worm is a reclusive, desert-dwelling creature content to spend its
life burrowing beneath the ground and
sustaining itself on a diet of sand and
earth. On occasion, it surfaces to devour
more substantial prey (animals such as camels,
desert dogs, and humanoids). The combination of its
ferocious teeth, acidic saliva that it spits with great accuracy,
and lightning generated by a mysterious organ in its head makes the death
worm a seldom-seen but much feared legend in the desert.

Death worms lay their eggs far beneath the surface of the earth.
Newborn death worms live on a diet of sand and earth; only when they
reach maturity (two to five years after hatching) do they surface in search
of their first living prey.

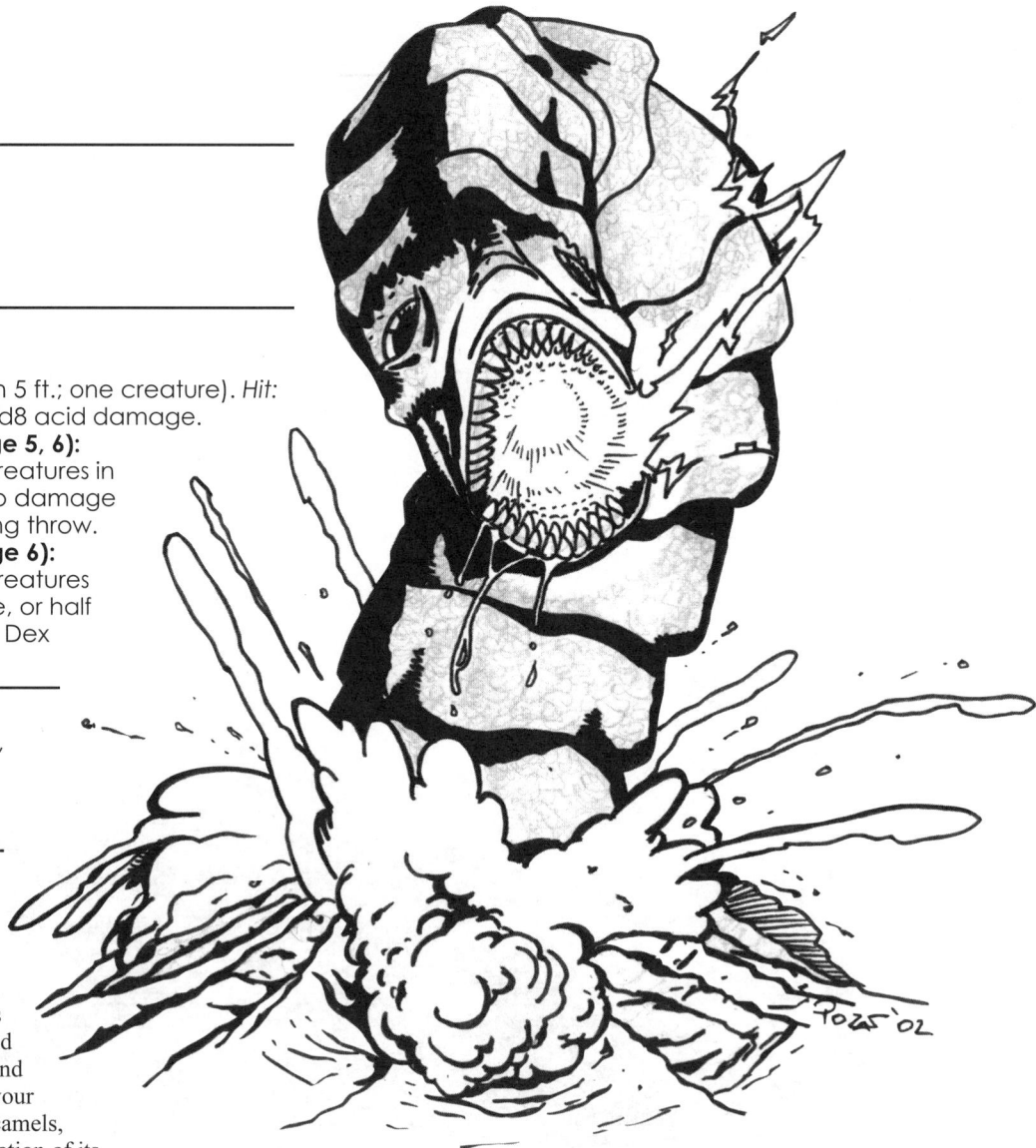

Decapus

This creature's body is a large spheroid sprouting ten tentacles. Hair grows in broken patches around its flesh. Its eyes are stark white with no visible pupils, and its large mouth sports long, yellow fangs.

Decapus

XP 450 (CR 2)
CE Medium aberration
Initiative +1

DEFENSE

AC 12 (natural armor)
hp: 44 (8d8 +8)

OFFENSE

Speed: 10 ft., climb 30 ft.
Multiattack: A decapus attacks four times, in any combination of tentacle slams and constriction.

Melee Attack—Tentacle Slam: +4 to hit (reach 10 ft.; one creature). *Hit:* 1d6 + 2 bludgeoning damage and the target is grappled and restrained.

Melee Attack—Constriction: automatic hit (one creature already grappled by a tentacle at the start of the decapus's turn). *Hit:* 1d6 + 2 bludgeoning damage and the target is grappled and restrained.

STATISTICS

Str 14 (+2), **Dex** 13 (+1), **Con** 15 (+2), **Int** 10 (+0), **Wis** 11 (+0), **Cha** 12 (+1)
Languages: Unique (decapus)
Skills: Deception +5, Stealth +3
Senses: Darkvision 60 ft.

TRAITS

Brachiation: A decapus can move through trees at its climb speed (30 feet per round) by using its tentacles to swing from tree to tree, provided the trees are no more than 10 feet apart.

Sound Imitation: A decapus can mimic the sounds of any creature it has previously encountered with uncanny accuracy, though it can't mimic humanoid speech patterns for more than two or three words at a stretch. The ruse can be detected with a contest between the decapus's Deception and a listener's Insight.

Spell-like Abilities: A decapus can use the following spell-like ability, using Charisma as its casting ability (DC 11). The decapus doesn't need material components to use this ability.
At Will: *major image*

ECOLOGY

Environment: Ruins, underground, and temperate or warm forests
Organization: Solitary (or a mated pair, rarely)

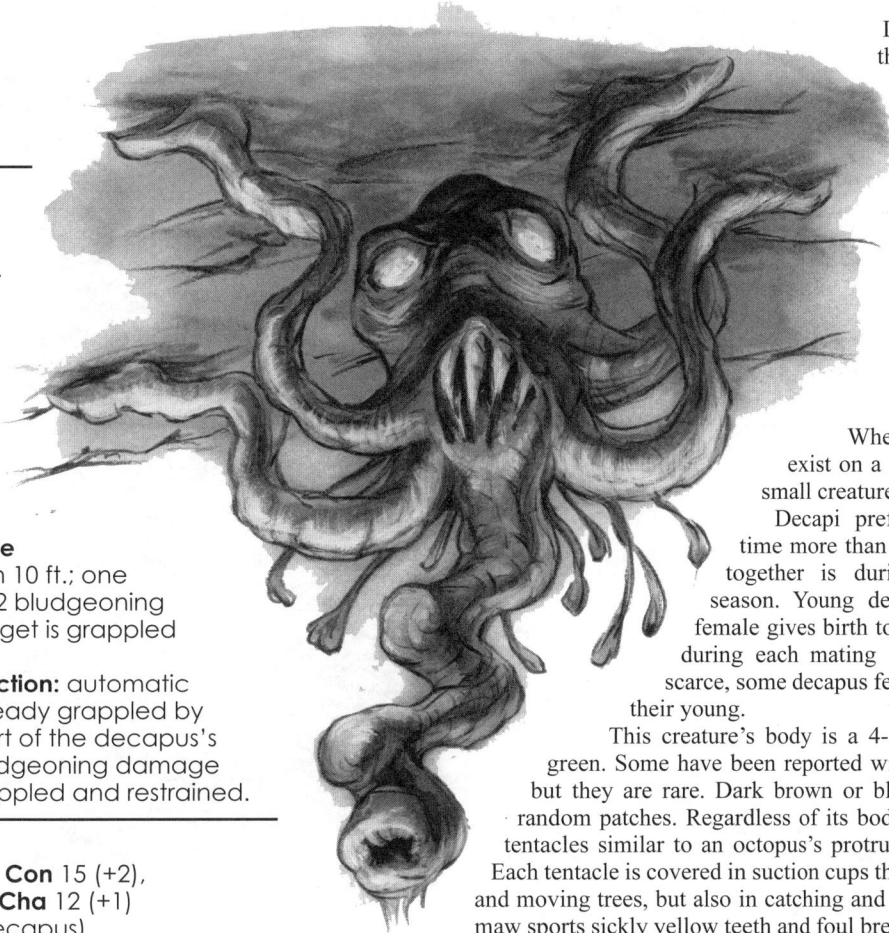

Decapi are solitary creatures that dwell in ruins, caverns, or dense forest (where their climbing ability gives them great mobility through the tree canopy for pursuing prey or evading predators). On the ground, decapi are slow-moving, so they spend most of their time among the tree tops or hanging from ceilings.

As nocturnal hunters, decapi are quite fond of human, elf, and halfling flesh. When food is scarce, they can exist on a diet of rats, snakes, and other small creatures or dungeon denizens.

Decapi prefer a solitary life; the only time more than one will ever be encountered together is during their infrequent mating season. Young decapi are born live, and the female gives birth to only a single young decapus during each mating season. If food is extremely scarce, some decapus females have been known to eat their young.

This creature's body is a 4-foot-diameter globe of pallid green. Some have been reported with purple or yellow coloring, but they are rare. Dark brown or black hair grows in seemingly random patches. Regardless of its body color, each decapus has 10 tentacles similar to an octopus's protruding from its spherical body. Each tentacle is covered in suction cups that aid the creature in climbing and moving trees, but also in catching and killing its prey. Its large wide maw sports sickly yellow teeth and foul breath. Decapi seem to be able to speak with others of their kind using guttural noises.

A decapus hunts with its *major image*. When it senses potential prey nearby, it creates an illusion intended to draw unwary creatures within reach of its tentacles. Usually this involves a creature that will elicit sympathy from the prey being threatened somehow. For example, when typical humanoid adventurers approach, the decapus is likely to create the image of a child surrounded by hungry wolves or of a young woman or man being terrorized by bandits.

Credit
The decapus originally appeared in the First Edition module *B3 Palace of the Silver Princess* (© TSR/Wizards of the Coast, 1981) and is used by permission.

Copyright Notice
Author Scott Greene, based on original material by Jean Wells.

Demon, Teratashia

*This mighty demon has the body of a cockroach topped by the head of a beautiful
but savage woman, made even fiercer by the bleached human skulls draped round her shoulders.
The only light near her is the sparks that crackle and dance around her claws.*

Teratashia, Demon Princess of Dimensions

XP 13,000 (CR 15)
CE Large fiend
Initiative +4

DEFENSE

AC 18 (natural armor)
hp: 161 (19d10 + 76)
Saving Throws: Dex +9, Con +9, Int +9, Cha +9
Resistance: Acid, cold, and psychic damage
Immunity: Lightning and poison damage; bludgeoning,
  piercing, and slashing damage from nonmagical
  weapons; charm, fright, poison

OFFENSE

Speed: 35 ft., fly 50 ft.
Multiattack: Teratashia attacks four times with her claws, or
  she attacks twice with claws and either uses one spell-like
  ability or one charge from her necklace.
Melee Attack—Claw: +9 to hit (reach 5 ft.; one creature).
  Hit: 3d8 + 4 slashing damage plus 2d6 lightning damage.

STATISTICS

Str 17 (+3), **Dex** 19 (+4), **Con** 18 (+4),
Int 19 (+4), **Wis** 15 (+2), **Cha** 18 (+4)
Languages: Abyssal
Senses: Truesight 120 ft.

TRAITS

Regeneration: Teratashia heals 10 hit points at the start of
  her turn if she is in darkness. She heals 5 hit points if she is in
  dim light, and no hit points if she is in bright light.
Light Avoidance: Teratashia's speed increases to 50 feet
  and her flying speed increases to 70 feet if she is in bright
  light at the start of her turn. Her speed returns to normal
  when she starts her turn in dim light or darkness.
Spell-like Abilities: Teratashia can use the following spell-
  like abilities, using Charisma as her casting ability (DC 17,
  attack +9). She doesn't need material components to use
  these abilities.
At Will: *clairvoyance, darkness, detect thoughts, dimension
  door, dispel magic, fear, suggestion*
3/day: *charm person, insect plague, telekinesis, wall of stone*
Teratashia's Necklace of Skulls: Teratashia's necklace is a
  powerful magic item. It is made from 13 skulls, and each
  skull has gems set into the eye sockets. Each gem stores
  one magic spell; the wearer of the necklace can use
  an action (or reaction for *counterspell*) to cast one of
  the spells. Spells are cast at their lowest level, using the
  caster's attack bonus and saving throw DC. The necklace
  recovers one expended charge per hour when worn
  by Teratashia; it doesn't recover charges when worn by
  anyone else.
> *arcane lock* (x2)
> *bestow curse* (x2)
> *cloudkill* (x2)
> *cone of cold* (x4)
> *counterspell* (x2)
> *cure wounds* (x4)
> *fireball* (x2)

> *hypnotic pattern* (x2)
> *knock* (x2)
> *mirror image* (x2)
> *witch bolt* (x2)

ECOLOGY

Environment: The Abyss
Organization: Solitary

The Demon-Princess Teratashia's dark palace in the depths of the Abyss
is a nexus of countless gaps between dimensions, a warren of tunnels
worming their way deep into a multitude of other realities. She is known in
some circles as the Mistress of Dimensions. From the center of this network
of connections, Teratashia sends her minions creeping and slithering through
the planes of existence to do her bidding. Any type of demon can be found
serving her, with or without the knowledge of any other masters it serves.
Besides demons, mortal creatures that hunt and hide in the dark nonplaces
between the true planes of existence can also be found in her service.

Teratashia resembles a huge, female-headed cockroach with a feral
visage, wearing a necklace of human skulls. The necklace is a powerful
magic item, but it functions at full effect only for Teratashia.

Teratashia seldom involves herself in the quarrels of the other great
demons. She is far more interested in controlling the nooks and crannies
between dimensions than with her political status in the Abyss. She is
inclined to leave the other demon princes alone to the same degree that
they extend that courtesy to her.

Demon, Thalasskoptis

*From a mass of writhing tentacles, the face of a boy emerges
—a boy with needle-sharp teeth and drowned eyes.*

Thalasskoptis, Demon Prince

XP 5,900 (CR 10)
CE Large fiend (aquatic)
Initiative +4

DEFENSE

AC 18 (natural armor)
hp: 168 (16d10 + 80)
Saving Throws: Dex +8, Con +9, Wis +7
Resistance: Bludgeoning, piercing, and slashing damage
from nonmagical weapons
Immunity: Cold, psychic, and thunder damage; charm,
fright, grappling, paralysis, prone, unconsciousness

OFFENSE

Speed: 30 ft., swim 60 ft.
Multiattack: Thalasskoptis attacks four times with tentacles,
or it attacks twice with tentacles and either uses one spell-
like ability or emits a toxic ink cloud.
Melee Attack—Tentacles: +8 to hit (reach 10 ft.; one
creature). *Hit:* 2d10 + 4 bludgeoning damage. If the
target of this attack is a stunned creature, the attack is
automatically a critical hit.

STATISTICS

Str 19 (+4), **Dex** 18 (+4), **Con** 20 (+5),
Int 15 (+2), **Wis** 17 (+3), **Cha** 18 (+4)
Languages: Abyssal, telepathy
Senses: Truesight 120 ft.

TRAITS

Spell-like Abilities: Thalasskoptis can use the following
spell-like abilities, using Charisma as its casting ability
(DC 16, attack +8). Thalasskoptis doesn't need material
components to use these abilities.
At Will: *animate dead, charm person, clairvoyance,
darkness, detect thoughts, dispel magic, fear, suggestion,
teleport*
3/Day: *dominate monster*
Toxic Ink (3/day): Thalasskoptis can squirt a cloud of
poisonous ink into air or water. The ink creates a sphere
60 feet in radius centered on Thalasskoptis, and it lasts
for one minute. The cloud is stationary; it doesn't move
with Thalasskoptis. The area inside the cloud is heavily
obscured. Creatures other than Thalasskoptis in the ink
cloud must make a successful DC 17 Con saving throw
against poison or be stunned for as long as they remain
inside the ink cloud.

LEGENDARY ACTIONS

Thalasskoptis can take up to three legendary actions per
round. Legendary actions are taken at the end of another
creature's turn, and only one can be taken after each
turn.
Bite: +8 to hit (one creature grappled by Thalasskoptis). *Hit:*
2d6 + 4 piercing damage and the target must make a
successful DC 17 Con saving throw or be poisoned for 1d6
rounds and take 2d8 poison damage.
Spell-Like Ability: Thalasskoptis uses one at-will spell-like
ability.
Tentacle Grab: Thalasskoptis makes one tentacle attack. If

this attack hits, the target is also grappled.

ECOLOGY

Environment: Any aquatic
Organization: Solitary

Thalasskoptis is a mass of writhing tentacles with a feral but boyish
face at the center. It is the lord of underwater corruption, of those who
die at sea, and of many horrific beasts of the dark, oceanic deeps. It is
an occasional rival of Orcus, who considers his domain to include all
death, without exceptions for death at sea. The two demons have many
overlapping interests, however, so they are allies more often than enemies
in the grim power struggles of the Abyss. Some of Thalasskoptis's enemies
dismiss this demon as an underwater minion of Orcus—a claim that incurs
a terrible vengeance from the sea-demon, if it hears such talk.

The lair of Thalasskoptis is a sprawling palace of coral that stretches
for miles across the sea floor and extends into deep subterranean tunnels
beneath the sea floor of the Abyss. It can sometimes be located by the
mass of rotting, bloated bodies of humanoids, whales, fish, sea monsters,
and seaweed that slowly revolves on the surface of the sea above the lair.
In its lair, Thalasskoptis spends much of its time slumbering at the heart of

a 300-foot-diamater sphere of corpses bound together by seaweed. While it slumbers, the demon is guarded by giant sharks, aquatic ghouls, sea serpents, and possibly even an undead kraken.

Thalasskoptis has scattered followings of human cultists in the Material Plane, predominantly in coastal communities. It is served in the deep oceans of the Material Plane by dark tritons. From time to time, dark ships of drowned, undead sailors rise from the sea to pillage treasure from coastal cities and transport it back to their dread lord's realm. Although they appear very rarely—seldom more than once in a single human lifetime—the visits of these ships are so feared that Thalasskoptis's cultists are allowed to quietly practice their dark rites lest the dread sea lord seek vengeance for them. When the dark fleets rise from the water, reeking of salt and rot, miles of coastline can be purged of life, the inhabitants dragged beneath the waves to serve the master they did not fear sufficiently.

Demonic Knight

This creature appears as a mansized humanoid dressed in black iron armor.
Its head is completely hidden by a dull black helm.

Demonic Knight
XP 1,800 (CR 5)
CE Medium fiend
Initiative +1

DEFENSE
AC 17 (*half plate armor +1*)
hp: 81 (10d8 + 36)
Resistance: Bludgeoning, piercing, and slashing damage from nonmagical weapons

OFFENSE
Speed: 20 ft.
Multiattack: A demonic knight attacks once with its *anarchic longsword* and once with either its breath of unlife or its fist.
Melee Attack—Anarchic Longsword: +9 to hit (reach 5 ft.; one creature). *Hit:* 1d10 + 6 slashing damage (treat as magic damage).
Melee Attack—Mailed Fist: +8 to hit (reach 5 ft.; one creature). *Hit:* 1d8 + 5 bludgeoning damage.
Ranged Attack—Breath of Unlife (recharge 5, 6): automatic hit (range 10 ft. cone; creatures in the cone). *Hit:* 6d10 necrotic damage, or half damage with a successful DC 15 Con saving throw. A creature reduced to 0 hit points by this attack dies instantly; see Create Spawn below.

STATISTICS
Str 20 (+5), **Dex** 13 (+1), **Con** 18 (+4),
Int 17 (+3), **Wis** 18 (+4), **Cha** 18 (+4)
Languages: Abyssal, Common
Skills: A demonic knight applies its proficiency bonus (+3) to all skill checks.
Senses: Truesight 60 ft.

TRAITS
Create Spawn: Any humanoid slain by a demonic knight's breath of unlife returns to life in 2d4 rounds as a shadow demon under the command of the demonic knight that created it. The new shadow demon remains enslaved to the demonic knight until the knight's death. They do not retain any of the abilities they had in life.
Spell-like Abilities: The demonic knight can use the following spell-like abilities, using Charisma as its casting ability (DC 15, attack +7). The demonic knight doesn't need material components to use these abilities.
At Will: *detect magic, see invisibility, wall of ice*
2/day: *dispel magic, symbol*
1/day: *fireball, power word stun*
Summon Demonic Aid (1/day): Once per day as an action, a demonic knight can summon additional demons to his side. He can summon 1d4 shadow demons, 2 glabrezus or hezrous, or 1 vrock or marilith. To complete the summoning, the demonic knight must make a successful DC 18 Cha check (normally a 50% chance). The summoned demons teleport into empty spaces within 60 feet of the demon knight, of his choosing, and remain until they're slain or for one hour.

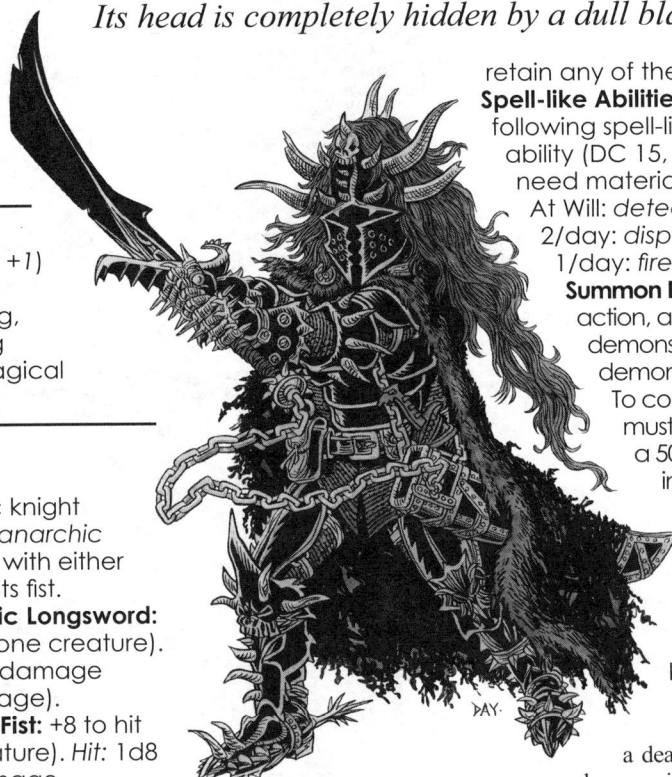

ECOLOGY
Environment: Any (Abyss)
Organization: Solitary or troupe (demonic knight plus 2–4 demons of CR 10 or lower)

The demonic knight—known incorrectly by some as a death knight—is rumored to be the creation of the great demon prince Orcus, the Prince of the Undead. Some sages doubt the validity of that claim, since demonic knights are not undead. It is known, however, that three of the most powerful demonic knights (Baruliis, Caines, and Arrunes) make their homes on the same plane of the Abyss as the Prince of the Undead, within the shadow of his great citadel. The true origins of the demonic knight lay hidden deep in the stinking pits of the Abyss, and those brave few who have dared search for these secrets have never returned.

Demonic knights serve their master (whoever it may be) with unswerving loyalty. They never question their orders and never question their superior. They are often sent to the Material Plane to recruit new bodies for their master's next plot or deception, or to punish those that have offended their lord. On some occasions, they are simply sent to another plane to corrupt and slay those that are just and good (to the delight of their master).

A demonic knight appears as a 6-foot-tall humanoid dressed in black iron half-plate armor. Its head is completely hidden beneath a helmet that it never removes. A black iron longsword is clutched in its mailed fist or sometimes slung at its hip. Some demonic knights don jet-black cloaks and other decorations as a badge of station. It is unknown how many demonic knights exist, but sages of such things claim that arcane logic dictates there can be no more than nine.

Denizen of Leng

Wrapped from head to toe in tattered leather robes, this creature appears almost human at first glance. The longer one looks, however, the more one becomes aware of strange and terrifying realities beneath the façade.

Denizen of Leng

XP 1,800 (CR 5)
CE Medium aberration
Initiative +4

DEFENSE

AC 16 (natural armor)
hp: 85 (10d8 + 40)
Saving Throws: Dex +7
Resistance: Cold and lightning damage
Immunity: Poison damage; poison, suffocation

OFFENSE

Speed: 40 ft.
Multiattack: A denizen of Leng bites once and attacks once with claws.
Melee Attack—Bite: +7 to hit (reach 5 ft.; one creature). *Hit:* 1d8 + 4 piercing damage and the target must make a successful DC 15 Con saving throw or immediately gain one level of exhaustion.
Melee Attack—Claws: +7 to hit (reach 5 ft.; one creature). *Hit:* 1d8 + 4 slashing damage.

STATISTICS

Str 14 (+2), **Dex** 18 (+4), **Con** 19 (+4), **Int** 18 (+4), **Wis** 17 (+3), **Cha** 21 (+5)
Languages: Deep Speech, Unique
Skills: Deception +9
Senses: Darkvision 60 ft.

TRAITS

Regeneration: At the start of its turn, a denizen of Leng recovers 5 lost hit points. This ability fails to function only if the creature is utterly cut off from Leng; e.g., if its ability to *plane shift* is negated. If a denizen of Leng is reduced to 0 hit points while it is still capable of regenerating, its body dissipates into vapor in 1d4 rounds, leaving only its clothing and equipment behind, and it returns to life on Leng.
Sneak Attack: Once per turn, a denizen of Leng can do an extra 4d6 damage with a claw or bite attack if the denizen has advantage on the attack or if one of its allies is within 5 feet of the target.
Spell-like Abilities: A denizen of Leng can use the following spell-like abilities, using Charisma as its casting ability (DC 16, attack +8). A denizen of Leng doesn't need material components to use these abilities.
Constant: *tongues*
3/day: *detect thoughts, hypnotic pattern, levitate, minor image*
1/day: *locate object, plane shift* (self only)

ECOLOGY

Environment: Any land
Organization: Solitary, gang (2–5), or crew (6–15)

Denizens of Leng are remote, alien, and inscrutable, much like their distant, well-hidden home realm. Scholars argue endlessly over whether Leng is a physical realm like other planes—secreted among the Outer Planes, according to some—or a more ephemeral dimension of dreams and shadows. What is known for certain is that its native inhabitants can travel freely among the planes, both individually using an innate power and also aboard great black-sailed ships. They venture out in search of exotic slaves, magic items, and gems, for which they have an insatiable greed. Gems always make up the greatest portion of their treasure. It is also known that the denizens of Leng are involved in an ages-old war against the monstrous, intelligent spiders that infest their homeland.

Travelers from Leng always go abroad in voluminous robes and head-wrappings similar to those of desert people, to disguise their true origin. In their disguises, they can readily pass as elves or short humans. Stripped of their robes and hoods, they reveal horned brows, clawed fingers, mouths ringed by tentacles, and cloven, double-jointed legs like a goat's.

Credit
The denizen of Leng is adapted from the *Pathfinder Roleplaying Game Bestiary 2*, © 2010, Paizo Publishing, LLC.

Dire Corby

This creature resembles a wingless, humanoid crow with slick black feathers, powerful arms that end in razor-sharp claws, and a gold beak.

Dire Corby
XP 100 (CR 1/2)
NE Medium monstrosity
Initiative +1

DEFENSE
AC 11
hp: 11 (2d8 + 2)

OFFENSE
Speed: 30 ft.
Multiattack: A dire corby attacks twice with claws.
Melee Attack—Claw: +5 to hit (reach 5 ft.; one creature). *Hit:* 1d6 + 3 slashing damage.

STATISTICS
Str 16 (+3), **Dex** 12 (+1), **Con** 13 (+1),
Int 6 (–2), **Wis** 10 (+0), **Cha** 8 (–1)
Languages: Deep Speech, Undercommon
Skills: Perception +2
Senses: Darkvision 60 ft.

ECOLOGY
Environment: Underground
Organization: Gang (2–5), flock (6–11), or community (10–60 plus 1 leader of 3rd to 5th level per 10 adults)

Dire corbies are humanoid, bipedal birdmen that dwell deep beneath the surface world. They make their homes in large, open caverns where they hollow out individual shelters in the walls. These creatures do not now have wings, but they almost certainly did in the remote past. Why their wings disappeared and were replaced by muscular arms with claws is unknown.

Dire corbies are omnivores but prefer a diet of fresh meat. They hunt and enjoy the flesh of subterranean rodents, animals, and even other races. They are particularly fond of the leathery flesh of bats.

Dire corbies hunt in flocks. They enjoy the thrill of the hunt and chasing down their prey. A typical hunt ends with the prey cornered and trapped, then cruelly tormented and tortured for many minutes before the dire corbies finally tear it to shreds with their claws.

Dire corbies always fight to the death and never flee, even when faced with overwhelming odds.

Credit
The dire corby originally appeared in the First Edition *Fiend Folio* (© TSR/Wizards of the Coast, 1981) and is used by permission.

Copyright Notice
Author Scott Greene, based on original material by Jeff Wyndham.

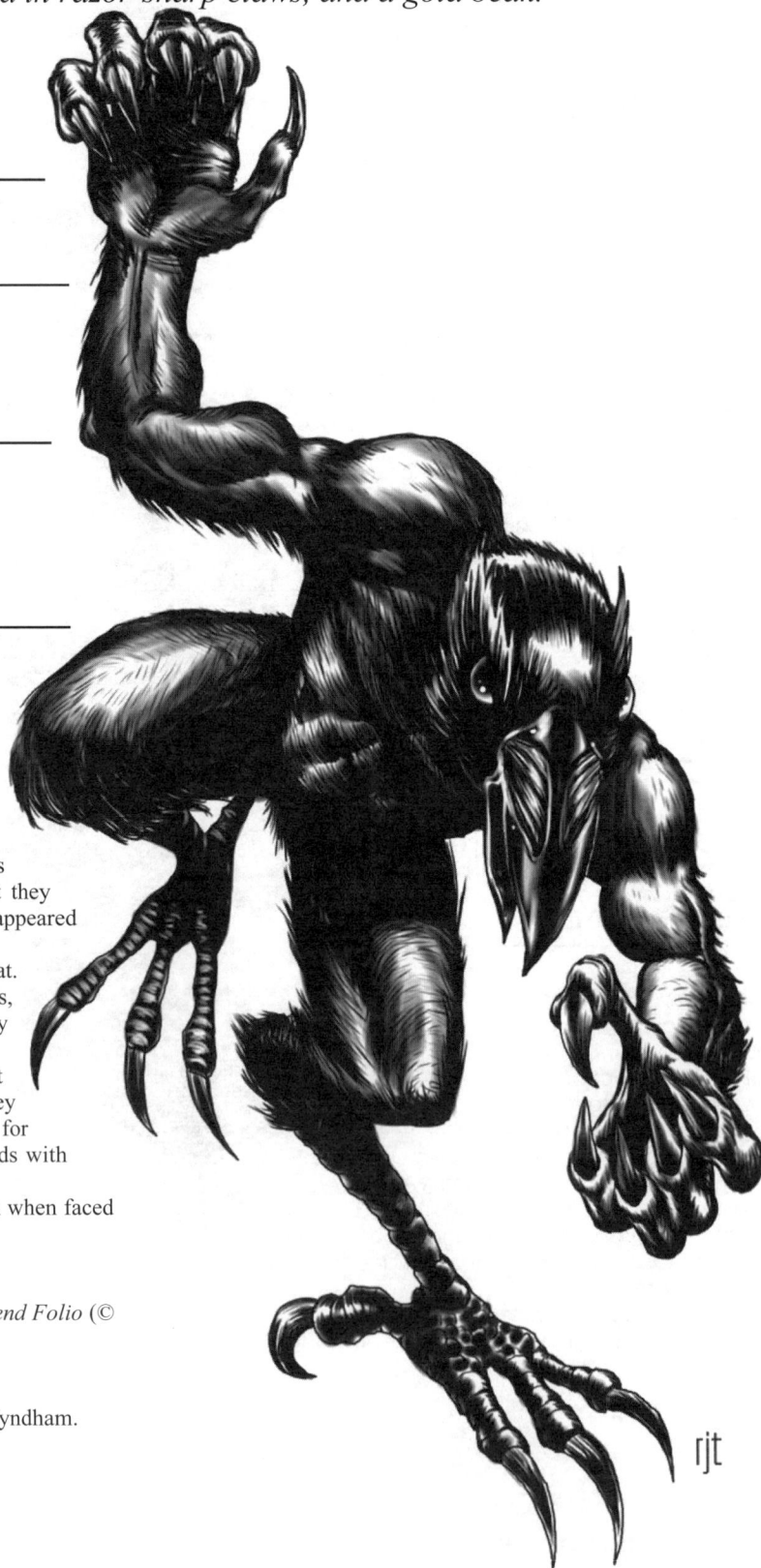

Dracolisk

This creature resembles a young six-legged dragon with glistening scales and gleaming eyes.

Dracolisk

XP 2,900 (CR 7)
Unaligned Large dragon
Initiative +1

DEFENSE

AC 17 (natural armor)
hp: 114 (12d10 + 48)
Immunity: Paralysis, petrification, one energy type (see Traits)

OFFENSE

Speed: 30 ft., fly 60 ft.
Multiattack: A dracolisk bites once and attacks once with claws, or it uses its breath weapon or its petrifying gaze.
Melee Attack—Bite: +8 to hit (reach 5 ft.; one creature). *Hit:* 2d8 + 5 piercing damage.
Melee Attack—Claws: +8 to hit (reach 5 ft.; one creature). *Hit:* 3d8 + 5 slashing damage.
Area Attack—Breath Weapon (recharge 5, 6): automatic hit (range varies; creatures in range). *Hit:* target takes the indicated damage, or half damage with a successful DC 16 Dex saving throw. See Breath Weapon, below, for variables.

STATISTICS

Str 21 (+5), **Dex** 12 (+1), **Con** 19 (+4),
Int 6 (−2), **Wis** 12 (+1), **Cha** 13 (+1)
Languages: Draconic
Skills: Perception +4

Senses: Darkvision 60 ft.

TRAITS

Breath Weapon: A dracolisk can use its breath weapon as an attack. Its breath characteristics are determined by its draconic background, as summarized on the table. Regardless of the type of breath weapon involved, targets in the area of effect take half damage with a successful DC 16 Dex saving throw. Lines are 5 feet wide.

Immunity to Energy: Each type of dracolisk is immune to the energy type inherent in its own breath weapon, as summarized on the table.

Dracolisk Variety	Breath Weapon	Damage	Immunity
Black	60-foot line	4d8 acid	acid
Blue	60-foot line	4d8 electricity	electricity
Green	30-foot cone	4d8 acid	acid
Red	30-foot cone	4d8 fire	fire
White	30-foot cone	4d8 cold	cold

Petrifying Gaze: As an attack, a dracolisk can target one living creature within 30 feet and line of sight with its petrifying gaze. If the targeted creature can see the dracolisk, then the targeted creature must make a successful DC 15 Con saving throw or begin turning to stone; it immediately becomes restrained, and it must make another DC 15 Con saving throw at the end of its next turn. Success on the second saving throw ends this effect. Failure on the second saving throw means the creature is petrified permanently. A creature that is capable of taking actions can, at the start of its turn, look away to avoid the dracolisk's gaze for one complete round. If it targets the dracolisk while averting its gaze, it suffers all the usual penalties for attacking an unseen target. Creatures that are blind, unconscious, or unable to see the dracolisk for any other reason are immune to this attack.

ECOLOGY

Environment: Varies
Organization: Solitary or colony (3–6)

The vicious dracolisk is a rare crossbreed of dragon and basilisk. No one is sure how the dracolisk species came to be, but all who have encountered it are well aware of its lethality. The only confirmed species of dracolisk is clearly the offspring of black dragons, but based on that evidence, sages hypothesize that a species of dracolisk could exist corresponding to every species of dragon.

At first glance, a dracolisk appears to be a juvenile dragon of its color, except the dracolisk has six legs instead of four. Thanks to the petrifying

gaze it inherited from its basilisk parent, most characters who encounter a dracolisk never get a second glance. A dracolisk has a scaled body the same color as its dragon parent that fades to a lighter shade on its underside. A short, curved horn, similar to a rhino's, juts from its nose. Its leathery wings match its body color but darken near the tips. All dracolisk's eyes are pale green with sparkles that match its dragon-parent color.

A dracolisk's environment varies based on its dragon heritage: black dracolisks can be found in warm marshes, deserts, or underground; blue dracolisks favor warm deserts and mountains, rarely being found underground; green dracolisks favor temperate or warm forests and underground settings; red dracolisks favor warm mountains and underground settings; and white dracolisks favor cold mountains, cold deserts, and underground.

The dracolisk always opens a fight with its breath weapon and gaze attack, resorting to its claws and teeth only afterward.

Credit
The dracolisk originally appeared in the First Edition module *S4 Lost Caverns of Tsojcanth* (© TSR/Wizards of the Coast, 1982) and later in the First Edition *Monster Manual II* (© TSR/Wizards of the Coast, 1983) and is used by permission.

Copyright Notice
Author Scott Greene, based on original material by Gary Gygax

Drake, Fire

This creature has the shape of a small red dragon, but its translucent scales are mottled mauve and burgundy. Heat and steam rise from its body. Its wings are mottled black, and its eyes are crimson.

Fire Drake
XP 200 (CR 1)
CE Small dragon
Initiative +1

DEFENSE
AC 13 (natural armor)
hp: 27 (6d6 + 6)
Immunity: Fire damage; paralysis, sleep
Vulnerability: Cold damage

OFFENSE
Speed: 20 ft., fly 60 ft.
Multiattack: A fire drake bites once and attacks once with claws, or it uses its breath weapon.
Melee Attack—Bite: +3 to hit (reach 5 ft.; one creature). *Hit:* 1d8 + 1 piercing damage.
Melee Attack—Claws: +3 to hit (reach 5 ft.; one creature). *Hit:* 2d6 + 1 slashing damage.
Area Attack—Fiery Breath (recharge 6): automatic hit (range 20 ft. cone; creatures in range). *Hit:* 2d10 fire damage, or half damage with a successful DC 11 Dex saving throw.

STATISTICS
Str 13 (+1), **Dex** 13 (+1), **Con** 13 (+1), **Int** 4 (−3), **Wis** 11 (+0), **Cha** 10 (+0)
Languages: Draconic
Skills: Stealth +3
Senses: Darkvision 60 ft.

TRAITS
Pyrophoric Blood: A fire drake's blood is highly flammable; it ignites in a burst of flame on contact with air. A creature that makes a successful melee attack with a slashing or piercing weapon (including natural weapons) against a fire drake must make a successful DC 11 Dex saving throw or take 1d6 fire damage from the splashing blood.

ECOLOGY
Environment: Temperate and warm hills and mountains
Organization: Solitary, pair, clutch (2–6), or family (6–8)

Fire drakes lair in caves and caverns deep within the hills and mountains. They are viciously territorial, fighting any other significant carnivores that move into their area. The only competitors they tolerate are other fire drakes, but even in those cases, very little provocation is needed to set them against their own kind. On occasion, a mated pair is encountered, but only in late summer or early autumn.

Fire drakes are often mistaken for young or miniature red dragons. A typical fire drake is 4 feet long, but some as much as 6 feet long have been reported. They prefer to open combat with their flame breath. Once expended, they rely on their bite and razor-sharp claws.

Credit
The fire drake originally appeared in the First Edition *Fiend Folio* (© TSR/Wizards of the Coast, 1981) and is used by permission.

Copyright Notice
Author Scott Greene, based on original material by Dave Waring.

Drake, Ice

This slender creature looks like a small or immature white dragon with icy white scales and sapphire eyes. A chill hangs in the air around the creature. Its teeth and claws are like sharpened icicles.

Ice Drake

XP 200 (CR 1)
CE Small dragon
Initiative +1

DEFENSE

AC 14 (natural armor)
hp: 22 (5d6 + 5)
Immunity: Cold damage; paralysis, unconsciousness
Vulnerability: Fire damage

OFFENSE

Speed: 20 ft., fly 50 ft.
Multiattack: An ice drake bites once and attacks once with claws, or uses its breath weapon.
Melee Attack—Bite: +3 to hit (reach 5 ft.; one creature). *Hit:* 1d8 + 1 piercing damage.
Melee Attack—Claws: +3 to hit (reach 5 ft.; one creature). *Hit:* 2d6 + 1 slashing damage.
Area Attack—Icy Breath (recharge 6): automatic hit (range 20 ft. cone; creatures in range). *Hit:* 2d10 cold damage, or half damage with a successful DC 11 Dex saving throw.

STATISTICS

Str 13 (+1), **Dex** 13 (+1), **Con** 13 (+1),
Int 7 (–2), **Wis** 7 (–2), **Cha** 10 (+0)
Languages: Draconic
Senses: Darkvision 60 ft.

TRAITS

Alternate Form (2/day): Twice per day as an action, an ice drake can assume the shape of a young white dragon for 2 hours. It gains no new abilities or statistics, only the appearance.
Spell-like Abilities: An ice drake can use the following spell-like abilities, using Charisma as its casting ability (DC 10). The ice drake doesn't need material components to use these abilities.
2/day: *fear, sleep*

ECOLOGY

Environment: Any cold land
Organization: Solitary, pair, clutch (2–6), or family (6–8)

Ice drakes are found in cold, mountainous caves and chasms. Most encounters are with a solitary drake. Only in the winter months is it common to find a mated pair or family. An ice drake's scales are white, and it is often mistaken for a young white dragon (especially when it chooses to appear as one). Ice drakes range from 3 feet to 6 feet long.

Credit
The ice drake originally appeared in the First Edition *Fiend Folio* (© TSR/Wizards of the Coast, 1981) and is used by permission.

Copyright Notice
Author Scott Greene, based on original material by Mike Ferguson.

Dust Digger

This creature looks like a man-sized, sandy brown starfish;
five long tentacles ring a central maw lined with sharp teeth.

Dust Digger

XP 700 (CR 3)
Unaligned Large aberration
Initiative +0

DEFENSE

AC 13 (natural armor)
hp: 38 (7d8 + 7)
Immunities: Prone, unconsciousness

OFFENSE

Speed: 10 ft., burrow 10 ft.
Multiattack: A dust digger attacks five times; no more than one of those attacks can be a bite.
Melee Attack—Tentacle Slam: +5 to hit (reach 10 ft.; one creature). *Hit:* 1d8 + 3 bludgeoning damage and the target is grappled.
Melee Attack—Tentacle Crush: automatic hit (one creature already grappled by a tentacle at the start of the dust digger's turn). *Hit:* 1d8 + 3 bludgeoning damage and the target is grappled and restrained.
Melee Attack—Bite: +5 to hit (one creature already grappled by a tentacle at the start of the dust digger's turn). *Hit:* 2d8 + 3 piercing damage and the target must make a successful DC 13 Str saving throw or be swallowed (see below).

STATISTICS

Str 16 (+3), **Dex** 10 (+0), **Con** 13 (+1),
Int 2 (−4), **Wis** 11 (+0), **Cha** 10 (+0)
Languages: None
Skills: Stealth +4
Senses: Tremorsense 60 ft.

TRAITS

Earth Glide: A dust digger can glide through sand, loose soil, or other loosely packed earth as easily as a fish swims through water. Its burrowing leaves behind no tunnel or hole and creates no ripple on the surface or other sign of its presence. A *move earth* spell cast on an area containing a burrowing dust digger flings the creature back 30 feet and stuns it for one round unless it makes a successful Con saving throw.
Earthy Camouflage: A dust digger has tactical advantage on Stealth checks while it's buried in the ground.
Sinkhole: A buried dust digger can deflate its body as a free action, causing the sand above it to slide toward its maw. A creature standing on the surface above the dust digger when it deflates must be checked for surprise. If it is surprised, it is attacked by all five tentacles during the dust digger's surprise round. If the creature is not surprised, roll initiative normally.
Swallow: A swallowed creature is blinded and restrained but no longer grappled. It takes 1d8 + 1 bludgeoning damage plus 1d8 acid damage automatically at the start of each of the dust digger's turns. One Medium creature or two Small creatures can be inside the dust digger at one time. A swallowed creature is unaffected by anything happening outside the dust digger or by attacks from outside it. A swallowed creature can get out of the dust digger by using 5 feet of movement, but only after the dust digger is dead.

ECOLOGY

Environment: Warm desert
Organization: Solitary, gang (4–8), or colony (9–20)

Dust diggers are desert carnivores about 10 feet in diameter. The creature spends most of its life buried under the sand, waiting for potential prey to wander too close or to actually wander directly over the buried dust digger.

A hunting dust digger inflates its body with air and buries itself under a layer of sand or dirt. When a living creature walks over the dust digger, the creature deflates its body, creating a sinkhole in the loose earth that's similar in effect to quicksand. It folds its tentacles around the flailing victim and tries to shove the prey into its mouth.

Credit
The dust digger originally appeared in the First Edition module *I3 Pharaoh* (© TSR/Wizards of the Coast, 1982) and later in the First Edition *Monster Manual II* (© TSR/Wizards of the Coast, 1983) and is used by permission.

Copyright Notice
Author Scott Greene, based on original material by Tracy and Laura Hickman.

Eblis

This creature strongly resembles an 8-foot-tall stork. Its feathers are grayish brown and its beak is dark brown, but its eyes are striking gold in color.

Eblis
XP 100 (CR 1/2)
NE Medium monstrosity
Initiative +2

DEFENSE
AC 12
hp: 22 (4d8 + 4)
Saving Throws: Dex +5
Resistance: Fire damage

OFFENSE
Speed: 30 ft., fly 30 ft.
Melee Attack—Beak: +5 to hit (reach 5 ft.; one creature). *Hit:* 1d8 + 2 piercing damage.

STATISTICS
Str 12 (+1), **Dex** 16 (+3), **Con** 13 (+1), **Int** 12 (+1), **Wis** 12 (+1), **Cha** 12 (+1)
Languages: Common, Unique (Eblis)
Skills: Acrobatics +5, Stealth +5
Senses: Darkvision 60 ft.

TRAITS
Combat Mobility: Opportunity attacks against a moving eblis always have tactical disadvantage.
Spellcasting: Each eblis flock has one individual capable of using arcane magic as a 6th-level spellcaster. An eblis spellcaster uses Int as its casting ability (DC 11, attack +3) and doesn't need material components to cast these spells. The spells it can cast are listed below.
At Will: *minor illusion* (sound only)
1st level (x4): *disguise self, fog cloud*
2nd level (x3): *blur, magic mouth*
3rd level (x2): *fear, hypnotic pattern*

ECOLOGY
Environment: Temperate and warm marshes
Organization: Flock (4–16)

Eblis form a semi-civilized society of storkmen that make their homes in desolate swamps and marshes. They rarely interact with other races, preferring the company of their own kind and the serenity of their marshland homes.

An eblis is a large bird that strongly resembles a stork—so much so that eblis are often called "stork men." An eblis stands about 8 feet tall, and its neck is extremely long and snakelike. With it, an eblis is capable of blindingly fast movement. Storkmen are very fast at shifting and striking, and their necks are very powerful despite their slenderness. They attack by stabbing with their beak, which is long, sharp, and deadly.

A male eblis has gray-brown feathers with reddish patches on its head, while a female lacks the red patch.

Credit
The eblis originally appeared in the First Edition module *EX2 Land Beyond the Magic Mirror* (© TSR/Wizards of the Coast, 1983) and later in the First Edition *Monster Manual II* (© TSR/Wizards of the Coast, 1983) and is used by permission.

Copyright Notice
Author Scott Greene, based on original material by Gary Gygax.

Ectoplasm

This creature, which appears to be a shimmering cloud of filaments, tendrils, and whips of eerie mist, gives off light with the approximate brightness of a candle. The form of the thing continuously roils and billows like a cloud, and it is eerily silent.

Ectoplasm

XP 450 (CR 2)
Unaligned Large ooze (incorporeal)
Initiative +1

DEFENSE
AC 12
hp: 39 (6d10 + 6)
Resistance:
 Bludgeoning, piercing, and slashing damage from nonmagical weapons
Immunity: Psychic damage; blindness, charm, fright, paralysis, poison, stun, unconsciousness

OFFENSE
Speed: fly 30 ft.
Melee Attack—Touch:
 +3 to hit (reach 5 ft.; one creature). *Hit:* 2d8 + 2 psychic damage and the target gains one level of exhaustion. This attack has tactical advantage against targets wearing medium or heavy armor.
Area Attack—Ectoplasm (recharge 4, 5, 6): automatic hit (range 20-ft. cone; all creatures in cone). *Hit:* targeted creatures must make a successful DC 11 Con saving throw or fall unconscious for 1d6 rounds. A successful save renders a creature immune to that creature's ectoplasm's attack for 24 hours.

STATISTICS
Str 5 (–3), **Dex** 12 (+1), **Con** 21 (+5), **Int** 1 (–5), **Wis** 1 (–5), **Cha** 1 (–5)
Languages: None
Skills: Stealth +5
Senses: Darkvision 60 ft.

TRAITS
Amorphous and Incorporeal: An ectoplasm can move through gaps as small as 1 square inch without penalty.

It can also move through solid objects and other creatures as if they were difficult terrain. The ectoplasm takes 1d10 force damage if it is still inside something solid at the end of its turn.
Glow: An ectoplasm continually gives off light with the approximate brightness of a candle. It can't consciously extinguish this light. When an ectoplasm is killed, its light fades to darkness.
Silent: An ectoplasm has tactical advantage on Stealth checks when those detecting it are depending chiefly on sound.
Undead Bane: An ectoplasm deals double damage against corporeal undead.

ECOLOGY
Environment: Any
Organization: Solitary

Many encounters with glowing, ghostly spheres can be attributed to ectoplasms rather than restless spirits. An ectoplasm, sometimes called a ghost ooze, is a faintly glowing orb of immaterial substance that lurks in catacombs and cemeteries. Although incorrectly assumed by many to be some form of incorporeal undead, ectoplasms are quite alive. They dwell in places of the dead because they consume dead flesh, slowly dissolving decaying bones and skin and absorbing the nutrients directly. The strange irony of the ectoplasm is that a cemetery 'haunted' by these creatures is almost certain to be free of any corporeal undead; the ectoplasm makes a meal of them as soon as it discovers them.

Although its primary diet consists of the dead, an ectoplasm is also a threat to the living. An ectoplasm attacks anything within the range of its senses that disturbs it. An ectoplasm that encounters a living opponent attacks for a few rounds before attempting to escape—it senses that it can get no sustenance from the opponent. If it finds an undead opponent, an ectoplasm continues to attack until it or the opponent has been destroyed.

Ectoplasms are native to the Ethereal Plane. While ethereal, they can't affect or be affected by anything in the material world. To consume carrion on the Material Plane, however, they must manifest themselves, becoming visible but incorporeal. An ectoplasm's insubstantiality makes it very dangerous to those who depend on heavy armor for protection, because its otherworldly touch passes right through such defenses.

Eel, Giant Moray

This creature looks like an 8-foot-long eel with yellow-brown splotches on its back.

Giant Eel

XP 450 (CR 2)
Unaligned Medium beast (aquatic)
Initiative +2

DEFENSE
AC 12
hp: 52 (7d8 + 21)
Saving Throws: Dex +4
Immunity: Disease

OFFENSE
Speed: 5 ft., swim 30 ft.
Melee Attack—Bite: +5 to hit (reach 5 ft.; one creature). *Hit:* 2d6 + 3 piercing damage and the target is grappled. The grapple is broken if the eel tries to bite a different target.
Melee Attack—Gnaw: automatic hit (one creature already grappled at the start of the eel's turn). *Hit:* 2d8 + 3 piercing damage, and the target must make a successful DC 13 Con saving throw or take 2d6 necrotic damage and lose 1 point of Charisma.

STATISTICS
Str 17 (+3), **Dex** 14 (+2), **Con** 16 (+3), **Int** 1 (−5), **Wis** 12 (+1), **Cha** 4 (−3)
Languages: None
Skills: Stealth +4
Senses: Darkvision 60 ft.

TRAITS
Water Dependency: Giant moray eels can survive out of water for 15 minutes. After that, they begin suffocating.

ECOLOGY
Environment: Warm aquatic
Organization: Solitary or school (4–8)

The moray eel is a ferocious predator, and its giant cousin even more so. It is capable of holding prey in its primary jaws while a smaller set of inner jaws in its throat takes bites out of the prey. These inner jaws carry a flesh-rotting poison that leaves disfiguring scars. Lost Charisma can be restored with a *greater restoration* spell.

Credit
The giant moray eel originally appeared in the First Edition *Monster Manual* (© TSR/Wizards of the Coast, 1977) and is used by permission.

Copyright Notice
Author Scott Greene, based on original material by Gary Gygax.

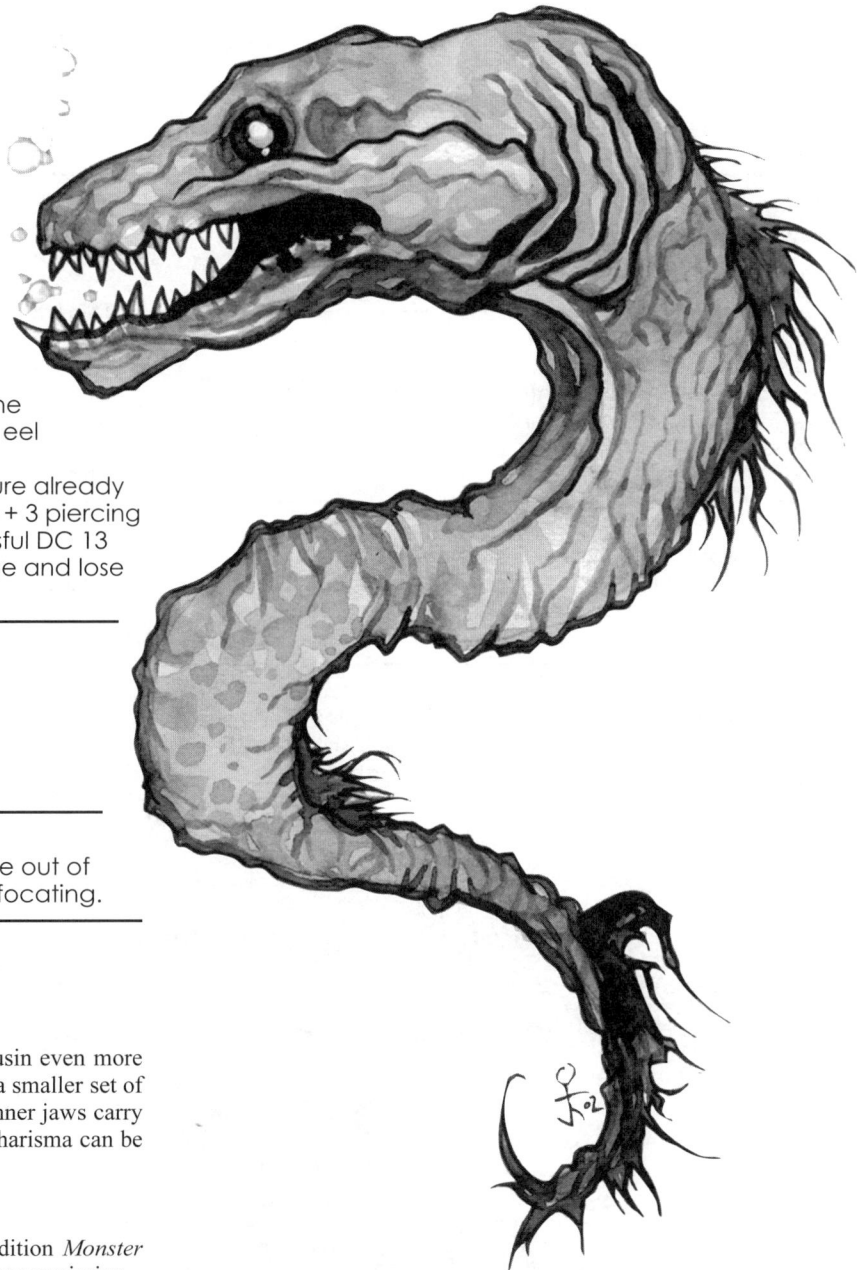

Eel, Gulper

This strange being of the depths appears to be little more than a large mouth, flaccid body, and dangling tail which glows with an eerie red light.

Gulper Eel

XP 700 (CR 3)
Unaligned Large beast (aquatic)
Initiative +2

DEFENSE
AC 14 (natural armor)
hp: 60 (8d10 + 16)
Immunity: Prone

OFFENSE
Speed: swim 50 ft.
Melee Attack—Bite: +5 to hit (reach 5 ft.; one creature). *Hit:* 2d8 + 3 piercing damage and the target must make a successful DC 13 Str saving throw or be swallowed (see below).

STATISTICS
Str 17 (+3), **Dex** 15 (+2), **Con** 14 (+2), **Int** 1 (−5), **Wis** 12 (+1), **Cha** 2 (−4)
Languages: None
Senses: Darkvision 60 ft.

TRAITS
Swallow: A swallowed creature is blinded and restrained. It takes 1d8 + 3 bludgeoning damage plus 1d8 acid damage automatically at the start of each of the gulper's turns. Up to four Medium creatures can be inside the gulper at one time; two Small or smaller creatures count as one Medium creature. A swallowed creature is unaffected by anything happening outside the gulper or by attacks from outside it. A swallowed creature can get out of the gulper by using 5 feet of movement, but only after the gulper is dead.

ECOLOGY
Environment: Any aquatic
Organization: Solitary

This larger version of the common eel makes its home in deep water: well below 3,000 feet of depth, and they seldom come above that level. At such depth, it cares little whether the weather above is tropical or arctic. The gulper spends its life dining on giant shrimp and any other creatures which happen to arouse its senses.

Solitary creatures by nature, during mating season (typically winter months), it is common to find a pair of these creatures together. The female deposits 2–8 eggs in the sea bottom, and they hatch within two months. Young gulper eels are dependent on their parents for survival for only about two weeks. After that, the family splits up again, everyone going their separate ways.

A gulper eel averages 10 feet in length but some as long as 30 feet have been reported, if such wild tales are to be believed. Its body is long, sleek, and black in color, and its tail ends in a luminous organ. The gulper's eyes are small for its body and very close to its snout. It massive mouth is lined with rows of needlelike teeth. Because a gulper eel can unhinge its jaw and stretch its stomach, it can swallow tremendous quantities of food and opponents as large as itself.

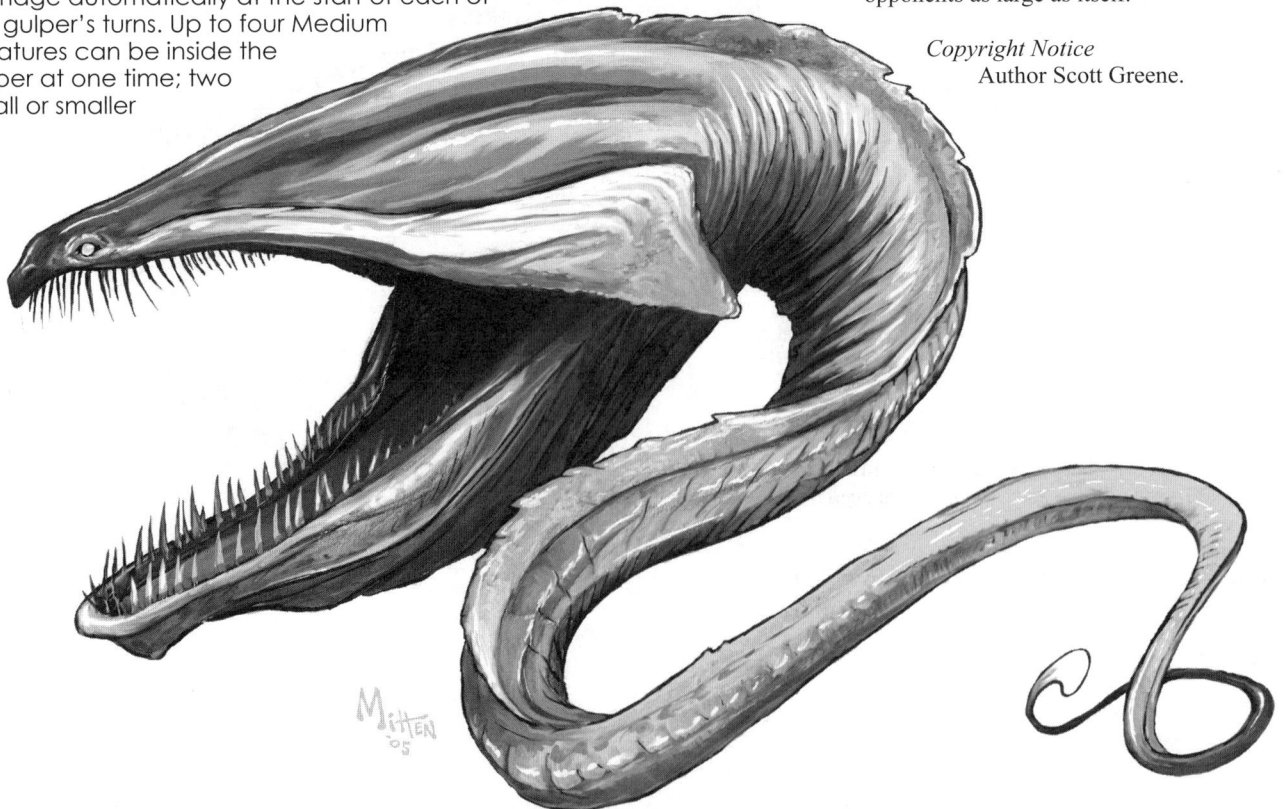

Elusa Hound

This powerful, wolf-like canine has coarse white fur, pale white skin, and a short, bushy tail. Its eyes are colored sickly yellow and its teeth are bone white.

Elusa Hound

XP 200 (CR 1)
Unaligned Medium monstrosity
Initiative +2

DEFENSE
AC 14 (natural armor)
hp: 26 (4d8 + 8)

OFFENSE
Speed: 50 ft.
Melee Attack—Bite: +4 to hit (reach 5 ft.; one creature). *Hit:* 1d8 + 2 piercing damage and the target must make a successful DC 12 Str saving throw or be knocked prone.

STATISTICS
Str 15 (+2), **Dex** 15 (+2), **Con** 15 (+2),
Int 6 (–2), **Wis** 12 (+1), **Cha** 8 (–1)
Languages: Understands Common but can't speak
Skills: Athletics +6, Perception +5, Survival +5
Senses: Darkvision 60 ft.

TRAITS
Arcane Sight: Elusa hounds detect magical auras as if they are under a permanent *detect magic* spell with a radius of 120 feet. This has the added benefit that an elusa hound can instantly identify any spellcaster within range.

Aura Tracking: Once an elusa hound has seen the magical aura of a living creature with its *arcane sight* ability, or has seen the magical residue of a spell or effect created by a particular spellcaster or other creature, it gets tactical advantage on Survival checks to follow that spellcaster's trail. The trail must be no more than three hours old for the elusa hound to get this bonus.

Stand Guard: When an elusa hound knocks a target prone, it can choose to grapple the target automatically. The target can't stand up unless it first escapes the grapple. While the hound has a target grappled, it can bite only that creature.

ECOLOGY
Environment: Temperate forests and plains
Organization: Solitary, pair, or pack (4–7)

Elusa hounds are kept and trained by many different types of creatures, but always for the same purpose: tracking (and sometimes killing) magic-wielders. These creatures can detect the emanations given off by arcane and divine spellcasters, and they follow this trail like bloodhounds following a scent.

The origin of elusa hounds has mystified even the most learned of sages. They seem to be born of magic, but no spellcaster in his or her right mind would ever create such a beast.

Renegade bands enthralled with the idea of ridding the world of spellcasters sometimes employ elusa hounds. Civilized towns and cities likewise use them in places where magic is forbidden or is policed by the local government, or where rogue magic-users often cause trouble. In other instances, they are used by spellcasters to ferret out rivals or to track down stolen magic items.

When given instructions to track and kill their target, a pack of elusa hounds uses tactics similar to other canines: they circle the prey and attack simultaneously from all sides. These beasts can be trained to pin or hold a foe rather than kill it. This tactic is often employed by handlers when they wish to capture and interrogate a renegade spellcaster. When using these tactics, the elusa hound attempts to trip its foe and then pins it with a bite.

Elusa hounds radiate a moderate aura of divination magic if examined with a *detect magic* spell or similar effect.

Encephalon Gorger

This creature is a hairless, pale-skinned humanoid with leathery white, semitranslucent flesh.
It is a bit taller than an average human, with features that are delicate and precise.
The creature's arms and legs are spindly, and each ends in just four digits.
It has an alarmingly long tongue and small eyes, with nictitating membranes.

Encephalon Gorger (Psilian)

XP 1,100 (CR 4)
CE Medium aberration
Initiative +3

DEFENSE

AC 13
hp: 65 (10d8 + 20)
Resistance: Cold damage

OFFENSE

Speed: 30 ft.
Multiattack: An encephalon gorger attacks twice with claws or once with mindfeed. A claw used to maintain a grapple can't attack.
Melee Attack—Claw: +5 to hit (reach 5 ft.; one creature). *Hit:* 2d8 + 3 slashing damage and the target is grappled.
Melee Attack—Mindfeed: automatic hit (one creature already grappled by the encephalon at the start of its turn). *Hit:* 2d6 + 5 Psychic damage and the encephalon gains 5 temporary hit points. The target must also make a successful DC 15 Int saving throw or lose 1 point of Intelligence. All drained Intelligence is recovered if *greater restoration* or comparable magic is used on the victim within 24 hours of the loss. After 24 hours, each casting of *greater restoration* restores just one point of Intelligence.

STATISTICS

Str 12 (+1), **Dex** 16 (+3), **Con** 14 (+2),
Int 21 (+5), **Wis** 15 (+2), **Cha** 15 (+2)
Languages: Common, Abyssal, Celestial, Infernal, Unique (Encephalon)
Skills: Insight +5, Perception +5
Senses: Darkvision 60 ft.

TRAITS

Adrenal Surge (2/day): Twice per day as a bonus action, an encephalon gorger can accelerate itself so that it gains speed 60 ft. and AC 15, it gets tactical advantage on Dex saving throws, and it can take one additional action on its turns. This effect lasts 1d4 rounds.
Combat Mobility: Opportunity attacks against a moving encephalon gorger always have tactical disadvantage.
Mind Screen: The mind of an encephalon gorger is an

alien and dangerous place. Should a creature attempt to scan the mind or read the thoughts of an encephalon gorger with magic or psionics (not just gauging intent with Insight skill), the creature making the attempt must make a successful DC 16 Int saving throw or be driven insane (Intelligence and Wisdom both reduced to 3). Even on a successful save, the creature suffers the effects of a *confusion* spell for 1d4 rounds.
Mindsense: An encephalon gorger instinctively senses the Intelligence of any creature within 60 feet.
Regeneration: At the start of its turn, an encephalon recovers 5 lost hit points. This ability fails to function if the creature took psychic damage since its previous turn.

ECOLOGY

Environment: Any land
Organization: Solitary, crowd (2–5), or array (4–7)

Encephalon gorgers (sometimes known as cranial vampires or psilians) are malevolent creatures from another dimension. They are greatly feared by intelligent creatures, because they use brain fluid to power the bizarre, alien technology of their great cities.

Encephalons are known to have constructed strongholds and outposts on the Material Plane for the purpose of collecting brain fluid. It is unknown when they first came to the Material Plane or where their true home lies.

Encephalon gorgers dislike direct sunlight, though they aren't harmed by it. When traveling in daylight, they usually cloak themselves in robes of gray or black. The gorger's leathery, whitish flesh is nearly translucent, and in older encephalon gorgers one can faintly see veins and other organs pushing grayish-brown blood through the body. They are completely hairless, and their eyes are small with nictitating membranes instead of eyelids. A psilian's mouth is lined with short, needlelike teeth, with pronounced canines (perhaps the reason these monsters are sometimes called cranial vampires).

In combat, encephalon gorgers focus on targets with the most potent brains (i.e., those with the highest Intelligence) in an effort to sink their teeth into the brain and suck out the precious cranial fluid. They do not drink this cranial fluid but rather store it in organs similar to a snake's poison glands. Back at their base, the cranial fluid is expelled into the weird, arcane machinery that is so vital to the life-pulse of an encephalon city.

Self-preservation is high on the encephalons' list of virtues, so they take few risks in combat. When encountering groups of adventurers, they've been known to make use of enslaved humanoids and trained beasts of many types to keep enemy warriors occupied while the encephalons deal with the most prized targets. If an encephalon can capture a highly intelligent foe and spirit it away from its allies without risking an all-out battle, it will do so. Captured prey is taken to one of the encephalons' bewildering cities, where it is handed over to other encephalons who tend the slave pits.

Although spellcasting encephalon gorgers are rare, they have been encountered.

Encephalon gorgers refer to themselves as *psilians*. Outposts in the Material Plane tend to be constructed beneath the surface world or hidden far from prying eyes (cloaked by dense forest, frequent fog, or hidden by magic). Underground lairs resemble domed cities, while those on the surface resemble iron fortresses of exquisite craftsmanship. Each lair, regardless of its location, has dozens of slave pits and breeding pens filled with captured, intelligent creatures. Slaves are maintained by a specialized group of psilians called breeders. It is their job to gauge the relative worth of captives and manage them to ensure that as much

precious cranial fluid as possible is harvested from each before its inevitable death.

Encephalon gorgers sometimes trade with other races, usually for slaves. While most slaves are handed over to the breeders for harvesting, less intelligent ones (Intelligence 7 or lower) are conditioned for menial work or as bodyguards and footsoldiers. Once any slave exhausts its usefulness, it is recycled as food for both the encephalons and other slaves.

Little is known regarding the gorger's society, reproduction, life cycle, lifespan, and so on. Most of what little is known comes from hardened adventurers who were captured and enslaved but managed to escape before too much damage was done to their minds.

Exoskeleton, Giant Ant

This creature looks much like any other giant ant, but it is actually a construct fashioned from a giant ant's exoskeletal husk. Dull flames can be seen flickering through its empty eye sockets and through cracks in its armored shell.

Giant Ant Exoskeleton

XP 100 (CR 1/2)
Unaligned Large construct
Initiative +1

DEFENSE
AC 16 (natural armor)
hp: 15 (2d10 + 4)
Resistance: Piercing and slashing damage from nonmagical weapons; necrotic damage
Immunity: Fire, poison, and psychic damage; charm, disease, exhaustion, fright, poison, stun, unconsciousness

OFFENSE
Speed: 30 ft., climb 20 ft.
Melee Attack—Bite: +4 to hit (reach 5 ft.; one creature). *Hit:* 1d8 + 2 piercing damage.

STATISTICS
Str 14 (+2), **Dex** 12 (+1), **Con** 14 (+2), **Int** 1 (−5), **Wis** 8 (−1), **Cha** 1 (−5)
Languages: None
Senses: Darkvision 60 ft.

TRAITS
Fiery Insides: Whenever a giant ant exoskeleton takes slashing or piercing damage, flames from its insides erupt through the wound. Everyone within 5 feet of where the attack struck must make a successful DC 12 Dex saving throw or take 1d6 fire damage.

ECOLOGY
Environment: Warm deserts and plains
Organization: Foraging gang (2–5) or column (3–30)

Giant ant exoskeletons can be animated into undead creatures through rare necromantic magic. The process burns out whatever remained of their organic insides and replaces it with magical fire. They can be turned by *turn undead*.

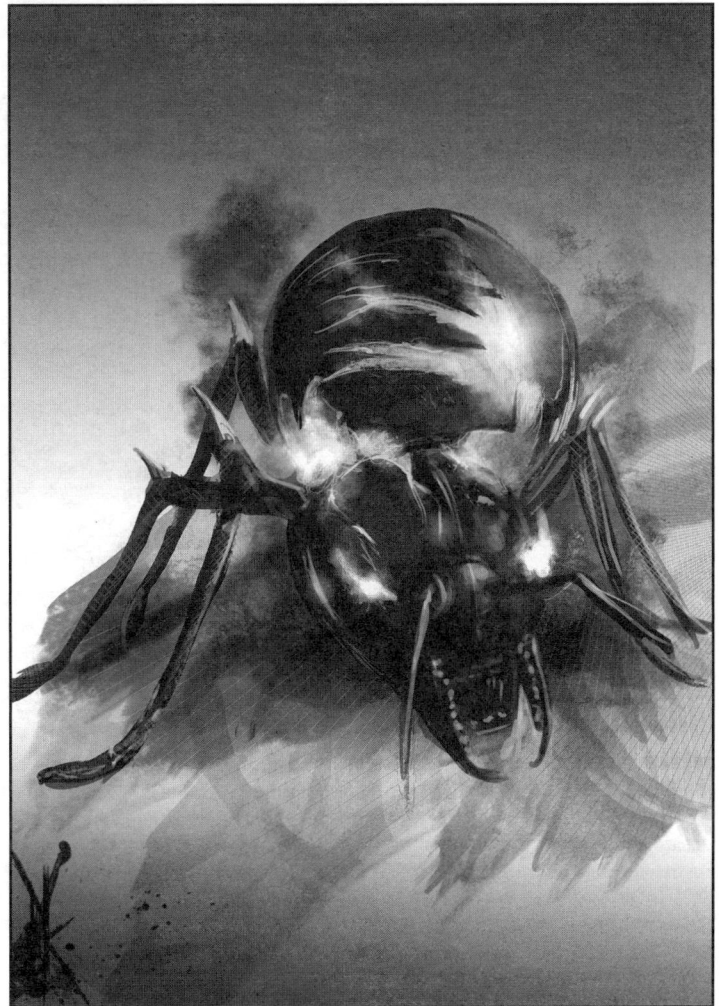

Exoskeleton, Giant Beetle

This creature resembles a normal giant beetle at first glance, but then pale green light is noticed flickering through its empty eye sockets and along mystic runes etched into its armored shell.

Giant Beetle Exoskeleton

XP 450 (CR 2)
Unaligned Large construct
Initiative +1

DEFENSE

AC 17 (natural armor)
hp: 42 (5d10 + 15)
Resistance: Piercing and slashing damage; necrotic damage
Immunity: Acid, poison, and psychic damage; charm, disease, exhaustion, fright, poison, stun, unconsciousness

OFFENSE

Speed: 20 ft., climb 20 ft.
Melee Attack—Bite: +5 to hit (reach 5 ft.; one creature). *Hit:* 1d8 + 3 piercing damage plus 1d8 acid damage.

STATISTICS

Str 16 (+3), **Dex** 11 (+1), **Con** 16 (+3),
Int 1 (−5), **Wis** 10 (+0), **Cha** 1 (−5)
Languages: None
Senses: Darkvision 60 ft.

TRAITS

Corrosive Insides: Whenever a giant beetle exoskeleton takes slashing or piercing damage, corrosive vapor from its insides erupts through the wound. Everyone within 5 feet of where the attack struck must make a successful DC 13 Dex saving throw or take 1d6 acid damage.

ECOLOGY

Environment: Any land
Organization: Solitary

Giant beetle exoskeletons are animated by secret necromantic magic quite different from that used in the standard *animate dead* spell. In the process, magical runes are etched onto the dead creature's husk which give them great staying power in the face of clerics who would turn them as undead. These same runes give giant beetle exoskeletons resistance to all piercing and slashing damage, including that from magical weapons.

In a few cases, the necromancer responsible for creating one of these creatures altered the process so that the exoskeleton remained empty inside instead of filling with poisonous vapor. It could then be carpeted and cushioned to become a comfortable, if somewhat slow-moving, vehicle for traveling across rugged or dreary terrain.

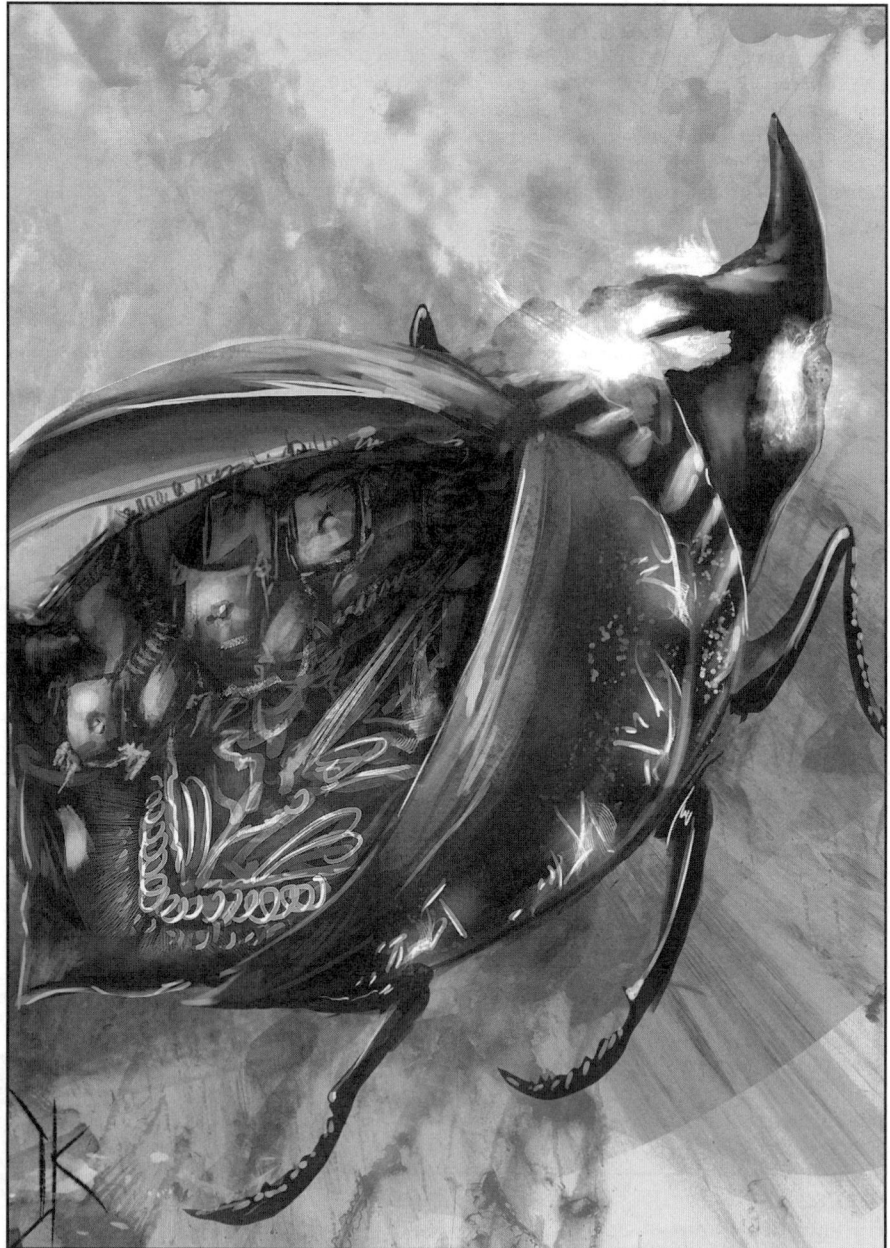

Exoskeleton, Giant Crab

What looks at first like a giant crab being ridden by a cloaked humanoid turns out to be only the former beast's exoskeleton, hollowed out and magically animated to become both a vehicle and a war machine.

Giant Crab Exoskeleton

XP 700 (CR 3)
Unaligned Large construct
Initiative +0

DEFENSE

AC 18 (natural armor)
hp: 57 (6d12 + 18)
Resistance: Piercing and slashing damage; necrotic damage
Immunity: Lightning, poison, and psychic damage; charm, disease, exhaustion, fright, poison, stun, unconsciousness

OFFENSE

Speed: 20 ft., swim 20 ft.
Multiattack: A giant crab exoskeleton attacks twice with claws or once with lightning.
Melee Attack—Claw: +7 to hit (reach 10 ft.; one creature). *Hit:* 1d8 + 5 slashing damage plus 1d8 lightning damage.
Area Attack—Lightning (recharge 5, 6): automatic hit (range 30-ft. line; all creatures in line). *Hit:* 3d8 + 3 lightning damage, or half damage with a successful DC 13 Dex saving throw.

STATISTICS

Str 20 (+5), **Dex** 10 (+0), **Con** 16 (+3),
Int 1 (–5), **Wis** 10 (+0), **Cha** 4 (–3)
Languages: None
Senses: Darkvision 60 ft.

TRAITS

Lightning Insides: Whenever a giant crab exoskeleton takes slashing or piercing damage, lightning from its insides erupts through the wound and ripples across its entire body. Every creature within 5 feet of the giant crab exoskeleton must make a successful DC 13 Dex saving throw or take 1d8 lightning damage. Anyone riding inside the creature is immune to this damage.

ECOLOGY

Environment: Any land
Organization: Solitary, team (1–3), or caravan (2–12)

Giant crab exoskeletons are animated by little-known necromantic spells cast on only the largest giant crab shells (10-foot diameter is typical; huge crab exoskeletons of 15-foot diameter are reported but unconfirmed). The process also involves etching magical runes onto the dead creature's husk which give them great staying power in the face of clerics who would turn them as undead. These same runes give giant beetle exoskeletons resistance to all piercing and slashing damage, including that from magical weapons.

In rare cases, the necromancer responsible for creating one of these creatures altered the process so that only the head of the exoskeleton filled with lightning while most of the body remained empty. The empty portion could then be fitted with seats for up to four people to use as a slow-moving vehicle. In ages past, at least one entire tribe of necromancers was known to migrate up and down the coast in such conveyances. Occasionally one of these giant crab exoskeletons is discovered in a tidal cave, abandoned but still perfectly functional after centuries of disuse and ready to resume duty—if a way can be found to take control of it.

Fear Guard

This incorporeal entity appears as a hooded humanoid figure clad in flowing robes of translucent gray over a suit of ghostly armor. Its facial features are a swirl of maddening images, fluctuating between a serene countenance and a visage twisted into a grimace of horror and fear.

Fear Guard

XP 700 (CR 3)
CE Medium undead
Initiative +2

DEFENSE

AC 17 (natural armor)
hp: 51 (6d8 + 24)
Resistance:
Bludgeoning, piercing, and slashing damage from nonmagical weapons; necrotic damage
Immunity: Poison damage; exhaustion, fright, poison, unconsciousness

OFFENSE

Speed: fly 30 ft.
Melee Attack—Greatsword:
+5 to hit (reach 5 ft.; one creature). *Hit:* 2d6 + 3 necrotic damage and the target must make a successful DC 14 Con saving throw or its maximum hit points are reduced by an amount equal to the necrotic damage.

STATISTICS

Str 17 (+3), **Dex** 15 (+2),
Con 18 (+4), **Int** 10 (+0),
Wis 12 (+1), **Cha** 18 (+4)
Languages: Common
Skills: Stealth +4
Senses: Darkvision 60 ft.

TRAITS

Create Spawn: Any living creature slain by a fear guard has tactical disadvantage on its death saving throws. If it dies, it will rise again as a fear guard under the control of its killer 1d6 rounds later.
Daylight Vulnerability: A fear guard suffers 2d6 points of radiant damage if it is exposed to true sunlight (not magical sunlight or artificial, bright light) at the start of its turn, and it is *slowed* (as the spell) until the start of its next turn.

Incorporeal: A fear guard can move through solid objects and other creatures as if they were difficult terrain. It takes 1d10 force damage if it is still inside something solid at the end of its turn.
Shadow Stealth: If the fear guard ends its turn in dim light or darkness, it can use a bonus action to make a Dex (Stealth) check to become hidden, with tactical advantage on the check. Because it is incorporeal and all of its movement is flight, it makes very little sound when moving and never leaves footprints or disturbs dust on the floor.
Spell-like Abilities: A fear guard can use the following spell-like abilities, using Charisma as its casting ability (DC 14, attack +6). The fear lord doesn't need material components to use these abilities.
At Will: *darkness, ray of enfeeblement*
2/day: *inflict wounds* (as 2nd-level slot)

ECOLOGY

Environment: Underground
Organization: Solitary or group (2–5)

Fear guards embody the ultimate joining of evil and loyalty. They are summoned from some unknown place by evil wizards and clerics to guard prized possessions or valued locations, and they serve that duty with the unwavering singlemindedness and eternal patience of the undead.

Shrouding themselves in preternatural darkness, fear guards fight using their life-draining greatswords and life-sapping magic. Because of their ability to spawn additional fear guards under their control, a location guarded by a single fear guard can become more secure as time goes by and grave robbers who fall to the fear guard's attacks join its ranks. If somehow exposed to natural sunlight, fear guards wrap themselves in magical darkness if they can. If they can't, they flee toward safety. Sunlight is the only force that can cause a fear guard to abandon its post.

Fen Witch

This creature appears as a female humanoid with one nostril, webbed feet and hands, and fiery red eyes. Her body is cloaked in tattered robes of gray or brown. Her hands sprout razor-sharp claws and her hair is long and unkempt.

Fen Witch

XP 450 (CR 2)
CE Medium monstrosity
Initiative +1

DEFENSE

AC 12 (padded armor)
hp: 33 (6d8 + 6)
Saving Throws: Con +3

OFFENSE

Speed: 30 ft.
Multiattack: A fen witch attacks twice with claws, or uses her mind probe or death speak ability.
Melee Attack—Claw: +4 to hit (reach 5 ft.; one creature). *Hit:* 1d6 + 2 slashing damage.

STATISTICS

Str 15 (+2), **Dex** 12 (+1), **Con** 13 (+1), **Int** 14 (+2), **Wis** 14 (+2), **Cha** 15 (+2)
Languages: Common, Deep Speech, Sylvan; telepathy 100 ft.
Skills: Deception +4, Insight +4, Perception +4, Stealth +3
Senses: Darkvision 60 ft.

TRAITS

Death Speak: A fen witch who knows the secret vibrations of an individual's name can speak that name as an attack. If the individual hears the fen witch speak its name, that creature must make a successful DC 12 Wis save or immediately drop to 0 hit points. If the save succeeds, that creature can't be affected again by the same fen witch's death speak for 24 hours. Note that the fen witch does not need to speak a language the creature understands in order to affect it; she only needs to speak its name with its secret vibrations. Other fen witches who hear the name spoken this way can't use it for their own death speak attacks (if the target's saving throw succeeds, other fen witches assume the name was vibrated incorrectly and won't copy it). Each fen witch must learn the vibrations independently by using her mind probe successfully on the target.
Horrific Appearance: The sight of a fen witch is so revolting that anyone who sets eyes on one within 60 feet must make a successful DC 11 Con save or be sickened, with effects identical to the poisoned condition, for 1 minute. Characters fighting a fen witch can instead avert their eyes at the start of their turn and take tactical disadvantage on attack rolls against the fen witch. Anyone who is surprised by a fen witch must attempt this saving throw immediately at the beginning of combat unless they can't see her for some other reason. This saving throw never needs to be attempted more than once per 24 hours. Fen witches and hags of all kinds are immune to this effect.
Mind Probe: As an attack, a fen witch can peer into the mind of a living creature within 60 feet in an attempt to extract the secret vibrations of the creature's name. The target resists the mental trespassing (and becomes immune to further mind probes by the same fen witch until after a long rest) with a successful DC 12 Wis saving throw. If the saving throw fails, the fen witch finds the information she sought and can use her death speak ability on a later turn. Creatures with an Intelligence score of 2 or less are immune to this ability, as are creatures that are immune to psychic damage.
Swamp Stride: A fen witch can move through any sort of natural difficult terrain at its normal speed while within a swamp. Magically altered terrain affects a fen witch normally.

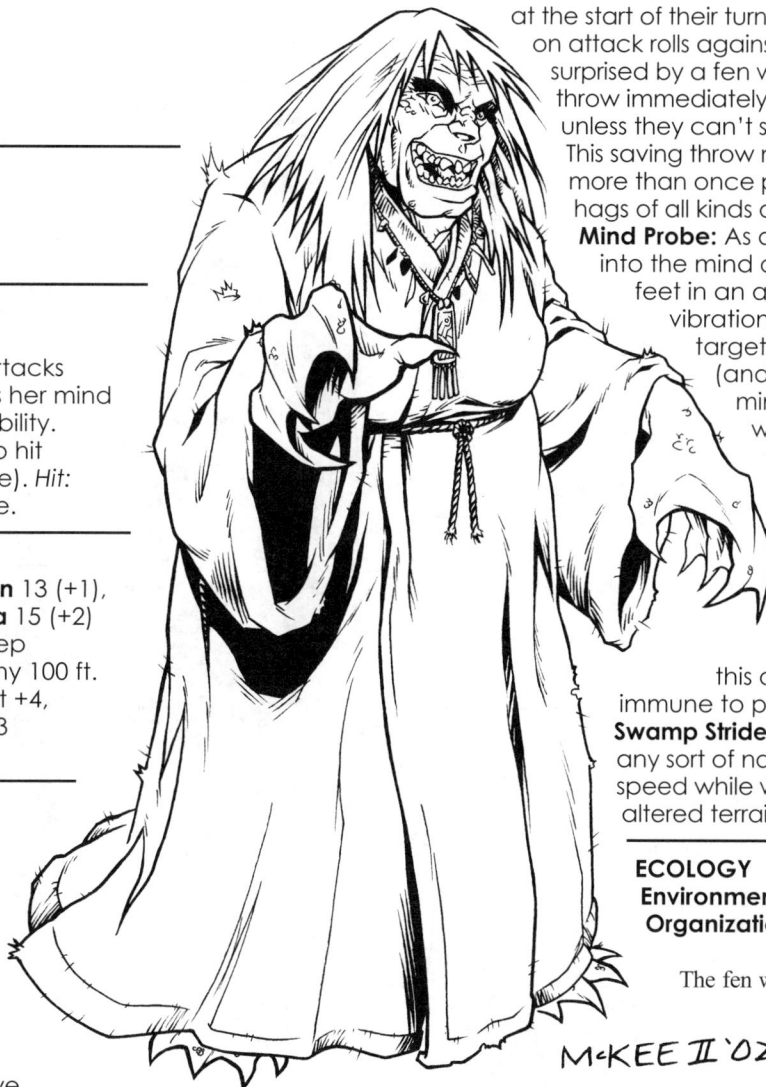

ECOLOGY

Environment: Temperate swamp
Organization: Solitary or coven (2–7)

McKEE II '02

The fen witch is a creature of legend, found only in the most remote of places. It is almost always a solitary creature—they despise others of their own kind almost as much as they hate strangers in their swamps—but they sometimes band together in larger groups for mysterious, evil rituals when omens command. Occasionally, fen witches with spellcasting ability are encountered. These tend to be the leaders of their small covens, by virtue of their greater ability to inflict suffering on their cohorts.

A fen witch is thoroughly evil and malign, speaking to those she encounters only to learn the "secret vibrations" of their true names in order to use that secret against them. Fen witches rarely engage in direct combat. Instead, they rely on their mind probe and death speak abilities to slay creatures almost instantaneously and drive off the victim's comrades (they hope) by instilling shock and fear in them. If this tactic fails, a fen witch will wade into the fight with her claws. It is not uncommon, however, for a fen witch to have trained or charmed swamp creatures such as giant crocodiles nearby that will come to her when needed.

Fetch

A ragged-looking and rotting humanoid leaps from the snow, its filthy nails slashing through the frosty air. Its eyes are stark blue and its skin is pale white. Ice hangs from its scraggly hair.

Fetch

XP 200 (CR 1)
LE Medium undead
Initiative +2

DEFENSE

AC 13 (natural armor)
hp: 16 (3d8 + 3)
Saving Throws: Wis +3
Resistance: Necrotic damage
Immunity: Cold and poison damage; exhaustion, fright, poison, unconsciousness
Vulnerability: Fire damage

OFFENSE

Speed: 30 ft.
Multiattack: A fetch attacks twice with claws.
Melee Attack—Claw: +5 to hit (reach 5 ft.; one creature).
Hit: 1d6 + 3 slashing damage plus 1d6 cold damage.

STATISTICS

Str 17 (+3), **Dex** 15 (+2), **Con** 13 (+1),
Int 10 (+0), **Wis** 12 (+1), **Cha** 15 (+2)
Languages: Common
Skills: Intimidation +4
Senses: Darkvision 60 ft.

ECOLOGY

Environment: Cold plains, hills, and mountains
Organization: Solitary

A murdered person who is buried in frozen ground sometimes returns from the grave as a fetch, an evil undead monster with a hatred for fire and life. Fetches seek out living creatures that wander too close to their grave, kill them, and bury them in the hope that the victim will also rise as a fetch. Not all foes are buried, however; some are dragged to the fetch's lair and devoured. Fetches savor the flesh of humanoids and monstrous humanoids—in particular humans, elves, and centaurs.

A fetch stands from 5 to 7 feet tall and weighs between 100 and 250 pounds. Its clothes are tattered and worn with age and exposure. Its rotting flesh is drawn tight around its bones and flushed grayish-white. Its hair is scraggly and frozen, and ice crystals cover its skin; the ice frozen onto and into its flesh gives it a small bit of armor protection. A fetch's eyes are stark blue.

A fetch is a ruthless opponent. They always fight to the death, unless they are threatened with fire. If they can't quickly defeat someone who attacks them with fire, they flee. Afterward, the fetch trails the hated foe (relatively easy across snow), waiting for a chance to take it by surprise and destroy the source of heat.

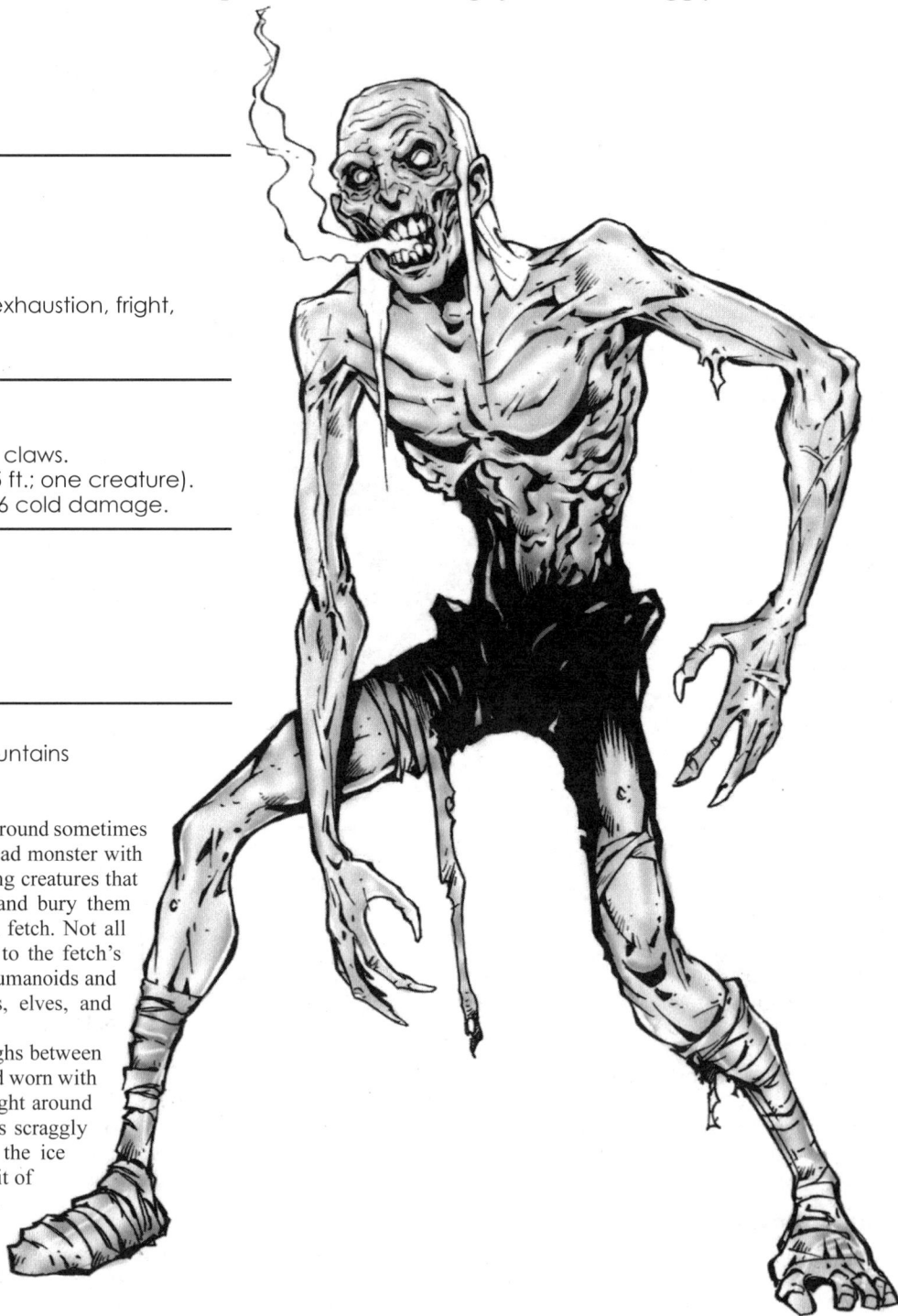

Fire Crab

*A massive crab with a square-shaped, reddish-brown carapace covered with
dark red and yellow markings scuttles forward, pincers raised.
Tiny flames lick its body, erupting at irregular intervals from its underbelly.
Its eyes are perched atop two long eyestalks that protrude from the center of the carapace.*

Greater Fire Crab

XP 450 (CR 2)
Unaligned Large monstrosity
Initiative +0

DEFENSE
AC 14 (natural armor)
hp: 34 (4d10 + 12)
Immunity: Fire damage
Vulnerability: Cold damage

OFFENSE
Speed: 30 ft., swim 30 ft.
Multiattack: A greater fire crab attacks twice, in any
combination of pincer and crush attacks.
Melee Attack—Pincer: +6 to hit (reach 5 ft.; one creature).
Hit: 1d8 + 4 slashing damage plus 1d4 fire damage and
the target is grappled.
Melee Attack—Crush: automatic hit (one creature already
grappled at the start of the fire crab's turn). *Hit:* 1d8 + 4
slashing damage plus 1d10 fire damage and the target is
grappled.

STATISTICS
Str 18 (+4), **Dex** 11 (+0), **Con** 16 (+3),
Int 1 (–5), **Wis** 11 (+0), **Cha** 2 (–4)
Languages: None
Senses: Darkvision 60 ft.

TRAITS
Ring of Fire: The body of a greater fire crab generates
intense heat. Any creature that starts its turn within 5 feet
of a greater fire crab takes 1d8 fire damage. This damage
is cumulative if more than one fire crab is within 5 feet of

the character.

ECOLOGY
Environment: Elemental Plane of Fire
Organization: Solitary, cluster (2–5), or colony (6–11)

Lesser Fire Crab

XP 25 (CR 1/8)
Unaligned Small monstrosity
Initiative +2

DEFENSE
AC 12
hp: 4 (1d6 + 1)
Immunity: Fire damage
Vulnerability: Cold damage

OFFENSE
Speed: 20 ft., swim 20 ft.
Multiattack: A lesser fire crab makes two pincer attacks.
Both must be against the same target.
Melee Attack—Pincer: +4 to hit (reach 5 ft.; one creature).
Hit: 1d4 + 2 slashing damage plus 1d4 fire damage and
the lesser fire crab latches onto the target with its burning
grip (see below).

STATISTICS
Str 10 (+0), **Dex** 14 (+2), **Con** 12 (+1),
Int 1 (–5), **Wis** 10 (+0), **Cha** 2 (–4)
Languages: None
Senses: Darkvision 60 ft.

TRAITS
Burning Grip: The body of a lesser fire crab generates intense

heat. Any creature that starts its turn with one or more lesser fire crabs latched onto it takes 2 fire damage for each of those lesser fire crabs. Once a lesser fire crab has latched onto a character, it moves with that character when the character moves, as if the character was moving a grappled character (half-speed). A lesser fire crab releases its grip when killed or when the character wins a Strength contest against it. Up to four lesser fire crabs can latch onto a Small character, and up to eight can latch onto a Medium character.

ECOLOGY
Environment: Elemental Plane of Fire
Organization: Solitary, cluster (4–7), or colony (11–20)

Fire crabs are invertebrates found roaming the fiery shores of the Elemental Plane of Fire, where they enjoy crawling and swimming through pools and lakes of liquid flame. They spend their time eating the superheated rocks and plants of their home plane. Their lairs take the form of large burrows under the fiery seas or along the shore, near their "water source." Such burrows are sometimes very large, housing up to 20 of these creatures. On the rare occasions when fire crabs are found on the Material Plane, they spend their time in or near active volcanoes and hot springs.

The most notable feature of fire crabs, besides the flames playing across their bodies, are their large pincers. Males can be distinguished from females because one of the male's claws is noticeably larger than the other. Fire crabs have six spindly, segmented legs, blackish-red in color.

Fire crabs are generally not aggressive creatures, but they can be highly territorial, especially if they feel that their lair is threatened. In that case, they attack without hesitation and fight to the death. Both greater and lesser fire crabs tend to focus all their effort against one enemy until it is dead, then shift to the next, and so on.

Copyright Notice
Author Scott Greene.

Fire Snake, Poisonous

This creature looks like a snake with reddish-orange scales and stark white eyes with no pupils.

Poisonous Fire Snake
XP 100 (CR 1/2)
Unaligned Small fiend
Initiative +3

DEFENSE
AC 13
hp: 13 (3d6 + 3)
Immunity: Fire damage
Vulnerability: Cold damage

OFFENSE
Speed: 20 ft., climb 20 ft.
Melee Attack—Bite: +5 to hit (reach 5 ft.; one creature). *Hit:* 1d6 + 3 piercing damage and the target must make a successful DC 11 Con saving throw against poison or be paralyzed for 1d6 rounds. A paralyzed creature takes 1d4 fire damage at the start of each of its turns while it is paralyzed.

STATISTICS
Str 10 (+0), **Dex** 17 (+3), **Con** 12 (+1), **Int** 1 (–5), **Wis** 12 (+1), **Cha** 7 (–2)
Languages: None
Skills: Acrobatics +5, Stealth +5
Senses: Darkvision 60 ft.

ECOLOGY
Environment: Elemental Plane of Fire
Organization: Solitary or pack (2–5)

A fire snake resembles a normal snake ranging from 2 feet to 6 feet in length, except for the dimly flickering flames visible inside its mouth and along its scales. Away from the Elemental Plane of Fire, fire snakes make their homes in fires and rarely journey more than 30 feet from an open flame. Sages conjecture that fire snakes might be some form of larval salamander.

A poisonous fire snake's preferred method of attack is to hide in a fire and surprise foes as they come nearby. They will sometimes crawl into a campfire that no one is paying close attention to, and attack while people are cooking or relaxing around the fire, without their weapons and armor, or even wait until the campers build up the fire for the night and go to sleep before creeping out and striking.

Credit
The Fire Snake originally appeared in the First Edition *Fiend Folio* (© TSR/Wizards of the Coast, 1981) and is used by permission.

Copyright Notice
Author Scott Greene, based on original material by Michael McDonagh.

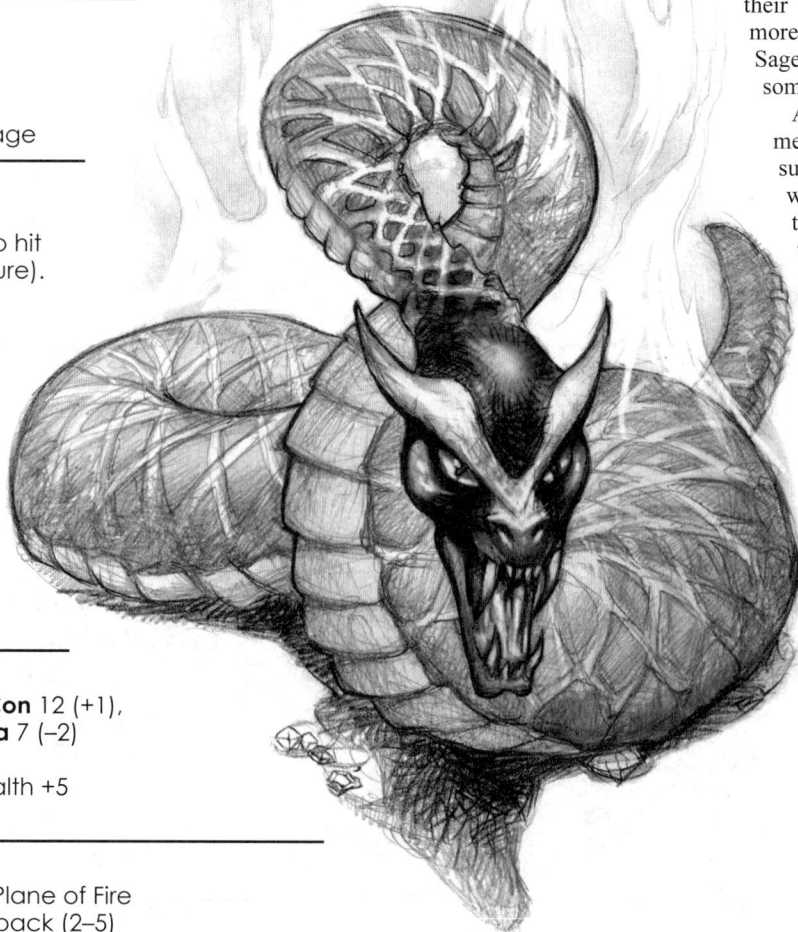

Flail Snail

*This creature looks like a massive version of a normal snail whose head has been replaced with
four tentacles as thick as a man's arm, each ending in a clublike ball.
Its shell is striped in bright hues of red, blue, yellow, and green, and its flesh is gray-blue.*

Flail Snail

XP 700 (CR 3)
Unaligned Large monstrosity
Initiative −1

DEFENSE

AC 16 (natural armor)
hp: 38 (4d10 + 16)
Resistance: Fire damage
Immunity: Poison damage; blindness,
poison, prone

OFFENSE

Speed: 10 ft., climb 10 ft.
Multiattack: A flail snail attacks four times
with tentacle clubs.
Melee Attack—Tentacle Club: +5 to hit
(reach 5 ft.; one creature). *Hit:* 1d8 + 3
bludgeoning damage.

STATISTICS

Str 16 (+3), **Dex** 8 (−1), **Con** 18 (+4),
Int 5 (−3), **Wis** 12 (+1), **Cha** 4 (−3)
Languages: Unique (flail snail)
Skills: Perception +3
Senses: Blindsight 60 ft.

TRAITS

Mucus: As a flail snail moves, it can leave a trail of mucus
along the ground that it travels across. It has two types of
mucus: slimy and sticky. Slimy mucus has the effect of a
grease spell (affected ground is difficult terrain; creatures
that enter affected ground must make a successful DC
12 Dex [Acrobatics] check or fall prone). Sticky mucus has
the effect of a *web* spell (creatures entering the affected
ground must make a successful DC 12 Str [Athletics] check
or become restrained; the check can be repeated as an
action, with success indicating the trapped creature broke
free). Both types last for 10 minutes, then dry out and are no
longer effective. Flail snails are immune to this mucus.
Retraction: Instead of moving, a flail snail can pull its fleshy
parts back into its shell, increasing its armor class to 22, but
it can't move or take actions while retracted. Extending

itself again also takes the place of any other movement
that turn.
Slime Rope: A flail snail can turn its mucus into a ropelike
strand up to 60 ft. long. If this strand is anchored to a
wall or ceiling, the flail snail and up to another 1,000
pounds can hang from it indefinitely. The flail snail
can climb up this strand 10 feet per round,
or lower itself down it 20 feet per round.
Other creatures can climb the strand
with a successful DC 20 Str (Athletics)
check. Once the snail breaks contact
with the strand, the slime dries out
and decomposes in 1d4 rounds,
after which it can't be used by
anyone.
Suction: A snail's foot adheres
to surfaces so well that
its 10-foot climb speed
applies even on
perfectly sheer surfaces
and ceilings, with no
chance to fall off unless
the foot is actively
peeled loose by external
force.
Warp Magic: Any spell that
targets a flail snail directly has an 80% chance of
producing a random effect instead of the desired affect.
Only spells that directly target the flail snail are warped;
area effect spells are not affected. When a spell is cast,
roll percentile dice and consult the table.

d100	Result
1–25	Spell misfires. For the next 1d4 rounds, the caster must make a successful DC 12 concentration check each time he or she tries to cast a spell or the spell can't be cast this turn and the action is wasted.
26–50	Spell misfires. The creature nearest the flail snail is affected instead, as if the spell had targeted it.
51–70	Spell fails. The spell slot is used but nothing happens.
71–80	Spell rebounds and targets the caster with its full effect.
81–100	Spell behaves and takes effect as intended.

ECOLOGY

Environment: Underground or ruins
Organization: Solitary, pair, or rout (3–30)

Flail snails are solitary omnivores that live in the deepest recesses of
caverns, caves, and dungeons, or occasionally aboveground in the ruins
of ancient, abandoned cities. They sustain themselves on a diet of fungus,
mold, and rodents. Although one would hardly suspect it on seeing a flail

Greater Flail Snail

A typical adult flail snail has 4 hit dice, but there is tremendous
variety among their population. In fact, flail snails can be found
with 1 to 12 hit dice, and they have one clublike tentacle per hit
die. Thus, a 6 HD flail snail has six tentacles; an 8 HD flail snail
has eight tentacles; a 12 HD flail snail has twelve tentacles; and
so on. A flail snail can attack with all of its tentacles. Flail snails
have 7.5 hit points per hit die, and the creature's CR increases by 1
for every two additional tentacles beyond the basic four. All other
statistics remain the same.

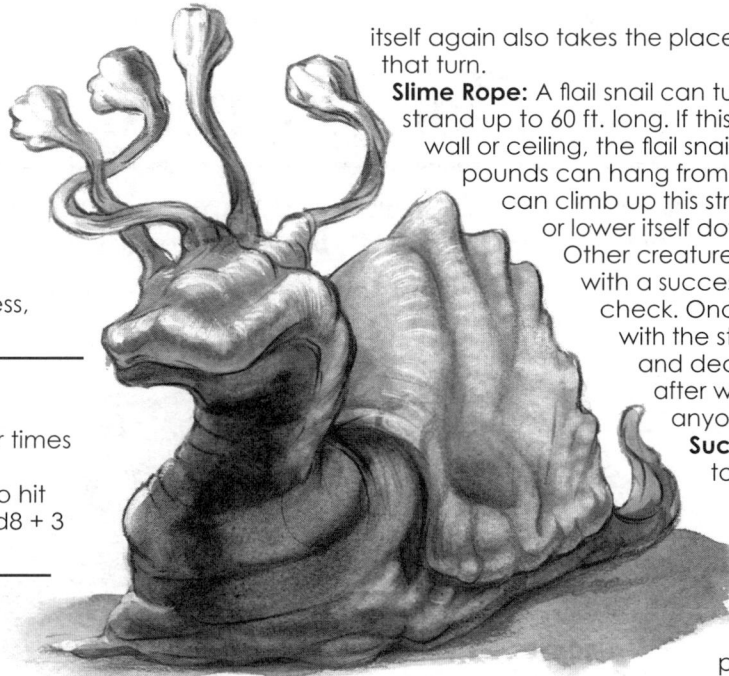

snail, they are intelligent creatures. They have no sound-producing organs, so their language is built around patterns created with their multipurpose mucus. Like most creatures, they are inoffensive when left alone, but they are tremendously paranoid about strangers; when someone intrudes into their normally abandoned territory, flail snails are prone to attack first and think up questions later.

They do not collect treasure, but the multi-hued shell of a flail snail can be sold to craftsmen, carvers, and collectors of strange and exotic curios for 80–120 gp, or possibly more for a particularly large or fine specimen.

Shell hunters may be the reason why flail snails are paranoid in the first place.

Credit

The flail snail originally appeared in the First Edition *Fiend Folio* (© TSR/Wizards of the Coast, 1981) and is used by permission.

Copyright Notice

Author Scott Greene, based on original material by Simon Tilbrook.

Flowershroud

This mass of bright flowers and leaves looks no different from any other carpet of spreading flowers—but it is.

Flowershroud

XP 200 (CR 1)
Unaligned Large plant
Initiative +1

DEFENSE
AC 11
hp: 19 (3d10 + 3)
Resistance: Bludgeoning and piercing damage from nonmagical weapons
Immunity: Psychic damage; charm, fright, prone, stun, unconsciousness

OFFENSE
Speed: 5 ft., climb 5 ft.
Multiattack: A flowershroud attacks three times with thorn strands.
Melee Attack—Thorn Strand: +3 to hit (reach 15 ft.; one creature). *Hit:* 1d6 + 1 piercing damage and the target must make a successful DC 11 Con saving throw or be affected by shroudblossom poison (see below).

STATISTICS
Str 6 (–2), **Dex** 12 (+1), **Con** 12 (+1),
Int 0 (–5), **Wis** 0 (–5), **Cha** 6 (–2)
Languages: None
Skills: Stealth +3
Senses: Tremorsense 60 ft.

TRAITS
Innocent Appearance: A patch of flowershroud looks completely natural to the untrained eye. They always have tactical advantage on Stealth checks, and their Stealth is opposed by the observer's Nature skill, not Perception.
Shroudblossom Poison: A character who fails a DC 11 Con saving throw when struck by a flowershroud's thorn strand attack falls prone and goes into convulsions lasting 1d6 rounds unless the poison effect is ended early with magic. During that time, the character can't stand up or move, is incapacitated, and takes 1d4 poison damage at the start of each of its turns.

ECOLOGY
Environment: Temperate and warm forest and prairie
Organization: Solitary or patch (2–9)

A flowershroud is a flowering plant that spreads across the ground and most other surfaces the same as any creeping plant. Its roots are extremely shallow, however, and it can pull them out of the ground in only a few seconds, then use them like tiny legs to literally creep across the ground and any other surface that a plant can cling to. They infest pleasant forest glades but also grow along game trails, where movement off the trail is difficult. They move so slowly that most animals can escape from the danger by simply walking away, but their tendrils can lash out to a surprising distance. Unlike adventurers traveling through the wilderness, flowershrouds never need to stop for rest. They present their greatest danger at night, when travelers have made camp and gone to sleep. Then, flowershrouds can creep into a campsite to attack sleeping prey.

Credit
Matt Finch

Foo Dog

This man-sized dog has a slightly oversized head and large, bulbous eyes.
Its paws carry sharp claws. Its golden fur fades to crimson on the creature's belly.

Foo Dog

XP 700 (CR 3)
CG Medium monstrosity
Initiative +2

DEFENSE

AC 13 (natural armor)
hp: 52 (7d10 + 21)
Saving Throws: See Resilient below

OFFENSE

Speed: 40 ft.
Melee Attack—Bite: +5 to hit (reach 5 ft.; one creature). *Hit:* 2d10 + 3 piercing damage.

STATISTICS

Str 17 (+3),
Dex 15 (+2),
Con 17 (+3),
Int 10 (+0),
Wis 14 (+2), **Cha** 10 (+0)
Languages: Celestial
Skills: Perception +4, Stealth +6
Senses: Darkvision 60 ft.

TRAITS

Aura: A foo dog is protected by an aura of goodness. An evil-aligned creature that attacks a foo creature takes a –1 penalty on attack and damage rolls.

Invisibility: A foo dog can become invisible as a bonus action. It becomes visible again when it attacks.

Planar Travel: A foo dog can shift between the Astral, Ethereal, and Material Planes during its move. Crossing the boundary from one plane to another costs the foo dog 30 feet of movement. It can transport only itself into or out of the Ethereal Plane, but it can bring up to eight other willing creatures with it across the Astral boundary, with effects and restrictions identical to the *astral projection* spell.

Resilient: A foo dog has tactical advantage on all saving throws.

Strike Evil: Foo dogs have a +2 bonus on attack and damage rolls when fighting evil-aligned creatures.

Summon Foo Creatures (1/day): Once per day as an action, a foo dog can summon up to four additional foo dogs by barking for them. Roll 4d4; one foo dog appears within 20 feet of the summoning foo dog for each die that rolls a 4. Foo dogs summoned this way can't summon more foo dogs.

ECOLOGY

Environment: Any good-aligned outer plane

Organization: Solitary or pack (5–12)

Foo dogs are extraplanar creatures that serve as guardians to those of good alignment. They are rarely encountered on the Material Plane, but when they are, they are always in the employ of a good-aligned creature, acting as either a companion or guardian. A foo dog never associates with creatures of evil alignment. It tolerates those of neutral alignment—barely.

A foo dog has the body of a large dog but its head is oversized, fierce, and distinctly un-canine in appearance. Some people say it more closely resembles a stylized lion, but others see a stronger resemblance to an ogre mage, or no resemblance to any other creature at all. It has large, intense, bulging eyes, outward-curving fangs, bushy eyebrows, a flattened nose, and pointed ears. Most foo dogs range in color from black to deep gold, though a few have been encountered that were pure white in color. They speak Celestial in a surprisingly deep voice. Sometimes they pick up other languages as well, depending on how widely they've traveled and who they've served.

Credit
The foo dog originally appeared in the First Edition *Monster Manual II* (© TSR/Wizards of the Coast, 1983) and is used by permission.

Copyright Notice
Author Scott Greene, based on original material by Gary Gygax.

Forester's Bane

This creature resembles an enormous, dark green shrub.

Forester's Bane

XP 1,800 (CR 5)
Unaligned Large plant
Initiative +0

DEFENSE

AC 10
hp: 103 (9d10 + 54)
Resistance:
Bludgeoning and piercing damage from nonmagical weapons
Immunity: Psychic damage; charm, fright, stun, unconsciousness

OFFENSE

Speed: 0 ft.
Multiattack:
Forester's Bane attacks four times with leaves and six times with stalks.
Melee Attack—Leaf: +5 to hit (reach 10 ft.; one creature of size Medium or smaller). *Hit:* the target is grappled and restrained.
Melee Attack—Stalk: +5 to hit (one creature grappled by a leaf). *Hit:* 1d6 + 3 slashing damage.

STATISTICS

Str 17 (+3), **Dex** 10 (+0), **Con** 22 (+6),
Int 0 (−5), **Wis** 13 (+1), **Cha** 8 (−1)
Languages: None
Skills: Stealth +4
Senses: Tremorsense 60 ft.

TRAITS

Grasping Tendrils: A creature grappled by a forester's bane can break free by winning a Strength contest against the plant or by inflicting 10 slashing damage against the grappling leaf, thereby severing it from the plant. Grappling leaves have AC 10. Damage done to a leaf is not subtracted from the plant's overall hit points. If a creature is grappled by more than one leaf, each leaf must be severed or overpowered individually. Severed leaves grow back in one week, if the forester's bane survives the fight.

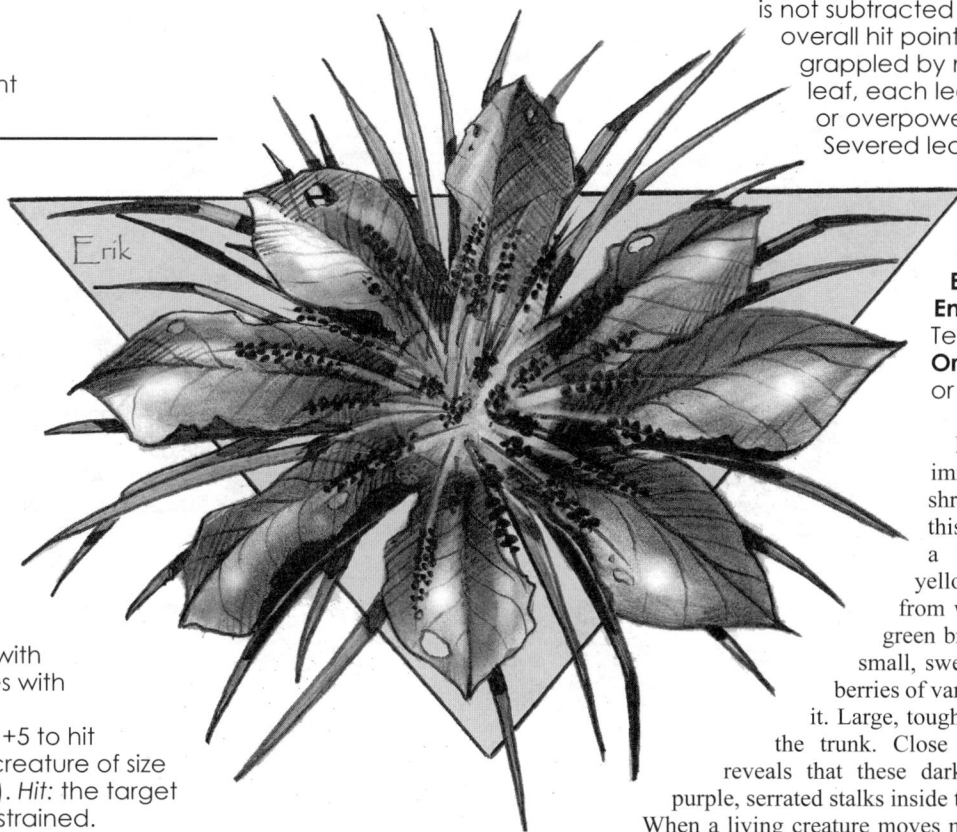

ECOLOGY

Environment: Temperate plains
Organization: Solitary or pair

Forester's bane is a huge, immobile, carnivorous shrub. At the center of this low-growing shrub is a 3-foot diameter, tough, yellowish, spherical "trunk" from which sprout many small green branches. Each branch has small, sweet smelling (and tasting) berries of various colors growing from it. Large, tough leaves also radiate from the trunk. Close inspection (if possible) reveals that these dark green leaves hide six purple, serrated stalks inside the plant's body.

When a living creature moves near a forester's bane, the plant tries to grab the creature. Trapped creatures are slashed and cut by the serrated stalks to make them bleed profusely into the ground around the plant. The plant makes no special effort to kill its victims; whether they're alive or dead after bleeding onto its roots is of no concern to the forester's bane. If one victim escapes, the plant would rather catch a fresh victim than try to squeeze more sustenance from a creature that's already low on blood.

Credit

The forester's bane originally appeared in the First Edition module *S3 Expedition to the Barrier Peaks* (© TSR/Wizards of the Coast, 1980) and later in the First Edition *Monster Manual II* (© TSR/Wizards of the Coast, 1983) and is used by permission.

Copyright Notice

Author Scott Greene, based on original material by Gary Gygax.

Froghemoth

This gigantic creature resembles a giant frog with four long tentacles in place of what would normally be two front legs. A single eyestalk juts from the top of its head. Its body is green, its underbelly is yellow, and its tentacles and legs are mottled green and yellow.

Froghemoth
XP 7,200 (CR 11)
Unaligned Huge aberration
Initiative +0

DEFENSE
AC 15 (natural armor)
hp: 200 (16d12 + 96)
Saving Throws: Dex +4
Resistance: Fire damage
Immunity: Lightning damage

OFFENSE
Speed: 20 ft., swim 30 ft.
Multiattack: A froghemoth attacks once with its tongue and four times with tentacles. Each tentacle can either grab or crush. In addition to these attacks, it can also bite one creature it grapples.
Melee Attack—Tentacle Grab: +11 to hit (reach 15 ft.; one creature). *Hit:* 1d8 + 7 bludgeoning damage and the target is grappled.
Melee Attack—Tentacle Crush: automatic hit (one creature already grappled by a tentacle at the start of the froghemoth's turn). *Hit:* 1d10 + 7 bludgeoning damage and the target is grappled.
Melee Attack—Tongue: +11 to hit (reach 30 ft.; one creature). *Hit:* 1d6 + 7 bludgeoning damage and the target is grappled and restrained.
Melee Attack—Bite: +11 to hit (reach 15 ft.; one creature grappled by the froghemoth's tentacles or tongue). *Hit:* 2d8 + 7 piercing damage and the target must make a successful DC 18 Dex saving throw or be swallowed (see below).

STATISTICS
Str 25 (+7), **Dex** 11 (+0), **Con** 22 (+6),
Int 2 (−4), **Wis** 13 (+1), **Cha** 10 (+0)
Languages: None
Skills: Perception +5, Stealth +4
Senses: Darkvision 60 ft.

TRAITS
All-Around Vision: A froghemoth's eyestalk allows it to scan quickly in all directions. Attackers never gain tactical advantage or bonus damage against it from the presence of nearby allies.
Slowed by Electricity: Although a froghemoth is immune to lightning damage, whenever it would otherwise take such damage, it is instead slowed for 1 round.
Swallow: A swallowed creature is blinded and restrained but no longer grappled. It takes 1d8 + 6 bludgeoning damage plus 2d8 acid damage automatically at the start of each of

the froghemoth's turns. Any number of creatures can be inside the froghemoth at one time. A swallowed creature is unaffected by anything happening outside the froghemoth or by attacks from outside it. A swallowed creature can get out of the froghemoth by using 10 feet of movement, but only after the froghemoth is dead.

ECOLOGY
Environment: Temperate marsh
Organization: Solitary

The froghemoth is a terrifying aberration that dwells in marshes and swamps. Its 30-foot-long tongue is agile and sticky, and it uses it to capture prey which it then swallows whole and digests alive. The froghemoth eats almost anything it can wrap its tongue or its tentacles around. Despite their size, froghemoths blend into their native swamps to a surprising degree, making them difficult to spot by people who haven't encountered one before.

A froghemoth has no use for treasure, but a fair amount of it accumulates in the beast's gut after the travelers and adventurers who carried it were digested. Many other useful items can be found around the creature's territory, where they were "deposited" after passing through the froghemoth's digestive tract.

Credit
The froghemoth originally appeared in the First Edition module *S3 Expedition to the Barrier Peaks* (© TSR/Wizards of the Coast, 1980) and later in the First Edition *Monster Manual II* (© TSR/Wizards of the Coast, 1983) and is used by permission.

Copyright Notice
Author Scott Greene, based on original material by Gary Gygax.

Fungoid

This tall, stocky, and powerful humanoid appears to be formed of mushroom flesh rather than normal muscle and tissue. Its rough facial features are barely discernible as crudely humanoid, and its long, thick arms end in immense, clawed hands. Instead of typical humanoid feet, its legs end in splayed, three-toed pads. Something akin to thick fur grows only on its chest, stomach, and lower back.

Fungoid

XP 450 (CR 2)
NE Medium plant (fungus)
Initiative +1

DEFENSE

AC 15 (natural armor)
hp: 45 (6d8 + 18)
Resistance: Lightning damage; piercing damage from nonmagical weapons
Immunity: Psychic damage; charm, fright, stun, unconsciousness

---

OFFENSE

Speed: 30 ft.
Multiattack: A fungoid attacks twice with fists.
Melee Attack—Fist: +6 to hit (reach 5 ft.; one creature).
Hit: 1d10 + 4 bludgeoning damage.

STATISTICS

Str 19 (+4), **Dex** 12 (+1), **Con** 17 (+3),
Int 4 (–3), **Wis** 11 (+0), **Cha** 6 (–2)
Languages: Understands Common but can't speak
Senses: Darkvision 60 ft., tremorsense 60 ft.

ECOLOGY

Environment: Temperate and warm marshes
Organization: Gang (2–4) or cluster (6–10)

Fungoids are man-sized humanoid creatures formed of mushroom flesh and leaves. Their coloration varies from brownish-green to brown to dark green to light gray with mottled brown splotches. Most weigh about 300 pounds. They are found in all but the coldest of swamps and marshes, where they delight in attacking creatures that wander too close to their lair.

Although related to fungi, fungoids are not scavengers but carnivorous hunters who consider the flesh of humans, elves, and goblins a delicacy. Only when live food is scarce do fungoids resort to scavenging for carrion.

Fungoids lair in the darkest and most dismal place they can find—the more devoid of light, the better. Typically a lair is beneath the densest tree canopy in the area and is ringed with mushrooms of many colors, shapes, and sizes. The lair itself is guaranteed to be well-hidden or camouflaged and difficult to get into. Creatures that wander close enough to actually spot the lair are already in trouble; by then the fungoids are certainly aware of the intruders' presence and are already considering how and when to eat them.

Fungoids do most of their hunting at night, when they travel up to 5 miles away from a lair in search of prey. Slain prey is carried or dragged back to the lair and devoured over several days' time. Fungoids often hunt in groups, but they never share their kill. "Each to its own" is the unspoken motto among fungoids.

These brutes are straightforward combatants that rush into melee swinging their powerful fists. Each fungoid selects a foe and pummels it relentlessly, single-mindedly ignoring all other threats until that one target is smashed. Multiple fungoids gang up against one foe only when that creature is obviously more powerful than any of them individually. Once the fight is over, the fungoids' cooperation ends, and it's back to "every creature for itself." Fungoids seldom retreat from a fight that's going against them unless a few believe they can reach the safety of their lair while others delay pursuit by continuing to fight (probably unaware that they've been abandoned).

Fungus Bat

A strange mass of what appears to be mushrooms trailing long, writhing tendrils flies out of the darkness toward you.

Fungus Bat

XP 50 (CR 1/4)
Unaligned Medium plant (fungus)
Initiative +1

DEFENSE
AC 11
hp: 16 (3d8 + 3)
Immunity: Psychic damage; fright, stun, unconsciousness

OFFENSE
Speed: 30 ft., fly 60 ft.
Melee Attack—Bite: +3 to hit (reach 5 ft.; one creature). *Hit:* 1d8 + 1 piercing damage and the target must make a successful DC 11 Con saving throw or suffer the effect of fungus bat poison (see below).

STATISTICS
Str 11 (+0), **Dex** 12 (+1), **Con** 13 (+1),
Int 1 (–5), **Wis** 10 (+0), **Cha** 1 (–5)
Languages: None
Senses: Blindsight 60 ft.

TRAITS
Fungus Bat Poison: A creature that fails a DC 11 Con saving throw against fungus bat poison suffers the usual effects of being poisoned. In addition, if the creature typically moves around on legs, it loses the use of its legs for 1d4 rounds. It falls prone immediately, and it can't stand up again until after the 1d4 rounds have elapsed. A successful saving throw against fungus bat poison does not impart any immunity against future poisonings.

ECOLOGY
Environment: Underground
Organization: Solitary, pair, patch (3–6), or field (6–15)

Fungus bats are found only in deep caves and more extensive regions of the subterranean world, for they are a very deep-dwelling species. They are uncommon everywhere, however; their colonies are small and few. It is believed they were more numerous in the distant past, but other creatures hunted them near to extinction.

A fungus bat resembles a mass of lumpy mushroom caps with leathery wings. A pair of long tails flap behind it when it flies, giving it a deceptively ungraceful appearance. Their bite carries a venom that affects the lower spine, paralyzing the legs. It's a short-lived effect, but dangerous—fungus bats tend to swarm creatures that are on the ground to the exclusion of other targets.

Credit
  Author Matt Finch

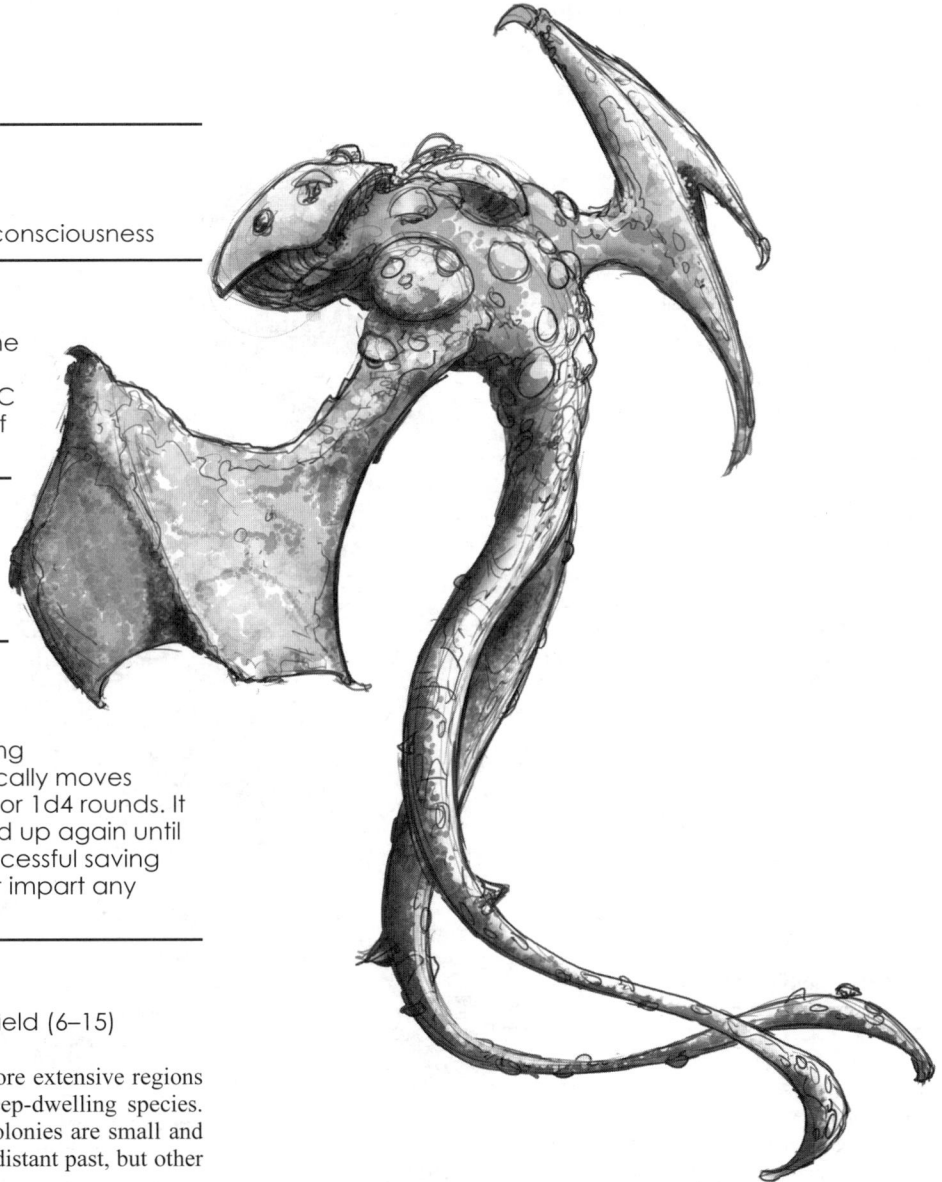

Fyr

This small, goat-headed humanoid combines long, backward-curving horns, goatlike legs, a brutish face, and a short, bushy tail with a very human-looking torso. Thick brown fur covers their legs, back, and head. They adorn themselves heavily with rings, necklaces, bracelets, earrings, and other such trinkets, and all fyrs, male and female, braid and decorate their beards.

Fyr

XP 50 (CR 1/4)
Neutral Small fey
Initiative +1

DEFENSE
AC 11
hp: 9 (2d6 + 2)
Saving Throws: See Resilient below
Resistance: Bludgeoning, piercing, and slashing damage from nonmagical weapons

OFFENSE
Speed: 30 ft.
Melee Attack—Battleaxe: +4 to hit (reach 5 ft.; one creature). *Hit:* 1d8 + 1 slashing damage.
Melee Attack—Headbutt: +3 to hit (reach 5 ft.; one creature). *Hit:* 1d6 + 1 bludgeoning damage and the target must make a successful DC 11 Dex saving throw or be knocked prone. If the target is knocked prone, the fyr can make an immediate battleaxe attack against it as a bonus action.

STATISTICS
Str 12 (+1), **Dex** 13 (+1), **Con** 12 (+1), **Int** 12 (+1), **Wis** 13 (+1), **Cha** 13 (+1)
Languages: Common, Sylvan
Skills: Animal Handling +3, Arcana +3, Deception +5, Insight +3, Nature +3, Stealth +5
Senses: Darkvision 60 ft.

TRAITS
Resilient: A fyr has tactical advantage on all saving throws.
Spell-like Abilities: All fyrs can use the following spell-like abilities, using Charisma as their casting ability (DC 11, attack +3). A fyr doesn't need material components to use these abilities.
At Will: *animal friendship, speak with animals*
3/day: *faerie fire, pass without trace*
2/day: *beast sense, conjure animals*
1/day: *dominate beast, invisibility*
Weapon Attunement: Fyrs have an ability to attune themselves with any wood-handled weapon, so that they get a +1 attack bonus with such a weapon once they've handled for at least 10 minutes. This bonus is already included in the battleaxe attack line above.

ECOLOGY
Environment: Any forests and mountains

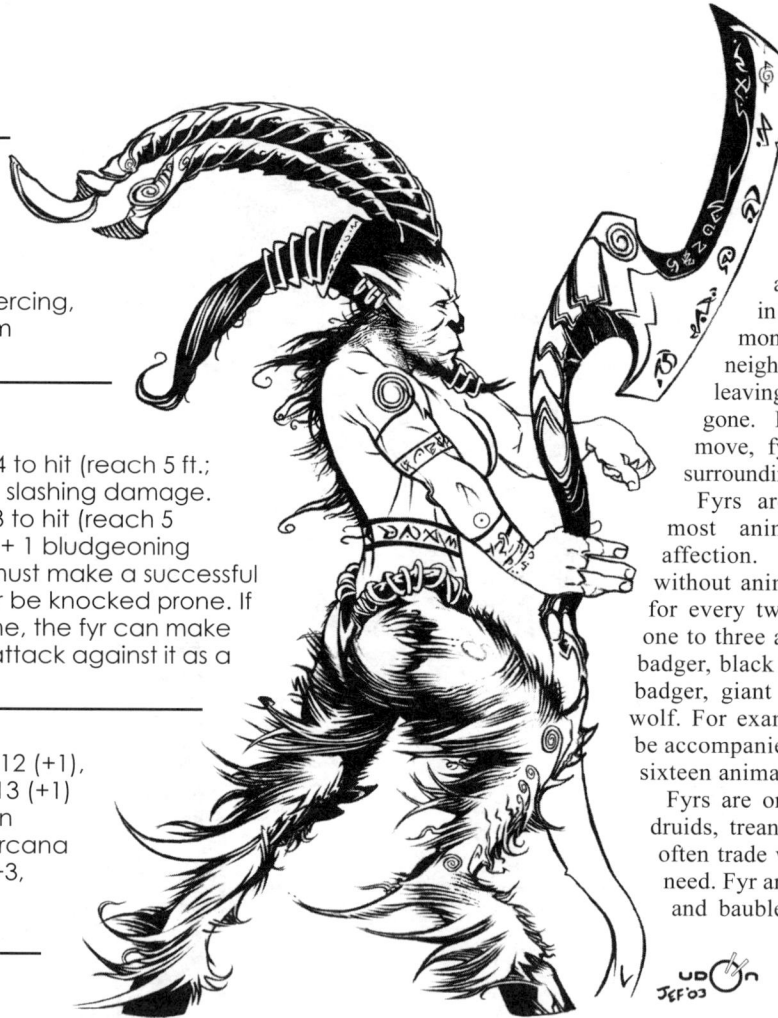

Organization: Solitary, band (2–5), or troop (6–11)

Fyrs are satyrlike creatures that make their homes in the mountainous wilds and dense forests, locating their lairs in secluded caves or caverns or under a dense covering of tangled branches and leaves. They are also a nomadic race, rarely staying in one place for longer than a few months before moving on. If they have neighbors, fyrs never give notice before leaving; one morning, they are simply gone. Despite being so often on the move, fyrs acclimate themselves to their surroundings very quickly.

Fyrs are great lovers of animals, and most animals instinctively return their affection. Fyrs are seldom encountered without animals in their company. Typically, for every two fyrs in a group, there will be one to three animal companions from this list: badger, black bear, boar, brown bear, elk, giant badger, giant weasel, goat, hawk, panther, or wolf. For example, a troop of eight fyrs could be accompanied by as few as four or as many as sixteen animal companions.

Fyrs are on good terms with most gnomes, druids, treants, elves, and halflings, and they often trade with them or aid them in times of need. Fyr are master jewelers, so their trinkets and baubles are highly sought by civilized races that appreciate fine jewelry. These fey tolerate humans and dwarves and likewise trade with them during those rare times when they are near a human settlement or dwarven stronghold. Fyr dislike orcs, goblins, bugbears, and other goblinoids, and avoid contact with them.

Fyrs are not great warriors, so they avoid combat if possible, but if their homeland or friends are threatened, they will fight. They prefer attacking from ambush, where their ability to become invisible gives them a great advantage. Fyrs use their natural ability to hide themselves in their terrain and attack from surprise. Fyrs like to knock their opponents prone—"bringing them down to size"—before using their axes with tactical advantage. Fyrs aren't hesitant to retreat if the tide of battle turns against them. *Pass without trace* usually allows them to escape without being tracked.

Gallows Tree

This creature appears as a massive, tall tree with thick branches from which hang several humanoid corpses tightly secured by their necks with greenish-brown ropes. Its canopy is thick and bushy, and its trunk is mottled brown.

Gallows Tree

XP 10,000 (CR 13)
Unaligned Huge plant
Initiative +0

DEFENSE

AC 15 (natural armor)
hp: 225 (18d12 + 108)
Resistance: Bludgeoning and piercing damage from nonmagical weapons; fire damage
Immunity: Psychic damage; fright, prone, stun, unconsciousness

OFFENSE

Speed: 20 ft.
Multiattack: A gallows tree attacks six times with branches. Grappling does not reduce the number of attacks the gallows tree can make; it can have any number of creatures grappled and still make six branch attacks.
Melee Attack—Branch: +10 to hit (reach 15 ft.; one creature). *Hit:* 2d8 + 5 bludgeoning damage and the target must make a successful DC 18 Dex saving throw or be grappled and restrained.

STATISTICS

Str 21 (+5), **Dex** 10 (+0), **Con** 23 (+6), **Int** 10 (+0), **Wis** 10 (+0), **Cha** 8 (−1)
Languages: Understands Common but can't speak
Skills: Perception +5
Senses: Tremorsense 60 ft.

TRAITS

Create Gallows Tree Zombie:
When a creature dies within 15 feet of a gallows tree, the tree uses a sharpened tendril to slice open the creature's abdomen, spilling the corpse's innards on the ground. The organs and fluids are absorbed by the tree's roots. Corpses of a size other than Medium or Large are simply left to rot. Medium or Large corpses are filled with a greenish pollen from one of the tree's branches. The abdominal wound heals in 1d4 days, and the slain creature then rises as a gallows tree zombie connected by a tether–vine to the gallows tree that created it. Gallows tree zombies possess none of their former abilities.
Staggering Critical: A gallows tree scores a critical hit if its attack roll is a natural 19 or 20. In addition to the standard critical hit effect, a creature hit by a gallows tree's critical hit must make a successful DC 17 Con saving throw or be stunned for 1d4 rounds.
Gallows Tree Zombies: Each gallows tree has several gallows tree zombies connected to it. A Huge gallows tree can have no more than seven gallows tree zombies connected to it at one time. A Gargantuan gallows tree can have up to 11 zombies connected to it. See the gallows tree zombie entry in this book for details on that monster.

ECOLOGY

Environment: Temperate and warm forest, hill, marsh, and plains
Organization: Grove (1 gallows tree plus 6–11 gallows tree zombies)

Gallows trees are sentient plants that sustain themselves on the internal organs and body fluids of slain creatures. They use deception to lure potential prey into range, at which time they unleash the gallows tree zombies attached to their branches to kill or capture prey.

While mobile, a gallows tree prefers to remain in one spot for an extended time—usually until the food supply in the area runs out. From this location, it simply waits for prey. Gallows trees do not collect treasure but occasionally the remnants of devoured prey can be found in the vicinity of a gallows tree.

A gallows tree normally stands idle, lowering its zombies to the ground when living prey approaches within 100 feet of the tree. If a foe comes within 15 feet of the tree itself, it lashes out with its sharpened branches and pummels the creature or wraps a branch around the foe. A grappled foe is always attacked by at least one other branch, and usually many more, because the gallows tree's goal is to kill creatures for food. Occasionally the tree works in concert with its zombies, grabbing a foe and holding it while its zombies pound the victim into goo. Slain creatures are sliced open and dragged close to the tree, where their innards are devoured by the tree's roots.

Gallows Tree Zombie

This creature is a humanoid with deathly gray skin stained green from grass and leaves, dressed in tattered and torn clothes. Small plants, weeds, and fungi grow on the creature. A long, sinewy, woody noose connects the creature to the massive tree behind it.

Gallows Tree Zombie

XP 450 (CR 2)
Unaligned Medium plant
Initiative +1

DEFENSE
AC 11
hp: 33 (6d8 + 6)
Immunity: Psychic damage; fright, stun, unconsciousness

OFFENSE
Speed: 30 ft.
Multiattack: A gallows tree zombie attacks once with its fists and can create one spore cloud.
Melee Attack—Fists: +6 to hit (reach 5 ft.; one creature). *Hit:* 2d8 + 4 bludgeoning damage.
Area Attack—Spore Cloud (recharge 5, 6): automatic hit (range 5 ft. cube adjacent to zombie; creatures in cube). *Hit:* a creature in the cloud of spores must make a successful DC 11 Con saving throw or suffer the effect of a *slow* spell lasting 6 rounds (no concentration required). When the *slow* effect ends, the target takes 1d8 poison damage, or half damage with a successful DC 11 Con saving throw.

STATISTICS
Str 19 (+4), **Dex** 13 (+1), **Con** 13 (+1), **Int** 4 (–3), **Wis** 10 (+0), **Cha** 1 (–5)
Languages: Understands Common but can't speak
Senses: Darkvision 60 ft.

TRAITS
Regeneration: At the start of its turn, a gallows tree zombie recovers 5 lost hit points. This ability fails to function if the creature has been severed from its gallows tree (see Tether Vine, below).
Tether Vine: A gallows tree zombie is connected to the gallows tree that created it by a sinewy vine. This vine can be lengthened to allow the zombie to move up to 100 feet from the tree. The vine has AC 14 and 10 hit points. Harming the vine deals no damage to the gallows tree zombie or the gallows tree, but if severed, does prevent the zombie from using its regeneration.

ECOLOGY
Environment: Temperate and warm forest, hill, marsh, and plains
Organization: Grove (6–11 gallows tree zombies plus 1 gallows tree)

Gallows tree zombies were once living humanoids, but they were slain and devoured by a gallows tree and reborn from its seedlings as one of its minions. Their new purpose is killing or capturing prey for the gallows tree that created them to devour.

These monsters retain small memories of their former lives, and these scenes sometimes manifest in the zombie's mind when they see living creatures similar to what the zombie once was. This triggers great anger that the zombie vents on the nearest living creature.

Gallows tree zombies appear as humanoid creatures with deathly gray skin that is coarse, like tree bark. A long, sinewy cord of greenish-brown wraps around the zombie's throat and connects it to the gallows tree.

Gallows tree zombies show no spark of life in their eyes, but they are not completely mindless. Neither are they undead, even though their name suggests otherwise; therefore, they can't be turned.

Gallows tree zombies hang motionless from the tree that created them, being lowered to the ground only when a living creature comes within 100 feet of the gallows tree they are connected to. They relentlessly pound their foes with their clublike fists while belching out clouds of choking spores. The zombies prefer uneven odds that favor them, so ganging up on an individual is their norm in battle. Slain foes are dragged to the gallows tree to be devoured, implanted with a seed, and eventually transformed into a gallows tree zombie to replace any that fell in battle.

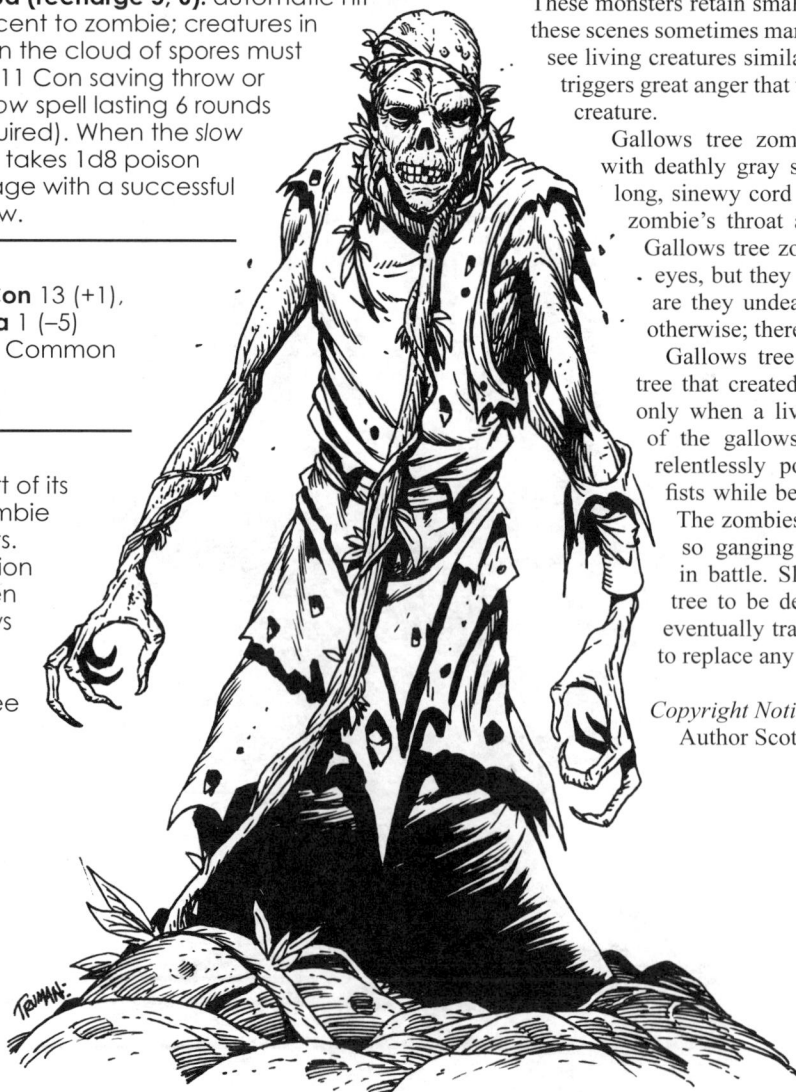

Gargoyles

Several varieties of gargoyles exist, and each is detailed below. For all their differences, gargoyles also share some common traits. They can remain utterly motionless for days, weeks, or even years, and they are indistinguishable from stone for as long as they remain still. Regardless of how long they've been inert, they can spring into sudden, savage action in an instant.

Gargoyle, Four-Armed

This creature appears to be a hideous and winged humanoid carved of stone. Its ears are oversized and pointed, and two large, backward-curving horns jut from its head above its eyes. It has four arms, and each ends in stony claws.

Four-Armed Gargoyle
XP 1,100 (CR 4)
CE Medium monstrosity
Initiative +2

DEFENSE
AC 15 (natural armor)
hp: 55 (10d8 + 10)
Resistance: Bludgeoning, piercing, and slashing damage from weapons that are nonmagical or not made of adamantine
Immunity: Poison damage; exhaustion, petrification, poison

OFFENSE
Speed: 30 ft., fly 60 ft.
Multiattack: A four-armed gargoyle attacks twice with claws, bites once, and gores once with its horns.
Melee Attack—Claws: +4 to hit (reach 5 ft.; one creature). *Hit:* 2d8 + 2 slashing damage.
Melee Attack—Bite: +4 to hit (reach 5 ft.; one creature). *Hit:* 1d8 + 2 piercing damage.
Melee Attack—Gore: +4 to hit (reach 5 ft.; one creature). *Hit:* 1d8 + 2 piercing damage.

STATISTICS
Str 15 (+2), **Dex** 14 (+2), **Con** 12 (+1), **Int** 6 (–2), **Wis** 11 (+0), **Cha** 7 (–2)
Languages: Terran
Senses: Darkvision 60 ft., tremorsense 60 ft. (while motionless)

TRAITS
Stony Appearance: While a four-armed gargoyle sits motionless, it is indistinguishable from natural stone and can't be detected as alive by any means.

ECOLOGY
Environment: Any land, aquatic, and underground
Organization: Solitary, pair, or wing (5–16)

Like their two-armed brethren, four-armed gargoyles often perch indefinitely without moving. Exactly why they do this is unknown: it may be no more than an ambush technique, or it might fulfill some unknown physiological need for the gargoyle. There seems to be no limit to how long a gargoyle can remain motionless, without food, water, or air.

Gargoyles are shockingly sadistic. When a four-armed gargoyle has the upper hand in battle, it often draws out the conflict as long as it can in its effort to inflict as much pain and fear as it can on foes.

Credit
The four-armed gargoyle first appeared in the First Edition module *S1 Tomb of Horrors* (© TSR/Wizards of the Coast, 1978) and is used by permission.

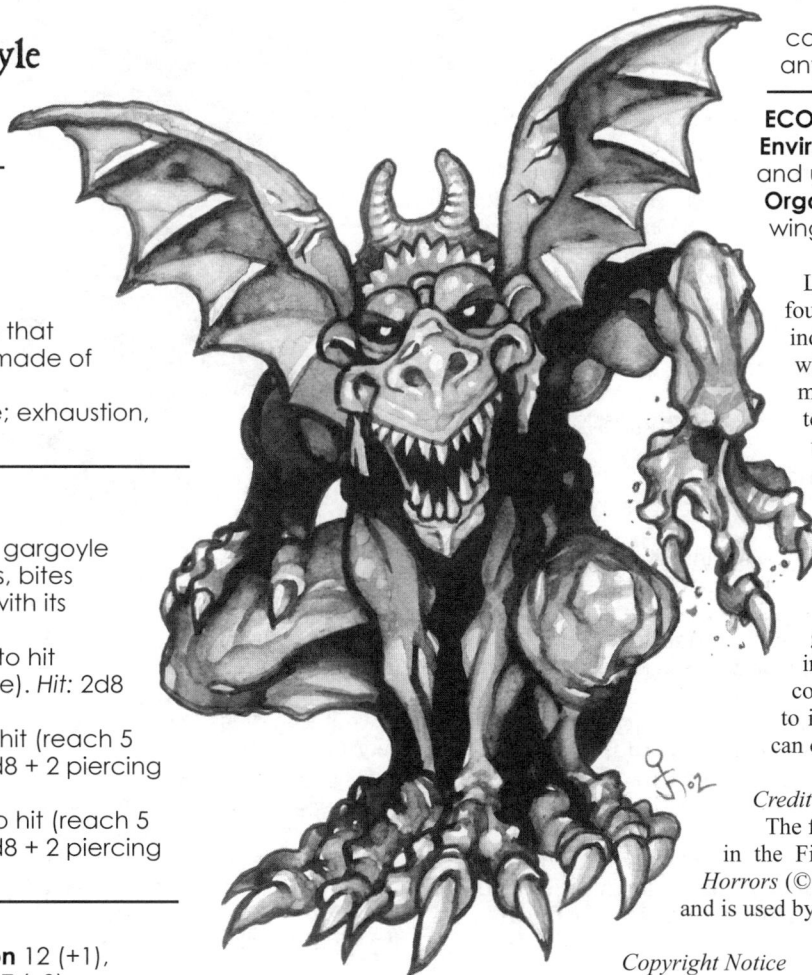

Gargoyle, Fungus

This creature looks like a winged statue, humanoid in shape, carved from molds, mushrooms, and other fungi. Its arms and legs end in clawed hands and feet, and its mouth is lined with fangs carved from the same substances as its body.

Fungus Gargoyle

XP 700 (CR 3)
NE Medium plant (fungus)
Initiative +2

DEFENSE

AC 14 (natural armor)
hp: 52 (7d8 + 21)
Saving Throws: Wis +2
Resistance: Bludgeoning and fire damage
Immunity: Psychic damage; fright, stun, unconsciousness

OFFENSE

Speed: 30 ft., fly 60 ft.
Multiattack: A fungus gargoyle attacks twice with claws or once with spore breath.
Melee Attack—Claw: +4 to hit (reach 5 ft.; one creature). *Hit:* 1d10 + 2 slashing damage.
Area Attack—Spore Breath (recharge 5, 6): automatic hit (range 10-ft. line; creatures in line). *Hit:* affected creatures must make a successful DC 13 Con saving throw or gain one level of exhaustion and suffer spore poisoning (see below).

STATISTICS

Str 14 (+2), **Dex** 14 (+2), **Con** 17 (+3),
Int 6 (−2), **Wis** 11 (+0), **Cha** 7 (−1)
Languages: Understands Common but can't speak
Skills: Stealth +4
Senses: Darkvision 60 ft., tremorsense 60 ft. (while motionless)

TRAITS

Sickening Aura: A fungus gargoyle stinks like rotting vegetable matter. Creatures that begin their turn within 10 feet of a fungus gargoyle must make a successful DC 13 Con saving throw or become poisoned for as long as they remain within 10 feet of any fungus gargoyle and for 1d4 rounds afterward.

Spore Poisoning: A creature affected by spore poisoning must make a DC 13 Con saving throw at the end of every hour. On a successful saving throw, there is no effect; on a failed saving throw, the creature adds one level of exhaustion to its current exhaustion level. A creature can't recover from exhaustion while suffering from spore poisoning. The character recovers from exhaustion by normal means once the poison is neutralized with magic.

ECOLOGY

Environment: Any non-arctic land
Organization: Solitary, pair, or patch (5–10)

Fungus gargoyles are thought to have once been normal gargoyles that were transformed into a fungoid state by an evil cult that pays reverence to demons of slime, ooze, and fungus. There is a link, in that these creatures are often found acting as guardians in temples dedicated to such demons.

Fungus gargoyles do not require food or air, though they still require water. They sometimes consume fallen enemies for the sheer pleasure of doing so.

A typical fungus gargoyle stands 5 to 6 feet tall (depending on how much it stoops) and weighs up to 200 pounds. Though their shape can vary, most resemble ugly, winged humanoids with diabolical features.

Fungus gargoyles behave much like normal gargoyles. They can stand motionless for seemingly endless lengths of time until they spring into action to ambush nearby prey. Unlike stony gargoyles, motionless fungus gargoyles are relatively easy to injure by cutting or stabbing, though this usually triggers an immediate response of claws to the face of the attacker. Once battle is joined, fungus gargoyles prefer to take flight and fight on the wing rather than on their feet.

Credit

The fungus gargoyle originally appeared in the First Edition *Fiend Folio* (© TSR/Wizards of the Coast, 1981) and is used by permission.

Copyright Notice

Authors Scott Greene and Clark Peterson, based on original material by Gary Gygax.

Gargoyle, Green Guardian

This winged humanoid is carved from a strange green stone, with eyes that are deep ebony in color.

Green Guardian Gargoyle

XP 200 (CR 1)
CE medium monstrosity
Initiative +2

DEFENSE

AC 13 (natural armor)
hp: 34 (4d8 + 16)
Resistance: Bludgeoning, piercing, and slashing damage from weapons that are nonmagical or not made of adamantine
Immunity: Poison damage; exhaustion, petrification, poison

OFFENSE

Speed: 30 ft., fly 60 ft.
Multiattack: A green guardian gargoyle attacks once with claws and gores once with its horns.
Melee Attack—Claws: +4 to hit (reach 5 ft.; one creature). *Hit:* 2d8 + 2 slashing damage. If both claw attacks hit the same target, the target is also grappled and restrained.
Melee Attack—Gore: +4 to hit (reach 5 ft.; one creature). *Hit:* 1d8 + 2 piercing damage.

STATISTICS

Str 15 (+2), **Dex** 14 (+2), **Con** 18 (+4),
Int 6 (–2), **Wis** 11 (+0), **Cha** 7 (–2)
Languages: Common, Terran
Skills: Stealth +4
Senses: Darkvision 60 ft., tremorsense 60 ft. (while motionless)

TRAITS

Reanimation: A green guardian gargoyle that is destroyed will reanimate 1d8 + 2 days later unless its eyes are removed, crushed, and disenchanted by casting both *dispel magic* (automatic) and *greater restoration* on them. If the eyes are taken away but not destroyed, they simply disappear from wherever they are and reappear in the green guardian's eye sockets at the moment it reanimates. The same applies to any other body parts that were demolished or removed.
Stony Appearance: While a green guardian gargoyle sits motionless, it can't be detected as a living creature by any means.

ECOLOGY

Environment: Any land, aquatic, and underground
Organization: Solitary, pair, or wing (5–16)

Green guardian gargoyles are carved from a strange, green stone. Their only features that are not this stone are their eyes, which are black jet; they can easily be appraised to have a value of 200 gp apiece by someone who knows gems, but they also detect as magic (conjuration) under a *detect magic* spell.

The green guardian gargoyles' preferred way to kill their victims is to direct all their attacks at the same foe and grab that creature so that they can then fly them 60 feet up into the air before releasing them, letting them take another 6d6 bludgeoning damage from the fall. Fortunately, a single green guardian can carry only 150 pounds while flying, so it takes two of them to lift most Medium-sized characters. The first one to attack must establish the grapple by hitting the same target with both claw attacks. The second gargoyle needs only one of its claw attacks to hit in order to grab an arm and help hoist the character into the air.

Green guardian gargoyles are mercifully rare. So far, they are known to exist only in the halls of Rappan Athuk, where they are employed as guards and gatekeepers. It's only a matter of time before they spread to other sites.

Credit
Green guardian gargoyles can be found in the Necromancer Games module *Rappan Athuk I: The Upper Levels* (©2000 Bill Webb and Clark Peterson, Necromancer Games, Inc.).

Copyright Notice
Authors Scott Greene and Clark Peterson, based on original material by Gary Gygax.

Gargoyle, Margoyle

This creature looks like a hideously ugly humanoid chiseled from brown stone. Two large horns protrude from its head, just above its eyes. Four large, stony spikes jut from its shoulder blades. Its hands and feet end in sharpened claws.

Margoyle

XP 1,800 (CR 5)
CE Medium monstrosity
Initiative +2

DEFENSE

AC 16 (natural armor)
hp: 114 (12d8 + 60)
Resistance: Bludgeoning, piercing, and slashing damage from weapons that are nonmagical or not made of adamantine
Immunity: Poison damage; exhaustion, petrification, poison

OFFENSE

Speed: 30 ft., fly 60 ft.
Multiattack: A margoyle attacks once with claws, bites once, and gores once with its horns.
Melee Attack—Claw: +6 to hit (reach 5 ft.; one creature). *Hit:* 2d8 + 3 slashing damage.
Melee Attack—Bite: +6 to hit (reach 5 ft.; one creature). *Hit:* 1d8 + 3 piercing damage.
Melee Attack—Gore: +6 to hit (reach 5 ft.; one creature). *Hit:* 1d8 + 3 piercing damage.

STATISTICS

Str 17 (+3), **Dex** 15 (+2), **Con** 20 (+5),
Int 8 (−1), **Wis** 12 (+1), **Cha** 8 (−1)
Languages: Common, Terran
Skills: Stealth +5
Senses: Darkvision 60 ft., tremorsense 60 ft. (while motionless)

TRAITS

Stony Appearance: While a margoyle sits motionless, it is indistinguishable from natural stone and can't be detected as alive by any means.

ECOLOGY

Environment: Any land, aquatic, and underground
Organization: Solitary, pair, or wing (1–2 margoyles and 4–6 gargoyles or four-armed gargoyles)

A margoyle is nothing more than a slightly larger version of a typical gargoyle. It is, however, meaner, deadlier, and even more evil than the normal gargoyle, if such a thing is imaginable. Margoyles are most often encountered in subterranean regions, where they typically have a pack of gargoyles accompanying them. In such cases, the margoyle is almost always looked upon as the master or leader of the group.

Credit

The margoyle originally appeared in the First Edition module *S4 Lost Caverns of Tsojcanth* (© TSR/Wizards of the Coast, 1982) and later in the First Edition *Monster Manual II* (© TSR/Wizards of the Coast, 1983) and is used by permission. It was called a "marlgoyle" in S4 (note the extra "l").

Copyright Notice

Authors Scott Greene and Clark Peterson, based on original material by Gary Gygax.

Genie, Hawanar

This being is twice as tall as a normal human and has reddish skin, no hair, and small fangs.
Its lower torso is shrouded in a cyclone of embers and flame.

Hawanar Genie
XP 2,900 (CR 7)
LN Large fiend
Initiative +2

DEFENSE
AC 17 (natural armor)
hp: 97 (13d10 + 26)
Saving Throws: Dex +5, Con +5
Immunity: Acid and fire damage
Vulnerability: Cold damage

OFFENSE
Speed: 20 ft., fly 50 ft.
Multiattack: A hawanar genie
attacks twice with fists or twice
with its falchion, or uses a spell-
like ability.
Melee Attack—Fist: +8 to hit (reach
5 ft.; one creature). *Hit:* 2d8 + 5
bludgeoning damage plus 1d8 fire
damage.
Melee Attack—Falchion: +8 to
hit (reach 5 ft.; one creature).
Hit: 2d8 + 5 slashing damage
plus 1d6 fire damage. This
attack scores a critical hit if the
hawanar's attack roll is a natural 18,
19, or 20.

STATISTICS
Str 20 (+5), **Dex** 14 (+2), **Con** 14 (+2),
Int 14 (+2), **Wis** 10 (+0), **Cha** 15 (+2)
Languages: Auran and Ignan
Skills: Deception +5, Intimidation +5,
Perception +3
Senses: Darkvision 60 ft.

TRAITS
Air Mastery: Airborne creatures have tactical disadvantage
on attacks against a hawanar.
Holocone: A hawanar can transform into a vortex of
embers and white-hot fire as a bonus action and can
remain in this form for up to six rounds. Once it changes
back to its normal form, it can't resume its holocone form
for another 10 minutes. In holocone form, the hawanar
genie can move through the air or along any surface
at its fly speed. It can move through spaces occupied
by other creatures; creatures of Medium size or smaller
must make a successful DC 13 Dex saving throw or
be swept into the vortex, taking 2d8 + 5 bludgeoning
damage plus 1d8 fire damage and being grappled by
the genie, which can then move the grappled creature
according to the normal grappling rules. The genie can't
end its move in the same space as a character it isn't
grappling.
Mobility: When a hawanar genie moves,
opportunity attacks against it have tactical
disadvantage.
Spell-like Abilities: A hawanar genie can
use the following spell-like abilities, using
Charisma as its casting ability (DC 13,
attack +5). The genie doesn't
need material components to
use these abilities.
At will: *plane shift* (willing
targets to elemental
planes, Astral Plane, or
Material Plane only)
1/day: *burning hands,
create wine and water*
(as *create food and
water*, but creates wine
instead of water),
*fireball, gaseous
form, invisibility* (self
only), *major image,
scorching ray* (3
rays), *wall of fire,
wind walk*

ECOLOGY
Environment: Any
(Plane of Elemental
Air or Plane of
Elemental Fire)
Organization: Solitary,
pair, company (2–4), or
band (6–15)

Hawanar are the unlikely union of an efreeti noble and
a djinni noble. Neither of the parent races truly accepts the hawanar;
the djinn are somewhat tolerant, while the efreet usually execute or enslave
hawanar offspring, viewing them as something unnatural.

A typical hawanar stands 12 feet tall and weighs about 1,100 pounds.

Hawanar society is ruled by a rajah who is served by a multitude of
beys, sheiks, sahibs, and sirdars The hawanar race has no true home and
can be found spread throughout the planes (most dwell on the Plane of Air
or a pocket plane of air and fire). Those that dwell on the Plane of Fire
generally avoid the City of Brass and efreeti patrols because of the disdain
the efreet have for them.

Hawanar wade into battle in a hail of fire and wind, relying on their
spell-like abilities and holocone form to vanquish opponents. If combat
goes against it, a hawanar slips into holocone form or becomes gaseous
and flees.

Copyright Notice
Author Scott Greene.

Ghost Ammonite

This large, nautilus-shaped spirit seemingly swims its way through the air to attack with its writhing, incorporeal tentacles.

Ghost Ammonite

XP 450 (CR 2)
Unaligned Medium undead
Initiative +2

DEFENSE

AC 10
hp: 33 (6d8 + 6)
Resistance: Bludgeoning, piercing, and slashing damage from weapons that are nonmagical or not made of adamantine
Immunity: Necrotic and poison damage; exhaustion, fright, poison, unconsciousness

OFFENSE

Speed: fly 30 ft., burrow 20 ft.
Multiattack: A ghost ammonite attacks three times with tentacles.
Melee Attack—Tentacle: +4 to hit (reach 5 ft.; one creature). *Hit:* 2d4 + 2 necrotic damage and the target's maximum number of hit points is reduced by an amount equal to the necrotic damage.

STATISTICS

Str 4 (–3), **Dex** 14 (+2), **Con** 12 (+1), **Int** 3 (–4), **Wis** 11 (+0), **Cha** 10 (+0)
Languages: None
Skills: Stealth +4
Senses: Darkvision 60 ft.

TRAITS

Lunge: A ghost ammonite can extend its reach to 15 feet at will, but if it does, attacks against it have tactical advantage until the start of the ghost ammonite's next turn.
Shell Retreat: If a ghost ammonite suffers radiant damage, it retreats into its shell for 1d6 rounds. While withdrawn inside its shell, its AC increases to 16 and it heals 1 hit point at the start of each of its turns, but it can't attack.

ECOLOGY

Environment: Any (but chiefly, the Plateau of Leng)
Organization: Solitary, haunt (2–5), or fossil bed (10–100)

Unlike Leng-fossils, which are virtually unique to the Leng Plateau, ghost-ammonites are the remnants of some unspeakably ancient race that once traveled freely through many planes of existence—or so believe those rare scholars who've dared to study the enigmatic realm of Leng. Their wide travels explain the fact that they can be found literally anywhere. In life, they possessed genius-level intellects, but their ghostly remnants have been reduced to idiocy, propelled by little more than hatred and instinct.

Ghost ammonites are truly undead, unlike the fossils of Leng. These six-tentacled creatures are incorporeal and almost invulnerable to damage of any kind, but their spiraling, fossilized shells are real stone. If the shell is destroyed, the ghost-ammonite inside is destroyed along with it.

For reasons unknown, ghost ammonites often lie quiescent for centuries, usually in layers of earth thick with fossils. They become active for as long as a century or two before returning to eons-long hibernation deep within the alien rock, where they dream of unknown, unquiet realities.

Giant Slug of P'nahk

An immense brain seems to hang in the air, tepidly rising and falling from unseen forces.
Slowly the hazy outline of a massive, transparent slug comes into focus.

Giant Slug of P'nakh

XP 1,100 (CR 4)
CE Large fiend
Initiative −1

DEFENSE

AC 11 (natural armor)
hp: 76 (9d10 + 27)
Saving Throws: Con +5, Int +6
Resistance: Piercing and slashing damage; acid damage
Immunity: Bludgeoning damage; blindness, deafness, prone

OFFENSE

Speed: 20 ft.
Multiattack: A giant slug of P'nahk bites once and crushes once, or uses its mind blast.
Melee Attack—Bite: +6 to hit (reach 5 ft.; one creature). *Hit:* 2d10 + 4 slashing damage.
Melee Attack—Crush: +6 to hit (reach 5 ft.; one creature). *Hit:* 2d10 + 4 bludgeoning damage and the target is knocked prone, grappled, restrained, and smothered (see below).
Area Attack—Mind Blast (recharge 6): automatic hit (range 60 ft. cone; creatures in cone). *Hit:* every creature in the affected area must make a successful DC 14 Int saving throw or be affected by the insanity of P'nahk (see below). Characters with Int 16 or higher have tactical disadvantage on the saving throw.

STATISTICS

Str 18 (+4), **Dex** 8 (−1), **Con** 16 (+3),
Int 19 (+4), **Wis** 10 (+0), **Cha** 4 (−3)
Languages: Abyssal, Deep Speech, Primordial
Skills: Arcana +6, History +6, Stealth +3
Senses: Tremorsense 60 ft.

TRAITS

Smothering: When a giant slug of P'nahk hits a creature with its crushing attack, it drops its body onto the creature, pinning it to the ground. Treat this as being grappled and restrained, but the creature must also make an immediate DC 14 Con saving throw. A successful saving throw indicates the creature inhaled a lungful of air before being trapped; a failed saving throw indicates the air was forced from the creature's lungs and it is suffocating. A suffocating creature can act normally for a number of rounds equal to its Con modifier (minimum of 1 round). Once those rounds expire, the creature drops to 0 hit points at the start of its next turn and it must make death saving throws.
Insanity of P'nahk: A giant P'Nahki slug can produce a momentary mental blast that transmits subliminal images of the nightmarish realm of P'nahk. All creatures in the affected area that fail a DC 16 Int saving throw recall these images and

must roll 1d4 to determine how they are affected (see below). In addition, affected characters repeat the saving throw at the end of each of their turns; the effect ends with a successful save (indicating the character managed to forget the images). Characters with Int scores of 16 or higher are peculiarly vulnerable to this attack; they make the saving throws with tactical disadvantage.

1d4	Effect
1	Paralyzed; the character strikes back instinctively with a melee attack or a cantrip (as a reaction) against anything that attacks him or her, but can take no other action and can't move.
2	Paranoid rage; the character attacks its nearest allies.
3	Self loathing; the character drops any held items and claws at his or her body, inflicting 1d4 slashing damage per round.
4	Awe of P'nahk; the character drops all held items, falls prone, and grovels in worship of the slug and all things P'nahki. The character is paralyzed.

Telepathy: Giant slugs of P'nahk are telepathic, so they can communicate with all creatures within 100 feet.
Transparency: Because of its transparent body, a giant slug of P'nahk always has tactical advantage on Stealth checks and it can attempt to hide anytime it is lightly obscured, such as when it is in dim light.

ECOLOGY

Environment: Any, but especially ancient ruins and underground
Organization: Solitary or pair

P'Nahki slugs are massive creatures with bodies so transparent that they are almost invisible. The only part of the slug's anatomy that can be clearly seen is its disturbingly human-looking brain, which appears at first glance to be floating in the air. Their soft, thick hide gives them excellent protection against melee weapons.

These creatures originated in a forgotten place called P'Nahk; whether this was an alien city now in ruins, a lost world, or an entirely different dimension is not known. It's entirely likely that even the slugs themselves don't know the full answer to the mystery of their origin.

The giant slugs of P'Nahk are highly intelligent, although this intellect is seldom put to use in a way that can be related to human motivation or logic. They are most commonly encountered in remote subterranean realms or in the ruins of ancient civilizations, where they sift through the rubble in search of forgotten tomes and lost relics. They have been known to possess startling knowledge about the distant past and about magical artifacts, if one can persuade them to share.

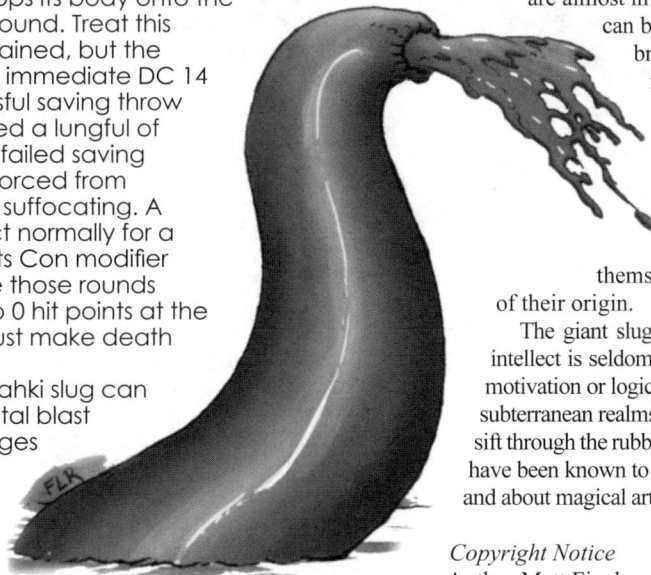

Giant, Jack-in-Irons

Brutish, warty, hairy, and stinking of oil and iron, this creature has jutting lower jaws and tusklike teeth, not unlike an orc or hobgoblin of huge size. It wears belts of skulls, rotting heads are strung on ropes around its throat and waist, and jangling iron chains enwrap its entire body.

Jack-in-Irons Giant

XP 2,900 (CR 7)
CE Huge giant
Initiative +1

DEFENSE

AC 14 (chains)
hp: 126 (11d12 + 55)
Saving Throws: Wis +4, Con +8

OFFENSE

Speed: 40 ft.
Multiattack: A jack-in-irons giant makes two melee attacks in any combination of club, chain, fist, and pound, or it makes two ranged attacks, or it shakes the earth (see below).
Melee Attack—Club: +9 to hit (reach 10 ft.; one creature). *Hit:* 3d10 + 6 bludgeoning damage and the target must make a successful DC 17 Str saving throw or be incapacitated until the start of the giant's next turn.
Melee Attack—Chain: +9 to hit (reach 15 ft.; one creature). *Hit:* 2d10 + 6 bludgeoning damage and the target must make a successful DC 17 Dex saving throw or be grappled and restrained until the start of the giant's next turn.
Melee Attack—Fist: +9 to hit (reach 10 ft.; one creature). *Hit:* 2d8 + 6 bludgeoning damage and the target must make a successful DC 17 Con saving throw or be knocked prone.
Ranged Attack—Rock: +9 to hit (range 60 ft./240 ft.; one creature). *Hit:* 3d10 + 6 bludgeoning damage.

STATISTICS

Str 22 (+6), **Dex** 12 (+1), **Con** 20 (+5),
Int 9 (−1), **Wis** 12 (+1), **Cha** 11 (+0)
Languages: Giant
Senses: Darkvision 60 ft.

TRAITS

Pound: A jack-in-irons that grapples an opponent of Medium size or smaller can smash the opponent into the ground or any other nearby solid object as an attack. This attack hits automatically and does 2d8 + 6 bludgeoning damage and the creature must make a successful DC 17 Con saving throw or be incapacitated until the start of the giant's next turn.
Shake the Earth: As an action, a jack-in-irons can stomp its foot on the ground, causing powerful vibrations to radiate out around the giant. Any creature within 10 feet of the jack-in-irons must make a successful DC 17 Dex saving throw or fall prone.

ECOLOGY

Environment: Temperate plains and forest
Organization: Solitary

A jack-in irons giant steal chains from gates, portcullises, and wherever else it can get them, and fastens them all around its body, with a special emphasis on the wrists, forearms, shins, throats, and shoulders. They collect the heads of their victims as trophies and fashion them into grisly belts and necklaces.

Most jack-in-irons giants dwell in ruined towers overlooking remote stretches of roads. From this base, they watch for lone travelers, pilgrims, and even guarded caravans to ambush and sack. Armored knights are their favored prey. They have been known to take prisoners and hold them for high ransom, but bargaining with a jack-in-irons is always a tricky undertaking; as often as not, they become bored or angry during the process and simply kill their captives, regardless of whether they've been promised or even paid a ransom for them.

Orcs and goblins sometimes follow a jack-in-irons as their king or leader because of its size, strength, and bottomless capacity for wickedness. Such a company almost never includes more than one jack-in-irons, however, because none will submit to the command of another.

A jack-in-irons stands about 18 feet tall. It prefers to dress in dark colors such as black or brown and always drapes itself in chains. Its hair is dark and matted, and many male jacks-in-irons sport thick, bushy beards. Its eyes are purplish-black with light green irises.

A jack-in-irons is not a clever opponent. They rely almost exclusively on brute strength until they run out of enemies. Most fight only to the death, because they believe themselves invincible—as indeed they are, until someone defeats and kills them.

Copyright Notice
Author Scott Greene.

Gillmonkey

*This small creature resembles a cross between a monkey and a fish,
with gangly arms and legs, bulging eyes, scaly skin, and webbed fingers and toes.*

Gillmonkey

XP 50 (CR 1/4)
CE Small beast (aquatic)
Initiative +2

DEFENSE

AC 12
hp: 7 (2d6)
Saving Throws: Dex +4

OFFENSE

Speed: 25 ft., swim 30 ft.
Multiattack: A gillmonkey bites once and attacks once with claws.
Melee Attack—Bite: +4 to hit (reach 5 ft.; one creature). *Hit:* 1d6 + 2 piercing damage.
Melee Attack—Claw: +4 to hit (reach 5 ft.; one creature). *Hit:* 1d6 + 2 slashing damage.

STATISTICS

Str 8 (–1), **Dex** 15 (+2), **Con** 10 (+0),
Int 10 (+0), **Wis** 12 (+1), **Cha** 9 (–1)
Languages: Unique (Gillmonkey)
Skills: Stealth +4
Senses: Darkvision 60 ft., tremorsense 60 ft. (when in water)

TRAITS

Amphibious: A gillmonkey can breathe equally well in air or underwater.

ECOLOGY

Environment: Saltwater or fresh water
Organization: School (2–20) or colony (20–200)

Gillmonkeys are nasty, monkeylike creatures that live in the sea. They are native to saltwater, but they sometimes swim up rivers and into lakes to hunt or raid. They have hairless, pinkish-brown skin that is lightly scaled. Short appendages like tentacles grow from the tops of their heads, but they seem to be used only for handling food.

Gillmonkeys never fight alone; if someone is attacked by one gillmonkey, they will be attacked by more. Individually, gillmonkeys are weak and cowardly (more generous observers might call them shy), but in groups they can be quite dangerous—and they always travel in groups. When they attack, they swarm over a ship's rails like waves crashing up from the sea.

Credit
Author Matt Finch

Gloom Crawler

This giant, squidlike beast has thirty to forty tentacles, each up to 30 feet long. From the end of each tentacle stares a small, round, lidless eye with a stark blue pupil. The creature's glossy flesh is inky-black with a slightly paler underside centered around a vicious, beaked mouth of monstrous size.

Gloom Crawler
XP 5,900 (CR 10)
N Huge monstrosity
Initiative +2

DEFENSE
AC 12
hp: 159 (13d12 + 75)
Immunity: Prone
Vulnerability: Radiant damage

OFFENSE
Speed: 20 ft., climb 20 ft.
Multiattack: A gloom crawler attacks ten times with tentacles and bites once. Each tentacle can either slam or constrict.
Melee Attack—Bite: +9 to hit (reach 5 ft.; one creature grappled by the gloom crawler). *Hit:* 1d10 + 5 piercing damage and the creature is dragged to the gloom crawler's mouth.
Melee Attack—Tentacle Slam: +9 to hit (reach 15 ft.; one creature). *Hit:* 1d8 + 5 bludgeoning damage and the target is grappled.
Melee Attack—Tentacle Constriction: automatic hit (one creature already grappled by the gloom crawler at the start of the gloom crawler's turn). *Hit:* 1d8 + 5 bludgeoning damage and the target is grappled and restrained.

STATISTICS
Str 20 (+5), **Dex** 14 (+2), **Con** 20 (+5),
Int 4 (–3), **Wis** 12 (+1), **Cha** 2 (–4)
Languages: None
Skills: Perception +9, Stealth +6
Senses: Darkvision 60 ft.

TRAITS
All-Around Vision: A gloomcrawler's many eyes allow it to scan quickly in all directions. Attackers never gain tactical advantage or bonus damage against it from the presence of nearby allies.

ECOLOGY
Environment: Temperate
Organization: Solitary

The gloom crawler is a solitary creature resembling a giant squid with ebony skin and dozens of writhing tentacles. It makes its lair in caves, dungeons, and other subterranean complexes far away from the hated light of the surface world. Most of its time is spent in dormant dreaming, waking only occasionally to eat.

The gloom crawler moves through its underground world by attaching to any surface with the suction cups on its tentacles. The average gloom crawler has from thirty to forty tentacles, each 15 to 30 feet long. Besides suction cups, each tentacle has a small eye near the tip that allows the creature to see in all directions at once and to peek around corners or over ledges while remaining almost completely concealed.

Gloom crawlers are omnivores; under normal conditions, they sustain themselves on a diet of plants, moss, rodents, and other subterranean fauna. They do not, however, turn down the chance for a larger meal, such as that offered by a foolhardy adventurer who stumbles into a gloom crawler's lair.

When a potential opponent approaches a gloom crawler, the creature lashes out with its tentacles to grab the foe. A gloom crawler can bring up to five tentacles to bear against a single target. It always chooses to bite the softest target available (the one with the lowest AC).

Gnarlwood

*This creature resembles a treant, but instead of the kindly, gentle face of the tree-folk,
its face is twisted into a grim scowl. Its deep-set eyes and jagged mouth give it an almost
skull-like grimace, and its four twisted arms are tipped with sharp, woody claws.
Its leaves are deep green, almost black, and have ghostly white markings on them.
Behind it, the skeletal remains of its unfortunate victims shamble through the undergrowth.*

Gnarlwood

XP 3,900 (CR 8)
NE Huge plant
Initiative -1

DEFENSE
AC 16 (natural armor)
hp: 132 (11d12 + 55)
Resistance: Bludgeoning and piercing damage
Vulnerability: Fire damage

OFFENSE
Speed: 30 ft.
Multiattack: A gnarlwood attacks four times with clawed
branches, or it uses a spell-like ability.
Melee Attack—Clawed Branch: +9 to hit (reach 5 ft.; one
creature). *Hit:* 2d8 + 6 slashing damage.

STATISTICS
Str 22 (+6), **Dex** 9 (−1), **Con** 20 (+5),
Int 13 (+1), **Wis** 13 (+1), **Cha** 8 (−1)
Languages: Common
Skills: Perception +4, Stealth +5
Senses: Darkvision 60 ft.

TRAITS
Protected from Good: Good-aligned creatures have tactical
disadvantage when attacking a gnarlwood, and it can't
be charmed, frightened, or possessed by a good-aligned
creature.
Rend: If a single target is hit by two of the gnarlwood's
clawed branch attacks in a single turn, that target
automatically takes an additional 2d8 + 6 slashing
damage and is grappled.
Spell-like Abilities: The gnarlwood can use the following
spell-like abilities, using Wisdom as its casting ability (DC
12, attack +4). The gnarlwood doesn't need material
components to use these abilities.
At Will: *ray of sickness*
3/day: *animate dead, blight, inflict wounds*
1/day: *circle of power, dispel evil and good*
1/week: *circle of death*
Unhallowed Aura: When an undead creature within 30 feet
of a gnarlwood attacks or makes a saving throw, it can roll
1d4 along with its d20 and add the results together.

ECOLOGY
Environment: Temperate forests
Organization: Solitary or band (2–4 plus 1d6 skeletons or
zombies per gnarlwood)

Gnarlwoods grow from the seeds of treants that had the misfortune of
sprouting in cursed ground. The good nature of the treant is subverted by the
evil nourishment it gains from the earth, and the evil suffuses into its every fiber.

Most gnarlwoods die before they are much larger than twiggy saplings,
since few creatures of nature can survive on a diet of pure evil. Those
that do survive grow into menacing, twisted mockeries of treants, with

four knobby arms that end in cruel barbed claws. Gnarlwoods are spiteful,
hateful beings that seek to destroy everything they see. Bereft of any
compassion, they tear through forests accompanied by the shambling
corpses of their victims, rending and clawing whatever they meet.

Some evil druidic temples secluded deep in ancient forests are protected
by entire groves of gnarlwoods. Unfortunately for the worshippers,
eventually not even they are spared the psychotic wrath of the gnarlwood.

A gnarlwood usually begins combat by sending its undead minions into
battle ahead of itself, to distract or soften up its foes. It uses its spell-like
abilities against targets it deems most hateful—clerics and paladins are
high priority, followed by other spellcasters. During battle, it tries to keep
its undead minions within range of its undead blessing aura. A gnarlwood
constantly howls and wails in its uncanny, hollow voice during battle, and
always fights to the death.

Gohl

This creature appears as a floating blob of mottled black and gray flesh. From its central form sprout six long tentacles and three snakelike heads, each head perched atop a thin, serpentine neck. Each head has a mouth lined with pointed fangs. Smaller tentacles constantly extend from the central mass only to disappear back into it as quickly as they appeared.

Gohl (Hydra Cloud)

XP 3,900 (CR 8)
CE Large aberration
Initiative +3

DEFENSE

AC 13
hp: 85 (10d10 + 30)
Saving Throws: Dex +6, Wis +4
Resistance: Bludgeoning, piercing, and slashing damage from nonsilver weapons
Immunity: Acid damage

OFFENSE

Speed: fly 30 ft.
Multiattack: A gohl bites three times and attacks six times with tentacles. Each tentacle can either slam or constrict.
Melee Attack—Bite: +7 to hit (reach 10 ft.; one creature). *Hit:* 1d6 + 4 piercing damage plus 1d8 acid damage.
Melee Attack—Tentacle Slam: +7 to hit (reach 5 ft.; one creature). *Hit:* 1d8 + 4 bludgeoning damage and the target must make a successful DC 15 Dex saving throw or be grappled.
Melee Attack—Tentacle Constriction: automatic hit (one creature already grappled by the gohl at the start of the gohl's turn). *Hit:* 1d10 + 4 bludgeoning damage.

STATISTICS

Str 18 (+4), **Dex** 17 (+3), **Con** 17 (+3), **Int** 6 (−2), **Wis** 12 (+1), **Cha** 6 (−1)
Languages: Understands Common but can't speak
Senses: Darkvision 60 ft.

ECOLOGY

Environment: Underground or ruins
Organization: Solitary

Gohls are nightmarish creatures that lurk in desolate ruins and subterranean caverns. No one is quite sure of their origin; some sages believe they traveled to the Material Plane from another dimension or even from the distant past or future. They are solitary creatures that favor humanoid prey above all else, but they are not above attacking and devouring any living thing that crosses their path.

A gohl is a 10-foot-wide, 10-foot-high, writhing mass of tentacles twined around three serpentine bodies with snakelike heads. Each head is gold with red eyes, and the mouths are lined with needle-sharp teeth. The snake bodies have gold-colored scales that shift to dark green near the central body mass, which can be any color. Gohls communicate with others of their kind by changing the colors of their tentacles and central body mass. They spend most of their lives alone, however, so when encountered by adventurers, a gohl's body is likely to be a plain, splotchy mass of black and gray.

In combat, a gohl can release a loud, metallic-sounding roar. It does this in an effort to scare adversaries—as if its horrific appearance isn't sufficient for that job.

Gohls make no effort to disguise themselves or to hide from opponents. They move to intercept intruders as soon as they detect something entering their territory. If it's not too badly outnumbered, a gohl tends to concentrate its bite attacks against a single target—preferably one that's also grappled. Foes that are killed or knocked unconscious by a gohl are carried to its lair, to be consumed later.

Copyright Notice
Author Scott Greene.

Golden Cat

This marvelous creature appears identical to any other small housecat, except for its sleek, golden fur and glowing, emerald eyes.

Golden Cat

XP 0 (CR 0)
Unaligned Tiny beast
Initiative +2

DEFENSE
AC 12
hp: 3 (2d4 – 2)

OFFENSE
Speed: 20 ft., climb 10 ft.
Melee Attack—Claws: +4 to hit (reach 5 ft.; one creature).
  Hit: 1 slashing damage.

STATISTICS
Str 6 (–2), **Dex** 15 (+2), **Con** 8 (–1),
Int 2 (–4), **Wis** 12 (+1), **Cha** 10 (+0)
Languages: Understands Common but can't speak
Senses: Darkvision 60 ft.

TRAITS
Escape Artist (1/day): The golden cat teleports up to 30 feet as a move.
Luck/Unluck (3/day): The owner of a golden cat can reroll one die and take the most favorable result, provided the golden cat is within 40 feet of its owner. Only one reroll is allowed per round. This ability is a power of the cat, which responds to its owner's telepathic request for luck. There is a downside, however. Each time the golden cat grants luck (a reroll) to its owner, it saps a bit of luck from other, nearby creatures. All other creatures (including the owner's allies) within 40 feet of the golden cat have tactical disadvantage on their first attack roll or ability check for one round.

ECOLOGY
Environment: Temperate land
Organization: Solitary

These fickle creatures are highly sought after for their magical ability to grant luck to the person fortunate enough to be selected as their owners. Some people have been known to spend extravagant amounts of gold trying first to locate a golden cat, and then to keep the cat lavishly protected, entertained, comfortable, and contented. Despite this, golden cats tend to grow bored easily with an owner. When that happens, they wander off on their own in search of someone new and interesting to bestow their good luck upon. It's important to note that a golden cat bestows luck on an owner only while it's pleased to belong to that creature. Nothing compels a golden cat to provide luck against its will, just because it was asked. Imprisoning a golden cat with the intention of forcing it to supply good luck is a sure way to lose its favor and guarantee that it provides no bonuses at all. Frequently carrying one into dangerous, frightening situations and cold, damp, lightless dungeons is another.

While prized by their owners for the luck they bestow, golden cats tend to be equally despised by the owner's allies for the bad luck they bring to everyone around their owner.

In the wild, golden cats tend to lair in forested areas or hilly terrain, usually near civilized lands where generous, indulgent owners are easy to find. They favor humans and elves as owners above other races, and never accept an orc, half-orc, goblin, or other savage as an owner.

A golden cat appears as a normal cat with rich golden fur and green eyes. Like all cats, a golden cat enjoys catching mice, rabbits and small birds. They fight larger creatures only if that's their only option.

Golem, Flagstone

What you thought was a section of ordinary stone floor unfurls itself before your eyes, assuming a humanoid form almost 10 feet tall. The words "You shall not pass" echo through the area as the creature advances.

Flagstone Golem

XP 2,900 (CR 7)
Unaligned Large construct
Initiative −1

DEFENSE

AC 15 (natural armor)
hp: 114 (12d10 + 48)
Resistance: Bludgeoning, piercing, and slashing damage from weapons that are neither magical nor adamantine
Immunity: Force, lightning, poison, psychic, radiant, and thunder damage; charm, fright, paralysis, petrification; any effect that would alter the golem's form

OFFENSE

Speed: 30 ft.
Multiattack: A flagstone golem attacks twice with fists.
Melee Attack—Fist: +7 to hit (reach 5 ft.; one creature). *Hit:* 2d10 + 4 bludgeoning damage. If both attacks hit the same target, the target must make a successful DC 15 Con saving throw or be knocked prone and stunned until the start of the flagstone golem's next turn.

STATISTICS

Str 19 (+4), **Dex** 9 (−1), **Con** 18 (+4), **Int** 3 (−4), **Wis** 11 (+0), **Cha** 1 (−5)
Languages: Understands its creator's language but can't speak
Senses: Darkvision 60 ft.

TRAITS

Camouflage: While lying flat on the ground, a flagstone golem can't be distinguished from normal floor.
Energy Absorption: If a flagstone golem is hit by an attack that causes damage of a type it is immune to, it takes no damage but instead heals 1 hit point per 3 points of damage the attack would have inflicted. Excess hit points are gained as temporary hit points.
Energy Burst: As an action, a flagstone golem can "release" temporary hit points as a blast of energy. All creatures within 20 feet of the flagstone golem take force damage equal to the number of temporary hit points being released, or half damage with a successful DC 14 Dex saving throw. This attack expels all of the flagstone golem's temporary hit points.
Flatten: As an action, a flagstone golem can flatten itself onto the ground and become indistinguishable from normal flagstone flooring or any other flat, stone surface. While flattened, the golem becomes immune to all the damage types it is normally resistant to. Resuming humanoid shape takes another action.
Magic Resistance: A flagstone golem has tactical advantage on saving throws versus spells and magical effects.

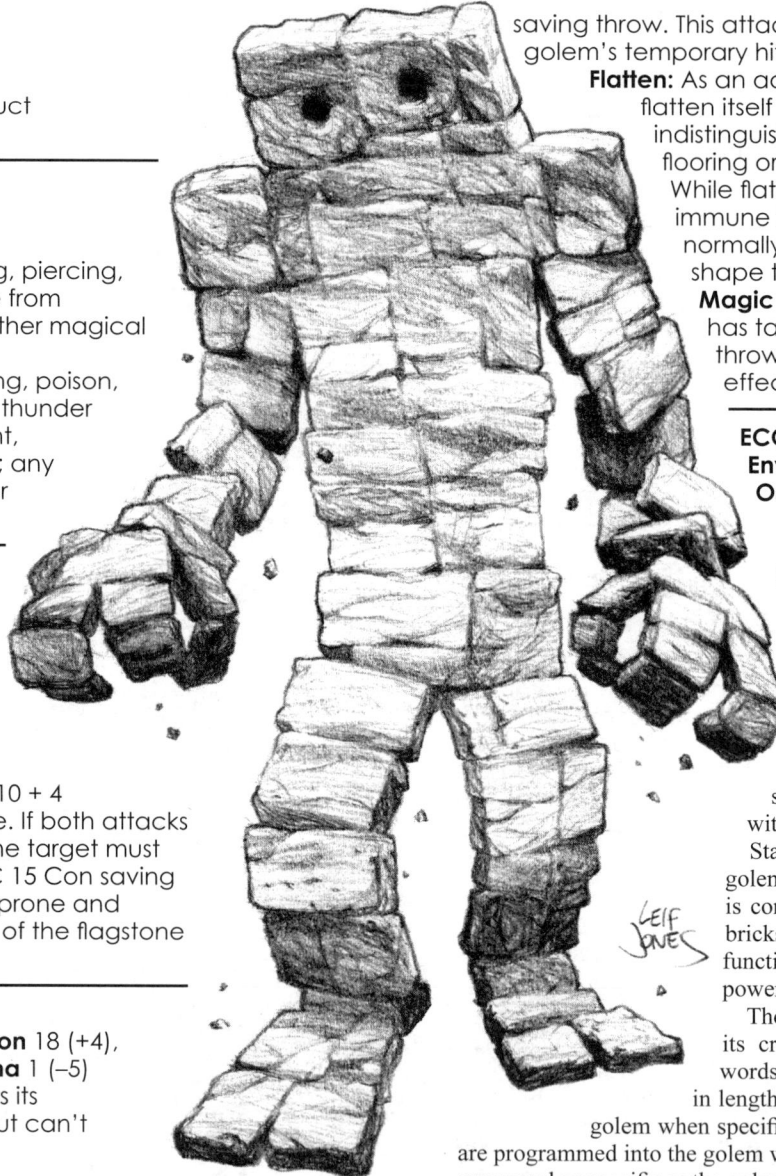

ECOLOGY

Environment: Any
Organization: Solitary

A flagstone golem is composed of flagstones—large, flat stones used in paving and flooring—jointed and fitted together so as to allow the creature to fold itself flat. They are created to serve as guardians or servants by powerful spellcasters, and have been the death of many an unsuspecting rogue. They are most useful in situations where something needs to be protected but without having obvious guards around it.

Standing unfolded and upright, a flagstone golem stands 10 feet tall. Its humanoid form is composed of flat stones (and occasionally bricks). Two darkened sockets on its head function as eyes. Its arms are thick and powerful and end in stony, clenched fists.

Though a flagstone golem can't converse, its creator can program up to four simple words or phrases (no more than four words in length) into it. Those words are spoken by the golem when specified conditions are met. These conditions are programmed into the golem when it is constructed. Conditions can be as general or specific as the golem's creator wants, but they must be fairly simple, such as "if anyone but me enters this room, say 'go back'," or "if anyone but me touches this book, say 'don't be foolish'."

A flagstone golem tasked with guarding or securing a location usually flattens itself onto the floor so it will go unnoticed until too late. For obvious reasons, those who create such golems usually design the rooms where the golems will stand guard with an eye toward giving the golem plenty of camouflage. When an interloper violates the conditions set out by the golem's creator, it rises into its humanoid form and attacks with powerful blows from its fists.

A flagstone golem is constructed from brick, stone, various powders, and exotic liquids totaling 2,500 gp in value.

Golem, Furnace

This 20-foot-tall construct looks like a humanoid clad in black iron armor.
A large grate-covered opening in its abdomen reveals a roaring fire in its innards.

Furnace Golem

XP 5,000 (CR 9)
Unaligned Large construct
Initiative –1

DEFENSE

AC 16 (natural armor)
hp: 152 (16d10 + 64)
Resistance: Cold damage
Immunity: Fire, poison, and psychic damage; bludgeoning, piercing, and slashing damage from weapons that are neither magical nor adamantine; charm, fright, paralysis, petrification; any effect that would alter the golem's form

OFFENSE

Speed: 20 ft.
Multiattack: A furnace golem attacks twice with fists or once with flame breath. It can't attack with its fists while it has a creature grappled.
Melee Attack—Fist: +10 to hit (reach 5 ft.; one creature). *Hit:* 2d8 + 6 bludgeoning damage plus 1d8 fire damage. If both attacks hit the same target, the target is grappled (see Furnace, below).
Area Attack—Flame Breath (recharge 6): automatic hit (50-ft. line; creatures in line). *Hit:* 10d8 fire damage, or half damage with a successful DC 16 Dex saving throw.

STATISTICS

Str 22 (+6), **Dex** 9 (–1), **Con** 19 (+4),
Int 3 (–4), **Wis** 11 (+0), **Cha** 1 (–5)
Languages: Understands its creator's language but can't speak
Senses: Darkvision 60 ft.

TRAITS

Cold and Fire Sensitivity: If a furnace golem takes cold damage, its speed is halved, it can't take bonus actions, and it can make only one attack until the end of its next turn. If it is attacked with fire, it takes no damage but instead heals 1 hit point per 3 points of fire damage the attack would have inflicted. Excess hit points are gained as temporary hit points.
Furnace: As a bonus action at the start of its turn, a furnace golem can try to shove a grappled opponent into its interior furnace. The furnace golem makes a Str check that is opposed by the grappled creature's Str (Athletics) or Dex (Acrobatics) check. If the grappled creature wins the contest, nothing happens. If the furnace golem wins the contest, the grappled creature is shoved into the furnace, where it is blinded and restrained. The trapped creature takes 2d8 + 4 fire damage and gains one level of exhaustion at the start of each of its turns. The creature remains trapped until it uses an action to win an opposed Str (Athletics) or Dex (Acrobatics) check against the furnace golem's Con check. Alternatively, a creature outside the furnace golem can attempt a Str (Athletics) or Dex (Acrobatics) check against the golem's Con check to drag the trapped character free, but the rescuer automatically takes 2d8 + 4 fire damage whether the attempt succeeds or fails. Only one creature of up to Medium size can be inside the golem's furnace.
Heat: A furnace golem's entire form is extremely hot. Creatures that attack a furnace golem with unarmed attacks or with natural weapons take 1d8 fire damage each time one of their attacks hits.
Magic Resistance: A furnace golem has tactical advantage on saving throws versus spells and magical effects.

ECOLOGY

Environment: Any
Organization: Solitary

Furnace golems are most often used to guard some arcane secret or treasure, though some are programmed to seek out objects or individuals. Those used as guards stand motionless, appearing as nothing more than a giant black iron statue, until activated.

Like other constructs, furnace golems obey their creator's commands to the best of their ability. Should the creator die or its commands be impossible to follow, the furnace golem becomes an uncontrolled rogue; it remains completely functional, but it follows no commands or orders from anyone, being driven purely by its own limited, erratic intelligence.

The fire powering a furnace golem is magical in nature; it needs no fuel to continue burning forever and it can't be extinguished except by more potent magic. If a furnace golem is destroyed, the fire in its innards continues burning for days before fading to a flicker and eventually dying.

A furnace golem's body is constructed from 8,000 pounds of iron mixed with rare ingredients and chemicals totaling 12,000 gp.

Copyright Notice
Author Scott Greene

Golem, Stone Guardian

This automaton looks to be carved from mud and stone. It stands as tall as a human, and where its heart would be—if it were alive—is a fist-sized, rounded, red stone.

Stone Guardian Golem

XP 450 (CR 2)
Unaligned Medium construct
Initiative -1

DEFENSE

AC 14 (natural armor)
hp: 42 (5d10 + 15)
Resistance: Cold, fire, and lightning damage
Immunity: Poison and psychic damage; bludgeoning, piercing, and slashing damage from weapons that are neither magical nor adamantine; charm, fright, paralysis, petrification; any effect that would alter the golem's form

OFFENSE

Speed: 20 ft.
Multiattack: A stone guardian golem attacks twice with fists.
Melee Attack—Fist: +5 to hit (reach 5 ft.; one creature). *Hit:* 1d10 + 3 bludgeoning damage.

STATISTICS

Str 17 (+3), **Dex** 9 (–1), **Con** 17 (+3), **Int** 6 (–2), **Wis** 8 (–1), **Cha** 2 (–4)
Languages: Understands its creator's language but can't speak
Senses: Truesight 60 ft.

TRAITS

Fortified: A stone guardian never takes additional damage from critical hits.
Ring Link: A stone guardian is linked to a magic ring. The construct will never attack any creature that wears this ring, or any creatures within 10 feet of the ringwearer, unless one of those creatures attacks the guardian first.

ECOLOGY

Environment: Any
Organization: Solitary or gang (2–4)

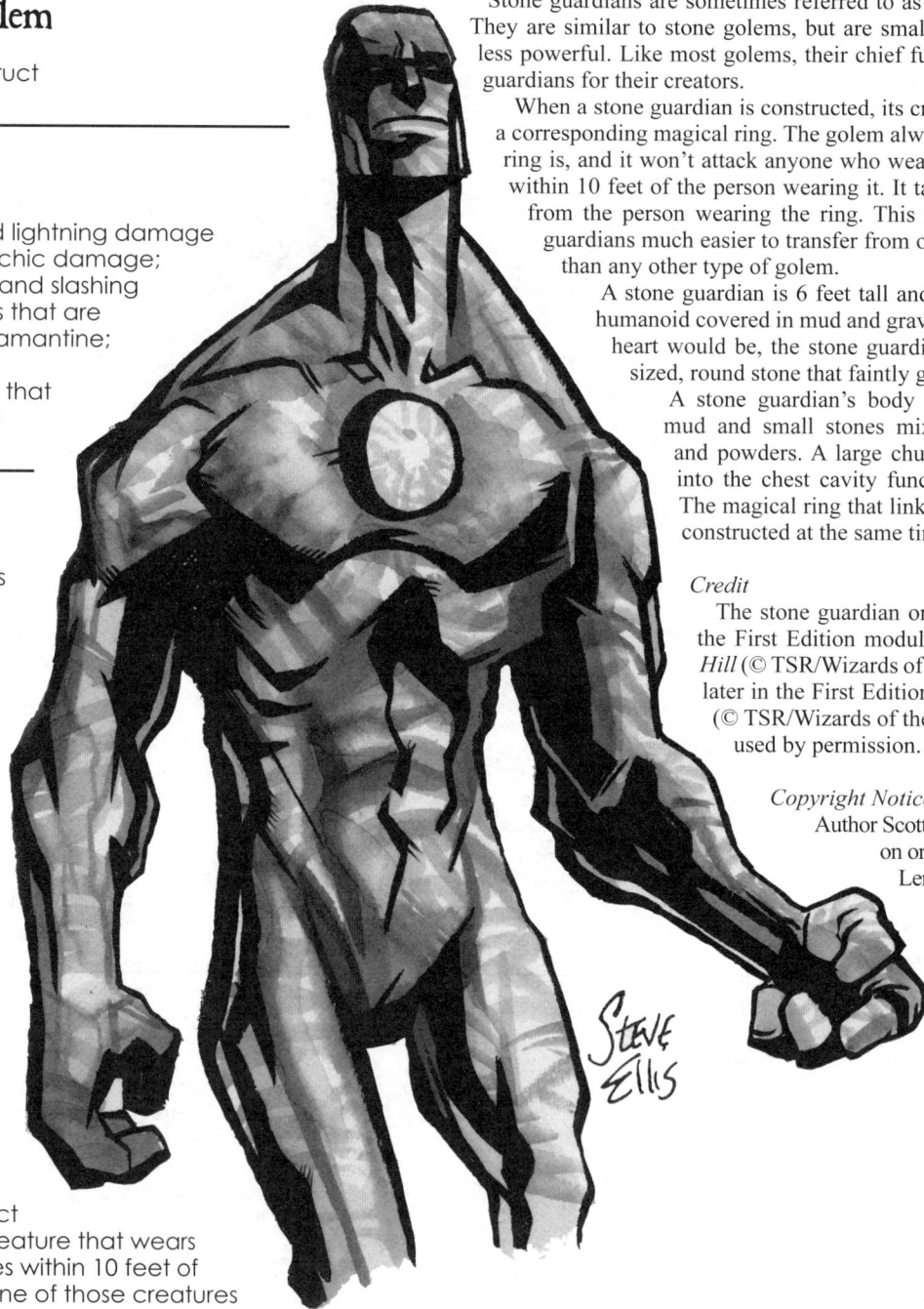

Stone guardians are sometimes referred to as lesser stone golems. They are similar to stone golems, but are smaller and considerably less powerful. Like most golems, their chief function is to serve as guardians for their creators.

When a stone guardian is constructed, its creator must also craft a corresponding magical ring. The golem always knows where the ring is, and it won't attack anyone who wears the ring or who is within 10 feet of the person wearing it. It takes commands only from the person wearing the ring. This feature makes stone guardians much easier to transfer from one master to another than any other type of golem.

A stone guardian is 6 feet tall and resembles a stocky humanoid covered in mud and gravel. Where a human's heart would be, the stone guardian golem has a fist-sized, round stone that faintly glows and pulses.

A stone guardian's body is constructed from mud and small stones mixed with rare herbs and powders. A large chunk of stone inserted into the chest cavity functions as its "heart." The magical ring that links a stone guardian is constructed at the same time.

Credit

The stone guardian originally appeared in the First Edition module *L1 Secret of Bone Hill* (© TSR/Wizards of the Coast, 1981) and later in the First Edition *Monster Manual II* (© TSR/Wizards of the Coast, 1983) and is used by permission.

Copyright Notice
Author Scott Greene, based on original material by Lenard Lakofka

Golem, Wooden

This automaton is human-sized and resembles an ornately carved wooden statue.

Wooden Golem

XP 700 (CR 3)
Unaligned Medium construct
Initiative −1

DEFENSE

AC 14 (natural armor)
hp: 60 (8d8 + 24)
Resistance: Bludgeoning, piercing, and slashing damage from weapons that are neither magical nor adamantine
Immunity: Cold, poison, psychic, and radiant damage; charm, fright, paralysis, petrification; any effect that would alter the golem's form
Vulnerability: Fire damage

OFFENSE

Speed: 30 ft.
Multiattack: A wooden golem attacks twice with longswords.
Melee Attack—Longsword: +6 to hit (reach 5 ft.; one creature). *Hit:* 1d8 + 4 bludgeoning damage.

STATISTICS

Str 18 (+4), **Dex** 9 (−1), **Con** 16 (+3), **Int** 3 (−4), **Wis** 9 (−1), **Cha** 1 (−5)
Languages: Understands its creator's language but can't speak
Senses: Darkvision 60 ft.

TRAITS

Alarm (1/day): All creatures with hearing and within 30 feet of a wooden golem when it howls an alarm must make a successful DC 13 Con saving throw or be deafened for 10 minutes.
Camouflage: While standing still, a wooden golem can't be distinguished from a wooden statue.
Magic Resistance: A wooden golem has tactical advantage on saving throws versus spells and magical effects.

ECOLOGY

Environment: Any
Organization: Solitary

Arcane spellcasters used several ancient texts to arrive at a process to create inexpensive yet still reasonably powerful golems. They had master craftsmen create wooden statues with articulated limbs and then performed the proper spells to animate and control them. The statues vary widely in shape and form, but most have weapons in both hands.

The original wooden golems were designed to act both as guards and as alarms, and most still do. Wooden golems can emit a deafening howl when intruders enter the area they've been set to guard. Besides deafening nearby intruders, this howl can be heard through 600 feet of winding corridor and carries for up to two miles in the open.

Wooden golems are usually programmed to seek cover against ranged weapons and spells, but lacking any real sense of self-preservation, they never break off combat simply because they're losing.

A wooden golem is assembled from blocks of fine wood and sprinkled during its construction with rare powders and crushed herbs worth at least 300 gp. The head of a destroyed wooden golem can be turned into a fine sculpture for a mantel or entryway, if it wasn't damaged in battle. Some collectors pay handsomely for such relics.

Credit
Wood golems originally appeared in the Necromancer Games adventure *Hall of the Rainbow Mage*.

Copyright Notice
Authors Scott Greene and Patrick Lawinger.

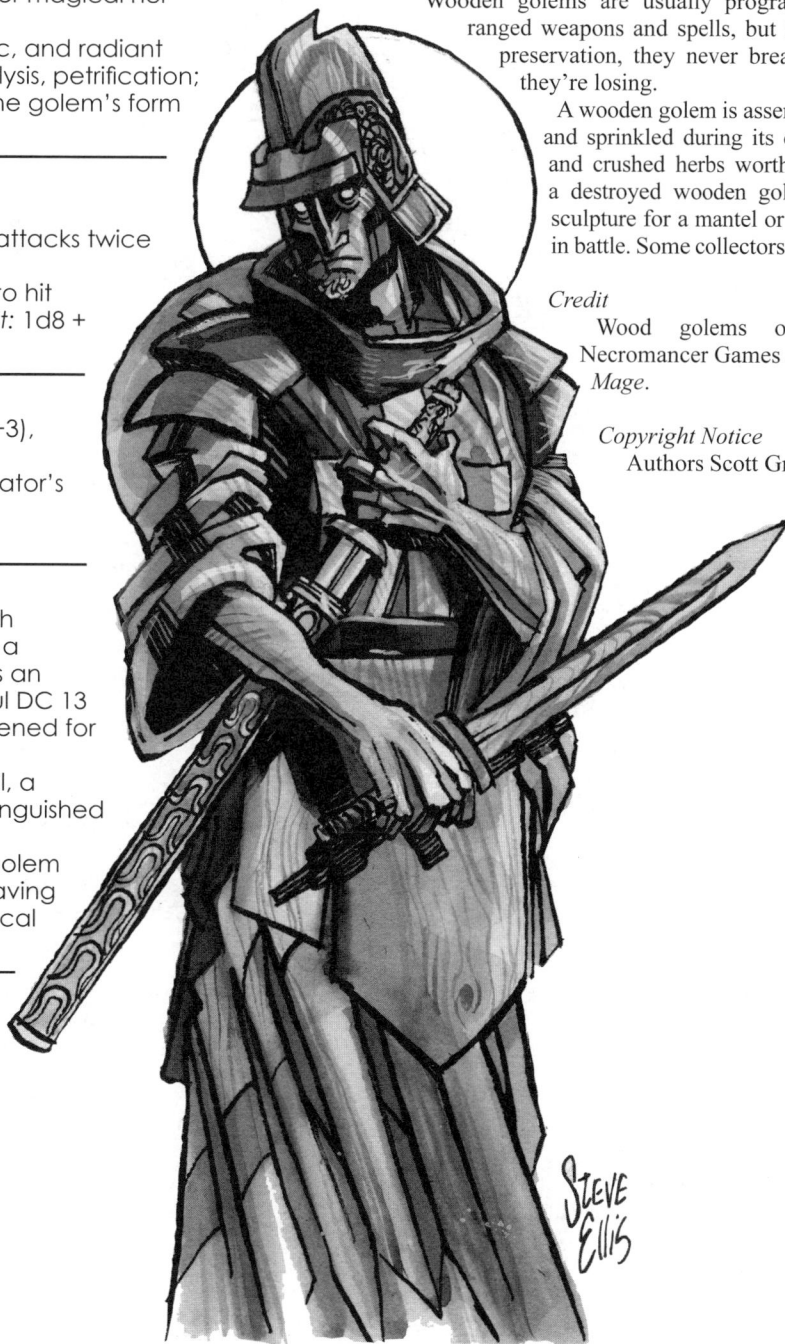

Gorbel

This bizarre creature is a small, floating orb with reddish skin.
Atop its round body are six eyestalks, each ending in a sapphire-colored eye.
Dangling beneath its body are two stubby, rubbery legs that end in claws.

Gorbel

XP 50 (CR 1/4)
N Small aberration
Initiative +2

DEFENSE

AC 12
hp: 11 (2d8 + 2)
Resistance: Bludgeoning damage

OFFENSE

Speed: 5 ft., fly 40 ft.
Multiattack: A gorbel bites once and attacks once with claws.
Melee Attack—Bite: +4 to hit (reach 5 ft.; one creature). *Hit:* 1d6 + 2 piercing damage.
Melee Attack—Claw: +4 to hit (reach 15 ft.; one creature). *Hit:* 1d4 slashing damage. A target of Small size or smaller is pulled to within 5 feet of the gorbel; if the target is Medium size or larger, the gorbel pulls itself to within 5 feet of the target.

STATISTICS

Str 12 (+1), **Dex** 14 (+2),
Con 12 (+1), **Int** 8 (–1), **Wis** 9 (–1),
Cha 8 (–1)
Languages: Deep Speech
Senses: Darkvision 60 ft.

TRAITS

Explosive: When a gorbel takes piercing or slashing damage, it must make a successful Con saving throw or it explodes. The DC for the saving throw equals 5 plus the damage taken from the attack. When it explodes, all creatures within 5 feet of it take 1d6 + 1 force damage, or half damage with a successful DC 11 Dex saving throw. The gorbel dies instantly, of course.

ECOLOGY

Environment: Warm forests
Organization: Solitary or swarm (2–10)

The gorbel is a strange creature approximately 3 feet in diameter, possibly related to the gas spore. Its reddish skin is a tough, rubbery membrane that is tragically thin. The spherical body of a gorbel is filled with a lighter-than-air gas that smells of rotten eggs (sulfur) and that reacts violently with air.

A gorbel eats, breathes, and excretes through an aperture best described as a mouth. This mouth is lined with a ring of sharp teeth that face inward to help it force food into its gullet.

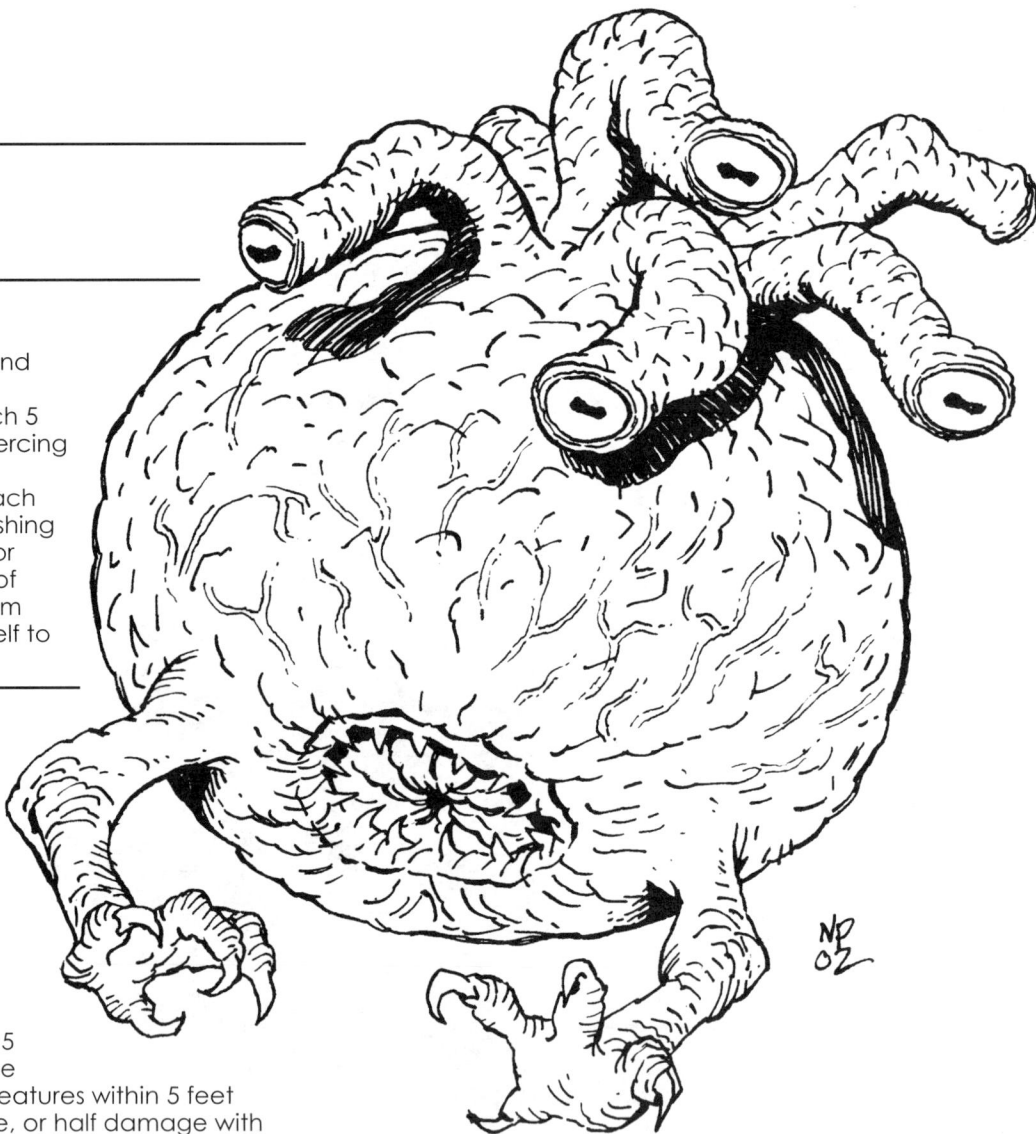

Gorbels primarily attack with their claws, which they can extend elastically to tremendous lengths and hook into prey. They then either drag the prey to their mouths, or drag their mouths to the prey. A gorbel will attack and try to eat whatever it suspects might be edible—generally, that covers anything that moves. The strange metabolic processes that produce the gorbel's light-than-air gas also instill it with an insatiable hunger.

Credit
The gorbel originally appeared in the First Edition *Fiend Folio* (© TSR/Wizards of the Coast, 1981) and is used by permission.

Copyright Notice
Author Scott Greene, based on original material by Andrew Key

Gorgimera

This hideous creature has leathery dragon wings and three heads; one each resembling a lion, a dragon, and a gorgon. The back half of its body resembles a gorgon's hindquarters, and the front half resembles a great lion.

Gorgimera

XP 2,900 (CR 7)
Unaligned Large monstrosity
Initiative +1

DEFENSE
AC 17 (natural armor)
hp: 95 (10d10 + 40)
Immunity: Petrification

OFFENSE
Speed: 30 ft., fly 50 ft.
Multiattack: A gorgimera bites once, and attacks once with its horns and twice with claws. The horn attack can be replaced by gorgon breath, and the bite attack can be replaced by dragon breath.
Melee Attack—Bite: +7 to hit (reach 5 ft.; one creature). *Hit:* 2d8 + 4 piercing damage.
Melee Attack—Claw: +7 to hit (reach 5 ft.; one creature). *Hit:* 1d8 + 4 slashing damage.
Melee Attack—Horns: +7 to hit (reach 5 ft.; one creature). *Hit:* 1d8 + 4 bludgeoning damage.
Area Attack—Dragon Breath (recharge 5, 6): automatic hit (range varies; creatures in area). *Hit:* 3d8 damage (type varies), or half damage with a successful DC 15 Dex saving throw.
Area Attack—Gorgon Breath (recharge 5, 6): automatic hit (range 30-ft. cone; creatures in cone). *Hit:* targets must make a successful DC 15 Con saving throw or be restrained as they begin turning to stone. A restrained creature attempts the saving throw again at the end of

its next turn. If the second saving throw succeeds, the effect ends. If the second saving throw fails, the target is permanently petrified; a *greater restoration* spell can reverse the petrification.

STATISTICS
Str 19 (+4), **Dex** 13 (+1), **Con** 19 (+4),
Int 4 (–3), **Wis** 13 (+1), **Cha** 10 (+0)
Languages: Draconic
Skills: Perception +4
Senses: Darkvision 60 ft.

TRAITS
Dragon Breath (recharge 5, 6): The breath weapon used by a gorgimera's dragon head depends on the color of its dragon head, as listed on the table below. Regardless of its type, a gorgimera's breath weapon deals 3d8 points of damage, or half damage to targets that make a successful DC 15 Dex saving throw. To determine a gorgimera's head color and breath weapon randomly, roll 1d10 and consult the table.

1d10	Head Color	Breath Weapon	Damage
1–2	Black	40-foot line	acid
3–4	Blue	40-foot line	lightning
5–6	Green	20-foot cone	gas (acid)
7–8	Red	20-foot cone	fire
9–10	White	20-foot cone	cold

ECOLOGY
Environment: Temperate hills and mountains
Organization: Solitary or pair

A gorgimera is a chimerical creature with the heads of a lion, a dragon, and a gorgon. It has the hindquarters of a gorgon and the forequarters of a lion. A gorgimera's dragon head can be that of any of the chromatic dragons. The lion head has no mane, and the scaled gorgon head is a deep navy blue with glowing red eyes.

These creatures are highly territorial predators, and their hunting range covers many square miles around their lairs. The creature makes its home inside deep caverns with openings atop high mountains. A typical lair contains a mated pair and one or two young.

A gorgimera prefers to attack from ambush or to plunge suddenly onto unsuspecting targets from high in the sky. It usually attacks by biting with its dragon head, butting with its gorgon head, and slashing with its leonine paws. The dragon and gorgon heads can also use their characteristic breath weapons.

Credit
The gorgimera originally appeared in the First Edition module *S4 Lost Caverns of Tsojcanth* (© TSR/Wizards of the Coast, 1982) and later in the First Edition *Monster Manual II* (© TSR/Wizards of the Coast, 1983) and is used by permission.

Copyright Notice
Author Scott Greene, based on original material by Gary Gygax

Gorilla Bear

This creature resembles a massive gorilla with shaggy, dark fur and the forepaws of a powerful bear. Its head and face mix the features of both a gorilla and a bear.

Gorilla Bear

XP 200 (CR 1)
Unaligned Medium monstrosity
Initiative +2

DEFENSE
AC 13 (natural armor)
hp: 26 (4d8 + 8)

OFFENSE
Speed: 40 ft., climb 30 ft.
Multiattack: A gorilla bear attacks twice with claws.
Melee Attack—Claw: +6 to hit (reach 5 ft.; one creature).
Hit: 1d6 + 4 slashing damage. If both claw attacks hit the same target, the target is grappled and restrained, and it takes an additional 2d6 bludgeoning damage. The grapple ends automatically at the start of the gorilla bear's next turn, if the creature hasn't escaped before then.

STATISTICS
Str 18 (+4), **Dex** 14 (+2), **Con** 14 (+2),
Int 4 (−3), **Wis** 12 (+1), **Cha** 7 (−2)
Languages: None
Skills: Athletics +6, Perception +3
Senses: Darkvision 60 ft.

ECOLOGY
Environment: Warm forests
Organization: Solitary, pair, or troop (3-6)

Gorilla bears are the result of the same, or similar, magical crossbreeding that created the owlbear. In this case, the creatures merged were an ape (not necessarily a gorilla, despite the name) and a black bear. The resulting creature is smaller than an owlbear, but somewhat more intelligent.

A gorilla bear's fur ranges in color from jet black to brownish-black. Older creatures have a distinct stripe of gray fur running down their backs. Their forepaws and hind feet end in bear claws, not a gorilla's nails. On its hind feet, a typical gorilla bear stands 8 feet tall, but they spend most of the their time on all fours.

Legends speak of an immensely powerful, white-furred gorilla bear with eyes the color of amethysts, but such a pelt has never been sold or displayed in any civilized land.

Gorilla bears make their lairs in caves hidden among the twisted tangle of trees and shrubs. A typical lair contains a single adult male, one to three adult females, and one to four young. Many adult males live alone. Gorilla bears are daylight hunters with a stronger taste for fresh meat than either bears or gorillas. They've been known to actually trail and hunt both goblins and elves, presumably because they enjoy the taste of those creatures' flesh more than any other.

Gorilla bears are highly aggressive. They seldom retreat from a fight, but they have been known to flee from fiery magic. Escaping from a pack of attacking gorilla bears is next to impossible, given their great speed both on the ground and through the treetops. If a gorilla bear gets both paws onto a foe, it's capable of delivering a crushing hug, but they always release the victim almost immediately to resume slashing with their claws.

Credit

The gorilla bear originally appeared in the First Edition *Fiend Folio* (© TSR/Wizards of the Coast, 1981) and is used by permission.

Copyright Notice

Author Scott Greene, based on original material by Cricky Hitchcock.

Gray Nisp

This creature is a tall, hairless humanoid with smooth, slick skin; its hands and feet are webbed and clawed, and its face has large, dark eyes with no visible pupils. It likewise has no nose or ears, and its wide, fishlike mouth is filled with sharp teeth.

Gray Nisp

XP 2,300 (CR 6)
CN Large fey
Initiative +3

DEFENSE

AC 15 (natural armor)
hp: 95 (10d10 + 40)

OFFENSE

Speed: 10 ft., swim 40 ft.
Multiattack: A gray nisp bites once and attacks twice with claws.
Melee Attack—Bite: +6 to hit (reach 5 ft.; one creature). *Hit:* 1d12 + 3 piercing damage.
Melee Attack—Claw: +6 to hit (reach 5 ft.; one creature). *Hit:* 1d10 + 3 slashing damage. If both claws hit the same target, it takes an additional 1d10 + 3 slashing damage.

STATISTICS

Str 17 (+3), **Dex** 17 (+3), **Con** 19 (+4),
Int 5 (–3), **Wis** 12 (+1), **Cha** 7 (–2)
Languages: Unique (Gray Nisp)
Senses: Darkvision 60 ft., tremorsense 180 ft.

TRAITS

Keen Scent: A gray nisp can taste blood in the surrounding water from a distance of up to 1 mile.
Spell-like Abilities: A gray nisp can use the following spell-like abilities, using Wisdom as its casting ability (DC 12, attack +4). The gray nisp doesn't need material components to use these abilities.
At Will: *confusion, detect thoughts, minor illusion* (auditory only), *hold monster, slow*
Water Dependent: A gray nisp can survive out of water for only 10 minutes. After that, it begins suffocating.

ECOLOGY

Environment: Temperate and warm aquatic
Organization: Solitary

Nisps are a race of water-based fey creatures that dwell in oceans, seas, lakes, rivers, and occasionally swamps, provided they can find deep enough water there. They are aggressive hunters that dine on anything they can catch and kill. This fearsome creature is 9 feet tall, with light gray skin and a white underbelly. It has large, wicked talons and a frighteningly large mouth that is filled with daggerlike teeth.

Gray nisps dwell alone in deep water; caves on the ocean floor or hollows at the bottom of large lakes are where they usually hide their lairs. They are solitary and territorial, and they have a keen sense of smell while underwater.

Nisps do not reason the way most creatures do. They have no concepts of love, duty, or hatred, and they seem completely unsympathetic to the pain and suffering of others. While they seldom leave their watery homes or interact with creatures on land, tremendous curiosity drives them to investigate whenever creatures stray too close to their lairs. To satisfy their curiosity, nisps are more likely to pull intruders apart limb by limb to see how they are built than to ask questions—or they will ask their questions as they are pulling someone apart, and become annoyed when the person doesn't answer clearly. They have enough intelligence to realize that most other humanoids are smarter than them, and this understanding also makes them irritable and unpredictable. Even other aquatic creatures such as kuo-toa and sahuagin tend to leave gray nisps alone, although sahuagin have been known to enlist their aid on rare occasions.

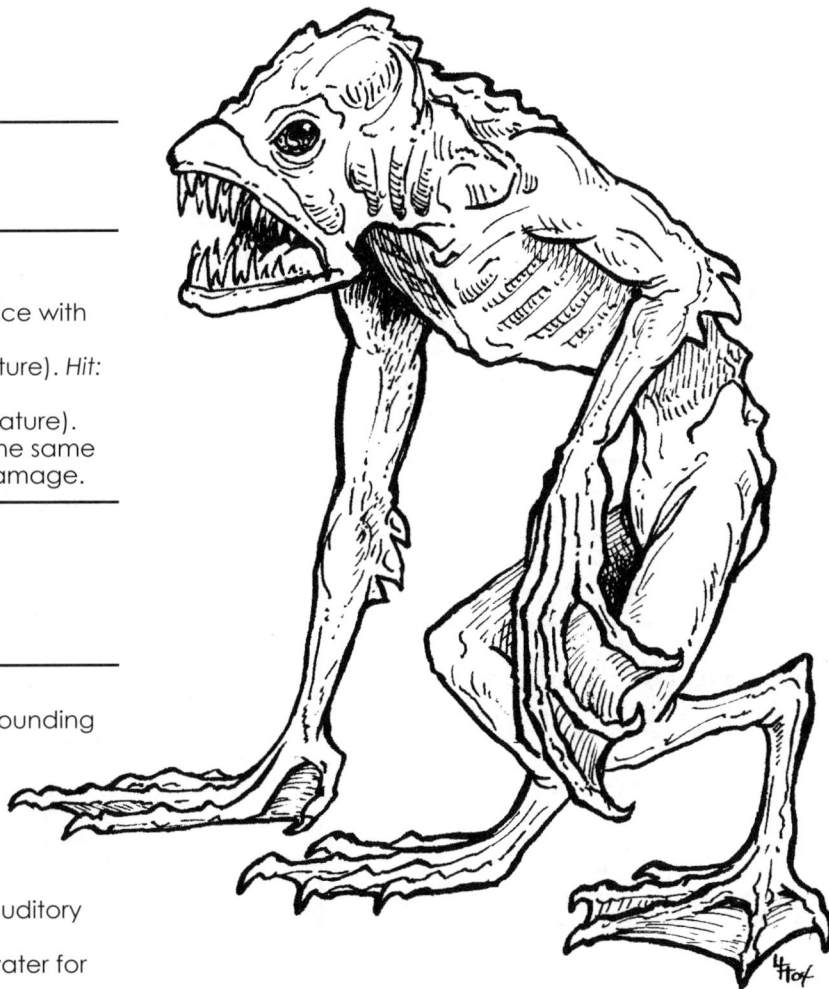

Gray nisps surprise intruders if they can. They are unpredictable in all things, including combat. They can be engaged in conversation if the stranger has something the gray nisp wants that can't easily be snatched away. Sadly, their innate stupidity usually leads to increasing frustration, and finally a burst into violence. It is never wise to goad or even drift too close to a nisp that is showing signs of impatience.

Green Brain

This creature resembles a walking cauliflower head—but instead of white cauliflower, its leaves wrap around a pulsing, fleshy brain.

Green Brain

XP 200 (CR 1)
LE Small plant
Initiative +2

DEFENSE

AC 12
hp: 17 (5d6)
Immunity: Psychic damage; fright, stun, unconsciousness

OFFENSE

Speed: 10 ft., fly 30 ft.
Ranged Attack—Psychic Bolt: automatic hit (range 50 ft.; one creature). *Hit:* 2d8 + 3 psychic damage, or half damage if the target makes a successful DC 13 Int saving throw.

STATISTICS

Str 6 (–2), **Dex** 14 (+2), **Con** 10 (+0), **Int** 7 (–2), **Wis** 12 (+1), **Cha** 16 (+3)
Languages: Telepathy
Senses: Truesight 60 ft.

TRAITS

Psychic Waves (1/day): As an action, a green brain can emit a pulse of psychic energy to debilitate and disarm potential foes. The pulse affects all creatures with Int 3 or higher within 50 feet of the green brain.

- Every creature in the affected area must make a successful DC 13 Int saving throw or be affected as if poisoned until the start of the green brain's next turn. This is a psychic effect, not poison, so resistance to poison provides no defense against it.
- Every creature in the affected area must make a successful DC 13 Dex saving throw or drop everything it is holding in its hands.
- Every spellcaster in the affected area must make a successful DC 13 Con saving throw or be unable to cast spells for 1d4 rounds.

ECOLOGY

Environment: Underground
Organization: Solitary or pair

Green brains are plant creatures grown by myconids and other malevolent races with aptitudes for magically altering and breeding plants. Green brains are reasonably intelligent, psychically potent, and entirely free of personal ambitions or thoughts of freedom, traits that make them useful to their masters for supervising and overseeing the activities of mindless or semi-intelligent creatures. Often the supervised species will be other plant creatures of some kind, but a green brain can also supervise brutish humanoids and other non-plant creatures of low intelligence.

The telepathy of green brains allows them to project mental commands and communication at a deep enough level that the brain's demands are clear even to mindless creatures such as oozes or monstrous plants. Indeed, the less intelligent the recipient of the orders, the stronger the green brain's hold over it.

Credit
Author Matt Finch

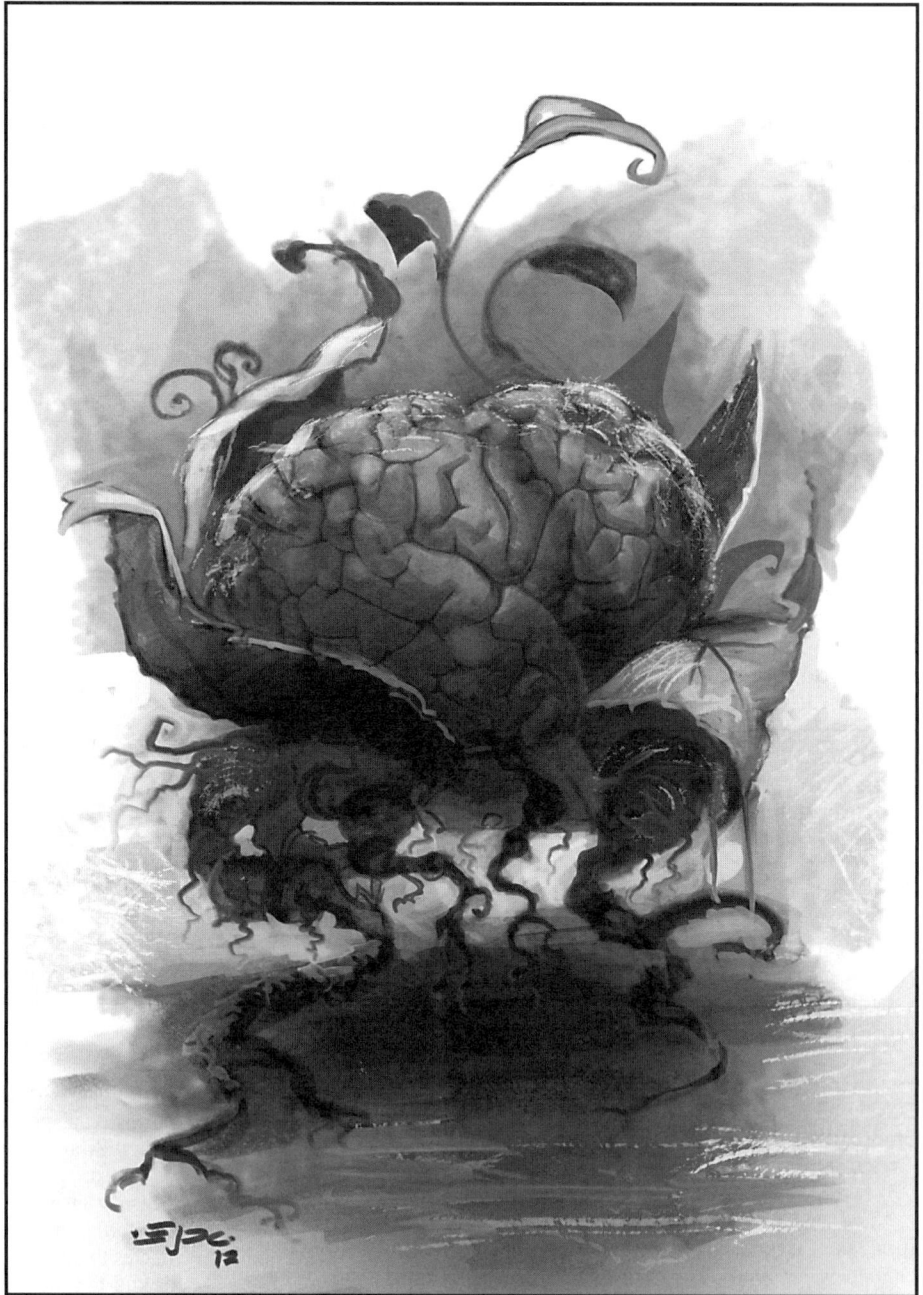

Grimm

This enormous humanoid stands well over 9 feet tall. Its flesh is a very dark blue-green and glistens as if coated with oil. Its head is oval and pointed, and its eyes show as dull, ivory-colored pits without visible pupils. Its mouth is almost too wide for its face and is crowded with two rows of fanglike teeth and a long, snaky tongue that flicks in and out past its thin, scaly lips. The monster's powerful arms and legs end in wicked claws that sport broken, jagged, yet incredibly sharp and tough fingernails.

Grimm

XP 2,900 (CR 7)
NE Large fey
Initiative +2

DEFENSE
AC 14 (natural armor)
hp: 104 (11d10 + 44)
Saving Throws: Con +7
Resistance: Bludgeoning, piercing, and slashing damage from weapons that aren't silver or good-aligned

---

OFFENSE
Speed: 30 ft.
Multiattack: A grimm attacks twice with its claws, then bites once.
Melee Attack—Claw: +8 to hit (reach 5 ft.; one creature). *Hit:* 1d10 + 5 slashing damage. If both claw attacks hit the same target, the grimm gains tactical advantage on its bite attack if it makes that attack immediately against the same target.
Melee Attack—Bite: +8 to hit (reach 5 ft.; one creature). *Hit:* 3d10 + 5 piercing damage. Also see devour, below.

STATISTICS
Str 20 (+5), **Dex** 14 (+2), **Con** 19 (+4),
Int 12 (+1), **Wis** 14 (+2), **Cha** 16 (+3)
Languages: Understands Common and Sylvan but can't speak
Skills: Stealth +5
Senses: Blindsight 10 ft., Darkvision 60 ft.

TRAITS
Aura of Evil: A grimm constantly exudes a miasma of evil around itself. Any creature that begins its turn within 5 feet of a grimm takes 2d6 radiant damage. Creatures of evil alignment are immune to this effect.
Diehard: A grimm does not die when it reaches 0 hit points. Instead, the creature continues fighting, but it must make a Con saving throw every time it takes damage while at 0 hit points. The DC of the saving throw equals the damage from the attack. The first time the grimm fails this saving throw, it gains tactical disadvantage on all its attack rolls and ability checks, but it keeps fighting. When it fails this saving throw for a second time, it dies instantly.

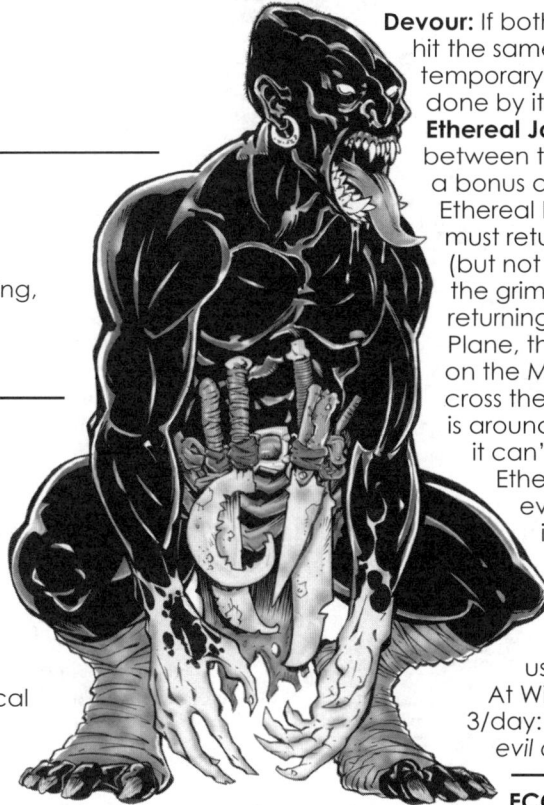

Devour: If both of a grimm's claw attacks and its bite attack hit the same target in a single turn, the grimm gains temporary hit points equal to the piercing damage done by its bite.
Ethereal Jaunt (recharge 5, 6): A grimm can shift between the Ethereal Plane and the Material Plane as a bonus action when it moves. It can remain on the Ethereal Plane only until ethereal jaunt recharges; it must return to the Material Plane on the first turn it can (but not necessarily as the first thing it does that turn; the grimm could move in the Ethereal Plane before returning to the Material Plane). While in the Ethereal Plane, the grimm can't be seen or harmed by anyone on the Material Plane except by magical effects that cross the planar boundary. It can see and hear what is around it (within 60 feet) on the Material Plane, but it can't harm anything in the Material Plane. While Ethereal, the grimm can move in any direction, even up or down and through solid objects, but it treats all space as difficult terrain.
Spell-like Abilities: A grimm can use the following spell-like abilities, using Charisma as its casting ability (DC 14, attack +6). The grimm doesn't need material components to use these abilities.
At Will: *blur*
3/day: *call lightning, darkness, detect fey* (as *detect evil and good* but detects fey only)

ECOLOGY
Environment: Mountains
Organization: Solitary

A grimm is one of the most evil of all fey. Conceived and created by members of the Unseelie Court, the monster's only purpose seems to be the destruction of life and that which is beautiful. Legends among the fairy folk say powerful members of the Unseelie Court created this fell beast (legends say a circle of powerful quickling sorcerers are responsible) to avenge the death of their kin who were slain when the Seelie and Unseelie Courts did battle.

Grimms dwell in the deepest and darkest mountains, making their lairs in deep recesses or hard to access caves and caverns, venturing forth only to kill and to eat. They eat only meat—the fresher the better, and the flesh of good-aligned fey creatures is their top choice. Any creature that crosses their path, however, is fair game. These creatures are highly territorial and do not associate with other creatures, even their own kind, for long without some force such as a powerful Unseelie noble compelling them to.

A grimm stands 9 feet tall and is stout and powerfully built. Its body ripples with muscles and is always covered in a glossy sheen.

In combat, grimm's focus their attacks on single opponents, hoping to gain temporary hit points by devouring part of their foe. If the tide of battle turns against it, a grimm will try to flee through the Ethereal Plane, but this is an unreliable gambit.

Copyright Notice
Author Scott Greene

Grippli

This creature looks like a bipedal tree frog, smaller than a halfling, and with delicate, dexterous hands in place of its forepaws. Its skin is grayish-green with dark green swirls and stripes.

Grippli

XP 50 (CR 1/4)
N Small humanoid
Initiative +3

DEFENSE
AC 13
hp: 9 (2d6 + 2)

OFFENSE
Speed: 30 ft., climb 30 ft., swim 20 ft.
Melee Attack—
Shortsword: +5 to hit (reach 5 ft.; one creature). *Hit:* 1d6 + 3 piercing damage.
Ranged Attack—
Dart: +5 to hit (range 20 ft./60 ft.; one creature). *Hit:* 1d4 + 3 piercing damage. If poison is used, see grippli poison, below.
Ranged Attack—Net: +5 to hit (range 5 ft./15 ft.; one creature). *Hit:* The target is restrained until it makes a successful DC 10 Str check or until 5 slashing damage is done to the net (AC 10). Targets of Huge size or larger are not affected.

STATISTICS
Str 10 (+0), **Dex** 16 (+3), **Con** 12 (+1),
Int 12 (+1), **Wis** 11 (+0), **Cha** 6 (–2)
Languages: Common, Unique (Grippli)
Skills: Perception +2, Stealth +4, Survival +4
Senses: Darkvision 60 ft.

TRAITS
Grippli Shaman: Any large group of gripplis (12 or more) will be accompanied by one or more tribal shamans. A grippli shaman has heightened Wisdom (13) and the ability to cast the following spells, using Wisdom as its spellcasting ability (DC 11, attack +3). It doesn't need material components to cast these spells.
Cantrips (at will): *druidcraft, guidance*
1st level (x4): *animal friendship, entangle, fog cloud, goodberry*
2nd level (x2): *lesser restoration, pass without trace*
Grippli Poison: A target hit by a poisoned grippli dart must make a successful DC 11 Con saving throw or become poisoned for 1d4 rounds. At the end of the last turn of poisoning, the target repeats the saving throw. A successful save means the target recovers, but a failed save means the target becomes paralyzed for 1d6 rounds. A successful saving throw does not make the target immune to later poisonings.
Swamp Stride: Gripplis can move across mud, muck, shallow water, and any other difficult terrain that arises from the presence of water without penalty.

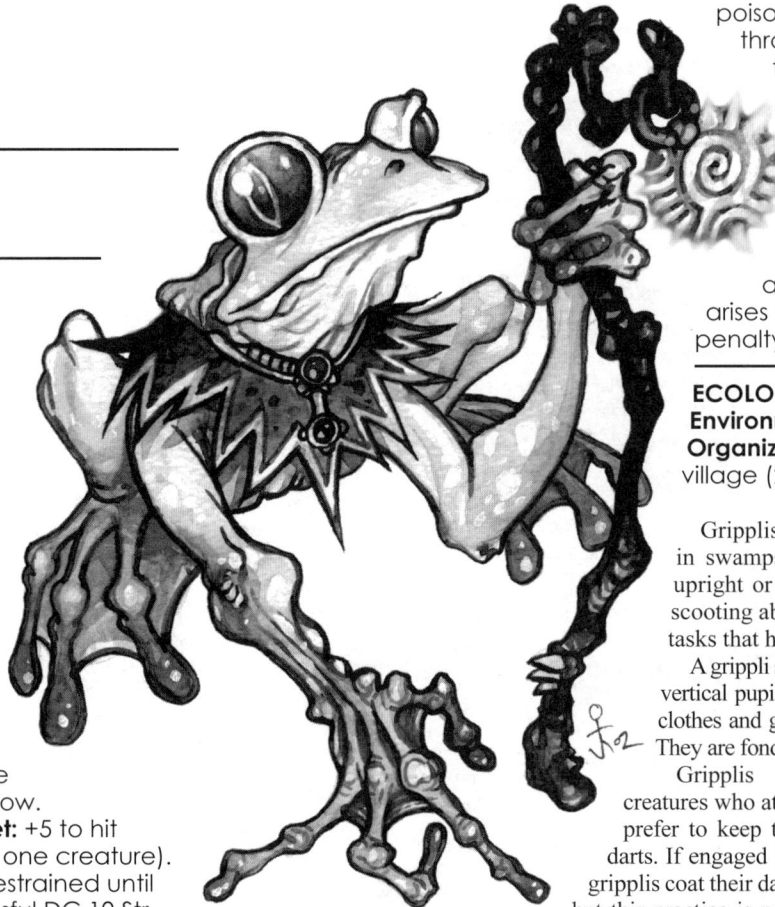

ECOLOGY
Environment: Warm forests and marshes
Organization: Gang (2–5), pack (6–11), or village (20–30 plus 6–11 noncombatants)

Gripplis are short, froglike humanoids that dwell in swamps, marshes, and rainforests. They can move upright or on all fours. They spend most of their time scooting about their community doing many of the same tasks that humans perform in their own towns.

A grippli stands 2 to 2–1/2 feet tall. Its eyes are yellow with vertical pupils of black. Gripplis often wear brightly colored clothes and gaudy, decorative jewelry and other adornments. They are fond of brightly colored items of all kinds.

Gripplis are peaceful, thoughtful, nonaggressive, creatures who attack only when threatened or frightened. They prefer to keep their distance and attack using their nets and darts. If engaged in melee, gripplis employ short swords. Some gripplis coat their darts with paralytic poison before entering battle, but this practice is not universal; it largely depends on how much trouble this tribe of gripplis has experienced from outsiders recently.

A grippli village is organized much like a human village. Each grippli family maintains its own dwelling. Their huts are small, constructed of wood and mud. Gripplis build them beneath the branches of large trees to shade themselves from long, hot, tropical days. Every grippli village is led by a tribal leader (usually a female) who is considered the wisest among them, and has one or more shamans (always female) who cast spells similar to druids.

Gripplis are enthusiastic traders with other more gregarious races such as elves and halflings and with peaceful fey. They are also skilled hunters in their swampy or forested territory. Gripplis are fond of fruit and insects (including the giant varieties), and they are very responsible about collecting and storing supplies in their villages against seasonal shortages and lean times.

Gripplis reproduce by laying eggs. They reproduce slowly, with a typical clutch containing but one egg. For this reason, the normally peaceful gripplis defend their young with a ferocity that surprises even those races of humanoids with a reputation for cherishing their children.

Credit
The grippli originally appeared in the First Edition *Monster Manual II* (© TSR/Wizards of the Coast, 1983) and is used by permission.

Copyright Notice
Author Scott Greene, based on original material by Gary Gygax

Grue (Type 1)

*This creature is seldom seen as anything more than an indistinct shape in the darkness,
until a stray beam of light glints off its enormous, fang-lined mouth.*

Grue, Type 1

XP 1,100 (CR 4)
Unaligned Large ooze
Initiative +0

DEFENSE

AC 15 (natural armor)
hp: 75 (10d10 + 20)
Immunity: Bludgeoning
and piercing damage from
nonmagical weapons; prone,
paralysis
Vulnerability: Radiant damage

OFFENSE

Speed: 20 ft.
Melee Attack—Bite: +3 to hit
(reach 5 ft.; one creature).
Hit: 2d8 + 1 piercing
damage and the
target must make a
successful DC 11
Str saving throw or
be swallowed (see
below).

STATISTICS

Str 13 (+1), **Dex** 10 (+0),
Con 15 (+2),
Int 1 (–5), **Wis** 8 (–1),
Cha 1 (–5)
Languages: None
Skills: Stealth +2
Senses: Darkvision 60 ft.

TRAITS

Amorphous: A type 1 grue can move
through gaps as small as 6 square
inches without penalty.
Blends Into Darkness: A grue has tactical
disadvantage on Stealth checks when not in darkness or
dim light.
Extinguish Light: As a bonus action, a grue can extinguish
one normal (nonmagical) light within 100 feet.
Swallow: A swallowed creature is blinded and restrained.
It takes 1d8 + 1 bludgeoning damage plus 1d8 acid
damage automatically at the start of each of the grue's
turns. Up to two Medium creatures or four Small creatures
can be inside the grue at one time. A swallowed creature
is unaffected by anything happening outside the grue
or by attacks from outside it. A swallowed creature can
get out of the grue by using 5 feet of movement, but only
after the grue is dead.

ECOLOGY

Environment: Underground
Organization: Solitary

A type 1 grue is a nasty, large thing with dark gray or green skin,
rather like a half-filled water balloon ten feet long, with a huge
mouth filled with needlelike teeth. Inside its leathery skin, the
grue is mostly gelatinous goo surrounding an enormous
stomach. Its rubbery hide is deceptively thick and tough.

Grues can't coexist with light; if they are exposed
to a light source, they instantly retreat into
the darkness. In the dark, however, they are
dangerous.

Once a grue swallows a victim, it is
satisfied. It will leave with a full stomach
if it is permitted to do so. They are
unintelligent, despite their evil
appearance, and they eat people
for nourishment, not out of malice.
Although they don't accumulate
treasure, valuable items can
sometimes be found in their
guts, depending on how
recently they've eaten a well-
supplied adventurer.

Credit
Author Matt Finch

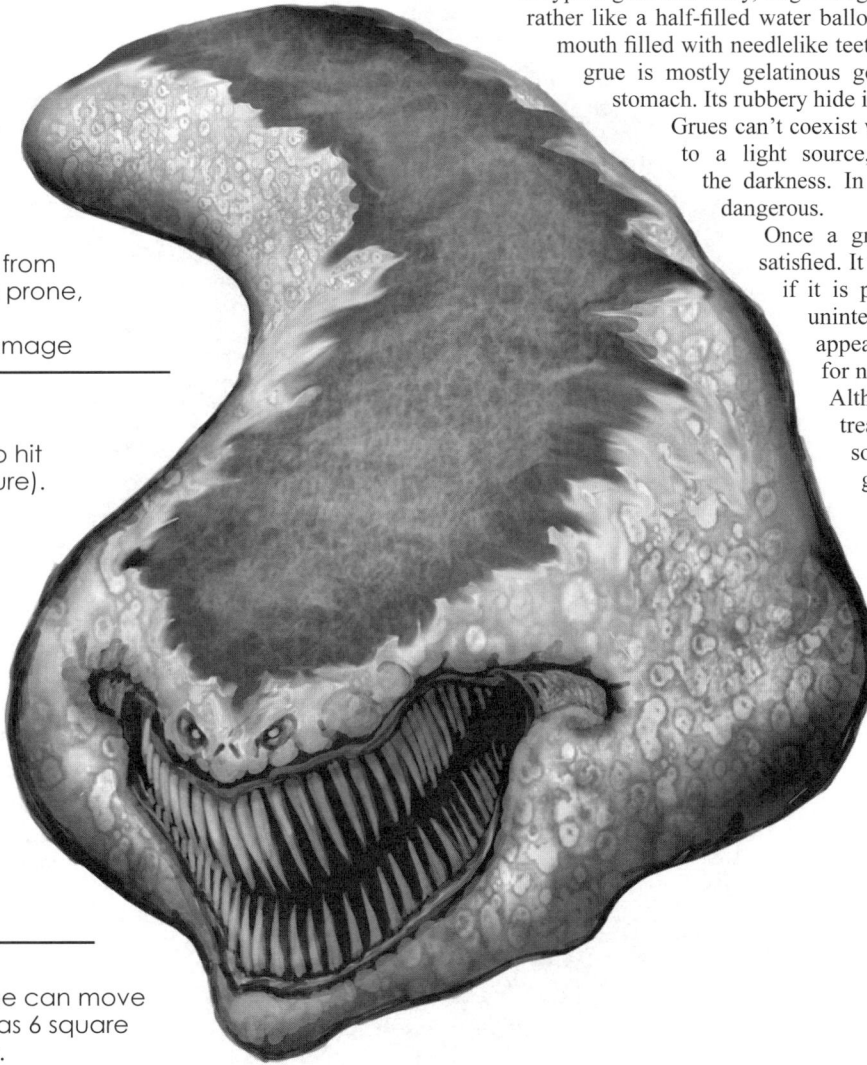

Grue (Type 2)

What can only be described as a blob of darkness moves menacingly up the corridor, seeming to swallow all light as it advances.

Grue, Type 2

XP 450 (CR 2)
CE Medium aberration
Initiative +3

DEFENSE

AC 13
hp: 36 (8d8)
Immunity: Bludgeoning, piercing, and slashing damage from nonmagical weapons; grappling, paralysis, petrification, poison, prone, restrained

OFFENSE

Speed: fly 30 ft.
Melee Attack—Bite: +5 to hit (reach 5 ft.; one creature). *Hit:* 2d8 + 3 piercing damage and the grue heals half as many hit points.

STATISTICS

Str 3 (–4), **Dex** 16 (+3),
Con 10 (+0), **Int** 8 (+0),
Wis 10 (+0), **Cha** 10 (+0)
Languages: Deep Speech
Senses: Truesight 60 ft.

TRAITS

Aura of Darkness: A type 2 grue is permanently enveloped by a sphere of darkness with a 15-foot diameter. Other than the aura's size and duration, it behaves exactly as the *darkness* spell.
Extinguish Light: As a bonus action, a grue can extinguish one normal (nonmagical) light within 100 feet.
Soul Devourer: The body of any creature killed by a grue, along with everything it wore or carried, fades from existence 1d6 x 10 minutes after its death unless it is protected by magic such as a *gentle repose* spell. Four days later, the vanished person's soul returns as a grue, and it becomes impossible for the slain creature to ever be raised.
Spell Immunity: The only spells that affect a type 2 grue are those that do radiant damage.

ECOLOGY

Environment: Temperate
Organization: Solitary

Found in the darkest recesses of dungeons or in the deepest corners of attics, grues are the essence of Chaos and Darkness given form and a ravenous appetite for living souls.

Grues are chaotic spirits that exist in a blot of pure darkness. Unlike type 1 grues, a type 2 grue does not flee from a light source; it extinguishes it and then attacks the light wielder.

Because of the nature of their darkness aura, grues are effectively invisible to anyone without magical sight. All that anyone typically sees is the blot of darkness surrounding the entity. With magical senses such as truesight, a grue can be seen for what it is: a set of grinning, slavering jaws filled with multiple rows of pointed teeth, with no other physical presence at all.

On rare occasions, type 2 grues have been known to converse with adventurers rather than attacking them. They have shown remarkably deep knowledge about tremendously narrow topics, and they seem to have a great sense of pride in this. They are also cruel and malicious, zeroing in on someone's fears and insecurities for use as conversational weapons. It's possible that adventurers could actually learn something from a type 2 grue, if they can establish communication with it and discover the subject of its interest.

Credit
Author Chgowiz

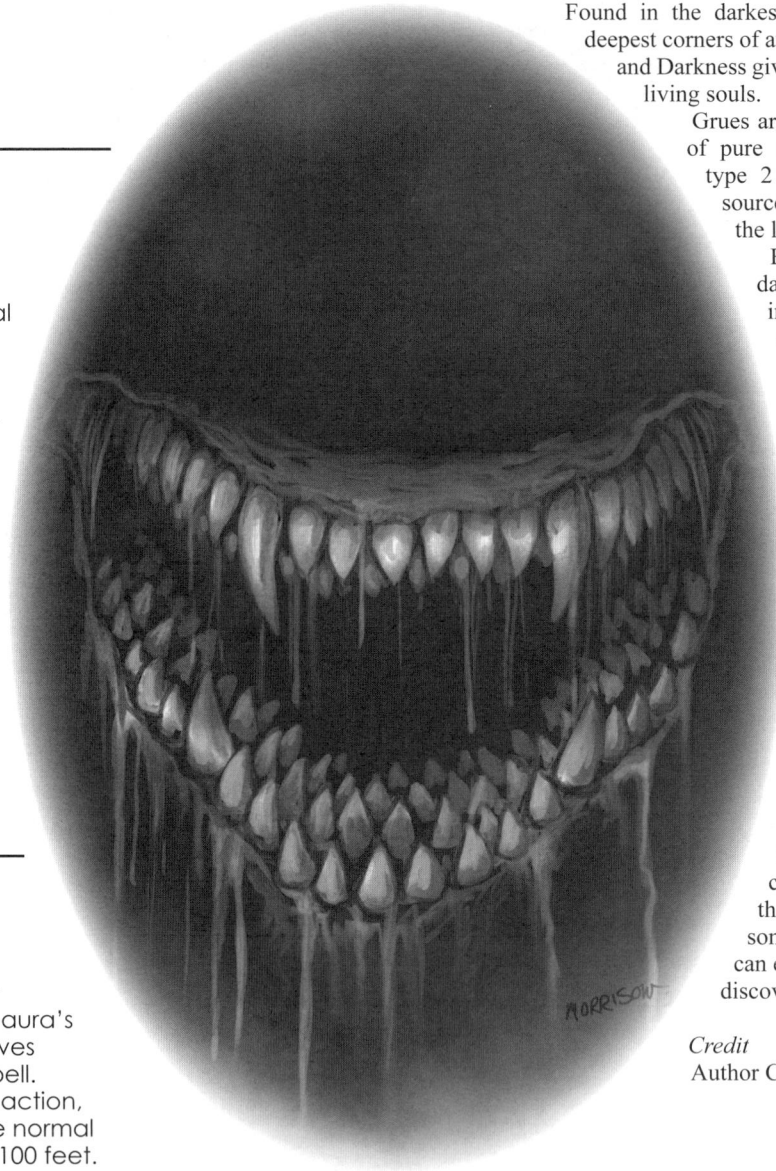

Hanged Man

This creature has pale skin pulled tight over its bones. Its head hangs at an odd angle, unsupported by a broken neck. A rotted noose and many feet of rope hang from its neck and trail behind it. Its lifeless eyes stare unblinking into eternity.

Hanged Man

XP 100 (CR 1/2)
CE Medium undead
Initiative +1

DEFENSE

AC 11
hp: 22 (4d8 + 4)
Saving Throws: Wis +2
Resistance: Piercing damage from nonmagical weapons; necrotic damage
Immunity: Charm, fright, poison, unconsciousness

OFFENSE

Speed: 30 ft.
Multiattack: A hanged man attacks once with claws and once with its rope.
Melee Attack—Claw: +4 to hit (reach 5 ft.; one creature).
Hit: 1d6 + 2 slashing damage.
Ranged Attack—Rope: +3 to hit (range 20 ft.; one creature).
Hit: 1d4 + 1 necrotic damage and the target is entangled (see below).

STATISTICS

Str 15 (+2), **Dex** 13 (+1), **Con** 12 (+1),
Int 9 (−1), **Wis** 11 (+0), **Cha** 13 (+1)
Languages: Understands Common but can't speak
Senses: Darkvision 60 ft.

TRAITS

Entangle: The hanged man's noose is a 20-foot length of rope that moves on its own like an animated object to entangle opponents of any size. An entangled creature is grappled and restrained. If it is not already adjacent to the hanged man, the rope initiates a Str contest against the entangled creature on each of the hanged man's turns. If the rope wins the contest, it pulls the entangled creature 10 feet closer to the hanged man. If the entangled creature wins the Str contest, it stays at its current range from the hanged man. Only one creature can be entangled at a time. The rope can be attacked directly (AC 13); it is destroyed by 15 points of slashing or fire damage but is immune to all other damage. If the rope is severed, both it and the hanged man are destroyed. The rope becomes nothing more than 20 feet of rotted rope if removed from the hanged man.

ECOLOGY

Environment: Any land
Organization: Solitary

A hanged man is the corpse of a hanged humanoid who was too evil to rest peacefully in the grave or who was wrongfully hanged for a crime that was actually committed by one of his or her executioners. It is a malevolent and vengeful entity that attacks living creatures on sight; it can't be reasoned with or placated. Like a ghoul, it devours the flesh of its victims, although it seems to draw no sustenance from them.

Hanged men are always encountered near the area where they were executed or where they were interred in a way that shames them (in unsanctified ground or in a mass grave for criminals, for example). Its "lair" is either this final resting place, if it is an accessible mausoleum, or a secluded area near the place of its death that is overgrown and choked with brush, thorns, and ancient trees. Its lair is marked by the scattered remains of its victims, including any treasure a former meal happened to be carrying.

The rope around the hanged man's neck is imbued with necrotic energy to such an extent that it acts like an extension of the undead creature. It is also the creature's weakness, however, because if the rope is cut, the creature is also destroyed.

Hangman Tree

A giant oak tree with few leaves and branches stands nearby.

Hangman Tree

XP 2,900 (CR 7)
NE Huge plant
Initiative −2

DEFENSE

AC 17 (natural armor)
hp: 92 (8d12 + 40)
Resistance: Bludgeoning and piercing damage
Immunity: Psychic damage; charm, fright, prone, stun, unconsciousness
Vulnerability: Lightning damage

OFFENSE

Speed: 10 ft.
Multiattack: A hangman tree attacks four times with vines and constriction in any mix, or it can release hallucinatory spores (see below).
Melee Attack—Vine: +8 to hit (reach 15 ft.; one creature). *Hit:* 1d8 + 5 bludgeoning damage and the target must make a successful DC 16 Dex saving throw or be grappled. Because the tree seizes targets by the neck, a creature grappled by the hangman tree can't speak or cast spells with verbal components.
Melee Attack—Constriction: automatic hit (one creature already grappled by the hangman tree at the start of the tree's turn). *Hit:* 1d8 + 5 bludgeoning damage and the target must make a successful DC 16 Str saving throw or be lifted off the ground and hanged (see below).
Area Attack—Hallucinatory Spores: automatic hit (range 50 ft. cloud centered on tree; creatures in range). *Hit:* creatures must make successful DC 16 Wis saving throws or be *charmed* by the tree for 2d6 minutes. Affected creatures believe the tree to be of some ordinary sort (or to be a treant or other friendly tree creature). An affected creature won't attack the hangman tree for any reason while charmed. A successful saving throw renders a creature immune to this tree's hallucinatory spores for 24 hours.

STATISTICS

Str 20 (+5), **Dex** 7 (−2), **Con** 20 (+5), **Int** 6 (−2), **Wis** 12 (+1), **Cha** 10 (+0)
Languages: Common
Senses: Darkvision 60 ft.

TRAITS

Hang: When a creature fails the saving throw from a constriction attack, the hangman tree hoists it off the ground by the vine around the target's neck. The creature is still grappled, and it runs out of breath and begins suffocating.
Paralyzed by Cold: A hangman tree is paralyzed for 1 round if it fails a Con saving throw after taking cold damage. The DC of the saving throw equals the spellcaster's standard DC.
Slowed by Darkness: Spells that engulf the hangman tree in darkness affect it as the *slow* spell for 1d4 rounds.
Vines: The vines of a hangman tree have AC 15 and 10 hit points. Only slashing damage affects them. Damage done to a vine is not subtracted from the hangman tree's overall total and does not reduce its number of vine attacks (the tree has plenty of vines to replace any that are severed).

ECOLOGY

Environment: Temperate and warm forests
Organization: Solitary or pair

The hangman tree looks like any other tree in its part of the forest. It is always a broadleaf hardwood; hangman trees never live among conifers or trees with needle-shaped leaves. Hidden among the tree's branches and leaves are its ropelike appendages that it uses to trap and strangle prey.

Strangled victims are hoisted high into the branches and then lowered into the creature's "mouth:" an opening at the top of the trunk through which the tree eats. The tree also appears to have a horizontal scar in its bark near the ground, but close inspection reveals it to be an orifice through which the tree expels bones, gear, and other undigestible bits of the creatures it eats.

Being plants, hangman trees are not subject to any of the emotions or sentiment of humanoids. They are not malicious killers, but they place no value on animal life beyond the food it provides. Most of them believe that animals (including humanoids) don't actually feel pain, so they see no reason to be gentle with their food.

Credit
The hangman tree originally appeared in *EX1 Dungeonland* (© TSR/ Wizards of the Coast, 1983) and is used by permission.

Copyright Notice
Author Scott Greene, based on original material by Gary Gygax.

Hawktoad

*The creature you see resembles a three-foot-long toad, but instead of hopping on the ground,
it swims through the air, propelled by a swishing, tadpole-like tail instead of back legs.
Its foreclaws are long and hooked, and its tongue lashes menacingly.*

Hawktoad
XP (CR 1/4)
Unaligned Small monstrosity
Initiative +2

DEFENSE
AC 12
hp: 5 (2d4)

OFFENSE
Speed: fly 30 ft.
Multiattack: A hawktoad attacks once with claws and once with its tongue.
Melee Attack—Claws: +4 to hit (reach 5 ft.; one creature). *Hit:* 1d4 + 2 slashing damage.
Melee Attack—Tongue: +4 to hit (reach 5 ft.; one creature). *Hit:* the target is grappled and strangled (see below).

STATISTICS
Str 8 (–1), **Dex** 14 (+2),
Con 10 (+0), **Int** 2 (–5),
Wis 10 (+0), **Cha** 3 (–4)
Languages: None
Senses: Darkvision 60 ft.

TRAITS
Strangling: When a hawktoad hits a target with its tongue, the monster wraps its tongue around the victim's neck. It then quickly maneuvers itself behind the target, landing on the target's back. The hawktoad digs in its claws and tries to strangle the victim with its tongue. If the targeted creature makes a successful DC 12 Dex saving throw, it gets an arm, a hand, or some other limb or object under the hawktoad's tongue and avoids any further danger from this specific tongue attack; the hawktoad can try again on coming turns. If the Dex saving throw fails, the creature is being strangled by the hawktoad; it runs out of breath and begins suffocating. As long as the hawktoad continues strangling it, the unconscious creature can't stabilize by making successful death saving throws. If the hawktoad is killed or its stranglehold is broken, the victim can recover normally. A creature has tactical disadvantage on attacks against a hawktoad that has grappled it and is clinging to its back. A hawktoad uses its Dex in contests to maintain its grapple, instead of Str.

ECOLOGY
Environment: Temperate and warm forest and swamp
Organization: Army (2–12)

Hawktoads are amphibians with the body of a very large toad, but their front paws have very long, hooked claws. Instead of back legs, they have a thick tail like that of a tadpole. The full length of a hawktoad is about 3 feet.

These bizarre creatures float in air and "swim" through it by lashing their tails, exactly the way a tadpole swims through water. Their sharp claws are dangerous, but the real threat comes from their tongues, with which they can strangle creatures up to Large size. Once a hawktoad gets its tongue around a potential victim's neck and latches onto the victim's back, it quickly transitions from pest to lethal threat.

A single hawktoad would be easy to deal with, but they always move and attack in packs. Hawktoads are most dangerous in spring, when they can be ravenous if the winter was particularly long or harsh.

There are rumors that some wizards have attained hawktoads as familiars, but most scholars discount them as legend. Even if such stories were true, the hawktoad's foul temper would make it an unpleasant companion.

Credit
Author Matt Finch

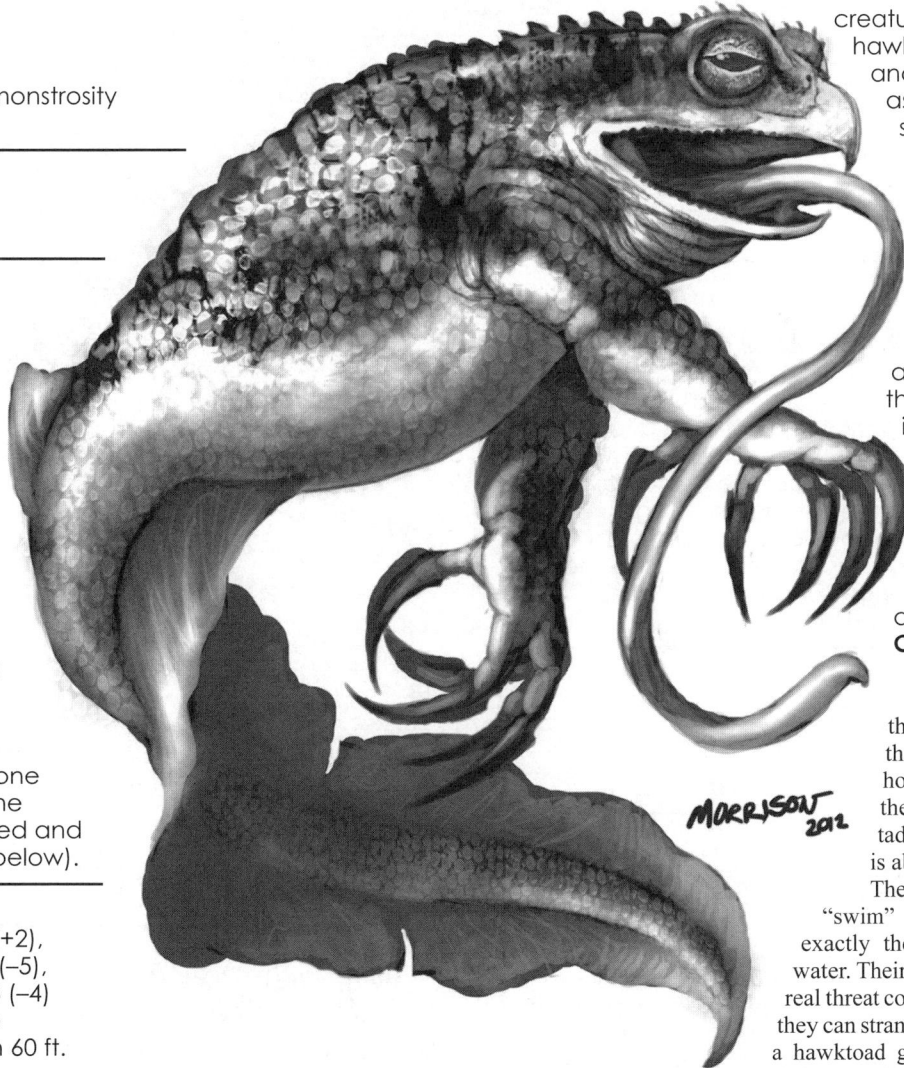

Helix Moth Adult

This 20-foot-long insect has a black abdomen wrapped with spiraling bands of varied color and a white underbelly. Three sets of translucent, bluish-violet wings extend from its body. A small black swordlike stinger protrudes from the end of its abdomen, and its maw clatters with large mandibles.

Helix Moth Adult

XP 2,300 (CR 6)
Unaligned Huge beast
Initiative +2

DEFENSE

AC 14 (natural armor)
hp: 114 (12d12 + 36)

OFFENSE

Speed: 20 ft., fly 60 ft.
Multiattack: An adult helix moth bites once and stings once.
Melee Attack—Bite: +5 to hit (reach 5 ft.; one creature).
  Hit: 2d8 + 2 piercing damage plus 1d8 acid damage and the target is grappled. If the helix moth has a target grappled at the start of the moth's turn, it can do 2d8 + 2 piercing damage plus 1d8 acid damage to that target automatically if it does not try to bite another target.
Melee Attack—Sting: +5 to hit (reach 5 ft.; one creature).
  Hit: 1d8 + 2 piercing damage and the target must make a successful DC 14 Con saving throw or take 2d8 poison damage (see Helix Moth Poison below).

STATISTICS

Str 13 (+1), **Dex** 15 (+2), **Con** 16 (+3),
Int 1 (–5), **Wis** 11 (+0), **Cha** 2 (–4)
Languages: None
Senses: Darkvision 60 ft.

TRAITS

Drone: The rapid beating of the helix moth's wings creates an incessant droning sound that clouds the minds of creatures capable of hearing it. All such creatures within 30 feet of the moth must make a successful DC 14 Wis saving throw or suffer a penalty identical to being poisoned (this is not a poison effect, however, so poison resistance and immunity don't apply). The effect lasts for 1 minute (10 rounds); at the end of that time, if the droning can still be heard, the saving throw can be repeated. A successful save renders a creature immune to the droning of helix moths for 12 hours.
Helix Moth Poison: If a player character drops to 0 hit points from a helix moth sting that caused poison damage (the character failed the saving throw), the character stabilizes automatically but remains unconscious for 2d6 hours. The character must attempt the saving throw even if the sting's piercing damage alone was enough to drop the character to 0 hit points. Healing the character above 0 hit points won't awaken the character before the 2d6 hours have elapsed. The character can awaken early only if the poison is neutralized by *lesser restoration* or similar magic.

ECOLOGY

Environment: Temperate forests
Organization: Solitary or pair

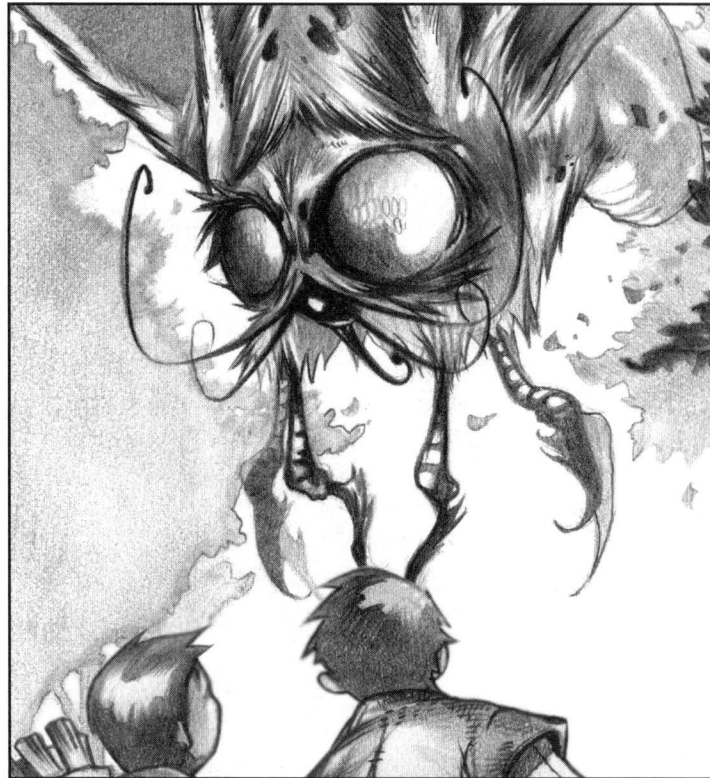

Helix Moth Larva

A monstrously large insect with a segmented body crawls on scores of stumpy legs. Its fleshy gray exterior glistens with slime, and its great gray mandibles click wildly.

Helix Moth Larva

XP 450 (CR 2)
Unaligned Large beast
Initiative +2

DEFENSE

AC 14 (natural armor)
hp: 65 (10d10 + 10)

OFFENSE

Speed: 10 ft.
Melee Attack—Bite: +4 to hit (reach 5 ft.; one creature). *Hit:* 1d10 + 2 piercing damage plus 1d8 acid damage.

STATISTICS

Str 10 (+0), **Dex** 10 (+2), **Con** 12 (+1), **Int** 1 (–5), **Wis** 11 (+0), **Cha** 2 (–4)

Languages: None
Senses: Tremorsense 60 ft.

ECOLOGY
Environment: Underground
Organization: Solitary or nest (2–12)

The lair of an adult helix moth usually can be found in a cave, a tunnel, a volcanic lava tube, or some other, similar structure. The entrances are difficult, if not impossible, for nonflying creatures to reach.

Helix moths are solitary creatures, though on rare occasions a mated pair might be encountered. When the time comes for a female helix moth to lay her eggs, she digs a tunnel down into the floor of her lair that is at least 15 feet long or longer. At its end, she hollows out a chamber at least 20 feet square, then she coats every surface of the tunnel and the chamber with thick, slightly acidic slime. The acid in the slime is weak enough to be harmless, but it tingles unpleasantly when it comes in contact with skin. In that chamber, she deposits up to twelve eggs.

The eggs hatch after just two weeks. If the mother is still around, she brings them food to keep them alive for the first few weeks. Otherwise, the hungry larvae attack and eat each other; this typically results in only half the larvae surviving their first weeks of life.

On rare occasions (1-in–6 chance), the secretions of the larvae react with the slime covering their chamber to form a vapor that's poisonous to other creatures who inhale it. Creatures other than helix moths breathing the fumes must make a successful DC 11 Con saving throw or take 1d8 poison damage. The saving throw must be repeated after every minute of continued exposure.

Despite their imposing size and ferocious appearance, helix moths are normally inoffensive creatures toward humanoids. They are nocturnal hunters, and their usual prey is deer, elk, pheasant, and boar. A helix moth journeys up to a mile from its lair in search of prey. Slain prey is carried back to the lair to be eaten.

The exception to this behavior is when a mother helix moth has a brood of larvae to feed. At those times, she becomes quite aggressive, attacking anything made of meat. Ideally, the mother brings something back for her larvae that is unconscious but still alive.

Copyright Notice
Author Scott Greene

Hieroglyphicroc

This creature has the size and shape of a crocodile, but it is shrunken, as if its insides are dried out or even removed entirely. Its eyes shine with an eerie yellow glow, and the rough scales of its sides and back are covered with faded hieroglyphs.

Hieroglyphicroc
XP 700 (CR 3)
LE Large undead
Initiative +0

DEFENSE
AC 13 (natural armor)
hp: 52 (7d10 + 14)
Resistance: Bludgeoning, piercing, and slashing damage from nonmagical weapons
Immunity: Necrotic and poison damage; charm, exhaustion, fright, paralysis, poison
Vulnerability: Fire damage

OFFENSE
Speed: 20 ft., swim 30 ft.
Melee Attack—Bite: +5 to hit (reach 5 ft.; one creature). *Hit:* 2d10 + 3 piercing damage. If the attack causes 16 or more damage to a Medium or smaller creature, the target must make a successful DC 13 Str saving throw or be swallowed by the hieroglyphicroc (see below).

STATISTICS
Str 16 (+3), **Dex** 11 (+0), **Con** 15 (+2), **Int** 5 (–3), **Wis** 10 (+0), **Cha** 6 (–2)
Languages: None
Skills: Stealth +2
Senses: Darkvision 60 ft.

TRAITS
Swallow: A swallowed creature is blinded and restrained. It takes 1d8 + 3 bludgeoning damage automatically at the start of each of the hieroglyphicroc's turns. Only one Medium creature or two Small creatures can be inside the hieroglyphicroc at one time. A swallowed creature is unaffected by anything happening outside the hieroglyphicroc or by attacks from outside it. A swallowed creature can get out of the hieroglyphicroc by using 5 feet of movement, but only after the hieroglyphicroc is destroyed. A humanoid that dies inside a hieroglyphicroc reanimates as a zombie 1d4 rounds later, and is regurgitated by the hieroglyphicroc.
Unholy Fortitude: Hieroglyphicrocs are highly resistant to turning. They have tactical advantage on saving throws against being turned.

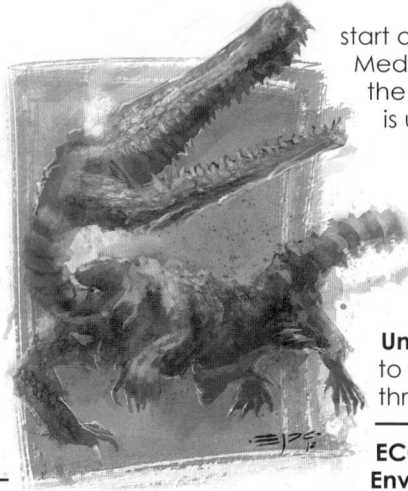

ECOLOGY
Environment: Arid tombs
Organization: Solitary or troop (2–7)

Raised by ancient methods long forgotten or suppressed, hieroglyphicrocs resemble zombie crocodiles. They are actually more akin to mummies than to zombies, largely because they are created by a similar process. A hieroglyphicroc's eyes glow with a yellow light, and they have rudimentary intelligence. Often they are created to serve as defenders of tombs where mummies are also found.

Because of their animal origin, these creatures are resistant to clerical turning. A tomb defended by hieroglyphicrocs is also likely to contain at least a few wandering zombies—the remains of unfortunate tomb robbers who ran afoul of the hieroglyphicroc guardians.

The skin of these undead creatures is often painted with hieroglyphs describing the terrible fates that await those who plunder the tomb and meant to give the hieroglyphicrocs endurance and resolve in their duties.

Credit
Author Matt Finch

Hippocampus

This strange creature appears to be half horse and half fish. The front half resembles a sleek stallion with a flowing mane and long, powerful legs ending in wide fins rather than hooves. The hindquarters are that of a great fish

Hippocampus
XP 200 (CR 1)
CG Large monstrosity
Initiative +2

DEFENSE
AC 12
hp: 34 (4d10 + 12)

OFFENSE
Speed: swim 60 ft.
Melee Attack—Bite: +5 to hit (reach 5 ft.; one creature). *Hit:* 1d6 + 3 bludgeoning damage.
Melee Attack—Tail Slap: +5 to hit (reach 5 ft.; one creature). *Hit:* 2d8 + 3 bludgeoning damage and the target is pushed 5 feet away from the hippocampus if it is Medium size or smaller.

STATISTICS
Str 16 (+3), **Dex** 14 (+2), **Con** 16 (+3),
Int 3 (–4), **Wis** 12 (+1), **Cha** 10 (+0)
Languages: None
Senses: Darkvision 60 ft.

TRAITS
Water Dependent: A hippocampus can breathe air for up to 15 minutes, but after that time, it begins suffocating.

ECOLOGY
Environment: Any aquatic
Organization: Solitary, pair, or herd (3–8)

A hippocampus is often called a merhorse or sea horse, for it is indeed half horse/half fish and lives entirely in the sea. The hindquarters of the animal are that of a great fish. The front (horse) portion of its body is covered in fine scales, and the rear (fish) portion is covered in large scales. The scales vary in color from ivory to deep green, mixed with shades of blue and silver.

Aquatic races sometimes tame these animals, because hippocampi make fine steeds. They are strong, swift, and smarter than horses; they can be taught hundreds of words, and some actually learn to speak the language of their riders. Hippocampi are docile creatures that fight only if they or an ally is threatened.

Credit
The hippocampus originally appeared in the First Edition *Monster Manual* (© TSR/Wizards of the Coast, 1977) and is used by permission.

Copyright Notice
Authors Scott Greene and Erica Balsley, based on original material by Gary Gygax.

Training a Hippocampus
A hippocampus requires training before it will carry a rider, in combat or otherwise. To be trained, a hippocampus must have a friendly attitude toward the trainer (this can be achieved through a successful Diplomacy check). Training a friendly hippocampus as a mount takes six weeks of work concluding with a successful DC 15 Wis (Animal Handling) check. A failed check can be retried after another three weeks of remedial training. If that fails, the hippocampus is untrainable.

Riding a hippocampus requires an exotic saddle. Riding a hippocampus in combat involves the rules for mounted combat and for fighting underwater.

Hippocampus eggs are worth 1,000 to 1,500 gp apiece, depending on local demand. A young, untrained hippocampus can fetch twice as much. Professional trainers (tritons sometimes specialize in this) charge 1,000 gp to rear or train a hippocampus.

Hoar Fox

This creature appears to be a silvery gray fox with sapphire-colored eyes.

Hoar Fox
XP 200 (CR 1)
Unaligned Small monstrosity
Initiative +3

DEFENSE
AC 14 (natural armor)
hp: 26 (4d8 + 8)
Immunity: Cold damage
Vulnerability: Fire damage

OFFENSE
Speed: 40 ft.
Multiattack: A hoar fox bites once or use its cold breath.
Melee Attack—Bite: +5 to hit (reach 5 ft.; one creature). *Hit:* 1d8 + 3 piercing damage.
Area Attack—Cold Breath (recharge 5, 6): automatic hit (range 30 ft. cone; creatures in cone). *Hit:* 2d8 + 2 cold damage, or half damage with a successful DC 13 Dex saving throw.

STATISTICS
Str 10 (+0), **Dex** 17 (+3), **Con** 14 (+2), **Int** 3 (–4), **Wis** 12 (+1), **Cha** 10 (+0)
Languages: None
Skills: Perception +3, Stealth +5
Senses: Darkvision 60 ft.

TRAITS
Winter Hunter: In natural, wintry surroundings, a hoar fox has tactical advantage on both Perception and Stealth checks.

ECOLOGY
Environment: Cold hills and forest
Organization: Solitary, pair, or pack (3–8)

Hoar foxes live and hunt in stable packs of up to eight animals. Although they are shy and generally not aggressive toward humanoids, they are also curious creatures, and their curiosity (and taste for easy food like chickens and young sheep) too often lead them to build their underground dens near humanoid settlements. They are hunted for their remarkably warm fur, which brings a handsome sum on the market.

When threatened, hoar foxes tend to bite a foe in an attempt to scare it away. Only if that fails (or they have prior experience with it failing against similar attackers) do they use their breath weapon.

While attacking a hoar fox with fire seems like an effective tactic, given their vulnerability to it, any fire damage destroys the fox's pelt and renders it worthless for sale.

Credit
The hoar fox originally appeared in the First Edition *Fiend Folio* (© TSR/Wizards of the Coast, 1981) and is used by permission.

Copyright Notice
Author Scott Greene, based on original material by Graeme Morris.

Horsefly, Giant

This creature looks like a common, hairy, black and green horsefly, except it is 8 feet long.

Giant Horsefly

XP 100 (CR 1/2)
Unaligned Large beast
Initiative +2

DEFENSE
AC 12
hp: 30 (4d10 + 8)

OFFENSE
Speed: 20 ft., fly 60 ft.
Melee Attack—Bite: +4 to hit (reach 5 ft.; one creature).
Hit: 1d8 + 2 piercing damage and the target is grappled.
Melee Attack—Fluid Drain: automatic hit (one creature already grappled by the giant horsefly at the start of the horsefly's turn). *Hit:* 1d6 + 2 piercing damage and the target must make a successful DC 12 Con saving throw or become paralyzed until it is no longer grappled by the giant horsefly.

STATISTICS
Str 15 (+2), **Dex** 15 (+2), **Con** 14 (+2),
Int 1 (−5), **Wis** 12 (+1), **Cha** 7 (−2)
Languages: None
Senses: Tremorsense 60 ft.

ECOLOGY
Environment: Any land
Organization: Solitary, pair, or nest (10–20)

Giant horseflies are aggressive relatives of the smaller, common horsefly, and they generally frequent the same types of habitats. Their underground lairs are always dug near water, where the lair will stay damp from water in the surrounding ground. A typical nest contains one female and up to 20 males.

During warmer months but especially when the temperature is high, a flurry of activity can be noticed around the nest. This is the horseflies preparing for the colder months and for the time when the female lays her eggs. One male is taken as a mate, and during the spring or fall months, the female lays a clutch of five to eight eggs. Larvae hatch within a few weeks and resemble giant grubs with segmented bodies. Each segment of the larvae's body has short protuberances that are used like stiff, unjointed legs to aid in movement.

Giant horseflies sustain themselves on a diet of nectar, pollen, blood, and other bodily fluids. Their hunting territory covers a range of several square miles around their nest. Any and all animals are targeted for their blood, from wild creatures to domesticated livestock to unlucky humanoids.

Except for their size, giant horseflies look like large, black, hairy flies. Their bodies are thick and their multifaceted eyes reflect many dark colors. Their wings are translucent and their legs are long and bristly. Females have a slightly longer mouth tube than males.

Giant horseflies attack by delivering a painful "bite" to their opponent that amounts to gripping it with their forelegs and stabbing it with their needlelike proboscis. The fact that an area is inside a nest of giant horseflies' hunting territory can sometimes be recognized by the bodies of animals and people that have been drained of fluid and left to rot on the ground; giant horseflies siphon out their victims' body fluids but do not eat any other part of them.

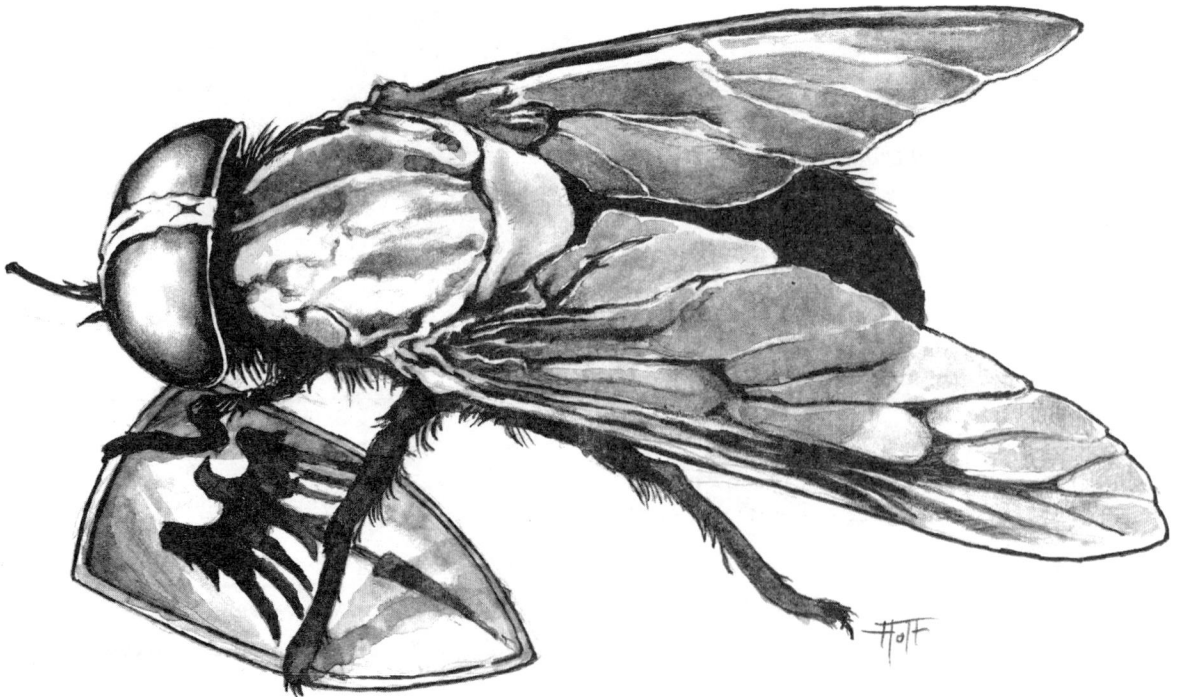

Huggermugger

This small humanoid stands no more than 4 feet tall. Its cropped, black hair is hidden beneath a floppy-brimmed black hat that's pulled low to hide its face. A long, dark robe conceals the rest of its body.

Huggermugger

XP 50 (CR 1/4)
CE Small humanoid
Initiative +3

DEFENSE
AC 13
hp: 7 (2d6)

OFFENSE
Speed: 30 ft.
Melee Attack—Shortsword:
+5 to hit (reach 5 ft.; one creature).
Hit: 1d6 + 3 piercing damage.
Ranged Attack—Sling: +5 to hit (range 30 ft./120 ft.; one creature). *Hit:* 1d4 + 3 bludgeoning damage.

STATISTICS
Str 11 (+0), **Dex** 16 (+3), **Con** 10 (+0), **Int** 11 (+0), **Wis** 13 (+1), **Cha** 12 (+1)
Languages: Unique
Skills: Stealth +5, Survival +5
Senses: Darkvision 60 ft.

TRAITS
Confusion Aura (1/ day): When three huggermuggers gather in a group, they automatically generate an aura of confusion. All creatures within 40 feet of any one of the huggermuggers must make a successful DC 11 Wis saving throw or be affected the same as if by a *confusion* spell for 1d6 rounds. Each of the huggermuggers generating the effect must be no more than 30 feet from both of the other two; if one of them moves outside that range or is killed, incapacitated, or knocked unconscious, the aura and the effect end immediately. If another huggermugger is within range of the other two, however, it can instantly assume the fallen huggermugger's role in maintaining the confusion aura, so there is no break in the aura's effect. An individual huggermugger can contribute to creating one confusion aura per day. A creature that successfully saves against the aura is immune to all huggermugger confusion auras until the end of their next long rest.

Cunning: Huggermuggers possess cunning and logical ability far beyond what their nominal Intelligence and Wisdom scores imply. They never lose their bearings in any setting, they are never surprised, and they can automatically follow any trail that's less than 24 hours old. They have tactical advantage on Wis (Survival) checks to follow a trail that's more than 24 hours old.

ECOLOGY
Environment: Underground
Organization: Band (4–9) or swarm (10–20)

Huggermuggers are small humanoids that dwell underground. They relish chaos, disorder, trickery, and the fine art of thieving. Outside their own subterranean territory, these degenerate humanoid creatures have only been encountered in large cities with extensive sewer systems for them to hide in and travel through secretly. Nothing is known about how their race developed or how widely spread they are. Unkind observers compare them to rats, swarming up from the filth to feed on human society like scavengers or parasites. A few fear-mongering city dwellers loudly speculate that the huggermuggers maintain vast tunnel complexes that connect all the large cities of the world and that some day this vile race will scramble up from the depths as an invading army. They have been known occasionally to work as bounty hunters; their tracking ability makes them amazing manhunters.

Huggermuggers chatter and mumble incessantly, but their sounds might or might not constitute an actual language. If it is a language, it has yet to be translated by sages, so what they call themselves remains a mystery. The term "huggermugger" is akin to "boogeyman," being a name used in stories to scare children into keeping close to home and not exploring the sewers and dark alleys of the city.

Curiously, the skin of a huggermugger is pale and cold to the touch, regardless of the actual temperature in the surrounding area. They are believed to be cold-blooded mammals.

A band of huggermuggers circles its opponents, chattering and mumbling so as to cause confusion. They seldom reveal themselves to a foe unless they have a significant advantage in numbers. If outnumbered or clearly outclassed, huggermuggers prefer to attack from ambush, confusing their opponents before robbing or slaying them.

Igniguana

If not for its glowing eyes and flickering skin that makes this creature look as if its insides are all glowing coals, this creature could be mistaken for any other giant lizard.

Igniguana

XP 200 (CR 1)
Unaligned Medium elemental
Initiative +0

DEFENSE
AC 12 (natural armor)
hp: 26 (4d8 + 8)
Immunity: Fire damage; prone
Vulnerability: Thunder damage

OFFENSE
Speed: 20 ft., burrow 30 ft.
Melee Attack—Bite: +4 to hit (reach 5 ft.; one creature). *Hit:* 1d4 + 2 piercing damage plus 1d8 fire damage.
Area Attack—Fire Breath (recharge 4, 5, 6): automatic hit (range 20 ft. cone; creatures in cone). *Hit:* 2d8 fire damage, or half damage with a successful DC 12 Dex saving throw.

STATISTICS
Str 14 (+2), **Dex** 11 (+0), **Con** 15 (+2), **Int** 3 (–4), **Wis** 11 (+0), **Cha** 7 (–2)
Languages: None
Senses: Darkvision 60 ft.

TRAITS
Earth Glide: The igniguana can move through any sort of earth or mineral except metal as easily as a fish swims through water. This movement leaves behind no tunnel or hole, nor does it create any ripple or other sign of the igniguana's presence. It provokes an opportunity attack if it leaves a creature's reach while on the surface, but not if it does so while gliding through solid earth. The igniguana can't breathe while surrounded by solid stone or earth, so it can remain underground only for as long as it can hold its breath (15 minutes).

ECOLOGY
Environment: Underground, Elemental Plane of Fire
Organization: Solitary or group (2–5)

Igniguanas resemble lizards, though whether there is a true relationship or the resemblance is only coincidence is unknown. It's been postulated that they could be relatives of the fire salamander.

An adult igniguana has a body that's about 4 feet long, plus a tail that adds another 3 to 5 feet. It has reddish hide that flickers live embers and glowing eyes. They are undoubtedly elemental in origin, coupling attributes of fire and earth, as evidenced by their ability to crawl through solid rock without digging even faster than they move on the surface and leaving no tunnel behind to mark their passage. They can exhale small but intense blasts of fire even more frequently than most dragons, making them a bit more dangerous than their size implies.

Credit
Author Matt Finch

Jackal of Darkness

This creature appears to be a jackal with jet-black skin, wearing gold ornaments on its collar and with intricate designs traced on its face and flanks with light-colored ink. Most striking of all is the aura of shadow that surrounds it, like flickering flames of translucent darkness.

Jackal of Darkness

XP 200 (CR 1)
NE Small undead
Initiative +2

DEFENSE

AC 13 (natural armor)
hp: 21 (6d4 + 6)
Saving Throws: Wis + 4
Resistance: Bludgeoning, piercing, and slashing damage from nonmagical weapons
Immunity: Necrotic and poison damage; charm, exhaustion, fright, paralysis, poison, unconsciousness

OFFENSE

Speed: 40 ft.
Multiattack: A jackal of darkness bites once and attacks once with black fire.
Melee Attack—Bite: +4 to hit (reach 5 ft.; one creature). *Hit:* 1d8 + 2 piercing damage.
Melee Attack—Black Fire: automatic hit (reach 50 ft.; one creature). *Hit:* the target must make a successful DC 12 Dex saving throw or take 1d6 + 2 necrotic damage immediately and again at the start of each of the jackal of darkness's turns until the jackal is destroyed, the jackal attacks a different target with black fire, the jackal is turned, or the jackal and the target are more than 50 ft. apart.

STATISTICS

Str 13 (+1), **Dex** 14 (+2), **Con** 12 (+1), **Int** 4 (−3), **Wis** 14 (+2), **Cha** 8 (−1)
Languages: None
Senses: Darkvision 60 ft.

TRAITS

Black Fire: Bright light fades to dim light, and dim light fades to darkness, within 5 feet of a jackal of darkness.

ECOLOGY

Environment: Arid tombs
Organization: Solitary or pack (2–12)

These creatures resemble black-furrred jackals, but they are limned with a flickering fire that appears to be burning shadow, and casts shadow instead of light. They haunt ancient tombs. Possibly they are shackled to such tombs as guardians by ancient magic, or possibly they are just drawn to the aura of death that permeates such places; the precise relation of the jackals to their tomb-lairs is not known. They are undead, but they do not decay like normal undead and they are fully corporeal.

These jackals are surrounded by a nimbus of shadow that looks exactly like flickering flames but casting only darkness instead of light. In combat, a 5-foot sphere of this darkness can detach itself from each creature and wander the battlefield almost like an independent entity. It engulfs the jackal's foes with necrotic energy and saps their life relentlessly.

Credit
Author Matt Finch

Jaculi

This creature appears as serpent with a long, muscular body and a squarish, flat head. Its head is encased in bony armor, and a fringe of sharp bone spikes rings its head like a mane.

Jaculi
XP 25 (CR 1/8)
Unaligned Medium monstrosity
Initiative +3

DEFENSE
AC 14 (natural armor)
hp: 4 (1d8)

OFFENSE
Speed: 30 ft.
Melee Attack—Bite: +5 to hit (reach 5 ft.; one creature). *Hit:* 1d8 + 3 piercing damage.

STATISTICS
Str 12 (+1), **Dex** 16 (+3), **Con** 11 (+0), **Int** 2 (−4), **Wis** 12 (+1), **Cha** 2 (−4)
Languages: None
Skills: Stealth +5
Senses: Darkvision 60 ft.

TRAITS
Ambush Leap: A jaculi can drop or fall as far as 30 feet without taking any damage. It takes normal damage for falling farther than 30 feet. A jaculi gets tactical advantage on an attack roll immediately after dropping 10 feet or more.

ECOLOGY
Environment: Temperate

Organization: Solitary

Jaculi average 8 feet long, but they can grow to a length of 12 feet. Its natural coloration is a deep green with dark brown stripes across its back; its underbelly is light gray.

Jaculi typically find a hiding spot high up in trees or on a rock wall above a pathway or game trail, then wait for prey to stroll beneath them. The jaculi then drops silently onto its victim and bites.

Credit
The jaculi originally appeared in the First Edition *Fiend Folio* (© TSR/Wizards of the Coast, 1981) and is used by permission.

Copyright Notice
Author Scott Greene, based on original material by Philip Masters.

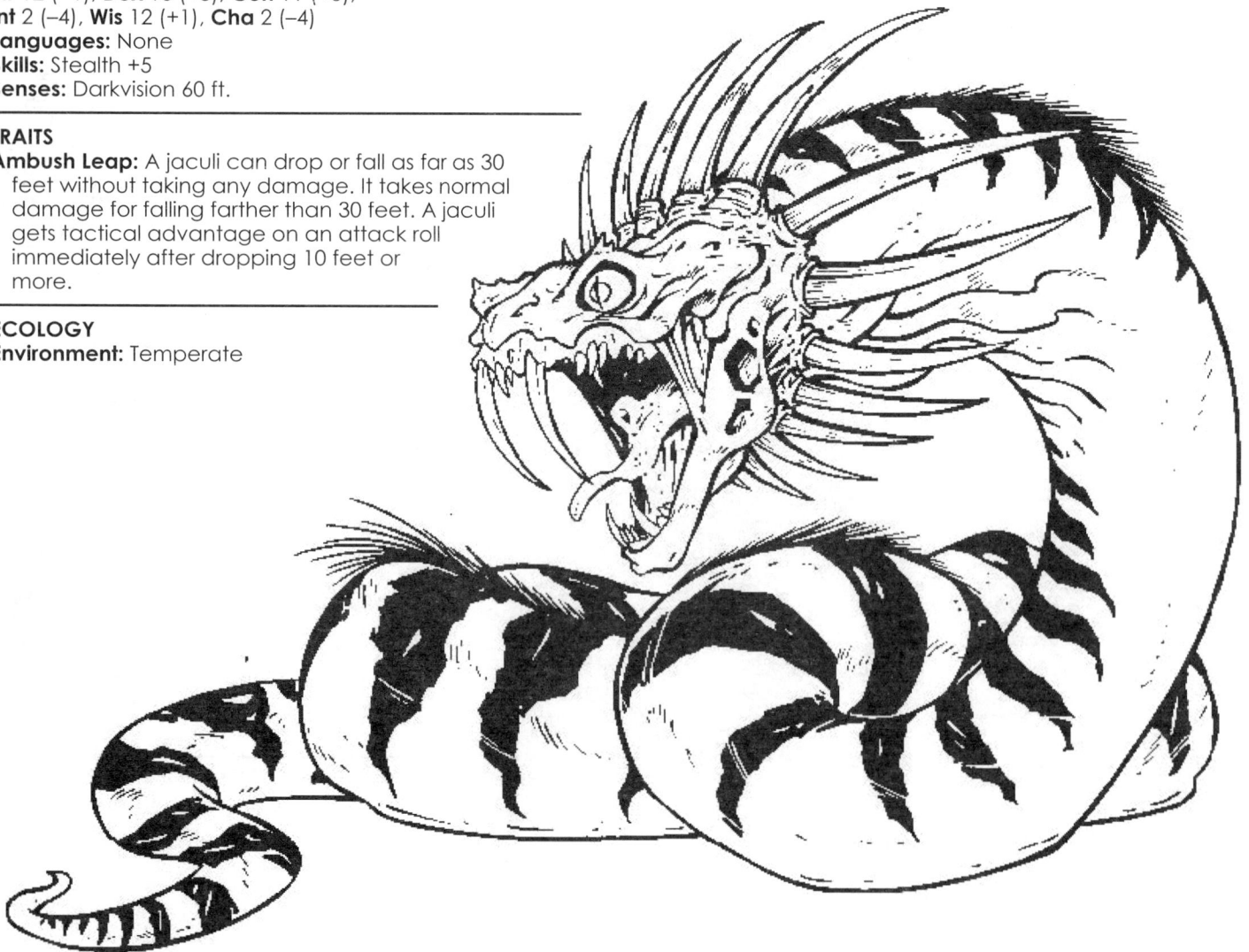

Jelly, Mustard

This creature appears to be an enormous, yellowish-brown amoeba.

Mustard Jelly

XP 1,800 (CR 5)
Unaligned Large ooze
Initiative +0

DEFENSE

AC 14
hp: 85 (10d8 + 40)
Resistance: Bludgeoning, piercing, and slashing damage from nonmagical weapons; cold damage
Immunity: Acid, lightning, and poison damage; grappling, paralysis, poison, restraint, stun, unconsciousness; *magic missile*

OFFENSE

Speed: 30 ft.
Multiattack: A mustard jelly makes one slam attack, plus up to five constriction attacks against grappled creatures.
Melee Attack—Slam: +5 to hit (reach 5 ft.; one creature). *Hit:* 2d6 + 2 bludgeoning damage plus 1d6 acid damage and the target must make a successful DC 13 Str saving throw or be grappled. A mustard jelly can have up to five creatures grappled at once and still make slam attacks; it can grapple a sixth creature, but it can't make slam attacks while it has six creatures grappled.
Melee Attack—Constrict: automatic hit (one creature already grappled by the mustard jelly at the start of the jelly's turn). *Hit:* 2d6 + 2 bludgeoning damage plus 1d10 acid damage.

STATISTICS

Str 15 (+2), **Dex** 10 (+0), **Con** 18 (+4),
Int 10 (+0), **Wis** 10 (+0), **Cha** 10 (+0)
Languages: None
Senses: Tremorsense 60 ft.

TRAITS

Blind: A mustard jelly has no eyes, so it is immune to effects that depend on sight such as illusions or gaze attacks.
Divide: As an action, a mustard jelly with more than 10 hit points can split itself into two identical jellies, each with half of the original's current hit points (rounded down). For the first minute (10 rounds) after dividing, the newly divided jellies have speed 40 feet.
Energy Absorption: When a mustard jelly is targeted by a *magic missile* spell or when it would take lightning damage, it takes no damage but instead gains temporary hit points equal to the damage the attack

should have caused.
Poison Aura: A mustard jelly exudes a poisonous vapor. Every creature that ends its turn within 10 feet of a mustard jelly must make a successful DC 15 Con saving throw or be restrained for as long as it remains within 10 feet of any mustard jelly and for 1d4 rounds afterward. This is a poison effect, not physical restraint.

ECOLOGY

Environment: Temperate marshes
Organization: Solitary

Mustard jelly appears to be a yellowish-brown form of the ochre jelly, and it's thought to be a distant relative of that creature. The mustard jelly, however, is more dangerous than its supposed relative, thanks to its intelligence. Though it possesses intelligence, a mustard jelly can't speak. They seem to have no inherent means of communication, but they do respond when contacted telepathically or with magic. Their intelligence is quite alien to that of most humanoids, but those who've "conversed" with mustard jellies say they have a surprisingly robust sense of humor.

The mustard jelly gives off a faint odor similar to that of the mustard plant, detectable to a range of 20 feet.

It attacks by forming a pseudopod from its body and either bashing or enveloping its foes. Mustard jellies prefer to attack from ambush, or at least in a situation where they have the upper hand. If combat goes against a mustard jelly, it does not hesitate to flee—after dividing to gain the speed bonus. They have also been known to feign a panicky retreat to lure overconfident or rash foes into prepared traps.

Credit

The mustard jelly originally appeared in the First Edition *Monster Manual II* (© TSR/Wizards of the Coast, 1983) and is used by permission.

Copyright Notice

Author Scott Greene, based on original material by Gary Gygax.

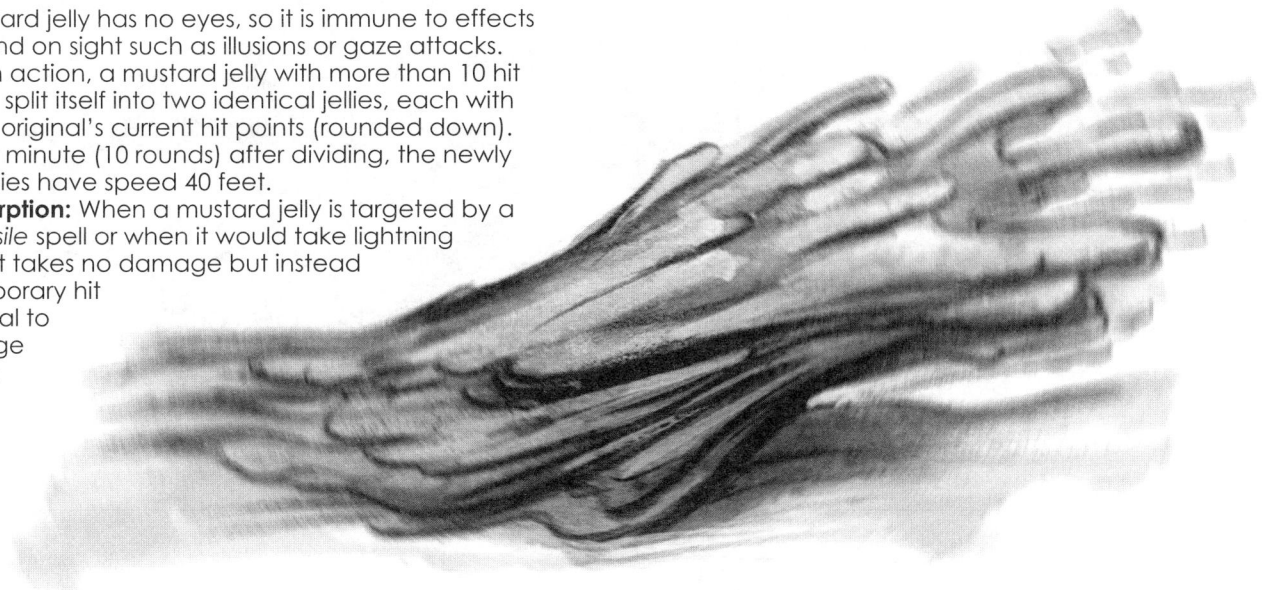

Jupiter Bloodsucker

This plant is a man-sized tangle of leaves and roots. Four large, dark green, serrated leaves top the roots laced with pulsing red veins.

Jupiter Bloodsucker

XP 200 (CR 1)
Unaligned Medium plant
Initiative –3

DEFENSE

AC 8 (natural armor)
hp: 26 (4d8 + 8)
Saving Throws: Con +4
Immunity: Psychic damage; charm, fright, stun, unconsciousness
Vulnerability: Fire damage

OFFENSE

Speed: 5 ft.
Multiattack: A Jupiter bloodsucker makes five melee attacks.
Melee Attack—Vine: +3 to hit (reach 5 ft.; one creature). *Hit:* 1d8 + 1 piercing damage and the target is grappled.
Melee Attack—Smother: +3 to hit (one creature grappled by the Jupiter bloodsucker). *Hit:* The target must make a successful DC 11 Con saving throw or it begins suffocating. Suffocation continues for as long as the creature is grappled by the Jupiter bloodsucker.

STATISTICS

Str 12 (+1), **Dex** 5 (–3), **Con** 14 (+2),
Int 1 (–5), **Wis** 10 (+0),
Cha 10 (+0)
Languages: None
Senses: Tremorsense 60 ft.

ECOLOGY

Environment: Temperate forests
Organization: Solitary, patch (2–5), or bed (6–10)

The Jupiter bloodsucker, or vampire plant, is a seemingly ordinary plant. A creature looking closely at the roots may notice that the stems are transparent and that blood seems to course through them. The vines are lined with leaves, and on the underside of each leaf are many small but very sharp, hollow thorns. When these are stabbed into a victim, the plant can siphon off the creature's blood.

The Jupiter bloodsucker attacks with its vines, trying to grapple a foe with the ropy vine and then gulp down its blood through the leaves. At the same time, leaves cover the victim's face to smother it and prevent it from escaping the plant's weak grip.

Credit

The Jupiter bloodsucker originally appeared in the adventure module *B3 Palace of the Silver Princess* (© TSR/Wizards of the Coast, 1981) and is used by permission. It appears in the orange-covered version (the original), not the revised green-covered module.

Copyright Notice

Author Scott Greene, based on original material by Jean Wells.

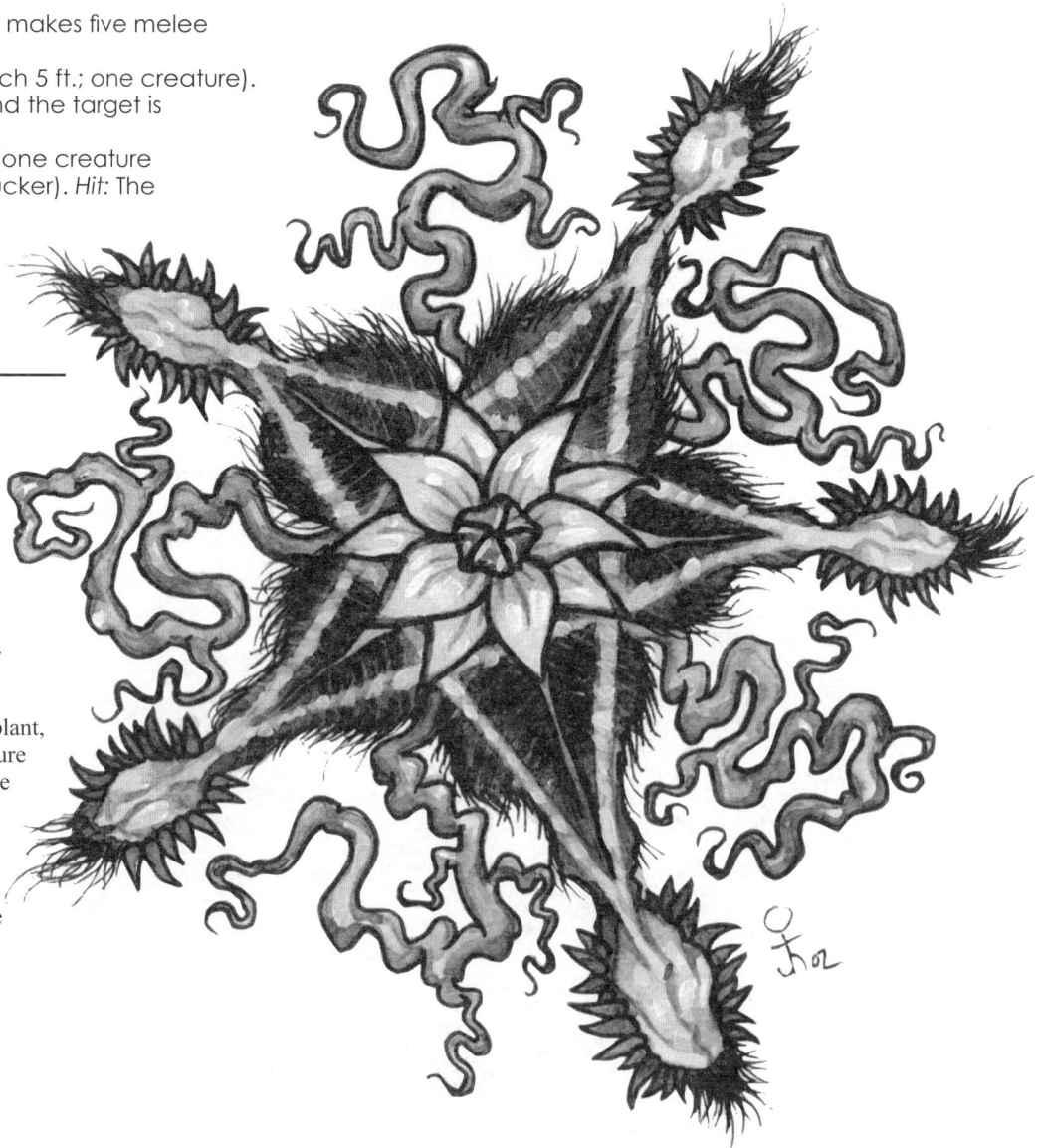

Kamadan

This creature resembles a large, leopardlike cat with green eyes. From its shoulders sprout six serpents that are blackish-green in color, each about twice the length of an adult human. The serpents' eyes are reddish-yellow.

Kamadan

XP 700 (CR 3)
Unaligned Large monstrosity
Initiative +2

DEFENSE

AC 14 (natural armor)
hp: 30 (4d10 + 8)

OFFENSE

Speed: 40 ft.
Multiattack: The kamadan attacks once with claws, twice with snake appendages, and either bites once or uses sleep breath.
Melee Attack—Bite: +6 to hit (reach 5 ft.; one creature). *Hit:* 1d10 + 4 piercing damage.
Melee Attack—Claws: +6 to hit (reach 5 ft.; one creature). *Hit:* 1d10 + 4 slashing damage.
Melee Attack—Snakes: +6 to hit (reach 5 ft.; one creature). *Hit:* 1d10 piercing damage.
Area Attack—Sleep Breath (recharge 5, 6): automatic hit (range 30 ft. cone; creatures in the cone). *Hit:* every creature in the cone must make a successful DC 12 Con saving throw or become unconscious for 2d4 rounds.

STATISTICS

Str 18 (+4), **Dex** 15 (+2), **Con** 15 (+2),
Int 5 (–3), **Wis** 12 (+1), **Cha** 9 (–1)
Languages: None
Skills: Stealth +6
Senses: Darkvision 60 ft.

ECOLOGY

Environment:
Temperate and warm land
Organization: Solitary

The kamadan is a felinelike predator. It is highly territorial and a fierce hunter that pursues just about anything that lingers in its territory, which encompasses an area of five to six square miles. A kamadan's lair usually is a shallow cave or a sheltered area surrounded by rocks.

The kamadan's body is identical to a standard leopard's, but it is much larger, being almost 9 feet long. It is covered with coarse yellow fur with brown spots. The snakelike appendages that protrude from the kamadan's shoulders can be up to 6 feet long.

The kamadan almost always uses its sleep breath as soon as possible, usually from ambush.

Poisonous Kamadan

A rare, poisonous kamadan is rumored to exist in remote regions. The poisonous kamadan has the same statistics as the normal kamadan, but creatures struck by its snake attack must make a successful DC 12 Con saving throw or take an additional 1d6 poison damage.

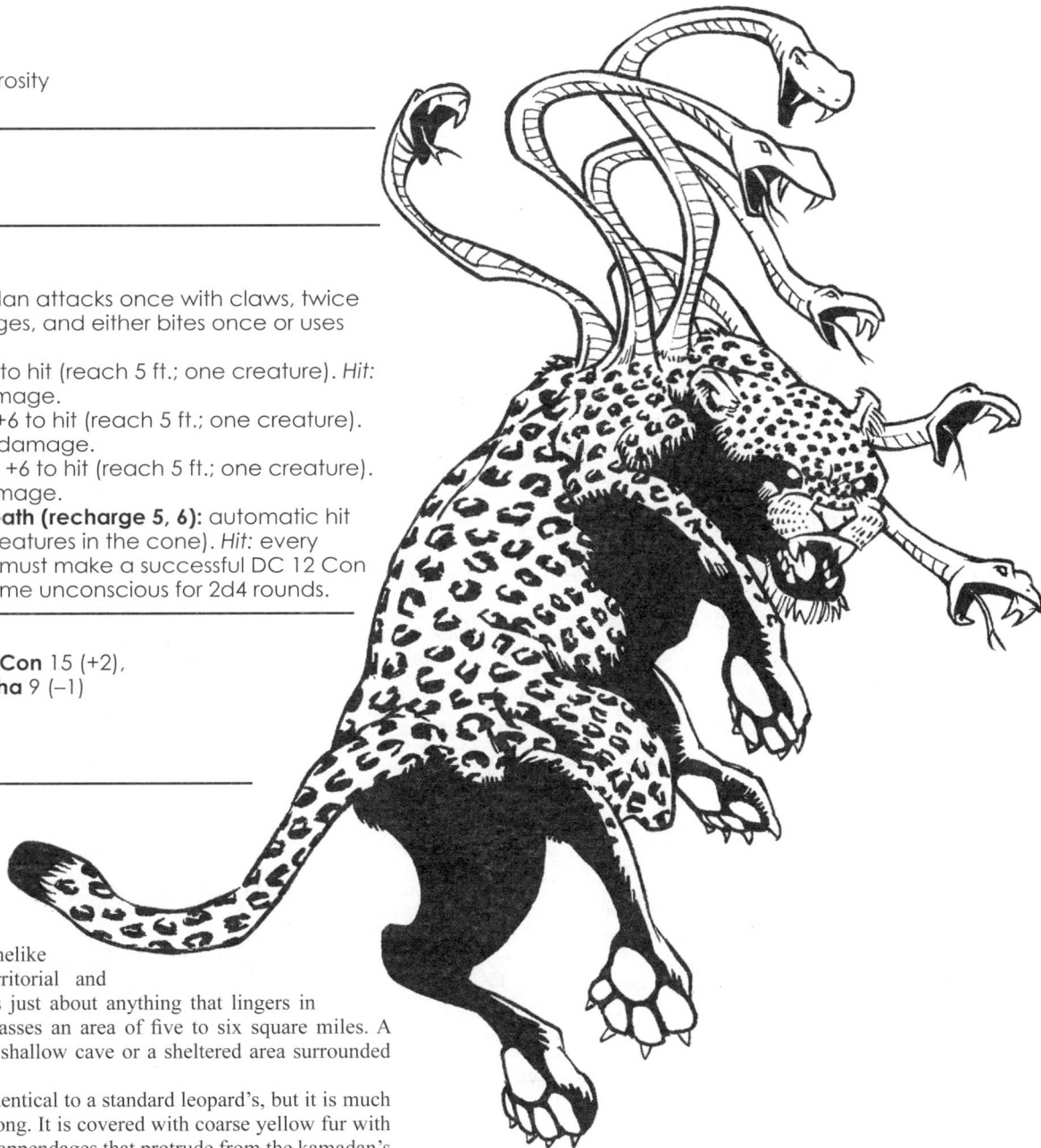

Credit
The kamadan originally appeared in the First Edition *Fiend Folio* (© TSR/Wizards of the Coast, 1981) and is used by permission.

Copyright Notice
Author Scott Greene, based on original material by Nick Louth.

Kampfult

This creature is a human-sized monster resembling nothing so much as a tree trunk with six thick, twisting, barren branches that are as flexible as vines. Six smaller "roots" at the base of the trunk drag it around slowly. Its coloration is similar to any tree's, but it has no leaves.

Kampfult
XP 450 (CR 2)
Unaligned Medium plant
Initiative +1

DEFENSE
AC 15 (natural armor)
hp: 32 (5d8 + 10)
Resistance: Bludgeoning damage from nonmagical weapons
Vulnerability: Fire damage

OFFENSE
Speed: 10 ft.
Multiattack: A kampfult attacks six times with branches. Each branch can either slam or constrict.
Melee Attack—Slam: +5 to hit (reach 5 ft.; one creature). *Hit:* 1d4 + 3 bludgeoning damage and the target must make a successful DC 13 Str saving throw or be grappled.
Melee Attack—Constriction: automatic hit (one creature already grappled by the kampfult at the start of the kampfult's turn). *Hit:* 1d8 + 3 bludgeoning damage and the target is grappled and restrained.

STATISTICS
Str 16 (+3), **Dex** 12 (+1), **Con** 14 (+2),
Int 6 (−2), **Wis** 12 (+1), **Cha** 6 (−2)
Languages: Understands Sylvan but can't speak
Senses: Tremorsense 60 ft.

ECOLOGY
Environment: Underground
Organization: Solitary or grove (2–12)

The kampfult is a plant creature that resembles a tree that's had all its leaves and secondary branches stripped off. It hunts subterranean realms for living creatures that it crushes to death and then slowly absorbs the liquids from their bodies for nourishment.

A kampfult stands 6 feet tall, but smaller and larger specimens have been encountered. They have no organs with which to speak, but they can be communicated with telepathically. They are not deep thinkers and they seldom have anything interesting to say, but they can provide useful information about the types of creatures roaming nearby tunnels.

A kampfult usually stands completely still, looking like nothing more than an oddly out-of-place dead tree, until potential prey approaches within reach. Then it lashes out and tries to get as many grappling tendrils as possible around a single target. They rarely attack creatures larger or more dangerous than themselves unless they're extremely hungry, since they can't run from a fight that's going against them. For a kampfult, every battle is to the death.

Credit
The kampfult originally appeared in the First Edition *Monster Manual II* (© TSR/Wizards of the Coast, 1983) and is used by permission.

Copyright Notice
Author Scott Greene, based on original material by Gary Gygax.

Kech

This man-sized, humanoid creature resembles a monkey, but it has sapphire blue eyes and its body is covered is covered in short, coarse fur that blends easily into foliage.

Kech
XP 100 (CR 1/2)
NE Medium monstrosity
Initiative +2

___

DEFENSE
AC 13 (natural armor)
hp: 27 (5d8 + 5)

___

OFFENSE
Speed: 40 ft., climb 20 ft.
Multiattack: A kech bites once and attacks once with claws.
Melee Attack—Bite: +4 to hit (reach 5 ft.; one creature). *Hit:* 1d8 + 2 piercing damage.
Melee Attack—Claws: +4 to hit (reach 5 ft.; one creature). *Hit:* 1d6 + 2 slashing damage. If the claw and bite attacks hit the same target, the second attack does an additional 1d6 damage.

___

STATISTICS
Str 13 (+1),
Dex 15 (+2),
Con 12 (+1),
Int 10 (+0),
Wis 13 (+1),
Cha 11 (+0)
Languages: Unique
Skills: Perception +3, Stealth +4, Survival +3
Senses: Darkvision 60 ft.

___

TRAITS
Leafy Camouflage: In leafy surroundings (trees, brush), a kech has tactical advantage on Stealth checks.
Mobility: Opponents have tactical disadvantage on opportunity attacks against a kech.
Pass Without Trace: A kech moving through natural terrain leaves no detectable trail.

___

ECOLOGY
Environment: Any forest
Organization: Pack (2–5) or band (2–8 plus 1–4 noncombatant young)

Kechs are monkeylike humanoids that stand about 6 feet tall and weigh as much as a lanky human. They make their homes in trees, and they spend most of their time in the branches, seldom coming down to the ground.

Their society and organization closely resembles that of primitive, tribal humans. Family units dwell in a single lair (usually a hollowed tree or a hut built on the branches of a leafy tree).

At a quick glance, a kech's leathery skin resembles a covering of leaves and foliage. Their coloration acts as natural camouflage in their typicaly surroundings.

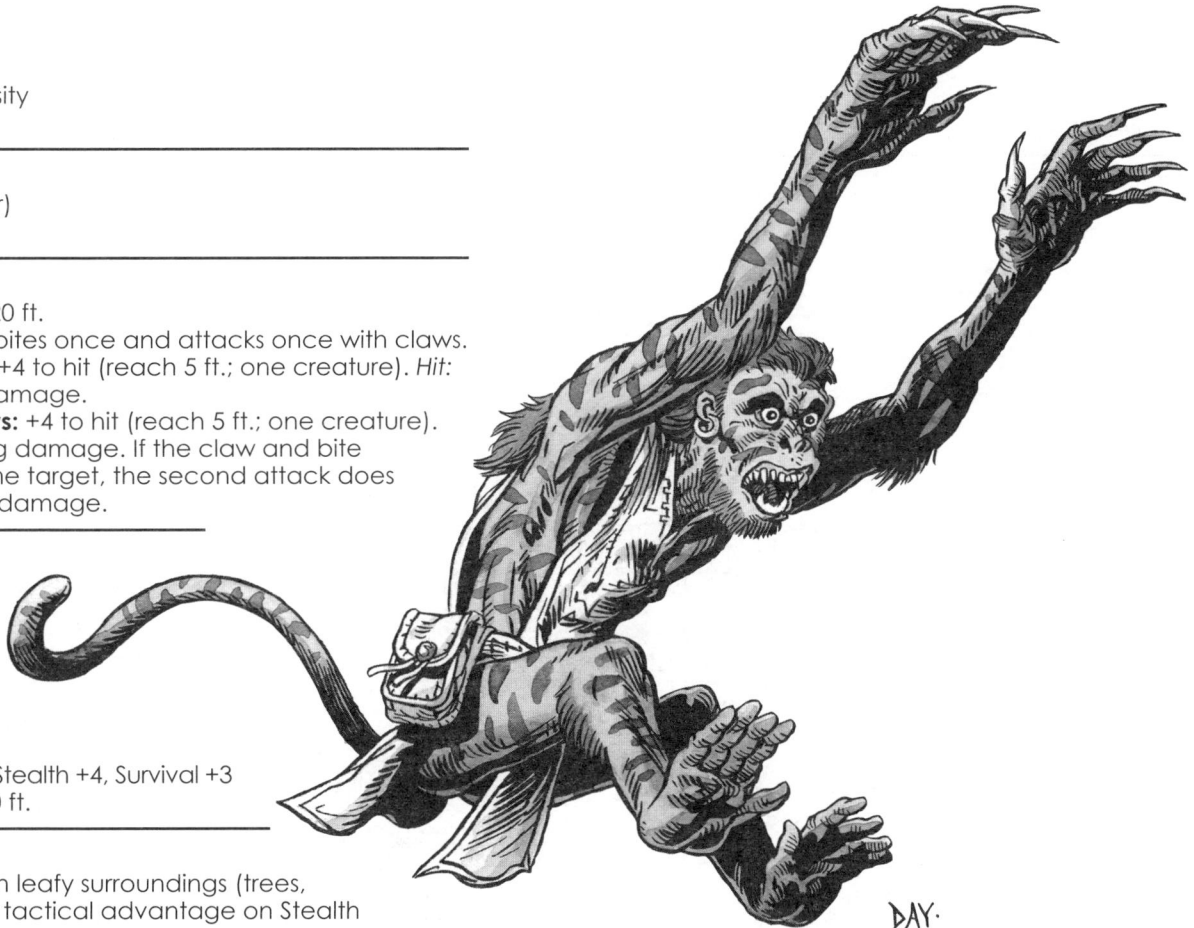

Kechs are notorious for surrounding their small villages with pits, snares, tripwires, and other types of traps and alarms. Their trapmaking skill rivals that of kobolds. It would be unfair to call them sadistic, because they don't derive any joy from causing pain. Even so, they have no concern for the suffering of creatures they capture, so being caught alive in a kech trap is a harrowing experience. Their traps are typically designed to maim and incapacitate rather than to kill or restrain.

Credit
The kech originally appeared in the First Edition *Monster Manual II* (© TSR/Wizards of the Coast, 1983) and is used by permission.

Copyright Notice
Author Scott Greene, based on original material by Gary Gygax.

Kelpie

A beautiful human female with long, flowing dark hair, emerald eyes, and milky-white skin sits nearby. She is cloaked in a robe of green seaweed.

Kelpie

XP 200 (CR 1)
NE Medium plant
Initiative +2

DEFENSE
AC 12
hp: 27 (5d8 + 5)
Resistance: Fire damage

OFFENSE
Speed: 20 ft., swim 30 ft.
Melee Attack—Claws: +4 to hit (reach 5 ft.; one creature). *Hit:* 1d6 + 2 slashing damage and a humanoid target must make a successful DC 13 Wis saving throw or be charmed by the kelpie. The effect is the same as the kelpie's charm ability (see below), but a humanoid charmed by this attack can repeat the saving throw at the end of each of its turns; the charm is broken by a successful save. Charming from the claw attack is unlimited.

STATISTICS
Str 13 (+1), **Dex** 14 (+2), **Con** 12 (+1), **Int** 8 (−1), **Wis** 13 (+1), **Cha** 17 (+3)
Languages: Common, Sylvan, telepathy
Skills: Deception +5, Persuasion +5
Senses: Darkvision 60 ft.

TRAITS
Amphibious: A kelpie can breathe equally well in air or underwater.
Charm (1/day): As an action, a kelpie can force a humanoid who can see the kelpie or hear her voice to make a DC 13 Wis saving throw. If the save succeeds, the creature is immune to kelpie charm for 24 hours. If the save fails, the victim is charmed by the kelpie for 24 hours (the saving throw is not repeated each round, as it is with the kelpie's claw attack). A charmed creature perceives the kelpie as a beautiful and alluring creature and wants nothing more than to sit adoringly by its side, even if that means diving underwater and staying there forever. The charm is broken if the kelpie is killed or knocked unconscious, or if *dispel magic, lesser restoration,* or comparable magic is used on the charmed creature.
Reshape Form: A kelpie can assume four different physical forms. The first is simply a mass of tangled seaweed. The second is a female of any Small or Medium humanoid race, or a semihuman form in which she appears as a

person from the waist up but from the hips down, she is still a tangle of seaweed. The third form is a hippocampus (see that entry). The fourth form is a Large horse. In each form, the kelpie retains all of her special abilities. Kelpies do not polymorph as true shapechangers do, they simply reshape the seaweed of their bodies. In all of her forms, a kelpie's flesh or fur has a greenish cast and her features are slightly distorted, but this distortion is usually perceived as a strikingly beautiful exoticness. A nearby observer can spot the true nature of the creature with a successful DC 13 Wis (Perception) check, provided they're suspicious in the first place and are not charmed.
Telepathy: A kelpie can communicate telepathically to a range of 1 mile with any creature she's touched who is not immune to her charm.

ECOLOGY
Environment: Any aquatic
Organization: Solitary or bed (2–5)

In their true form, kelpies are indistinguishable from seaweed. They live in saltwater and freshwater, lakes and swamps, flowing water and stagnated pools. Sages and scholars believe kelpies were created by an evil water goddess or an unusually powerful elemental entity.

In her human guise, a kelpie appears as a beautiful woman of any humanoid race, with flowing dark hair, emerald eyes, and soft, pale skin with a slight greenish tint. She is cloaked in robes of seaweed or wears nothing at all, and has normal humanoid limbs. Kelpies can pose as merfolk if they stay in the water so their legs are hidden. Kelpies enjoy luring people to a drowning death. They lie in wait along regular shipping lanes or the banks of rivers and lakes. When a vessel or a shore party approaches, they reshape themselves as women and begin acting as if they're drowning, or floating unconscious on a piece of wreckage from a lost ship. If the ruse is not detected and observers come to their aid, they try to charm their rescuers. Kelpies aren't interested in fighting to the death; their method is to charm a few victims, lure them into the water, then dive and swim down into deep water while their victims swim down after them and drown.

Credit
The kelpie originally appeared in the First Edition module *S2 White Plume Mountain* (© TSR/Wizards of the Coast, 1979) and later in the First Edition *Fiend Folio* (© TSR/Wizards of the Coast, 1981) and is used by permission.

Copyright Notice
Author Scott Greene, based on original material by Lawrence Schick.

Khargra

This creature resembles a man-sized cylinder covered in metallic scales. It sports three large "fins" spaced even around its circumference. Between each fin is a metal sheath from which slide long, clawlike arms. A large hole in the front of the cylindrical body is lined with many small, inward-curving, metallic teeth; this appears to function as the creature's mouth.

Khargra

XP 450 (CR 2)
Unaligned Small fiend
Initiative +2

DEFENSE

AC 16 (natural armor)
hp: 33 (6d6 + 12)
Immunity: Cold, fire, and poison damage; paralysis, poison, stun, unconsciousness

OFFENSE

Speed: 10 ft., burrow 30 ft.
Multiattack: A khargra attacks once with claws and bites once.
Melee Attack—Claws: +4 to hit (reach 5 ft.; one creature). *Hit:* 1d6 + 2 piercing damage and the target is grappled. If the target is using a shield, it is not grappled but it must make a successful DC 12 Str saving throw or the khargra pulls the shield away and drops it.
Melee Attack—Bite: +4 to hit (reach 5 ft.; one creature). *Hit:* 1d10 + 2 piercing damage, plus 1d8 fire damage if the target is grappled by the khargra.

STATISTICS

Str 14 (+2), **Dex** 14 (+2), **Con** 15 (+2), **Int** 10 (+0), **Wis** 11 (+0), **Cha** 10 (+0)
Languages: Common, Ignan (understands but can't speak)
Senses: Darkvision 60 ft.

TRAITS

Earth Glide A khargra can glide through stone, dirt, and almost any other sort of earth, including metal, as easily as a fish swims through water. Its burrowing leaves behind no tunnel or hole and does not create a ripple or other sign of its presence. A *move earth* spell cast on an area containing a burrowing khargra flings the khargra back 30 feet and stuns the creature for 1 round unless it makes a successful Con saving throw.
Metal Attunement: A khargra has tactical advantage on attack rolls against targets wearing metal armor (chain shirt or better) or carrying a metal shield.
Vulnerable to Heat: A khargra takes maximum damage from a *heat metal* spell.

ECOLOGY

Environment: Elemental Plane of Earth
Organization: Solitary or pack (2–5)

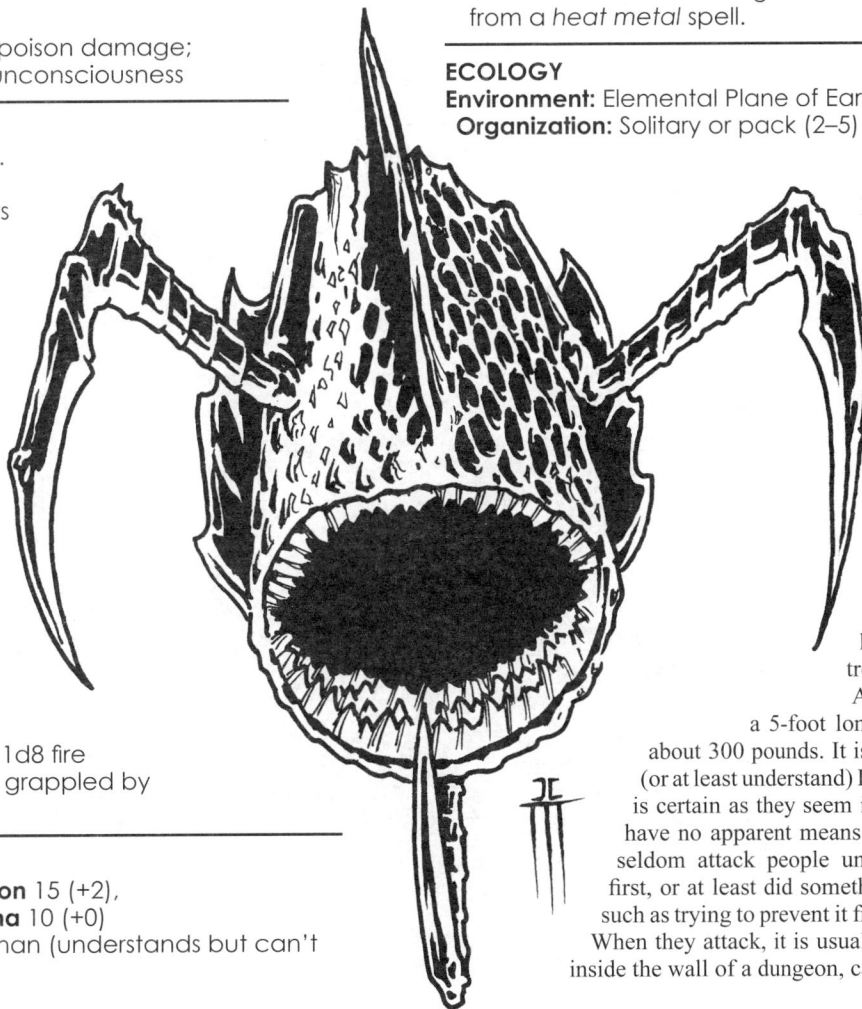

Khargras are native to the Elemental Plane of Earth and they seldom leave there willingly. When one is encountered on the Material Plane, it probably was summoned there. Occasion, however, a khargra slips through a tear in the planar fabric and enters the Material Plane to digest ores and metals not normally found on its native plane. It especially loves coins and other refined metal; a single khargra loose in a counting house can cause tremendous trouble.

A khargra is little more than a 5-foot long metal cylinder that weighs about 300 pounds. It is believed that khargras speak (or at least understand) Ignan and Common, but no one is certain as they seem immune to telepathy and they have no apparent means of forming speech. Khargras seldom attack people unless someone attacked them first, or at least did something that the khargra disliked, such as trying to prevent it from devouring valuable metal. When they attack, it is usually from ambush while hiding inside the wall of a dungeon, cavern, or castle.

Credit
The khargra originally appeared in the First Edition *Fiend Folio* (© TSR/Wizards of the Coast, 1981) and is used by permission.

Copyright Notice
Author Scott Greene, based on original material by Lawrence Schick.

Korred

This creature has the upper torso of a small humanoid and the lower torso of a goat, giving it an appearance similar to a satyr's. It has a long, flowing beard that, like its hair, is dark and wild, tangled and matted into frightful knots. It wears a simple leather tunic and a large leather pouch. Its brown eyes have an almost feral gleam.

Korred

XP 200 (CR 1)
CN Small fey
Initiative +2

DEFENSE

AC 13 (leather armor)
hp: 27 (6d6 + 6)
Resistance: Bludgeoning, piercing, and slashing damage from nonmagical weapons.
Immunity: Charm, stun, unconsciousness

OFFENSE

Speed: 30 ft.
Melee Attack—Club: +4 to hit (reach 5 ft.; one creature). *Hit:* 1d6 + 2 bludgeoning damage.
Melee Attack—Shears: +4 to hit (reach 5 ft.; one creature). *Hit:* 1d8 + 2 slashing damage. A korred scores a critical hit with shears if its attack roll is a natural 18, 19, or 20.
Ranged Attack—Stone: +4 to hit (range 20 ft./60 ft.; one creature). *Hit:* 1d4 + 2 bludgeoning damage.
Area Attack—Laugh (recharge 5, 6): automatic hit (range 60 ft.; all creatures in range). *Hit:* creatures in range that can hear the laugh must make a successful DC 12 Wis saving throw or be stunned for 1d3 rounds.

STATISTICS

Str 15 (+2), **Dex** 15 (+2), **Con** 12 (+1), **Int** 12 (+1), **Wis** 12 (+1), **Cha** 14 (+2)
Languages: Common, Sylvan
Skills: Sleight of Hand +4, Stealth +4
Senses: Darkvision 60 ft.

TRAITS

Animated Hair: A korred carries cuttings of its own hair, braided into ropes, in its leather pouch. It can quickly splice these short hair ropes into a longer rope and magically animate it to entangle foes. The time it takes to weave together enough rope for the job depends on the size of the creature to be entangled, as shown below. A korred's animated hair rope has AC 14,

8 hp, is immune to all but slashing damage, and flies with a speed of 30 feet. When it attacks its target, the target creature must make a successful DC 12 Dex or Str saving throw or be restrained. A restrained creature can repeat the saving throw at the end of each of its turns. The hair rope is destroyed by a successful Str saving throw, but a successful Dex save leaves it unaffected and it continues attacking.

Target Size	Time to Create	Duration
Up to Tiny	1 round	9 rounds
Small or Medium	2 rounds	6 rounds
Large	3 rounds	3 rounds

Mobility: An opponent has tactical disadvantage on opportunity attack rolls against a korred.
Spell-like Abilities: Korreds can use the following spell-like abilities, using Charisma as their casting ability (DC 12). A korred doesn't need material components to use these abilities.
At Will: *animate objects* (stones only), *shatter*, *speak with stone* (functions identically to *speak with plants*, but with stones instead), *stone shape*
Stone Stride: A korred can step into a stone and emerge from any other stone within 30 feet as part of normal movement. The stones must be at least as large as the korred. It can't end its turn inside a stone.

ECOLOGY

Environment: Temperate forests and hills
Organization: Solitary or gang (2–4)

A korred is a satyrlike creature that dwells deep in the forest or in remote, stony hills. Korreds keep all their meager belongings in a large, leather pouch. The contents of every korred's pouch varies with the tastes of the individual, but one thing all korreds carry is a pair of shears with which to cut their fast-growing, matted hair when it becomes too long.

Laughing is typically the first thing and the last thing a korred does in combat. It laughs at the start of the fight to stun its foes and gain the upper hand. It laughs at the end either to rub the losers' face in it, or to make possible a quick retreat. They prepare their entangling hair ropes just before the fight begins, if given the chance, but the limited duration of their animating magic makes it impossible for them to create these weapons any more than a few seconds in advance.

If korreds snare foes with their hair ropes, they love to administer a quick, embarrassing haircut with their shears before laughing in their victims' faces and quickly escaping through the stones while triumphantly waving the captured locks of hair.

Credit

The korred originally appeared in the First Edition *Monster Manual II* (© TSR/Wizards of the Coast, 1983) and is used by permission.

Copyright Notice

Author Scott Greene, based on original material by Gary Gygax.

Kurok-spirit

This ghostly creature resembles an enormous crocodile burning with flames of unlife as it swims out of the darkness toward you.

Kurok-spirit

XP 200 (CR 1)
CN Large fiend
Initiative +3

DEFENSE
AC 13
hp: 19 (3d10 + 3)
Immunity: Bludgeoning, piercing, and slashing damage from nonmagical or nonsilver weapons

OFFENSE
Speed: fly 30 ft.
Melee Attack—Bite: +5 to hit (reach 5 ft.; one creature). *Hit:* 1d8 necrotic damage and the target must make a successful DC 11 Wis saving throw or take 1d6 + 3 psychic damage.

STATISTICS
Str 1 (–5), **Dex** 16 (+3), **Con** 13 (+1),
Int 7 (–2), **Wis** 10 (+0), **Cha** 12 (+1)
Languages: Abyssal
Senses: Darkvision 60 ft.

TRAITS
Ghost Flames: Every creature that ends its turn within 5 feet of a kurok-spirit must make a successful DC 11 Con saving throw or take 1d4 necrotic damage. The creature's maximum number of hit points is reduced by an amount equal to the necrotic damage, and the kurok-spirit gains the same number of temporary hit points.
Incorporeal: A kurok-spirit can move through solid objects and other creatures as if they were difficult terrain. The kurok-spirit takes 1d10 force damage if it is still inside something solid at the end of its turn.
Soul Eater: A creature slain by a kurok-spirit can't be raised from the dead; its soul was devoured by the kurok-spirit and no longer exists.

ECOLOGY
Environment: Any
Organization: Solitary or bask (2–5)

A kurok-spirit is a fiendish spirit that manifests as a ghostly crocodile, seeming to "swim" through the air. Its most startling feature is the gray, ghostly fire that swirls and churns around it constantly. This fire drains life from living beings and transfers it to the kurok, which is ravenous for the stuff.

The most frightening aspect of the kurok-spirit, however, is that they devour the souls of the dead. A person slain by a kurok is lost forever; no magic short of divine intervention can return them to life. It's hypothesized that the souls consumed by a kurok aren't really destroyed but would be released if the kurok itself was tracked down and destroyed. These creatures are so rare, however, that this notion has never been tested or confirmed.

Credit

Author Matt Finch

Land Lamprey

This creature is a 3-foot-long, blackish-green eel with a large mouth lined with sharpened teeth that look as if they'd be hard to extract from flesh once they were sunken in.

Land Lamprey

XP 50 (CR 1/4)
Unaligned Small beast
Initiative +2

DEFENSE
AC 12
hp: 2 (1d6 −1)
Vulnerability: Fire damage

OFFENSE
Speed: 40 ft.
Melee Attack—Bite: +4 to hit (reach 5 ft.; one creature).
Hit: 1d4 + 2 piercing damage and the lamprey enters the target's space and attaches itself to the target. While attached, the lamprey doesn't attack but automatically inflicts 1d4 + 2 piercing damage at the start of its turn. The lamprey can't move on its own while attached, but it moves with the other creature. To get free from the lamprey, the target creature uses its action to make a Str (Athletics) check contested by the lamprey's Dex check. The lamprey has tactical advantage on this check. It can't use its bite attack again until it is pulled free or it releases the target, either of which automatically moves it out of that creature's space. A lamprey detaches immediately if it caused 5 or 6 damage that turn.

STATISTICS
Str 6 (−2), **Dex** 14 (+2), **Con** 9 (−1),
Int 1 (−5), **Wis** 10 (+0), **Cha** 2 (−4)
Languages: None

Senses: Tremorsense 60 ft.

ECOLOGY
Environment: Temperate land or underground
Organization: Solitary, pack (2–5), or swarm (6–11)

Land lampreys can be found in all but the hottest and the coldest environments. They prefer the darkness and dampness of the underground world and are most often encountered there, but they also hunt on the surface near fissures and caves that lead into deeper subterranean realms.

A school of land lampreys wriggling across the ground as if they're swimming can be a startling sight the first time they're encountered. Some people find them amusing, even comical, until the creatures leap onto people, bite through their clothing and armor, and start sucking out a person's blood, fluids, and other organs. Thankfully, they hate fire, and will often release a victim if they're struck with a torch—assuming the fire doesn't kill the creature outright.

Credit
The land lamprey originally appeared in the First Edition *Monster Manual II* (© TSR/Wizards of the Coast, 1983) and is used by permission.

Copyright Notice
Author Scott Greene, based on original material by Gary Gygax.

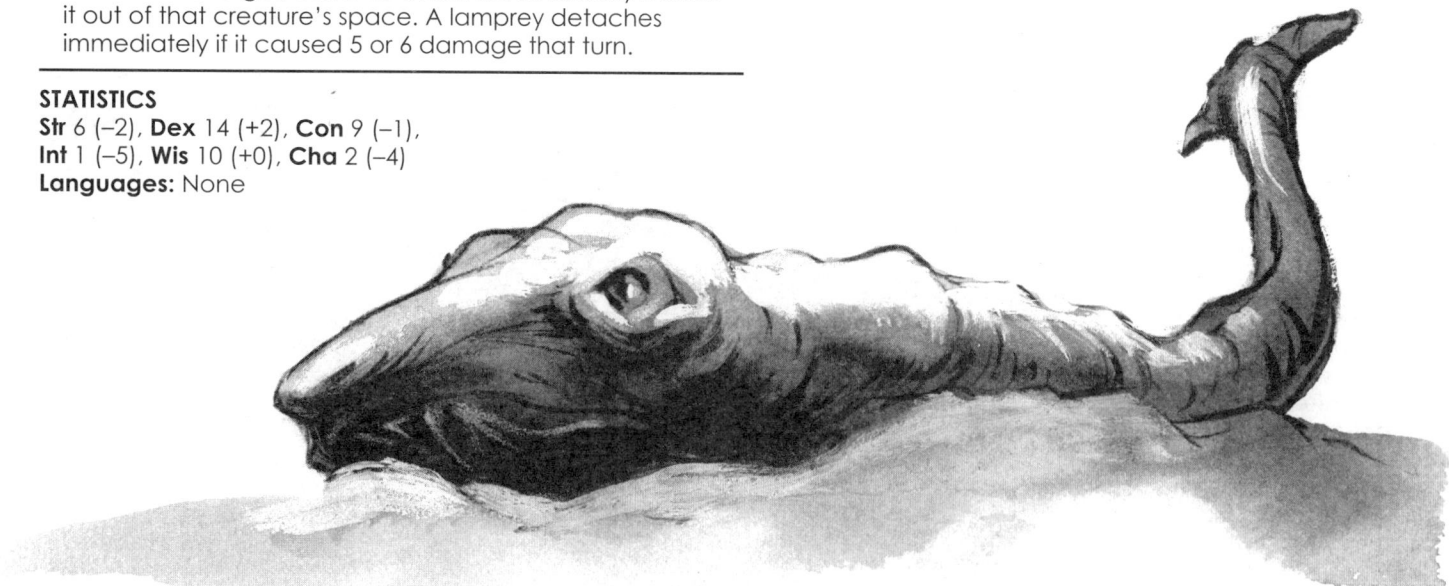

Lava Child

This creature is a stocky humanoid standing 5 or 6 feet tall with sooty black hair, green eyes, and flesh that ranges from pink to crimson. It sometimes wears clothing crudely fashioned from hides, and sometimes goes naked. Its face has a curious, almost childlike appearance and seems to be imprinted with a permanent, unchanging smile.

Lava Child

XP 200 (CR 1)
N Medium humanoid (elemental)
Initiative +0

DEFENSE
AC 11 (natural armor)
hp: 22 (4d8 + 4)
Immunity: Fire damage; damage from metal weapons
Vulnerability: Cold damage

OFFENSE
Speed: 25 ft.
Multiattack: A lava child bites once and attacks once with claws.
Melee Attack—Claws: +3 to hit (reach 5 ft.; one creature). *Hit:* 1d8 + 1 slashing damage.
Melee Attack—Bite: +3 to hit (reach 5 ft.; one creature). *Hit:* 1d6 + 1 bludgeoning damage. If the lava child bites the same creature that it hit with its claws this turn, its bite does an additional 1d8 fire damage.

STATISTICS
Str 13 (+1), **Dex** 11 (+0), **Con** 13 (+1), **Int** 10 (+0), **Wis** 11 (+0), **Cha** 11 (+0)
Languages: Ignan
Senses: Darkvision 60 ft.

TRAITS
Elemental Vulnerability: Lava children take 1 extra damage per damage die from spells of the tempest domain. They are unaffected (either directly or indirectly) by spells of the transmutation school.
Metal Immunity: Lava children are completely unaffected by metal. They can walk through metal doors or bars as if the metal wasn't there, and metal objects and weapons, including magic weapons, pass right through a lava child's body without affecting it in any way. Because of this, a lava child also has tactical advantage on melee attack rolls against targets wearing armor that is predominantly metal.

Lava Child Shaman: Every band of lava children includes one arcane spellcaster. A lava child spellcaster has heightened Charisma (13) and the ability to cast the following spells, using Charisma as its spellcasting ability (DC 11, attack +3). It doesn't need material components to cast these spells. The shaman is CR 1 (200 XP).
Cantrips (at will): *fire bolt, dancing lights*
1st level (x4): *burning hands, comprehend languages, magic missile*
2nd level (x2): *continual flame, scorching ray*

ECOLOGY
Environment: Underground
Organization: Gang (3–6) or band (7–14 plus 1 shaman and 1–8 noncombatants)

Lava children make their lairs deep underground and usually in warm areas—the warmer, the better. Volcanoes, hot springs, thermal vents, and other geothermal areas are the most likely to attract lava children. They are reclusive and rarely have dealings with other races. The exceptions are those races with a similar elemental structure and tolerance for extreme heat, such as magmin, salamanders, and azers.

When they're drawn into combat, lava children attack with their clawed hands and vicious bite. When they claw and bite the same target, their red-hot breath causes extra damage. Their melee fighters don't shy away from enemies in heavy armor, because metal armor offers little protection against lava children claws and teeth. Quick-moving, agile foes and those that dish out cold damage are among their chief worries.

Credit
The Lava Children originally appeared in the First Edition *Fiend Folio* (© TSR/Wizards of the Coast, 1981) and is used by permission.

Copyright Notice
Author Scott Greene, based on original material by Jim Donohoe.

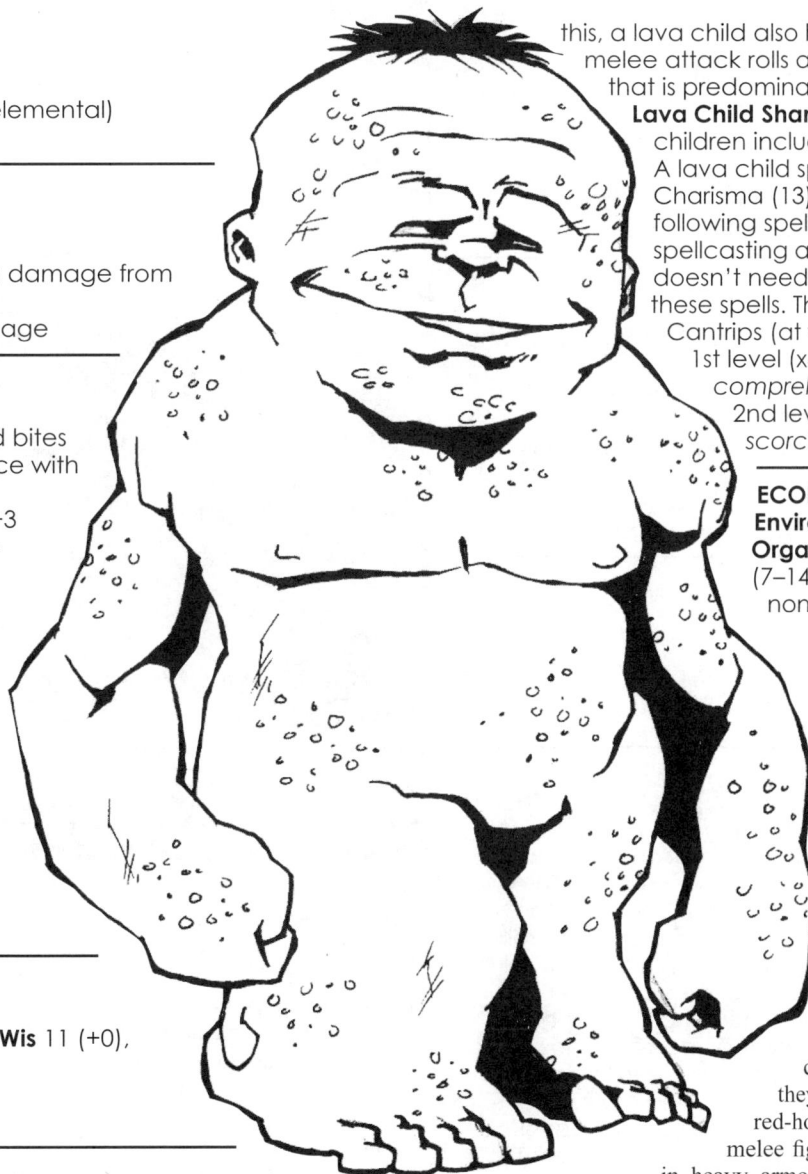

Leng Spider

This creature resembles an enormous spider with the glint of malevolent intelligence in its multifaceted eyes. Its bloated, purple body moves with surprising grace on seven legs.

Leng Spider

XP 2,300 (CR 6)
CE Huge aberration
Initiative +3

DEFENSE

AC 15 (natural armor)
hp: 97 (15d12)
Resistance: Cold damage
Immunity: Poison damage; poison, suffocation

OFFENSE

Speed: 40 ft.
Multiattack: A Leng-spider bites once and attacks once with web flails.
Melee Attack—Bite: +6 to hit (reach 5 ft.; one creature). *Hit:* 2d10 + 3 piercing damage and the target must make a successful DC 11 Con saving throw or be poisoned by Leng venom (see below).
Melee Attack—Web Flails: +6 to hit (reach 5 ft.; one creature). *Hit:* 2d10 + 3 bludgeoning damage.

STATISTICS

Str 14 (+2), **Dex** 16 (+3), **Con** 10 (+0),
Int 18 (+4), **Wis** 15 (+2), **Cha** 16 (+3)
Languages: Deep Speech, Unique
Skills: Arcana +7, Stealth +6
Senses: Darkvision 60 ft.

TRAITS

Leng Venom: A Leng spider's venom causes flesh to blister and rot, reducing the target's Charisma score by 1 point. It also triggers vivid and horrific hallucinations. A poisoned creature suffers the effect of the poisoned condition and must act as if affected by the *confusion* spell. The *confusion* effect ends the second time the creature rolls a 9 or 10 at the start of its turn (allowing it to act normally that turn). The poisoned condition persists until after the creature's next long rest, or until the poison is neutralized magically. Lost Charisma can be regained through magic.
Spell-like Abilities: A Leng-spider can use the following spell-like abilities, using Intelligence as its casting ability (DC 16, attack +8). The Leng-spider doesn't need material components to use these abilities. It can cast *dispel magic* as a bonus action.
At Will: *dispel magic*
3/day: *invisibility*, *phantasmal force*
1/day: *dominate monster*

ECOLOGY

Environment: Any land
Organization: Solitary or gang (2–5)

The immense purple spiders of Leng are hideously bloated, yet they move with a fluid grace. A Leng-spider's body can grow up to 15 feet long, and they weigh several tons. Most leng-spiders possess seven legs, but some have nine, eleven, or five. They never have an even number, and the legs are positioned according to the rules of some alien symmetry that is unfathomable to human minds.

The spiders of Leng have long warred with that realm's more humanoid denizens, but this does not make the spiders allies of sane life. Leng-spiders see themselves as the only entities truly deserving of power. The only creatures they do not continually plan to destroy, apart from their kin, are their magically controlled slaves—most of whom probably would prefer death to the nightmare of servitude to the spiders of Leng. Fortunately, Leng-spiders have no intrinsic way to travel to the Material Plane. They must use meticulously-constructed portals or other methods to visit this world.

Despite their legendary cruelty, Leng-spiders build lairs with haunting beauty from their own webbing and other natural material. Their webs are similar to those of ordinary giant spiders, but they don't burn easily. The spiders' artistry extends to traps as well; their homes are laced with devices that are doubly deadly to the unwary because of their disarming beauty.

In addition to their poisonous bite, a Leng-spider's webs are also used as weapons. The spider attaches a weight (often nothing more complicated than a rock or a skull) to a length of webbing, which it then swings like a flail. Leverage from the spider's long limbs turn these makeshift flails into deadly weapons.

Credit
Author Matt Finch

Leopard, Snow

Grayish fur covers this large cat, allowing it to blend in with the high-contrast light and shadow of snow drifts.

Snow Leopard

XP 50 (CR 1/4)
Unaligned Medium beast
Initiative +2

DEFENSE
AC 12
hp: 16 (3d8 + 3)

OFFENSE
Speed: 50 ft.
Multiattack: A snow leopard attacks once with its claws. If that attack hits, it bites the same target.
Melee Attack—Claws: +4 to hit (reach 5 ft.; one creature). *Hit:* 1d4 + 2 slashing damage.
Melee Attack—Bite: +4 to hit (reach 5 ft.; one creature). *Hit:* 1d6 + 2 piercing damage.

STATISTICS
Str 15 (+2), **Dex** 15 (+2), **Con** 12 (+1), **Int** 3 (−4), **Wis** 14 (+2), **Cha** 7 (−2)
Languages: None
Skills: Perception +4, Stealth +4
Senses: Darkvision 60 ft.

TRAITS
Snow Camouflage: A snow leopard has tactical advantage on Stealth checks in an arctic or snowy environment.
Snow Mobility: Because of its large, fur-covered paws, a snow leopard never treats snowy or icy ground as difficult terrain.

ECOLOGY
Environment: cold forests, plains, and mountains
Organization: Solitary, pair, or den (1–2 adults plus 1–4 cubs)

Snow leopards are relatives of the common leopard. They're found in the coldest regions of the world, inhabiting mountain ranges, taiga, and snowy coniferous forests. Their lairs are typically rocky shelters lined with their own fur for warmth.

Snow leopards are strong, agile, nocturnal hunters. Their diet consists of livestock, wild boars, hares, and deer. Like most other big cats, they stalk and ambush their prey. Slain prey is dragged back to the lair and devoured over a period of several days.

Snow leopards are generally solitary, but a pair can be encountered during mating season. A den typically contains up to four cubs. Captured snow leopard cubs can be sold on the exotic-animal market for up to 500 gp.

A snow leopard is about five feet long, with light gray or smoky gray fur that turns to white on its underbelly. Its fur is marked with large rings that contain smaller and darker spots of dark gray or black. The fur is over an inch thick, providing the snow leopard with warmth against the extreme cold of its environment. Eyes are gray or dark blue. The cat's paws are large and thickly furred, enabling it to maintain its footing on normally treacherous ice and to move quickly across deep snow.

Snow leopards are hunted by many races for their fur, which is both visually striking and warm.

Unlike other great cats, snow leopards do not roar. Their only vocalization is a low, soft moan.

Copyright Notice
Author Scott Greene.

Leucrotta

This hideous, staglike creature has the head of a badger,
yellow-gray fangs, and demonically glowing eyes.

Adult Leucrotta

XP 450 (CR 2)
CE Large monstrosity
Initiative +2

DEFENSE

AC 14 (natural armor)
hp: 39 (6d10 + 6)

OFFENSE

Speed: 40 ft.
Multiattack: A leucrotta bites once and kicks once.
Melee Attack—Bite: +4 to hit (reach 5 ft.; one creature). *Hit:* 1d8 + 2 piercing damage.
Melee Attack—Kick: +4 to hit (reach 5 ft.; one creature behind the leucrotta). *Hit:* 1d6 + 2 bludgeoning damage and the target is knocked prone.

STATISTICS

Str 14 (+2), **Dex** 14 (+2), **Con** 12 (+1),
Int 8 (–1), **Wis** 9 (–1), **Cha** 12 (+1)
Languages: Unique (Leucrotta)
Skills: Acrobatics +4, Deception +5, Stealth +4
Senses: Darkvision 60 ft.

TRAITS

Armor-Piercing Bite: The bony ridges that a leucrotta has for teeth can chew through metal or wood. When a leucrotta scores a critical hit with its bite attack, the target's armor or shield (GM's choice), if any, loses one point of armor protection; e.g., a damaged shield provides just one point of AC instead of two, or a chain shirt provides AC 12 + Dex mod instead of AC 13 + Dex mod. This damage is cumulative, but it can be repaired by an armorer for 20% of the armor or shield's new cost per critical hit inflicted on it. Magical properties continue to function while the armor or shield is damaged.
Kicking Retreat: When a leucrotta turns to flee, it instinctively kicks with both rear legs as a bonus action before racing away. The leucrotta still provokes an opportunity attack when it leaves a character's reach.
Mimic Voice: A leucrotta can mimic the voice of a man, woman, child, or a domestic animal in pain. This is often used to lure a victim into attack range. To mimic a voice, the leucrotta must make a Cha (Deception) check opposed by the passive Wis (Perception) of any listeners. Characters who expressly try to determine whether the sound is mimicry can make an active Wis (Perception) check instead.

ECOLOGY

Environment: Temperate or tropical forests or hills
Organization: Solitary, pair, or pack (3–12)

Young Leucrotta

XP 50 (CR 1/4)
CE Medium monstrosity
Initiative +2

DEFENSE

AC 13 (natural armor)

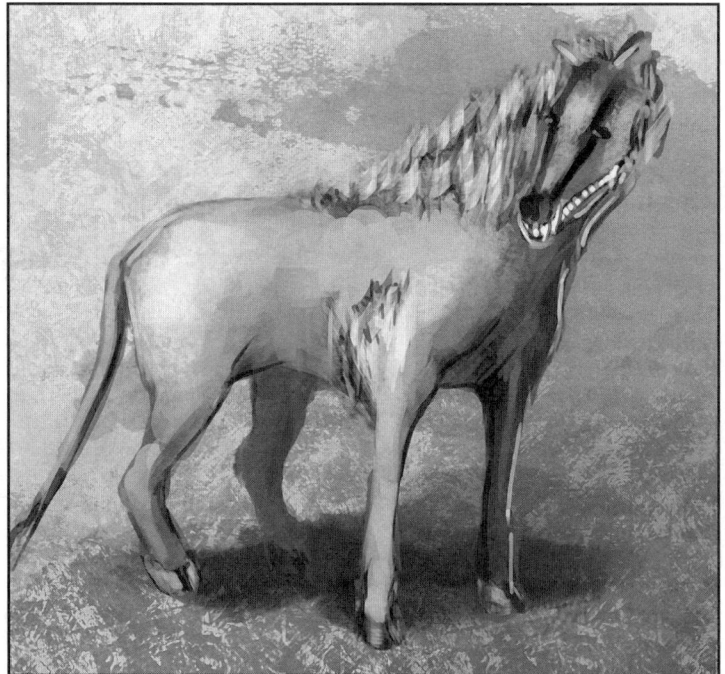

hp: 10 (3d8 – 3)

OFFENSE

Speed: 30 ft.
Melee Attack—Bite: +2 to hit (reach 5 ft.; one creature). *Hit:* 1d4 piercing damage.
Melee Attack—Kick: +2 to hit (reach 5 ft.; one creature behind the leucrotta). *Hit:* 1d6 bludgeoning damage and the target must make a successful DC 10 Str saving throw or be knocked prone.

STATISTICS

Str 10 (+0), **Dex** 15 (+2), **Con** 8 (–1),
Int 8 (–1), **Wis** 9 (–1), **Cha** 10 (+0)
Languages: Unique (Leucrotta)
Skills: Acrobatics +4, Deception +4, Stealth +4
Senses: Darkvision 60 ft.

TRAITS

Armor-Piercing Bite: Armor-piercing bite: The bony ridges that a leucrotta has for teeth can chew through metal or wood. When a leucrotta scores a critical hit with its bite attack, the target's armor or shield (GM's choice), if any, loses one point of armor protection; e.g., a damaged shield provides just one point of AC instead of two, or a chain shirt provides AC 12 + Dex mod instead of AC 13 + Dex mod. This damage is cumulative, but it can be repaired by an armorer for 20% of the armor or shield's new cost per critical hit inflicted on it. Magical properties continue to function while the armor or shield is damaged.
Kicking Retreat: When a leucrotta turns to flee, it instinctively kicks with both rear legs as a bonus action before racing away. The leucrotta still provokes an opportunity attack when it leaves a character's reach.
Mimic Voice: A leucrotta can mimic the voice of a man,

woman, child, or a domestic animal in pain. This is often used to lure a victim into attack range. To mimic a voice, the leucrotta must make a Cha (Deception) check opposed by the passive Wis (Perception) of any listeners. Characters who expressly try to determine whether the sound is mimicry can make an active Wis (Perception) check instead.

ECOLOGY
Environment: Temperate or tropical forests or hills
Organization: Solitary, pair, or pack (3–12)

A leucrotta is a horrible, unbearably ugly beast. It has the body of a stag, the head of a badger, and a leonine tail. It has bony, yellow-gray ridges for teeth and burning, feral red eyes. Their bodies are tan, darkening to black at the head. The stench of rotting corpses surrounds the beast, and its breath reeks of the grave. A full-sized male can reach seven feet tall at the shoulder, though they average six feet. Other animals shun this foul creature.

Leucrotta are intelligent and speak their own language. They are evil and malicious. Because of their mountain goat-like surefootedness, leucrotta normally make their lairs in treacherous, rocky crags accessible only to them.

Lithonnite

*What appeared to be a submerged, moss-covered boulder turns out
to be some type of monstrous crustacean, with slashing, crushing tentacles.*

Lithonnite
XP 700 (CR 4)
Unaligned Large monstrosity
Initiative +1

DEFENSE
AC 18 (natural armor)
hp: 68 (8d10 + 24)
Resistance: Psychic damage

OFFENSE
Speed: 10 ft., swim 30 ft.
Multiattack: A lithonnite attacks twice with tentacles.
Melee Attack—Tentacles: +5 to hit (reach 5 ft.; one creature). *Hit:* 1d10 + 3 slashing damage. If both attacks hit the same target, it takes an additional 2d6 bludgeoning damage and is grappled and restrained. While the lithonnite has a target grappled, it can attack only that target.

STATISTICS
Str 16 (+3), **Dex** 13 (+1), **Con** 17 (+3),
Int 4 (–3), **Wis** 10 (+0), **Cha** 4 (–3)
Languages: None
Skills: Stealth +3
Senses: Darkvision 60 ft.

TRAITS
Soft Underbelly: A lithonnite's shell has AC 18. If it can be attacked from underneath, where its body is exposed, its AC is only 11. Its soft body has resistance to bludgeoning damage from nonmagical weapons.
Stony Camouflage: While sitting motionless in water, a lithonnite is impossible to distinguish visually from a moss-covered boulder.

ECOLOGY
Environment: Temperate and warm aquatic, underground
Organization: Solitary or pair

Lithonnites are enormous creatures related to mollusks. They live in shallow water both on the surface and underground. When the lithonnite's body is at rest in shallow water (2 to 6 feet of depth is its preferred environment), the shell is nearly indistinguishable from any other boulder or natural rock. A lithonnite is always covered with barnacles, moss, seaweed, starfish, and other aquatic life, adding to its camouflage.

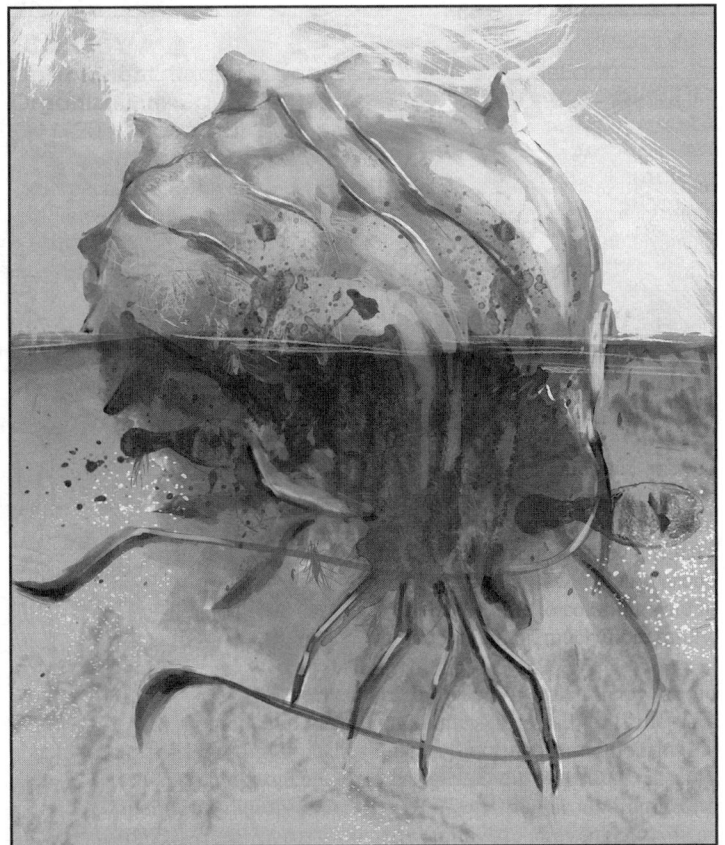

Most of a lithonnite's body is encased in a hard shell that rivals plate armor for toughness. Even its eyes are protected by heavy, rocklike protrusions. This shell is nearly as hard as stone, giving the lithonnite excellent protection against enemies. The creature's tentacles are long enough to reach around the shell and strike effectively in any direction.

It is not possible for the lithonnite to draw its soft body entirely into the shell. If attackers can get underneath the lithonnite, where its squishy flesh is exposed, it's quite vulnerable. The lithonnite tries to protect itself by staying in shallow water, where it can use the stony lake bottom or a coral reef for protection. A lithonnite can be rolled onto its back with a successful DC 25 Str (Athletics) check, but it will right itself again on its next turn unless it's somehow prevented from doing so.

Credit
    Author Matt Finch

Magmoid

This elemental appears to be a massive sphere of swirling fire and superheated, liquid rock.

Magmoid

XP 1,100 (CR 4)
Unaligned Large elemental
Initiative +2

DEFENSE

AC 16 (natural armor)
hp: 75 (10d10 + 20)
Resistance: Bludgeoning and slashing damage from nonmagical weapons
Immunity: Fire damage
Vulnerability: Cold damage

OFFENSE

Speed: 40 ft.
Melee Attack—
Slam: +5 to hit (reach 5 ft.; one creature). *Hit:* 2d8 + 3 bludgeoning damage plus 1d8 fire damage, and the creature takes 1d8 fire damage at the start of its next turn.
Area Attack—Magma Blast (recharge 5, 6): automatic hit (range 40 ft. line; creatures in line). *Hit:* Each target must make a successful DC 12 Dex saving throw or take 2d8 + 2 fire damage plus 1d8 fire damage at the start of its turn for 1d3 turns.

STATISTICS

Str 17 (+3), **Dex** 14 (+2), **Con** 15 (+2), **Int** 4 (–3), **Wis** 11 (+0), **Cha** 10 (+0)
Languages: Ignan (understands but can't speak)
Skills: Athletics +5
Senses: Blindsight 60 ft.

TRAITS

All-Around Awareness: A magmoid "sees" perfectly in all directions. Attackers never gain tactical advantage or bonus damage against it from the presence of nearby allies.
Magma Body: Every time a magmoid is struck by a melee weapon, the weapon's wielder must make a successful DC 12 Dex saving throw or the weapon is destroyed by the heat of the magmoid's body. Magical weapons and bludgeoning weapons have tactical advantage on the saving throw, piercing weapons have tactical disadvantage, and magical piercing weapons have neither advantage nor disadvantage. Missiles are destroyed automatically. Creatures that attack a magmoid unarmed or with natural weapons take 1d8 fire damage each time one of their attacks hits.

ECOLOGY

Environment: Elemental Plane of Fire
Organization: Solitary

Magmoids are giant balls of elemental fire and magma that burn everything they come in contact with. Though they are typically found only on the Elemental Planes of Fire and Earth, or the Plane of Molten Skies (see the ***City of Brass*** by **Necromancer Games** for details on this demiplane), one occasionally slips through a portal or nexus into the Material Plane (usually in the heart of a volcano) where it wreaks havoc on everything that cross its path until something destroys it. The magmoid leaves a scorched wake of flaming buildings, seared foliage, burned creatures, and even melted rocks wherever it rolls across the landscape. Attempts by arcane spellcasters (foolish ones, some would say) to control or harness the power of a magmoid thus far have failed.

Magmoids are thought to be living extensions of the Elemental Plane of Fire. A giant magmoid measuring 30 feet across is rumored to exist near the Sea of Fire, but no one has ever brought back a first-hand account of having actually seen it. What role these creatures fulfill in their native environment is unknown.

Bubbling pockets and glowing blisters on the magmoid's form serve as sensory organs, but they change size and position continually.

A magmoid can eject a spray of superheated magma, or it can simply hurl itself against foes. It has no fear of opponents who fight with melee weapons, for obvious reasons. They've been known to attack humanoids armed with swords and spears first, and to ignore them entirely while seeking out spellcasters with their magma blasts. In short, they are unpredictable and dangerous.

Copyright Notice
Author Scott Greene.

Mandragora

This small, vaguely humanoid plant-creature is mottled green and brown.
Its body, if it could be called that, is a solid mass of vegetable matter covered in lumps.
Beneath that, its roots twist into ropy, grasping arms and gangly legs with splayed feet.

Mandragora

XP 25 (CR 1/8)
NE Small plant (fungus)
Initiative +1

DEFENSE

AC 11
hp: 4 (1d6 + 1)
Resistance: Fire damage
Immunity: Psychic damage; charm, fright, stun, unconsciousness

---

OFFENSE

Speed: 30 ft., burrow 15 ft.
Melee Attack—Tentacles: +3 to hit (reach 5 ft.; one creature). *Hit:* 1d4 + 1 bludgeoning damage and the target must make a successful DC 11 Dex saving throw or be grappled.
Melee Attack—Strangulation: automatic hit (one creature already grappled by the mandragora at the start of the mandragora's turn). *Hit:* 1d6 + 1 bludgeoning damage.

STATISTICS

Str 11 (+0), **Dex** 13 (+1), **Con** 13 (+1),
Int 8 (−1), **Wis** 10 (+0), **Cha** 9 (−1)
Languages: None
Senses: Darkvision 60 ft., tremorsense 60 ft.

ECOLOGY

Environment: Temperate forests
Organization: Solitary, gang (2–5), or colony (3–18)

The mandragora is a small, vaguely humanoid fungus that prefers to hunt and kill its own carrion rather than scavenging for creatures that are already dead. If the mandragora goes more than three days without fresh meat, it burrows into the ground and attaches to local tree roots, from which it draws sustenance until living prey wanders nearby.

The mandragora stands about 4 feet tall. Most of them have two "arms" and two "legs," but that isn't universal; some have more than four limbs, and the frequently have unequal numbers of arms and legs.

This creature's chief attack is by strangulation. Once it wraps its arm-roots around a foe's throat, it hangs on until the prey is dead or the mandragora itself is killed. They tend to strip off all of a slain creature's clothing and belongings to lighten the body before dragging it away to a quiet spot, where it is covered in a thick layer of slime and dissolved at the mandragora's leisure. The digestive process leaves behind a pile of softened, rubbery bones that are the tell-tale spoor of mandragoras.

Credit

The mandragora originally appeared in the First Edition *Monster Manual II* (© TSR/Wizards of the Coast, 1983) and is used by permission.

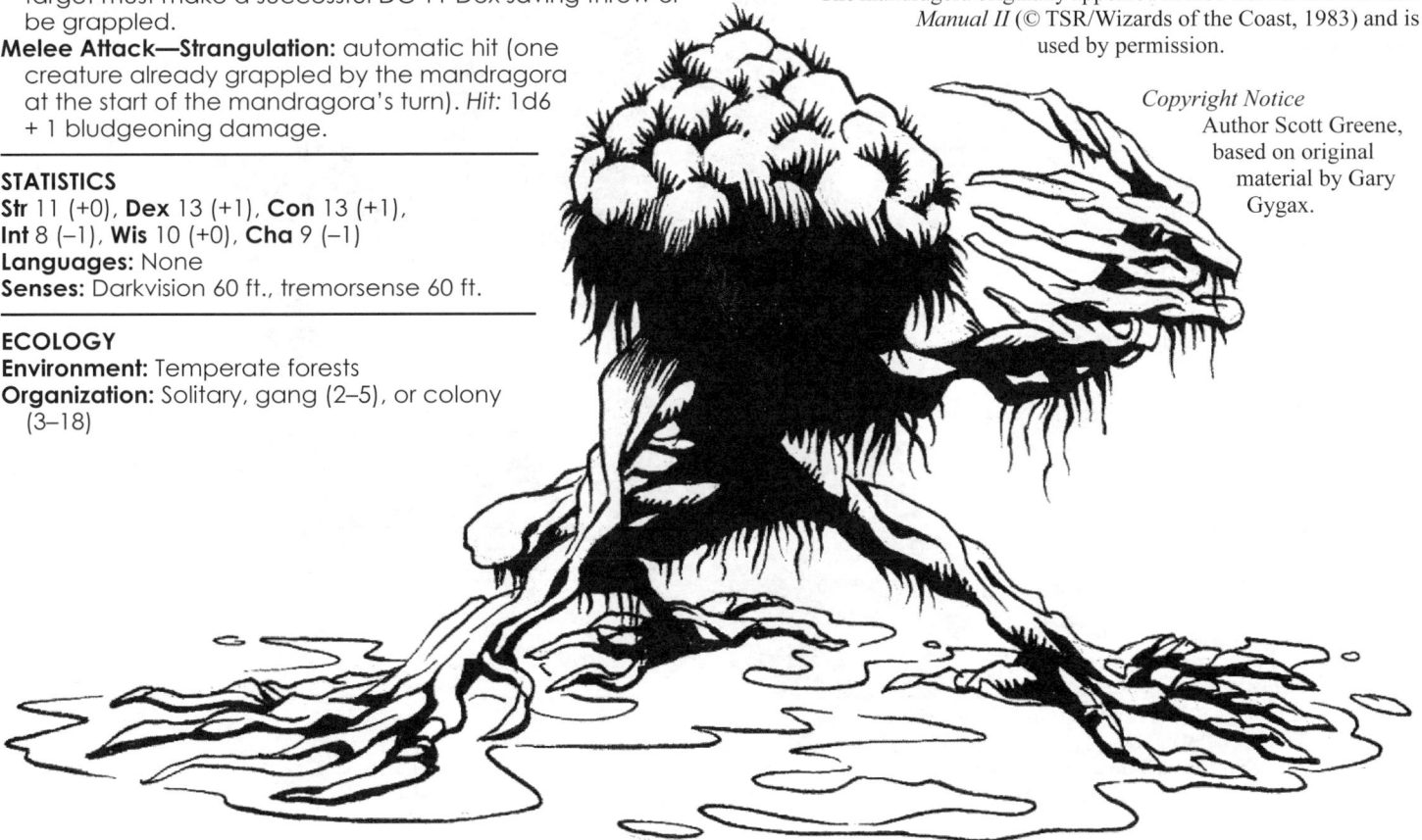

Mandrill

This brightly-colored primate has a bushy mane, dense fur, and a long ridged snout.

Mandrill

XP 25 (CR 1/8)
Unaligned Small beast
Initiative +2

DEFENSE

AC 12
hp: 9 (2d6 + 2)

OFFENSE

Speed: 30 ft., climb 30 ft.
Melee Attack—Bite: +4 to hit (reach 5 ft.; one creature). *Hit:* 1d4 + 2 piercing damage.
Ranged Attack—Thrown Object: +4 to hit (range 20 ft./50 ft.; one creature). *Hit:* 1d4 + 2 bludgeoning damage.

STATISTICS

Str 10 (+0), **Dex** 15 (+2),
Con 12 (+1), **Int** 4 (–3),
Wis 12 (+1), **Cha** 6 (–2)
Languages: None
Senses: Darkvision 60 ft.

ECOLOGY

Environment: Warm forests
Organization: Solitary, foraging pack (2–5), group (4–9 adults plus 4–10 young) or colony (10–40 adults plus 15–160 young)

Mandrills are primates found in warm forests. They are active during the day, when mandrills spend their time hunting and foraging on the forest floor. At night, the animals seek shelter in the trees. They subsist on a diet of fruits, nuts, berries, small insects, seeds, roots, and occasionally grass. The typical group has a foraging territory of 5 to 8 square miles. A mandrill often stores food in its cheeks while it continues hunting or climbing; it can store an entire meal in its pouchy cheeks.

The average adult mandrill reaches a height of just under 3 feet tall and weighs around 35 pounds. A mandrill's fur is olive brown fading to a paler color on its underbelly. Adult males have a bright blue and red snout and a yellowish "beard." Females and young mandrills have similar but duller coloration.

Mandrills are generally passive creatures that rarely fight. When danger threatens, they prefer to climb into the trees and either dash away or pelt the intruder with fruit and branches. That situation can change suddenly if mothers believe that their young are threatened. Likewise, a foraging pack defends its food tenaciously.

Mantari

This creature looks like a man-sized flying manta ray, dark gray in color.

Mantari

XP 25 (CR 1/8)
NE Medium monstrosity
Initiative +2

DEFENSE
AC 12
hp: 4 (1d8)

OFFENSE
Speed: 5 ft., fly 50 ft.
Melee Attack—Tail Sting: +4 to hit (reach 5 ft.; one creature). *Hit:* 1d8 + 2 piercing damage.

STATISTICS
Str 12 (+1), **Dex** 14 (+2), **Con** 11 (+0), **Int** 2 (–4), **Wis** 11 (+0), **Cha** 6 (–2)
Languages: None
Senses: Darkvision 60 ft.

ECOLOGY
Environment: Underground
Organization: Solitary or pack (2–4)

Mantari appear as large manta rays, gray in color, with a long smooth tail that ends in a sharpened barb. The mantari flies silently through its underground world in search of prey, and when encountered, it is often hungry and immediately attacks.

Mantari sustain themselves on a diet of rats, carrion, and subterranean plants, but prefer the taste of fresh meat—particularly humans and gnomes.

The mantari attacks by slashing and stinging with its tail. Its preferred method of attack is to circle in the air near the ceiling of a high cavern, where it is hidden by darkness, and then dive onto a target by surprise.

Credit
The mantari originally appeared in the First Edition *Fiend Folio* (© TSR/Wizards of the Coast, 1981) and is used by permission.

Copyright Notice
Author Scott Greene, based on original material by David Wormell.

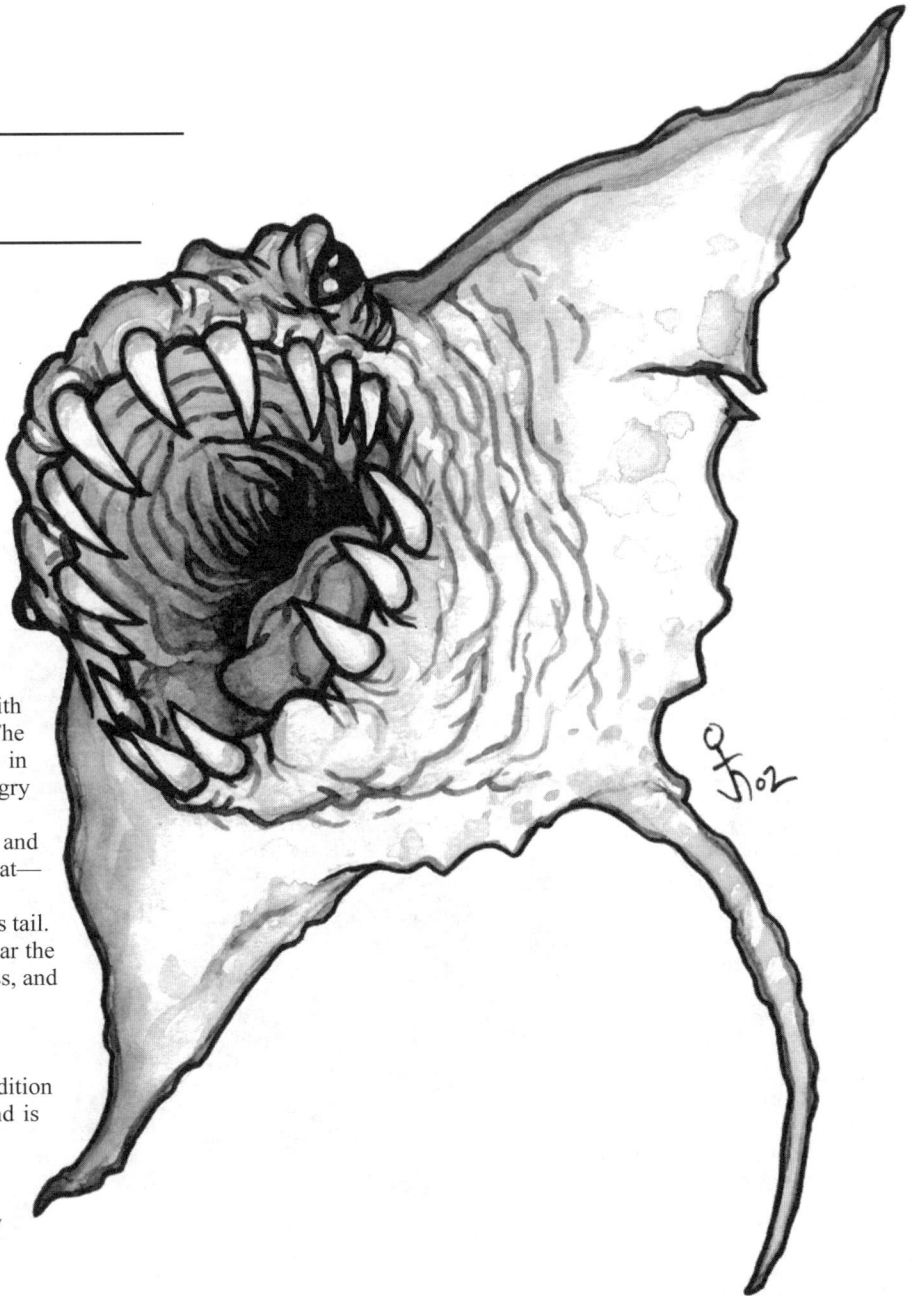

Midnight Peddler

This creature appears as a human cloaked in a gray, hooded robe. A long sharp jaw protrudes from under the hood. It moves with a shuffling gait, pushing a wooden cart that squeaks as it rolls along.

Midnight Peddler

XP 100 (CR 1/2)
N Medium fey
Initiative +1

DEFENSE
AC 11
hp: 45 (7d8 + 14)
Saving Throws: Con +4

OFFENSE
Speed: 20 ft.
Melee Attack—Deathly Touch: +3 to hit (reach 5 ft.; one creature). *Hit:* 1d6 + 1 necrotic damage. The target's maximum number of hit points is reduced by an amount equal to the necrotic damage, and the midnight peddler gains the same number of temporary hit points.

STATISTICS
Str 11 (+0), **Dex** 13 (+1), **Con** 15 (+2), **Int** 15 (+2), **Wis** 16 (+3), **Cha** 13 (+1)
Languages: Common
Senses: Darkvision 60 ft.

TRAITS
Divination: The peddler provides good advice or a correct answer to one question asked of him by a creature who buys something from his cart. This ability functions similarly to a *divination* spell.
Plane Shift: The midnight peddler can use the *plane shift* spell at will. He can shift only himself, his cart, and the nonliving contents of his cart; he can't bring along willing companions or banish other creatures.

ECOLOGY
Environment: Any land
Organization: Solitary

The midnight peddler wanders city streets, where he is most often encountered on fog-shrouded nights. He is first detected by the audible squeaking of the cart he pushes. The midnight peddler moves with a slow gait as he pushes his noisy wooden cart. The contents of the cart vary each time he visits the Material Plane, and anyone looking into the cart sees nothing but junk: dented pots and pans, dull utensils, tattered gloves, chipped crockery. With a few moments of searching beneath the junk, however, the midnight peddler can find any item on the Adventuring Gear, Tools, Trade Goods, and Trinkets lists with a value of 50 gp or less. No one else will ever find anything but junk. He sometimes charges standard prices for his items and sometimes refuses to sell for any price—but will accept a favor.

Even more valuable than the items in his cart is the knowledge in the midnight peddler's head. He will answer one question for someone who buys an item from his cart, and the answer is invariably correct. The answer is likely to be cryptic, and the midnight peddler doesn't advertise this ability at all; it's up to customers to ask questions.

The midnight peddler shuns combat. If forced into battle, his chief concern will be simply plane shifting to safety. Afterward, characters who attacked the midnight peddler might find themselves oddly unwelcome in certain taverns and markets, and beggars and street thieves will be distinctly unfriendly toward them.

Copyright Notice
Author Scott Greene.

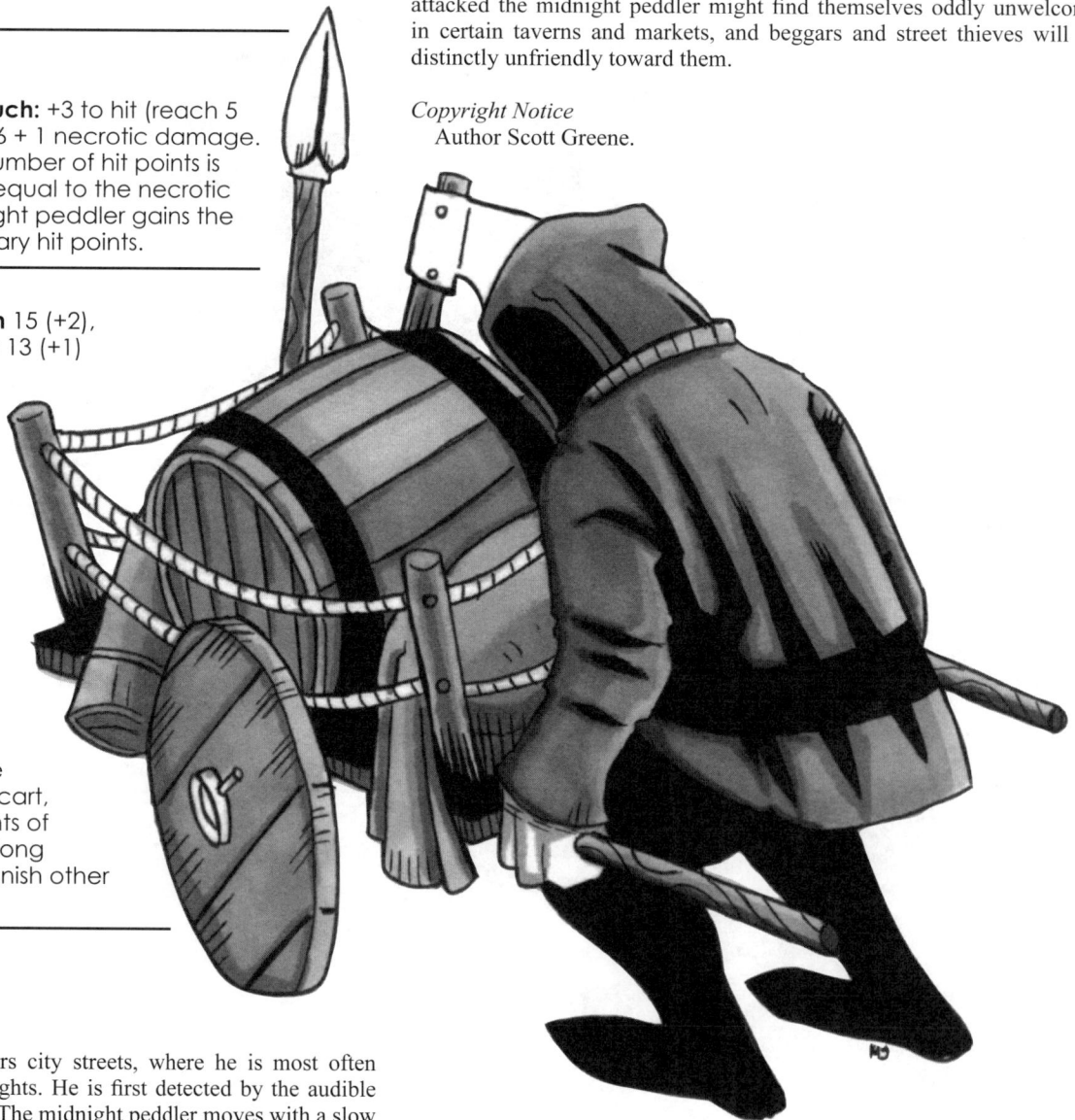

Mite

*This creature is an ugly humanoid about 2 feet tall.
It has long, pointed ears, a large round nose, and grayish-brown skin.*

Mite

XP 25 (CR 1/8)
LE Small fey
Initiative +1

DEFENSE
AC 11
hp: 3 (1d6)

OFFENSE
Speed: 20 ft., climb 20 ft.
Melee Attack—Dagger:
+3 to hit (reach 5 ft.; one creature). *Hit:* 1d4 + 1 piercing damage.
Ranged Attack—Dart: +3 to hit (range 20 ft./60 ft.; one creature). *Hit:* 1d4 + 1 piercing damage.

STATISTICS
Str 8 (−1), **Dex** 13 (+1),
Con 11 (+0), **Int** 8 (−1),
Wis 13 (+1), **Cha** 10 (+0)
Languages: Deep Speech
Skills: Stealth +3
Senses: Darkvision 60 ft.

TRAITS
Hatred: Mites have tactical advantage on attack rolls against dwarves, gnomes, and svirfneblin.
Spell-like Abilities: A mite can use the following spell-like abilities, using Charisma as its casting ability (DC 10). The mite doesn't need material components to use these abilities.
At Will: *prestidigitation*
1/day: *fear*
Vermin Empathy (1/day): As an action, a mite can summon a swarm of bats, a swarm of rats, 1d4 giant centipedes, 1d4 giant wasps, or 1d2 giant wolf spiders. The summoned creatures arrive 1d4 rounds after being summoned and stays near the mite for one hour. The mite has telepathic communication with the creatures and can give them simple commands such as "attack" and "enter that building."

ECOLOGY
Environment: Underground
Organization: Solitary, band (2–8), or mob (9–20 plus 2–6 summoned vermin)

Descended from even smaller fey, mites are among the most pitiful and craven dwellers of the dark. They are so ugly that even goblins mock mites for their appearance—mockery that the insecure mites take to heart and brood on for weeks, months, or even years until their distress and anger finally overcome their natural cowardice and launch them on short-lived bouts of bloody vengeance.

Their diminutive stature places them at the bottom of the pecking order in the dangerous caverns where they live. Their traditional enemies are dwarves, gnomes, and especially svirfneblin. The one thing that gives them an edge in a fight is their ability to summon certain types of vermin. Since they live in areas infested with such vermin, this is a handy ability.

Mites make their homes underground in deep, dark dungeons and caverns, where they survive largely by stealing from other creatures that live nearby or that wander near their lair. A mite lair consists of a large central chamber from which many small, winding tunnels lead. All mite lairs are littered with garbage and refuse. Cleanliness and sanitation are virtually unknown among mites. A typical lair contains young mites but they are almost never encountered; they scatter into deep hiding places whenever intruders appear.

Mites have a reputation for almost animal-like stupidity, but they are more canny than their reputation suggests. Trickery and surprise are the forte of the

mite. They avoid melee, preferring to attack from ambush with thrown darts and stones, or better yet, with traps. The first telltale sign that mites may be nearby often is the plethora of traps, snares, and tripwires in an area. Mites focus their attacks on the weakest foes first. Powerful opponents are more likely to be allowed through an area without interference.

A typical mite ambush involves the creatures digging narrow tunnels parallel to a dungeon's corridors. When a foe traverses these corridors, the mites burst from the walls and strike quickly with their daggers. Opponents are rarely killed; instead they are knocked unconscious and relieved of coins, weapons, and other items of value. If forced into an ongoing or disadvantageous melee, mites try to escape at the first possible opportunity.

Although they have lost the supernatural ability to tinker with magic items or mechanical objects possessed by their more sinister and dangerous gremlin kin, mites retain the ability to perform minor magical tricks. When faced with dangerous foes, a mite uses its *fear* ability, primarily to give itself an opportunity to escape. A mite's eyes bulge hideously when it uses this ability. A single mite using *fear* isn't greatly effective, but six or eight using it at once can drive off much more powerful threats.

Mite, Pestie

This creature is an ugly humanoid about 3 feet tall. It has long, pointed ears, a large round nose, and grayish-brown skin wrapped in filthy rags.

Pestie

XP 50 (CR 1/4)
LE Small fey
Initiative +2

DEFENSE
AC 12
hp: 7 (2d6)

OFFENSE
Speed: 40 ft., climb 20 ft.
Melee Attack—Dagger: +4 to hit (reach 5 ft.; one creature). *Hit:* 1d4 + 2 piercing damage.
Ranged Attack—Dart: +4 to hit (range 20 ft./60 ft.; one creature). *Hit:* 1d4 + 2 piercing damage.

STATISTICS
Str 8 (−1), Dex 15 (+2), Con 11 (+0),
Int 6 (−2), Wis 13 (+1), Cha 10 (+0)
Languages: Deep Speech (understands but can't speak)
Skills: Acrobatics +4, Sleight of Hand +6, Stealth +6
Senses: Darkvision 60 ft.

TRAITS
Combat Mobility: Opportunity attacks against a moving pestie always have tactical disadvantage.
Hatred: Pesties have tactical advantage on attack rolls against dwarves, gnomes, and svirfneblin.
Sneak Attack: A pestie's dagger attack does an extra 1d6 piercing damage if the pestie has advantage on the attack or if one of its allies is within 5 feet of the target.
Spell-like Abilities: A pestie can use the following spell-like abilities, using Charisma as its casting ability (DC 10). The pestie doesn't need material components to use these abilities.
At Will: *prestidigitation*
1/day: *fear*

ECOLOGY
Environment: Underground
Organization: Solitary or squad (2–8)

Pesties are the larger cousins of the mites. They stand taller—as much as 3 feet tall—but also tend to be leaner, with elongated limbs, slender fingers, and large, pointed ears.

Pesties communicate only through body language and crude hand signals, even with others of their own race. Sages who've examined pesties state that the creatures have vocal chords, but they remain silent except when terrified or in terrible pain. Whether their lack of speech is caused by a mental condition or is a cultural choice is unknown.

Where mites focus on stealth and surprise in combat, pesties rely on their speed and agility to evade and bewilder their foes.

Pesties are found working with and living among common mites and (less often) goblins. They seldom band together into large communities of their own.

All pesties are kleptomanics. This tendency often leads to pesties being driven out of whatever community they were living in when their allies' patience with their pilfering finally reaches an end. However, the trapmaking skills of the mites complement the pesties' agility and speed, so that invariably the two groups end up cooperating again. Pesties who wear out their welcome in a goblin community face a grimmer fate; either they succeed at outrunning their pursuers or they end up in a goblin cook pot.

Credit
The mite and pestie originally appeared in the First Edition *Fiend Folio* (© TSR/Wizards of the Coast, 1981) and are used by permission.

Copyright Notice
Authors Scott Greene and Skeeter Green, based on original material by Ian Livingstone and Mark Barnes.

Mummy of the Deep

This rotting and bandaged humanoid shuffles and slides as it moves. Its body is covered in tattered and torn bandages. Seaweed hangs from its limbs and water drips constantly from its desiccated form.

Mummy of the Deep

XP 450 (CR 2)
NE Medium undead (aquatic)
Initiative +0

DEFENSE

AC 11 (natural armor)
hp: 33 (6d8 + 6)
Saving Throws: Wis +2
Resistance: Bludgeoning, piercing, and slashing damage from nonmagical weapons
Immunity: Necrotic and poison damage; charm, exhaustion, fright, paralysis, poison

OFFENSE

Speed: 20 ft., swim 20 ft.
Melee Attack—Fist: +5 to hit (reach 5 ft.; one creature). *Hit:* 1d10 + 3 bludgeoning damage and a target of Medium size or smaller must make a successful DC 13 Dex saving throw or be grappled; see Curse of the Deep below.

STATISTICS

Str 16 (+3), **Dex** 10 (+0), **Con** 12 (+1),
Int 6 (−2), **Wis** 10 (+0), **Cha** 12 (+1)
Languages: Common
Senses: Darkvision 60 ft.

TRAITS

Control Water (1/day): A mummy of the deep can *control water* as the spell by using an action.

Curse of the Deep: When a mummy of the deep grapples a creature, it immediately uses a bonus action to press its mouth against the opponent's and spew sea water into the opponent's lungs. It then releases its grapple. The affected creature must make a successful DC 11 Con saving throw at the start of each of its turns. An affected creature can act normally on a round when it makes a successful saving throw; if the saving throw fails, the creature takes 1d6 necrotic damage and is stunned until the start of its next turn. The effect ends when the affected creature makes a third successful save. It can also be ended by a spell or other magical effect that neutralizes a curse.

Despair: At the sight of a mummy of the deep within 60 feet, the viewer must make a successful DC 11 Wis saving throw or be frightened for 1d4 rounds. If the saving throw result is 5 or less, the creature is paralyzed instead. A successful saving throw renders the creature immune to any mummy of the deep's despair for 24 hours.

ECOLOGY

Environment: Any aquatic

Organization: Solitary or gang (2–4)

A mummy of the deep is an undead creature that resides in the depths of the sea, a lake, or a slow-moving river, usually in the ruins of a submerged and forgotten city, palace, or tomb. It is the corpse of an evil creature that was cursed for its sins in life and buried in shame, possibly while still alive, and the wickedness of its life revived the soul as a mummy of the deep.

Although most mummies of the deep were created accidentally and thus are solitary, there are cases of these mummies being created intentionally to guard a sunken treasure or flooded tomb. They are much more dangerous *en masse* than individually, of course, but the presence of a group of mummies of the deep is a clue that something of great value might be hidden nearby.

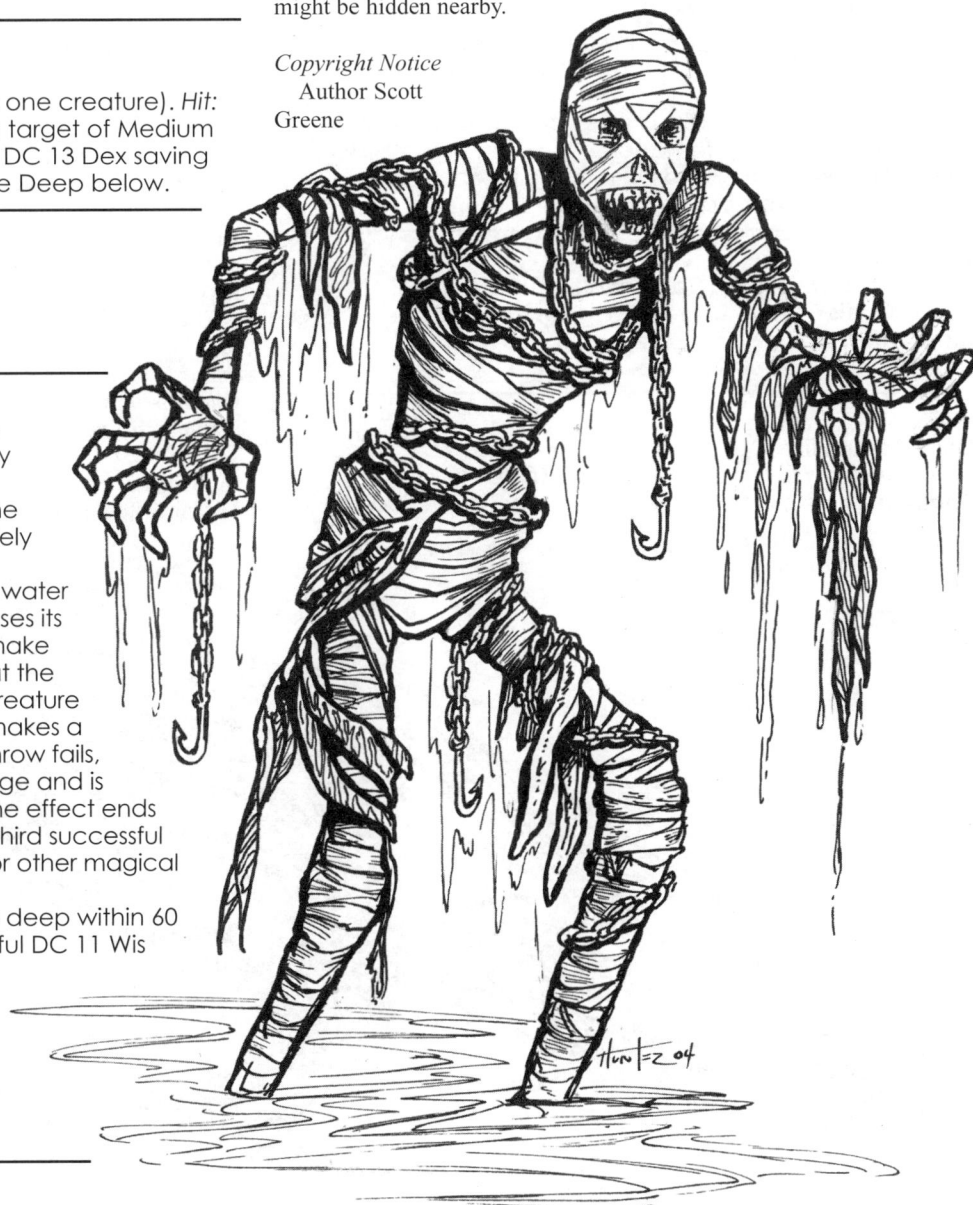

Murder Crow

This creature appears to be a massive crow about 4 feet tall. Its feathers are tattered, blood-soaked, and matted against its rotting form. A stench of decay emanates from it as it circles overhead.

Murder Crow

XP 700 (CR 3)
CE Medium undead
Initiative +3

DEFENSE

AC 15 (natural armor)
hp: 52 (8d8 + 16)
Resistance: Piercing damage from nonmagical weapons
Immunity: Necrotic and poison damage; charm, exhaustion, fright, poison, unconsciousness

OFFENSE

Speed: 10 ft., fly 50 ft.
Multiattack: A murder crow attacks once with claws and once with its beak. If both attacks hit the same target, see Eye Rake below.
Melee Attack—Claws: +5 to hit (reach 5 ft.; one creature).
  Hit: 1d8 + 3 slashing damage.
Melee Attack—Beak: +5 to hit (reach 5 ft.; one creature).
  Hit: 1d6 + 3 piercing damage.

STATISTICS

Str 10 (+0), **Dex** 17 (+3), **Con** 14 (+2),
Int 2 (−4), **Wis** 14 (+2), **Cha** 12 (+1)
Languages: None
Senses: Darkvision 60 ft.

TRAITS

Combat Mobility: Opportunity attacks against a moving murder crow always have tactical disadvantage.
Death Throes: If a murder crow is reduced to 0 hit points, it explodes into a swarm of ravens that continues to relentlessly attack all living creatures within sight. These ravens are undead, and they have tactical advantage on saving throws against being turned.
Eye Rake: If a murder crow hits the same target with its claws and beak in the same round, the target must make a successful DC 13 Dex saving throw or be blinded for 1d4 rounds. If a creature is blinded more than once during an encounter, the condition lasts until the creature is healed of all damage or the blindness is removed magically.

ECOLOGY

Environment: Temperate
Organization: Solitary

Murder crows are undead avians that haunt cemeteries, graveyards, and charnel houses, where they dig up and feast on carcasses. These creatures arise where the formless souls of birds condense into a single creature—a murder crow. Murder crows attack with their gore-spattered beaks and sinister talons. Rarely does a murder crow face its adversaries on the ground, preferring instead to fight on the wing.

Murder crows might be mistaken for normal crows from a long distance, where their astounding size can't be accurately judged. Standing 4 feet tall and with a wingspan of 9 feet, they can't be mistaken for normal crows once someone gets a good look at one.

Their tattered feathers are black and carry the stench of death. The eyes of a murder crow are bleak and hollow, showing no signs of emotion or life. There is no indication that the murder crow actually comprises hundreds of smaller creatures until it "dies" and bursts into a cloud of normal-sized but undead ravens.

Copyright Notice
  Author Lance Hawvermale.

Naga, Hanu-naga

The creature twined around a crumbling stone obelisk resembles an enormous python,
but instead of the head of a great serpent, its body is topped by the head of a great ape.
It stares at you with deep, intelligent, almost human eyes, then begins a hypnotic dance.

Hanu-naga

XP 450 (CR 2)
CE Large monstrosity
Initiative +2

DEFENSE

AC 14 (natural armor)
hp: 39 (6d10 + 6)
Saving Throws: Dex +5
Immunity: Poison damage; charm, poison

OFFENSE

Speed: 40 ft.
Melee Attack—Bite: +5 to hit (reach 5 ft.; one creature). *Hit:*
1d8 + 3 piercing damage plus 2d6 poison damage, or
half as much poison damage with a successful DC 11 Con
saving throw. A creature has tactical disadvantage on this
saving throw if it is grappled by the hanu-naga.
Melee Attack—Constrict: +5 to hit (reach 5 ft.; one creature).
Hit: 1d6 + 3 bludgeoning damage and the target is
grappled and restrained.

STATISTICS

Str 14 (+2), **Dex** 16 (+3), **Con** 12 (+1),
Int 11 (+0), **Wis** 14 (+2), **Cha** 15 (+2)
Languages: Common, telepathy (with charmed primates)
Senses: Darkvision 60 ft.

TRAITS

Dominate Apes: A hanu-naga can dance in a writhing,
hypnotic way that charms apes, baboons, mandrills,
and other primates with Intelligence scores of 5 or
less (including humanoids). It can perform this dance
even while fighting. When it dances, all primates
within 60 feet are charmed by the hanu-naga, and
all other primates within one mile are drawn to the
hanu-naga's location at top speed. It can have up
to 20 creatures charmed this way at one time. The
hanu-naga has telepathic communication with the
creatures it's charmed, and they do their utmost to
carry out its simple commands as if they are affected
by a *dominate beast* spell. Its control lasts for as long
as the hanu-naga continues dancing. Humanoids of
Intelligence 5 or less who are within 60 feet of a dancing
hanu-naga must make a successful DC 12 Cha saving
throw to avoid the hanu-naga's charm. One successful
save renders a humanoid immune to this charm effect
for 24 hours.

ECOLOGY

Environment: Tropical and subtropical forest and mountains
Organization: Pack (1–4)

Hanu-nagas are a form of naga with the head and face of an ape instead
of a human or other creature. They are less magical than the human-
headed variety but more savage.

These nagas lair in jungles and rainforests, where they haunt overgrown
temples and ancient ruins. In these remote regions, many hanu-nagas are
worshipped by tribes of wild primates. The most intelligent hanu-nagas
sometimes even have followings of more advanced humanoids such as
cavemen and primitive tribesmen.

The stylized, writhing dance of a hanu-naga allows it to exert a mystic
control over nearby primates, including simple-minded humanoids. This
might explain their influence over tribes of primitive humans.

Although they're no geniuses, hanu-nagas are more intelligent than
their brutish features suggest they are. They also live for centuries,
meaning they sometimes have first-hand knowledge about the history of
the ruins they inhabit. They've been known to teach themselves to read the
inscriptions carved on crumbling temple walls and vine-choked edifices.
Such knowledge makes hanu-nagas excellent allies for adventurers
looking to explore or plunder ancient jungle sites, if a way can be found to
placate the creatures' bloodlust and their deep mistrust of strangers.

Olive Slime

The walls, ceiling, and floor of the cavern ahead are coated with glistening, dripping slime.

Olive Slime

XP 0 (CR 0)
Unaligned Large
plant (fungus)
Initiative +1

DEFENSE
AC 11
hp: 14 (4d10 – 8)
Immunity: Lightning, piercing, and psychic damage; charm, fright, prone, stun, unconsciousness
Vulnerability: Acid, cold, and fire damage

OFFENSE
Speed: 0 ft.
Melee Attack—Drop: +3 to hit (reach 30 ft.; one creature beneath the olive slime). *Hit:* target creature must make a successful DC 15 Wis saving throw to notice the olive slime that dripped onto it. If the olive slime is noticed and removed immediately, it has no effect. If the olive slime is not noticed and removed within two minutes, the creature loses 1 point of Constitution and is infested with olive slime; see below.

STATISTICS
Str 1 (−5), **Dex** 12 (+1), **Con** 6 (−2),
Int 1 (−5), **Wis** 10 (+0), **Cha** 4 (−3)
Languages: None
Skills: Stealth +5
Senses: Tremorsense 30 ft.

TRAITS
Olive Slime Defenses: The armor class and hit points listed above are for a Large patch of olive slime in its native environment. Olive slime on a victim has the victim's AC and hit points equal to the number of Constitution points the victim has lost.

Olive Slime Infestation: Any amount of olive slime that remains in contact with a potential victim for more than two minutes *charms* the victim and alters his or her thinking patterns so that the host's main concern becomes feeding and protecting the olive slime—including keeping the slime hidden from companions. If anyone tries to remove the olive slime from the host, the host does whatever is required to protect the slime, whether it's running away or fighting back. As long as the host is alive and conscious, it will do everything in its power to protect the slime, including knocking out or even killing its friends. An infested creature suffers the following effects.

• It loses 1 point of Constitution immediately when the infestation begins and another 1d6 points of Constitution at the end of each 24-hour period, as the growing olive slime replaces the creature's skin, muscle, and organs

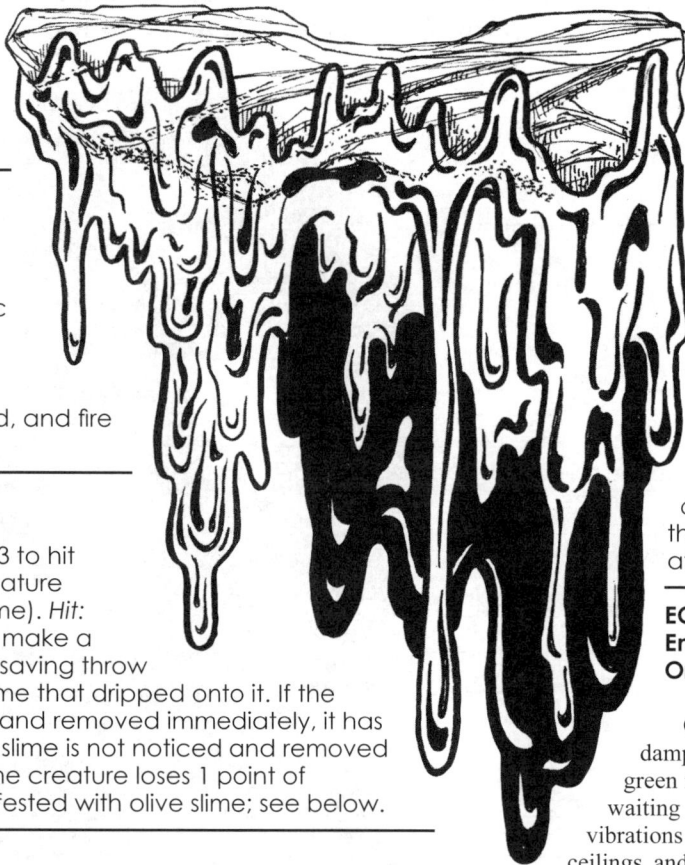

with olive slime. The olive slime gains hit points equal to the number of Constitution points lost by the victim.

• The host must double its normal food intake or lose 1 extra point of Constitution after each 24 hours. Also, the host does not recover hit points or hit dice after a long rest if it didn't double its food intake.

• If the host's Constitution drops to 0, the host dies. Five minutes later, its body reanimates as an olive slime zombie. Olive slime can be burned, cut away, or frozen. Anything that damages the olive slime deals half damage to its host (before doubling for vulnerability in the case of acid, cold, or fire damage). *Greater restoration* ends the olive slime's *charm* effect for two minutes; during that time, the victim can cooperate with attempts to remove the slime.

ECOLOGY
Environment: Underground
Organization: Solitary or colony (2–5)

Olive slime is a fungal growth that thrives in dark, damp, underground areas. It is sticky, gloppy, and drab green in color. It grows across ceilings, floors, and walls, waiting for live prey to pass nearby. Olive slime detects vibrations and drops gobs the size of a chicken egg from ceilings and walls when it detects movement beneath it, or oozes up the sides and over the tops of boots and shoes that step in it. Once on a victim, the gob of slime oozes through gaps in armor and clothes until it contacts skin, where it immediately secretes a numbing poison to hide its presence from its new host. As time goes by, the olive slime slowly digests the victim's body, replacing its flesh and organs with olive slime, until the victim is entirely transformed into an olive slime zombie.

The slime instinctively seeks a patch of flesh that's hidden from view to begin its work of transformation: the small of the back and the armpit are favorite spots. Unless the victim strips to bathe, other characters aren't likely to notice the infestation—at least, not right away.

The GM should keep track of the victim's Constitution loss. Other characters can notice the change taking place in their companion with passive Perception. The DC for noticing the creeping transformation is 8 plus the number of Constitution points the victim has left. For example, if an infested character has been reduced to Con 7, characters with passive Perception 15 notice the olive slime growing across his or her skin; when the character's Con drops to 3, the condition can be noticed by characters with passive Perception 11.

Credit

Olive slime originally appeared in the First Edition module *S4 Lost Caverns of Tsojcanth* (© TSR/Wizards of the Coast, 1982) and later in the First Edition *Monster Manual II* (© TSR/Wizards of the Coast, 1983) and is used by permission.

Copyright Notice

Author Scott Greene, based on original material by Gary Gygax.

Olive Slime Zombie

*This creature appears humanoid, but its skin is translucent
and its face has no features beyond asymmetrical lumps.*

Olive Slime Zombie

XP 100 (CR 1/2)
NE Medium plant
Initiative −1

DEFENSE

AC 9
hp: 26 (4d8 + 8)
Immunity: Lightning, piercing, and psychic damage; charm,
   fright, stun, unconsciousness
Vulnerability: Acid, cold, and fire damage

OFFENSE

Speed: 20 ft.
Melee Attack—Fist: +3 to hit (reach 5 ft.; one creature).
   Hit: 1d8 + 1 bludgeoning damage and the target must
   make a successful DC 15 Wis saving throw to notice the
   olive slime smeared on it. If the olive slime is noticed
   and removed immediately, it has no effect. If the
   olive slime is not noticed and removed within
   two minutes, the creature loses 1 point of
   Constitution and is infested with olive slime;
   see below.

STATISTICS

Str 12 (+1), **Dex** 8 (−1), **Con** 14 (+2),
Int 3 (−4), **Wis** 6 (−2), **Cha** 4 (−3)
Languages: None
Senses: Darkvision 60 ft.

TRAITS

Death Throes: When a slime zombie
   is reduced to 0 hit points, it
   collapses into a full-strength
   puddle of olive slime.
Telepathic Bond: A
   slime zombie is linked
   telepathically with the
   patch of olive slime that
   created it and with all
   other slime zombies
   linked to that patch
   of olive slime.
   This link has a
   maximum range of
   20 miles. The slime
   zombie and olive
   slime must be on the same
   plane of existence.
Olive Slime Infestation:
   Any amount of olive
   slime that remains
   in contact with a
   potential victim for
   more than two minutes *charms*
   the victim and alters his or her
   thinking patterns so that the
   host's main concern becomes

feeding and protecting the olive slime—including keeping
the slime hidden from companions. If anyone tries to
remove the olive slime from the host, the host does
whatever is required to protect the slime, whether it's
running away or fighting back. As long as the host is alive
and conscious, it will do everything in its power to protect
the slime, including knocking out or even killing its friends.
An infested creature suffers the following effects.

- It loses 1 point of Constitution immediately when the
infestation begins and another 1d6 points of Constitution
at the end of each 24-hour period, as the growing olive
slime replaces the creature's skin, muscle, and organs with
olive slime. The olive slime gains hit points equal to the
number of Constitution points lost by the victim.
  - The host must double its normal food intake or lose
  1 extra point of Constitution after each 24 hours.
  Also, the host does not recover hit points or hit dice
  after a long rest if it didn't double its food intake.
  - If the host's Constitution drops to 0, the host dies.
  Five minutes later, its body reanimates as an olive
  slime zombie.

Olive slime can be burned, cut away, or
frozen. Anything that damages the olive
slime deals half damage to its host
(before doubling for vulnerability in the
case of acid, cold, or fire damage).
Greater restoration ends the olive
slime's *charm* effect for two minutes;
during that time, the victim can
cooperate with attempts to remove
the slime.

ECOLOGY

Environment: Underground
Organization: Mob (1–20)

Olive slime zombies (or slime
creatures) are created when a living
creature dies from olive slime
infestation. The slime zombie's sole
purpose in existence is to capture or
kill new prey for its master (i.e., the
olive slime that created it).

A slime zombie resembles a
humanoid blob, olive drab in color.
The creature has no distinguishing
marks or facial features; its face has the
rough shape of a humanoid face, but it is
lumpy and gelatinous. The same applies
to its entire body; the skin is translucent,
revealing outlines of interior shapes
that resemble the creature's original
bones and organs, but it is olive
slime throughout.

An olive slime zombie can
communicate telepathically with
the olive slime that controls it and with
others of its kind, but it never speaks or
makes any other sound.

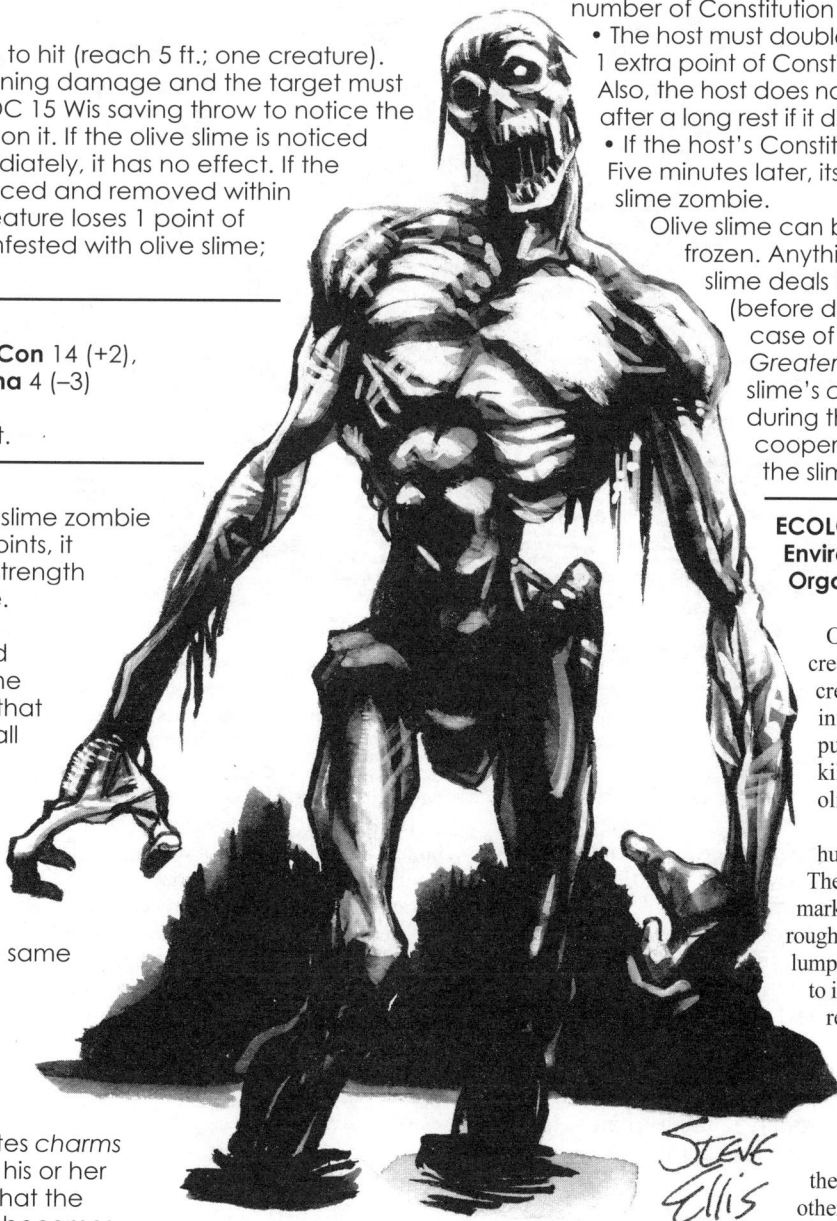

Ooze, Glacial

What appeared at first glance to be a snow bank or mound of snow reveals itself to be a sentient creature formed of clear ice.

Glacial Ooze

XP 200 (CR 1)
Unaligned Large ooze
Initiative −5

DEFENSE
AC 5
hp: 57 (6d10 + 24)
Resistance: Bludgeoning, piercing, and slashing damage from nonmagical weapons
Immunity: Cold and psychic damage; blindness, exhaustion, fear, paralysis, poison, prone, stun
Vulnerability: Fire damage

OFFENSE
Speed: 20 ft., swim 20 ft.
Melee Attack—Slam: +4 to hit (reach 5 ft.; one creature). *Hit:* 2d6 + 2 bludgeoning damage plus 1d6 cold damage.

STATISTICS
Str 15 (+2), **Dex** 1 (−5), **Con** 19 (+4),
Int 0 (−5), **Wis** 1 (−5), **Cha** 1 (−5)
Languages: None
Senses: Tremorsense 60 ft.

TRAITS
Amorphous: A glacial ooze can move through gaps as small as 1 square foot as if it's difficult terrain.
Freezing Embrace: As it moves, a glacial ooze can enter spaces occupied by Large or smaller creatures. If the creature whose space is being entered makes a successful DC 12 Dex saving throw, the creature can move safely out of the glacial ooze's path. If the saving throw fails, the creature is engulfed: it takes 2d6 cold damage immediately, is restrained, can't breathe, and takes 4d6 cold damage at the start of each of the glacial ooze's turns. An engulfed creature can use an action on its turn to try to escape from the glacial ooze; the creature escapes if it makes a successful DC 14 Str check. A creature adjacent to the glacial ooze can use an action to try to pull one engulfed creature free. The rescue succeeds if the creature makes a successful DC 14 Str check, and the creature making the check takes 2d6 cold damage whether it succeeds or fails. A glacial ooze can contain up to four creatures that are Medium or smaller, or one Large creature.
Superchilled: A glacial ooze's form is extremely cold. Creatures that hit a glacial ooze with natural weapons or with an unarmed attack take 1d6 cold damage per hit.
Transparent: A glacial ooze is hard to spot, even under ideal conditions. A DC 15 Wis (Perception) check is needed to notice one, and if the ooze is drifting in water or is surrounded by blowing snow (as it usually is), this check is made with tactical disadvantage. Creatures who blunder into the glacial ooze's space are treated exactly as if the ooze had attacked them with its freezing embrace, but they make the Dex saving throw with tactical disadvantage.

ECOLOGY
Environment: Any cold
Organization: Solitary

A glacial ooze is an arctic relative of the gelatinous ooze. Like its cousin, the glacial ooze is nearly invisible. When it can be seen, it appears as no more than a block or wall of clear ice. The desiccated, shriveled remains of creatures can sometimes be seen frozen inside.

Glacial oozes of Huge or even Gargantuan size have been conjectured, but their existence is so far only a rumor.

The glacial ooze is equally at home in an ice cave, prowling the blizzard-riven tundra, or drifting in frigid arctic seas and rivers like a small iceberg. Like most oozes, the glacial ooze is a scavenger that feeds primarily on whatever frozen carcasses it finds—but it doesn't see much difference between a frozen carcass and a living creature. A glacial ooze doesn't digest its food, but rather absorbs all fluids and liquids from the body, leaving behind a frozen, shrunken husk.

A glacial ooze prefers to acquire food by just moving onto it and engulfing it. If the food resists, the ooze forms a pseudopod and batters the meal into submission.

Copyright Notice
Author Scott Greene.

Ooze, Magma

This creature appears to be no more than a normal pool of bubbling and churning molten rock.

Magma Ooze

XP 1,800 (CR 5)
Unaligned Large ooze
Initiative −5

DEFENSE

AC 14 (natural armor)
hp: 115 (10d10 + 60)
Resistance: Bludgeoning, piercing, and slashing damage from nonmagical weapons
Immunity: Fire, poison, and psychic damage; blindness, exhaustion, fear, paralysis, poison, prone, stun
Vulnerability: Cold damage

OFFENSE

Speed: 10 ft., climb 10 ft.
Melee Attack—Slam: +6 to hit (reach 5 ft.; one creature). *Hit:* 2d6 + 3 bludgeoning damage plus 2d6 fire damage, and the target must make a successful DC 14 Dex saving throw or be grappled (see Superheated, below).

STATISTICS

Str 16 (+3), **Dex** 1 (−5), **Con** 23 (+6),
Int 1 (−5), **Wis** 1 (−5), **Cha** 1 (−5)
Languages: None
Senses: Tremorsense 60 ft.

TRAITS

Amorphous: A magma ooze can move through gaps as small as 6 square inches as if it's difficult terrain.
Split: If an attack does 10 or more slashing damage to a magma ooze, a chunk of the ooze is sliced off and becomes an independent magma ooze. The new ooze has hit points equal to the slashing damage caused by the attack, and the parent ooze's hit points are reduced by an equal amount (in addition to the damage caused by the attack). The new ooze makes one slam attack immediately as a reaction against one adjacent foe, then joins the initiative order at the same point as its parent.
Superheated: A magma ooze's form is extremely hot and composed entirely of magma. Creatures that hit a magma ooze with natural weapons or with an unarmed attack take 1d6 fire damage per hit. If a hit from a metal weapon causes the minimum possible damage, the weapon melts and is destroyed. A creature grappled by a magma ooze takes 2d6 fire damage at the start of its own turn.

ECOLOGY

Environment: Warm mountains, underground
Organization: Solitary

Magma oozes are thought to have originated on the Plane of Fire, but they are now encountered primarily on the Material Plane. They are found in or near volcanoes, hot geysers, sulfuric springs, and other uncomfortably warm places where the world vents its internal heat. They never approach water and are never found near it. Magma oozes can grow to a length of 10 feet, and they can squeeze themselves down to a thickness of about 6 inches.

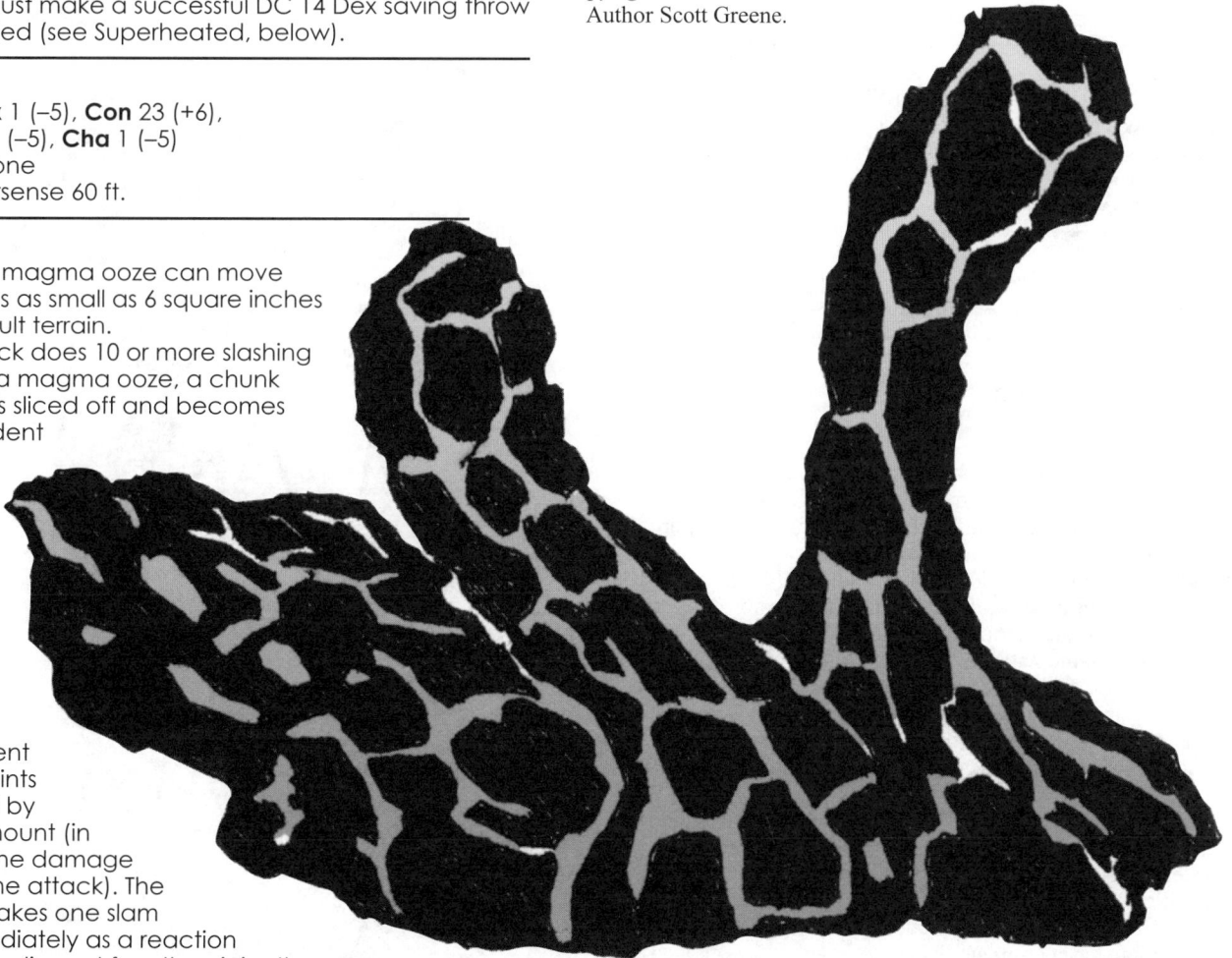

Origami Warrior

*The creature appears to be an armed and armored human warrior,
but it is made entirely of folded paper.*

Origami Warrior

XP 25 (CR 1/8)
Unaligned Medium construct
Initiative +3

DEFENSE
AC 15 (natural armor)
hp: 9 (2d8)
Resistance: Bludgeoning damage from nonmagical
 weapons
Immunity: Necrotic, piercing, poison, and psychic damage;
 disease, fright, poison, stun, unconsciousness
Vulnerability: Fire damage

OFFENSE
Speed: 40 ft.
Melee Attack—Paper Longsword: +5 to hit (reach 5 ft.; one
 creature). *Hit:* 1d8 + 3 slashing damage.

STATISTICS
Str 8 (−1), **Dex** 16 (+3), **Con** 10 (+0),
Int 8 (−1), **Wis** 10 (+0), **Cha** 10 (+0)
Languages: Understands Common but can't speak
Skills: Acrobatics +5
Senses: Darkvision 60 ft.

TRAITS
Mobility: An opponent has tactical disadvantage on
 opportunity attack rolls against an origami warrior.

ECOLOGY
Environment: Any land
Organization: Squad (1–10)

An origami warrior is a magical creation made of intricately folded
paper with the shape and size of a humanoid warrior. They can be made
to resemble any type of humanoid, but humans and elves are the most
common. Except in dim light or darkness, however, no one would ever
mistake an origami warrior for a living creature. They are flat and angular,
just like the small paper sculptures they're named for. They range from
very simplistic in their structure to tremendously complex and intricate,
but all have the same statistics.

The magic for creating origami warriors is not widely known, but it
doesn't seem much of a leap from making origami creatures that resemble
humans to making origami trolls, ogres, bulettes, or even dragons.
Somewhere, an ambitious or curious wizard undoubtedly is working on
that, if it hasn't been done already.

Like most constructs, origami warriors have limited autonomy. They
wait for orders from their creators, then follow those orders narrowly and
to the letter, but also patiently and for as long as they survive.

A "typical" origami warrior is armed with a longsword, but they can be
given any weapon. The only restriction is that their creator must be able to
fold paper into the appropriate shape.

Pech

This small humanoid has the same height and rough build of a dwarf, but with gangly arms and legs. Its hands are broad and its skin is ochre-colored with lighter shades on its palms and feet. Its hair is a mix of reds and light browns. Its large, bulbous eyes are stark white with no apparent pupil or iris.

Pech

XP 50 (CR 1/4)
NG Small fey
Initiative +1

DEFENSE

AC 11
hp: 18 (4d6 + 4)
Resistance: Bludgeoning, piercing, and slashing damage from nonmagical weapons
Immunity: Petrification

OFFENSE

Speed: 20 ft.
Multiattack: A pech attacks twice with its pick or twice with stones, or uses one spell-like ability.
Melee Attack—Pick: +6 to hit (reach 5 ft.; one creature). *Hit:* 1d4 + 4 piercing damage.
Ranged Attack—Stone: +3 to hit (range 30 ft./90 ft.; one creature). *Hit:* 1d4 + 1 bludgeoning damage.

STATISTICS

Str 18 (+4), **Dex** 12 (+1), **Con** 12 (+1),
Int 11 (+0), **Wis** 12 (+1), **Cha** 11 (+0)
Languages: Terran, Undercommon
Skills: Perception +3, Survival +3
Senses: Darkvision 60 ft.

TRAITS

Earthbound: A pech has tactical disadvantage on attack rolls against targets that are entirely surrounded by an element other than earth; i.e., foes that are flying or swimming.
Light Blindness: A pech has tactical disadvantage on attack rolls and Wis (Perception) checks in bright light.
Spell-like Abilities: A pech can use the following spell-like abilities, using Wisdom as its casting ability (DC 11, attack +3). The pech doesn't need material components to use these abilities.
4/day: *stone shape*, *speak with stone* (functions identically to *speak with plants*, but with stones instead)
A pech can also use the following spell-like abilities as part of a group. All members of the group must be within 20 feet of all other members of the group, and all must use an action simultaneously to trigger the spell-like effect. An individual pech can use each ability once per day. Only one pech needs to maintain concentration to keep an effect ongoing.
4 pechs: *wall of stone*
8 pechs: *greater restoration* (only to remove petrification)
Stone Knowledge: A pech's extensive knowledge of stone gives it tactical advantage on attack rolls against creatures made of stone, earth, or clay.

ECOLOGY

Environment: Underground, Elemental Plane of Earth
Organization: Gang (2–4), pack (5–20), or tribe (21–40 plus 11–20 noncombatants)

A pech is a fey creature believed to have its origins on the Elemental Plane of Earth. On the Material Plane, peches dwell deep underground in places rarely seen even by dwarves, drow, or other subterranean races.

They are unexcelled as stonemasons, a talent that leads to them sometimes being employed by other subterranean races for their skill at stoneworking. Peches seek isolation for their lairs, however, and their skill at stonecarving lets them blend their dwellings into the natural surroundings so perfectly that they are almost impossible to find.

Peches never wear armor; most are arrayed in nothing more than a simple leather apron or a loincloth of brown or black fur. Peches speak Terran as their primary language, but a few in any group will also be able to communicate in Undercommon or, much more rarely, Common.

Peches are a peaceful folk. They avoid combat and hostile encounters if possible. If they are forced to fight, peches rely on their picks and their magic to dispatch opponents or to escape. Their favorite trick is to cooperate in rapidly erecting a *wall of stone* around attackers to trap them, or across a narrow tunnel to prevent pursuit as the peches and their families escape into the caverns they know perfectly.

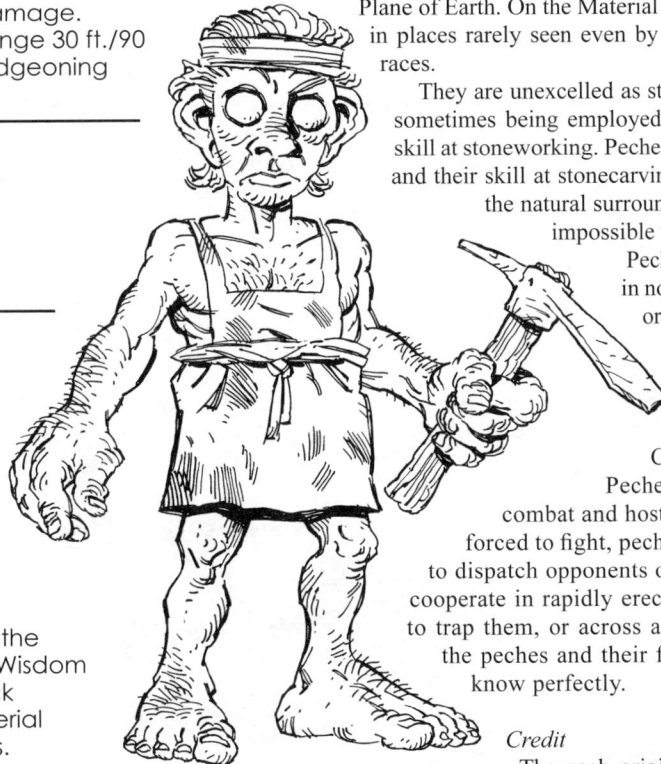

Credit
The pech originally appeared in S4 *Lost Caverns of Tsojcanth* (© TSR/ Wizards of the Coast, 1982) and is used by permission.

Copyright Notice
Author Scott Greene, based on original material by Gary Gygax.

Phycomid

A small blob of decomposing matter covers the ground, with mushrooms sprouting from the patch.

Phycomid

XP 100 (CR 1/2)
NE Small plant (fungus)
Initiative +0

DEFENSE
AC 10
hp: 22 (5d6 + 5)
Immunity: Psychic damage; charm, fright, prone, stun, unconsciousness

OFFENSE
Speed: 10 ft.
Ranged Attack—Fluid Glob: +2 to hit (range 20 ft.; one creature). *Hit:* 1d8 acid damage and the target must make a successful DC 11 Con saving throw or be infected by phycomid spores (see below).

STATISTICS
Str 8 (–1), **Dex** 10 (+0), **Con** 13 (+1),
Int 0 (–5), **Wis** 11 (+0), **Cha** 1 (–5)
Languages: None
Senses: Tremorsense 30 ft.

TRAITS
Spore Infection: A creature that fails the DC 11 Con saving throw against a phycomid's fluid glob attack is infected with the plant's spores. Tiny mushroomlike growths sprout from the creature's body. These look like fine, white hairs at first, but after 10 minutes they become recognizable as distinct mushroom shapes. An infected creature takes 1 acid damage and its maximum number of hit points declines by 1 at the start of each of its turns, until the infestation is ended with a *lesser restoration* spell or comparable magic, or by spending 2d4 rounds burning away the phycomid spores or scraping them off with a dagger or other edged weapon. Scraping or burning causes 1d4 slashing or fire damage per round. A creature can't take any other actions during a round when it is destroying a spore infection. If a creature dies while infected, its body immediately sprouts a new, full-strength phycomid.

ECOLOGY
Environment: Underground
Organization: Solitary or patch (2–5)

A patch of phycomids is often found growing in garbage heaps, refuse pits, and other such dark, moist places with plenty of rotting organic material for the phycomid to feed on. A typical patch covers an area of 4 to 5 square feet. The exact number of mushroom growths making up a patch varies wildly.

Phycomids themselves are highly variable. The caps of phycomid mushrooms can be white, red, purple, or yellow, but the stalk of the plant is always milky white or off-white. The mushrooms range from less than an inch tall to a foot or more, with an average of 8 inches.

What all phycomids have in common, and what makes them unique among fungi, is that the body of the plant forms a hollow tube, similar in some ways to a clam's siphon. This tube opens through the cap of the mushroom, but the opening usually is kept tightly closed. It opens only when the phycomid "attacks" by "spitting" an oozy, liquidy glob of slime at a nearby living creature. This slime contains the phycomid's reproductive spores. The acid of the slime eats into the target, allowing the spores to take root in the wound and then spread quickly throughout the creature, inside and out.

Credit
The phycomid originally appeared in *Dragon #68* (© TSR/Wizards of the Coast, 1982) and later in the First Edition *Monster Manual II* (© TSR/Wizards of the Coast, 1983) and is used by permission.

Copyright Notice
Author Scott Greene, based on original material by Gary Gygax.

Pleistocene Animals

Pleistocene animals, also known as megafauna, are from a time just prior to recorded history.

Pleistocene Animal, Brontotherium

This massive beast vaguely resembles a rhinoceros with a forked horn on its nose. Its powerful body is covered in tough hide with short, bristly hair.

Brontotherium

XP 2,300 (CR 6)
Unaligned Huge beast
Initiative +0

DEFENSE
AC 13 (natural armor)
hp: 128 (10d12 + 50)

OFFENSE
Speed: 40 ft.
Melee Attack—Gore: +9 to hit (reach 5 ft.; one creature). *Hit:* 2d10 + 6 piercing damage.

STATISTICS
Str 23 (+6), **Dex** 10 (+0),
Con 20 (+5), **Int** 2 (–4),
Wis 13 (+1), **Cha** 6 (–2)
Languages: None
Senses: Darkvision 60 ft.

TRAITS
Wounded Fury: While a brontotherium's hit points are below half of its starting number, the brontotherium has tactical advantage on attack rolls, the DC to avoid its trample increases to 19, and it rerolls all 1s, 2s, and 3s rolled on its damage dice.

Trample: As the brontotherium moves, it can enter spaces occupied by enemies up to Large size. Creatures in spaces the brontotherium enters can attempt DC 17 Dex saving throws. On a failed save, the creature takes 2d10 + 6 bludgeoning damage and is knocked prone; on a successful save, the creature moves 5 feet out of the brontotherium's path and can make an opportunity attack if it's allowed to react. A brontotherium can attempt to trample any number of creatures during its move, but it can't trample the same creature more than once per round and it can't end its movement in another creature's space.

ECOLOGY
Environment: Temperate
Organization: Solitary

Brontotheriums (also called thunder beasts by some primitive tribes) are found on lost continents and large islands far from civilization. They dwell in primeval forests bordering broad plains where there is plenty of vegetation for these herbivores to feast on. They generally forage at night, in the early morning hours, or early evening hours so as to avoid the midday heat.

Herds are highly territorial and tend to keep to themselves. Occasionaly, they clash with other herds of their kind, except on mutual common ground (water holes, foraging areas, and so on). When two herds meet on ground that both consider theirs, the males quickly charge, butting heads and goring with their horns in an attempt to force the other herd to leave the area.

A brontotherium is about 14 feet long and stands eight feet tall at the shoulder. Its fur is dark brown or grayish-brown. When a herd is in danger, they charge, tearing up everything in their path and trampling any creatures that stand in their way.

Pleistocene Animal, Hyaenodon

This spotted canine resembles a normal hyena, but it has a blunt face, longer teeth, and is overall much larger and more vicious than its cousin.

Hyaenodon

XP 200 (CR 1)
Unaligned Large beast
Initiative +2

DEFENSE
AC 13 (natural armor)
hp: 44 (8d10)

OFFENSE
Speed: 50 ft.
Melee Attack—Bite: +6 to hit (reach 5 ft.; one creature). *Hit:* 2d6 + 4 piercing damage and the target must make a successful DC 14 Dex saving throw or be grappled; see Scrapping for Food, below. A hyaenodon can't bite while it has a target grappled.

STATISTICS
Str 18 (+4), **Dex** 14 (+2), **Con** 11 (+0), **Int** 7 (−2), **Wis** 12 (+1), **Cha** 6 (−2)
Languages: None
Skills: Perception +3
Senses: Darkvision 60 ft.

TRAITS
Keen Senses: Hyaenodons have tactical advantage on Perception checks based on smell.
Pack Tactics: A hyaenodon has tactical advantage on its attack roll if the target is already grappled by at least one other hyaenodon.
Scrapping for Food: A creature that is grappled by one or more hyaenodons takes damage automatically at the start of its turn. It takes 1d6 + 4 piercing damage from the first grappling hyaenodon, 2d6 + 4 from the second hyaenodon, 3d6 + 4 from the third hyaenodon, and so on. Up to four hyaenodons can grapple the same Small or Medium creature. Up to six can grapple a Large creature.

ECOLOGY
Environment: Temperate and arid plains
Organization: Solitary, pair, or pack (3–18)

The hyaenodon, sometimes called the short-faced hyena, is a larger relative of the common hyena. Hyaenodons (and hyenas) are generally thought of as scavengers, but they are skilled hunters capable of taking down large prey—very large prey, in the case of the hyaenodon. When food is scarce, hyaenodons cover large areas individually in search of food, relying primarily on their sense of smell to locate potential prey.

Hyaenodons hunt both alone and in packs led by a single leader. They eat carrion they find lying on the ground or abandoned by other carnivores, but such treasure is scarce in the hyaenodons' world, and their size and ferocity enable them to fill their bellies with their own kills. Favored meals include deer, elk, moose, zebras, bison, lions, brontotheriums, and even mastodons.

Hyaenodons up to Huge size have been reported, but never in packs. They are solitary hunters. Aside from these monsters, the largest typical hyaenodons grow to lengths of 8 feet.

Pleistocene Animal, Mastodon

This elephantine beast has a coat of thick fur and stands longer and lower to the ground than a typical pachyderm. Its long, curved tusks are formidable natural weapons.

Mastodon

XP 1,100 (CR 4)
Unaligned Huge beast
Initiative −1

DEFENSE

AC 13 (natural armor)
hp: 105 (10d12 + 40)

OFFENSE

Speed: 35 ft.
Melee Attack—Gore: +8 to hit (reach 5 ft.; one creature). *Hit:* 3d10 + 6 piercing damage.

STATISTICS

Str 22 (+6), **Dex** 9 (−1),
Con 19 (+4), **Int** 3 (−4),
Wis 12 (+1), **Cha** 5 (−3)
Languages: None

TRAITS

Trample: As the mastodon moves, it can enter spaces occupied by enemies up to Large size. Creatures in spaces the mastodon enters can attempt DC 16 Dex saving throws. On a failed save, the creature takes 3d10 + 6 bludgeoning damage and is knocked prone; on a successful save, the creature moves 5 feet out of the mastodon's path and can make an opportunity attack if it's allowed to react. A mastodon can attempt to trample any number of creatures during its move, but it can't trample the same creature more than once per round and it can't end its movement in another creature's space.

ECOLOGY

Environment: Cold forests, hills, and plains
Organization: Solitary or herd (5–20 plus 5–30 calves)

The great mastodon is a distant relative of the elephant, and is linked to that creature through the woolly mammoth. It is a herbivore that lives primarily in northerly, forested areas. Its diet includes grasses, fruit, and berries, but also leaves, twigs, and branches of trees. A mastodon herd stays in an area long enough to deplete it of food, then moves on.

The mastodon has few natural predators, thanks to its great size. Humanoids who hunt the creatures for meat, for their tusks, or to train them as beasts of burden or war pose the greatest threat.

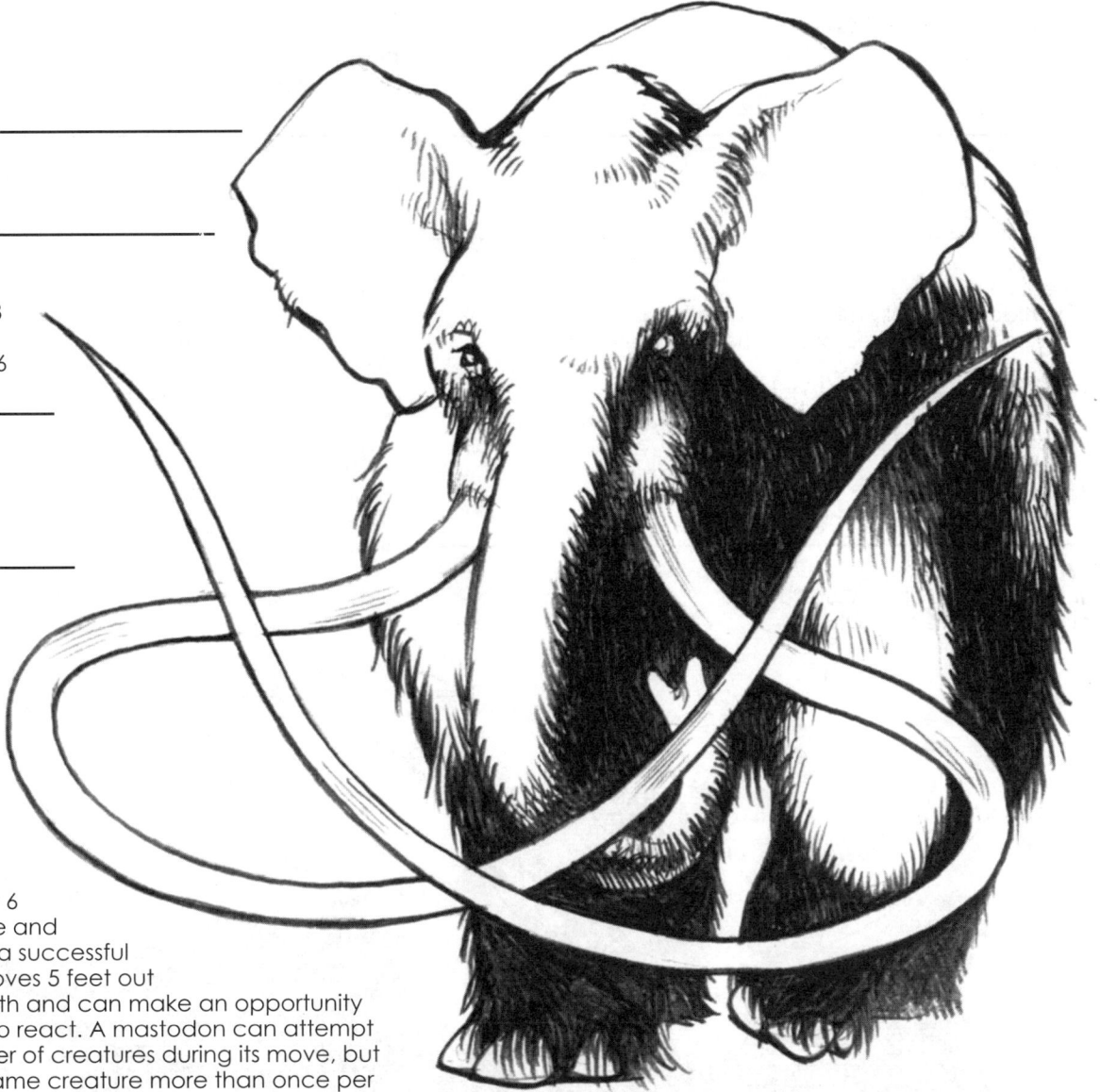

Young mastodons taken into captivity can be trained to drag great loads and to carry riders. With enough training, they can even serve as war leviathans, but they are unpredictable and impossible to control when injured.

The mastodon is slightly longer and lower than its distant relative, the elephant. Its head is longer and taller than an elephant's, and the mastodon's entire body is covered in thick fur.

Mastodons are generally peaceful creatures that avoid combat. They have no natural fear of any creature. If threatened, and especially if their young are threatened, mastodons fight by goring with their tusks and trampling. They are ferocious combatants when angered or wounded.

Pleistocene Animal, Wooly Rhinoceros

This creature has massive legs and a stout body covered with a thick coat of brown fur. From the tip of its elongated nose rise two curving horns.

Woolly Rhinoceros

XP 2,300 (CR 6)
Unaligned Large beast
Initiative –1

DEFENSE
AC 14 (natural armor)
hp: 136 (13d10 + 65)

OFFENSE
Speed: 35 ft.
Multiattack: A woolly rhinoceros attacks once by goring. If the target is knocked prone, the rhino stomps the same creature as a bonus action.
Melee Attack—Gore: +9 to hit (reach 5 ft.; one creature). *Hit:* 2d10 + 6 piercing damage and the target must make a successful DC 17 Dex saving throw or be knocked prone and stomped.
Melee Attack—Stomp: +9 to hit (reach 5 ft.; one creature). *Hit:* 3d10 + 6 bludgeoning damage.

STATISTICS
Str 23 (+6), **Dex** 8 (–1), **Con** 20 (+5),
Int 3 (–4), **Wis** 12 (+1), **Cha** 5 (–3)

Languages: None

TRAITS
Nearsighted: A woolly rhinoceros has tactical disadvantage on Perception checks involving sight.

ECOLOGY
Environment: Temperate and cold forests, marshes, and plains
Organization: Solitary or herd (2–8)

The woolly rhino is an herbivore of the Pleistocene era and of remote, lost worlds. It always lives near areas with plentiful water, such as along rivers, near lakes, and even in marshes and swamps. It does most of its foraging in the morning, so encounters are more common at this time. Although these beasts spend much time on their own, they gather in herds around watering holes when females have young that need protection.

The woolly rhino averages 11 feet long. The two horns on its snout grow to three feet in length. Its body is covered in a thick, dark fur that enables it to withstand harsh climates. The creature has poor eyesight, which only makes it more likely to overestimate the threat from an intruder and attack.

Pudding, Blood

A three-foot-tall spherical blob of blood-red protoplasm seeps a sticky, foul smelling slime.

Blood Pudding
XP 450 (CR 2)
Unaligned Medium ooze
Initiative +0

DEFENSE
AC 10
hp: 42 (5d8 + 20)
Resistance: Fire damage
Immunity: Poison and psychic damage; blindness, exhaustion, fright, paralysis, poison, prone, stun

OFFENSE
Speed: 30 ft.
Melee Attack—Slam: +3 to hit (reach 5 ft.; one creature). *Hit:* 1d6 + 1 bludgeoning damage plus 1d6 acid damage and a Medium or Large target is grappled and restrained (see Infusion below). A blood pudding can grapple one creature at a time.

STATISTICS
Str 12 (+1), **Dex** 11 (+0), **Con** 18 (+4),
Int 0 (–5), **Wis** 10 (+0), **Cha** 7 (–2)
Languages: None
Senses: Blindsight 60 ft.

TRAITS
Amorphous: A blood pudding can move through gaps as small as 1 square inch without penalty.
Cold Vulnerability: A blood pudding that takes cold damage has its speed halved, it can't grapple (a grappled creature is immediately released), and damage from disgorgement is halved.
Disgorgement: When a blood pudding starts its turn infused in a host creature (see Infusion), it uses its action to force out the creature's blood and bodily fluids through the creature's eyes, ears, nose, mouth, open wounds, and pores. The host creature takes 2d6 + 4 bludgeoning damage. If the creature dies, the blood pudding stays put, feeding on the corpse from the inside. When sated, the pudding oozes out; to onlookers, it appears as if the slain creature is bleeding profusely.
Infusion: A blood pudding that starts its turn grappling a creature forces itself into that creature's body through osmosis. The blood pudding quickly disappears as it oozes into wounds and through skin. This is an action on the part of the blood pudding. It causes no damage to the target but does turn the host's eyes blood red and gives it an overall swollen, flushed appearance.

A creature infused with a blood pudding can use an action on its turn trying to eject the creature by coughing it up, vomiting, and so on. The blood pudding is expelled with a successful DC 14 Con saving throw. *Lesser restoration* and comparable magic gives the host tactical advantage on its next Con saving throw to expel the pudding. Drinking alcohol has the same effect. If the host creature takes damage from an external cause (not from the blood pudding), the blood pudding takes half as much. It does not get saving throws against attacks that allow them, but simply takes half as much damage as the host creature. If a blood pudding is killed while inside a host creature, the creature is considered poisoned until *greater restoration* is cast on it.

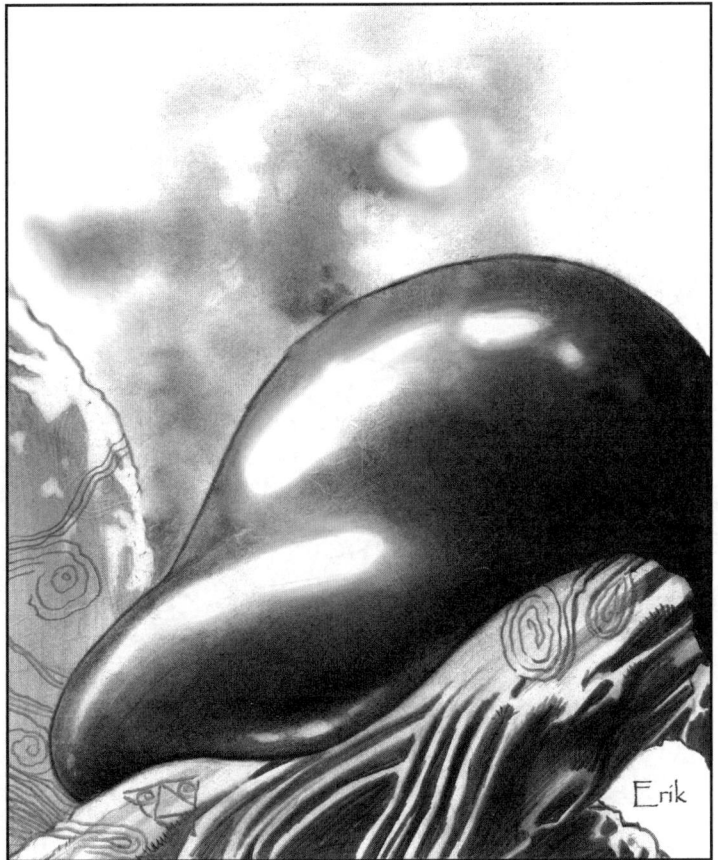

If the blood pudding is still infused in the creature at the start of the pudding's turn, it disgorges (see Disgorge).
Vinegar Vulnerability: Drinking vinegar forces an infused blood pudding to abandon a host's body immediately. The host takes 2d6 + 4 bludgeoning damage from the pudding rapidly forcing itself out and must make a successful DC 14 Con saving throw or be stunned for 1d4 rounds. The blood pudding is poisoned for 2d6 rounds.

ECOLOGY
Environment: Temperate marshes and underground
Organization: Solitary

This monster rolls through dark corridors and marshes looking for sustenance. Its method of eating is repulsive and alarming to see. In marshes and swamps, the blood pudding feeds on whatever living creatures wander by. In underground settings, it tends to hunt for vermin and for the humanoid denizens that share its environment.

A blood pudding strikes by forming a long pseudopod that winds around a creature multiple times, pinning the creature's limbs. Unless the pudding can be forced out of the victim's body quickly, it will kill the host and then consume the corpse's soft organs from the inside out. It's an unpleasant way to die.

Copyright Notice
Author Scott Greene.

Pyrolisk

This creature resembles a rooster with thinning feathers and leathery, batlike wings covered thinly in red-tinged feathers. Its tail feathers are yellow-brown save for one bright red feather.

Pyrolisk

XP 100 (CR 1/2)
NE Small monstrosity
Initiative +2

DEFENSE
AC 12
hp: 21 (6d6)
Immunity: Fire damage
Vulnerability: Cold damage

OFFENSE
Speed: 20 ft., fly 40 ft.
Melee Attack—
Beak: +4 to hit (reach 5 ft.; one creature). *Hit:* 1d4 + 2 piercing damage and the target must make a successful DC 12 Con saving throw or burst into flames, taking 1d6 fire damage immediately plus 1d6 fire damage at the start of each of the pyrolisk's turns for as long as the flames burn. A creature can extinguish flames on itself or on an adjacent creature by using an action to make a successful DC 10 Dex (Survival) check.

STATISTICS
Str 6 (−2), **Dex** 15 (+2), **Con** 11 (+0),
Int 3 (−4), **Wis** 13 (+1), **Cha** 9 (−1)
Languages: Understands Common but can't speak
Senses: Darkvision 60 ft.

TRAITS
Pyrotechnics (1/day): As an action, a pyrolisk can cause an ordinary fire within 120 feet of it to flare into a burst of sparks and light. This burst is so bright that all creatures able to see the fire and within 60 feet of it must make a successful DC 10 Wis saving throw or be blinded for 1d4 rounds. Pyrolisks are immune to this effect.

ECOLOGY
Environment: Temperate and warm lands, underground
Organization: Solitary, flight (2–4), or flock (6–13)

The pyrolisk closely resembles a cockatrice and is often mistaken for that creature. A character who makes a successful DC 15 Int (Nature) check spots the difference, which lies in the coloration of the pyrolisk's tail feathers and wings. The pyrolisk has a single red feather in its tail and a reddish tinge to its wings. Otherwise, it appears identical to the cockatrice.

Pyrolisks are attracted to firelight, such as campfires at night and glowing forges in dimly-lit blacksmiths' shops. If it detects other creatures around the fire, it uses its pyrotechnics ability to blind them before entering the circle of light and attacking. These birds are intelligent enough to take turns causing a fire to flare round after round, guaranteeing that the maximum number of foes are blinded for as long as possible.

Credit
The pyrolisk originally appeared in the First Edition *Monster Manual II* (© TSR/Wizards of the Coast, 1983) and is used by permission.

Copyright Notice
Author Scott Greene, based on original material by Gary Gygax.

Quadricorn

This creature is a two-headed bull-like monstrosity, armed with four sharp-tipped, glistening horns.

Quadricorn

XP 1,100 (CR 4)
NE Large monstrosity
Initiative +1

DEFENSE
AC 12 (natural armor)
hp: 59 (7d10 + 21)
Saving Throws: Con +5
Immunity: Charm, stun

OFFENSE
Speed: 30 ft.
Multiattack: A quadricorn attacks twice with its horns. The two attacks must be made against separate targets.
Melee Attack—Horns: +6 to hit (reach 5 ft.; one creature). *Hit:* 1d8 + 4 piercing damage.

STATISTICS
Str 18 (+4), **Dex** 12 (+1), **Con** 17 (+3), **Int** 10 (+0), **Wis** 12 (+1), **Cha** 9 (−1)
Languages: Common
Senses: Darkvision 60 ft.

TRAITS
Charge: A quadricorn does extra damage with a horn attack if it moved at least 20 feet in a straight line toward the target of the attack. It can trample another target during this move. If the horn attack hits, the target creature takes an extra 3d8 piercing damage and must make a successful DC 14 Str check or be pushed 5 feet away from the quadricorn and knocked prone.

Magic Horns: A quadricorn's horns are treated as magic weapons.

Trample: As it moves, a quadricorn can trample one Medium or smaller creature. The target creature must make a DC 14 Dex saving throw when the quadricorn moves adjacent. If the saving throw succeeds, the target can move 5 feet to either side, the quadricorn continues moving, and the trample attack has no effect. If the saving throw fails, the target is knocked prone, takes 1d8 + 4 bludgeoning damage, and the quadricorn can move through the target's space but can't end its turn there.

ECOLOGY
Environment: Temperate and warm hills and prairies
Organization: Solitary

Quadricorns resemble two-headed bulls, although the body is more massive than that of a normal bull, to accommodate the two heads. Unlike unicorns, with their attraction toward virgins, quadricorns have somewhat the reverse propensity; they are known to sometimes charge into towns to find houses of ill repute, where they batter through walls and doors in an attempt to carry off one or two captive "soiled doves."

In general, quadricorns live in barren wilderness areas, and can even be found making their lairs in caves, although they are not generally found in deep catacombs. The wilderness around a quadricorn's lair shows signs of the creature's presence: stretches of ground that are heavily trampled and torn up by hooves, trees with their bark torn off and with deep gouges from horns, even boulders split cleanly in half from unimaginably heavy impact.

Quickwood

This creature resembles an oak tree with a humanlike visage on its trunk. Its bark is dark and withered with age. A great maw filled with jagged teeth opens in its trunk.

Quickwood

XP 3,900 (CR 8)
N Huge plant
Initiative +2

DEFENSE

AC 14 (natural armor)
hp: 149 (13d12 + 65)
Saving Throws: Dex +4, Con +5
Resistance: Bludgeoning and piercing damage
Immunity: Lightning and psychic damage; charm, stun, unconsciousness
Vulnerability: Fire damage

OFFENSE

Speed: 10 ft.
Multiattack: A quickwood bites once and attacks four times with its roots.
Melee Attack—Bite: +8 to hit (reach 5 ft.; one creature). *Hit:* 3d8 + 5 piercing damage. This attack roll has tactical advantage against a target that's grappled by the quickwood.
Melee Attack—Root: +8 to hit (reach 30 ft.; one creature). *Hit:* 1d10 + 5 bludgeoning damage and the target must make a successful DC 16 Dex saving throw or be grappled and dragged 15 feet closer to the quickwood. This attack roll has tactical advantage against a target that's already grappled by the quickwood.

STATISTICS

Str 20 (+5), **Dex** 7 (–2), **Con** 20 (+5), **Int** 10 (+0), **Wis** 13 (+1), **Cha** 11 (+0)
Languages: Common, Sylvan
Senses: Darkvision 60 ft.

TRAITS

Fear Aura: If a quickwood makes a successful saving throw against a spell that would have damaged it, the quickwood takes no damage but instead absorbs some of the spell's energy and immediately releases it as a *fear* spell in a 30-foot radius instead of a cone. Saving throws against this fear are made against DC 12.
Grasping Roots: A creature grappled by a quickwood can break free with a successful DC 16 Str (Athletics) or Dex (Acrobatics) check or by inflicting 10 slashing damage against the grappling root, thereby severing it from the plant. Roots have AC 14. Damage done to a root is not subtracted from the plant's overall hit points, and severing a root doesn't reduce the quickwood's number of root attacks. If a creature is grappled by more than one root, each root must be severed or overpowered individually.
Remote Sensing: A quickwood can see and hear through any normal oak tree within 360 feet of the quickwood. It can see and hear through up to ten oak trees at a time, and it can drop one tree and add another as a bonus action once per round. An oak tree utilized as a magical sensor develops a vaguely humanlike visage on its trunk that seems to peer around itself.

ECOLOGY

Environment: Temperate forests, hills, and mountains
Organization: Solitary

Quickwoods appear as nothing more than common oak trees, and are indistinguishable from them at distances greater than 30 feet. Closer inspection can reveal a humanlike visage in the trunk, but unless the quickwood moves, even this "face" is likely to be dismissed as nothing more than an unusual arrangement of bark and knots.

Quickwoods are carnivorous, and they prefer the taste of human and elven flesh above all others.

Quickwoods usually root themselves to a particular location and rarely move. When they do move, they pull themselves along slowly with their roots.

Quickwoods use their remote sensing ability to keep close tabs on their surroundings. If trespassers are detected, the creature simply waits until one or more potential victims come within range of its roots before striking. A grabbed opponent is pulled close enough for the quickwood to bite it.

Four root attacks matches up to the "typical" quickwood, but larger and smaller versions can make more or fewer attacks.

Credit
The quickwood originally appeared in the First Edition *Monster Manual II* (© TSR/Wizards of the Coast, 1983) and is used by permission.

Copyright Notice
Author Scott Greene, based on original material by Gary Gygax.

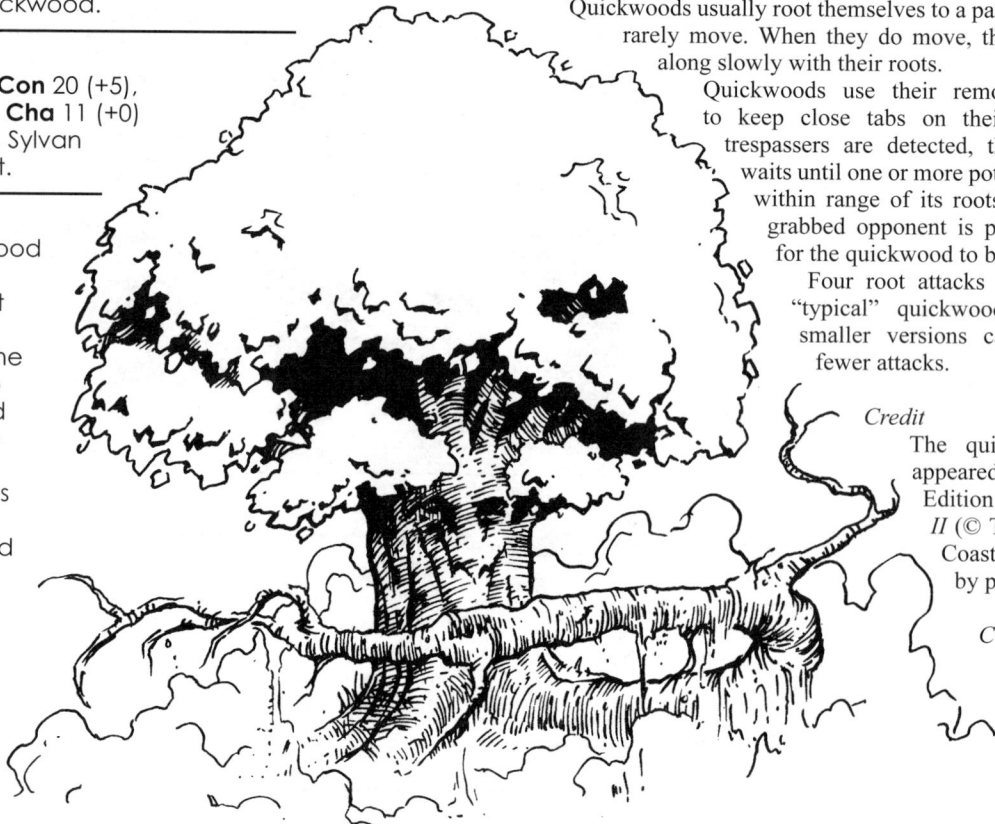

Rat, Shadow

This creature appears as a rat with rotting flesh, torn and matted fur, and blazing red eyes.
Its semitranslucent skin reveals the rat's discolored bones and muscles.

Shadow Rat
XP 10 (CR 0)
Unaligned Tiny undead
Initiative +2

DEFENSE
AC 12
hp: 1 (1d4 – 1)
Immunity: Poison damage; exhaustion, fright, poison, unconsciousness

OFFENSE
Speed: 40 ft., climb 15 ft.
Melee Attack—Bite: +4 to hit (reach 5 ft.; one creature). *Hit:* 1 piercing damage and the target may be infected with cadaver fever (see below).

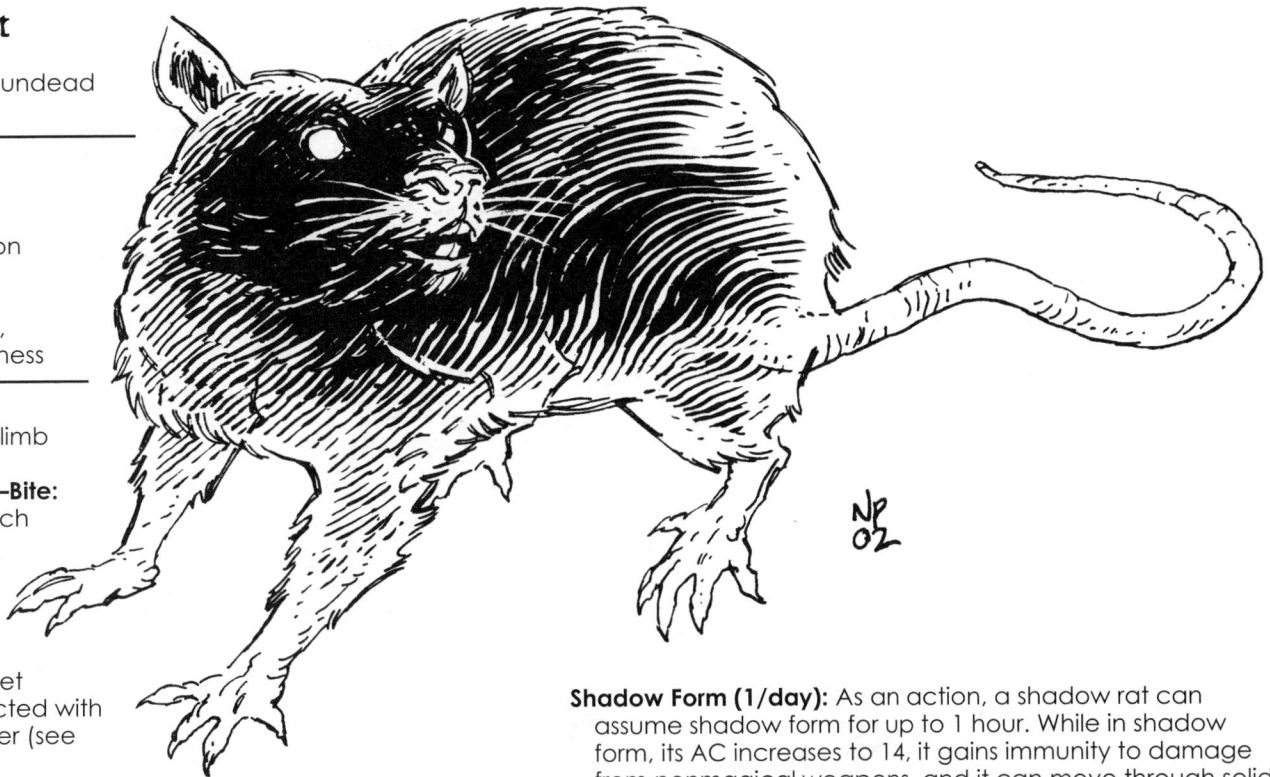

STATISTICS
Str 6 (–2), **Dex** 15 (+2), **Con** 9 (–1), **Int** 2 (–4), **Wis** 12 (+1), **Cha** 12 (+1)
Languages: None
Senses: Darkvision 60 ft.

TRAITS
Cadaver Fever: At the end of a battle against shadow rats, anyone who was bitten by a shadow rat must make a DC 9 Con saving throw against disease. Failure indicates the character is infected with cadaver fever. An infected character gains one level of exhaustion immediately and must repeat the saving throw at the end of every long rest. Each failed saving throw adds one more level of exhaustion; a successful saving throw at the end of a long rest means only that the character's condition doesn't worsen. The character recovers fully when he or she makes successful saving throws at the ends of two consecutive long rests or when *lesser restoration* or comparable magic is used on the character.

Shadow Form (1/day): As an action, a shadow rat can assume shadow form for up to 1 hour. While in shadow form, its AC increases to 14, it gains immunity to damage from nonmagical weapons, and it can move through solid objects and other creatures as if they were difficult terrain. The shadow rat is destroyed if it is still inside something solid at the end of its turn.

Shadow Blend: A shadow rat becomes invisible when it moves into darkness, dim light, or any other space where it is heavily obscured.

ECOLOGY
Environment: Temperate
Organization: Solitary

Shadow rats are undead rats that can blend effortlessly into shadows and even reduce their physical form to shadows for a limited time. Other than their semitranslucent skin (which they have even in shadow form), they resemble normal rats in every other aspect.

Shadow rats attack relentlessly with their bite attack. Unlike normal shadows, shadow rats do not create spawn.

Red Jester

A horrid walking corpse appears, arrayed in brightly colored clothes, floppy shoes, and a bright red jester's hat complete with jingling bells sewn to the ends of the cap. Rigor mortis has permanently pulled the creature's face into a broad yet horrifying grin.

Red Jester

XP 1,800 (CR 5)
CN Medium undead
Initiative +3

DEFENSE

AC 14 (natural armor)
hp: 67 (15d8)
Saving Throws: Dex +6
Resistance: Bludgeoning, piercing, and slashing damage from nonmagical weapons
Immunity: Necrotic and poison damage; exhaustion, fright, poison, unconsciousness

OFFENSE

Speed: 30 ft.
Multiattack: A red jester attacks twice with fists, or once with its jester's deck, or twice with its mace.
Melee Attack—Fist: +6 to hit (reach 5 ft.; one creature). *Hit:* 1d12 + 3 bludgeoning damage.
Ranged Attack—Jester's Deck: +6 to hit (range 20 ft.; one creature). *Hit:* the target creature is affected as if he or she drew a random card from the *Deck of Many Things*. In the hands of anyone but a red jester, the jester's deck acts as a normal, nonmagical deck of playing cards.
Melee Attack— +2 Mace of Merriment: +7 to hit (reach 5 ft.; one creature). *Hit:* 2d8 + 4 bludgeoning damage and the target must make a successful DC 14 Wis saving throw or be paralyzed with merriment for 1d3 rounds. In the hands of anyone but a red jester, the weapon acts as a *+1 mace.*

STATISTICS

Str 15 (+2), **Dex** 17 (+3), **Con** 10 (+0), **Int** 15 (+2), **Wis** 14 (+2), **Cha** 16 (+3)
Languages: Common and any two others
Skills: Acrobatics +6, Deception +6, Sleight of Hand +6
Senses: Darkvision 60 ft.

TRAITS

Fear Cackle (1/day): As an action, a red jester can unleash a fear-inducing cackle. All creatures within 60 feet that hear the cackle must make a successful DC 14 Wis saving throw or be frightened for 2d4 rounds. A frightened creature has a 50% chance of immediately dropping everything it holds in its hands.
Unassailable Mind: The mind of a red jester is a twisted and dangerous place to peer into. If a living creature targets a red jester with an attack that normally causes psychic damage, or tries to use telepathy on a red jester, that creature must make a successful DC 13 Int saving throw or be cursed, with an effect identical to a permanent *confusion* spell. The *confusion* effect can be ended only by magic that lifts the curse.

ECOLOGY

Environment: Any
Organization: Solitary

Red jesters are thought to be the undead form of court jesters who were executed for telling bad jokes, for making fun of their lord and master, or who died in some other violent, untimely manner. Legend speaks of the red jesters as being the court jesters of Orcus, Demon Prince of the Undead, sent to the Material Plane to "entertain" those the demon prince singled out for special attention. The real truth behind their origin remains a mystery.

While they can be encountered from the coldest to the warmest regions of the world and on any type of terrain, a red jester is generally encountered near civilization. They are the only undead that show any sign of retaining a sense of humor that living persons might relate to (as opposed to the sorts of things some undead appear to find amusing, such as sadism, horror, and death). Red jesters seem to actually enjoy entertaining the living, at least briefly. They can turn murderous at the drop of a hat, however, if their act doesn't get exactly the reaction the red jester expected or hoped for.

Most red jesters don masks or wear heavy makeup to disguise their deathly features. They engage in humorous patter during their acts, lapsing between languages apparently without regard for the audience—and failing to get a laugh is sure to send a red jester into a rampage, even if it's his own fault for telling the joke in a language no one in the audience understands. This patter of jokes, riddles, and bad puns keeps up even while the red jester is murdering everyone within reach.

The trouble usually begins when the strange entertainer does something inexplicable that fails to get a laugh, then grits his teeth and says, "Maybe you'd prefer to see . . . a card trick?"

Copyright Notice
Author Scott Greene.

Ronus

A horrific creature steps forth, its body that of a great gray wolf and its head resembling a tremendous falcon covered with light brown feathers. It sits poised to pounce, gnashing its black, razor-sharp beak.

Ronus
XP 50 (CR 1/4)
Unaligned Medium monstrosity
Initiative +3

DEFENSE
AC 14 (natural armor)
hp: 16 (3d8 + 3)

OFFENSE
Speed: 60 ft.
Melee Attack—Bite: +5 to hit (reach 5 ft.; one creature). *Hit:* 1d6 + 3 piercing damage.

STATISTICS
Str 14 (+2), **Dex** 16 (+3), **Con** 12 (+1), **Int** 4 (–3), **Wis** 13 (+1), **Cha** 7 (–2)
Languages: None
Skills: Perception +3, Stealth +5
Senses: Darkvision 60 ft.

ECOLOGY
Environment: Temperate forest
Organization: Pack (3–8) or lair (6–14)

When the sound of a falcon's shriek and a wolf's howl mix together in the night air, chances are good that a ronus is nearby and about to strike. Turning and running won't help; that only incites the pack, because they know few normal creatures can outrun them.

Ronuses always hunt in packs. The only time a runus is encountered alone is if it is injured, sick, old, or cast out of its pack. Such a creature won't attack unless provoked and fights only to defend itself.

Ronuses live by hunting for fresh meat. They will eat anything from mice to rabbits to goblins to ogres; anything they can catch and kill is food. Prey is attacked and dispatched as quickly as possible, before it has a chance to mount a defense against the pack. Prey is eaten where it falls. The pack ravenously devours most of the meat, but enough is left behind on the bones for other scavengers—which encourages creatures the ronuses can eat to live in their territory.

A ronus lair is always hard to find, being camouflaged with boulders, leaves, fallen trees, and broken tree limbs. Although they hunt in forests, they prefer rocky areas for their lairs, because stony ground makes it harder for enemies to follow the ronuses' tracks to their lair's entrance. In areas where hunting is good, several ronus packs might share the same lair. They are smart enough to understand that there's safety in numbers.

Ronuses are blazingly fast sprinters. They use their speed to great advantage when hunting. While one portion of the pack stalks prey noisily to keep it moving and to keep its attention focused on what's behind, another portion races ahead at top speed and waits for the prey to stumble into their ambush, where they'll be caught with no way forward and no way back.

Russet Mold

This plant appears to be a normal rust stain formed by iron-rich water trickling across the stone for ages.

Russet Mold
XP 100 (CR 1/2)
Unaligned Medium plant (fungus)
Initiative +2

AC 8
hp: 9 (2d8)
Immunity: Bludgeoning, piercing, and slashing damage; Cold, fire, necrotic, poison, and psychic damage; all conditions
Vulnerability: Acid damage
Speed: 0 ft.
Area Attack—Spores: automatic hit (range 5 ft. radius; all creatures in radius). *Hit:* each target must make a successful DC 12 Con saving throw or take 2d6 poison damage and become poisoned. While poisoned, a creature repeats the saving throw at the end of each of its turns. On a successful save, the poisoned condition ends; on a failed save, the creature takes another 2d6 poison damage. A creature that dies from this poison damage reanimates 24 hours later, transformed into a vegepygmy commoner. The spores remain active in a dead creature's body, so if a creature is restored to life before it reanimates, it is still poisoned and it continues taking poison damage until the poison is neutralized magically or by a successful save.

TRAITS
Camouflage: From a distance of 10 feet or more, russet mold is indistinguishable from the normal rust stains that are often seen in damp dungeons

and caves. On closer inspection (within 10 feet), it can be identified with a successful DC 15 Int (Nature) check. Once characters are familiar with it (they've had a prior encounter with russet mold), it can be identified automatically, but this identification still requires close inspection.

ECOLOGY
Environment: Underground
Organization: Solitary or patch (2–5)

Russet mold thrives in dark, wet areas. It looks nearly identical to the rust streaks and stains that can be found in every cave or dungeon where water trickles down the walls and forms puddles on the floor. When a living creature gets within 5 feet, however, the russet mold "coughs" out a burst of spores that forms a cloud 15 feet in diameter, centered on the russet mold. This cloud contains a deadly, mutagenic poison that not only kills creatures unfortunate enough to be caught in it, but transforms them into vegepygmies.

A patch of russet mold is 5 to 7 feet in diameter.

Acid is by far the most effective way to kill a patch of russet mold. If none is available, alcohol can also be used, but it does just 2 points of damage per gallon, or 1 point per gallon if beer or wine are used.

Credit
Russet mold originally appeared in the First Edition module *S3 Expedition to the Barrier Peaks* (© TSR/Wizards of the Coast, 1980) and later in the First Edition *Monster Manual II* (© TSR/Wizards of the Coast, 1983) and is used by permission.

Copyright Notice
Author Scott Greene, based on original material by Gary Gygax.

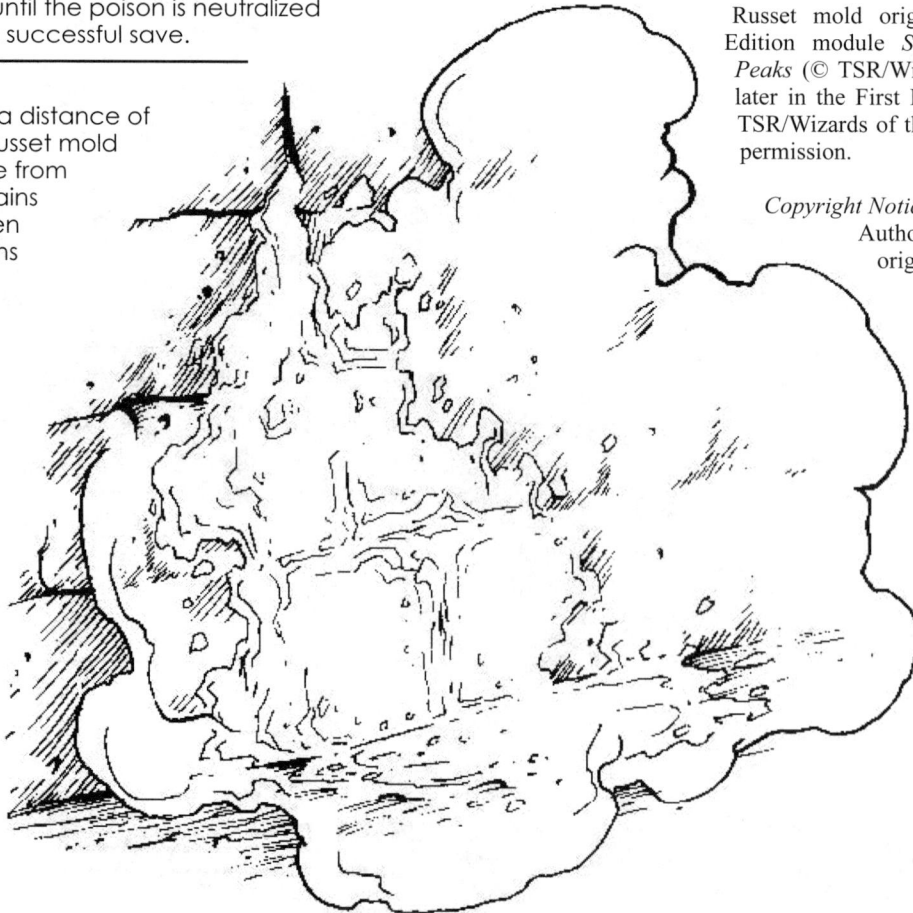

Ryven

This humanoid resembles an anthropomorphic badger. It stands nearly as tall as a human, but its body is broader and covered with gray fur, with a white stripe running across the top of its head and down its back to its bushy tail. A ryven has long, sharp claws on its fingers and toes alike.

Ryven

XP 200 (CR 1)
Neutral Medium humanoid
Initiative +2

DEFENSE

AC 13 (natural armor)
hp: 19 (3d8 + 6)

OFFENSE

Speed: 30 ft., burrow 5 ft.
Multiattack: A ryven normally makes one melee attack or one ranged attack. When berserk, it bites once and attacks once with claws.
Melee Attack—Bite: +4 to hit (reach 5 ft.; one creature). *Hit:* 2d6 + 2 piercing damage.
Melee Attack—Claw: +4 to hit (reach 5 ft.; one creature). *Hit:* 1d6 + 2 slashing damage; also see White and Black Death, below.
Melee Attack—Shortsword: +4 to hit (reach 5 ft.; one creature). *Hit:* 1d6 + 2 piercing damage; also see White and Black Death, below.
Ranged Attack—Light Crossbow: +4 to hit (range 80 ft./320 ft.; one creature). *Hit:* 1d8 + 2 piercing damage; also see White and Black Death, below.

STATISTICS

Str 12 (+1), **Dex** 14 (+2),
Con 14 (+2), **Int** 8 (−1),
Wis 12 (+1), **Cha** 10 (+0)
Languages: Common
Skills: Perception +3, Survival +3
Senses: Darkvision 60 ft.

TRAITS

Rage: When a ryven is reduced to 12 or fewer hit points in combat, it flies into a berserk rage lasting ten rounds (one minute). While berserk, the ryven has tactical advantage on bite attacks, it uses both its bite and claw attacks, all of its attacks do 2 extra points of damage, and it gains resistance to bludgeoning, piercing, and slashing damage. It drops whatever it held in its hands and fights solely with tooth and claw. Ryven shamans are immune to rage.
Ryven Shaman: Any large group of ryvens (seven or more) will be accompanied by one or more tribal shamans. A ryven shaman has heightened Wisdom (16) and the ability to cast the following spells, using Wisdom as its spellcasting ability (DC 13, attack +5). It doesn't need material components to cast these spells. The listed spells are suggestions only; others can be chosen instead. Ryven shamans are immune to rage.
Cantrips (at will): *druidcraft, guidance, resistance*
1st level (x4): *cure wounds, faerie fire, goodberry, speak with animals*
2nd level (x2): *beast sense, moonbeam*
White and Black Death: Some ryven (approximately 1 in 5) coat their weapons and claws with a poison known as "the white and black death." A living creature struck by a poisoned weapon or claw must make a successful DC 12 Con saving throw or take 1d6 poison damage immediately and be poisoned for 1d6 rounds.

ECOLOGY

Environment: Temperate forests
Organization: Solitary, pair, raiding party (4–9), or tribe (11–30 plus 2–16 noncombatants, 1–3 shamans, and 2–6 giant badgers)

Ryven are known as badger-folk by other races. They resemble man-sized, bipedal badgers. They are a battle-hardened race, having waged war for generations with elves and centaurs. Ryven warriors carry the scars from their battles with pride.

Most ryvens carry weapons—shortswords and spears are among their favorites—but their use of weapons is really a type of cultural shorthand that tells other ryvens, "I am under control; see, I'm using a sword!" When berserk rage seizes them, they instinctively drop whatever weapons they held and resort to their teeth and claws: "the old weapons," as they refer to them.

Some (mostly those who've been in the wars for a long time) coat their weapons, crossbow bolts, and sometimes even their claws with a specially formulated poison called "the white and black death." These poison-users are not casual killers but a distinct cult within ryven society. The feelings of other ryven toward them is complicated. They are admired for their prowess in battle and their ability to protect the pack, but at the same time, most ryven have a general unease about the use of poison as being somehow less than courageous.

Ryvens attack with surprise whenever possible. They've been known to burrow into ambush positions, then burst up out of the ground in a blast of rock and dirt when an enemy enters their killing zone.

As tribal folk, ryvens dig extensive burrows deep into hillsides and riverbanks. The largest, strongest members of a tribe invariably become its leaders, and the wiliest become its shamans. It is not uncommon to find more than one tribe sharing the same burrow complex. Each usually has its own, sometimes secret, entrances and living chambers, but all of the tunnels are interconnected for rapid movement and defense. Entrances and exits are well camouflaged so enemies and predators can't easily find them. Although ryvens aren't especially religious, they consider their shrines and temples to be the most important chambers in their warrens, so they are always guarded. In most cases, the temple doubles as a final redoubt in case the burrow is overrun.

Thanks to the efforts of their shamans, all ryven tribes count giant badgers among their friends. Sometimes giant badgers live in a warren alongside the ryvens; other times, they live nearby.

The favorite meals of ryvens include sheep, goat, deer, and snakes, but they aren't above consuming the flesh of humanoid enemies. They consume massive quantities of meat, much more than one would expect for creature of their size.

Ryvens are primarily nocturnal, so most encounters with them occur at night. They have no difficulty hunting and fighting during the day; they just prefer nighttime.

Sandling

This creature appears to be a large snake formed of earth and sand.
A simple slit functions as the creature's mouth.

Sandling

XP 200 (CR 1)
Unaligned Large elemental
Initiative +1

DEFENSE

AC 15 (natural armor)
hp: 26 (4d10 + 4)
Resistance: Piercing and slashing damage from nonmagical weapons
Immunity: Poison damage; paralysis, poison, prone, stun, unconsciousness

OFFENSE

Speed: 30 ft., burrow 20 ft.
Melee Attack—Bite: +5 to hit (reach 5 ft.; one creature). *Hit:* 2d8 + 3 bludgeoning damage.

STATISTICS

Str 17 (+3), **Dex** 13 (+1), **Con** 13 (+1),
Int 4 (–3), **Wis** 11 (+0), **Cha** 11 (+0)
Languages: Understands Terran but can't speak
Senses: Darkvision 60 ft., tremorsense 60 ft.

TRAITS

Vulnerability to Water: A sandling that is hit by at least two gallons of water has its speed halved, its AC reduced by 2, and it can't use reactions for one round.

ECOLOGY

Environment: Elemental Plane of Earth
Organization: Solitary

Sandlings are creatures from the Elemental Plane of Earth. A sandling in its natural form resembles a mound of sand that covers a 10-foot area. A typical sandling is 10 feet long but can grow to a length of 20 to 25 feet.

If one visits the Material Plane, it probably was summoned by a spellcaster of some type. Occasionally a sandling slips through a vortex between the planes, but that's a rare occurrence. Sandlings live on a diet of minerals only. They can't digest plants, herbs, meat, or any other substance that has ever been alive. Creatures killed by a sandling are left where they fall.

Sandlings are entirely solitary, and they have no societal structure of any kind. Though they harbor no ill-will toward others of their kind, it is very rare to find two or more sandlings even near one another, let alone cooperating. It is believed that a new sandling is created when one grows large enough to divide in half.

Credit

The sandling originally appeared in the First Edition module *A4 In the Dungeons of the Slave Lords* (© TSR/Wizards of the Coast, 1981) and later in the First Edition *Monster Manual II* (© TSR/Wizards of the Coast, 1983) and is used by permission.

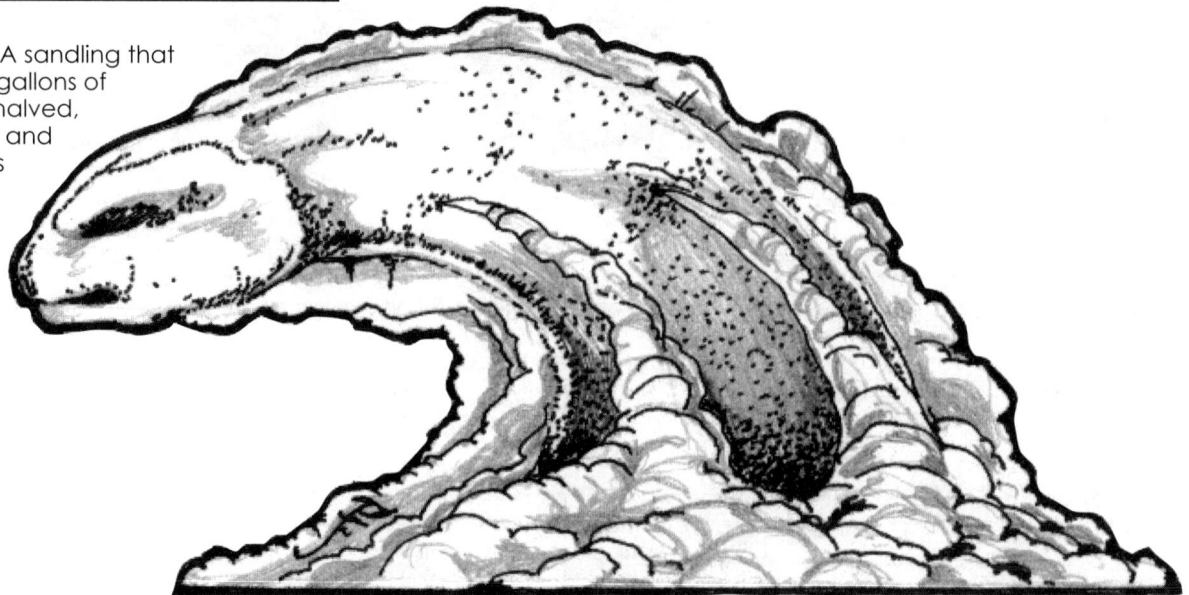

Screaming Devilkin

This winged creature is humanoid in appearance, with frail, spindly arms and legs.
It also has a long, thick tail that ends in a wicked barb.

Screaming Devilkin

XP 50 (CR 1/4)
LE Small fiend
Initiative +2

DEFENSE
AC 12
hp: 13 (3d6 + 3)

OFFENSE
Speed: 5 ft., fly 30 ft.
Melee Attack—Tail Barb: +4 to hit
   (reach 5 ft.; one creature). *Hit:*
   1d4 + 2 piercing damage.

STATISTICS
Str 6 (−2), **Dex** 13 (+2), **Con** 12 (+1),
Int 6 (−2), **Wis** 11 (+0), **Cha** 12 (+1)
Languages: Infernal
Senses: Darkvision 60 ft.

TRAITS
Scream: A screaming devilkin
   continuously emits a painful howl.
   Creatures with hearing must make a
   successful DC 11 Con saving throw every
   time they start their turn within 60 feet of
   a screaming devilkin or be incapacitated
   and deafened until the start of their
   next turn. It doesn't matter how many
   screaming devilkin are within range; only
   one saving throw needs to be made each round.
   A *silence* spell can negate devilkin screaming for the
   duration of the spell.

ECOLOGY
Environment: Any
Organization: Solitary or pack (2–5)

Shrill wails echoing through the night signal the arrival of a screaming devilkin. Screaming devilkins are small creatures, humanoid in appearance but with frail, spindly arms and legs. These weak limbs are nearly useless for combat and locomotion, but the screaming devilkin makes up for this disability by flying everywhere with its batlike wings. Screaming devilkins are fast fliers but not particularly agile on the wing.

Screaming devilkins also have a long, muscular, barbed tail that is their primary means of physical attack.

Screaming devilkins are tireless foes. They attack mortals on sight and never back down no matter how a fight is progressing.

A typical screaming devilkin is 3 feet tall and has a wingspan of about 5 feet. Its skin is reddish-brown and its eyes are entirely black. Their barbed tails are up to 4 feet long.

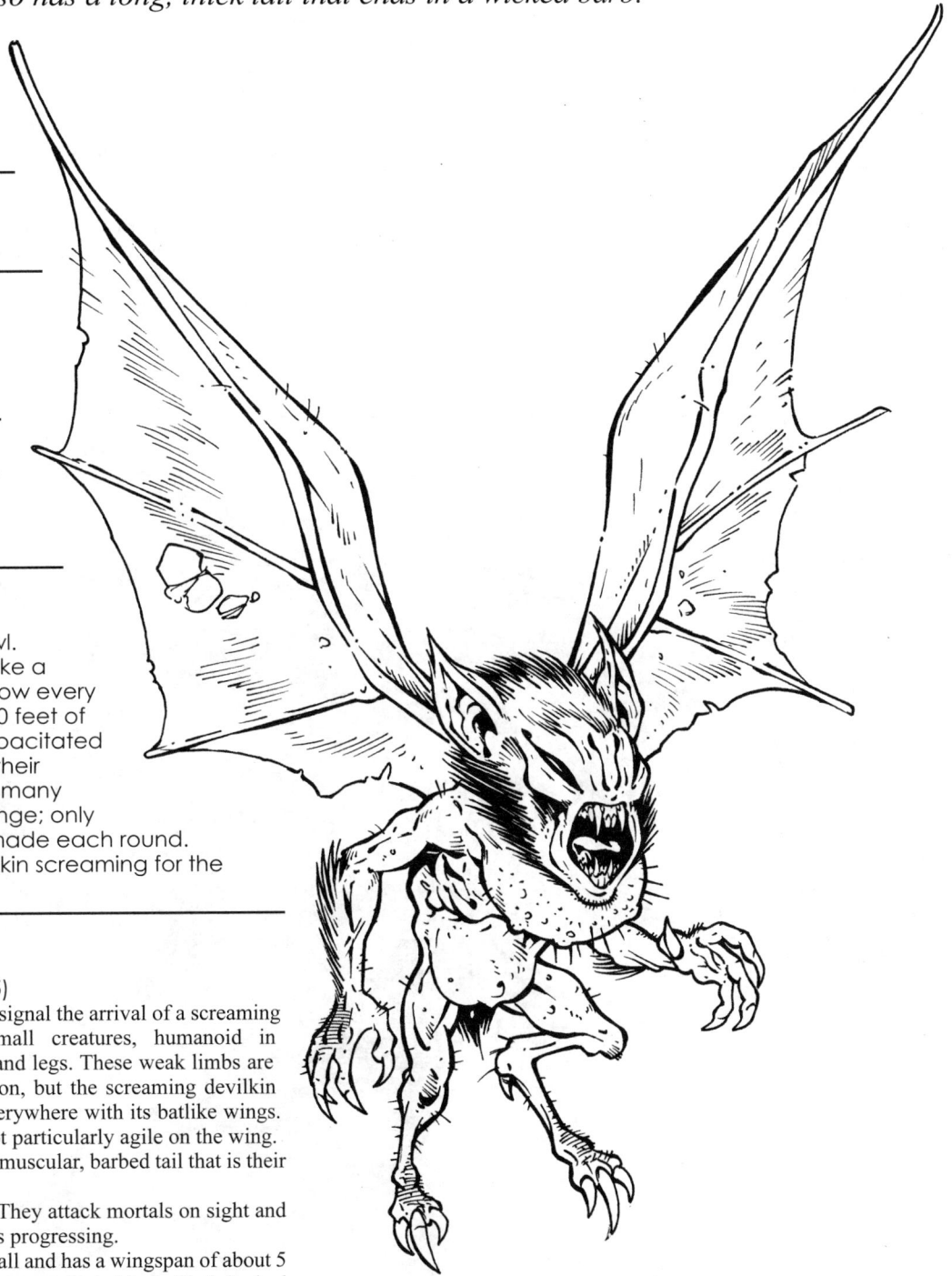

Credit
   The screaming devilkin originally appeared in the First Edition *Fiend Folio* (© TSR/Wizards of the Coast, 1981) and is used by permission.

Copyright Notice
   Author Scott Greene, based on original material by Philip Masters.

Scythe Tree

This twisted tree has many branches but few leaves. In the center of its trunk is a long, deep scar. Its roots are twisted and blackened as if by fire.

Scythe Tree

XP 1,800 (CR 5)
CE Huge plant
Initiative −1

DEFENSE

AC 14 (natural armor)
hp: 76 (8d12 + 24)
Saving Throws: Con +6
Resistance: Bludgeoning and piercing damage from nonmagical weapons
Immunity: Psychic damage; charm, fright, prone, stun, unconsciousness
Vulnerability: Fire damage

OFFENSE

Speed: 20 ft.
Multiattack: A scythe tree attacks three times with branches.
Melee Attack—Branch: +8 to hit (reach 10 ft.; one creature). *Hit:* 2d6 + 5 slashing damage. A scythe tree scores a critical hit if the attack roll is a natural 19 or 20.

STATISTICS

Str 20 (+5), **Dex** 8 (−1),
Con 17 (+3), **Int** 10 (+0),
Wis 13 (+1), **Cha** 12 (+1)
Languages: Sylvan, Treant

Senses: Darkvision 60 ft.

ECOLOGY

Environment: Temperate forest
Organization: Solitary or grove (4–7)

Scythe trees are malevolent plants that live in dense forest, where they blend in with normal trees around them. Scythe trees are carnivorous by nature and draw very little sustenance from sun, air, or earth, preferring a diet of dryad or elf flesh.

Scythe trees average 20 feet in height, but they can reach or even exceed heights of 30 feet, with a trunk diameter of 3 feet. Their bark is dark brown, becoming darker near the roots. What few leaves a scythe tree has are reddish-brown year-round; they don't change color or fall off as the seasons change.

The branches of a scythe tree curve like scythes (hence the tree's name). The scar on its trunk is the tree's mouth.

Scythe trees hate treants and dryads. They attack dryads on sight, but they steer clear of treants unless the scythe trees have a significant numbers advantage.

A scythe tree stands motionless, appearing to be a normal tree, until prey comes within range. Then it slashes with its scythe-like limbs in an effort to cut its foe into bite-size pieces.

Copyright Notice
Author Scott Greene.

Sea Serpents

The sea serpents, great snakelike creatures that have roamed the oceans for ages, are nearly as old as the dragons that roam the sky. Unlike dragons, these great, scaly, serpentine beasts are products of natural evolution, though many scholars suspect magical influence, either deliberate or natural, somewhere in their evolution.

Sea serpents display great variation in size, color, intellect, and temperament. All of them, however, bear certain similarities. They are long, serpentine, warmblooded creatures that resemble snakes in appearance, though they also have two sets of flippers. On some sea serpents, these flippers are large and powerful, while on others they are so small and atrophied as to be almost unnoticeable. All sea serpents are aquatic, as their name implies, but they can survive for extended times out of water and some can even make their way about on land. Furthermore, all sea serpents are sentient, with intellects ranging from that of a smart dolphin to levels rivaling the smartest humans.

One trait that sea serpents share with dragons is a sense of innate superiority, a feeling that they are unequalled, unchallenged masters of the sea.

Unlike dragons, sea serpents are not distinguished by color or age. A few species are as acquisitive as dragons, but most have no interest in hoarding wealth or surrounding themselves with worshipful, lesser creatures. All sea serpents can speak and understand Aquatic, and many know Draconic as well. The more intelligent among them often learn the languages of nearby marine civilizations or the languages of seagoing surface dwellers.

In combat, most sea serpents use similar tactics. All have venomous bites, and all have the ability to trap prey in their coils and crush the life out of them the way a giant constrictor snake does. The largest sea serpents can even crush ships this way; mariners in their smoky dens delight in recounting tales of horror about great serpents that splintered mighty hulls and then gulped down the helpless sailors as they splashed in the water or sank into the brine.

Because they are intelligent, sea serpents can often be reasoned with or bargained with, if the bargainer has something the sea serpent wants and approaches as a supplicant, not an equal. They are adaptable to circumstances and never throw themselves into battle rashly.

Sea Serpent, Brine

This serpentine creature is about 20 feet long from nose to tail, with two sets of large flippers and a body that's somewhat wider side-to-side than top-to-bottom. A finned crest runs the length of its back. The body is dark blue with a lighter underbelly, often tinged with rust or green highlights, and the head is marked with notable, almost batlike ears.

Brine Sea Serpent
XP 5,900 (CR 10)
CE Huge dragon (aquatic)
Initiative +2

DEFENSE
AC 17 (natural armor)
hp: 168 (16d12 + 64)
Saving Throws: Dex +6, Con +8, Str +9
Immunity: Paralysis, prone, stun, unconsciousness

OFFENSE
Speed: swim 60 ft.
Multiattack: A brine sea serpent attacks once with its tail and either bites or uses its brine blast.
Melee Attack—Bite: +9 to hit (reach 5 ft.; one creature). *Hit:* 2d10 + 5 piercing damage plus 2d6 poison damage, and the target must make a successful DC 17 Str saving throw or be grappled and restrained. If the target of this attack is already grappled by the sea serpent, the attack hits automatically but the target repeats the saving throw, escaping from the grapple and restraint if the save succeeds. A brine serpent can have one creature grappled at a time.
Melee Attack—Tail Slap: +9 to hit (reach 15 ft.; one creature). *Hit:* 2d8 + 5 bludgeoning damage and the target is pushed 10 feet away from the sea serpent.
Area Attack—Brine Blast (1/day): automatic hit (range 50-ft. cone; creatures in cone). *Hit:* 10d8 acid damage, or half damage with a successful DC 16 Dex saving throw.

STATISTICS

Str 21 (+5), **Dex** 15 (+2), **Con** 18 (+4),
Int 7 (–2), **Wis** 13 (+1), **Cha** 14 (+2)
Languages: Aquan, Draconic
Skills: Athletics +9, Perception +5
Senses: Darkvision 60 ft.

LEGENDARY ACTIONS

The sea serpent can take up to three legendary actions per round. Legendary actions are taken at the end of another creature's turn, and only one can be taken after each turn.

Coiling Maneuver: +9 to hit (reach 5 ft.; one creature). *Hit:* the target must make a successful DC 16 Str saving throw or be grappled and restrained by the sea serpent. A brine serpent can have one creature grappled at a time.

Concentrate Brine: The sea serpent can try to recharge its brine blast attack. Roll 1d6; the attack recharges on a roll of 5 or 6.

Tail Attack: The sea serpent uses its tail attack against a target within reach.

ECOLOGY

Environment: Any aquatic
Organization: Solitary

The brine sea serpent is an aggressive but relatively stupid (compared to other sea serpents) predator of the deeps. It is the only sea serpent able to attack in a manner similar to a dragon's breath weapon. The brine sea serpent has a special organ that harvests sodium from seawater and stores it in concentrated form in a gland in its cheek. Unlike a dragon's breath, this weapon takes an hour or more to recharge after it's used, but the brine serpent can speed the process by gulping enormous quantities of seawater.

The brine serpent lives in a cave on the ocean floor, where it maintains a hoard, much as a dragon does. The brine serpent's hoard is scavenged from sunken ships, so it often lives in seas known for their storm dangerous storms; besides the potential for treasure, storms also send tasty sailors sinking down into the brine serpent's territory. A brine serpent will attack a ship directly if it is hungry enough.

The eyes of a brine serpent are small, but it possesses large ears that give it exceptional hearing. In quiet seas, it can detect sounds from many miles away.

Against lone prey, the brine serpent likely just rushes in and attack with its bite, saving the brine blast in case a bigger target becomes available. When confronting a group, it uses its brine blast first.

Copyright Notice
Authors Scott Greene and Patrick Lawinger.

Sea Serpent, Deep Hunter

The serpent is about 60 feet long and 10 feet thick. Its body scales are smooth, each about the size of a large shield, and the entire serpent is deep green to jet black in color, with eyes a nearly solid, deep scarlet.

Deep Hunter Sea Serpent

XP 11,500 (CR 14)
LN Gargantuan dragon (aquatic)
Initiative +2

DEFENSE

AC 18 (natural armor)
hp: 232 (16d20 + 64)
Saving Throws: Str +10, Dex +7, Con +9
Immunity: Paralysis, prone, stun, unconsciousness

OFFENSE

Speed: swim 60 ft.
Multiattack: A deep hunter attacks once with its tail and either bites or uses its swallow attack.
Melee Attack—Bite: +10 to hit (reach 5 ft.; one creature). *Hit:* 2d12 + 5 piercing damage plus 2d10 poison damage, and the target must make a successful DC 18 Str saving throw or be grappled and restrained. If the target of this attack is already grappled by the sea serpent, the attack hits automatically but the target repeats the saving throw; if the save succeeds, the target escapes from the grapple and restraint, but if the save fails, the target is swallowed (see below). A deep hunter can have up to two creatures grappled at a time.
Melee Attack—Swallow (recharge 5, 6): automatic hit (reach 5 ft.; one creature grappled by the deep hunter). *Hit:* the target must make a successful DC 18 Str saving throw or be swallowed. A swallowed creature is blinded and restrained. It takes 2d12 +5 piercing damage

immediately, and another 3d8 bludgeoning damage plus 2d8 acid damage automatically at the start of each of the sea serpent's turns. Up to two Large creatures and any number of smaller creatures can be inside the deep hunter at one time. A swallowed creature is unaffected by anything happening outside the deep hunter or by attacks from outside it. A swallowed creature can get out of the deep hunter by using 15 feet of movement, but only after the sea serpent is dead.

Melee Attack—Tail Slap: +10 to hit (reach 15 ft.; one creature). *Hit:* 2d10 + 5 bludgeoning damage and the target is pushed 10 feet away from the sea serpent.

STATISTICS

Str 21 (+5), **Dex** 15 (+2), **Con** 18 (+4),
Int 7 (–2), **Wis** 13 (+1), **Cha** 14 (+2)
Languages: Aquan, Draconic
Skills: Athletics +10, Perception +6
Senses: Darkvision 60 ft.

LEGENDARY ACTIONS

The sea serpent can take up to three legendary actions per round. Legendary actions are taken at the end of another creature's turn, and only one can be taken after each turn.

Coiling Maneuver: +9 to hit (reach 5 ft.; one creature). *Hit:* the target must make a successful DC 18 Str saving throw or be grappled and restrained by the sea serpent. A deep hunter can have up to two creatures grappled at a time.

Unhinge Jaw: The sea serpent can try to recharge its swallow attack. Roll 1d6; the attack recharges on a roll of 5 or 6.

Tail Attack: The sea serpent uses its tail attack against a target within reach.

ECOLOGY

Environment: Any aquatic
Organization: Solitary

The immense deep hunter sea serpent lives in the deepest parts of the ocean, where it delights in hunting down and killing the most fearsome creatures of the sea. Its preferred prey is giant squids, the largest whales, and sometimes even other sea serpents—only the long-slumbering kraken is more feared than this monstrous predator of the sea. Its lair usually is near thermal vents or underwater volcanoes, where the water is very warm. When hunting, however, it can be encountered anywhere at sea.

Thankfully, the deep hunter seldom comes to the surface, because its favorite prey sticks to deep water. When one is sighted on the surface, rumors of its presence can cause shipping to reroute thousands of miles out of its way to avoid deep hunter-infested water, or to not venture out of port at all. Such a sighting is a calamity for commerce, but also a great opportunity for the few sea captains brave enough to risk a trip through a deep hunter's territory (and charismatic enough to find a crew that will share the risk).

Sea Serpent, Fanged

This serpent is 12 to 15 feet long and 5 feet thick. Its body scales are thick and hard, making it somewhat slower than other sea serpents but also giving it excellent armor. This serpent's most notable feature, however, is multiple rows of long, sharp teeth that line its jaws beneath large, lidless red eyes with white pupils.

Fanged Sea Serpent

XP 1,800 (CR 5)
NE Large dragon (aquatic)
Initiative +1

DEFENSE

AC 18
hp: 85 (10d10 + 30)
Saving Throws: Dex +4
Immunity: Paralysis, prone, stun, unconsciousness

OFFENSE

Speed: swim 30 ft.
Melee Attack—Bite: +7 to hit (reach 5 ft.; one creature). *Hit:* 1d12 + 4 piercing damage plus 2d6 poison damage. The target must make a successful DC 14 Con saving throw or be poisoned for 1d4 rounds. The fanged sea serpent scores a critical hit if its attack roll is a natural 18, 19, or 20; see Impale, below.

STATISTICS

Str 18 (+4), **Dex** 13 (+1), **Con** 16 (+3),
Int 5 (–3), **Wis** 11 (+0), **Cha** 6 (–2)
Languages: Aquan, Draconic

Skills: Athletics +7, Perception +3
Senses: Darkvision 60 ft.

TRAITS

Impale: When a fanged sea serpent delivers a critical hit, it drives its fangs completely through the creature's body or limbs. An impaled creature is grappled and takes 1d12 + 4 piercing damage at the start of each of the fanged sea serpent's turns. It

also takes 1d12 piercing damage when it escapes from the grapple. A fanged sea serpent can have up to one Medium or two Small creatures impaled at one time.

ECOLOGY
Environment: Any aquatic
Organization: Solitary, pair, or swarm (3–20)

The fanged sea serpent is a vicious predator of the sea. Although it is much smaller than other sea monsters such as the bine serpent or the deep hunter, it is greatly feared for its tendency to travel in packs that swarm over creatures or vessels much larger than any individual member of the pack.

Fanged sea serpents are nomadic. They follow the ocean currents year-round, which means they can be found all around the world—but only for part of the year. Fishermen often take their vacations during the season when fanged sea serpents are swarming in nearby water.

An attack by fanged sea serpents is a terrifying sight. They close in on selected prey from all sides, and the water boils and foams red from the writhing, splashing bodies tearing at the unfortunate victim. Fanged sea serpents have been known to attack their own kind, but only when starving.

Fanged sea serpents on their own usually live on large fish and avoid confronting intelligent creatures of any kind unless they are desperate or believe it's a fight they can't lose. They are fearless and aggressive in a group, however. Packs of fanged sea serpents are known to attack creatures much larger than themselves. Once a target is surrounded—and in water, "all sides" includes above and below, too—few marine creatures can stand up to a determined assault by these ferocious predators.

Sea Serpent, Shipbreaker

This devastating serpent is over 120 feet long and 15 feet thick. Its scales are dark gray or brown, festooned with seaweed, barnacles, lampreys, and other sea life. Its maw is the size of a wagon, with teeth the size of greatswords.

Shipbreaker Sea Serpent
XP 25,000 (CR 20)
CN Gargantuan dragon (aquatic)
Initiative +1

DEFENSE
AC 19 (natural armor)
hp: 310 (20d20 + 100)
Saving Throws: Dex +7, Con +11, Str +14
Immunity: Paralysis, prone, stun, unconsciousness

OFFENSE
Speed: 10 ft., swim 40 ft.
Multiattack: A shipbreaker can bite once, attack with its tail, and ram a ship (if its ram attack is available).
Melee Attack—Bite: +14 to hit (reach 5 ft.; one creature). *Hit:* 2d12 + 8 piercing damage plus 2d10 poison damage, and the target must make a successful DC 22 Str saving throw or be grappled and restrained. A ship breaker can have up to two creatures grappled at a time. This attack scores a critical hit if the attack roll is a natural 19 or 20.
Melee Attack—Tail Slap: +14 to hit (reach 15 ft.; one creature). *Hit:* 2d10

+ 8 bludgeoning damage and the target is pushed 20 feet away from the sea serpent.

Melee Attack—Ram (recharge 6): automatic hit (one ship). *Hit:* the vessel makes a Hull saving throw, using the most appropriate DC from the table below, based on the ship's type. The vessel sinks when it has failed the listed number of saving throws. The proficiency bonus of the ship's captain can be added to the saving throw.

Ship Type	Hull DC	Sinks after
Rowboat	20	1 failed save
Barge	19	1 failed save
Oared Galley, small	18	2 failed saves
Oared Galley, large	16	2 failed saves
Sailing Merchant, small	17	2 failed saves
Sailing Merchant, large	15	3 failed saves
Sailing Warship	13	3 failed saves

STATISTICS

Str 26 (+8), **Dex** 13 (+1), **Con** 21 (+5), **Int** 11 (+0), **Wis** 17 (+3), **Cha** 17 (+3)
Languages: Understands Aquan and Draconic but seldom speaks
Skills: Athletics +14, Perception +9
Senses: Darkvision 60 ft.

LEGENDARY ACTIONS

The sea serpent can take up to three legendary actions per round. Legendary actions are taken at the end of another creature's turn, and only one can be taken after each turn.

Coiling Maneuver: +14 to hit (reach 5 ft.; one creature). *Hit:* the target must make a successful DC 22 Str saving throw or be grappled and restrained by the sea serpent.

It's Coming 'Round!: The shipbreaker can try to recharge its ram attack. Roll 1d6; the attack recharges on a roll of 5 or 6.

Tail Attack: The sea serpent uses its tail attack against a target within reach.

ECOLOGY

Environment: Any aquatic
Organization: Solitary

The legendary shipbreaker is believed (and hoped!) to be the largest of the sea serpents, a true behemoth that rules the seas. It is a fearless hunter that enjoys attacking seagoing vessels and tearing out their hulls or capsizing them by ramming. It is believed by many sailors and seafarers that only one of these mighty beasts exists. Thankfully, it seems to spend most of its time hibernating.

A shipbreaker attacks ships and huge-sized creatures as its primary prey. It ignores smaller creatures except as snacks, or if directly threatened by one. Its favorite tactic is to either smash a ship's hull with the shipbreaker's massive snout or armored spine, or to crush the vessel by coiling the shipbreaker's massive body around it, or to swamp it with a might slap of the creature's tail. Once the vessel is destroyed and sinking, the shipbreaker feasts on the drowning sailors in the water.

The shipbreaker is most often sighted well out of sight from land. It has been known to shadow a ship for hours or days, letting its mere presence instill terror in the crew, as they know there's no escape from the coming calamity.

It is unknown what language the shipbreaker speaks or understands, if any, because no one has ever reported hearing anything but terrifying bellows from it. In fact, the creature understands and can speak both Aquan and Common, but it almost never does. What could a mortal possibly say that would merit a response from the shipbreaker?

A shipbreaker can drag itself across reefs and even onto dry land with its broad, flat flippers, but it seldom has any reason to. If the shipbreaker is bent on destroying a ship and its crew, even taking shelter in a shallow lagoon or abandoning the ship entirely to seek safety on an island won't stave off the shipbreaker's fury.

Copyright Notice
Authors Scott Greene and Patrick Lawinger.

Sea Serpent, Spitting

The bodies of these serpents are 15 to 18 feet long, with a girth of up to 3 feet. They are covered with serrated scales of brown, green, or blue, giving their hides a mottled, shimmery appearance. Their heads are short, with thick, muscular necks concealed beneath a webbed fringe.

Spitting Sea Serpent

XP 1,800 (CR 5)
CE Large dragon (aquatic)
Initiative +4

DEFENSE

AC 14
hp: 97 (13d10 + 26)
Saving Throws: Dex +7, Con +5
Immunity: Paralysis, prone, stun, unconsciousness

OFFENSE

Speed: 10 ft., swim 40 ft.
Multiattack: A spitting sea serpent spits once and bites once, or it can make a constrict attack.
Melee Attack—Bite: +7 to hit (reach 5 ft.; one creature). *Hit:* 2d8 + 4 piercing damage and the target must make a successful DC 13 Con saving throw or take 1d8 poison damage.
Ranged Attack—Spit: +7 to hit (range 60 ft.; one creature). *Hit:* 3d6 + 4 acid damage. This attack functions underwater with no penalty.
Melee Attack—Constrict: +7 to hit (range 5 ft.; one creature). *Hit:* the target must make a successful DC 15 Dex saving throw or be grappled and restrained and take 4d8 + 4 bludgeoning damage.

STATISTICS

Str 13 (+1), **Dex** 18 (+4), **Con** 14 (+2), **Int** 8 (−1), **Wis** 13 (+1), **Cha** 6 (−2)
Languages: Understands Aquan but seldom speaks
Skills: Athletics +4, Perception +4
Senses: Darkvision 60 ft.

ECOLOGY

Environment: Any aquatic
Organization: Solitary or pair

Spitting sea serpents are a fiercely territorial if not terribly intelligent species that can be a great hazard along coastlines. They are renowned for their ability to spit gobs of acidic spittle onto creatures that threaten them. Their spittle is just as dangerous underwater as through the air—and they have been known to spit at people on the decks of ships and on docks, wharfs, and beaches. Being able to move (slowly) on land, they sometimes hunt along the shore, killing creatures with their spit and then crawling onto land to retrieve the carcass and drag it back to the sea.

Spitting sea serpents dwell in shallow coastal water and and avoid deep water, where they sometimes fall prey to larger sea serpents and other gigantic sea predators such as giant squids or octopi. They are most often found in water well away from high-traffic shipping lanes, because sailors kill them on sight, too. Remote stretches of coast are where spitting sea serpents are most likely to be encountered.

Copyright Notice
Authors Scott Greene and Patrick Lawinger.

Seahorse, Giant

This aquatic creature resembles an ordinary seahorse with a vaguely equine-shaped head, fins emerging from the base of its head, and a curling tail that extends to a length of 8 feet or more.

Giant Seahorse

XP 100 (CR 1/2)
Unaligned Large beast
Initiative +2

DEFENSE
AC 12
hp: 26 (4d10 + 4)

OFFENSE
Speed: swim 30 ft.
Melee Attack—Tail Slap: +4 to hit (reach 5 ft.; one creature).
Hit: 1d8 + 2 bludgeoning damage.

STATISTICS
Str 14 (+2), **Dex** 15 (+2), **Con** 13 (+1),
Int 2 (–4), **Wis** 13 (+1), **Cha** 10 (+0)
Languages: None
Senses: Darkvision 60 ft.

ECOLOGY
Environment: Temperate and warm aquatic
Organization: Solitary, pair, or herd (20–40)

Giant seahorses are larger versions of the common seahorse that spend their days swimming slowly while dining on crustaceans and other small, aquatic life. The average giant seahorse is about eight feet long and weighs 300 pounds.

Giant seahorses reproduce four times a year through internal fertilization. During reproduction, the female giant seahorse lays between 300 and 700 eggs in the male's incubation pouch (which resembles the pouch of a kangaroo). After 20 days, the eggs hatch, and the young remain in the pouch until they are capable of swimming on their own (about ten days). Newborn giant seahorses are about 1-foot long and reach maturity in 8 months. Giant seahorses are monogamous and mate for life.

A giant seahorse's body is covered in fine scales. It's head has a long snout that gives it an eerie resemblance to a horse. Its back is lined with small dorsal fins. Giant seahorses range in color from yellow to dull green to brown. Their eyes are almost always brown; the rare seahorse with blue eyes is prized by mermen, tritons, and other underwater races.

Giant seahorses are not aggressive. They attack only if cornered or if a member of the herd is threatened. In combat, a giant seahorse slaps an opponent with its powerful tail or occasionally butts with its bony head. Most simply flee when confronted.

Training a Giant Seahorse

A giant seahorse requires training before it can bear a rider, and even more training before it can serve as a mount in combat. Creatures who train giant seahorses (mermen and tritons, mainly) like to start with a seahorse that shows curiosity about other creatures rather than fear. Training a seahorse as an aquatic mount takes six weeks of work followed by a successful DC 20 Wis (Animal Handling) check. Riding a seahorse calls for an exotic saddle.

Seahorse eggs are worth 500 gp apiece on the animal market, while young are worth 800 gp each. Professional trainers charge 1,000 gp to rear or train a giant seahorse.

Sepulchral Guardian

A humanoid wearing iron armor stands before you. In its hands it holds a wickedly sharp halberd.
Its eyes show no signs of life.

Sepulchral Guardian

XP 700 (CR 3)
Unaligned Medium construct
Initiative +0

DEFENSE
AC 14 (scale mail)
hp: 65 (10d8 + 20)
Resistance: Acid and lightning damage; bludgeoning, piercing, and slashing damage from non-adamantine weapons
Immunity: Cold, fire, necrotic, poison, and psychic damage; charm, disease, fright, paralysis, petrification, poison, stun, unconsciousness

OFFENSE
Speed: 30 ft.
Melee Attack—Glaive: +5 to hit (reach 10 ft.; one creature). *Hit:* 1d10 + 3 slashing damage and the target must make a DC 12 Con saving throw or be infected with crypt fatigue (see below).

STATISTICS
Str 17 (+3), **Dex** 10 (+0), **Con** 14 (+2),
Int 5 (–3), **Wis** 11 (+0), **Cha** 12 (+1)
Languages: None
Senses: Darkvision 60 ft.

TRAITS
Crypt Fatigue: A creature infected with crypt fatigue gains one level of exhaustion immediately, and gains one more level every time it fails the DC 12 Con saving throw after taking damage from a sepulchral guardian. An infected creature must make a DC 12 Con saving throw at the end of every long rest; with a successful save, it recovers from one level of exhaustion, but with a failed save, it gains one level of exhaustion. The disease is cured when the victim no longer has any levels of exhaustion.
Dread: Living creatures with line of sight to one or more sepulchral guardians and within 50 feet of them must make a successful DC 11 Wis saving throw or be frightened for 2d4 rounds. A successful save renders the target immune to any guardian's dread for 24 hours.

ECOLOGY
Environment: Temperate
Organization: Solitary

Sepulchral guardians are constructs created from the preserved corpses of dead humanoids that have been encased in iron. They are created for one purpose only: to guard the final resting place of a dead creature. Once activated, a sepulchral guardian performs its task until it is destroyed. Even the death of its creator does not disrupt a sepulchral guardian: many are created to guard the final resting places of their creators.

A sepulchral guardian appears as a humanoid standing just over 6 feet tall. Its entire body except for its face is encased in a suit of banded iron. Its face, while humanoid, shows no sign of life, and its eyes are filled with the emptiness of an automaton. Most sepulchral guardians wield glaives or halberds, and the touch of the weapon transmits a wasting disease from the guardian into the target of the attack. When creatures are affected by a sepulchral guardian's dread, the guardian tries to corner the victim so it can attack from 10 feet away with its pole weapon while the frightened creature cowers under the blows, unable to get close enough to use its weapons. These constructs are intelligent enough to pursue an intruder through nearby corridors and chambers of a tomb, but they seldom leave the immediate structure they've been set to guard, even to chase down a thief who stole something.

Sepulchral guardians can't speak; they are incapable of uttering any sound, but their armor scrapes and grinds loudly when they move. As they stand perfectly still on guard, however, they are also perfectly silent.

A sepulchral guardian' body is constructed from 500 pounds of iron mixed with rare chemicals totaling 1,000 gp and fashioned into armor that is fused to the preserved corpse of a humanoid.

Shadow Mastiff

This creature resembles an enormous dog, but with shadow-stuff for flesh.

Shadow Mastiff
XP 100 (CR 1/2)
CE Medium fiend
Initiative +2

DEFENSE
AC 12
hp: 22 (5d8)
Resistance: Bludgeoning, piercing, and slashing damage from nonmagical weapons
Immunity: Necrotic and poison damage; poison
Vulnerability: Radiant damage

OFFENSE
Speed: 45 ft.
Melee Attack—Bite: +4 to hit (reach 5 ft.; one creature). *Hit:* 2d6 + 2 piercing damage.

STATISTICS
Str 12 (+1), **Dex** 14 (+2), **Con** 10 (+0), **Int** 4 (–3), **Wis** 12 (+1), **Cha** 14 (+2)
Languages: None
Skills: Stealth +6
Senses: Darkvision 60 ft.

TRAITS
Frightful Howl: As an action, a shadow mastiff can emit a terrifying, otherworldly howl that conjures nightmare visions in those who hear it. All living creatures within 300 feet of the shadow mastiff that hear its howl must make a successful DC 12 Wis saving throw or be frightened for 3d6 rounds. While frightened, the creature must move away from the shadow mastiff as rapidly as possible, until it's far enough away that it can't hear the howling at all (not just beyond the howl's effective 300-foot range).

Shadow Affinity: A shadow mastiff has tactical advantage on Dex (Stealth) checks in dim light or darkness, and it can make a Stealth check to become hidden as a bonus action anytime it is in darkness or dim light. A shadow mastiff suffers the effect of being poisoned while in bright light.

ECOLOGY
Environment: Any land
Organization: Hunting pack (4–16)

Shadow mastiffs are large dogs resembling normal mastiffs but seemingly composed of solid shadow. The existence of these and similar shadow creatures leads some scholars to posit the existence of an entire Plane of Shadow, but such conjectures are scoffed at by more experienced travelers of the multiverse. There's no denying, however, that the glossy black coats and powerful jaws of these creatures have the look of shadow about them. What's more, when a shadow mastiff is killed, its body rapidly "evaporates" into wisps of ectoplasmic darkness that flow into any nearby shadows and disappear.

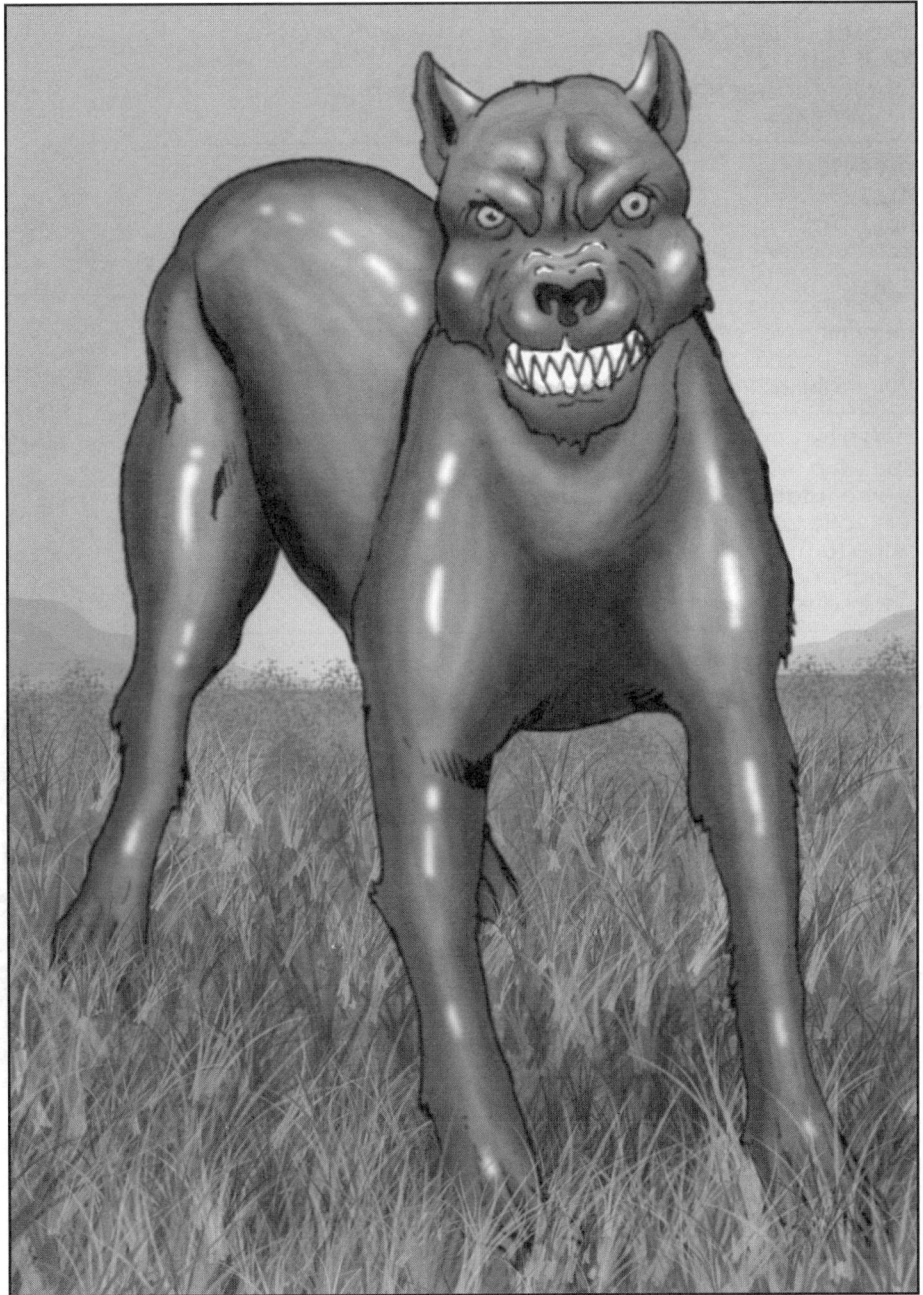

Shadow mastiffs are hunters of the night. They always travel in packs, and except when they are trying to sneak up on prey, their fearful howling is constant. On a quiet night, they can be heard baying from more than a mile away; farther if the wind is right.

Shadow, Lesser

This creature appears to be a humanoid constructed of living darkness.

Lesser Shadow

XP 25 (CR 1/8)
CE Medium undead
Initiative +2

DEFENSE
AC 12
hp: 7 (2d8 – 2)
Resistance: Acid, cold, fire, lightning, and thunder damage; bludgeoning, piercing, and slashing damage from nonmagical weapons
Immunity: Necrotic and poison damage; poison, prone, stun, unconsciousness
Vulnerability: Radiant damage

OFFENSE
Speed: fly 40 ft.
Melee Attack—Strength Damage: +4 to hit (reach 5 ft.; one creature). *Hit:* 1d6 + 2 necrotic damage and the target's Strength is reduced by 1. If its Strength is reduced to 0, the target dies. Lost Strength is recovered fully after a long or short rest.

STATISTICS
Str 5 (–3), **Dex** 15 (+2), **Con** 9 (–1),
Int 5 (–3), **Wis** 10 (+0), **Cha** 14 (+2)
Languages: None
Skills: Stealth +4
Senses: Darkvision 60 ft.

TRAITS
Shadow Affinity: A lesser shadow has tactical advantage on Dex (Stealth) checks in dim light or darkness, and it can make a Stealth check to become hidden as a bonus action anytime it is in darkness or dim light.

ECOLOGY
Environment: Temperate
Organization: Solitary

According to ancient texts, an arcane creature known only as the Shadow Lord created beings of living darkness to aid him and protect him. These beings, called shadows, were formed through a combination of darkness and evil. He also created lesser beings of darkness, not as powerful as his favored creations. These creatures are known as lesser shadows. Though not as powerful as shadows, lesser shadows are every bit as evil. Until it moves, a lesser shadow is indistinguishable from any mundane shadow.

Lesser shadows hide in darkness, springing to attack when living opponents wander too close. They are often led in combat by a shadow. Unlike full shadows, lesser shadows do not spawn additional shadows. It is rumored that such a lesser shadow might exist, but none have been proven.

Shroom

This creature is about the size and stature of a gnome, but for the enormous mushroom cap atop a cylindrical head. Two dark, piercing eyes drill into you from beneath flaring eyebrows on an otherwise featureless face.

Shroom
XP 1,100 (CR 4)
CE Small plant (fungus)
Initiative +0

DEFENSE
AC 12 (natural armor)
hp: 49 (11d6 + 11)
Saving Throws: Int +7, Cha +5
Resistance: Bludgeoning, piercing, and slashing damage from nonmagical weapons
Immunity: Psychic damage; charm, fright, stun, unconsciousness

OFFENSE
Speed: 25 ft.
Melee Attack—Slam: +2 to hit (reach 5 ft.; one creature). *Hit:* 1d6 bludgeoning damage.
Ranged Attack—Psychic Thrashing: +6 to hit (range 100 ft.; one creature). *Hit:* 2d10 + 4 psychic damage and the target must make a successful DC 14 Int saving throw or be stunned until the end of its next turn.

STATISTICS
Str 9 (–1), **Dex** 10 (+0), **Con** 12 (+1), **Int** 19 (+4), **Wis** 16 (+3), **Cha** 15 (+2)
Languages: Common, Deep Speech, Sylvan, Undercommon
Skills: Arcana +6, Nature +6, Medicine +5, Perception +5, Persuasion +4
Senses: Darkvision 60 ft.

TRAITS
Animate Plants (1/day): As an action, a shroom can magically animate plants within 50 feet of itself. The effect is identical to the *animate objects* spell, but only live plants can be animated and the duration is 24 hours.
Awaken Plants (1/month): A shroom can magically awaken one plant it touches. The effect is identical to the *awaken* spell, but only live plants can be awakened.
Spellcasting: The shroom is an arcane and divine spellcaster that uses Intelligence as its spellcasting ability (DC 14, attack +6). It doesn't need material components to cast spells. The spells listed below are suggestions; individual shrooms can have different spell selections.
Cantrips (at will): *druidcraft, poison spray, thorn whip*
1st level (x4): *charm, detect magic, entangle, sleep, thunderwave*
2nd level (x3): *barkskin, enlarge/reduce, pass without trace, spike growth*
3rd level (x2): *plant growth, speak with plants, stinking cloud*
Toxic Flesh: Any creature that tastes the flesh of a shroom must make a DC 13 Con saving throw. If the save succeeds, the creature detects the poison and spits out the morsel before any damage is done. If the save fails, the character is overwhelmed by the deliciousness of the shroom and immediately downs a mouthful, then continues eating in a normal manner until full or until someone stops him or her. An hour after consuming even one bite of shroom flesh, the eater is affected as if by a *feeblemind* spell. The effect of the toxin can actually turn out to be beneficial in the long run; there is a 5 percent chance that a character who recovers or is restored to sanity after being *feebleminded* by shroom flesh permanently gains 1 point of Intelligence from the experience. A character can gain this benefit only once.

IN-LAIR ACTIONS
At "20" in the initiative countdown, a shroom defending its lair can take one of the following actions.
Entangle: The shroom selects a 20-foot-by–20-foot area of ground, and entangling roots and vines erupt from it, turning it into difficult terrain. Every creature in the area when the effect is triggered must make a successful DC 15 Str saving throw or be restrained until it uses an action on its turn to make a successful DC 15 Str saving throw. The plants wither and die after five minutes.
Plant Stride: The shroom can step into a Medium or larger plant it is adjacent to and emerge immediately from another Medium or larger plant within 50 feet of the first plant.

ECOLOGY
Environment: Underground, temperate and warm forests
Organization: Solitary (but usually accompanied by 2–7 animated plants or charmed, feebleminded adventurers)

Shrooms are evil toadstool creatures with genius intellects and considerable magical power. They lurk in the deep places of the earth and in dank forests, plotting ruin against surface dwellers and scheming to gain power for themselves by any means possible. They are highly adept with magic that influences plants, and most of them are knowledgeable in various forms of arcane study of other kinds, such as alchemy. Many, too, will surround themselves with strange minions that they have created, grown, or bred.

Shrooms are highly individual and their schemes are wide-ranging, but always sinister. They can be gracious hosts, but they always want something in return for their hospitality. They are master manipulators; many adventurers have "stumbled upon" the lair of a shroom and been treated to an evening (or several days) of fine dining, engaging conversation, and whimsical entertainment, only to discover later that the shroom pre-arranged all of it—right down to their traveling through that area to begin with—because it wanted to enlist their unwitting aid in one of its intricate plots.

The flesh of a shroom is delectable but deadly. Shrooms have been known to slice off portions of their own bodies (painful, but it grows back) and feed these morsels to unsuspecting diners, then *charm* the *feebleminded* victims into acting as their bodyguards.

Although one might expect to find an affinity between shrooms and myconids, they are not natural allies. Shrooms have little patience for or understanding of the myconids' spirituality and introspection. If myconids could be hammered into a conquering army, the situation might be different.

Copyright
Author Matt Finch

Skeleton Warrior

The armor clanks loosely against the bony form that wears it, an ancient warrior in archaic harness. It raises its sword in salute and assumes a fighting stance.

Skeleton Warrior
XP 11,500 (CR 14)
NE Medium undead
Initiative +1

DEFENSE
AC 19 (splint mail +2)
hp: 150 (20d8 + 60)
Saving Throws: Con +8, Wis +6, Cha +7
Resistance: Piercing and slashing damage from nonmagical weapons
Immunity: Necrotic and poison damage; exhaustion, fright, poison, unconsciousness

OFFENSE
Speed: 30 ft.
Multiattack: A skeleton warrior attacks three times with its greatsword or twice with its longbow.
Melee Attack—Greatsword +2: +12 to hit (reach 5 ft.; one creature). *Hit:* 2d6 + 7 slashing damage plus 2d6 necrotic damage.
Ranged Attack—Longbow: +6 to hit (range 150 ft./600 ft.; one creature). *Hit:* 1d12 + 1 piercing damage plus 2d6 necrotic damage, and the target must make a successful DC 16 Con saving throw or be infected with crypt fatigue (see below).

STATISTICS
Str 20 (+5), **Dex** 13 (+1), **Con** 16 (+3),
Int 10 (+0), **Wis** 13 (+1), **Cha** 14 (+2)
Languages: Common, any other language the warrior knew in life
Skills: Insight +6, Intimidate +7, Perception +6
Senses: Truesight 60 ft.

TRAITS
Crypt Fatigue: A creature infected with crypt fatigue gains one level of exhaustion immediately, and gains one more level every time it fails the DC 16 Con saving throw after taking damage from a skeleton warrior's longbow. An infected creature must make another DC 16 Con saving throw at the end of every long rest; with a successful save, it recovers from one level of exhaustion, but with a failed save, it gains one level of exhaustion. The disease is cured when the victim no longer has any levels of exhaustion.
Legendary Resistance (3/day): The skeleton warrior can

Skeleton Warrior's Circlet

In the process of transforming into a skeleton warrior, the dying warrior's soul is trapped in a golden circlet. Anyone possessing one of these circlets can exert control over the skeleton warrior whose soul the circlet contains. To establish control, the controller must be within 300 feet of the skeleton warrior, must wear the circlet, and must spend one full round doing nothing but concentrating on the skeleton warrior. If the controller is not interrupted during this time, resolve a Cha (Intimidation) contest between the skeleton warrior and the creature with the circlet (note that the skeleton warrior adds its proficiency bonus to Intimidation skill checks). If the wearer of the circlet wins the contest, the skeleton warrior is charmed, views that character as an ally, and interprets any of the character's suggestions in the most positive light. It is not dominated or controlled, but it doesn't feel the urge to immediately kill the wearer of the circlet and recover its soul, either. It would like its soul back eventually, but it can wait until its new ally is slain by some other creature or dies naturally.

While within 300 feet of the charmed skeleton warrior, a person wearing the circlet can exert the following types of influence over the skeleton warrior. He or she can:

• choose to see through the skeleton warrior's eyes;

• try to force the skeleton warrior to attack something by making a successful DC 15 Cha check (failing the check means the skeleton warrior acts as it chooses);

• try to force the skeleton warrior to take some other action—search an area, move across a room, etc.—by making a successful DC 10 Cha check (failing the check means the skeleton warrior acts as it chooses);

• try to place the skeleton warrior in "inert mode" by making a successful DC 15 Cha check. If this check succeeds, the skeleton warrior stands motionless, effectively unconscious and paralyzed, until the wearer of the circlet wills it back into wakefulness. If this check fails, the skeletal warrior is no longer charmed.

While forcing the skeleton warrior to do anything, the circlet wearer can't move or take any other action. If the circlet wearer moves more than 300 feet away from the skeleton warrior or removes the circlet from his or her head while the skeleton warrior is active (not inert), the skeleton warrior is no longer charmed. If someone else becomes the circlet's owner, the skeleton warrior knows instantly; if it was charmed, it's not anymore, and if it was inert, it becomes active again.

If a skeleton warrior ever gains control of the circlet containing its soul, it places the circlet on its head and "dies," vanishing in a flash of light. The circlet falls to the ground and crumbles to dust.

choose to change a failed saving throw to an automatic success.

Track Circlet: A skeleton warrior can track and find its circlet unerringly. It can also find the last person who possessed the circlet.

Unholy Fortitude: Skeleton Warriors are highly resistant to turning. They have tactical advantage on saving throws against being turned.

LEGENDARY ACTIONS

The skeleton warrior can take up to three legendary actions per round. Legendary actions are taken at the end of another creature's turn, and only one can be taken after each turn.

Attack: The skeleton warrior attacks once with its greatsword or longbow.

Drain Life: +10 to hit (reach 5 ft.; one creature). *Hit:* the target must make a successful DC 16 Con saving throw or be infected with crypt fatague. If already infected, a failed saving throw causes the creature to gain another level of fatigue.

Instill Dread: One living creature within 50 feet of the skeleton warrior, which the skeleton warrior can see, must make a successful DC 15 Wis saving throw or be frightened for 2d4 rounds. A successful save renders the target immune to this skeleton warrior's dread for 24 hours.

ECOLOGY

Environment: Any land, underground
Organization: Solitary

The skeleton warrior is an undead creature that was once a powerful fighter of at least 8th level. Legend says that skeleton warriors were forced into their undead state by a powerful demon prince who trapped each of their souls in a golden circlet. A skeleton warrior's only purpose is to search for and regain the circlet containing its soul.

A skeleton warrior appears as a desiccated humanoid corpse dressed in the same armor and clothes it wore during life, but showing the signs of great age and wear. Aside from its armor and weapons, a skeleton warrior could easily be confused for a lich.

Stygian Skeleton

This creature looks like a skeleton with glistening black bones, seemingly constructed of blackened steel. Small red pinpoints of light burn in its hollowed eye sockets.

Stygian Skeleton

XP 2,900 (CR 7)
CE Medium undead
Initiative +3

DEFENSE
AC 16 (chain mail)
hp: 97 (15d8 + 14)
Saving Throws: Wis +3
Resistance: Piercing and slashing damage from nonmagical weapons; necrotic damage
Immunity: Poison damage; exhaustion, fright, poison, unconsciousness

OFFENSE
Speed: 35 ft.
Multiattack: A stygian skeleton makes two melee attacks or two ranged attacks.
Melee Attack—Shortsword: +6 to hit (reach 5 ft.; one creature). *Hit:* 3d6 + 3 piercing damage plus 1d8 necrotic damage and the target must make a successful DC 13 Con saving throw or be poisoned by Stygian poison (see below).
Melee Attack—Claw: +6 to hit (reach 5 ft.; one creature). *Hit:* 2d6 + 3 slashing damage plus 1d12 necrotic damage and the target must make a successful DC 13 Con saving throw or be poisoned by Stygian poison (see below).
Ranged Attack—Shortbow: +6 to hit (range 80 ft./320 ft.; one creature). *Hit:* 2d6 + 3 piercing damage plus 1d8 necrotic damage and the target must make a successful DC 13 Con saving throw or be poisoned by Stygian poison (see below).

STATISTICS
Str 11 (+0), **Dex** 17 (+3), **Con** 14 (+2), **Int** 12 (+1), **Wis** 10 (+0), **Cha** 10 (+0)
Languages: Abyssal, Common
Senses: Darkvision 60 ft.

TRAITS
Stygian Poison: A Stygian skeleton's weapons are caked with Stygian poison. A creature affected by Stygian poison has the poisoned condition and takes 1d12 + 3 necrotic damage at the start of the Stygian skeleton's turn. At the end of each of its turns while poisoned, the creature makes a DC 13 Con saving throw; a successful save ends the poisoning.

ECOLOGY
Environment: Underground
Organization: Squad (2–12) or troop (10–100)

Stygian skeletons were first encountered in Rappan Athuk (see the adventure, **Rappan Athuk** from **Necromancer Games** and **Frog God Games**). Much more powerful than standard skeletons, these minions of evil are often employed as guardians over ancient knowledge that is best left undiscovered. They are intelligent, free-willed monsters, unlike zombies and lesser skeletons. They are known to sometimes act against the commands of those they serve, if doing so benefits the Stygian skeleton, preserves its existence, or furthers its mission.

Stygian skeletons are the remnants of creatures that were slain in an area saturated with evil. The bodies of fallen heroes become contaminated and polluted by the ambient evil and, within days after their death, rise as Stygian skeletons, leaving their former lives and bodies behind. Stygian skeletons maintain some memories of their former lives, but the retention is random and the skeletons themselves are often not aware of the memories' significance (undead, as a group, are not known for deep introspection) until an event or a person reminds them.

Stygian skeletons wear whatever clothes and armor they wore in life. Some still carry the same ancient gear and weapons, but they tend to swap their deteriorating weapons for newer ones taken from victims whenever they can. For an unknown reason, Stygian skeletons favor fighting with two short swords or with one short sword and their own filthy, infected claws.

Having been veteran warriors in life, Stygian skeletons are excellent tacticians. They employ enveloping maneuvers, timing, and even ruses in combat. They are smart enough to know when a battle is lost and withdraw to save themselves. Most, however, simply fight until one side or the other is destroyed, driven by some unseen hatred for the living.

Skelzi

This creature is humanoid but shorter and slighter than a human, and its face is birdlike with a long, sharp beak—but you only get a glimpse before it fades from view and blends into the background!

Skelzi

XP 200 (CR 1)
CE Medium humanoid
Initiative +2

DEFENSE
AC 14 (natural armor)
hp: 44 (8d8 + 8)

OFFENSE
Speed: 30 ft.
Multiattack: A skelzi attacks once with claws and once with its blood whip.
Melee Attack—Blood Whip: +4 to hit (reach 10 ft.; one creature). *Hit:* 1d4 + 2 slashing damage and the target must make a successful DC 12 Con saving throw or take continuing damage from bleeding (see Blood Whip, below).
Melee Attack—Claws: +4 to hit (reach 5 ft.; one creature). *Hit:* 1d8 + 2 slashing damage.

STATISTICS
Str 14 (+2), **Dex** 15 (+2), **Con** 12 (+1),
Int 10 (+0), **Wis** 10 (+0), **Cha** 10 (+0)
Languages: Common, Unique
Skills: Stealth +4

TRAITS
Blood Whip: A skelzi's vicious blood whip causes wounds that bleed profusely. A creature must make a DC 12 Con saving throw every time it takes damage from a blood whip. If the saving throw fails, the wound is bleeding freely and the creature takes 1d4 + 2 damage at the start of each of its turns. Bleeding continues for 1d6 rounds unless it is ended early with magical healing. Bleeding is also stopped if the affected creature or another creature adjacent to it binds the wound by spending an action and making a successful DC 12 Wis (Medicine) check. Every bleeding wound causes additional damage and must be treated separately; a character that was struck three times by blood whips, for example, takes 3d4 + 6 damage at the start of its next turn if none of those wounds are treated before then. A blood whip behaves as a normal whip when wielded by anyone who is not a skelzi.
Chameleonic Hide: If they shed their garments, skelzis can hide when they are lightly obscured, their Stealth bonus increases to +6, and they have tactical advantage on Stealth checks and on initiative rolls.

ECOLOGY
Environment: Any land
Organization: Solitary, flight (10–13), or squadron (20–120)

Skelzis originate from beyond the Material Plane. They have humanoid bodies with leathery skin, but their human appearance is rendered alien by the long, sharp beak that protrudes from the birdlike skelzi face. Moreover, a skelzi's hide is chameleonic, changing to blend with its surroundings. The creatures usually travel robed and masked so that they are less alarming to other races and to conceal their chameleonic power until the need for it arises.

A typical skelzi stands 6 feet tall and weighs 160 pounds. They speak their own language (a strange patter of clicks and whispered crooning), the

language of skulks, and the Common tongue.

They often employ skulks and doppelgangers as spies or even as trusted agents in skelzi plans. Every skelzi outpost, colony, and expedition is well-supplied with weredactyls.

Skelzis are aggressively expansionistic, so countless colonies and more than a few empires exist across the infinite planes of existence. Many of these domains are located in pocket dimensions and limited offshoots of the Material Plane. Great skelzi empires tend to be decadent, corrupt, torpid, and slow to respond to threats—but when they do respond, it is likely to be with overwhelming force. Smaller and younger societies are more energetic. All skelzi societies are organized around a many-tiered caste system in which lower-ranking skelzis serve those above them. Promotion is possible and highly sought. The fact that skelzis are willing to serve other skelzis who outrank them should not be confused with an attitude of obedience or with any sense of loyalty. Death creates openings for advancement, whether it comes naturally or through an assassin's poison. On the rare occasions when skelzis serve another race as mercenaries or spies, it is purely for monetary gain; they never swear allegiance to anyone who is not a skelzi.

Noble skelzis make it a point to wear extravagant headdresses and rich clothing, deliberately drawing attention to themselves and to their high positions (emphasizing the fact that many skelzis are below them and few are above them). Skelzis of lower rank prefer to avoid notice as much as possible.

Skelzi hide is surprisingly tough. It is possible, although somewhat gruesome, to fashion thin, flexible leather armor from skelzi skin so that it retains a vestige of the living skelzi's chameleonic properties.

Skulk

This creature appears to be a human, but entirely hairless and with slender, graceful limbs. Their skin, however, can change color like a chameleon's.

Skulk

XP 100 (CR 1/2)
CN Medium humanoid
Initiative +3

DEFENSE

AC 13
hp: 18 (4d8)

OFFENSE

Speed: 30 ft.
Melee Attack—Shortsword: +5 to hit (reach 5 ft.; one creature). *Hit:* 1d6 + 3 piercing damage.
Ranged Attack—Sling: +5 to hit (range 30 ft./120 ft.; one creature). *Hit:* 1d4 + 3 bludgeoning damage.

STATISTICS

Str 10 (+0), **Dex** 16 (+3), **Con** 10 (+0),
Int 12 (+1), **Wis** 12 (+1), **Cha** 6 (–2)
Languages: Unique
Skills: Acrobatics +5, Stealth +5
Senses: Darkvision 60 ft.

TRAITS

Chameleonic Hide: If they shed their garments, skulks can hide when they are lightly obscured, their Stealth bonus increases to +7, and they have tactical advantage on Stealth checks and initiative rolls.
Sneak Attack: A skulk's attack does an extra 1d6 damage if the skulk has advantage on the attack or if one or more of its allies is within 5 feet of the target.
Untrackable: Anyone trying to follow skulks through forest or underground territory has tactical disadvantage on skill checks for trailing or tracking.

ECOLOGY

Environment: Any land, underground
Organization: Solitary or gang (2–20)

Skulks are a race of humanoids that dwell on the fringe of other societies. They are a parasitic race—the humanoid equivalent of rats that survive by theft, subterfuge, and the occasional outright murder. Skulks are consummate cowards, sneaking into humanoid communities under cover of darkness to take what they desire but fleeing if they are interrupted or spotted. Skulks are physically very close to human in appearance, but they are hairless and lightly built with slender, graceful arms and legs. Their eyes are usually pale blue or pink.

In its "relaxed" state, the leathery skin of a skulk is a medium gray color. All skulks have a natural, chameleonic ability to vary their skin tone to match almost any environment. This gives them a tremendous ability to infiltrate areas with minimal cover and to "disappear" when the situation turns ugly, and they are almost impossible to track. They speak their own whispered language and the Common tongue.

Skulks have also been enslaved in great numbers by the warlike skelzi race, with whom they share their chameleonlike blending ability. These creatures live across all across the multiverse and in many nooks and crannies between the worlds.

Credit
The skulk originally appeared in the First Edition *Fiend Folio* (© TSR/ Wizards of the Coast, 1981) and is used by permission.

Copyright Notice
Author Scott Greene, based on original material by Simon Muth.

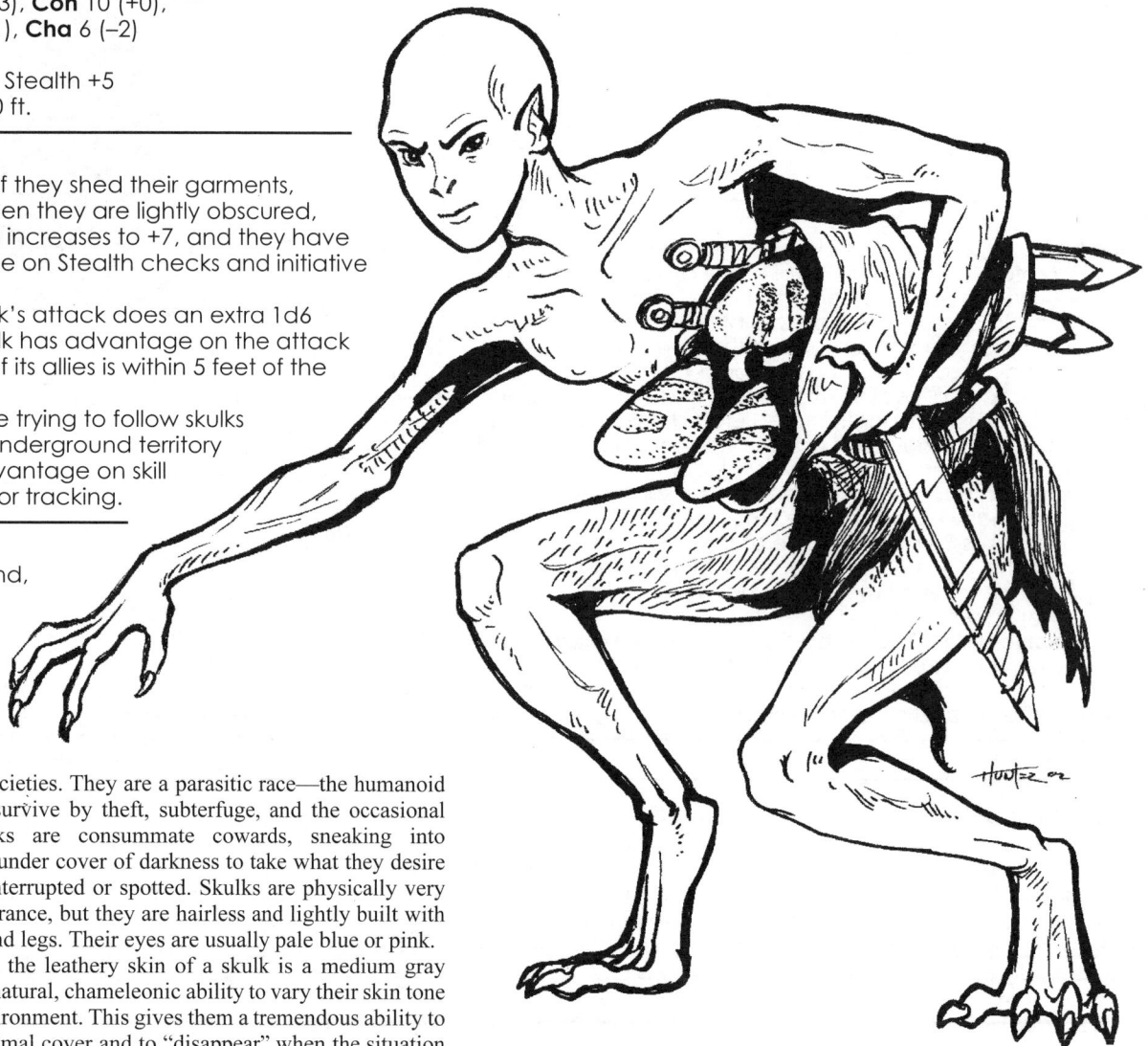

Slithering Tracker

This creature looks like a long, thin, transparent protoplasm, almost snakelike in form.

Slithering Tracker

XP 200 (CR 1)
Unaligned Small ooze
Initiative +4

DEFENSE

AC 14
hp: 32 (5d6 + 15)
Immunity: Poison and psychic damage; blindness, charm, exhaustion, paralysis, poison, prone, stun

OFFENSE

Speed: 30 ft., climb 30 ft.
Melee Attack—Slam: +4 to hit (reach 5 ft.; one creature). *Hit:* 2d6 + 2 bludgeoning damage and the target must make a successful DC 13 Con saving throw or be paralyzed for 1d4 hours.

STATISTICS

Str 14 (+2), **Dex** 18 (+4), **Con** 16 (+3),
Int 8 (−1), **Wis** 10 (+0), **Cha** 1 (−5)
Languages: None
Skills: Stealth +6
Senses: Blindsight 60 ft.

TRAITS

Amorphous: A slithering tracker can move through gaps as small as 1 square inch without penalty.
Engulf: As an action, a slithering tracker can enter the space of a Medium or smaller paralyzed creature and completely cover it with a thin, transparent film. The engulfed creature loses 1 point of Constitution every 5 minutes. The creature dies if its Constitution drops to 0. If a slithering tracker is attacked while it is engulfing a victim, damage is split evenly between the slithering tracker and the engulfed victim. A slithering tracker can't make melee attacks while it is engulfing a creature.
Transparent: A slithering tracker is hard to spot even under ideal conditions. Spotting one that is sitting still takes a successful DC 15 Wis (Perception) check. The creature is spotted automatically if it moves, attacks, or is engulfing someone. Creatures that blunder into an unseen slithering tracker are automatically hit by its slam attack.

ECOLOGY

Environment: Any underground
Organization: Solitary

The slithering tracker is an amorphous and transparent creature that inhabits dark underground areas. Unlike other oozes, the slithering tracker does not feed on carrion. It eats only living tissue.

A typical slithering tracker is 3 to 4 feet long and has a thickness of about 6 inches. Very old ones can grow to a length of 8 feet.

A slithering tracker prefers to attack helpless or immobile opponents. They've been known to ooze through tiny cracks between stones into an underground campsite that's foolishly believed to be secure against attack, where they paralyze a sleeping victim, engulf it, drain it of life, and ooze away again, leaving behind the shrunken husk of the victim to be discovered in the morning by its alarmed comrades.

Credit
The slithering tracker originally appeared in the *Strategic Review #5* (© TSR/Wizards of the Coast, 1975) and later in the First Edition *Monster Manual* (© TSR/Wizards of the Coast, 1977) and is used by permission.

Copyright Notice
Author Scott Greene, based on original material by Gary Gygax.

Soul Reaper

This sinister figure appears shrouded in a long, black, hooded robe. Its face is hidden from view and its wickedly-curved claws are night-black in color. The gleaming, silver-bladed scythe in its grip completes the image of death.

Soul Reaper

XP 15,000 (CR 16)
NE Large undead
Initiative +3

DEFENSE

AC 19 (natural armor)
hp: 152 (16d10 + 64)
Saving Throws: Con +9, Wis +9, Cha +10
Resistance: Bludgeoning, piercing, and slashing damage from nonmagical weapons
Immunity: Necrotic and poison damage; exhaustion, fright, poison, restraint, stun, unconsciousness

OFFENSE

Speed: fly 40 ft.
Multiattack: A soul reaper attacks three times with its scythe.
Melee Attack—Scythe +1: +10 to hit (reach 5 ft.; one creature). *Hit:* 2d8 + 5 slashing damage plus 1d10 necrotic damage. If this attack hits a creature with 0 hit points, the target dies instantly. The scythe scores a critical hit if the attack roll is a natural 19 or 20. A critical hit causes an additional 1d8 slashing damage and 1d10 necrotic damage, and see Soul Slash below.

STATISTICS

Str 19 (+4), **Dex** 17 (+3), **Con** 18 (+4),
Int 16 (+3), **Wis** 19 (+4), **Cha** 20 (+5)
Languages: None
Skills: Insight +9, Intimidation +10, Perception +9
Senses: Truesight 60 ft.

TRAITS

Aura of Evil: A soul reaper constantly exudes a miasma of evil around itself. Any creature that begins its turn within 15 feet of a soul reaper takes 2d6 necrotic damage. Creatures of evil alignment are immune to this effect.
Inseparable Weapon: If separated from its scythe, the soul reaper can summon the weapon back into its hands as a bonus action. If someone else is holding the weapon when the reaper summons it, that opponent and the soul reaper engage in a contest pitting the opponent's Strength (Athletics) against the soul reaper's Charisma (Intimidation). If the soul reaper wins the contest, the scythe returns to its hands and the opponent takes damage as if struck by the scythe. If the opponent wins the contest, it takes 2d8 + 5 slashing damage.

Soul Slash: If a soul reaper scores a critical hit with its scythe, the target must make a successful DC 18 Con saving throw or its soul is torn from its body and into the soul reaper's scythe, and the creature dies immediately. A victim's soulless body collapses into a desiccated husk and crumbles to dust after 24 hours. To release a captured soul, the reaper must be destroyed and its scythe shattered on consecrated ground. When the scythe is shattered, all trapped souls are released. If a soul's body hasn't crumbled into dust, the soul returns to the body and the body returns to life. Souls without a body are left to wander formlessly, but they can be returned to life through powerful magic (*wish, true resurrection*).

Spell-like Abilities: The soul reaper can use the following spell-like abilities, using Charisma as its casting ability (DC 18, attack +10). The soul reaper doesn't need material components to use these abilities.
At Will: *darkness, bane, inflict wounds*
1/Day: *contagion, hold person, insect plague*

ECOLOGY

Environment: Any
Organization: Solitary

Soul reapers are vile undead with a fierce hatred for the living. They take great pleasure in slaying any living creature they encounter. They kill without guilt, without remorse, and without emotion, trapping the souls of their victims to insure they never return to life.

Soul reapers have no ties to the world of the living. Their origins are shrouded in unknowable antiquity, but scholars speculate that soul reapers stepped directly from the great void at the beginning of creation. It is believed that very few—perhaps only six or seven—of these creatures exist (and most living beings are thankful for that).

A soul reaper has a mystic connection to its scythe. Barring incredible circumstances, it can't be separated from the weapon for more than a few seconds.

Soul reapers are humanoid creatures shrouded in long, black, hooded cloaks, but standing 12 feet tall. Though they are corporeal, their form is either shrouded in utter darkness or formed of the stuff of shadows. They are not skeletal; no discernible facial features of any kind are visible under the hood. The creature's "hands" are wicked claws of inky blackness that are always wrapped tightly around its gleaming scythe.

These creatures never speak; no one knows if they even can. If they could, what would one say to a soul reaper?

Soul reapers haunt civilized lands, searching for the next victim who will fall prey to the deadly, soul-drinking scythe. They have been known to attack lone travelers in remote areas, and to wade through towns or cities, reaping souls left and right. No one knows why a soul reaper appears in a certain area, or why it leaves.

Stegocentipede

This creature resembles a gigantic centipede covered with plates of chitin with spikes that can be raised or lowered along its back and flanks. Its tail ends in a wicked, whiplike stinger.

Stegocentipede

XP 1,100 (CR 4)
Unaligned Huge beast
Initiative +2

DEFENSE

AC 14 (natural armor)
hp: 76 (9d12 + 18)
Immunity: Charm, prone, restraint

OFFENSE

Speed: 40 ft.
Multiattack: A stegocentipede bites once and stings once.
Melee Attack—Bite: +6 to hit (reach 5 ft.; one creature). *Hit:* 1d8 + 4 piercing damage.
Melee Attack—Sting: +6 to hit (reach 10 ft.; one creature). *Hit:* 2d8 + 4 piercing damage and the target must make a successful DC 12 Con saving throw or be poisoned for 2d4 rounds. While poisoned, the creature takes 2d6 poison damage at the start of each of its turns

STATISTICS

Str 19 (+4), **Dex** 15 (+2), **Con** 14 (+2),
Int 1 (−5), **Wis** 10 (+0), **Cha** 6 (−2)
Languages: None
Senses: Darkvision 60 ft.

TRAITS

Spines: Creatures adjacent to a stegocentipede must make a successful DC 12 Dex saving throw each time they make a melee attack against it or take 1d8 + 2 slashing damage from spines on the stegocentipede's carapace.

ECOLOGY

Environment: Temperate forest, underground
Organization: Solitary

Stegocentipedes are arthropods that have grown to stunning size. They are rumored among sages to have come to the Material Plane from another plane or dimension, though no proof has been found to support this theory. It is based chiefly on the fact that nothing else like it exists. Whatever their origin, they are greatly feared by adventurers and dungeon dwellers.

A stegocentipede raises its spines instinctively when it enters combat, and it moves constantly in a back-and-forth, sawing motion as it fights.

A typical stegocentipede is 18 feet long, but there is much variety among the species. The color of a stegocentipede's carapace depends on its environment; in wooded areas, they tend toward green and brown, but in underground areas, they tend toward gray and black.

Credit
The stegocentipede originally appeared in the First Edition *Monster Manual II* (© TSR/Wizards of the Coast, 1983) and is used by permission.

Copyright Notice
Author Scott Greene, based on original material by Gary Gygax.

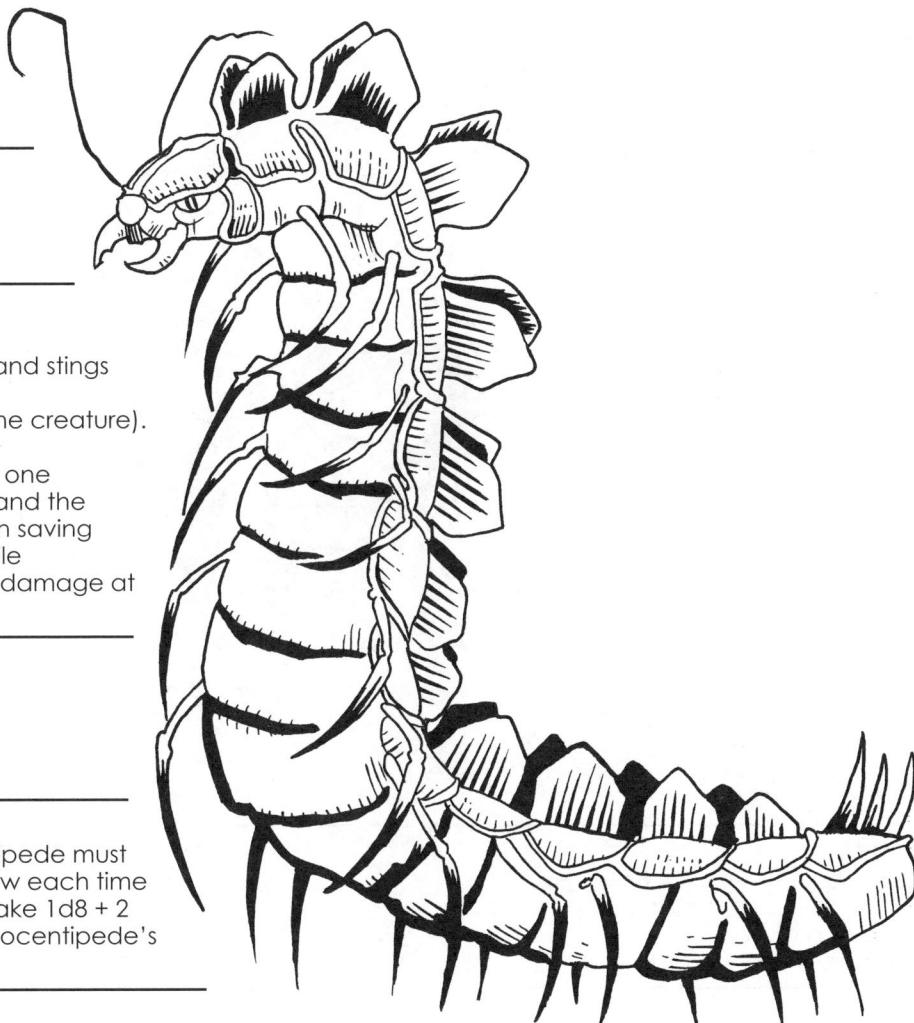

Strangle Weed

This mass of writhing vines and leaves looks like a large patch of seaweed.
Several long fronds protrude from the center of it.

Strangle Weed

XP 450 (CR 2)
Unaligned Large
plant (aquatic)
Initiative +0

DEFENSE
AC 10
hp: 34 (4d10 + 12)
Resistance: Fire
damage
Immunity: Psychic
damage; charm,
fright, prone, stun,
unconsciousness

OFFENSE
Speed: Swim 5 ft.
Multiattack: A strangle weed
makes 1d4 melee attacks.
The number of attacks is
determined each round.
Melee Attack—Frond: +4
to hit (reach 20 ft.; one
creature). *Hit:* 1d6 + 2
bludgeoning damage and the
target must make a successful DC 12
Dex saving throw or be grappled. Also see
Strangling, below.

STATISTICS
Str 14 (+2), **Dex** 10 (+0), **Con** 16 (+3),
Int 2 (–4), **Wis** 12 (+1), **Cha** 6 (–2)
Languages: None
Senses: Tremorsense 30 ft.

TRAITS
Camouflage: Because strangle weed looks like normal
seaweed, it can be recognized as hazardous before it
attacks only with a successful DC 20 Int (Nature) or Wis
(Survival) check.
Strangling: As a bonus action, a strangle weed can
strangle one creature that was already grappled at
the start of the strangle weed's turn. The strangle weed
drags the grappled creature underwater and wraps 1d6
additional fronds around the target, which becomes
grappled and restrained. The DC to escape from this

grapple equals 10 plus
2 per frond restraining
the creature. A
restrained creature
takes 1d8 + 2
bludgeoning damage
at the start of each
of its turns, and it can
also be targeted by
frond attacks. Strangling
fronds have AC 10
and can be severed
individually by 4 slashing
damage each.

ECOLOGY
Environment: Temperate and
warm aquatic, underground
aquatic
Organization: Solitary or patch
(2–5)

Strangle weed is an extensive,
floating plant that resembles a patch
of seaweed. Strangle weed, however, is
an ambush predator. It floats quietly and
inconspicuously until prey wanders near, then
lashes out with fronds to grapple foes and drag them into
the water, where they are strangled and drowned.

This deadly plant thrives in warm and temperate bodies of water,
and also in underground seas and pools.

A typical strangle weed is 10 feet in diameter, dark green, and slimy.
Suspended beneath the central mass of seaweed are dozens of long,
ropelike prehensile fronds up to 20 feet long.

Although strangle weed has no interest in treasure, coins and valuable
items can sometimes be found among the bones and rotted gear of the
plant's victims that sink into the muck where creatures were killed.
Strangle weed drifts on the current, however, so victims won't necessarily
be found at the plant's current location. Finding this lost treasure might
take many hours' or days' of underwater searching.

Credit
Strangle weed originally appeared in the First Edition *Monster Manual*
(© TSR/Wizards of the Coast, 1977) and is used by permission.

Copyright Notice
Author Scott Greene, based on original material by Gary Gygax.

Tabaxi

This creature appears as a tall, thin, felinelike humanoid with cinnamon-colored fur with black stripes like those of a tiger. It wears no clothing or armor. Its eyes are a piercing yellow, and it has pointed ears and a long tail.

Tabaxi

XP 25 (CR 1/2)
CN Medium humanoid
Initiative +2

DEFENSE
AC 12
hp: 11 (2d8 + 2)

OFFENSE
Speed: 40 ft., climb 20 ft.
Multiattack: A tabaxi attacks twice with claws or once with a weapon.
Melee Attack—Claw: +4 to hit (reach 5 ft.; one creature). *Hit:* 1d4 + 2 slashing damage. If both attacks hit the same target, the second attack does an additional 1d6 slashing damage.
Melee Attack—Shortsword: +6 to hit (reach 5 ft.; one creature). *Hit:* 1d6 + 2 piercing damage.
Ranged Attack—Javelin: +5 to hit (range 30 ft./120 ft.; one creature). *Hit:* 1d6 + 1 piercing damage.

STATISTICS
Str 13 (+1), **Dex** 14 (+2), **Con** 12 (+1),
Int 10 (+0), **Wis** 12 (+1), **Cha** 10 (+0)
Languages: Common, Unique
Skills: Acrobatics +4, Stealth +4
Senses: Darkvision 60 ft.

TRAITS
Weapon Aptitude: Tabaxis have an instinctive affinity for weapons. They add twice their proficiency bonus to attack rolls with one-handed weapons and thrown weapons. This bonus is included in the attack modifiers listed above.

ECOLOGY
Environment: Warm forests
Organization: Solitary or pride (2–8)

The tabaxi (called cat-people or tigerfolk by some) are a reclusive race of feline humanoids that dwell far from settled areas, making their homes deep in remote forests and jungles. They rarely engage in trade or dealings with other races, preferring to keep to themselves most of the time.

Tabaxis are catlike and very graceful in their movements. They resemble humanoids with feline characteristics akin to tigers. Their hands and feet sport vicious claws that can inflict significant damage.

Although tabaxis have little use for clothing or most other material possessions, they have a great fascination for and aptitude with weapons. A tabaxi can pick up almost any weapon and immediately use it with great skill.

Tabaxis are also skilled at fighting with their claws. They specialize in a one-two attack that involves striking with both claws and then raking the target with the claws of one foot.

Tabaxis live in small groups called prides. A typical pride consists of one to three each of adult males, adult females, and young. Females tend to be slightly larger than males and usually are the dominant members of a pride. Tabaxis live a nomadic lifestyle, prowling through their chosen range and hunting in groups of three to five. They carry little in the way of possessions, other than the small armory of weapons they've captured from enemies and intruders. Unless they are desperately hungry, most tabaxi prides leave other intelligent creatures alone. They might attack, however, if intruders are carrying especially interesting-looking weaponry.

Credit
The tabaxi originally appeared in the First Edition *Fiend Folio* (© TSR/Wizards of the Coast, 1981) and is used by permission.

Copyright Notice
Author Scott Greene, based on original material by Lawrence Schick.

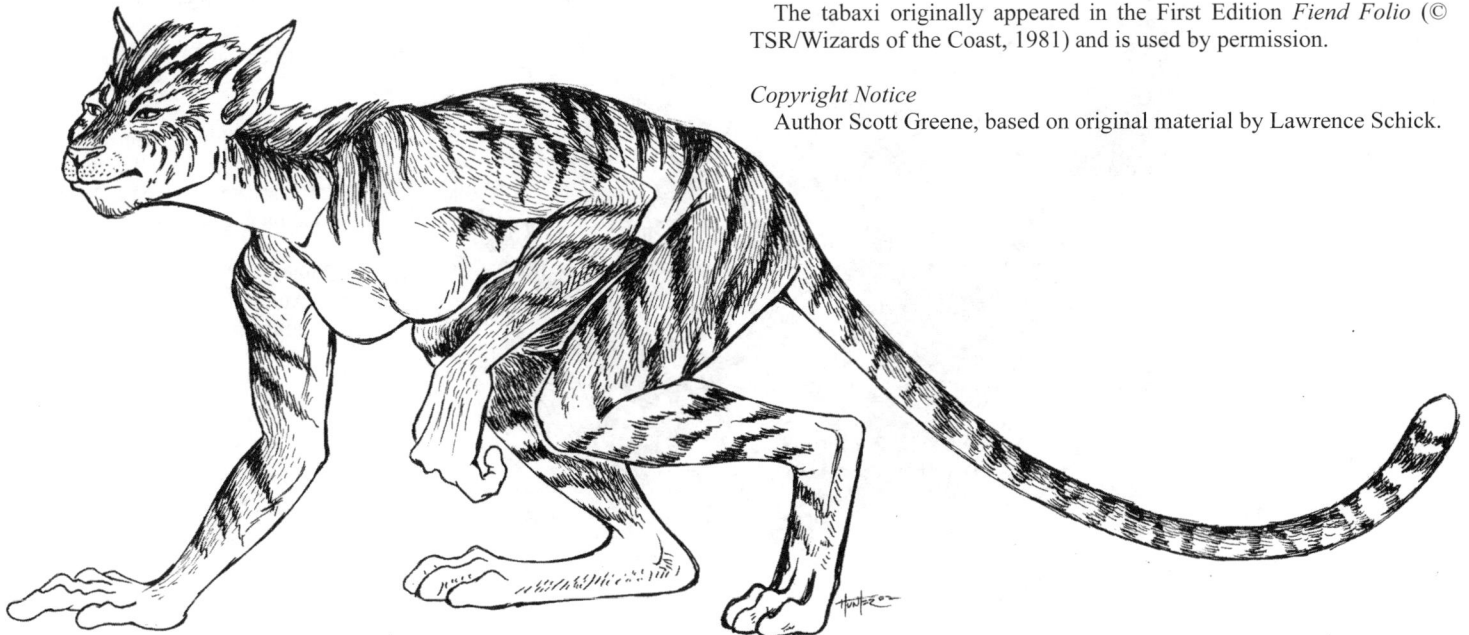

Taer

This hulking, shaggy brute has a large, sloping head, icy blue eyes, and overall apelike appearance. Its body is covered in thick, snow-white fur, and its fists are massive and powerful.

Taer

XP 200 (CR 1)
N Medium humanoid
Initiative +2

DEFENSE
AC 14 (natural armor)
hp: 26 (4d8 + 8)
Immunity: Cold damage
Vulnerability: Fire damage

OFFENSE
Speed: 35 ft.
Multiattack: A taer bites once and attacks once with fists, or it throws two stones or two javelins.
Melee Attack—Bite: +5 to hit (reach 5 ft.; one creature). *Hit:* 1d6 + 3 piercing damage.
Melee Attack—Fists: +5 to hit (reach 5 ft.; one creature). *Hit:* 1d6 + 3 bludgeoning damage.
Ranged Attack—Javelin or Stone: +5 to hit (range 20 ft./60 ft.; one creature). *Hit:* 1d6 + 3 piercing (javelin) or bludgeoning (stone) damage.

STATISTICS
Str 16 (+3), **Dex** 15 (+2),
Con 15 (+2),
Int 6 (–2),
Wis 12 (+1),
Cha 6 (–2)
Languages:
Unique
Skills: Athletics +5, Survival +3

ECOLOGY
Environment:
Cold mountains
Organization:
Solitary, band (2–12), or clan (10–40)

Taers are primitive, fur-covered humanoids that may be related to yetis. They resemble apelike, bestial, prehistoric ancestors of humans. Taers never wear clothing, although they do sometimes wear necklaces and bracelets made of tooth and horn. Their fur is coated with an oily, fatty substance that keeps out moisture and increases their fur's insulation—very important advantages in the frigid, snowy environments where taers live.

Taers can see clearly even in heavy snowstorms thanks to a second, transparent eyelid that protects their eyes from icy wind and blowing snow.

Taers do not have a fully-developed verbal language; they communicate through grunts, hooting, and yelling, as well as with body language similar to that used by apes.

Taers attack by punching and biting. Rarely, they use heavy clubs or even stone-tipped spears in combat. Being both fearless and highly territorial, they attack any creature that wanders into their tundra. Taers use their knowledge of the land to great advantage during combat by creating avalanches, burrowing under the snow to set up ambushes, and digging pits in the snow and ice that are skillfully camouflaged with branches and snow to trap the unwary. Despite their ferociousness, taers prefer to drive away intruders rather than kill them.

Bands of taers are nomadic hunters and gatherers. They follow herds of game animals and ripening fruits and nuts across their harsh landscape. Though they do eat meat, taer do not hunt or eat humanoids.

Taer are extremely superstitious. They have an irrational fear of metal and of clothing, and they also fear creatures that use metal weapons and wrap themselves in clothing. No taer will use metal weapons or tools or wear any sort of cloth.

Taer clans worship a snow god to whom they offer sacrifices (of food, which is precious in their world) for protection and guidance. Each clan has a stone idol of this snow god that is hidden somewhere in its territory, often near a warm spring, a sheltered valley, or a hidden cave.

Credit
The taer originally appeared in the First Edition *Monster Manual II* (© TSR/Wizards of the Coast, 1983) and is used by permission.

Tangtal

A large feline creature approaches, covered in stiff, short, brown fur. Small white flecks cover its head, throat, neck, and shoulders, and its long, upward curving tail ends with a white tip. It stands on muscular legs with huge paws and razor claws.

Tangtal

XP 200 (CR 1)
NE Medium monstrosity
Initiative +3

DEFENSE

AC 13
hp: 19 (3d8 + 6)

OFFENSE

Speed: 40 ft.
Multiattack: A tangtal bites once and attacks once with claws.
Melee Attack—Bite: +5 to hit (reach 5 ft.; one creature). *Hit:* 1d6 + 3 piercing damage.
Melee Attack—Claws: +5 to hit (reach 5 ft.; one creature). *Hit:* 1d8 + 3 slashing damage.

STATISTICS

Str 16 (+3), **Dex** 17 (+3), **Con** 15 (+2), **Int** 12 (+1), **Wis** 13 (+1), **Cha** 10 (+0)
Languages: Common, Sylvan
Senses: Darkvision 60 ft.

TRAITS

Duplicate (1/day): As an action, a tangtal creates 2d4 images of itself. The images can move up to 30 feet away from the tangtal, but each must stay within 10 feet of at least one other image. Images have the same AC and speed as the tangtal and 1 hit point apiece; an image disappears when it takes any damage. An image can be damaged only by an attack that targets and damages it specifically; images aren't affected by area attacks or nondamaging effects. An attack that targets the tangtal has a chance to hit an image instead, in exact proportion to the number of images; e.g., if there are six images, an attack against the tangtal has a 1-in–7 chance to hit it and a 6-in–7 chance to hit an image.

ECOLOGY

Environment: Temperate forests and plains
Organization: Solitary

Tangtals, or dupli-cats, have the appearance and ferocity of normal panthers, but they are far more intelligent and they have a magical ability to project illusory images of themselves. They roam haunted woodlands or plains, but also often lair near civilized areas.

Tangtals are solitary creatures; no recorded encounter has ever been with more than one of these creatures. Tangtal young are unknown; none have ever been killed, captured, or even seen.

Tangtals are carnivores that prefer to dine on rabbits, squirrels, grouse, and other small game. When food is scarce, it is not unheard of for a tangtal to sneak into a civilized area and carry off chickens, sheep, calves, dogs, cats, and even children.

A tangtal is about 7 feet long from nose to tail and weighs 350 to 400 pounds.

Tangtals are ferocious on the attack, but they are also smart enough to know when a fight is lost. If combat goes against one, it flees, usually while it still has images remaining to distract the enemy.

Tazelwurm

This creature looks like a long serpent with grayish scales and a leonine head resembling a female lion with gray and tan fur. Two long, powerful humanoid arms extend from its serpentine body, each ending in vicious talons.

Tazelwurm

XP 450 (CR 2)
Unaligned Large monstrosity
Initiative +2

DEFENSE
AC 12
hp: 45 (7d10 + 7)
Immunity: Fire damage

OFFENSE
Speed: 40 ft.
Multiattack: A tazelwurm bites once and attacks once with claws.
Melee Attack—Bite: +4 to hit (reach 5 ft.; one creature). *Hit:* 2d8 + 2 piercing damage.
Melee Attack—Claws: +4 to hit (reach 5 ft.; one creature). *Hit:* 1d6 + 2 slashing damage.

STATISTICS
Str 16 (+2), **Dex** 14 (+2), **Con** 16 (+1),
Int 2 (+0), **Wis** 15 (+2), **Cha** 15 (+2)
Languages: Common
Skills: Stealth +6
Senses: Darkvision 60 ft., tremorsense 60 ft.

TRAITS
Ambush: A tazelwurm has tactical advantage on initiative rolls. Against an opponent that hasn't yet taken a turn in the current combat, the tazelwurm has tactical advantage on attack rolls and each of its attacks causes an additional 1d6 damage.
Frightening Exuviation: If an attack that hits a tazelwurm includes fire damage, the tazelwurm takes no damage. Instead, its skin, scales, and flesh burn away in just a few seconds, reducing the tazelwurm to a living skeleton. A creature viewing this (other than another tazelwurm) must make a successful DC 12 Wis saving throw or be frightened for 1d4 rounds. A creature that saves successfully can't be affected by this ability until after its next long rest. If the tazelwurm survives the encounter, it regenerates all of its flesh and organs in 24 hours.

ECOLOGY
Environment: Any mountains
Organization: Solitary or pair

A tazelwurm is an aggressive, flesh-eating monster with a serpentine body, a feline head, and two long, powerful arms equipped with razor-sharp claws. Their flesh has the mottled appearance of stone and gravel, giving them excellent camouflage. They haunt mountain passes and prey on travelers passing through their territory.

Tazelwurms are masters of camouflage. Very old tazelwurms sometimes have lichens and mosses growing on them, enhancing their rocky appearance. They plan elaborate ambushes to gain devastating first strikes against intruders. They are diurnal hunters and are most active in the morning hours. Their hunting grounds cover several square miles of rocky terrain. Should a tazelwurm be detected in another's territory, it is quickly driven away. Tazelwurms eat just about anything, but they are especially fond of mountain lions and mountain goats. Downed prey is dragged to the tazelwurm's lair, which is usually a well-hidden and nearly inaccessible depression or cave. The kill is devoured over a period of several days.

Tazelwurms rarely interact with other creatures, including their own kind. When more than one is encountered, they will be a mated pair. Young are born live and left to the care of the mother. Young tazelwurms reach maturity and are driven out of their parents' territory after two years.

After choosing a likely ambush spot, a tazelwurm conceals itself among stones and scree along a path or a game trail, then waits for a meal to pass by. Being lone hunters, tazelwurms generally ignore large groups; they prefer to attack lone travelers, a single straggler from a large group, or a one-or-two-member scouting party moving ahead of a larger body. A hungry or desperate tazelwurm will attack just about anything, however.

Temporal Crawler

A six-foot-long, hairy, gray spider crawls from the darkness. An hourglass-shaped patch of silver fur stands out on its back, and light reflects from its silvery, metallic mandibles beneath red-glowing eyes.

Temporal Crawler

XP 450 (CR 2)
NE Medium aberration
Initiative +3

DEFENSE
AC 14 (foresight bonus)
hp: 45 (7d8 + 14)

OFFENSE
Speed: 35 ft., climb 25 ft.
Melee Attack—Bite: +5 to hit (reach 5 ft.; one creature). *Hit:* 1d6 + 3 piercing damage and the target must make a successful DC 12 Con saving throw or take 1d6 poison damage and be paralyzed for a number of rounds equal to the poison damage.
Ranged Attack—Webs (recharge 5, 6): automatic hit (range 50 ft.; one creature. *Hit:* the target must make a successful DC 12 Dex saving throw or be restrained. A restrained creature can escape by using an action to make a successful DC 12 Str (Athletics) check. Alternatively, the restraining webs can be destroyed by 10 points of slashing or fire damage (AC 10).

STATISTICS
Str 14 (+2), **Dex** 17 (+3), **Con** 14 (+2),
Int 5 (–3), **Wis** 13 (+1), **Cha** 10 (+0)
Languages: Unique, telepathy
Skills: Stealth +5
Senses: Darkvision 60 ft., tremorsense 30 ft. while in webs

TRAITS
Foresight: A temporal crawler can see a few seconds into the future. This ability prevents a temporal crawler from ever being surprised and grants it an AC bonus equal to its Wisdom modifier (already factored into its AC). In addition, attackers never gain tactical advantage or bonus damage against it from the presence of nearby allies.
Immunity to Temporal Magic: Temporal crawlers are unaffected by magic that alters or manipulates time in any way.
Slowing Webs: Creatures other than temporal crawlers that are within 10 feet of the webbing in a temporal crawler's lair must make a successful DC 12 Con saving throw or

suffer the effects of a *slow* spell. The slowing effect ends 1d4 rounds after the creature leaves the affected area.
Webbing Trap (1/day): The approach to a temporal crawler lair usually is trapped by a concealed net of webbing. The trap, which covers a 20-foot-by–20-foot area, can be spotted with a DC 15 Int (Nature) or Wis (Survival) check. Each creature entering the trapped area has a 1-in-3 chance to set it off. When the trap is triggered, the webbing drops and each creature in the trapped area must make a successful DC 12 Dex saving throw or be restrained. A restrained creature can escape by using an action to make a successful DC 12 Str (Athletics) check. Alternatively, the webs restraining one creature can be destroyed by 10 points of slashing or fire damage (AC 10).

ECOLOGY
Environment: Elemental Plane of Time, any land
Organization: Solitary or cluster (2–5)

Temporal crawlers are man-sized spiders from the distant and little-known Elemental Plane of Time. How and why they first came to the Material Plane is unknown; some sages believe they jumped through a portal opened by a time elemental.

These carnivorous aberrations prey on the flesh of intelligent creatures. They build their well-hidden lairs near populated areas where the food supply is plentiful. They can be found in the decaying slums and sewers of large, old cities, along remote stretches of well-traveled caravan routes, near lawless boom-towns of all sorts, and anywhere else that people can disappear without causing much alarm or triggering a well-organized search.

Because of their manner of hunting, their distant origins, the magical nature of their lairs, and their deep, piercing eyes, it is easy for victims to conclude that these creatures are more intelligent than they are. Sadly, all efforts to communicate with them have met with failure, and scholars have concluded that they are not reticent geniuses but just very clever beasts.

The silver hourglass-shaped marking on a temporal crawler's back is animated: sand actually appears to flow from one chamber to the other. If a temporal crawler is slain, the marking fades and the "sand" stops flowing.

Copyright Notice
Author Scott Greene.

Tendriculos

*What you thought was nothing more than another haystack in the field
just sprouted tentacles and a fanged mouth!*

Tendriculos

XP 1,100 (CR 4)
Unaligned Large plant
Initiative −2

DEFENSE
AC 8
hp: 93 (11d10 + 33)
Resistance: Bludgeoning and slashing damage
Immunity: Poison and psychic damage;
charm, fright, poison, prone, restraint, stun,
unconsciousness
Vulnerability: Fire damage

OFFENSE
Speed: 20 ft.
Multiattack: A tendriculos attacks twice with
tendrils and makes one swallow attack, if it can.
Having creatures grappled doesn't reduce the
tendriculos's number of tendril attacks.
Melee Attack—Tendril: +4 to hit (reach 10 ft.; one
creature). *Hit:* 1d8 + 2 bludgeoning damage and
the target must make a successful DC 12 Dex
saving throw or be grappled. A creature grappled
by more than one tendril is also restrained.
Melee Attack—Swallow: automatic hit (one
creature already grappled by the tendriculos
at the start of the tendriculos's turn). *Hit:* the
grappled creature is dragged to the tendriculos's
mouth and swallowed (see Swallow, below).

STATISTICS
Str 14 (+2), **Dex** 6 (−2), **Con** 16 (+3),
Int 2 (−4), **Wis** 10 (+0), **Cha** 4 (−3)
Skills: Athletics +4
Languages: None

TRAITS
Camouflage: Until it attacks or is set afire, a
tendriculos is indistinguishable from a normal
haystack.
Swallow: A swallowed creature is blinded and
restrained. It takes 1d8 + 3 bludgeoning damage
plus 1d8 acid damage automatically at the start of each
of the tendriculos's turns. One Medium creature or two
Small creatures can be inside the tendriculos at one
time. A swallowed creature is unaffected by anything
happening outside the tendriculos or by attacks from
outside it, with one exception; if the tendriculos takes
fire damage, creatures inside it take half as much fire
damage. A swallowed creature can get out of the
tendriculos by using 5 feet of movement, but only after the
tendriculos is dead.

ECOLOGY
Environment: Temperate
Organization: Solitary

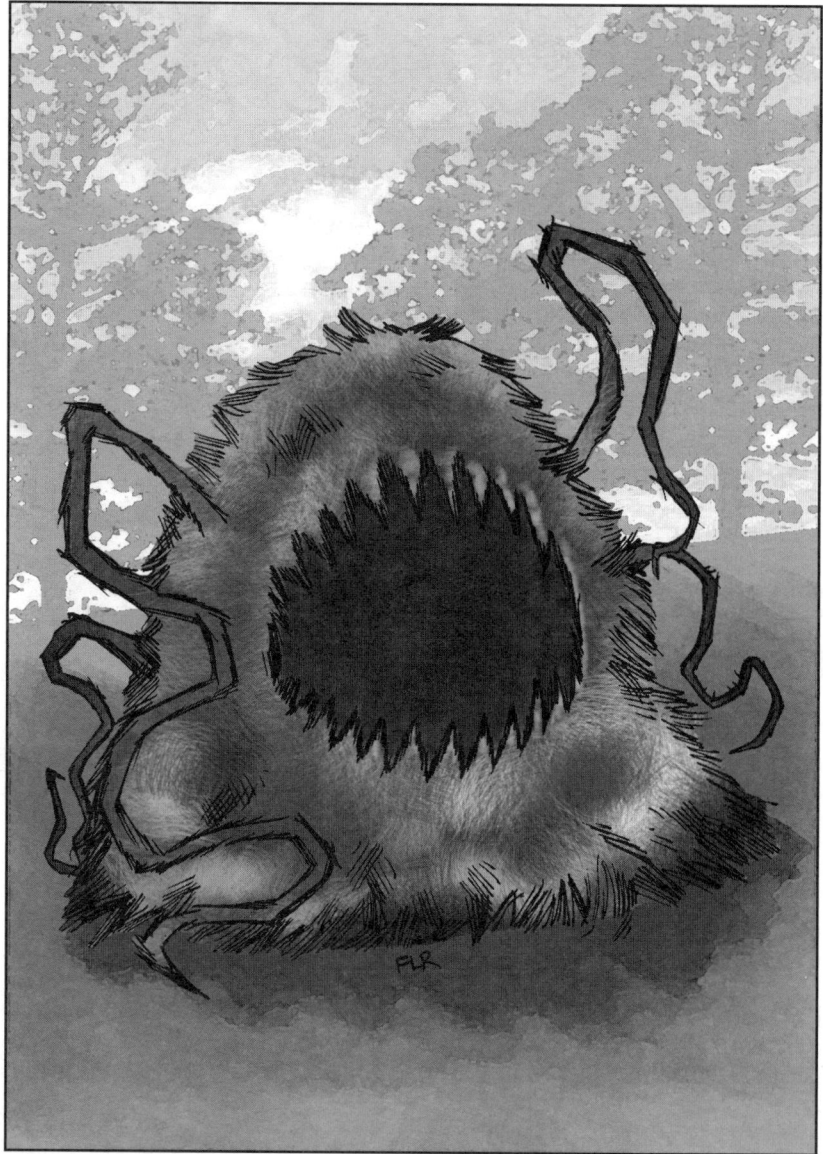

A tendriculos is a plant creature with an uncanny resemblance to
a haystack (or in rare cases, a grassy hillock). In fact, it is a voracious
predator that uses powerful tendrils to grab creatures and stuff them
into its enormous maw. These creatures are the bane of remote farming
communities. Any creature that wanders too near, whether it's a sheep,
a dog, a cow, a child, or a farmer, can be snatched and swallowed so
quickly that even people standing nearby won't realize that something
terrible just happened behind their backs. When the disappearance is
noticed, all that will be seen is a broken pitchfork or a dropped toy and a
seemingly normal, harmless haystack—probably just one of many that all
look identical. Most of them will be normal and harmless, but even one
tendriculos hidden in a field can eat many animals and people before it's
caught—if it ever is.

Tentacled Horror

Four tentacles emerge from the torso of this massive, misshapen creature. Above these are a tooth-lined maw and a single glaring, red eye. Atop the hideous head is a glistening, black horn.

Tentacled Horror

XP 7,200 (CR11)
CE Huge aberration
Initiative −1

DEFENSE
AC 17 (natural armor)
hp: 171 (18d12 + 54)
Saving Throws: Cha +7, Con +7, Str +10
Resistance: Acid damage

OFFENSE
Speed: 15 ft., swim 30 ft.
Multiattack: A tentacled horror attacks three times with tentacles.
Melee Attack—Tentacle: +10 to hit (reach 10 ft.; one creature). *Hit:* 2d6 + 6 bludgeoning damage and the target must make a successful DC 18 Dex saving throw or be grappled.

STATISTICS
Str 22 (+6), **Dex** 8 (−1), **Con** 16 (+3),
Int 7 (−2), **Wis** 10 (+0), **Cha** 16 (+3)
Languages: Telepathy
Senses: Darkvision 120 ft.

TRAITS
Horn: The source of a tentacled horror's power is its horn. If a tentacled horror's horn is removed or destroyed, the creature loses its regeneration ability, can't take legendary actions, and has disadvantage on attack rolls. The horn can be attacked specifically with targeted attacks but not area affects; it has AC 20, 30 hit points, and is immune to all damage types except slashing, bludgeoning, and force damage from spells or magic weapons. The horn can be torn off with a successful DC 25 Str (Athletics) check made by a creature that is grappling the tentacled horror. Damage done to the horn does not reduce the tentacled horror's hit points.
Regeneration: A tentacled horror heals 10 hit points at the start of each of its turns. This ability doesn't function if it took cold or fire damage since its previous turn or if its horn is destroyed or removed. If the horn is damaged, regeneration heals it first.
Insanity Toxin: Creatures poisoned by insanity toxin must roll 1d10, add their Intelligence modifier, and find the result on the table below. Affected creatures can repeat the saving throw if the tentacled horror's horn is torn off. A successful save ends the insanity. Otherwise, these effects are permanent until removed by magic that can end a curse.

Die	Result
3-	Frightened—The creature flees from the tentacled horror and from any creature not of its own species.

Die	Result
4	Incapacitated—The creature wanders aimlessly, dropping its items, staring at whatever catches its fancy, giggling and weeping, incapable of speech or intelligent action.
5	Poisoned
6	Blinded
7	Stunned
8	Dominated—The creature falls completely under the tentacled horror's control and does its best to kill any creatures that aren't worshiping the tentacled horror.
9	Overcome by Self-Loathing—The creature draws a dagger or similar weapon and inflicts the weapon's damage to itself automatically on each of its turns. If the creature has no suitable weapon or can't use weapons, it bashes its head against a wall or floor instead, doing 1d4 + Str mod damage. Aside from performing this attack against itself, the creature is effectively stunned.
10+	Overcome by Worshipfulness—The creature wants nothing but to worship the tentacled horror. It prostrates itself and tosses one possession on each of its turns to the tentacled horror, beginning with the most valuable possession and working down. Aside from making these offerings, the creature is effectively stunned.

LEGENDARY ACTIONS
A tentacled horror can take up to three legendary actions per round. Legendary actions are taken at the end of another creature's turn, and only one can be taken after each turn.
Bite: +10 to hit (one creature grappled by the tentacled horror). *Hit:* 1d12 + 6 piercing damage and the target must make a successful DC 15 Con saving throw or suffer the effect of insanity toxin (see above).
Escape: The tentacled horror attempts to escape from a grapple.
Tail Slap: +10 to hit (reach 10 ft.; one creature). *Hit:* 2d8 + 6 bludgeoning damage.

ECOLOGY
Environment: Underground
Organization: Solitary

Ancient and evil, a tentacled horror is a monstrosity from unknown depths of the earth. This monster is most often found inhabiting deep dungeons or ancient ruins far from the reaches of civilization.

Tentacled horrors are egotistical creatures that themselves above all others they encounter. A tentacled horror that finds its way into a subterranean society tries to set itself up as a god. Lesser creatures such as troglodytes, kuo-toas, and kobolds sometimes accept this false god and offer it living victims as sacrifices. Once ensconced as a ruler-deity, a tentacled horror is content to remain in one place and be served by its subjects. A tentacled horror that has been in power for a long time is surrounded by a pool of its own filth and the heaped bones of its victims.

A tentacled horror has a bloated but powerful, vaguely humanoid torso sitting atop a thick, sluglike foot. Sprouting from the torso are four tentacles lined with suction cups and tipped with cruel barbs. Most horrifying of all is its face. A tentacled horror has a lumpy, asymmetrical head dominated by a yawning chasm of a mouth, filled with spiky and broken teeth eager to sink into living flesh. Somewhere above it is a single, huge, unblinking eye that seems to drift languidly through the flesh of the head. Above the

eye is a glistening, black 2-foot-long horn—the source of much of the tentacled horror's power.

Although the origins of these horrors are unknown, their physical similarity to aboleths suggests that they may be mutant, idiotic relatives of that creature. Unlike the aboleth, the tentacled horror lacks both the intelligence and the ambition to dominate much more than it can see. Unfortunately, what it lacks in mental prowess, it makes up for with physical ferocity.

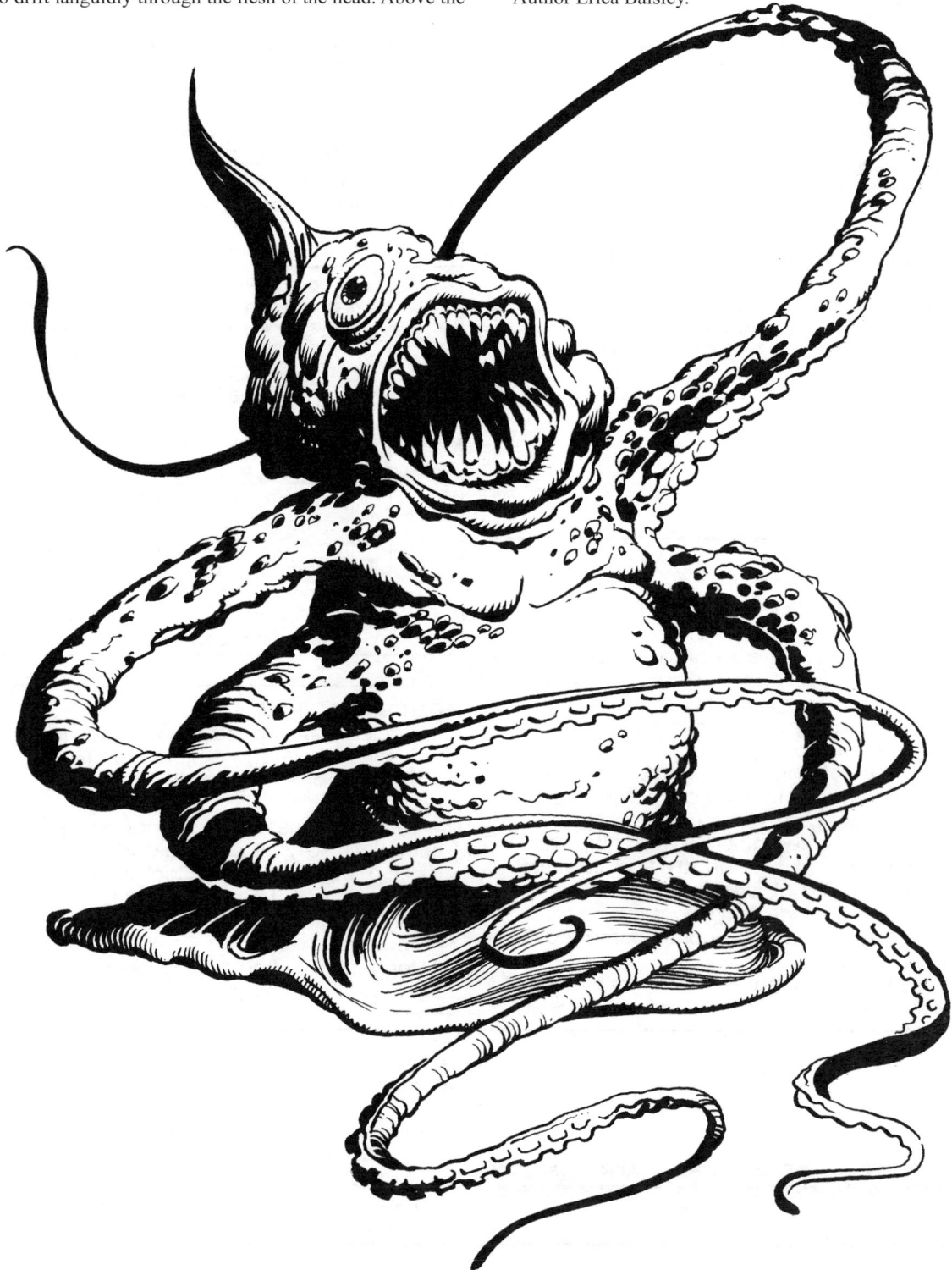

Therianthropes

Therianthropes (sometimes called anthromorphs or weretherions) are creatures whose natural form is of a normal animal, but they can also assume human form or a hybrid form that combines traits of both forms. Although they are shapechangers like lycanthropes, therianthropes are not cursed or diseased and they can't "infect" anyone else with their ability. In human form, therianthropes have slightly feral characteristics, such as slightly larger than normal canine teeth, extended fingernails, slightly pointed ears, or a barely noticeable covering of very fine hair on their entire bodies.

Therianthrope, Foxwere

This fox-headed humanoid stands 5 feet tall and is covered in reddish fur. A sleek, white stripe runs along its back.

Foxwere
XP 100 (CR 1/2)
LE Small monstrosity (shapechanger)
Initiative +2

DEFENSE
AC 12
hp: 13 (3d8)
Resistance: Bludgeoning, piercing, and slashing damage from nonmagical or nonadamantine weapons

OFFENSE
Speed: 40 ft. in fox form, 30 ft. in human or hybrid form
Multiattack: In hybrid form, a foxwere bites once and attacks once with its shortsword. In human or fox form, it makes one melee attack and can also use its charming gaze.
Melee Attack—Bite (fox and hybrid form): +4 to hit (reach 5 ft.; one creature). *Hit:* 1d4 + 2 piercing damage.
Melee Attack—Shortsword (human and hybrid form): +4 to hit (reach 5 ft.; one creature). *Hit:* 1d6 + 2 piercing damage.

STATISTICS
Str 10 (+0), **Dex** 14 (+2), **Con** 10 (+0), **Int** 11 (+0), **Wis** 12 (+1), **Cha** 14 (+2)
Languages: Common
Skills: Deception +4
Senses: Darkvision 60 ft.

TRAITS
Charming Gaze: As a bonus action, a foxwere in fox or human form can target one living creature within 30 feet and line of sight with its charming gaze. If the targeted creature can see the foxwere, then the targeted creature must make a successful DC 12 Cha saving throw or be charmed for one hour. A creature that is capable of taking actions can, at the start of its turn, look away to avoid the foxwere's gaze for one complete round. If it targets the foxwere while averting its gaze, it suffers all the usual penalties for attacking an unseen target. Creatures that are blind, unconscious, or unable to see the foxwere for any other reason are immune to this attack.

Shapechanger: The foxwere can change from its fox form or human form to its hybrid form as a bonus action. Changing from fox form directly to human form or vice versa takes an action. The foxwere is Small in fox form but Medium in human or hybrid form. In fox form, it is indistinguishable from a normal fox, but is noticeably larger than other foxes.

ECOLOGY
Environment: Temperate and cold forests, and underground
Organization: Solitary, gang (2–5), pack (1 plus 5–8 foxes)

Foxweres in humanoid form are indistinguishable from normal humanoids. Most have red hair.

Foxweres are very aggressive creatures; when hunting, they usually chase and attack potential prey on sight. They spend most of their time in fox form, switching to humanoid form chiefly to trick humanoids and lure them into traps. Once within range, they assume hybrid or animal form and attack.

Therianthrope, Lionwere

*This powerful creature appears as a lion-headed humanoid with a large, golden mane.
Its body is covered in golden-brown fur and its piercing eyes are greenish-gray.*

Lionwere

XP 450 (CR 2)
CE Large monstrosity (shapechanger)
Initiative +3

DEFENSE
AC 13
hp: 30 (4d10 + 8)
Resistance:
Bludgeoning,
piercing, and slashing damage from
nonmagical or nonadamantine weapons

OFFENSE
Speed: 40 feet in lion form, 30 ft. in human or hybrid form
Multiattack: In hybrid form, a lionwere attacks twice with
claws or once with its greatsword. In human form, it
attacks once with its greatsword. In lion form, it makes
two melee attacks and can also use its lethargy ability.
Melee Attack—Bite (lion form): +6 to hit (reach 5 ft.; one
creature). *Hit:* 1d6 + 4 piercing damage.
Melee Attack—Claws (lion and hybrid form): +6 to
hit (reach 5 ft.; one creature). *Hit:* 1d6 + 4 slashing
damage.
Melee Attack—Greatsword (human and hybrid form):
+6 to hit (reach 5 ft.; one creature). *Hit:* 2d8 + 4
slashing damage.

STATISTICS
Str 18 (+4), **Dex** 17 (+3), **Con** 14 (+2),
Int 10 (+0), **Wis** 12 (+1), **Cha** 15 (+2)
Languages: Common
Skills: Deception +4, Stealth +5
Senses: Darkvision 60 ft.

TRAITS
Lethargy: By speaking, singing, or roaring,
the lionwere causes all creatures
that can hear it and that are within
60 feet of it to make a successful
DC 12 Con saving throw or suffer
the effect of a *slow* spell lasting
1d6 rounds. A creature that saves
successfully is immune to lethargy until after its next long
rest. Therianthropes are immune to lethargy.
Shapechanger: The lionwere can change from its lion
form or human form to its hybrid form as a bonus action.
Changing from lion form directly to human form or vice
versa takes an action. The lionwere is Large in lion form
but Medium in human or hybrid form. In lion form, it is
indistinguishable from a normal lion.

ECOLOGY
Environment: Warm plains and underground
Organization: Solitary, gang (2–5), or pack (1 plus 5–8 lions)

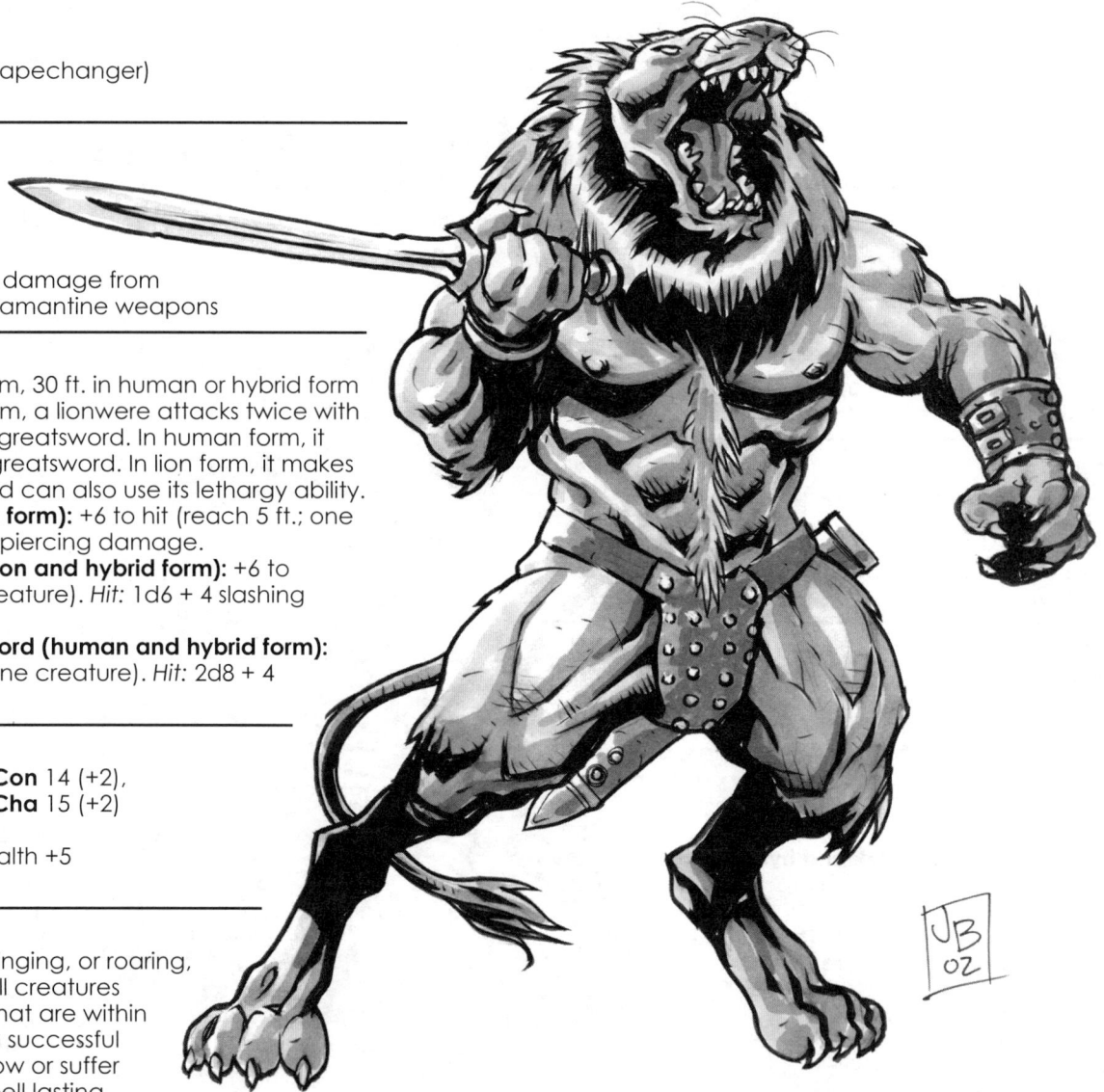

Lionweres appear as very stocky, muscular humanoids when in
humanoid form. They have a tendency to brag and to bully people who
can't fight back; the more helpless the victim, the more vicious the bullying
will be and the more it will amuse the lionwere. A lionwere bullies because
it's sadistic, not because it's cowardly, so a lionwere doesn't back down
when challenged by someone; in fact, it relishes the fight. They sometimes
seek work in civilized areas as bodyguards and bouncers, where their size,
strength, and lack of empathy come in handy.

Therianthrope, Owlwere

This creature appears as a small, lithe, owl–headed humanoid with brownish–yellow feathers and large white eyes.

Owlwere

XP 25 (CR 1/2)
CE Small monstrosity (shapechanger)
Initiative +3

DEFENSE

AC 13
hp: 13 (3d8)
Resistance: Bludgeoning, piercing, and slashing damage from nonmagical or nonadamantine weapons

OFFENSE

Speed: 10 ft., fly 60 ft. in owl form; 30 ft., fly 30 ft. in hybrid form; 30 ft. in human form
Melee Attack—Beak (owl form): +7 to hit (reach 5 ft.; one creature). *Hit:* 1d4 + 3 piercing damage.
Melee Attack—Talons (owl and hybrid form): +5 to hit (reach 5 ft.; one creature). *Hit:* 1d6 + 3 slashing damage and the target must make a successful DC 10 Con saving throw or be poisoned for 1d4 rounds.
Melee Attack—Shortsword (human and hybrid form): +5 to hit (reach 5 ft.; one creature). *Hit:* 1d6 + 3 piercing damage.

STATISTICS

Str 10 (+0), **Dex** 17 (+3), **Con** 11 (+0), **Int** 12 (+1), **Wis** 14 (+2), **Cha** 12 (+2)
Languages: Common
Skills: Deception +4, Perception +4
Senses: Darkvision 60 ft.

TRAITS

Shapechanger: The owlwere can change from its owl form or human form to its hybrid form as a bonus action. Changing from owl form directly to human form or vice versa takes an action. The owlwere is Small in owl form but Medium in human or hybrid form. In owl form, it is indistinguishable from a normal owl, but is noticeably larger than other owls.

ECOLOGY

Environment: Warm plains and underground
Organization: Solitary, gang (2–5), or flock (1 plus 5–8 owls)

Owlweres appear as normal humanoids in human form. They tend to have large eyes, and they are shy and quiet. In settled areas, they can be found working as aides to scholars or as crafters in trades where their high dexterity and amazing eyesight are assets, such as jewelry-making and clockwork. But most owlweres prefer solitude over any sort of town life. The sometimes rent their services as independent mercenaries specializing in scouting out enemy forces, a function at which they excel.

Therianthrope, Wolfwere

This humanoid has a wolf's head and a body covered in short gray fur.
Its hands bear sharp, lupine claws.

Wolfwere

XP 200 (CR 1)
CE Medium monstrosity
(shapechanger)
Initiative +3

DEFENSE

AC 14 (natural armor)
hp: 19 (3d8 + 6)
Resistance: Bludgeoning,
piercing, and
slashing damage
from nonmagical or
nonadamantine weapons

OFFENSE

Speed: 50 ft. in wolf form, 30 ft.
in hybrid or form
Multiattack: In hybrid form, a
wolfwere makes two melee
attacks, one of which can be
with its scimitar. In human or fox
form, it makes one melee attack
and can also use its mesmerizing
gaze.
Melee Attack—Bite (wolf form): +5
to hit (reach 5 ft.; one creature).
Hit: 2d4 + 3 piercing damage and
the target must make a successful
DC 11 Str saving throw or be knocked
prone.
Melee Attack—Claws (hybrid form): +5 to hit
(reach 5 ft.; one creature). *Hit:* 1d6 + 3
slashing damage.
**Melee Attack—Scimitar (human and
hybrid form):** +5 to hit (reach 5 ft.;
one creature). *Hit:* 1d6 + 3 slashing
damage.

STATISTICS

Str 13 (+1), **Dex** 17 (+3), **Con** 11 (+0),
Int 12 (+1), **Wis** 14 (+2), **Cha** 12 (+2)
Languages: Common
Skills: Deception +4, Perception +4
Senses: Darkvision 60 ft.

TRAITS

Mesmerizing Gaze: As a bonus action, a wolfwere in wolf or
human form can target one living creature within 30 feet
and line of sight with its mesmerizing gaze. If the targeted
creature can see the wolfwere, then the targeted
creature must make a successful DC 12 Cha
saving throw or be stunned for 1d4 rounds. A
creature that is capable of taking actions
can, at the start of its turn, look away
to avoid the wolfwere's gaze for
one complete round. If it targets
the wolfwere while averting
its gaze, it suffers all the usual
penalties for attacking an unseen
target. Creatures that are blind,
unconscious, or unable to see the
wolfwere for any other reason are
immune to this attack.
Shapechanger: The wolfwere can
change from its wolf form or
human form to its hybrid form
as a bonus action. Changing
from wolf form directly to
human form or vice versa
takes an action. In wolf
form, it is indistinguishable
from a normal wolf.

ECOLOGY

Environment: Cold or
temperate plains and
underground
Organization: Solitary,
gang (2–5), or pack (1
plus 5–8 wolves)

In humanoid form, a wolfwere
appears as a normal humanoid,
often with gray or gray-streaked
hair and dark gray eyes. Unlike most
other therianthropes, wolfweres are
social and gregarious. They love
boisterous company, whether their
companions are other wolfweres,
normal wolves, or a tavern full
of humanoids. They never stay in one
place for very long (an attribute they share with many adventurers),
because they're afflicted with incurable wanderlust, always wondering
what's beyond the bordering forest or in the next valley across the hills.
Fortunately for them, their sense of direction is unerring. A wolfwere
might not always know precisely where it is, but it can always find its way
back to where it came from—assuming it's ever interested in retracing its
steps and seeing the same sites twice.

Treant, Lightning

This creature looks like an animated, yet dead, moss-covered tree.
Its bark is darkened with age, and no leaves cling to its branches.

Lightning Treant

XP 2,300 (CR 6)
NE Huge plant
Initiative −2

DEFENSE

AC 15 (natural armor)
hp: 105 (10d12 + 40)
Saving Throws: Dex +1, Con +7
Resistance: Bludgeoning, fire, and piercing damage
Immunity: Lightning and psychic damage; charm, fright, stun, unconsciousness

OFFENSE

Speed: 30 ft.
Multiattack: A lightning treant attacks twice with limbs.
Melee Attack—Limb: +8 to hit (reach 5 ft.; one creature). *Hit:* 1d8 + 5 bludgeoning damage plus 1d6 lightning damage.

STATISTICS

Str 20 (+5), **Dex** 7 (−2), **Con** 19 (+4),
Int 10 (+0), **Wis** 14 (+2), **Cha** 10 (+0)
Languages: Common, Deep Speech, Sylvan
Senses: Darkvision 60 ft.

TRAITS

Electric Healing: A lightning treant is immune to lightning damage, but for every 3 points of lightning damage an attack should cause, the lightning treant heals 1 hit point. Excess healing is gained as temporary hit points.
Regeneration: A lightning treant heals 5 hit points at the start of each of its turns.
Spell-like Abilities: The lightning treant can use the following spell-like abilities, using Wisdom as its casting ability (DC 13, attack +5). The lightning treant doesn't need material components to use these abilities.
At Will: *enlarge/reduce, faerie fire*
3/day: *call lightning, lightning bolt, protection from energy*
1/day: *chain lightning*

ECOLOGY

Environment: Temperate forests
Organization: Solitary, pair, or grove (3–8)

This creature appears to be a dead, moss-covered tree, with bare, tangled branches stretching toward the sky. Often living in the shade of larger trees or in the wasteland of a destroyed or burned-over forest, lightning treants are strange, angry creatures whose powers and talents are almost elemental in nature. Especially twisted, stunted examples of this creature have been confused with shambling mounds, but lightning treants are much larger, and the mossy vegetation covering them is only a thin layer over their hard, barklike flesh.

While treants are generally willing to talk to strangers, hear what they have to say, and consider their requests or their plight, lightning treants tend to attack first and never ask questions at all. These creatures can be a serious bane to travelers who must cross the lightning treants' territory, especially those who don't recognize the nature of the danger facing them.

Lightning treants have an inherent hatred of all humanoids. Anyone armed with an axe is especially likely to anger them and incite them to violence just by being in their neighborhood. If combat goes against them, lightning treants will happily toss lightning at each other, to gain its healing benefits.

Tri-flower Frond

*This man-sized plant is deep green with trumpet-shaped flowers
of red, yellow, and orange topping its stalks.*

Tri-flower Frond
XP 100 (CR 1/2)
Unaligned Medium plant
Initiative +0

DEFENSE
AC 12
hp: 19 (3d8 + 6)
Immunity: Psychic damage; charm, fright, prone, stun, unconsciousness

OFFENSE
Speed: 0 ft.
Multiattack: A tri-flower frond makes two melee attacks.
Melee Attack—Tranquilizing Tendrils: +4 to hit (reach 5 ft.; one creature). *Hit:* 1d4 + 2 piercing damage and the target must make a successful DC 12 Con saving throw or become unconscious. This is a poison effect; resistance or immunity to sleep effects don't apply against it. The creature remains unconscious for one hour or until wakened with a successful DC 10 Wis (Medicine) check.
Melee Attack—Digestive Juice: automatic hit (reach 5 ft.; one unconscious creature). *Hit:* 1d6 acid damage.
Melee Attack—Fluid Drain: automatic hit (reach 5 ft.; one unconscious creature). *Hit:* the target is grappled and its Constitution score is reduced by 1d3 points. A creature dies if its Constitution is reduced to 0.

STATISTICS
Str 14 (+2), **Dex** 10 (+0), **Con** 14 (+2), **Int** 0 (−5), **Wis** 10 (+0), **Cha** 2 (−4)
Languages: None
Senses: Tremorsense 30 ft.

TRAITS
Camouflage: A tri-flower frond looks like a normal, if exotic, flowering plant. Until it attacks, its dangerous nature can be recognized only with close inspection and a successful DC 15 Int (Nature) check. Once characters have fought these plants, they can be recognized again on sight.

ECOLOGY
Environment: Warm forests and hills
Organization: Solitary, patch (2–5), or grove (6–11)

Tri-flower fronds are carnivorous plants found in warm forests and hilly regions. Rarely, they extend their range into mild temperate zones. They are immobile, but they reproduce readily by releasing seeds into the air. The seeds drift on the wind or hitch rides on passing creatures. They take root rapidly once they touch the ground, and reach full maturity within a few months.

These creatures are active round the clock. They dine on fresh meat of any kind, having no preference for one kind over any other. When a potential meal falls victim to the tri-flower's narcotic poison, the plant droops a frond over the fallen creature, allowing its yellow bloom to drip a shower of highly caustic digestive enzymes onto the sleeping victim. It then inserts a needlelike tendril from its red bloom deep into the victim's body and drains its fluids and dissolving organs.

A tri-flower frond stands 5 to 8 feet tall. A combination of orange, red, and yellow flowers is most common, but varieties with other color combinations exist, including white, gray, and pearly silver-gray, and golden brown, deep brown and russet.

Tri-flower fronds are popular in the gardens of wizards and alchemists, because their narcotic poison and digestive juices are useful in many concoctions. They are also planted defensively around the homes of many magic-users, wealthy merchants, and potentates in areas where they'll flourish, because they never sleep and thieves or assassins trying to creep silently past them make perfect targets for their tranquilizing tendrils.

Credit
The tri-flower frond originally appeared in the First Edition module *S3 Expedition to the Barrier Peaks* (© TSR/Wizards of the Coast, 1980) and later in the First Edition *Monster Manual II* (© TSR/Wizards of the Coast, 1983) and is used by permission.

Copyright Notice
Author Scott Greene, based on original material by Gary Gygax.

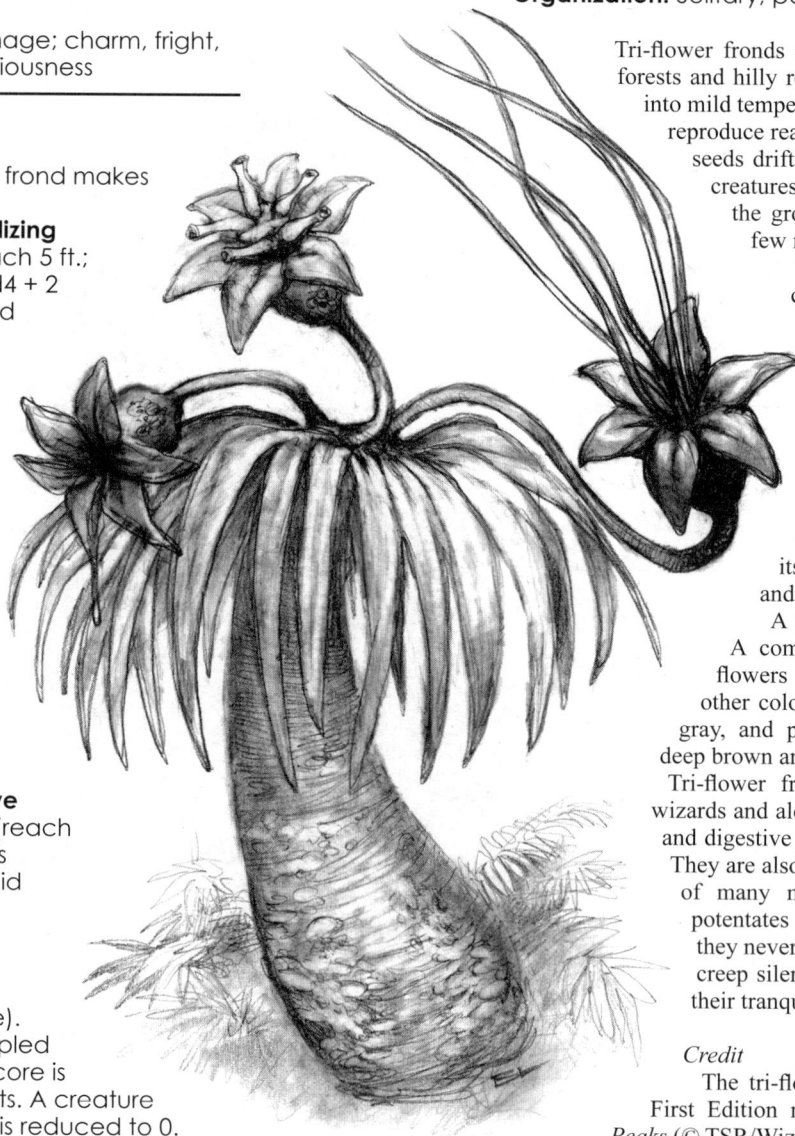

Triton, Dark

This creature has the upper body of a giant human, but from the waist down, it's all squirming tentacles.

Dark Triton

XP 200 (CR 1)
CE Large monstrosity (aquatic)
Initiative +0

DEFENSE

AC 12 (studded leather)
hp: 30 (4d10 + 8)

OFFENSE

Speed: 5 ft., swim 40 ft.
Melee Attack—Trident: +4 to hit (reach 5 ft.; one creature).
Hit: 2d6 + 2 piercing damage.

STATISTICS

Str 15 (+2), **Dex** 11 (+0), **Con** 14 (+2),
Int 10 (+0), **Wis** 11 (+0), **Cha** 13 (+1)
Languages: Aquan
Senses: Darkvision 60 ft., tremorsense 60 ft. in water

TRAITS

Summon Sea Creatures (1/day): All triton leaders (those with 50 or more hit points) have the ability to summon sea creatures as an action. Roll 2d6: one die indicates how many rounds later the creatures arrive, and the other determines what type of creatures respond.

Die	Creatures
1	1–3 giant octopi
2	3–10 sharks
3	1 fanged sea serpent
4	3–6 aquatic ghouls
5	1–4 aquatic trolls
6	1 drowned wight (a standard wight with a swim speed of 30 ft.) leading 3–8 aquatic ghouls

Triton Shaman: Any group of 10 or more dark tritons can be accompanied by one or more triton shamans. A triton shaman has heightened Wisdom (15) and the ability to cast the following spells, using Wisdom as its spellcasting ability (DC 12, attack +4). It doesn't need material components to cast these spells. The spell selection listed below is only a suggestion; different shamans can have different spell lists.
Cantrips (at will): *guidance, mending, resistance, thaumaturgy*
1st level (x4): *bane, inflict wounds, protection from evil and good, sanctuary*
2nd level (x3): *blindness/deafness, hold person, protection from poison, spiritual weapon*
3rd level (x2): *bestow curse, dispel magic, mass healing word*

ECOLOGY

Environment: Any aquatic
Organization: Squad (2–8) or school (6–60)

Dark tritons resemble their more benevolent cousins, the normal tritons, but they are malevolent creatures. Just as the normal tritons are rumored to be servants of a sea god, the dark tritons are servants of oceanic demons of various types, most commonly the demon-prince Thalasskoptis.

Dark tritons have tentacles rather than the fishlike "legs" of normal tritons. They often ride giant moray eels as mounts when traveling in the dark depths of the sea, where they dwell in their castlelike lairs on the sea floor.

For every 10 dark tritons, either in their lair or in a hunting party, there will be a lieutenant with 50 hit points and two melee attacks per round (CR 3). For every two lieutenants, there will be a captain with 70 hit points and three melee attacks per round (CR 5). Roll a die for each leader; for each even result, add one triton shaman to the group (CR 2).

Troll, Spectral

Spectral trolls resemble normal trolls but are jet-black in color, and translucent.

Spectral Troll

XP 1,100 (CR 4)
CE Large undead
Initiative +1

DEFENSE

AC 15 (natural armor)
hp: 52 (8d10 + 8)
Immunity: Necrotic and poison damage; all nonmagical damage; exhaustion, fright, poison, unconsciousness

OFFENSE

Speed: 30 ft., fly 30 ft.
Melee Attack—Corrupting Touch: +6 to hit (reach 5 ft.; one creature). *Hit:* 4d8 + 4 necrotic damage. Creatures immune to aging are immune to this attack.

STATISTICS

Str 18 (+4), **Dex** 13 (+1), **Con** 20 (+5),
Int 7 (–2), **Wis** 10 (+0), **Cha** 13 (+1)
Languages: Understands Giant but doesn't speak
Senses: Truesight 60 ft.

TRAITS

Create Spawn: A humanoid killed by a spectral troll rises one to three days later as a free-willed specter unless a cleric of the victim's religion casts *gentle repose* or comparable magic on the corpse before it rises.
Incorporeal: A spectral troll can move through gaps as small as 1 square inch without penalty. It can also move through solid objects and other creatures as if they were difficult terrain. The spectral troll takes 1d10 force damage if it is still inside something solid at the end of its turn.
Rejuvenation: Unless it is permanently destroyed by having its spirit laid to rest, a "destroyed" spectral troll's spirit restores itself to unlife in 2d4 days.
Silent: A spectral troll makes no sound whatsoever; it is undetectable by purely audial means.
Unholy Fortitude: Spectral trolls are highly resistant to turning. They have tactical advantage on saving throws against being turned.
Vanish in Sunlight: A spectral troll that begins its turn in bright sunlight is banished to a remote, unknown dimension. It returns, near the same spot, when that location is no longer in direct sunlight. Only true sunlight has this effect; magical light does nothing.

ECOLOGY

Environment: Any
Organization: Solitary

Spectral trolls are a unique form of undead. They are the undying spirits of slain trolls whose regenerative ability, for unknown reasons, continues functioning long after the troll's physical form is utterly destroyed. Such undead creatures are tormented by snatches of memory from their former lives. They detest all living creatures, including other trolls—possibly other trolls more than anything else.

Being undead, spectral trolls can be turned, but not easily.

By nature, they are creatures of darkness. Direct, bright sunlight banishes a spectral troll to an unknown realm. When daylight fades, the spectral troll returns, near the same spot but not necessarily at the exact location.

It's impossible to destroy a spectral troll through simple combat. Even the most potent spells (*wish*, *true resurrection*) offer temporary solutions at best. The spectral troll's spirit is so powerfully compelled by hatred to regenerate that it restores itself to unlife in 2d4 days. The only way to destroy a spectral troll permanently is to determine the reason for its existence and set right whatever prevents it from resting in peace or from traveling on to whatever spirit realm would claim it. The exact means for doing this vary with each spirit and usually can be discovered only with extensive research—including long hours of searching and investigating in the obviously dangerous area the spectral troll haunts.

Credit
The spectral troll originally appeared in the Second Edition *Monstrous Manual* (© TSR/Wizards of the Coast, 1993) and is used by permission.

Copyright Notice
Author Scott Greene, based on original material by Wizards of the Coast.

Troll, Two-headed

The most distinctive feature of this massive brute is the fact that it has two heads. Each head is identical: red eyes, drooping nose, and yellow fangs. Its arms and legs end in razor-sharpened claws, and its hide is mottled green-gray and covered in coarse, splotchy, dark hair.

Two-headed Troll

XP 2,300 (CR 6)
CE Large giant
Initiative +1

DEFENSE
AC 15 (natural armor)
hp: 105 (10d10 + 50)

OFFENSE
Speed: 30 ft.
Multiattack: A two-headed troll attacks twice with claws or weapons and bites twice.
Melee Attack—Bite: +7 to hit (reach 5 ft.; one creature). *Hit:* 1d8 + 4 piercing damage.
Melee Attack—Claw: +7 to hit (reach 5 ft.; one creature). *Hit:* 2d6 + 4 slashing damage.

STATISTICS
Str 19 (+4), **Dex** 12 (+1), **Con** 20 (+5), **Int** 8 (−1), **Wis** 8 (−1), **Cha** 6 (−2)
Languages: Giant
Skills: Perception +5
Senses: Darkvision 60 ft.

TRAITS
Regeneration: A two-headed troll heals 5 hit points at the start of each of its turns. This ability doesn't function if the troll took fire damage since its previous turn. To be killed, the troll must be prevented from regenerating for at least one round while it has 0 hit points.

ECOLOGY
Environment: Any mountains and underground
Organization: Solitary, gang (2–5), or warband (1–2 two-headed trolls plus 2–6 trolls)

The two-headed troll is thought to be the hideous offspring of an ettin and a female troll. Sages contend that no other explanation is possible (or bears thinking about) concerning this monster. They do not associate with ettins, but two-headed trolls are often found leading normal trolls during raids or wars. They are greatly feared, being bigger than and twice as cruel as other trolls.

Two-headed trolls make their lairs underground and, thankfully, far from civilization.

A two-headed troll stands 10 feet tall. Its hide is mottled green or gray, and its facial features resemble that of a standard troll. They dress in rags and uncured hides, and adapt battered armor from fallen foes to their own piecemeal use. Their feet and hands sport enormous claws. The two-headed troll has the gait of a normal troll but walks fully upright, not hunched over, so they tower above other trolls.

On occasion, two-headed trolls have been known to wield captured or crudely-made clubs, axes, longswords, or even greatswords (one-handed).

Credit

The two-headed troll originally appeared in the First Edition *Fiend Folio* (© TSR/Wizards of the Coast, 1981) and is used by permission.

Copyright Notice
Author Scott Greene, based on original material by Oliver Charles MacDonald.

Tunnel Prawn

You hear the clicking sound first for several moments, Then the walls and ceiling are suddenly crawling with dozens of what appear to be enormous lobsters.

Tunnel Prawn

XP 25 (CR 1/8)
Unaligned Small beast
Initiative +2

DEFENSE

AC 14 (natural armor)
hp: 7 (2d6)

OFFENSE

Speed: climb 25 ft.
Melee Attack—Pincers: +4 to hit (reach 5 ft.; one creature). *Hit:* 1d4 + 2 slashing damage.

STATISTICS

Str 12 (+1), **Dex** 14 (+2), **Con** 11 (+0), **Int** 1 (–5), **Wis** 9 (–1), **Cha** 3 (–4)
Languages: None
Senses: Darkvision 60 ft.

TRAITS

Crowding: Up to five tunnel prawns can occupy a single 5-foot-square space.

ECOLOGY

Environment: Underground
Organization: Group (1–4) or cluster (2–12)

Tunnel prawns are scavengers resembling very large lobsters. These creatures wander through subterranean caverns eating bugs and fungi from the wall, floor, and ceiling. A tunnel prawn can scale walls and move along ceilings with no more difficulty than walking along a floor.

These dungeon vermin consider everything food, and they are easily antagonized. They attack almost any creature they encounter, alive or dead, regardless of its size.

Tunnel prawns are edible, and each one is large enough to provide a day's rations for a Small or Medium humanoid. The meat is tough and chewy, but tasty (somewhat surprisingly, considering their diet). It becomes inedible after 24 hours, however. Some taverns—usually those located near well-known dungeon entrances—serve tunnel prawns, and will pay up to 3 gp apiece for fresh ones. An adult tunnel prawn weighs up to 20 lbs.

Tunnel Worm

This massive creature is a 30-foot-long, sleek black centipede with segmented armor covering its body. Its huge mandibles are serrated and razor-sharp. Heavy plates of chitin protect its oversized head.

Tunnel Worm

XP 3,900 (CR 8)
Unaligned Huge monstrosity
Initiative +1

DEFENSE

AC 16 (natural armor)
hp: 115 (11d12 + 44)
Saving Throws: Con +7
Resistance: Bludgeoning, piercing, and slashing damage from nonmagical weapons

OFFENSE

Speed: 20 ft., burrow 20 ft.
Melee Attack—Bite: +8 to hit (reach 5 ft.; one creature). *Hit:* 3d8 + 5 piercing damage and the target must make a DC 16 Dex saving throw or be grappled.
Melee Attack—Severing Bite: automatic hit (one creature already grappled by the tunnel worm at the start of the tunnel worm's turn). *Hit:* 4d10 + 5 slashing damage and the target's armor class is reduced by 2. A successful DC 15 Dex or Str saving throw reduces damage by half and reduces armor loss to 1. Armor reduced to AC 10 is destroyed. If the target isn't wearing armor, its armor class is not affected in any case.

STATISTICS

Str 20 (+5), **Dex** 13 (+1), **Con** 19 (+4),
Int 1 (−5), **Wis** 8 (−1), **Cha** 4 (−3)
Languages: Common
Skills: Perception +5, Stealth +4
Senses: Tremorsense 60 ft.

TRAITS

Armored Skull: Only the tunnel worm's head has resistance to bludgeoning, piercing, and slashing damage. Attacks against any other portion of its body aren't affected by that resistance.

ECOLOGY

Environment: Underground
Organization: Solitary or cluster (2–5)

The tunnel worm is a burrowing creature related to certain other enormous, subterranean monstrosities (the monstrous centipede, the purple worm). It can sustain itself by scavenging, but it is a very aggressive predator and hunter. Its preferred food is fresh, raw meat.

Tunnel worms attack anything that enters their territory. They live in winding, disorienting complexes of 3-foot-wide tunnels that they've chewed through earth and stone. These burrows are often filled with the rotting remains of past prey; the

worm's offspring incubate in carrion.

The favorite tactic of the tunnel worm is to lurk in a spot where one of its tunnels passes very near a dungeon passage until it senses live prey passing nearby. Then it cuts through the last remaining bit of wall, snatches a creature, and retreats into the tunnel so that only its well-armored head is exposed to attack. Thus protected, it chews through its prey's "protective covering" before devouring the gooey portions inside.

A tunnel worm that has lost more than half its hit points retreats to its lair if possible, taking along anything it's grappled. If it can't retreat, it fights to the death.

A typical tunnel worm is 30 feet long, but they've been known to grow to a length of 60 feet.

Credit
The tunnel worm originally appeared in the First Edition *Monster Manual II* (© TSR/Wizards of the Coast, 1983) and is used by permission.

Copyright Notice
Author Scott Greene, based on original material by Gary Gygax.

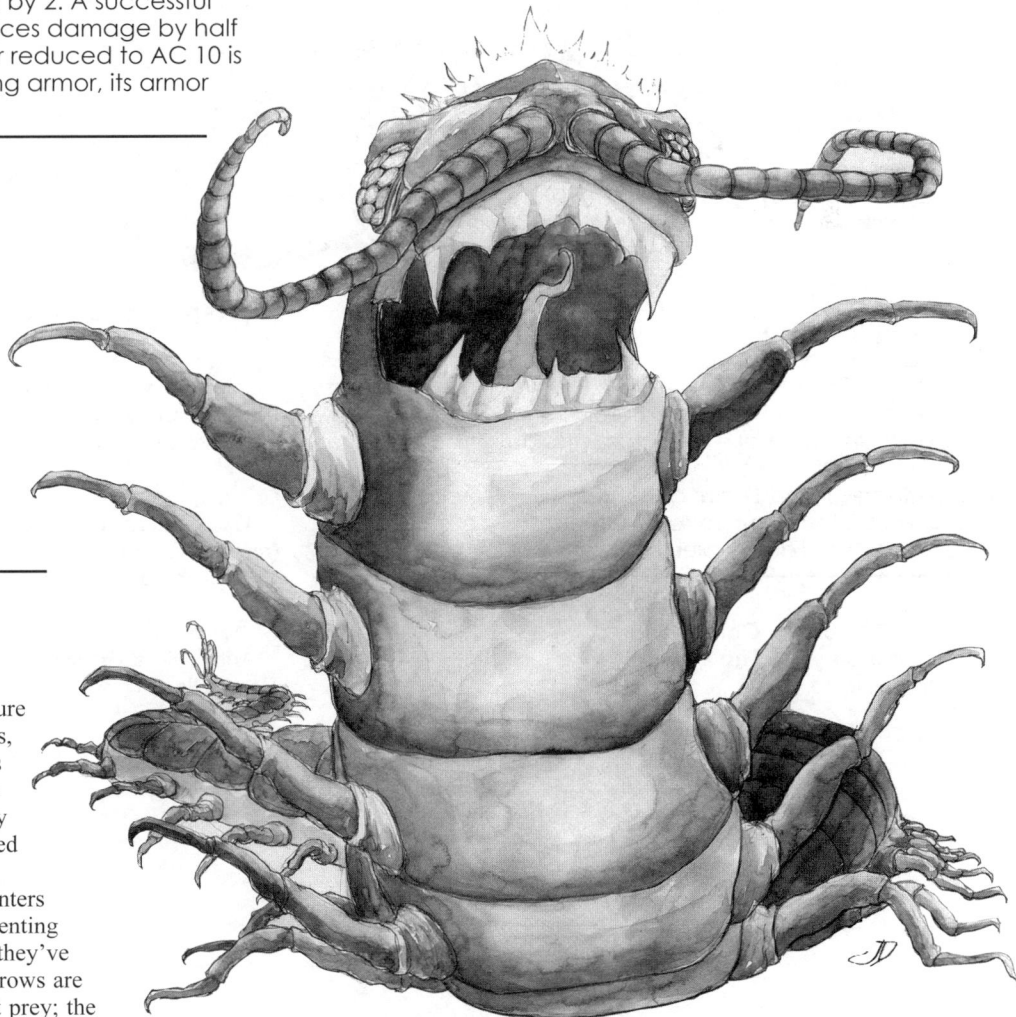

Vampire Rose

This bush has many flowering white bulbs and petals, green stems lined with tiny thorns, and small, viny branches of greenish-brown.

Vampire Rose

XP 50 (CR 1/4)
Unaligned Small plant
Initiative −1

DEFENSE

AC 9
hp: 27 (5d6 + 10)
Resistance: Bludgeoning damage from nonmagical weapons
Immunity: Piercing and psychic damage; charm, fright, prone, stun, unconsciousness
Vulnerability: Slashing damage

OFFENSE

Speed: 5 ft.
Multiattack: A vampire rose makes one thorn attack, and it drains blood from every creature it has grappled.
Melee Attack— Thorns: +3 to hit (reach 5 ft.; one creature). *Hit:* 1d4 + 1 piercing damage and the target is grappled. The vampire rose can have any number of creatures grappled and still make one thorn attack per turn. The DC to escape this grapple is 11.
Melee Attack—Blood Drain: automatic hit (all creatures grappled by the vampire rose at the start of the vampire rose's turn). *Hit:* 1d6 + 1 piercing damage.

STATISTICS

Str 12 (+1), **Dex** 8 (−1), **Con** 14 (+2), **Int** 1 (−5), **Wis** 13 (+1), **Cha** 10 (+0)
Languages: None
Senses: Tremorsense 60 ft.

Skills: Athletics +5

TRAITS

Camouflage: A vampire rose is indistinguishable from a normal rose bush until it moves or attacks.

ECOLOGY

Environment: Temperate land
Organization: Solitary, patch (2–5), or tangle (3–18)

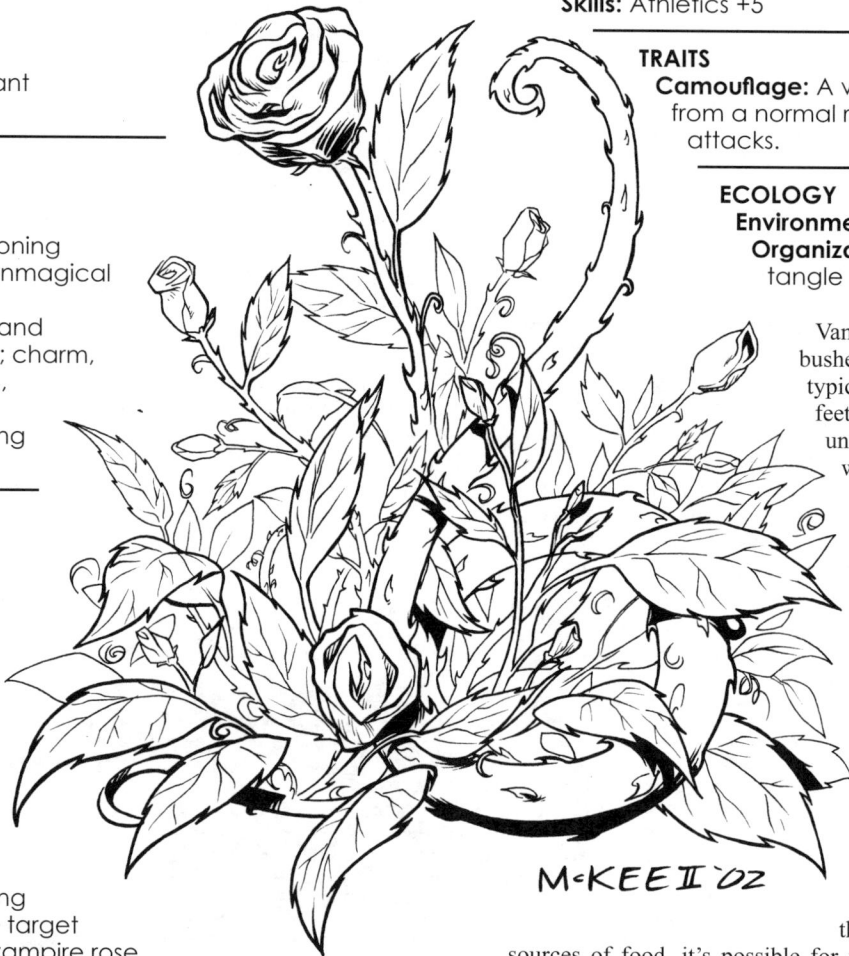

Vampire roses look like normal white rose bushes and are often mistaken for such. The typical vampire rose bush stands about 3 feet tall. The plant remains motionless until its prey moves within range, when it "strikes" with a thorny stalk. This attack is almost imperceptible and easily mistaken for simply becoming snagged by the thorny vines of a normal rose bush. It's only on the vampire rose's next turn, when the vine tightens its grip and thorns really dig into the victim's flesh and begin siphoning out blood, that the true nature of the plant becomes apparent.

When fully sated with blood, a vampire rose's petals flush red.

Vampire roses spreading out of control have been known to render entire valleys and stretches of forest impassable. Because they can uproot themselves and move to find fresh sources of food, it's possible for fully grown vampire roses to appear literally overnight in areas that were clear the day before, closing roads or even encircling a farm or a hamlet and cutting it off from its neighbors.

Credit

The vampire rose originally appeared in the First Edition module (revised edition) *B3 Palace of the Silver Princess* (© TSR/Wizards of the Coast, 1981) and is used by permission.

Copyright Notice

Author Scott Greene, based on original material by Tom Moldvay and Jean Wells.

Vegepygmy

This creature has a humanoid shape, but it otherwise appears to be composed entirely of vegetable matter. It has a wide mouth, large yellow eyes, and a topknot of dark leaves. In addition to two arms and two legs, leafy tendrils protrude from its shoulders, midsection, arms, and legs.

Vegepygmy Commoner and Worker

XP 25 (CR 1/8)
Unaligned Small plant (fungus)
Initiative +2

DEFENSE

AC 12
hp: 10 (3d6)
Resistance: Piercing damage from nonmagical weapons
Immunity: Lightning and psychic damage; charm, fright, stun, unconsciousness

OFFENSE

Speed: 25 ft.
Melee Attack—Claws: +4 to hit (reach 5 ft.; one creature). *Hit:* 1d4 + 2 slashing damage.
Melee Attack—Javelin: +2 to hit (reach 5 ft.; one creature). *Hit:* 1d4 piercing damage.

STATISTICS

Str 10 (+0), **Dex** 14 (+2), **Con** 11 (+0),
Int 7 (−2), **Wis** 11 (+0), **Cha** 10 (+0)
Languages: Unique; understands Undercommon but doesn't speak
Skills: Stealth +4
Senses: Darkvision 60 ft.

TRAITS

Camouflage: A vegepygmy has tactical advantage on Stealth checks in areas with dense vegetation.

ECOLOGY

Environment: Underground
Organization: Gang (2–5) or work crew (5–10)

Vegepygmy Guard

XP 100 (CR 1/2)
Unaligned Small plant (fungus)
Initiative +2

DEFENSE

AC 13 (plant fiber armor)
hp: 28 (6d6 + 6)
Resistance: Piercing damage from nonmagical weapons
Immunity: Lightning and psychic damage; charm, fright, stun, unconsciousness

OFFENSE

Speed: 25 ft.
Multiattack: A vegepygmy guard makes two melee attacks or two ranged attacks.
Melee Attack—Claws: +3 to hit (reach 5 ft.; one creature). *Hit:* 1d6 + 1 slashing damage.
Melee Attack—Javelin: +3 to hit (reach 5 ft.; one creature). *Hit:* 1d6 + 1 piercing damage.

Ranged Attack—Javelin: +4 to hit (range 30 ft./120 ft.; one creature). *Hit:* 1d6 + 1 piercing damage.

STATISTICS

Str 12 (+1), **Dex** 14 (+2), **Con** 13 (+1),
Int 10 (+0), **Wis** 12 (+1), **Cha** 10 (+0)
Languages: Unique; understands Undercommon but doesn't speak
Skills: Stealth +4
Senses: Darkvision 60 ft.

TRAITS

Camouflage: A vegepygmy has tactical advantage on Stealth checks in areas with dense vegetation.

ECOLOGY

Environment: Underground
Organization: Pair or patrol (2–8)

Vegepygmy Chief

XP 700 (CR 3)
Unaligned Medium plant (fungus)
Initiative +2

DEFENSE

AC 14 (wicker armor)
hp: 60 (8d8 + 24)
Resistance: Piercing damage from nonmagical weapons
Immunity: Lightning and psychic damage; charm, fright, stun, unconsciousness

OFFENSE

Speed: 25 ft.
Multiattack: A vegepygmy chief makes two melee attacks, or two ranged attacks, or one spores attack.
Melee Attack—Claws: +5 to hit (reach 5 ft.; one creature). *Hit:* 2d4 + 3 slashing damage.
Melee Attack—Spear: +5 to hit (reach 5 ft.; one creature). *Hit:* 1d8 + 3 piercing damage.
Ranged Attack—Spear: +5 to hit (range 20 ft./80 ft.; one creature). *Hit:* 1d8 + 3 piercing damage.
Area Attack—Spores (recharge 5, 6): automatic hit (40 ft. cone; creatures in cone). *Hit:* targets must make successful DC 13 Con saving throws against poison or be paralyzed for 2d6 rounds. When paralysis ends, affected creatures take 3d6 poison damage, or half damage with a successful DC 13 Con saving throw. Creatures that die from the poison damage reanimate 24 hours later as vegepygmy guards. The paralysis can be ended early by magic that neutralizes poison; ending the effect early also eliminates the second saving throw. Plant creatures are immune to this effect.

STATISTICS

Str 16 (+3), **Dex** 14 (+2), **Con** 16 (+3),
Int 11 (+0), **Wis** 14 (+2), **Cha** 14 (+2)

Languages: Unique; understands Undercommon but doesn't speak
Skills: Stealth +4
Senses: Darkvision 60 ft.

TRAITS
Camouflage: A vegepygmy has tactical advantage on Stealth checks in areas with dense vegetation.

ECOLOGY
Environment: Underground
Organization: Band (1 chief, 2–16 guards, and 3–24 workers) or tribe (2–4 chiefs, 3–24 guards, 3–300 commoners and workers, 1–4 patches of russet mold)

Vegepygmies are low-intelligence plant creatures that make their homes deep in forests or underground regions far from areas settled by humanois. They are carnivorous hunter/scavengers, but their usual prey is small game. They don't bother larger creatures or other intelligent species except in times of great need.

Vegepygmies are most dangerous when they experience a sudden surge in population. At those times, their growing numbers outstrip the local food supply and force them to march into new territory. Although they are capable of fighting larger, stronger creatures for dominance, they prefer to let russet mold do most of the work, converting the prior inhabitants of their new territory into more vegepygmy commoners and workers.

Most vegepygmies are 2 to 4 feet tall. They continue growing throughout their lives, "maturing" from commoners to workers to guards. Only chiefs grow to 5 feet or more. It's logical to assume that chiefs are the ultimate developmental form of guards, but their rarity calls this into question. Some scholars hypothesize that chiefs are created when needed, in a manner similar to the way ants create queens when needed.

They have no apparent ears, but it's well known that vegepygmies can hear. Their mouths are used only for eating. Vegepygmies never speak; they communicate with others of their kind by thumping their chests and rapping their spears on rocks, earth, or some other solid surface. They appear to understand Undercommon, but whether they have some means of communicating with other species is unknown.

Credit
The vegepygmy originally appeared in the First Edition module *S3 Expedition to the Barrier Peaks* (© TSR/Wizards of the Coast, 1980) and later in the First Edition *Monster Manual II* (© TSR/Wizards of the Coast, 1983), and is used by permission.

Copyright Notice
Author Scott Greene, based on original material by Gary Gygax.

Volt

This repulsive creature appears to be a small, spherical beast with a long, sinewy tail. Its body is covered with thick gray bristles. Two large eyes resembling those of a fly dominate its head. Small horns protrude above these from its head.

Volt (Bolt Wurm)

XP 50 (CR 1/4)
Unaligned Small
   aberration
Initiative +3

DEFENSE
AC 13
hp: 13 (3d6 + 3)
Immunity: Lightning
   damage

OFFENSE
Speed: fly 30 ft.
Melee Attack—Bite:
   +5 to hit (reach 5
   ft.; one creature).
   Hit: 1d6 + 3 piercing
   damage and the
   volt enters the target's
   space and grapples the
   target. The volt can't use its
   bite attack while it is grappling
   a creature.
Melee Attack—Tail Slap: automatic hit (one creature
   already grappled by the volt at the start of the
   volt's turn). *Hit:* 1d6 + 2 lightning damage. A
   creature reduced to 0 hp by this attack is
   unconscious and stable, not dying.

STATISTICS
Str 10 (+0), **Dex** 16 (+3), **Con** 12 (+1),
Int 2 (–4), **Wis** 10 (+0), **Cha** 6 (–2)
Languages: None
Skills: Acrobatics +5
Senses: Darkvision 60 ft.

TRAITS
Agile Grappler: A volt uses its Dex (Acrobatics) score to
   oppose attempts to escape from its grapple. The volt
   can't move a creature it grapples, but it moves with
   the grappled creature. If the grapple is broken, the volt
   immediately moves 5 feet into an adjacent, empty space.

ECOLOGY
Environment: Underground
Organization: Mob (2–12) or swarm (10–20)

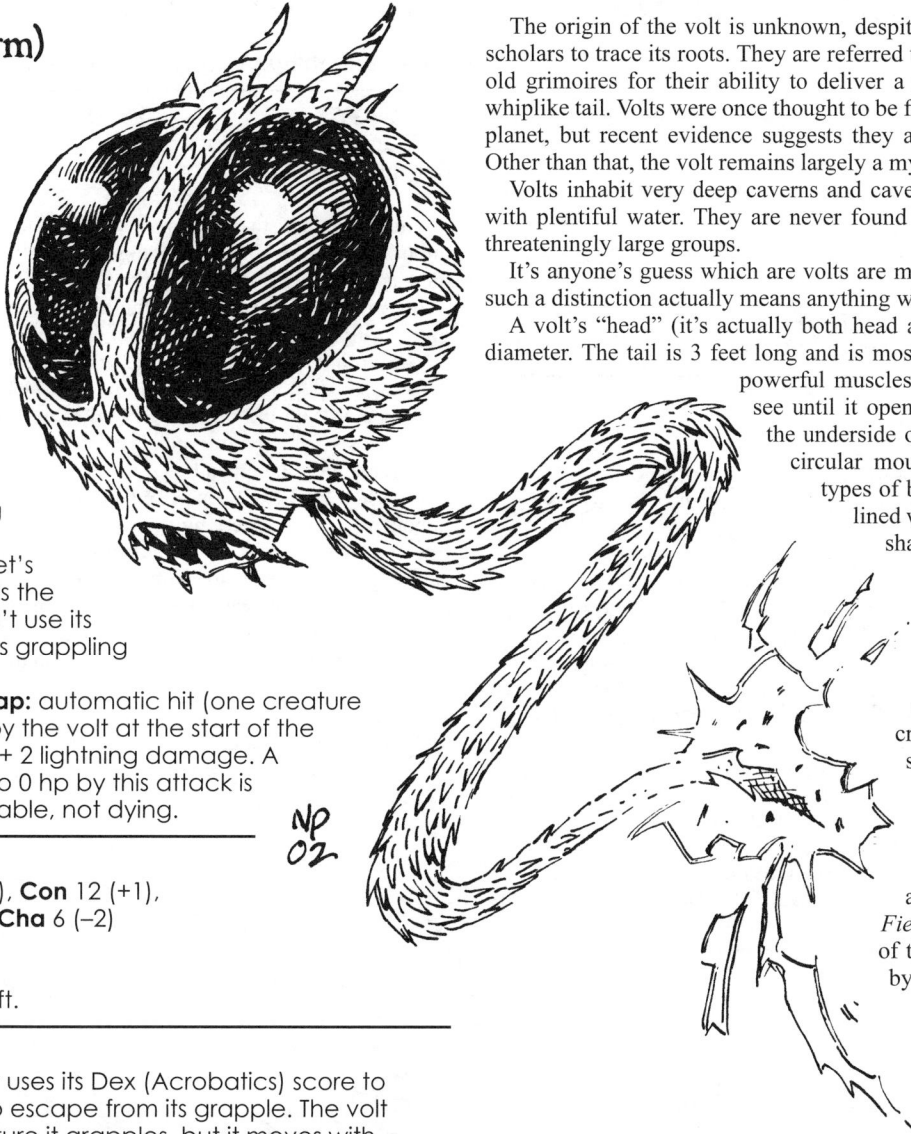

The origin of the volt is unknown, despite the effort of many learned scholars to trace its roots. They are referred to as "bolt wurms" in certain old grimoires for their ability to deliver a jolt of electricity with their whiplike tail. Volts were once thought to be from another plane or another planet, but recent evidence suggests they are from the Material Plane. Other than that, the volt remains largely a mystery.

Volts inhabit very deep caverns and caves, preferring to lair in areas with plentiful water. They are never found alone, and usually travel in threateningly large groups.

It's anyone's guess which are volts are male and which are female, if such a distinction actually means anything where volts are concerned.

A volt's "head" (it's actually both head and body) is about 2 feet in diameter. The tail is 3 feet long and is mostly tough cartilage and thin, powerful muscles. Its mouth is impossible to see until it opens; then it can be spotted on the underside of the body. It resembles the circular mouth of a lamprey or certain types of blood-sucking worms, and is lined with multiple rows of needle-sharp teeth.

Volts are very aggressive. They attack by latching onto a foe, then shocking the creature repeatedly with their electrified tails until it passes out. Once the creature is unconscious, they suck out its blood and other fluids at their leisure.

Credit
   The Volt originally appeared in the First Edition *Fiend Folio* (© TSR/ Wizards of the Coast, 1981) and is used by permission.

Copyright Notice
   Author Scott Greene, based on original material by Jonathon Jones.

Vorin

This creature is an immense, greenish-black, wormlike thing with intense yellow eyes. It is 30 feet long and a foot thick. The body is a ropy mass of pulpy flesh with several gill-like apertures along its length with which the creature propels itself through the water. The front of the beast has a long trunk similar to that of an elephant. Its skin glistens as if coated with oil.

Vorin

XP 5,000 (CR 9)
CE Huge monstrosity (aquatic)
Initiative +4

DEFENSE

AC 14
hp: 149 (13d12 + 65)
Saving Throws: Dex +8
Resistance: Fire and bludgeoning damage
Immunity: Acid damage; charm, prone

OFFENSE

Speed: 20 ft., swim 40 ft.
Multiattack: A vorin attacks three times. It spits, then bites, directing both attacks at the same target if it can. It also stings, and that attack can be aimed at any target within reach.
Ranged Attack—Spit: +8 to hit (range 25 ft.; one creature). *Hit:* the target must make a successful DC 17 Con saving throw or be incapacitated. An incapacitated creature repeats the saving throw at the end of its next turn. A successful save ends the incapacitation, but if the saving throw fails, the creature is paralyzed for 1d4 hours. If the target creature is wearing armor, see Seeping Poison, below.
Melee Attack—Bite: +9 to hit (reach 10 ft.; one creature). *Hit:* 2d10 + 5 piercing damage.
Melee Attack—Sting: +9 to hit (reach 10 ft.; one creature). *Hit:* 3d10 + 5 piercing damage and the target must make a successful DC 17 Con saving throw or be incapacitated. An incapacitated creature repeats the saving throw at the end of its next turn. A successful save ends the incapacitation, but if the saving throw fails, the creature is paralyzed for 1d4 hours.

STATISTICS

Str 20 (+5), **Dex** 18 (+4), **Con** 21 (+5),
Int 2 (–4), **Wis** 10 (+0), **Cha** 6 (–2)
Languages: None
Senses: Darkvision 60 ft.

TRAITS

Camouflage: A vorin that's submerged in water or mud can be spotted with a successful DC 15 Int (Nature) or Wis (Survival) check.
Seeping Poison: If the target of the vorin's spit attack is wearing armor, then the poison needs one round to seep through gaps in the armor and contact the target's skin. The target or an adjacent ally can use an action to make a DC 15 Dex check; success indicates the poison was scraped off completely before it penetrated the armor. An edged weapon or tool must be used. Any slashing weapon and most piercing weapons will do the job. Note that only the vorin's spit needs to seep through armor; poison from its sting does not.

Water Breathing: A vorin breathes equally well in air or water.

ECOLOGY

Environment: Any marsh
Organization: Solitary or knot (2–5)

Vorins live in dismal swamps and bogs, where they lurk in the murk and the mire. Only its slightly bulging eyes protrude above the water or the mud as it watches for potential prey.

A vorin is difficult to injure with blunt force; its squishy, boneless body gives easily under heavy blows that don't break its thick hide.

The vorin's proboscis contains muscular tubes that are used to spit gobs of sticky, poisonous saliva up to 25 feet. Each gob is the size of a small melon, and the substance seems almost to have a mind of its own as it oozes across an armored surface seeking a way through to the soft, vulnerable flesh underneath.

A vorin relies heavily on its spit attack in combat, hoping to incapacitate opponents before emerging from the slime to finish them off with its bite and its stinger. If its spit attacks aren't having the desired effect, it submerges and appears to swim away. In fact, it probably is shadowing its prey from a distance while keeping out of sight, waiting for an opportunity to try again under more favorable circumstances. Although the creature is dumb as a post in most ways, it is a wily hunter.

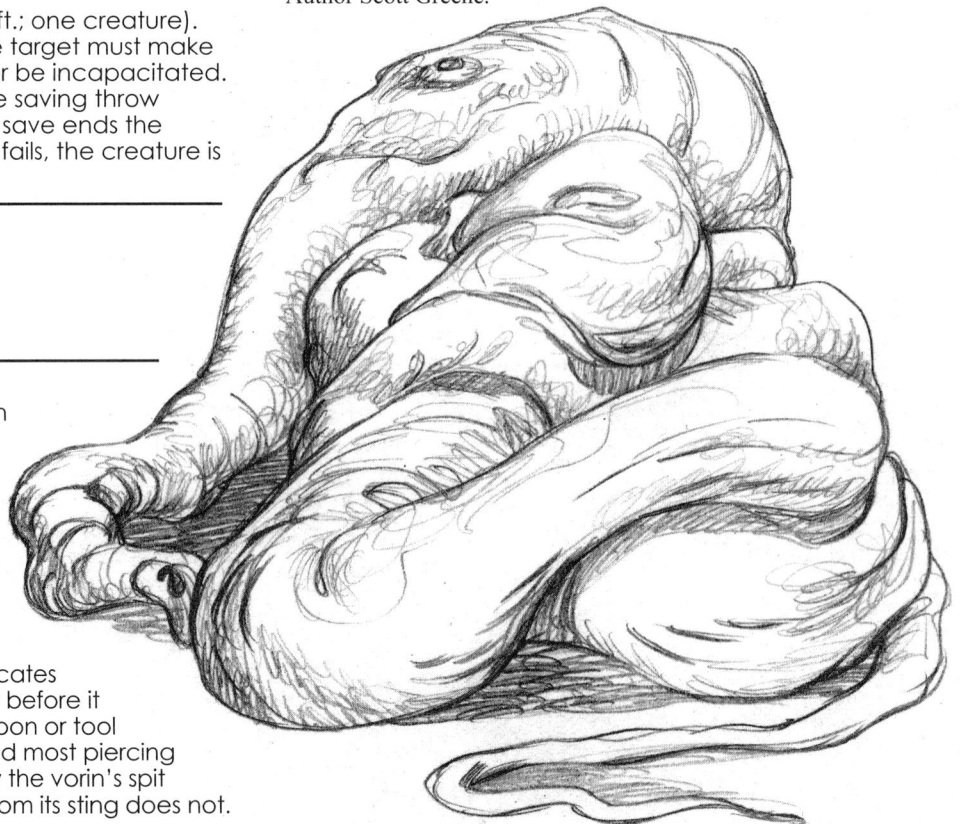

Vulchling

This creature looks like a man-sized vulture with inky black feathers, a gray beak, and jet black talons.

Vulchling

XP 25 (CR 1/8)
CE Medium monstrosity
Initiative +2

DEFENSE

AC 12
hp: 9 (2d8)

OFFENSE

Speed: 20 ft., fly 50 ft.
Melee Attack—Bite: +4 to hit (reach 5 ft.; one creature). *Hit:* 1d4 + 2 piercing damage. The vulchling uses this attack when it is grounded.
Melee Attack—Talons: +4 to hit (reach 5 ft.; one creature). *Hit:* 1d6 + 2 slashing damage. The vulchling uses this attack when it is flying.

STATISTICS

Str 9 (–1), **Dex** 14 (+2), **Con** 11 (+0),
Int 7 (–2), **Wis** 11 (+0), **Cha** 10 (+0)
Languages: Unique, Undercommon
Senses: Darkvision 60 ft.

ECOLOGY

Environment: Underground
Organization: Solitary or flock (2–16)

Vulchlings are a malevolent race of avian creatures akin to vultures, but larger and much more intelligent. Their faces are clearly birdlike, yet something about them seems oddly human.

Vulchlings are scavengers and predators. They hunt any creatures they believe they can kill. They tend to avoid hunting intelligent humanoids—not from any sense of ethics or revulsion over killing intelligent beings, but simply because intelligent prey is more dangerous.

Vulchlings can be found in the company of harpies and vrocks, sometimes as servitors and sometimes as mercenaries. Most of their time is spent in their large nests hidden deep inside the earth.

Vulchlings always attack from ambush if possible. They hide on shadowy ledges high up on cavern walls, then dive silently onto unsuspecting prey.

Credit

The vulchling originally appeared in the First Edition *Monster Manual II* (© TSR/Wizards of the Coast, 1983) and is used by permission.

Copyright Notice

Author Scott Greene, based on original material by Gary Gygax.

Weird, Lava

This serpentine horror coils beneath a haze of shimmering heat waves. As the outer layer of its form cools into hard, black plates, the cracks between these plates give off the cherry glow of molten rock.

Lava Weird

XP 1,100 (CR 4)
CE Large elemental
Initiative +2

DEFENSE

AC 16 (natural armor)
hp: 76 (9d10 + 27)
Resistance: Piercing and slashing damage from nonmagical weapons
Immunity: Fire and poison damage; paralysis, poison, stun, unconsciousness
Vulnerability: Cold damage

OFFENSE

Speed: 35 ft.
Melee Attack—Bite: +4 to hit (reach 5 ft.; one creature). *Hit:* 2d8 + 2 fire damage and the target must make a successful DC 12 Dex saving throw or be grappled. A grappled creature takes 1d8 + 2 fire damage at the start of its turn. If the save succeeds, the target is not grappled but it does catch fire if it is wearing or carrying combustible material or is itself flammable. While the fire burns, the creature takes 1d8 fire damage at the start of each of its turns. The fire is extinguished automatically when the creature or an adjacent ally spends an action to put it out.
Melee Attack—Drag Into Lava: automatic hit (one creature grappled by the lava weird). *Hit:* the lava weird and the grappled creature engage in a Strength (Athletics) contest. If the lava weird wins, the grappled creature is dragged into the lava pool; see Lava Pool below.

STATISTICS

Str 15 (+2), **Dex** 14 (+2), **Con** 16 (+3),
Int 11 (+0), **Wis** 12 (+1), **Cha** 16 (+3)
Languages: Ignan, Terran
Skills: Athletics +4
Senses: Darkvision 60 ft.

TRAITS

Control Elemental: Lava weirds have the ability to dominate elementals of the "earth" or "fire" type. When the lava weird uses an action to issue a command to an elemental within 50 feet, the elemental must make a successful DC 13 Wis saving throw or be dominated. The effect is permanent, but the elemental is allowed to repeat the saving throw if it is commanded to do something that will clearly result in its own destruction. An elemental that makes a successful save is not dominated and is immune to this effect for 24 hours. There's no limit to the number of elementals a lava weird can control. Once domination is established, it has no range limitation, provided the lava weird and the elemental remain on the same plane of existence. Lava weirds are immune to this effect.

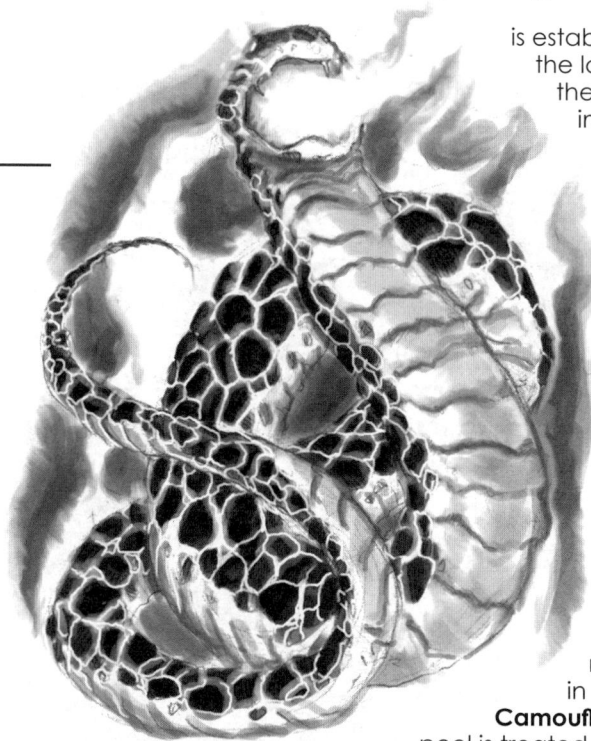

Lava Pool: A creature that's dragged into a lava pool (or that falls in, or winds up in lava for any reason at all) is restrained and takes 2d8 fire damage at the start of each of its turns. To escape from the lava, the creature or an adjacent ally must use an action and make a successful DC 15 Str (Athletics) check. If the check succeeds, the creature moves 5 feet out of the lava pool, is prone, and is on fire. While on fire, the creature takes 1d8 fire damage at the start of each of its turns. The fire is extinguished automatically when the creature or an adjacent ally spends an action to put it out.

Reform: When reduced to 0 hit points, a lava weird dissolves into its lava pool. One minute later, it reforms with full hit points minus any hit points it lost to cold damage in the preceding 24 hours.

Camouflage: Until it attacks, a lava weird in its lava pool is treated as invisible.

ECOLOGY

Environment: Elemental Plane of Fire, Plane of Molten Skies
Organization: Solitary, pack (2–5)

Weirds are creatures from the elemental planes. They are sometimes encountered on the Material Plane, often in the employ of a powerful spellcaster. They are much more intelligent than typical elementals, however, and they do not take kindly to deception or forced servitude, so summoning these creatures against their will is a risky undertaking. Even so, their ability to command elementals is legendary and highly useful to anyone who has a need for an army of such beings.

Weirds speak the elemental languages of earth and fire. Those that spend time on the Material Plane usually pick up enough words of Common to engage in simple conversations.

Lava weirds have serpentine bodies about 10 feet long formed of elemental magma. No matter what plane they reside on, they spend their time swimming in pools of molten rock and liquid fire. On the Material Plane, they are only found in active volcanoes and other sources of magma. The air of the Material Plane is painfully cold to them, so they never leave their lava pools willingly or for very long. Anyone who hopes to employ these creatures as guards or as elemental commanders must provide them with lava pools to swim in. Because their range of control over elementals is unlimited, they can control any number of them from the safety of their lava pools in a remote volcano while the elementals wreak havoc halfway across the world.

A lava weird hides in its bubbling lava pool, where it is effectively invisible, until enemies come within range. Once a target is within reach, the weird lashes out. If it can, it will pull an intruder into the lava pool and let the molten rock do most of its dirty work. Being of a naturally vicious and malign nature, lava weirds are prone to attack just about any creature that wanders too close to their pools.

Were-mist

An unusual mist flows across the ground and swirls around your companion's feet before seeming to climb up his body and envelop him. Then, as the mist takes on the vague outline of a wolflike monster, your companion begins changing into a werewolf!

Were-mist
XP 450, 700, or 1,100 (CR 2, 3, or 4)
CE Large aberration
Initiative +2

DEFENSE
AC 7
hp: 16 (3d10)
Immunity: Bludgeoning and slashing damage from nonmagical or nonsilver weapons; acid, necrotic, piercing, and poison damage; all conditions

OFFENSE
Speed: 30 ft.
Melee Attack—Domination: automatic hit (reach 5 ft.; one creature). *Hit:* the target must make a successful DC 13 Cha saving throw or the were-mist enters the target creature's space and the target is dominated and transformed by the were-mist; see Transformation, below.

STATISTICS
Str 0 (−5), **Dex** 4 (−3), **Con** 10 (+0),
Int 10 (+0), **Wis** 16 (+3), **Cha** 10 (+0)
Languages: Common
Senses: Darkvision 60 ft.

TRAITS
Transformation: A dominated creature is completely under the were-mist's control. At the start of its next turn, as a bonus action, the dominated creature transforms into the hybrid form of a wereboar, wererat, or werewolf (the form is chosen by the were-mist). The transformed creature has the stats and abilities of its new form, but it can't cause lycanthropy. Transformation into a beast heals all lost hit points the same as a long rest, but doesn't affect damaging conditions such as poisoning or disease. The domination and transformation are permanent until the were-mist is killed, is driven off, or leaves voluntarily. The were-mist can be attacked with weapons and with targeted spells without endangering the enveloped creature, but the transformed victim is subject to area affects as normal. The were-mist leaves the transformed creature and seeks a new victim when the transformed creature drops to 10 or fewer hit points. When the were-mist leaves or is killed, the transformed creature immediately transforms back into its normal form, with the same number of hit points it had in were-form. The creature is also stunned until it makes a successful DC 13 Con saving throw at the start of its turn. Killing or knocking out the transformed creature has no effect on the were-mist; it simply moves on to another victim.
Variable CR: The challenge rating of a were-mist is the same as the type of beast it transforms victims into; CR 2 for wererats, CR 3 for werewolves, or CR 4 for wereboars. If it transforms victims into more than one type in an encounter, use the highest value.

ECOLOGY
Environment: Any
Organization: Solitary

Despite its name, a were-mist is not a true lycanthrope, but is a monster than can inflict involuntary shapechange upon other creatures. The were-mist attacks by enveloping its chosen victim and trying to transform it. If the surrounded creature fails to resist the were-mist's assault, the creature transforms into a ravening, wolflike beast completely under the were-mist's control.

The only clue that the victim is not a real lycanthrope is that the were-mist remains wrapped around the victim, giving the creature an eerie, almost ethereal appearance. The mist can be attacked without risk to the controlled creature, but it is resistant to many types of attack. Magic is the best offense.

When the were-mist's victim is weakened by combat, the mist simply abandons it and moves on to a new victim. As soon as it departs, its control is broken and the slave returns to normal shape, but it usually takes several moments before it recovers from the shock of the experience. In battle, the were-mist moves from victim to victim, transforming them and forcing them to attack their allies, discarding each puppet when it becomes weak and moving to another.

Were-mists are solitary because of their rarity more than through any unwillingness to congregate. In rare instances, a lair containing more than one of these creatures might be found. They have no known means of reproduction, so such a lair probably could exist only near whatever force or source creates these malign entities.

Weredactyl

This creature closely resembles a pterodactyl, but for the human fingers rather than claws extending from its wing joint, and its very human-lookiing eyes.

Weredactyl

XP 450 (CR 2)
NE Medium humanoid (shapechanger)
Initiative +2

DEFENSE
AC 12
hp: 44 (8d8 + 8)
Immunity: Bludgeoning, piercing, and slashing damage from nonmagical and nonsilver weapons

OFFENSE
Speed: 30 ft. in human or hybrid form; 10 ft., 50 ft. flying in pterodactyl form
Multiattack: A weredactyl makes two melee attacks.
Melee Attack—Peck (pterodactyl form): +5 to hit (reach 5 ft.; one creature). *Hit:* 1d6 + 3 piercing damage.
Melee Attack—Claws (hybrid form): +5 to hit (reach 5 ft.; one creature). *Hit:* 1d6 +3 slashing damage. If both claw attacks hit the same target, the creature must make a successful DC 12 Dex saving throw or be grappled.
Melee Attack—Handaxe (human or hybrid form): +5 to hit (reach 5 ft.; one creature). *Hit:* 1d6 + 3 slashing damage.

STATISTICS
Str 16 (+3), **Dex** 15 (+2), **Con** 12 (+1), **Int** 7 (–2), **Wis** 10 (+0), **Cha** 8 (+0)
Languages: Common, Unique
Senses: Darkvision 60 ft.

ECOLOGY
Environment: Temperate
Organization: Solitary, patrol (2–5), or one per skelzi when encountered with their masters

Weredactyls in their "human" form are fat, slouching humanoids with protruding faces, low foreheads, and sagittal crests. Their were-form is a pterodactyl with long human fingers at the wing-joint and human eyes. In hybrid form, their arms and legs are more developed, and their wings and beaks are small; too small to enable flight, in the case of the wings.

Weredactyls live in servitude to the evil skelzis. They are naturally stupid even in human form. Weredactyls without skelzis to command them have been known to throw all their axes at approaching enemies, leaving themselves weaponless in the following melee. If they spend more than six continuous hours in pterodactyl form, they go completely feral and must be retrained from scratch to be of any use to their skelzi masters.

Obviously, the skelzis go to great lengths to prevent this from happening—just one reason why weredactyls are almost never encountered without skelzis nearby.

All but a few of the many skelzi hegemonies and empires use weredactyls as aerial mounts. They are most useful only in astral, ethereal, and other extraplanar environments, however, because in those planes, a weredactyl can carry a skelzi rider aloft. In the Material Plane, a weredactyl can fly with a Small rider, but it isn't strong enough to carry a Medium rider in flight. *Enlarge/reduce potions* are highly valued by skelzis visiting the Material Plane, because they can use the potions to become small enough for their weredactyl mounts to carry them, then return to normal size at the conclusion of their journey.

Widow Creeper

This creature resembles a monstrous spider about twice the size of a human, but constructed of weeds, vines, and leaves. Two writhing tentacles sprout from its eight-legged body, each ending in a sharpened talon. An hourglass-shaped pattern of leaves and brush can be seen on its back.

Widow Creeper

XP 7,200 (CR 10)
Unaligned Large plant
Initiative +1

DEFENSE

AC 13 (natural armor)
hp: 133 (14d10 + 56)
Saving Throws: Wis +4
Resistance: Bludgeoning and piercing damage from nonmagical weapons
Immunity: Psychic damage; charm, fright, stun, unconsciousness

OFFENSE

Speed: 30 ft., climb 20 ft.
Multiattack: A widow creeper attacks twice.
Melee Attack—Vines: +9 to hit (reach 15 ft.; one creature). *Hit:* 3d10 + 5 piercing damage. If both vine attacks hit the same target, the creature must make a successful DC 17 Dex saving throw or be grappled.
Melee Attack—Brain Fluid Drain: +9 to hit (reach 5 ft.; one restrained or grappled creature). *Hit:* 3d8 + 5 piercing damage and the target loses 1 point of Intelligence.
Ranged Attack—Webs (recharge 5, 6): +5 to hit (range 30 ft./60 ft.; one creature). *Hit:* The target is restrained by plant-fiber webs. A webbed creature can use its action to attempt a DC 17 Str (Athletics) check to escape. The web can also be destroyed by 15 points of slashing or fire damage against AC 10.

STATISTICS

Str 21 (+5), **Dex** 12 (+1),
Con 18 (+4), **Int** 5 (–3),
Wis 10 (+0), **Cha** 13 (+1)
Languages: None
Skills: Perception +8, Stealth +3
Senses:
  Darkvision 60 ft., plantsense 120 ft.

TRAITS

Charm Plants: All plant creatures with Intelligence 3 or higher that come within 50 feet of a widow creeper must make a successful DC 12 Wis saving throw or be charmed by it for 24 hours.
Entangle (recharge 6): As a bonus action, a widow creeper can cast the spell *entangle* (DC 13 to escape).
Plantsense: A widow creeper can pinpoint the location of anything within 120 feet that is in contact with vegetation.
This ability functions identically to tremorsense, but uses plants as its medium instead of earth.
Woodland Stride: A widow creeper can move through thorns, briars, dense brush, and similar terrain at its normal speed without being hindered, slowed down, or injured. This includes terrain that is magically manipulated.

ECOLOGY

Environment: Temperate forests
Organization: Solitary

Widow creepers are spiderlike plant creatures that make their lairs deep in tangled forests. When widow creepers are in a region, they are a constant danger to woodsmen, foresters, and other denizens of the forest.

Widow creepers spend much of their time in their nests, which are built of plant-fiber webs strung high in the trees and stretching to a diameter of 50 yards or more. When they venture out for food, however, they can cover a tremendous amount of territory in their lethal hunt.

A widow creeper sustains itself on a diet of brain fluid and blood. Corpses drained of fluids are left where they fell; the widow creeper does not devour the flesh, bones, or muscle of its prey.

A widow creeper looks like a giant (8 feet tall) black widow spider, but it is a plant, not an animal. Its body is formed from stems, small leaves, and tightly twisted vines, all dark green or brown in color. Two long, sinewy, tentacle-like vines protrude from its body and serve as both the creature's primary weapons and its primary manipulative limbs.

A widow creeper utters no sounds; it is believed they neither speak nor understand any humanoid languages.

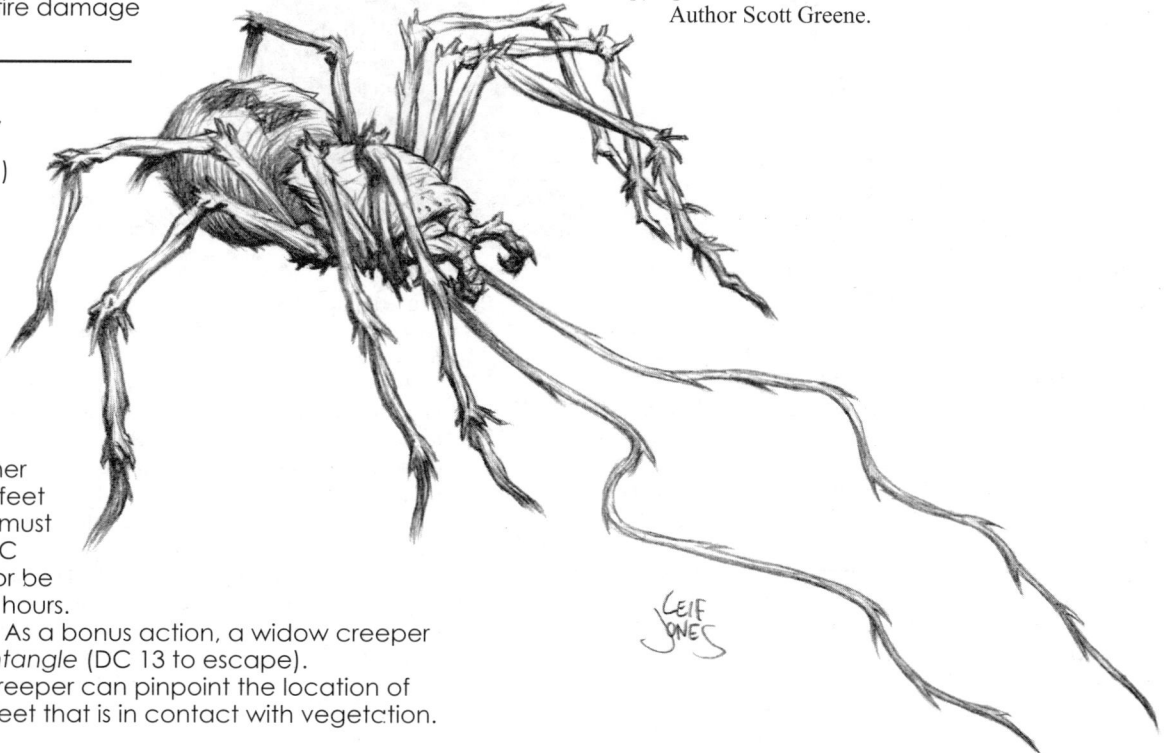

Witch Grass

These plants, growing to a height of about 2 feet, have a bulbous root and a bushy, leafy crown of purple leaves.

Witch Grass

XP 0 (CR 0)
Unaligned Small plant

AC 5
hp: 3 (1d6)
Immunity: All conditions
Speed: 0 ft.

TRAITS

Defenseless: Witch grass plants automatically fail saving throws.

Magic Damping: When an arcane spellcaster tries to cast an arcane spell within 20 feet of a patch of witch grass, the caster must make an Int or Cha saving throw; use the ability most appropriate to the spellcaster's class. The DC equals 10 + the size of the patch in 10-ft. squares (see Organization, below). For example, if a wizard tries to cast a spell near a 30-square-foot patch of witch grass, she must make a successful DC 13 Int saving throw. If the save succeeds, the spell is cast normally. If the saving throw fails, the spell is not cast but the spell slot is not expended. Only arcane magic is affected.

Seeds: Witch grass seeds attach themselves to anything they come in contact with. Seeds have the same magic damping effect as the plants, but their range is only 10 feet and the DC to overcome their effect is always 11. The effect lasts for 12 hours, then the seeds lose their potency. A close inspection of clothing and gear, plus a successful DC 8 Int (Nature) check, reveals the presence of the seeds. Once they're identified, seeds can be eliminated by spending an hour washing and thoroughly cleaning clothes, animals, and equipment.

ECOLOGY

Environment: Temperate or warm forests, hills, and plains
Organization: Patch (1d6 × 10 sq. ft.)

Witch grass is a summer-blooming, broad leaved plant that stands 2 feet tall at maturity. Its leaves and branches are very bushy, with a purplish

hue that extends to the plant's base and roots. A patch of witch grass covers an area of 10 to 60 square feet. It is only found in temperate or warm forests, hills and plains.

Witch grass is completely harmless in most ways, but it has an inhibiting effect on arcane magic. Something about the plant causes the intricate memorization patterns in an arcane spellcaster's mind to become muddled, making it difficult for them to cast spells properly. Only arcane magic is hampered; divine spellcasters aren't bothered by the plants.

When anything brushes past a witch grass plant, the plant's tiny seeds attach themselves to clothing, fur, boots, saddles, hooves, and whatever else they come in contact with. Once they get into a spellcaster's clothing or gear, or that of his or her companions, they can cause almost as much trouble as an entire patch of witch grass. The seeds are easily eliminated by cleaning, but the job must be thorough.

Copyright Notice
Author Scott Greene.

Witherstench

This creature resembles a mangy yellow skunk with very little fur, whose body is splotched with tiny purple spots. Patchy, dark fur grows here and there across its body.

Witherstench
XP 0 (CR 0)
Unaligned Small monstrosity
Initiative +2

DEFENSE
AC 12
hp: 1 (1d6 – 2)

OFFENSE
Speed: 20 ft.
Melee Attack—Claws: +4 to hit (reach 5 ft.; one creature).
Hit: 2 slashing damage.

STATISTICS
Str 6 (–2), **Dex** 14 (+2), **Con** 6 (–2),
Int 2 (–4), **Wis** 10 (+0), **Cha** 3 (–4)
Languages: None
Senses: Darkvision 60 ft.

TRAITS
Stench: A witherstench has a putrid stench that nearly every form of animal life finds offensive. All living creatures (except witherstenches) that start their turn within 30 feet of a witherstench must make a successful DC 8 Con saving throw or be incapacitated for as long as they remain within 30 feet of the creature. Even after leaving the affected area, the creature has tactical disadvantage on attack rolls and ability checks until the end of its next turn. Creatures that save successfully are immune to this stench until after their next long rest. Spells and effects that neutralize poison are effective against stench. Creatures that are immune to poison are immune to this effect, and those that are resistant to poison have tactical advantage on their saving throw.

ECOLOGY
Environment: Temperate
Organization: Solitary

A witherstench (also called a skunk beast) is a mutant relative of the common skunk. It grows to the size of a large dog. Its diet consists of carrion, and the creature is always found in areas where such food is plentiful.

Witherstenches shun combat, but they will fight if cornered.

Credit
The 2itherstench originally appeared in the First Edition *Fiend Folio* (© TSR/Wizards of the Coast, 1981) and is used by permission.

Copyright Notice
Author Scott Greene, based on original material by Jonathon Jones.

Yellow Musk Creeper

This plant is a large, clinging ivy with leaves of dark green.
Small, dark bulbs and bright yellow flowers with purple mottling adorn the plant.

Yellow Musk Creeper
XP 200 (CR 1)
Unaligned Large plant
Initiative +2

DEFENSE
AC 12
hp: 25 (3d10 + 9)
Immunity: Psychic damage; charm, fright, prone, stun, unconsciousness

OFFENSE
Speed: 5 ft.
Multiattack: A yellow musk creeper attacks twice with tendrils and sprays pollen once.
Melee Attack—Tendril: +6 to hit (reach 5 ft.; one creature). *Hit:* 1d4 + 2 piercing damage. If the target is charmed by the yellow musk creeper, it also loses 1d4 Intelligence points; see Create Yellow Musk Zombie, below.
Ranged Attack— Pollen: automatic hit (range 30 ft.; one creature). *Hit:* the target must make a successful DC 13 Con saving throw or be incapacitated and charmed by the yellow musk creeper for 1d4 minutes. Charmed creatures must approach the yellow musk creeper and don't resist its attacks; the creeper's tendril attacks have tactical advantage against them.

STATISTICS
Str 18 (+4), **Dex** 14 (+2), **Con** 17 (+3), **Int** 0 (–5), **Wis** 10 (+0), **Cha** 8 (–1)
Languages: None
Senses: Darkvision 60 ft.

TRAITS
Create Yellow Musk Zombie: A creature that is charmed by a yellow musk creeper and reduced to Intelligence 0 becomes a yellow musk zombie under the control of the creeper that created it. The transformation takes 1 hour. If the yellow musk creeper is slain before the transformation is complete, the transformation can be prevented by *lesser restoration, protection from poison,* or comparable poison-negating magic.
Rejuvenation: A yellow musk creeper can be killed only if its root is dug up and burned, hacked apart, or otherwise destroyed. Reducing the creeper to 0 hit points puts it out of commission so that its root can be dug up safely. The root is a Small bulb with AC 5 and 10 hit points. If the root is not destroyed, the plant regrows in two weeks.

ECOLOGY
Environment: Temperate and warm forests and underground
Organization: Patch (1 yellow musk creeper plus 1–6 yellow musk zombies)

The yellow musk creeper is a slow-moving plant that attacks living creatures and feeds on their intelligence, eventually turning them into yellow musk zombies. Creepers can be found in moderate to warm climates and underground, but are rarely encountered elsewhere.

The root of the plant is a bulbous, brown sac that lies deep beneath the ground where the yellow musk creeper grows. When a potential humanoid victim approaches within 10 feet, the flowers of the creeper shoot out a seed pod that bursts into a puff of musky-smelling, fine powder when it hits a target. These spores have a mesmerizing effect on living creatures. Once entranced, they want only to stand as near to the yellow musk creeper as possible—which is exactly what the plant needs them to do, so it can insert its strands into their braincase and draw out their cerebral fluid.

Yellow musk creepers are never encountered alone. They always have at least one yellow musk zombie somewhere nearby. These creatures remain hidden for as long as possible, to avoid tipping off potential victims to the danger the plant presents.

Credit
The yellow musk creeper originally appeared in the First Edition *Fiend Folio* (© TSR/Wizards of the Coast, 1981) and is used by permission

Copyright Notice
Author Scott Greene, based on original material by Albie Fiore.

Yellow Musk Zombie

*This shambling corpse has pale yellow skin and stark white eyes.
Its clothes hang in tatters around its decaying form.*

Yellow Musk Zombie
XP 50 (CR 1/4)
NE Medium plant
Initiative −1

DEFENSE
AC 9
hp: 19 (3d8 + 6)
Immunity: Psychic damage; charm, fright, stun, unconsciousness

OFFENSE
Speed: 20 ft.
Melee Attack—Fist or Weapon: +4 to hit (reach 5 ft.; one creature). *Hit:* 1d8 + 2 bludgeoning damage (type can vary by weapon)

STATISTICS
Str 15 (+2), **Dex** 8 (−1), **Con** 14 (+2),
Int 2 (−4), **Wis** 10 (+0), **Cha** 1 (−5)
Languages: None
Senses: Darkvision 60 ft.

TRAITS
Link to Creator: A yellow musk zombie can never move more than 200 feet away from the yellow musk creeper that created it. If it is forced to do so, it dies. The exception to this restriction is when the yellow musk creeper separates from the zombie so the zombie can seek out a location for a new creeper to take root.

ECOLOGY
Environment: Temperate and warm forests and underground
Organization: Solitary (when spreading) or patch (1 yellow musk creeper plus 1–6 yellow musk zombies)

Yellow musk zombies are creatures that have been transformed into their current state by a yellow musk creeper. The yellow musk zombie appears much as it did in life, wearing the same clothes and carrying the same weapons it had at the time of its transformation. Yellow musk zombies have pale yellow skin and stark white eyes. They are attuned to the yellow musk creeper that created them by the many thin, ivylike vines growing from their flesh. This attunement prevents them from moving more than 200 feet away from the creeper. If a zombie is forced to exceed that distance, it dies.

About two months after its transformation, the zombie is "ripe." At that time, the yellow musk creeper turns it loose, and the zombie wanders up to a mile away from its parent creeper and dies. Where it falls, new yellow musk seedlings sprout from the corpse, and within one hour, a fully grown yellow musk creeper blooms.

Credit
The yellow musk zombie originally appeared in the First Edition *Fiend Folio* (© TSR/Wizards of the Coast, 1981) and is used by permission.

Copyright Notice
Author Scott Greene, based on original material by Albie Fiore.

Zombie Raven

*Among the flock of ravens passing overhead are many birds that appear tattered,
rotted, and eyeless—flying zombie ravens!*

Zombie Raven

XP 10 (CR 0)
CE Tiny undead
Initiative +1

DEFENSE
AC 11
hp: 3 (1d4 + 1)
Saving Throws: Wis +0
Immunity: Poison damage; exhaustion, fright, poison,
unconsciousness

OFFENSE
Speed: 10 ft., fly 50 ft.
Melee Attack—Beak: +3 to hit (reach 5 ft.; one creature).
  Hit: 1 piercing damage.

STATISTICS
Str 4 (–3), **Dex** 12 (+1), **Con** 10 (+0),
Int 3 (–4), **Wis** 6 (–2), **Cha** 5 (–3)
Languages: None
Senses: Darkvision 60 ft.

TRAITS
Disintegration: Zombie ravens disintegrate into dust
  and feathers when destroyed. Whenever five zombie
  ravens have been destroyed in a confined space (or
  10 in the open), all living creatures involved in the fight
  must make successful DC 10 Con saving throws. The
  saving throw must be repeated every time another
  five (or 10 in the open) zombie ravens are destroyed.
  The first failed saving throw causes a creature to have
  tactical disadvantage on attack rolls against targets
  that are more than 5 feet away (if the attack is a spell
  that relies on a saving throw, the target has tactical
  advantage on the saving throw). The second failed
  saving throw applies tactical disadvantage to all
  attacks, regardless of range. The third failed saving
  throw blinds the creature. These penalties last until the
  affected creature leaves the confined space (or the
  area) where the fight occurred, or until five minutes
  have passed.
Mobility: An opponent has tactical disadvantage on
  opportunity attacks against a flying zombie raven.
Unholy Fortitude: Zombie ravens care nothing about the
  deities of humanoids, so they have tactical advantage on
  saving throws against being turned.

ECOLOGY
Environment: Any land
Organization: Flock (6–36)

Zombie ravens are created *en masse* by certain necromantic spells.
They make excellent aerial scouts for undead armies and evil wizards,
because they can fly tremendously long distances without tiring. Although
they aren't very dangerous individually, they present some danger in a
flock. There's very little to a zombie raven, and what there is amounts to
little more than brittle bones, feathers, and dust. When they're destroyed
by weapons or spells, they tend to "explode" into small clouds of filthy
feathers and choking dust. Kill enough of them in a small space, and the
air becomes clouded with obscuring feathers and stinging, burning dust.

Zombie ravens do most of their fighting on the wing, instinctively
understanding that this gives them an advantage against foes on the
ground. They've been known to fall in with flocks of live ravens and fly
with them, to make their presence harder to notice by observers on the
ground, or to flock around one or several murder crows.

Appendix A: Monsters by Type

Aberrations

Creature	CR
Adherer	2
Artificer of Yothri	5
Blood Orchid	5
Blood Orchid Grand Savant	9
Blood Orchid Savant	7
Bone Cobbler	2
Bonesucker	4
Brume	6
Carbuncle	1/8
Cerebral Stalker	5
Clamor	2
Crimson Mist	7
Decapus	2
Denizen of Leng	5
Dust Digger	3
Encephalon Gorger	4
Froghemoth	11
Gohl (Hydra Cloud)	8
Gorbel	1/4
Grue, Type 2	2
Leng Spider	6
Temporal Crawler	2
Tentacled Horror	11
Volt	1/4
Were-mist	2

Beasts

Creature	CR
Ant Lion	4
Assassin Bug	5
Beetle, Giant Rhinoceros	4
Beetle, Giant Slicer	3
Beetle, Giant Water	1/2
Boalisk	1
Boneedle, Greater	1
Boneedle, Lesser	1/4
Catfish, Giant Electric	3
Cave Cricket	1/4
Cave Eel	1/4
Cave Leech	6
Centipede Nest	1/2
Chain Worm	12
Clam, Giant	1/4
Crayfish, Monstrous	2
Eel, Giant Moray	2
Eel, Gulper	3
Gillmonkey	1/4
Golden Cat	0
Helix Moth, Adult	6
Helix Moth, Larva	2
Horsefly, Giant	1/2
Land Lamprey	1/4
Leopard, Snow	1/4
Mandrill	1/8
Pleistocene: Brontotherium	6
Pleistocene: Hyaenodon	1
Pleistocene: Mastodon	4
Pleistocene: Woolly Rhinoceros	6
Seahorse, Giant	1/2
Stegocentipede	4
Tunnel Prawn	1/8

Constructs

Creature	CR
Amphoron of Yothri: Juggernaut	6
Amphoron of Yothri: Warrior	2
Amphoron of Yothri: Worker	1/2
Brass Man	6
Caryatid Column	1
Exoskeleton: Giant Ant	1/2
Exoskeleton: Giant Beetle	2
Exoskeleton: Giant Crab	3
Golem, Flagstone	7
Golem, Furnace	9
Golem, Stone Guardian	2
Golem, Wooden	3
Origami Warrior	1/8
Sepulchral Guardian	3

Dragons

Creature	CR
Dracolisk	7
Drake, Fire	1
Drake, Ice	1
Sea Serpent, Brine	10
Sea Serpent, Deep Hunter	14
Sea Serpent, Fanged	5
Sea Serpent, Shipbreaker	20
Sea Serpent, Spitting	5

Elementals

Creature	CR
Igniguana	1
Lava Child	1
Magmoid	4
Sandling	1
Weird, Lava	4

Fey

Creature	CR
Fyr	1/4
Gray Nisp	6
Grimm	7
Korred	1
Midnight Peddler	1/2
Mite	1/8
Mite: Pestie	1/4
Pech	1/4

Fiends

Creature	CR
Aerial Servant	9
Astral Shark	5
Burning Dervish	3
Chaos Knight	4
Dagon	20
Demon: Teratashia	17
Demon: Thalasskpotis	10
Demonic Knight	5
Fire Snake, Poisonous	1/2
Genie: Hawanar	7
Giant Slug of P'nakh	4
Khargra	2
Kurok-spirit	1
Screaming Devilkin	1/4
Shadow Mastiff	1/2

Giants

Creature	CR
Biclops	6
Giant, Jack-in-Irons	7
Troll, Two-headed	6

Humanoids

Creature	CR
Aaztar-Ghola	4
Chupacabra	1
Dark Creeper	1/4
Dark Stalker	2
Grippli	1/4
Huggermugger	1/4
Ryven	1
Skelzi	1
Skulk	1/2
Tabaxi	1/2
Taer	1
Weredactyl	2

Monstrosities

Creature	CR
Ape, Flying	2
Aranea	3
Arcanoplasm	4
Astral Moth	1/8
Aurumvorax	5

Appendix B: Monsters by CR

CR 0

Creature	Type
Golden Cat	beast
Olive Slime	plant
Rat, Shadow	undead
Witch Grass	plant
Witherstench	monstrosity
Zombie Raven	undead

CR 1/8

Creature	Type
Astral Moth	monstrosity
Carbuncle	aberration
Cat, Feral Undead	undead
Fire Crab, Lesser	monstrosity
Jaculi	monstrosity
Mandragora	plant
Mandrill	beast
Mantari	monstrosity
Mite	fey
Origami Warrior	construct
Shadow, Lesser	undead
Tunnel Prawn	beast
Vegepygmy Commoner, Worker	plant
Vulchling	monstrosity

CR 1/4

Creature	Type
Blood Hawk	monstrosity
Boneneedle, Lesser	beast
Cave Cricket	beast
Cave Eel	beast
Clam, Giant	beast
Dark Creeper	humanoid
Fungus Bat	plant
Fyr	fey
Gillmonkey	beast
Gorbel	aberration
Grippli	humanoid
Hawktoad	monstrosity
Huggermugger	humanoid
Land Lamprey	beast
Leopard, Snow	beast
Leucrotta, Young	monstrosity
Mite, Pestie	fey
Pech	fey
Ronus	monstrosity
Screaming Devilkin	fiend
Vampire Rose	plant
Volt	aberration
Yellow Musk Zombie	plant

CR 1/2

Creature	Type
Amphoron of Yothri (Worker)	construct
Beetle, Giant Water	beast
Cadaver	undead
Centipede Nest	beast
Death Dog	monstrosity
Dire Corby	monstrosity
Eblis	monstrosity
Exoskeleton, Giant Ant	construct
Fire Snake, Poisonous	fiend
Hanged Man	undead
Horsefly, Giant	beast
Kech	monstrosity
Midnight Peddler	fey
Olive Slime Zombie	plant
Phycomid	plant
Pyrolisk	monstrosity
Russet Mold	plant
Seahorse, Giant	beast
Shadow Mastiff	fiend
Skulk	humanoid
Tabaxi	humanoid
Therianthrope, Foxwere	monstrosity
Therianthrope, Owlwere	monstrosity
Tri-Flower Frond	plant
Vegepygmy Guard	plant

CR 1

Creature	Type
Boalisk	beast
Boneneedle, Greater	beast
Caryatid Column	construct
Chupacabra	humanoid
Church Grim	monstrosity
Cooshee	monstrosity
Corpsespun	undead
Crabman	monstrosity
Drake, Fire	dragon
Drake, Ice	dragon
Elusa Hound	monstrosity
Fetch	undead
Flowershroud	plant
Gargoyle, Green Guardian	monstrosity
Gorilla Bear	monstrosity
Green Brain	plant
Hippocampus	monstrosity
Hoar Fox	monstrosity
Hyaenodon	beast
Igniguana	elemental
Jupiter Bloodsucker	plant
Kelpie	plant

Creature	Type
Korred	fey
Kurok-spirit	fiend
Lava Child	elemental
Ooze, Glacial	ooze
Ryven	humanoid
Sandling	elemental
Skelzi	humanoid
Taer	humanoid
Tangtal	monstrosity
Therianthrope, Wolfwere	monstrosity
Triton, Dark	monstrosity
Yellow Musk Creeper	plant
Jackal of Darkness	undead

CR 2

Creature	Type
Adherer	aberration
Amphoron of Yothri (Warrrior)	construct
Ape, Flying	monstrosity
Bloody Bones	undead
Bone Cobbler	aberration
Cave Fisher	monstrosity
Cimota	undead
Clamor	aberration
Cobra Flower	plant
Coffer Corpse	undead
Crayfish, Monstrous	beast
Dark Stalker	humanoid
Darnoc	undead
Decapus	aberration
Ectoplasm	ooze
Eel, Giant Moray	beast
Exoskeleton, Giant Beetle	construct
Fen Witch	monstrosity
Fire Crab, Greater	monstrosity
Flail Snail	monstrosity
Foo Dog	monstrosity
Fungoid	plant
Gallows Tree Zombie	plant
Ghost Ammonite	undead
Golem, Stone Guardian	construct
Grue, Type 2	aberration
Helix Moth Larva	beast
Kampfult	plant
Khargra	fiend
Leucrotta, Adult	monstrosity
Mummy of the Deep	undead
Naga, Hanu-naga	monstrosity
Pudding, Blood	ooze
Slithering Tracker	ooze
Strangle Weed	plant
Tazelwurm	monstrosity
Temporal Crawler	aberration

Therianthrope, Lionwere.......monstrosity
Weredactyl ....humanoid
Were-Mist ....aberration

CR 3

Creature	Type
Algoid	plant
Aranea	monstrosity
Ascomoid	plant
Basilisk, Crimson	monstrosity
Bat, Doombat	monstrosity
Beetle, Giant Slicer	beast
Bloodsuckle	plant
Borsin	monstrosity
Burning Dervish	fiend
Cadaver Lord	undead
Catfish, Giant Electric	beast
Crypt Thing	undead
Death Worm	monstrosity
Dust Digger	aberration
Eel, Gulper	beast
Exoskeleton, Giant Crab	construct
Fear Guard	undead
Gargoyle, Fungus	plant
Golem, Wooden	construct
Hieroglyphicroc	undead
Kamadan	monstrosity
Murder Crow	undead
Sepulchral Guardian	construct
Vegepygmy Chief	plant

CR 4

Creature	Type
Aaztar-Ghola	humanoid
Ant Lion	beast
Arcanoplasm	monstrosity
Beetle, Giant Rhinoceros	beast
Bonesucker	aberration
Caterprism	monstrosity
Chaos Knight	fiend
Churr	monstrosity
Cimota, Guardian	undead
Corpse Rook	monstrosity
Encephalon Gorger	aberration
Gargoyle, Four-Armed	monstrosity
Giant Slug of P'nahk	fiend
Grue, Type 1	ooze
Lithonnite	monstrosity
Magmoid	elemental
Mastodon	beast
Quadricorn	monstrosity
Shroom	plant
Stegocentipede	beast
Tendriculos	plant
Troll, Spectral	undead
Weird, Lava	elemental

CR 5

Creature	Type
Artificer of Yothri	aberration
Assassin Bug	beast
Astral Shark	fiend
Aurumvorax	monstrosity
Basilisk, Greater	monstrosity
Blood Orchid	aberration
Catoblepas	monstrosity
Cerebral Stalker	aberration
Corpsespinner	monstrosity
Demonic Knight	fiend
Denizen of Leng	aberration
Forester's Bane	plant
Gargoyle, Margoyle	monstrosity
Mustard Jelly	ooze
Ooze, Magma	ooze
Red Jester	undead
Scythe Tree	plant
Sea Serpent, Fanged	dragon
Sea Serpent, Spitting	dragon

CR 6

Creature	Type
Amphoron of Yothri (Juggernaut)	construct
Biclops	giant
Brass Man	construct
Brontotherium	beast
Brume	aberration
Cave Leech	beast
Cimota, High	undead
Gray Nisp	fey
Helix Moth Adult	beast
Leng Spider	aberration
Treant, Lightning	plant
Troll, Two-Headed	giant
Wooly Rhinoceros	beast

CR 7

Creature	Type
Blood Orchid Savant	aberration
Crimson Mist	aberration
Dracolisk	dragon
Genie, Hawanar	fiend
Giant, Jack-in-Irons	giant
Golem, Flagstone	construct
Gorgimera	monstrosity
Grimm	fey
Hangman Tree	plant
Stygian Skeleton	undead

CR 8

Creature	Type
Gnarlwood	plant
Gohl	aberration
Quickwood	plant
Tunnel Worm	monstrosity

CR 9

Creature	Type
Aerial Servant	fiend
Blood Orchid Grand Savant	aberration
Golem, Furnace	construct
Vorin	monstrosity

CR 10

Creature	Type
Demon: Thalasskoptis	fiend
Gloom Crawler	monstrosity
Sea Serpent, Brine	dragon
Widow Creeper	plant

CR 11

Creature	Type
Froghemoth	aberration
Tentacled Horror	aberration

CR 12

Creature	Type
Chain Worm	beast

CR 13

Creature	Type
Gallows Tree	plant

CR 14

Creature	Type
Sea Serpent, Deep Hunter	dragon
Skeleton Warrior	undead

CR 15

Creature	Type
Demon: Thalasskpotis	fiend

CR 16

Creature	Type
Soul Reaper	undead

CR 20

Creature	Type
Dagon	fiend
Sea Serpent, Shipbreaker	dragon

Legal Appendix

Reusing the Monsters in *Fifth Edition Foes*

This book contains two types of Open Game Content. Some of the Open Game Content was originally released under a specific license from Wizards of the Coast for Necromancer Games's *Tome of Horrors* and *Tome of Horrors Revised*, and contains restrictions that are not applicable to normal Open Game Content. Other Open Game Content in the book is ordinary Open Game Content, unrestricted by anything other than the provisions of the Open Game License.

Ordinary Open Game Content

The following monsters not subject to any special, pre-existing license with Wizards of the Coast, and the Open Game Content portions of these monsters may be used as normal, subject to our designation of Open Game Content and Product Identity:

Aaztar-Ghola
Amphoron of Yothri: Worker
Amphoron of Yothri: Warrior
Amphoron of Yothri: Juggernaut
Ape, Flying
Aranea
Arcanoplasm
Artificer of Yothri
Assassin Bug
Astral Moth
Basilisk, Crimson
Beetle, Giant Water
Biclops
Blood Orchid
Blood Orchid Savant
Blood Orchid Grand Savant
Bloodsuckle
Boneneedle, Greater
Boneneedle, Lesser
Borsin
Brass Man
Brume
Burning Dervish
Cadaver
Cadaver Lord
Cat, Feral Undead
Caterprism
Catfish, Giant Electric
Catoblepas
Cave Eel
Cave Leech
Centipede Nest
Cerebral Stalker
Chain Worm
Chaos Knight
Church Grim
Churr
Cimota
Cimota Guardian
Cimota, High
Clamor
Corpse Rook
Corpsespinner
Corpsespun
Crimson Mist
Demon Prince: Teratashia
Demon Prince: Thalasskoptis
Denizen of Leng

Ectoplasm
Eel, Gulper
Elusa Hound
Encephalon Gorger
Exoskeleton: Giant Ant
Exoskeleton: Giant Beetle
Exoskeleton: Giant Crab
Fear Guard
Fetch
Fire Crab, Greater
Fire Crab, Lesser
Flowershroud
Fungoid
Fungus Bat
Fyr
Gallows Tree
Gallows Tree Zombie
Gargoyle, Fungus
Genie: Hawanar
Ghost-Ammonite
Giant Slug of P'nakh
Giant, Jack-in-Irons
Gillmonkey
Gloom Crawler
Gnarlwood
Gohl (Hydra Cloud)
Golden Cat
Golem, Flagstone
Golem, Furnace
Gray Nisp
Green Brain
Grimm
Grue, Type 1
Grue, Type 2
Hanged Man
Hawktoad
Helix Moth
Hieroglyphicroc
Horsefly, Giant
Huggermugger
Igniguana
Jackal of Darkness
Kurok-spirit
Lava Weird
Leng Spider
Leopard, Snow
Leucrotta, Adult
Leucrotta, Young
Lithonnite
Magmoid
Mandrill
Murder Crow
Naga: Hanu-naga
Ooze, Glacial
Ooze, Magma
Origami Warrior
Pleistocene Animals: Brontotherium
Pleistocene Animals: Hyaenodon
Pleistocene Animals: Mastodon
Pleistocene Animals: Woolly Rhinoceros

Pudding, Blood
Quadricorn
Red Jester
Ronus
Ryven
Sea Serpent, Brine
Sea Serpent, Deep Hunter
Sea Serpent, Fanged
Sea Serpent, Shipbreaker
Sea Serpent, Spitting
Sepulchral Guardian
Shadow Mastiff
Shroom
Skeleton, Stygian
Skelzi
Soul Reaper
Tangtal
Tazelwurm
Temporal Crawler
Tendriculos
Tentacled Horror
Treant, Lightning
Triton, Dark
Tunnel Prawn
Vorin
Were-mist
Weredactyl
Widow Creeper
Witch Grass
Zombie Raven

"Special" Open Game Content

The following monsters contain Open Game Content that is subject to additional rules about how to use the Open Game Content in a publication (see below for instructions):

Adherer
Aerial Servant
Algoid
Ant Lion
Ascomoid
Astral Shark
Aurumvorax
Basilisk, Greater
Bat: Doombat
Beetle, Giant Rhinoceros
Beetle, Giant Slicer
Blood Hawk
Bloody Bones
Boalisk
Bone Cobbler
Bonesucker
Carbuncle
Caryatid Column
Cave Cricket
Cave Fisher
Clam, Giant
Cobra Flower
Coffer Corpe
Cooshee
Crabman
Crayfish, Monstrous
Crypt Thing
Dagon
Dark Creeper
Dark Stalker
Darnoc
Death Dog
Death Worm
Decapus
Demonic Knight
Dire Corby
Dracolisk
Drake, Fire
Drake, Ice
Dust Digger
Eblis
Eel, Giant Moray
Fen Witch
Fire Snake
Flail Snail
Foo Dog
Forester's Bane
Froghemoth
Gargoyle: Four-Armed
Gargoyle, Green Guardian
Gargoyle: Margoyle
Golem, Stone Guardian
Gorbel
Gorgimera
Gorilla Bear
Grippli
Hangman Tree
Hippocampus
Hoar Fox
Jaculi
Jelly, Mustard
Jupiter Bloodsucker
Kamadan
Kampfult
Kech
Kelpie
Khargra
Korred
Land Lamprey
Lava Child
Mandragora
Mantari
Midnight Peddler
Mite
Mite, Pestie
Mummy of the Deep
Olive Slime
Olive Slime Zombie
Pech
Phycomid
Pyrolisk
Quickwood
Rat, Shadow
Russet Mold
Sandling
Screaming Devilkin
Scythe Tree
Shadow, Lesser
Skeleton Warrior
Skulk
Slithering Tracker
Stegocentipede
Strangle Weed
Tabaxi
Taer
Therianthrope: Foxwere
Therianthrope: Lionwere
Therianthrope: Owlwere

Therianthrope:
  Wolfwere
Tri-flower Frond
Troll, Spectral
Troll, Two-headed
Tunnel Worm

Vampire Rose
Vegepygmy Commoner,
  Worker
Vegepygmy Guard
Vegepygmy Chief
Volt

Vulchling
Witherstench
Yellow Musk Creeper
Yellow Musk Zombie

How to Use the "Special" Open Game Content

To use the "Special" Open Game Content listed above, you must put the following identifying information in the Section 15 Copyright Notice of *your* book for each monster used (remember: this does not apply to the ordinary Open Game Content):

> "[Insert the name of monster used — incorporated here by this reference — in place of this bracketed text, with each monster used requiring a separate entry in Section 15], from the *Tome of Horrors Complete*, Copyright 2011, Necromancer Games, Inc., published and distributed by Frog God Games."

Does that mean you have to do a whole new entry in your Section 15 for *every* monster you use? Yes: this is because our agreement many years ago with Wizards of the Coast provided that the original authors of the material would be credited, and this is how it was done.

Important Reminder

Remember, at no time can you use or refer to any of the content in the "Credit" section of any monster. That content is provided to us by prior permission, and we do not have the right to contribute it as Open Game Content. If you use any content from the "Credit" section of any monster, you will be in violation of the license.

Disclaimer

The above is not legal advice. It is a helpful summary to aid you in reusing the content contained in this book. Though the above language warrants that Necromancer Games, Inc. and Frog God Games will not allege you have failed to comply with the Open Game License if you follow the above instructions, this does not prevent third parties from possibly making such a claim. If you have concerns, please consult an attorney.